The Serpent Bearer

The Serpent Bearer

A Novel

Jane Rosenthal

SHE WRITES PRESS

Published 2025
Printed in the United States of America
Print ISBN: 978-1-64742-850-1
E-ISBN: 978-1-64742-851-8
Library of Congress Control Number: 2024918851

For information, address:
She Writes Press
1569 Solano Ave #546
Berkeley, CA 94707

Interior Design by Kiran Spees

She Writes Press is a division of SparkPoint Studio, LLC.

Company and/or product names that are trade names, logos, trademarks, and/or registered trademarks of third parties are the property of their respective owners and are used in this book for purposes of identification and information only under the Fair Use Doctrine.

This is a work of fiction. Names, characters, places, and incidents either are the product of the author's imagination or are used fictitiously. Any resemblance to actual persons, living or dead, is entirely coincidental.

For my parents
Sanford and Elizabeth Rosenthal

1

Solly

Havana, Cuba
August 1941

You could put Solly Meisner in a glued-together Soviet Tupolev bomber, flying somewhere between Barcelona and Madrid, dodging Franco's antiaircraft fire, ascending and descending like a rubber ball, and he wouldn't break a sweat. Didn't break a sweat, as a matter of fact. But force him to sit around with nothing to do but kill time, twiddling his thumbs? Now that gave him the heebie-jeebies. Too much time on his hands and he'd start to think, and too much thinking always brought him right back to Spain, to that dank basement, waiting for radio communication from the front while Nationalists' bombs pounded Madrid, a communiqué that never came. Turns out you could raise your fist and shout *No pasarán!* all you wanted, and it wouldn't make a damn bit of difference.

Solly knew he'd never forget that night, never forget the smell, all those men crammed together, perspiring like dogs in the dark cellar of a villa near the Parque del Buen Retiro. The villa's owner, some *marqués* who'd met his match in the form of a Republican firing squad, was no longer around to enjoy his wine collection stacked along the walls, the rare bottles of rioja Solly's *camaradas* were indulging in. Solly had been too wound up to swill from the bottles.

The smell of piss where the men had urinated in the corner, the sweat, and the sharp whiff of wine had nauseated him.

He'd bolted, claustrophobic and desperate for some fresh air, leaving his post in the hands of a kid from Boston named Howie, telling him he just needed five minutes. When the bomb hit the villa, he'd been sitting on a park bench with his eyes closed, thinking he had all the time in the world. For that simple fact, he was still alive, waiting once again for an unknown danger and a chance to make it up to Howie and all the others. There were so goddamn many of them, weren't there?

Solly lay on the bed and stared at the rotating ceiling fan in his room, a jazzy rumba drifting up from the veranda cocktail lounge five stories below, waiting, his heart hammering in his chest as it had been from the moment he'd pushed his passport across the reception desk at the Hotel Nacional and signed in. Seven in the evening Cuba time.

He had waved away a disappointed bellhop who'd been hoping for a big tip and lifted his own suitcase. It was light, and if anyone had really been paying attention at customs, his clothing would have raised suspicions: a warm coat, a heavy sweater, hardly a wardrobe for the tropics. But customs officials hadn't even opened it. To them he was just one more American ready to enjoy the playground of the Caribbean.

Good, he'd thought. *I've passed that test.*

Back in the States, he'd been told they would contact him when they were ready, and now he wondered who *they* were, wondered if he should be worried as he filled up the thick glass ashtray on the nightstand with one Pall Mall cigarette after another. Maybe this was some kind of setup. He closed his eyes, better to remember every face, every encounter he'd had since last night, searching them for clues.

Which one was his handler? The desk manager? Nope, not him. Too much hair pomade to be a contact, too flashy. The waiter who'd delivered his room service meal? Hadn't he looked at Solly a certain way, as if to memorize his face should he need to? Solly sat up and pulled open the nightstand's drawer. Jesus, the Gideon Bible even here. He slammed the drawer shut and stared at the black phone beside the bed. He'd been in Havana for twenty hours now and was starting to fear that it never would ring, that this rendezvous would end, just like the other one had ended three years ago in Lisbon when it dawned on him with sickening clarity that Estelle wouldn't be joining him, that the ship's passage he'd secured for her was for naught, and that after all that had happened in Spain, he would return to the States defeated and alone, one more death to mourn.

Estelle.

Solly shook himself as if he'd just walked through cobwebs, got up, headed to the window, and peered down to the garden below where women in gauzy picture hats floated like water lilies in the damp air, lifting their champagne coupes to their painted lips, their laughter as buzzy as their drinks. All things come to those who wait, his mother used to say, back when he was in knee pants when *things to come* were always good things. He'd learned that lesson—that they weren't—the hard way.

It was dusk by the time Solly heard the knock on the door. His wait, or at least this part of it, was over. The concierge was all smiles as he carried a garment bag to Solly's closet, chattering that the Hotel Nacional had the best presser, that he hoped his shoes were polished sufficiently, and oh, here was a note from this evening's hosts, and was there anything else he would need?

"Nothing," Solly said, reaching into his pocket for a few Cuban pesos, quite a few more than was probably necessary. He wasn't exactly sure what he was buying with his generosity, but better to be on the safe side.

As soon as he'd shut the door, he tore open the envelope and read the letter, unsigned of course. The instructions were scant, but they were instructions that he would follow to a tee. He sat on the bed and stared at the closet for a moment before he got up and checked his tuxedo and dress shirt. And, just as he'd been told to do in the note, he paid special attention to the gold cuff links gleaming on his dress shirt's sleeves. He stuck his fingernail into the ridge along the side of one. Sure enough, it opened. Inside was just enough chloral hydrate to knock someone out. He knew from Spain that it could come in handy.

At 11:00 p.m. Solly Meisner, no longer an Abraham Lincoln *brigadista* but now a spy, dressed in his tuxedo and cummerbund, resplendent from his black tie to his black brogues, his hair slicked back, his mustache trimmed, pushed through the polished brass doors of the Hotel Nacional's gilded casino. The roar of spinning roulette wheels washed over him like a wave. He wandered the elegant gaming room with a studied nonchalance, taking in the enormous crystal chandeliers that scattered light over the gamblers, the heavy gold brocade curtains swooning above Jazz Moderne style window frames, the rich, flocked wallpaper, and the well-heeled, perfumed ladies like any tourist enthralled by Cuba's corrupt glamour. All the while, he assumed his presence would be made known to whomever was there to collect him.

After a few rounds, he headed to the cashier's cage to buy his chips. Solly hadn't felt this full of adrenaline and maybe even fear in, well, he didn't know how long. And considering all he'd been through the past year, the deadness he'd slogged through each day, fear was a relief. He had a gun in his suitcase and he had his marching orders:

get a pocketful of chips and place an inside bet—a split, just enough risk and a high payout. The chandeliers sparkled, the laughter ebbed and flowed, the click of the roulette wheels sounded like bullets, and Solly knew just who he was aiming for: Eton, his British *camarada* from Spain, a Nazi-sympathizing agent all along. The bastard.

"Eleven and twenty-three, split," he told the croupier.

"Hedging your bets I see," said a voice from behind his shoulder, a woman's voice, one he'd never expected. "Don't turn around," she said. "It's bad luck. Just let the wheel spin."

2

Izzy

Waxhaw, North Carolina
July 2008

"**Y**ou better get over here," the voice on the phone insisted. I rolled over and glanced at the time on the clock by the bed: 6:49 a.m. "Your father is about to drive me out of my mind. He's saying he's got to to the office. What office is Mr. Solly talking about?"

Oh dear. I sat up and felt the weight of my father's age fall on my shoulders. It was Linda, my father's caregiver. *What is he up to now?* I wondered, eyeing the clothes I'd thrown on the chair by the bed when I'd finished reviewing some postdocs' papers last night. It was a task I did regularly as a retired archaeology professor, all the while stifling my jealousy at their adventures, their new discoveries in the field, their futures before them.

I told Linda I'd grab a coffee at Starbucks on the way over. "I'll be there as soon as I can." And fifteen minutes later, fully caffeinated, the air conditioner blasting because it was July in the Carolinas, I pushed the code on the security gate of his upscale retirement community—Carson Lake—and let myself into the inner sanctum. Who Carson was, I had no idea, and lake was stretching it. Still, it wasn't a bad place to end up at age ninety-five, all landscaped Georgian homes with a residents' club, weeping willows leaning into the lake water and benches underneath them. Behind the club and pool, tucked away in a discreet area, was the assisted living facility, and behind that was the memory care unit for those who needed a higher level of care. These were all buildings I'd promised my dad I'd keep him out of. It was an easy promise to make until it wasn't. He was becoming more challenging every day. I really couldn't fathom how Linda did it. The woman was a saint.

"Hello," I pushed open the door and called out. The sight of my mother's paintings and antiques, the lamps on the hall entryway table made from eighteenth-century Spanish colonial candlesticks, and the deep reds and blues of the oriental runner leading to the sunroom in the back of the house all conspired to make me feel like a child again. You'd think none of the years had passed and I was just coming home from school, looking for a place to drop my book bag. But today something was different. An old Panama fedora rested against the candlesticks. I lifted it and looked at the sweaty liner but could only make out the letters *mer*, or something like that. The hat smelled like mothballs. Old.

"We're in here, in your dad's study," Linda shouted.

And that's where I found Solly Meisner of Meisner, Klein, Rosenbaum, and Blum, one of the Carolinas' biggest labor and civil rights law firms. He was stretched out on his recliner, a towel over his face.

"What happened?" I asked.

"Nosebleed is what happened," Linda clucked. "He was running around trying to get himself dressed. Had his Brooks Brothers suit and tie out on the bed and everything. Then he got frustrated and his pressure went up. Wanted me to get that old hat from a box he had in his safe, but for the longest time he couldn't remember the numbers. Who keeps an old hat in a safe?"

"My father, apparently—Isn't that right, Dad?—for some reason we mere mortals can't decipher." I sighed, looked around, and saw the blood pressure cuff on the lamp table by his chair, the pulse oximeter, and the amber-colored plastic pill bottles, the only weapons he had left to fight against the inevitable. I glanced at the chart we kept of my father's vitals. "BP–152/95," Linda had written.

"We're going to do what my old gran used to do." Linda waved a serving spoon around, one from my mother's wedding silver.

"What's that for?" I asked as she slipped it behind my father's neck.

My father yanked the towel off his face, "Superstition. She says a silver spoon stops the bleeding." He shook his head and mopped up the shockingly bright blood coming from his right nostril.

"Put that back on your face, Mr. Solly," Linda ordered. "That's right. Superstition. Well, Black people got all the superstition, and white people got all the money. Let's see which one works now."

I sat down in my dad's office chair and couldn't believe it when, not five minutes later, the bleeding stopped. "I told you," Linda said.

"Does it have to be silver?" I asked. "Could it be stainless steel? Is it the cold metal on a nerve that does it?"

Linda rolled her eyes like I was missing the point, and what did it matter. "I have no idea, honey," she said, wrapping the gray blood pressure cuff around my father's arm again. "Must be just superstition like y'all think it is." By y'all I knew she meant white people, only some of whom she was willing to tolerate. Fortunately, my father was one of them. She grabbed a baby wipe from a box on the lamp table and washed off his face. "You're all right." She patted my dad's knee. "But you are not going anywhere, not with your blood pressure," she said, unwrapping the cuff.

My father pushed himself up and reached for his cane. "I need you to drive." He pointed his cane in my direction. "I have to go to the office. Let's go."

I looked over at Linda, who was shaking her head. "It's the middle of July, Dad. You know what Dr. Pasquale told you. When the heat is over ninety and the humidity is very high, you need to stay inside in the air conditioning."

My father pulled an extra set of keys out of his pocket. "My license is still good for five more years. They renewed it."

"You are kidding," I said.

"I am not." He relayed the fact that the state of North Carolina had just reissued a ninety-five-year-old man's driver's license without so much as an eye test like it was the most normal thing in the world. To him it was because, in spite of all evidence to the contrary, my father didn't consider himself old. This was just more proof. "So, either you drive or I do. I have to go to the office." He wobbled into the hallway on his cane, picked up the straw hat, and, checking himself in the mirror, set it at a jaunty angle on his head.

I had no idea what had gotten into him, but I did a quick calculation. Presbyterian Hospital was right on the way to downtown Charlotte. I figured I'd humor him all the way down Providence Road and then swing into the ER. "Call Pasquale's office," I whispered to Linda on the way out.

I got him in the car, cranked up the AC, headed to the black iron gates that separated Carson Lake's residents from the hoi polloi, and was about to turn right, heading to downtown, when my dad said, "Go left."

"Dad, your office is downtown in the NCNB building."

"For your information, I know where my office is. It's in Pennington. Across the state line."

My vision started to blur and a sick chill descended over me. I'd been warned by the doctors that as his heart failed, his kidneys would too, and that confusion would be one of the signs. Were we at that point now? He never told me about an office in Pennington, South Carolina. Maybe he had one when he first came south, back when he lived in Pennington for a brief while, but this is the first I'd ever heard of it.

"What are you waiting for?" He pounded his cane on the floorboard. "Go."

I didn't move. "Dad, remember how we took a drive down to Pennington last spring like we always do? We went out to lunch. Remember?" By now I was squinting into the rearview mirror, wondering if I should back up. Then I thought of his extra set of keys and his determination to drive and changed my mind.

"Of course I remember," he huffed. "Do I look senile to you? I want to go down to Pennington. That's all. And I'm tired of you and Linda mother-henning me to death, telling me what I can and can't do, where I can and can't go. Now, drive."

I weighed my options. I could do what he said, or I could resist and have him fly into a rage, one that would only spike his blood pressure again. I checked the gas gauge—almost a full tank—and opted for the former, turned left, and headed to Pennington just over the South Carolina line.

For each of the five springs since my mother, of blessed memory, passed away, I would drive my dad over the North Carolina border to Pennington to have lunch in the old Pennington Mill building, now a fancy mall with shops that sold Italian leather handbags, designer dresses, and Jo Malone perfumes. He liked to get out, see the scenery, he said, and there was nothing in the world like a Carolina spring day.

All the way to Pennington, he would ask about the flowers and trees in bloom. That's an azalea, I'd tell him, a dogwood, a redbud.

"Your mother would have known," he always responded. He'd never really gotten over her death. Not that other people would know, because he was still a terrible flirt. Linda called him a babe magnet and said I wouldn't believe how all the old ladies in the retirement community were throwing themselves at him. Not so old either, some of them, and I should watch out.

On our annual spring pilgrimages to Pennington he would start regaling me with stories of the old days once we had crossed into South Carolina. How back then they had a circuit-riding rabbi and how they had to brown-bag their booze because it was a dry county. He'd tell me again how, when he got here, there was nothing but woods all the way from Charlotte to Pennington, nothing but kudzu and poison ivy. How Mo Blumberg convinced him to buy up land anyway. Not cotton fields or dairy pastures, he would say. "No, Solly," Mo had told him. "Buy all the poison ivy you can. They're practically giving it away. It'll be worth a fortune one day."

"Now look." My father would point to the large housing developments, brick homes resembling English manors, pillars in front of each subdivision with House of Windsor sounding names like Canterbury Woods, or Salisbury Plantation. "All this, nothing but kudzu and poison ivy." He would shake his head.

We'd end up at the Pennington Mill Bistro and Wine Bar for lunch, and every year my father would complain about the prices. Every year I'd hear how a club sandwich at the Rexall drugs on Main Street, which had been restored to its vintage glory a few years ago and now served ice cream sodas made with Häagen-Dazs, used to cost fifteen cents. He'd sip his iced tea and stare out of the twelve-foot multipaned windows, gaze through the trees to the Catawba River, and remind me again that back in the forties when the mill was running, these windows were so covered with lint that you couldn't see a thing out of them and how the noise of the knitting machines was deafening. He'd tell me again about the terrible working conditions and how when the union came in sometime in the fifties, old man Pennington had a stroke. "Now look," he would point to his sea bass garnished with a hibiscus flower. "Who would have ever believed it?"

But this trip was different. Once we got on the road, my father didn't seem to want to talk; he just gripped his cane between his knees and stared ahead. Every now and then he'd tell me to drive faster, to stop driving like an old lady. I ignored him, and he seemed to forget that I wasn't exactly zipping down the road, just stared ahead like he knew where he was going, like he had a job to do.

We reached the roundabout with the fancy fountain and the elaborate sign that let us know we were entering Pennington, South Carolina, a "Historic South Carolina Mill Town." I turned left on Main Street, slowed to the required fifteen miles an hour, and waited for my father's complaints about my driving. Only when we got to the Pennington Mill Shoppes and I started to pull in did my father speak up. "Keep going. I have to go to my office. It's three miles out of town on Old Catawba Bridge Road."

I glanced at the temperature gauge, which read ninety-two degrees. I had no more business driving my father into the middle of nowhere, the *yenevelt*, as Mo Blumberg would have called it, than I had flying to Jericho. "Dad do you have an address for this office?" I thought that would put a stop to this nonsense.

"Of course I have an address. It's on all my stationery. Solomon Meisner, attorney-at-law, 42 Old Catawba Bridge Road."

Stationery? I looked over at him. He didn't seem pale or sweaty, nothing out of the ordinary, so just to maintain the peace, I kept driving down Main Street, past the gentrified parts of town and into the country, all the while wondering what was wrong with me. Why was I being so protective of his pride at the expense of his heart? Maybe it was because I thought that was all he had left. I thought I was being kind, but I could be killing him. Meanwhile, the houses were getting shabbier by the minute. Where the hell were we?

"There it is," he shouted. "You passed it. Turn around. Go back."

I pulled into a red dirt driveway just as two dogs came barreling from the side of a trailer home, managed to back up before I hit one, and turned right on Old Catawba Bridge Road. About a half mile down the road, I got into addresses in the thirties, a few old mill houses, a new manufactured home. An abandoned mobile home was number forty, and next to it, in an ancient filling station, weeds growing up through the crumbling asphalt parking lot, was Garcia's Auto Repair. That was number forty-two, a place my father called his office, an old gas station from the year one. "That's it," my father shouted. "Over to the left."

Attached to the filling station, where my father was pointing, was some sort of studio or outbuilding, now a storage shed. I came to a stop and kept the car running, the AC blowing cool air. Before I knew it, he had unsnapped his seat belt, opened the door, and was walking toward the building like a much younger man, hardly using his cane at all. I could hear the sound of a Mexican radio station from the back of the shop, and a couple of men came around from the body of a truck they had up on a lift, stopped in their tracks, and stared at him. I hopped out of the car, calling, "Dad? Wait." He couldn't hear me. I started to run.

"*Camaradas,*" my father shouted to the men. "*Dónde está ella?*" He tipped his Panama hat and waved.

I reached my father just as he stepped up to the garage. By now the men were looking toward the back door and were possibly panicked.

I wanted to say, "Not immigration. Don't worry." But it should have been obvious to them that we were just one demented old man and his frazzled older daughter.

"*Mexicano*?" One of the men asked.

"*Mexicano*, no," I said. "He doesn't speak much Spanish, really. My father." I put my arm around my dad. "His office. Here. Many years ago." And then I repeated the words in Spanish.

They seemed to relax, smiled, and nodded. One of the men put down his rag and wrench and pulled out a folding chair from the garage. "Sir, you sit, please. You sit."

"*Dónde está ella*? What happened to her? Where has she gone?" My father kept demanding, pounding his cane on the asphalt.

The men looked at me. I shrugged and shook my head. "I don't know," I told them, because I didn't. I hadn't the faintest idea what he was talking about. I'd never even heard him speak Spanish before except when he lifted his five o'clock bourbon and said, "*Salud*."

Suddenly, I felt my father crumple under my arm like an empty sack. "Hospital? Near here? In Pennington?" I asked the men as I maneuvered my father into the chair before I ran to the car to grab a bottle of water.

He had taken off his hat, was staring into it, and when I got back, he wouldn't look up or take the bottle. It was a while before he straightened his shoulders, his eyes stunned, wounded. I didn't have words for what I saw in them. Then, it occurred to me. A faraway look. That's what people called it. Far away.

"They told me she was here. I thought I'd see her again," he said.

"Who, Dad? Who did you think you'd see again?"

One of the mechanics slipped me a piece of paper with the address of the hospital ER on it.

By then, my father had stopped talking and began to sip the water.

He looked around and handed the bottle back to me, seeming bewildered, lost. "Do you know where we are?" he asked.

The mechanic helped me get him up and walk him to the car, where I buckled him in. "We went to your old office, Dad, but it had changed so much you didn't recognize it." It seemed like the kindest thing to say.

I got in the car, looked over, and saw that he was asleep, but I waited to back up just to make sure he was breathing, to see his chest rise and fall as he did. Then I pulled away from Garcia's Auto Repair, much to their relief, I'm sure, and headed home, wondering all the way past the flowering crepe myrtle and under the shade of the looming, dense oaks who *she* was and if he would tell me or if I should ask. I decided we were all haunted by something in our lives and not to mention anything one way or the other. *Let the past stay in the past,* I told myself, but in the end, it didn't work out that way at all, did it?

3

Solly

Pennington, South Carolina
August 1941

"**G**et rid of it," Moses Blumberg told Solly, aiming his cigar at the pale yellow 1938 Pontiac Silver Streak convertible with red leather interior, Solly's pride and joy, the car he'd spent almost all his life savings on. "You look like you're flying around in Zeus's goddamn chariot." They were standing in the parking lot outside the Cardinal Club where they'd been playing poker, Solly flush with his winnings, enjoying the cooler night air, and listening to frogs. It's what amounted to nightlife in Pennington. "Get a Ford, Solly," Mo told him.

"I wouldn't buy a tin can from that Jew hater."

"You think he's the only one? The boys in the white hoods don't like it when Jews get too big for their britches down here. I've lived my whole life in South Carolina. I know the ropes. Trust me. Get a Ford." He puffed on his cigar and stared out at the kudzu-covered field next to the parking lot. "You want to show off? Go to the Catskills. Listen to me: no nice Jewish girl's father is going to let her parade around Pennington in that vehicle, calling attention to herself. It's too dangerous, Solly. And we do need to find you a nice girl, or so my wife tells me. Half of the ladies in Hadassah are talking about it." He patted Solly's cheek. "We don't want you to get lonely."

Too late for that, Solly thought, pushing his foot down hard on the accelerator a few minutes later, speeding down a one-lane road, top down, the longleaf pines whizzing by, a river of stars overhead. He should be driving Estelle to a beach hotel. Instead, well, instead, he wasn't.

Solly's rearview mirror filled with the unwelcome color of blue lights. "Oh, for Christ's sake." He pulled over and waited.

The copper took his time sauntering over to the car. "You have any idea how fast you was going?"

"Aren't you up past your bedtime, Officer?" Solly flashed a smile at the cop, no more than an eighteen-year-old kid, his blue uniform still too big for him. The officer wasn't amused.

"Get out of the car. I know who you are. Everyone knows who you and your friends are. We keep an eye on y'all over at the Cardinal Club. Know it's a high-stakes game. Must be nice to be able to play with money instead of having to earn it like the rest of us. Get out of the car. Give me your license."

Solly stood by the car, patted his pockets like he was looking for his wallet, pulled out a deck of cards, and fanned them in front of the cop. "Pick a card," he said. "Any card."

His joke hadn't gone over, but a five-dollar bill went a long way toward making amends. Back on the road, Solly reached for the radio dial, hoping for Sinatra singing "I'll Never Smile Again," not some twangy, hillbilly music, but no luck. *When in Rome,* Solly sighed, *or Pennington, as the case was, do as the local Johnny Rebs do.* The tune "Tears On My Pillow" and advertisements for Tube Rose Snuff would have to do. "Take Me Back to Tulsa." Solly whistled along with Bob

Wills as he turned on Old Catawba Bridge Road, but he stopped as soon as he saw the girl. Who was she? What was she doing there?

Then he remembered. She was the singer, a girl they called Alma, from the Cardinal Club, but what she was doing standing in front of his office door at this time of night, he had no idea. He thought about driving right by, afraid the cop had followed him, but changed his mind. It was too late. She'd seen him, and both he and she knew it wasn't safe for her, a Negro woman, or a colored girl as they would call her down here, to stand there in the dark very long, not in front of a white lawyer's office, not here in Pennington. He pulled into the lot, cut the engine, hit the lights, and lit a cigarette. He'd let her make the first move. When she didn't, Solly got out, walked to the road, and looked left and right. No copper. He went back to the car, leaned against the hood, and asked, "Are you lost? Do you need me to call someone?"

"One of those," she said, pointing to his cigarette. "That would be nice."

He hoped they weren't being watched. He gave her a cigarette, struck a match, and lit it. "What's this all about?"

Alma inhaled, blew smoke out the side of her mouth, looked at him, and said, "We've heard you do work for coloreds." She let that statement hang in the night air for a while, waiting for an answer.

Solly hadn't been in Pennington long enough to pick up all the nuances of Jim Crow, but from the little he'd seen and heard, he knew Alma was taking a risk. He was going to make a joke about the color of the money being green and how that was the only thing that mattered. But it wasn't, and this was probably no joking matter.

She set a basket of peaches on the hood. "Mr. Pearson, you know, the man who owns the Cardinal Club, right? He needs you to do some legal work for him. Nobody can know. It's in there, what he needs, under the peaches. If you say yes, just bring the basket round to the Penningtons, where I clean house." She started to walk away.

"Wait," Solly called after her. "Don't you need a ride?"

She didn't turn around. "Not with a white man, I don't, and not in a big yellow car like I'm in a parade."

Solly closed the door to his office, a cottage that doubled as his studio apartment, and set the basket down on the table. Feeling almost buried under the heavy scent of ripe peaches that filled the over-heated room, he pushed open all the windows that weren't swollen stuck with humidity, grabbed a bowl from the cabinet, and placed the too-soft fruit in the yellowed ceramic. Once the basket was empty, he saw the envelope. Walking back to the cabinet, he reached for the bourbon he kept behind the Wheaties and poured himself a couple of fingers. Then he sat down and read the letter.

Dear Mr. Meisner,

I am writing to request your services related to a legal matter. For reasons you may have discerned by now, as a Negro in the South I have but few resources at my disposal. I hope you may be able to advise me with your expertise and that you can assure me of your complete discretion.

Sincerely,

Robert B. Pearson

Professor of History

Solly had had no idea that Pearson, who owned the Cardinal Club, was a professor of anything, but it was the line about having few resources at his disposal in spite of being an educated man and a business owner that burned the back of his throat as much as the whiskey. Jesus. He'd thought being Jewish down here, anywhere, actually, was rough. He could still hear the young cop's sneering comment, "We know who you are." Well, try being a Negro in the South, as Mr. Pearson had put it. Solly took another swallow of bourbon and thought of all the signs that said "No Coloreds Allowed." So, sure, he knew what he would do. He took the glass to the sink, rinsing it while the frogs outside the screened window croaked. He'd use his expertise to help the professor. Complete discretion assured.

The next day, Solly took off during his lunch hour and drove up the winding drive to what was known as Pennington Manor, the stately home of B. D. Pennington. Standing on the front steps, the oh-so-familiar taste of envy rose in his throat, sour and hot. If he'd been one of Sherman's soldiers at that moment, he would have been the first to throw a torch to the roof. Envy, revenge—he knew in his gut that had been half the reason the *brigadistas* had been on the losing side in Spain. Every last one of the Republican peasants, out for revenge, killing and looting. Look where that had led.

His pops, born a peasant himself, had never felt bitter. Hell, the old man thought he was a king because he had two trees in his yard in America and he could swing up a hammock between them. Who cared what the goyim thought? That was his attitude. They were *ein andersh kesl*, a different kettle of fish. Solly, on the other hand, had been born in America, the land of restless strivers. He was always looking for the next frontier to cross. In this case, it seemed to be the Penningtons' doorstep.

Solly shielded his eyes and gazed over the broad lawn that swept downhill to a stand of weeping willows where glossy camellias stood out against the Georgian-style brick wall. Next to him, he could smell gardenias under the long, many-paned dining room windows. Nice life if you were born to it, which he wasn't. Well, he wasn't going to let that stop him. He pushed the brass doorbell next to the leaded side windows. The tones inside sounded like Caruso singing to a prima donna. Solly slouched against one of the windows. He wasn't standing at attention for anyone, least of all one of the Penningtons or their soon-to-be-wed starlet daughter. The wedding preparations had been on the front page of the Pennington Gazette for weeks. Who cared? He pushed the doorbell again and heard someone yell, "Alma, where the hell are you?"

And then there she was, Martha Ann Pennington in all her half-dressed glory, her silky nightgown clinging to all she was offering. She took a drag on a cigarette. "Yes?" she asked.

Solly slouched even more against the window and looked her up and down. "Late night?" he asked, looking at his watch and then pointing at the numbers: 12:30. "That's in the p.m., Miss Pennington."

"What's it to you?"

"Nothing. Absolutely nothing. I'm here to deliver this to Miss Collins." Solly lifted the basket.

"You mean the colored girl?"

"I mean Miss Collins, the talented young lady who sings at the Cardinal Club and whom you are fortunate enough to employ."

"Oh, I get it. I've been in Hollywood, you know. I know your type."

Solly straightened up and looked Miss Pennington in the eye. "And what type would that be? The Hebrew type?"

"No, the Bolshevik type." And with that she grabbed the basket and slammed the door.

Solly saw no point in waiting around to see if Miss Pennington remembered her manners. He lit a cigarette and headed down the walk to his car when the door opened again and someone called out, "Oh dear me, Mr. Meisner, isn't it? The new lawyer?" Solly turned to see a svelte and perfectly coiffed ash-blond with only a few crow's feet around her sparkling blue eyes. In her smooth, pale hands, studded with several dazzling rings, she held a bunch of gladioli and pruning shears. "Forgive my daughter. Prewedding jitters, you know. Would you mind giving something to Mr. Blumberg, your employer I believe?" She shut the door, and when she returned several minutes later, she was carrying a file of papers. "I'm sure he'll understand, but the architecture committee thinks y'all's church is just not going to fit in. It's back to the drawing board, as they say. We like to be accommodating, Mr. Meisner. We like to think of ourselves as very open-minded here in Pennington, you know, but up to a point. I'm sure you understand."

Solly reached for the file. "Sure thing. Mrs. . . ." He hesitated.

"Pennington," she said, raising herself up to her full five-foot-and-some-inches height. "Mrs. B. D. Pennington." And with that, like her daughter, she shut the door in his face.

Y'all's church. That was a good one. Solly chuckled all the way to the car, wondering if he should have corrected her, should have said synagogue, or if that was too big and foreign-sounding a word for her to handle. But the sight of the younger female member of the Pennington family in the passenger seat of his car, feet on the dashboard, stopped him in his tracks.

"I got dressed," she said, showing off tanned, shapely legs in a tennis outfit. "I need a ride to the club."

Miss Pennington could have walked, but Solly figured she would have gotten all sweaty. And that probably would not have done. Other than that, he had no idea why she wanted him to drive her to the club. "You're willing to risk your life with a Bolshevik?" he quipped.

"Some Bolshevik with this car. I'm supposed to meet Dray at the club, and I want to make him jealous, driving up in a flashy car with a dark, handsome stranger like some Rudolph Valentino."

"And I suppose Dray," he dragged out the name, "is your intended."

"Has been since we were babies in the cradle. Drayton Scott III. His family owns the low country. My people the up-country." She turned to face Solly. "It's the South, honey. Goes way back to the day of the *dreadful surrender*, as my grandfather called it. Families like mine and Dray's? We keep what we have for *our kind*. I'm just doing my little old bit to help the South rise again."

Solly started up the car. "Sort of like Ferdinand of Aragon and Isabella of Castile merging dynasties. You know the king and queen of Spain?"

"I'm not a complete idiot, Mr. Meisner. I spent a year at Sweet Briar."

"A whole year?"

"And then I got discovered, and the rest is . . . well, the rest is Hollywood, and we all know that isn't real. Nobody pays for real." She leaned her head back on the seat and closed her eyes, making Solly wonder what Hollywood had done to be so disappointing because, while her movie star story was every small-town girl's dream, she didn't seem too enthusiastic about any of it. On the other hand, given Miss Pennington's bleary-eyed state earlier, maybe that was just the way a hangover made everything, even Hollywood, feel in the bright light of day.

The Pennington Country Club wasn't far, and if Pennington Manor had been grand, the country club was an even grander Greek Revival mansion. On its front veranda, men, half-hidden behind massive Doric columns, relaxed in rockers with what looked like mint juleps.

A Negro doorman in a dashing and also sweltering red jacket rushed down the steps to open Miss Pennington's door. "Get Mr. Scott for me, will you?" she warbled, and off he went. Miss Pennington walked over to Solly's driver's side and leaned in a little too close, too suggestively. "I can't go in there without a male companion, Mr. Meisner, and you know what? That really burns my biscuits, but it suits Dray to a tee."

4

Solly

Pennington, South Carolina
August 1941

"I'm not a religious man, Mo. No shul, no davening." Solly shuffled the cards from a deck Mo had passed him. "Still, it doesn't seem right that Mrs. Pennington's architectural committee won't let you build your church, as she called it." Solly rolled his eyes. "Freedom of religion and all that."

Mo pointed to the file Solly had dropped on his desk. "You think we were going to build that monstrosity? Now that she's said no, showed us who holds the cards, so to speak," he waved the cards Solly had just dealt, "we'll show her the smaller version, and she'll say yes." He squinted at his cards and moved one to the left side of the hand he was holding. "Some fancy-schmancy modern architect my wife heard of who studied with that Frank Lloyd somebody or the other."

"What's modern about religion, Mo? I don't want any part of it," Solly said, pulling a card from the deck on top of Mo's desk and throwing another card down. "Saw enough religion in Spain to last a lifetime." He leaned back in his chair to catch the breeze from a fan perched on a file cabinet. It was the middle of August and Mo's office, the two-room headquarters of Blumberg Agricultural Freight Company, was hot enough to bake bagels.

"Stop, please, Mr. Karl Marx, with the opiate of the people. Tell Hitler you're not religious and see if he cares. No one is asking you to be religious. Just to come to Shabbos services. We need a minyan." Mo looked over his glasses. "Why'd you throw down the jack of spades? I was sure you were holding spades." Mo glanced at his cards. "I'm knocking with five." He pulled a pencil from behind his ear and wrote the score. "It's not all about you, Solly, about what you want." He reached for the bottle of Coca-Cola on his desk and waved it in Solly's direction before swilling half of it down. "Edelstein? He's religious. Berger? He's religious. Once a month, Rabbi Schoenfeld comes to Pennington, and for that, we need a minyan. That means ten men, so you're number ten."

One of the three phones on Mo's desk rang. He grabbed the handset and barked into the mouthpiece, "Where are you now?" Swiveling his chair to face a map of the Eastern Seaboard on the wall behind his desk, he pulled a pin from the bulletin board. "Richmond. Okay, find a place in the shade, wait a few hours, and then go to Pittsburgh. Call me tomorrow when you get there." He stuck the pin in the black letters that spelled Pittsburgh on the map and yelled through the open door to his secretary, "Eileen, honey, get Charlie at the A&P in Pittsburgh on the line. Tell him to call me."

"Helluva business, Solly. That trucker's got to get those peaches to the A&P by tomorrow morning or the fruit rots, and he's gotta drive at night so the temperatures are lower. Peach and tomato season is when I don't sleep at night." Mo took another swig of Coca-Cola, set the bottle on his desk, and walked to his secretary's office. "After you call Charlie, it's time to go, Eileen. It's too hot to work." He lumbered back to his desk, sagged in his chair, and reached for a handkerchief in his pants pocket. Swabbing the perspiration on his face, he held up a finger as if to say there was something he wanted to talk about but that Solly should wait.

Solly lifted a newspaper from a side table and fanned himself, the raspy sound of its pages and Eileen's heels clicking on the floor as she walked from her desk, the only sounds in the room beside the rattling desk fan. After Mo's secretary called out "Night y'all," and the door closed behind her, Solly set the newspaper down and asked, "Something you want to tell me? Something maybe Eileen shouldn't hear?"

Mo reached into his lower desk drawer, pulled out a manila folder, and took out a newspaper clipping. "Something I want you to read."

Solly glanced at the clipping. "It's an obituary, Mo. The guy, this Mr. Moore, killed himself. Terrible thing when a man wants to end his life." He handed the obituary back.

"He was a loan officer at the local bank. A friend of mine, a cotton merchant named Ezekiel Hurwitz, a nice family man, did business with him. Like you, Ezekiel tells me suicide is a terrible thing, but it's even worse when someone wants to maybe help you do it."

"What are you telling me, Mo?"

The older man stood, walked to the rack where his jacket hung, and lifted it off the hook. "Come on, enough already. We should go home too. You come to Shabbos at my house, you meet Mr. Hurwitz, you talk, and he tells you. He thought it was something I should know. Maybe it's something you should know too."

Solly figured he'd been cornered. He didn't want to let on that he was curious, maybe even concerned, about this loan officer's death. Why would Mo want him to know about it? All he said was, "I don't even own a kippah. Haven't put one on since my Bar Mitzvah."

Mo waved his hand, reached down, and pulled the plug on the fan. "The rabbi has a suitcase full, tallit, siddurim, the whole nine yards. Quit making excuses. Let me ask you this. What would your father want you to do? Your mother?"

Solly shrugged.

"That's what I thought." Mo slapped Solly on the back. "So, you'll come for Shabbos dinner with Rabbi Schoenfeld, and we'll see you on Saturday morning. It's a mitzvah. You'll do it. You can pray I don't beat you at gin the next time."

A day later, Solly found himself climbing the steps of Moses Blumberg's large bungalow on the banks of the Catawba River with a bouquet of flowers and a Whitman's Sampler of chocolates for Mo's wife Helen. "She'll be thrilled," Mo had grinned when Solly agreed to come, like he had much choice. "She'll be calling around to see what pretty girl is home, one who wouldn't mind sitting next to you at the table."

It was just dinner after all, Solly had reasoned, and his weekends weren't all that exciting around here anyway. "Tell her I'm not looking for a girlfriend, Mo. You know that. I'm not available."

Now standing on the porch, the setting sun a fiery, red globe over the green, murky river, he felt how far away he was from the sunsets in Spain, his glory days fighting the good fight, far from Estelle wherever she was, if she even was. What had Mo said? "Every young man your age is available, so this mystery woman? Until I see her, she doesn't exist. Anyway, that's the past. Cleveland, Spain, or somewhere. *Yehupetzville*, for all I know. You can't hold on to the past forever."

Ah, but he could, Solly knew, or he should. He owed Estelle that, he reminded himself as he squared his shoulders and pushed the doorbell.

From inside the house, he heard shouts and footsteps, and soon Helen Blumberg, in a pretty cotton dress, appeared, her hair curled and rose-scented with Bandoline just like his mother's when she came home from the beauty parlor. "Darling Solly, *Gut Shabbos*." She hugged him. "The men are having a schnapps on the porch."

Taking the flowers and the chocolates, she led him to the back of the house. "Look, Mo, flowers and chocolates. You have competition. Such a good son." She patted Solly's cheek like she could be his long-lost *bubbe*. "Your mother would be proud."

Helen turned and floated back into the kitchen, leaving Solly with Mo and the rabbi. And someone else. Sitting in a wicker chair by the screen door was a woman, a stunning-looking woman, as a matter of fact, with long black hair—a pageboy he remembered his mother calling that hairstyle—and bright-red lipstick that only drew more attention to the little mole on the right side of her upper lip. She crossed her shapely dark legs, lifted her highball glass, and mouthed the words *gut Shabbos*.

"Solly, this is Grace Weintraub, my niece from California." Mo waved at the bar cart and said, "Pick your poison. Scotch, bourbon, gin. The rabbi and I are going to my study and let you two young people get to know each other."

"We've been ambushed, I'm afraid," Grace said once Mo and the rabbi left, her voice deeper than Solly had expected. She swirled the bourbon around in her glass, making the ice cubes clink, and stared into the bottom before taking a sip.

"So, what's California like?" Solly walked over to the bar cart and poured a couple of fingers of bourbon into a glass, no ice. He needed it straight, and he needed it to hit fast.

"Sunny." She looked up from her drink.

"That's what they tell me." He sounded like an idiot. Why the hell was he nervous? Something about her eyes, almost as black as her hair. She was staring right through him.

"Uncle Mo's been bragging about you. Says you have a *yiddishe kopf*. I guess that means you win all your cases."

"Better than that. We don't even have to go to court. They settle."

"He didn't tell me you were so modest."

"I'm not. I'm a lawyer. What do you do in California?"

"I'm with the industry. Hollywood."

"That makes sense. You don't look like a longshoreman. Actress?"

She handed Solly her glass. "Fix me another, will you. One finger and one ice cube."

Solly took the glass and poured himself another while he was at it. "L'chaim." He clinked her glass, then took a swig out of his own.

"No, not an actress. Not unless you count the role I'll be playing this week." She turned and looked over her left shoulder, staring at the pinewoods just past the screened porch. "Bridesmaid. The Pennington wedding."

"I didn't know they let the members of our tribe inside the Pennington Presbyterian church." The whole caste system down here was starting to rub him the wrong way. Places white Christians could go, places Negroes could go, places Jews could go. And no one really rocking the boat. Even Mo acting like this was just the way of the world.

"The studio didn't give her a choice." Grace stopped his train of thought with her throaty voice. "Martha Ann tends to be unpredictable. My job, since Miss Pennington 'trusts me like a sister'"—Grace made air quotes with her red-tipped nails—"is to make sure that the movie magazines see only a blushing bride and a groom who isn't too drunk to cut the cake. That sort of thing." Grace turned from the woods, leaned over, and looked toward the dining room where the rabbi was standing at the table and pointing to his watch. "It's almost time," she said. "Sundown. We should join them."

Solly stood and motioned for Grace to go before him. "So that's what you do? Babysit movie stars?"

Grace stood, walked a few steps, turned back, and glared. "No, I'm a writer."

"You write movies?"

"Does that surprise you? That's why Martha Ann Pennington trusts me like a sister, if you get my drift. I have more power than you might imagine."

"I didn't mean to be insulting. I don't know anything about Hollywood. The industry."

"Obviously. And no, I don't write the movies. I fix the junk other people write for the movies."

Solly stopped. "Junk?"

"Do I sound too arrogant to be ladylike? Believe me, Solly, there was a much less ladylike word I could have used, but it's not my style."

Solly watched as she turned and walked into the dining room, but then she stopped, pivoted, and faced him. "I know a little about you, Mr. Lawyer. You were some kind of hero in Spain, weren't you? Radio operator, right?"

"How do you know that? I never told Mo what I did."

"It's Hollywood. Well, my kind of Hollywood. After a few drinks, that's all they talk about. Spain. Hemingway. What it was like in the Hotel Florida. I called a few friends. You're famous, you know."

"Really?" Solly rolled his eyes. "It was another time, another place." He pointed to the dining room and saw all the expectant faces beaming happily, thinking they'd made a match. Helen was ready to light the Sabbath candles and say the *b'rucha*. "Can't be a minute too late. The rabbi's here."

Solly knew the drill. After Helen said the prayer to the "King of the universe, Who has sanctified us with His commandments," Mo would bless the wine and the challah, and the rabbi would stand in the flickering light of the candles to chant the "Lekha Dodi." "Come, my beloved, to meet the bride; let us welcome the Sabbath."

He tried not to let it affect him, but whether he liked it or not, he was tied to all this: the polished silver Kiddush cup, the braided loaf of bread, and, yes, all the Jews dying—if what they were starting to hear was true—because they were different and practiced these handed-down-through-the-ages rituals.

"Sit, sit." Mo patted him on the back and pulled out a chair next to Grace.

So tonight maybe Solly should just forget what an outsider he was, how they were all outsiders and had been for centuries. It would never change, and for one minute he should just enjoy what life offered him: the borscht, the cold salmon, and the company of a beautiful girl.

Solly didn't see Grace again until the day of Martha Ann Pennington's wedding. He'd been sitting in the shady park across the street from the church with his drugstore bag lunch and his camera, the statue of some dead Confederate soldier looming over him. His mother would appreciate a few pictures of the local swells, the bride in her fancy gown, the bridesmaids, maybe even a minor movie star or two. From the crowd gathering in the park, you would have thought it was the coronation of King George VI.

For the past hour, the Caddys and Lincolns had been arriving, bearing their passengers all the way from Charlotte, across the state line, where he'd heard the Penningtons had commandeered the Barringer Hotel for the wedding guests and where the reception was to take place.

He'd finished his egg salad sandwich and was throwing the bag away when the church bells began to ring. The crowd rushed to the sidewalk to get a better view of the newly married Mrs. Drayton Scott as she emerged in her finery.

The studio had stationed a bunch of reporters in front of the church, with even two men shooting film. Solly jogged across the street and inserted himself in the press corps. Martha Ann Pennington was a beautiful bride, but just as beautiful was Grace Weintraub in her pink gown and picture hat. Mrs. Pennington kept scanning the bridal party with the expression of a general about to issue orders on a battlefield, and the men in their formal attire all looked like versions of the Prince of Wales, just bigger, blonder, American. He even got a picture of the state senator, Clay Wright, one of those America First Committee boys, and his friends who were huddling around him, which soured Solly on the whole lot and reminded him of the story Zeke Hurwitz had told him over coffee and poppy seed cake after shul about the senator and Drayton Scott, the banker's son. The bunch of them made him think of Lindbergh, the darker side of those corn-fed American men. Still, he hung around long enough to see the rice thrown and to watch Grace climb into a Cadillac LaSalle and head out to the reception before he wandered back to his car and drove without the top down or the Motorola on toward his rented rooms, wondering what the hell he was doing with his life. *You were some kind of hero*, Grace had said. She didn't know about the basement near the Parque del Buen Retiro, how he'd been told it was safe, had it on good authority that Franco himself had promised not to bomb those villas. The Distrito Salamanca was filled with Falangists, whole blocks of them.

Work would keep him busy and dull his bad memories, he figured as he pulled up to his cottage office next to the gas station. He'd throw himself into it. Once inside, he put on the coffee pot and waited to hear it percolate, and when it did, he poured a big cup just to keep himself going.

First, there was the question of Mr. Pearson's will, the legal work Pearson had asked him to look into. Pretty much boilerplate stuff. Pearson had a wife, one son, some real property, quite a bit actually, and even more surprising, an impressive little stock portfolio, equity he bought at rock-bottom prices in the thirties. No wonder he didn't want some white lawyer knowing that around these parts. A colored man could get lynched if that got around and it rubbed some white boys the wrong way. Next, there was a shipment of some sheet metal, odd lots Mo had bought that had never been delivered. It never ceased to amaze Solly what people thought they could get away with. Finally, there was Hurwitz's lawsuit, something Solly looked forward to digging his teeth into. He'd promised Mo he'd do it as a favor. It would be Mo's payback to Hurwitz for the information about a shady bank.

He set a stack of blank paper next to his Remington typewriter, which took up half the kitchen table, rolled one sheet in, and began drafting a letter, threatening to sue Middleton Cotton Processers for attempting to sell Ezekiel Hurwitz, a local cotton broker, shoddy goods. They might have gotten away with it had Zeke not taken his family to the beach for the week while the shipment sat there in the heat. Eventually, he'd gotten a phone call from the train station, saying that he'd been shipped a carload of cotton that was leaking water all over the tracks.

Some Johnny Reb at Middleton Cotton Processors had decided that since they were getting paid by the pound, he'd add water to the middle bales. More water, more weight, more money, or so he must have thought. Solly looked up from his typewriter and pictured all those blond groomsmen and the state senator and his friends yukking it up at the Pennington wedding. It could have been a meeting of the American Bund, and for all Solly knew, one of them might have even been from Middleton Cotton, thinking he'd pulled a fast one on the Jew with the funny accent.

Tomorrow morning, he would discover otherwise. Solly would give Middleton's counsel a choice. His clients were crooks, stupid, or both, and he was sure the judge would agree. On the other hand, Middleton Cotton Processors could forgo court and compensate Mr. Hurwitz adequately for the now mildewed, unsellable cotton, as well as for the rental fee on his beach house plus a few other things since his family vacation had been unfortunately brought to a halt due to their malfeasance. His client, Mr. Hurwitz, would hold no grudge and just chalk it up to a mistake. Let bygones be bygones.

Solly wasn't exactly shooting down Luftwaffe bombers, but it was something.

It was something, too, that story Zeke had told him Saturday morning after Shabbos services at Mo's about Mr. Moore, the bank loan officer who'd committed suicide. "He had a drinking problem," Zeke had whispered as if the dead could hear. "Okay," Zeke had added. "He had a gambling problem too. Bad combination. Sometimes he came to me for money to cover his debts. Sometimes he slept in his office on the sofa if his wife locked him out."

Turned out one night when Moore was sleeping it off, he heard some commotion. Drayton Scott and another man, plus none other than the state senator, were opening the brass doors to the safe deposit boxes.

Since Moore was trying to lie low, literally, he got off the sofa and crouched on the floor. He couldn't see anything, but he heard enough, and he recognized Scott's and the senator's voices. According to what Moore told Zeke, Drayton had said, "Damn, these things are heavy."

The senator told him to pipe down, and then the other man said to hurry up. Only not really hurry up. He'd said, "You now make it fast, *schnell.*" The other man was German.

"You sure of that?" Solly had asked Hurwitz. "How could Moore know?"

"So maybe he was Swiss," Hurwitz had shrugged. "Except South Carolina State Bank is not exactly the place for a Swiss banker to store gold bars or whatever they were, so the best guess is German. And then, Moore turns up dead in the woods. Killed himself with a hunting rifle. Except he didn't hunt, and how can a man even do that? But what do I know about guns? Anyway. I thought Mo should know. Maybe stop banking there if there was some funny business with Germans."

Funny business with Germans. Solly didn't know whether to laugh or cry. Nothing was funny about business with the Germans, he thought, staring out the window toward some corn fields, bright green in the evening light. He leaned back in his chair, stretched his arms behind his back, and closed his eyes, and when he opened them, he blinked hard. There was Grace Weintraub, still in her pink, flouncy gown, standing at the screen door, holding a covered dish in one hand and a bottle of champagne in the other.

He didn't move for a while. "I think your fairy godmother gave you the wrong address, Cinderella. They're holding the ball a few miles down the road."

"I heard differently. Heard you had a radio and that Saturday night was sacred to you. Your night to listen to Toscanini on NBC." She walked in, set the dish on the table, and handed him the champagne bottle. "It'll be very romantic."

Solly held up his hand to stop her. "I'm not available. Just so you know."

"Neither am I, just so you know. Although I could maybe be persuaded by the right guy. You're checking all my mother's boxes— Jewish, lawyer. But then," she said, laughing and nodding at the champagne, "I'm not my mother. Anyway, I meant romantic as in not baroque, not classical. Toscanini is conducting Brahms's Violin Concerto in D Major Opus 77 tonight. Why don't you pop the cork? Let's just enjoy Western civilization while it lasts."

Four days had gone by since Solly had spent the evening sipping champagne and listening to music with Mo Blumberg's niece, and he still found himself thinking about her. In spite of himself and his loyalty to Estelle, he'd been drawn to Grace's good looks—he was human, right? Her chutzpah, her education—she sure knew her music—they didn't hurt, either. Even now, as he stood in Mr., no Dr. Pearson's office, staring out the window over a lush green quad, he was imagining Grace in California, palm trees, sunshine, typing away in her office, fixing the junk other people wrote, as she'd said.

The quad outside the window, thousands of miles away from Grace, from Estelle, too, was studded with magnolia trees. What else had Solly expected? To tell the truth, he had no idea what he'd expected. A Negro college in the South? Certainly not something this bucolic, this ivy-covered, this quiet and peaceful. If Solly had wanted to escape his past, escape the war in Spain—and he did—he'd accomplished that much at least.

The window was opened as far as it would go, and Solly heard birds squabbling, leaves rattling on the large willow oak outside, Pearson having excused himself to attend to a pressing matter. Behind him a desk fan hummed, pulling in even more soggy heat from the August afternoon. Other than that, the campus was quiet, as no students had arrived. What had Pearson said most of them were studying?

The girls planned to go into teaching, the boys into medicine or the ministry. Options, as Pearson had told him, were limited.

Dr. Pearson sure had been something of a surprise. Until a few days ago, Solly had spent no time thinking about the owner of the Cardinal Club and had not once wondered how Pearson had come to be one of the proprietors or why. He had not given the colored man one moment's thought, other than to be courteous, circumspect, and careful not to bring unwanted attention to his establishment. That bothered Solly now, how invisible Pearson had been to him, that he had looked right past a fellow human being as if he didn't really matter. It was a pretty crappy thing to do.

This sudden meeting with Pearson in his book-lined office had been one of the more unexpected encounters he'd had since his arrival in Pennington, and even the drive out here was an eye-opener, a window on how Negroes lived in the South eighty-plus years after the Civil War. Their houses could still be slave quarters. Looking at them, he'd shuddered, chilled even in the summer heat by their poverty.

Solly had followed Pearson's directions to get to the college, driving down an overgrown, badly paved country road past tar paper shacks to the left and right, red dirt front yards, sometimes an old, colored man sitting on the stoop, sometimes a dead tree covered with hanging bottles. Suddenly, in the midst of these ramshackle dwellings and kudzu-covered pines, a narrow, manicured lawn appeared, carved out of this near jungle and bordered by a hedge of azaleas and low-growing flowers.

A plaque on one of the brick walls that supported a wrought iron gate read James B. Morehead University. Though he doubted that any self-appointed Klan member with nothing better to do with his time had followed him, Solly glanced in the rearview mirror just to make sure before turning up the drive to the college. It wasn't technically illegal for a white man to discuss business, as it were, with a member of the Negro race, but what Mo had told him when he brought race laws up was, "Legal schmegal." You had to be careful. He hoped he had been.

The professor's office was more elegant than anything his professors in Ohio had inhabited. There were two club chairs in front of the bookcases, a low tea table, and a mahogany desk with two upholstered desk chairs for student conferences. He'd never set foot in the Ivy League schools. The quotas limiting Jews had put the kibosh on those aspirations, but this office had to be just as elegant as anything at Yale.

Solly lifted his cup from the tea table, part of the tea service a secretary had brought in, sat down on one of the club chairs, and nibbled a slice of Dr. Pearson's wife's lemon pound cake, all the while running through what Pearson had told him about his biography, how he'd ended up here.

Pearson's father had been the wealthy publisher of a widely circulated Negro newspaper called the *Directory*. Its distribution network turned out to be members of the Pullman Porter's Union who spread the newspaper far and wide on colored sections of trains. Pretty clever how they'd turned segregation into an advantage, Solly thought. The *Directory* journalists could write whatever they wanted and no white person would be the wiser. With his inheritance, Pearson had invested in the Cardinal Club; his partners were the waiters and the chef at Pennington Country Club. In short, the ones who really knew how to run the business. Mo Blumberg had also invested, Solly had been told, and had been a white, albeit Jewish, face to present to the bank. That way nothing would call attention to the Negro primary owners—Pearson and the waiters. Hence, the card-playing privileges.

Solly wondered if Pennington's white residents had any idea what was going on in the shadows around them, shadows their own blinding arrogance prevented them from seeing, which was all just as well.

Solly turned in his chair and glanced at the bookcase—Aeschylus, Euripides, the Greeks, Homer, you name it. What had Pearson told him about why he'd settled here, besides the fact that his wife couldn't stand the cold? Oh yes. He'd said something about the North not being much more of a welcoming environment for Negroes than the South. And the weather was terrible. The difference between Northern whites and Southern whites, Pearson had told him, was this: Northern whites didn't care how high up the Negroes got as long as they didn't get too close. Down South it was the opposite. White folks didn't care how close you got as long as you didn't get too high up. Clearly, a former freed slaves' school and a shabby juke joint didn't count as high up. Therefore, the secrecy surrounding his estate had to be maintained at all costs. Did Mr. Meisner understand that?

Solly started turning something around in his head. If an educated Negro professor like Dr. Pearson could make a life here, could he, an outsider, a Yankee, and, even worse, a Jew, do the same? Up until this moment, he'd just been running away, from Spain, from Estelle's disappearance—he couldn't call it her death. Not yet, at least. He would just call it her absence.

Cleveland held no pull for him. He could relocate his parents here to warmer climes, and New York, where he'd assumed he would go eventually, was, as Pearson had said, too cold. Not that Solly had any intention of growing tropical plants, but being as far from Spain as he could possibly get seemed like a good thing. Maybe he should keep himself far away.

The door opened, and Solly, expecting to see Dr. Pearson returning to notarize the documents, was brought up short when a white man, slightly built, sporting a clipped mustache and equally short hair, walked toward him, extending his hand.

"Hello, Mr. Meisner," he said. "I'm John Smith. May I join you? Smith didn't wait for an answer. He removed his seersucker jacket and draped it over Pearson's chair, set his briefcase on the desk, snapped open the clasp, and pulled out two blue manila folders. "Professor Pearson has kindly lent me his office. I'm with the COI, Office of the Coordinator of Information. You won't have heard of us, I'm afraid. We just set up shop about a month ago under Roosevelt's handpicked man, Bill Donovan, 'Wild Bill' Donovan." Smith chuckled at his inside joke. "The President thought we needed, or will most certainly need in the future, something like the Brits' MI6 and their SOE. Wild Bill is the man to do it, and so here we are. Ready to get to work. Let's talk, shall we, Mr. Meisner?"

"Where's Pearson? I didn't sign up to work for Roosevelt, just Pearson."

"And that's just the problem, don't you see Mr. Meisner? Your reluctance, shall we say, to serve your country."

Solly glanced over at the closed door, and the same suffocating feeling he always got in closed spaces descended on him, making him want to run. He stood, heart fluttering, the three long steps to the door a race against nausea, a sensation that only slightly abated when the doorknob turned in his hand and he could step into the hall toward freedom. "If you see Pearson," he said over his shoulder. "Tell him to arrange another time to notarize the documents. Unless he was just blowing smoke, if you know what I mean?"

Mr. Smith lifted one of the folders and waved it at Solly. "I wouldn't leave just yet, Mr. Meisner. Not a good idea at all. Claustrophobia is it?" He flipped through the pages in the folder. "At least that's what your father told one of Hoover's boys when they interviewed him."

Solly turned back to face Smith. "What the hell are you talking about?"

Smith motioned for Solly to sit, "You see Hoover has quite a bit of information on you," he said, waving the blue FBI folder. "We could say he's very, very interested in your comings and goings. You might want to take a look." Smith flipped open the folder and looked down. "Right. So, you joined the Communist Party in 1936. Is old J. Edgar right about that? Because if he is, you might be getting a call from his outfit, or Mr. B. D. Pennington—his nibs, himself—might be getting one just as your father did." Smith raised his head from the pages and looked up at Solly like a man who knew he was holding all the cards. "Apparently, your father says claustrophobia saved your life in a bombing in Madrid. You might want to take a look-see at what else is in here."

Rage rose up in Solly, quickly replacing the nausea he'd felt, rage at the thought of his father being interviewed by government goons, at the terror that interview would have created for him, an elderly Jew, a man who'd kept his head down all his life, modesty his only means of survival in a world full of anti-Semites. He was a man who never really trusted that America's invitation to the world's tired, hungry, and poor was meant to include Jews on a permanent basis, even if Emma Lazarus, a Jew herself, wrote the damn poem. When had anything ever been permanent? From Spain to Syria, Amsterdam to England, Germany and Poland, where had Jews ever been safe? Now, with the FBI coming to the house? Solly clenched his fists, keeping them at his side so he didn't punch Smith in the face.

When Solly had finally calmed down enough to unclench his fists and take the folder Smith extended to him, he sank down in the club chair and stared at the FBI seal and his name written in black ink below the seal in large letters: Meisner, Solly. Opening the dossier, he saw that his passport photos filled half a page, followed by a typed description of his attendance at an anti-lynching rally where Eleanor Roosevelt spoke, a write-up about a meeting he had organized with the Socialist Scott Nearing, a sentence noting that Solly was a registered Democrat. He knew that if he went further, he would soon read about pamphlets he created against Father Coughlin, about meetings he organized in support of the Republican government in Spain, and finally his joining the Communist Party, a requirement to sign up with the Abraham Lincoln Brigade. "This is what taxpayer money is going for?" he glared at Smith.

"Just turn the page, Mr. Meisner, please."

And that was the shock. The past knocking him low with the force of a blast.

They were all there, all his dead comrades, alive once again in this picture, passing a bottle around. Solly could still hear their hopeful voices singing "Ay Carmela," hear the bombs that killed them in the raid he'd managed to escape. He passed his hands over his face, closed his eyes, tried to focus on the sound of the birds chirping outside, the rustle of leaves, tried to feel a bit of the breeze from the inadequate fan. He was here in South Carolina, not in Spain.

"That's the past, dead and buried." Solly handed the dossier back to Smith.

"Well, the past has a way of rising up from the grave, doesn't it? I'd carry on reading if I were you." He pushed the dossier back across Pearson's desk.

Solly turned the heavy pages, noting that the file was typed on expensive bond paper, nothing too shabby for Hoover's FBI, he supposed. "You want to tell me why the agency isn't investigating Coughlin or those goons in the American Bund?" Smith said nothing.

More trivial information about Solly followed, the ship he sailed to Lisbon, the train he took to Barcelona. And then the file got closer to the heart of the matter, closer to Solly's heart, as well. He turned another page and stared at another picture, this time of Solly with Phillips, or Eton, as they called him, the British *brigadista* with the posh accent and the upper-class pedigree, the two of them sitting at a table in an outdoor café in Barcelona with Orwell. Solly remembered that afternoon like it was yesterday, how sophisticated he'd felt as Solly Meisner from Cleveland dining with a famous writer and a member of the British aristocracy. That was when Spain was still glamorous and exciting and not a bloody disaster. He turned the page, hoping the nostalgia would pass. It did. In its place a stab of heartbreak tore into his chest. He could barely breathe.

Estelle.

Her picture, her blond hair backlit by the sun as if it were a gold orb and she a goddess.

He'd met her at a party at Eton's Las Ramblas apartment in Barcelona. It had been a warm June evening, and the plane trees were in bloom, their lemony smell wafting in from the terrace's open doors. The large salon was filled with laughter, young men and women in high spirits as the gin and conversation flowed. A stylish crowd from the International Brigades hovered around Estelle like bees in a flower garden. Needless to say, he had been surprised— okay, flattered—when she came out to the terrace where he'd been smoking and asked for a cigarette. It was only after she choked trying to inhale that she admitted she only used the cigarette as a pretext. She'd wanted to meet him.

Estelle, tall, elegant, the proverbial English rose, had taken his breath away at that moment, but he rallied, leaned back on the railing, trying to mimic Cary Grant in some romantic movie, and said, "You've met me. Now what?" Remembering that moment now, he realized he'd probably sounded like a jerk, not like Cary Grant at all, but she hadn't seemed to mind, hadn't laughed in his face.

He could see all this as if it were happening once again right here and now, how she raised her martini glass in salute before she turned, leaned on the wrought iron railing, and looked at the demonstrators below. It was 1937 Spain and there were always demonstrators. "Las Ramblas," she'd sighed. "Lorca said it was the only street in the world he wished would never end." She'd straightened up, looked him in the eye, and said, "We're young, there's a war going on. Considering all that, I think we should make the most of whatever time we have left, don't you?"

"And what does making the most of the time we have left look like to you?" Solly took her martini glass and sipped, not sure he was ready for an answer. He was still a virgin. Clearly, this woman was not.

"Well," Estelle drawled the words, "I suppose we should fall in love. What else is there? And, to me, falling in love looks a bit like this." She took his cigarette, crushed it on the balcony with her shoe, and kissed him. When they finally stopped she said, "Now that we've settled that, I should probably know your name don't you think?"

After that day, they'd been inseparable, until the night of the bombing, until he never saw her again. He'd left messages everywhere and had even bought her ship's passage to the States, but he'd heard nothing. She was the woman he'd left behind in the rubble of Madrid.

That is, she was until today, where in this sweltering office, with the drone of the desk fan whirring in his ears, she had returned, in the form of a recent photograph, very much alive and hanging on to Eton's arm as they stood on the steps of a German consulate somewhere tropical. And with them? A Nazi officer, grinning like a jackal.

"What do you know about these people?" Smith asked.

Solly reached into his shirt pocket for his cigarettes, anything to take his attention away from the fact that he wanted to weep or ram his fist into a wall. Walking to the open window, he fiddled with the cigarette before striking a match and blowing smoke between the slats in the blinds, all the while keeping his back to Smith, trying to hold himself together.

"Nothing, apparently," Solly responded to Smith's question in as few words as possible. Still, it was the truth, wasn't it? A truer answer than the recruiter seemed willing to believe.

"The time for dithering about has passed, Mr. Meisner. We need whatever information you can give us."

Mr. Smith may have wanted more, but it looked like Solly didn't know his friend Eton, his *camarada*, at all, did he? So there wasn't much he could tell him except that he'd been a fool. As it turned out, he didn't know his lover Estelle either, because here she was, the woman of his dreams, on the steps of the German consulate in— where did Smith say?—Mérida, Mexico, that was it, looking like she didn't have a care in the world.

"I'm sure you thought these people were probably dead and buried, as so many were. Am I correct?" Smith prodded.

Solly said nothing. The room spun around him.

"That bombing raid you escaped? Ever wonder how they knew to hit that mansion? Hadn't Franco said he wouldn't bomb that district, so you thought you were safe? That was why you were there, we've been told."

Solly straightened up, knowing where this was going. How *had* Solly managed to escape? Had he known all along and passed the information to the right person in exchange for favors? Of course he hadn't. But who had? "Your point is, Mr. Smith?"

"Yes, let's get to the point. We can agree on that."

"Let's." Solly shrugged. He'd been running, haunted by the demons of Spain, and all the while it turned out the ghosts that had haunted him weren't even dead.

"Mr. Meisner, the COI could use your help. And here's what we're prepared to offer in exchange. Donovan can make this FBI dossier with your communist past disappear. How does that sound to you? The alternative is Hoover puts you on the Alien Enemy Control list with the other commies, and your life will be a living hell. Looks like an easy decision to me."

Solly said nothing, and except for a door slamming down the hall and the sound of the fan, the room was silent as a tomb. Finally, Mr. Smith spoke. "You go to Mexico, find out about these people, and you'll be a free man, Mr. Meisner."

Smith rattled on, the words whirling around Solly like the rotating fan on Pearson's desk. Eton wasn't a communist *brigadista* at all. He was a Falangist spy in Spain and now a Nazi-sympathizing fifth columnist high up in the British foreign service, working as a German agent in Mexico. And Estelle? A voluntary agent of the Reich. In fact, she may have sent the bomber meant to kill him. Maybe she had been the one to pass the information. The documents didn't say, but Solly had told her where he'd be, hadn't he? Estelle, and possibly Eton, because maybe she had told him about his work in radio communications, about the hideout. Or maybe they had known all along.

Solly tried to snap out of it, tried to focus on what Smith was saying. Estelle and Eton, one or both of them, tried to kill him in Spain. He might want to find out. The recruiter repeated what he'd just said, "They failed last time. They might try again. Is that a risk you're willing to take?"

Solly refused to believe any of this, certainly not about Estelle.

Not that he would say that to this Smith fellow, and he didn't care about what Hoover had on him; getting answers about Estelle and Spain would be worth any risk. And if she were a Nazi spy, after all? At least he'd know the truth.

"Where'd you come up with the name Smith? Not very original, is it?" Solly tried a clever riposte, buying time, but Smith said nothing, his face impassive. "Okay, another question. Do I have a choice?"

"Not really. I hear Hoover's putting together a little blacklist. Wants to have a few show trials. So, if I were you, I'd take our offer. You're the right man in the right place. Lucky for both of us I'd say. We just lost our last operative."

"How?" Solly asked, already guessing the answer.

"Wrong man in the wrong place, I'm afraid. Murdered it would seem."

So that was the real offer. He'd be a free man. Or a dead one. Whichever came first.

5
Solly

Havana, Cuba
August 1941

Don't turn around. It's bad luck. The roulette wheel had stopped spinning, but the threat of being jinxed swirled around Solly in the glittering, smoky air. He'd hedged his bets right, won on the reds, lost on the blacks, and proved to whoever was behind him that he was a savvy gambler. Or so he'd thought until he defied the order, turned around, and found himself face to face with none other than Martha Ann Pennington, now Mrs. Drayton Scott. At that moment, all bets were off.

She embraced him, cooing, "Well, Solly Meisner, aren't you a sight for sore eyes," kissed his cheek, and whispered, "I'm your contact. You can lift your jaw off the floor now."

This was either some kind of joke or an FBI trap set for him by the natty Mr. Smith, or possibly both. Solly scanned the hall to see if any of Hoover's goons were lurking around the doors in case he decided to bolt.

"Surprised to see me?" she drawled, taking his arm and leading him across the crowded casino floor to the cashier. "Do you know, Mr. Meisner, that if you add all the numbers on a roulette wheel you will come up with 666?"

"Excuse me?" Solly stopped, pulling his arm away. "Aren't you supposed to be on your honeymoon, Mrs. Scott?"

She took his arm again, still chattering like a debutante. "And that the numbers 666 are known as the Number of the Beast. That's from the book of Revelation. Something you might not be familiar with. Please don't make a scene. The car is waiting. Cash in your chips, and we'll go like any normal couple."

Solly leaned against the cashier's grille and pushed his chips through the opening. "Ah, but we aren't a normal couple. This is something of a surprise." The cashier pushed some bills Solly's way. He counted them out, put them in his wallet, and turned to Martha Ann Pennington. "You want to tell me what's going on here?"

She took his arm again, leading him away from the cashier, this time to the large brass-embellished exit doors, and continued her chatter. "Now, some gamblers will tell you that the number 666 is code for the Roman emperor Nero, but others say that triple sixes are the numbers used to signify the Antichrist. In your line of work, I imagine that numbers will come in handy." She paused, waiting for him to open the door for her. Once they were in the foyer she looked around to make certain no one was near. "We'll get in the car that's waiting under the portico. Your things will be delivered to the boat. Just make small talk or no talk at all. Who knows whether we can trust the driver."

Solly stared out the window as the driver pulled out of the Hotel Nacional's long drive and headed north to the Malecón, swerving west, past the dark sea, its foam-topped waves rolling onto the shore. The newly married Mrs. Drayton Scott lit a cigarette, rolled down the window, and turned to look at the pastel buildings lining the shore as warm, tropical air blew past them. As they drove toward the elaborate mansions of Miramar, huge palms fanning out overhead, she stubbed her cigarette out in the ashtray and pointed to the German Embassy as they whizzed by. "Dray's in there," she said. "Some dinner for Americans. Germans trying to butter us up."

"Fraternizing with the enemy?"

"He says they're not the enemy yet, and maybe they won't be."

Not your enemy, Solly wanted to say and then thought better of it. Why bother? He doubted German food and song would keep the war at bay, but what did he know? He'd thought the Lincoln Brigade could win in Spain, that he could help them. And now, here he was, officially a spy, cruising to an uncertain assignation with a B-list movie star by his side. The world was a crazy place.

The driver turned into the circular drive of the Havana Yacht Club, drove under the portico, and jostled for a space along with other shiny luxury cars before pulling up to the entrance. A couple of valets rushed up to open the doors, and Solly pulled out a few bills from his roulette winnings.

Martha Ann looked right at home among the glamorous ladies, draped with fox capes and dripping with diamonds. "That was generous of you." She tilted her head toward the valets.

"What can I say? I'm a big spender, Mrs. Scott."

"Well, spend some of that getting me a daiquiri, would you? I'm dying for a drink. By the way, it's Mattie. My stage name. It took a while, but I'm used to it now."

A couple of cocktails later, Solly started to ask what the plan was, but Mattie stood up.

"Dance with me," she said, pulling Solly from the table to the wide marble floor. "You do dance, don't you?"

The band had started up the Tommy Dorsey tune "East of the Sun (West of the Moon)," and couples swirled by under the enormous chandeliers. Solly heard the rustle of taffeta and caught the scent of tuberose and damp face powder. "Sure, I dance," he said, wondering what this was leading to and why. Still, he slipped his right hand around Mattie's waist, placed it lightly onto her back, a true gentleman, and led her into a lively little foxtrot, gliding them in between the other couples as they passed. He and the woman in his arms were turning heads. People knew she was somebody they'd seen. Maybe they weren't like Frank and Ava, but they were somebody to know. Solly liked the feeling.

"Well say, did anyone ever tell you that you dance divinely?" Mattie moved a little closer.

Solly let her. "Many times, yes. At every Bar Mitzvah I ever went to." They glided by the French doors that led to the grand terrace and the sea beyond. Later that night, out there on the water somewhere, Solly had a date with destiny—or so Smith had told him. Another chance to be a hero if he didn't screw it up. Solly knew the other dancers didn't see that part. They glimpsed only a tan, dark-haired man dressed in evening clothes, with a blonde, resplendent in something silvery and low cut, in his arms. *Hitler should see me now,* he thought, letting out a low chuckle.

"What's so funny?"

Solly led her into the center of the floor. "Me dancing with a movie star at the Havana Yacht Club. First yacht club that ever let me in." He lifted his arm and guided her into an underarm turn.

"Well, you don't look Jewish. Maybe that's it. You look Cuban, like a rich Cuban."

Solly burst out laughing. "To be sure. A rich Cuban." He couldn't believe she was serious, but then again, he wasn't dancing with her because of her brains. He'd just pretend to be a rich Cuban and see how that felt. "Where'd the monkey suit come from, anyway? Sure fits like a dream."

"I got the information from Clyde's Dry Cleaners and Laundry on Main Street. That COI recruiter, Mr. Smith, had me measure the clothes you dropped off there a couple of weeks ago. Do you think his real name is Smith?"

"Probably not. Like you. How'd Hollywood come up with Mattie?" Solly twirled her again.

"Oh, Mattie sounded like the girl next door, which is how they pegged me."

Solly pulled her a little closer. "See what I mean? You're not the girl next door, are you?"

"Not at all."

"Well, does your husband know that?"

"There's a lot Dray doesn't know and probably even more he doesn't care to know. Anyway, it'll do him good to be a little jealous when he finds out I was dancing with a tall, dark stranger."

"You call five-ten tall?"

"Tall enough." She passed under his arm again. "That's why you're such a good dancer. Panache, that's what you've got. Clever word for a movie star, right?"

"You're full of surprises this evening."

"You have no idea."

The band moved into a rumba and so did Mattie, shifting effortlessly into a little forward, then side, then feet together box step, her hips swaying as the claves beat the rhythm. It had been a long time since Solly had felt a woman's hips move like that so close to his. He looked up at the chandeliers to get his mind off her. "Kind of a funny way to spend your honeymoon, don't you think? Does Mr. Pennington mind?"

"Don't call him that."

"He'd better get used to it."

"Nah, he'll be in uniform once he gets to Long Beach. Everyone will salute him. I'll be the good little military wife. The movie magazines will love it." Mattie turned her head to the right just as one of those barroom photographers popped a flash in their faces.

Solly had the strong sense she knew he was going to do that. Had she paid him? Was this part of the setup he'd been worried about at the casino? Another trap he'd fallen into? "Don't let Hoover see that."

"Why not? Gambling and dancing in Havana? What's more capitalist than that? We just proved that you abandoned your Bolshie past."

The music swelled around him, claves knocking like gunshots, horns blaring like air raids, the maracas hissing like a gas leak somewhere. Solly started to sweat. The old heebie-jeebies again.

"Let's get some air, shall we, Mattie?" He nodded to the French doors, and as they got near, he slipped out of the circle of dancers and onto the terrace, letting go of her hand. He walked quickly to the balustrade and pulled a cigarette case out of his suit pocket, hoping his hand didn't shake.

"Nice touch," he said, pointing to his initials monogrammed into the silver plate as he pulled out a smoke. "This Mr. Smith's idea too?" He didn't care about the cigarette case. It could have come off one of Meyer Lansky's mobsters down here. He was just fishing for how much of his life she had sniffed out and if he could really trust her. The COI might, but Solly was not so sure.

"Honestly, that guy Smith was so specific about everything. Sheesh." Mattie took the case, pulled out a cigarette, and waited for Solly to give her a light. "He could have been sent from Universal Pictures's costume department."

Solly lifted his cigarette to his lips, making sure the cuff links loaded with chloral hydrate were right in her line of sight. Nothing from Mattie. If she knew anything about them, she wasn't letting on, but it was too late now to worry about what Mattie was hiding behind her dumb bunny act. In for a penny, in for a pound. He stretched out his arm, admiring how the cuffs of his dress shirt were a perfect half inch from the tux jacket, how the cuff links sparkled. Again, no response from Mattie, which maybe meant bubkis. She was hardly Mata Hari, and how she had ended up on the COI payroll was going to have to remain a mystery at this point.

He crushed his cigarette on the stone. "Time to tell me what the hell is going on, don't you think?"

Mattie dragged on her cigarette, lifting her chin toward the docks. "The boat's called *La Orquidea*. Berth number 49. Your pilot will be waiting for you. My part of Roosevelt's little plan is over, I guess. Toodle-oo." She turned, waving her fingers in a goodbye.

Solly watched her walk away, then straightened up, breathing in the briny sea air. Down along the docks, the rigging on the boats clanged as they knocked against their moorings in the night breeze. He jogged down the curved staircase, his patent leather shoes clicking on the stone, and walked a short way in the dew-covered grass to the docks. Where he was going, his damp pant legs and muddied shoes would be the least of his worries.

He hadn't even reached berth 49 before a short, squat figure stepped onto the dock in front of him, calling out, "*Quién es? Ay, carajo! Cómo te va? Un verdadero cabrón burgués!*" Look at you. A real bourgeois bastard. This was a voice he'd never forget. It belonged to Adrian, the Mexican ambulance driver for the *brigadistas*, the man who'd saved his life, pulling him away from machine gun fire when he had run back to the bombed and burning building, screaming as his friends went up in smoke.

"*Pásale, camarada.*" Adrian wrapped his arm around Solly's shoulder. "Come and meet the rest of the crew."

By eleven on the second morning of this voyage, the sun had been up for three hours, blasting the *Orquidea* like a blow torch. If there was a place hotter than Mo Blumberg's office in Pennington, South Carolina, on a summer afternoon, the deck of a fishing boat in the middle of the ocean was it. Even the so-called sea breeze felt like a steam bath, and the shade on the starboard side wasn't much of a relief. Solly felt like he was soaking in the sweat of all the mariners past and present who had crossed this part of the ocean, and out of the blue, he remembered a poem he'd had to memorize in high school. *Water, water, everywhere, Nor any drop to drink.* Why rich people cruised around the world he would never know. *Give me a swimming pool on dry land any day,* Solly thought, scanning the western horizon for the first sign of palm trees and the shore, anything to relieve this endless, monotonous blur.

Two nights before, once they had pulled up anchor, the first thing he'd done was grab a blanket off his bunk and climb out of the galley and onto the main deck, where he'd spent the night sitting on a crate. Anything had been better than being cooped up below deck, breathing in gas fumes and listening to the sound of the engines droning as they pushed the *Orquidea* on toward the coast of Mexico. And after shivering all night on the deck, the first dawn had been a welcome sight, the gray sky turning blue, replacing the ink-black sea with clear water, wiping out the stars that had seemed less like celestial guidance and more like darts aimed straight at Solly. That is until the heat started bearing down on him like the wrath of God and all he could do was wait for sunset. Still, he shouldn't carp, as this might be as good as it was going to get, and after what he'd been told about being a spy in Mexico, he had other things to worry about. Let's just say he wasn't headed for a garden party.

"Come and meet the rest of the crew," Adrian had said as Solly gripped the metal shrouds on the side of the boat and lowered himself onto the deck.

"Rogelio and Hector." Adrian had waved to two men up the stairs on the flybridge, one man too young, the other too old. "*Son buenos marineros*," Adrian had told him. "They can read the sea and sky like a book." He lit a cigarette, laughed, and said that was the only thing they could read. They were *analfabetos*, completely illiterate. "They tell me the water is still cold, so no hurricane for at least forty-eight hours, the time it will take us to get Chichan, the smuggler's cove near Puerto Progreso. The men say they can smell hurricanes in the air. Other than that?" Adrian shrugged. "*Estamos en manos de Dios, camarada.*" He then pointed to the cabin below, and just past the stairs Solly saw there were others on board, someone wearing cuffed seersucker slacks and white tassel loafers and another sporting peekaboo heels and brightly painted toenails.

"They've been waiting for you." Adrian aimed his cigarette toward the galley. "Make it quick. We've got a two-day trip." With that, Adrian bounded up to the wheelhouse, leaving Solly rocking on the deck.

It wasn't much of a surprise that the ever-so-snazzy Mr. John Smith was lounging in the cabin. Why wouldn't the COI send the recruiter to give him his final marching orders here on the spot, making sure Solly came through in the end? Smith had left everything rather vague back in Pennington, not giving anything away until the last minute. He had only told Solly he was supposed to go into Mexico through Cuba, avoid Mexican customs, and leave no trace that he'd ever been there. So far, so good.

But Grace Weintraub? Waiting below deck? Well, that set him back. What was she doing here? Last time he'd seen her they'd been drinking champagne and listening to Brahms on the radio. Now here she was opening a shortwave radio spy set, and without even looking at him, she asked if he knew how to use it. It wasn't what he'd used in Spain, was it? Well, he had a few questions of his own. What about Mo? Does he know about this? What about her Hollywood job? But as he started to open his mouth, she waved him off.

"We don't have time," she said. "Your contact is meeting this boat the day after tomorrow at 1:00 p.m., thirty-eight hours from now. He can't be seen lurking around the coast. There are German spies all over Latin America and Mexico. That's why we need you."

"We? So, you're with him?" Solly pointed to Smith.

Smith cleared his throat. "Just so we're clear, this radio is a Whaddon Mark V from the Brits. Heavy as stone." He handed Solly a manual. "Think you can figure it out?"

Solly shrugged. "I'll have to."

"That's the spirit. Let's cut the lights. The fewer people who know we're here, the better."

Smith ran him through his paces quickly, which was good. The cabin was beginning to close in on him and the heat, the darkness, and the rocking of the boat as Adrian and the crew prepared to cast off didn't help. Smith chattered on about how Solly would be holed up with a bunch of refugees at an old henequen hacienda south of Mérida owned by a French filmmaker named Jean-Pierre Cordier, a resistance fighter who needed a visa. He knew all about Solly and why he'd be bivouacked there. He was trading Solly's safety for said visa. Smith seemed to think this was all hunky-dory. Solly was not so sure.

"A man on the run from the Reich, as it turns out, so a safe bet we think," Smith told Solly, sounding more like he was rattling off an itinerary for a grand tour or a pleasure trip with a hotel full of fascinating characters instead of a bunch of desperate exiles. "We don't believe all of them are who they say they are. Just be aware. But then who of us is in this world these days? Even you. Your cover story is that you are buying sisal rope for the US Army."

Monsieur Cordier would meet Solly's boat on a dock east of a place called Puerto Progreso, Smith continued, a remote cove called Puerto Chichan that Captain Adrian knew about. Solly felt the walls close in around him and leaned back against the counter, pressing his palms against the shelf door to steady himself, to keep the claustrophobia at bay, to keep himself from bolting up the stairs.

He should have been concentrating on what Smith was telling him and not on the creepy-crawlies going up and down his back. He would be receiving and decrypting only. Well, at least at first. There was a numbers station outside of Mexico City that was transmitting coded messages from Germany to Latin America and back. (More troubling was the fact that messages were being received in the States, but Smith was not at liberty to say more.) *At first*—those words again—Solly's job would be to write down the messages, usually strings of numbers, and hand them off to the courier. Then the essential job was to locate the code, whatever it was and wherever it was. It could be a book, a shopping list, anything. Solly was to find it, or them—there could be more than one. A layer of sweat formed under Solly's fancy-schmancy tux. Well, the duds were something they could bury him in, a savings on his funeral expenses, that is if there was much left of him after the Germans found out he'd located the code.

Maybe it was the feeling of being closed in, but Smith's hoity-toity accent, full of upper-class vowels, was getting on his nerves. It made

him think of a saying about Boston that went, "The Lowells talk
only to the Cabots and the Cabots talk only to God." He wouldn't
have been surprised if Smith was more used to talking to a Lowell
or a Cabot than some Jewish commie running from his past, and
this only drove home to Solly that Smith, Donovan, and ultimately
Hoover were holding all the aces. Solly didn't have much of a hand
to play. That's the way blackmail worked after all. Finding the code
was a long and very dangerous shot. He knew from Spain what could
happen to you once someone figured out what you were up to. It was
pretty much *adiós*.

Now, after more than thirty hours out in the middle of the ocean
with plenty of time to go over what he'd been told, he'd finally
wrapped his mind around the danger he'd signed up for. He wondered if he was up to the job, something he should have considered
back in Pennington. His bravery hadn't won the day in Spain, and
he'd been an idiot to think that was all the *brigadistas* needed. Well,
he was older and wiser than he'd been in Spain back when he thought
he couldn't lose. He reached in his pocket for the pill bottle Grace
had given him, unscrewed the cap, and stared at the white disk at the
bottom of the amber glass bottle.

"You may need this," she'd said. "I hope not."

"Don't worry," Solly had laughed. "I don't get seasick."

"It's not for that, Solly," she said, stopping at the stairs and turning
to face him. "It's cyanide."

The boat rocked, water slapping the sides, and the rigging clanged
in the wind. Grace waited. "Let's just hope the Germans, or whoever
they have working for them, don't get you."

Solly was surprised but not shocked. The Nazis were winning. No
one knew how long the Brits could hold out. Roosevelt seemed to
be holding off getting the US involved, so it was going to be up to a

bunch of freelancers like him and Grace and Smith to win this thing. Solly had leaped onto the stairs, grabbed Grace around the waist, and whispered in her ear, "Tell me you'll miss me when I'm gone. Tell me you'll be heartbroken." He'd meant it as a joke, but she didn't laugh.

"The last thing the world needs, Solly," she said, pulling away, "is one more dead Jew. So be careful." She headed across the hull, stopped, walked back to him, took his face in her hands, and kissed him, whispering once more, "Be careful, please." And then she hurried to the side of the boat, grabbed the railing, and lowered herself down to the dock.

Well, it was a little too late to be careful now, kiss or no kiss. That ship, in this case the *Orquidea*, had sailed two nights ago, along with him in it. Solly glanced at his watch—a little past 11:00 a.m.—and, wondering how close you had to be to the coastline before you could see land, he pushed himself up, heading to the wheelhouse to ask.

"*Cuando Dios quiere.*" When God wills it was all he could get out of Adrian.

Solly pointed to the control panels, not that they meant anything to him, and said, "What's God saying there, *camarada*? You don't sound like much of a communist anymore."

"Who is after Spain? Anyway, I'm a Mexican and a capitalist now. My own boat, my own workers. Anyway, *para que sepas. Los Rusos,*" Adrian sneered. He turned to Solly, one hand on the wheel. "The Russians *nos chingaron*. They fucked us in Spain, those bastards."

Solly stared out the wheelhouse windows at 360 degrees of vast blue water stretching around him and wondered what kind of person risked crossing back and forth from Mexico to Cuba, carrying spies like himself and who knew what else. The answer was pretty obvious. Adrian was a smuggler. He'd probably take anything or anyone for a price. What else could you be out here these days with a war going on, goods in short supply, and people desperate to get away from danger? The Cubans knew it. The COI knew it. Ergo, the Germans knew it. "So, you've gone from being a *brigadista* to a *contrabandista*, hey *Capitán*? You're not worried you're going to get caught?"

"The people I carry—mobsters, *revolucionarios*, men running from shotgun weddings—they got bigger problems. Like you. You got bigger problems than worrying about what I do to make a living."

"Ever bring in any Germans?"

"*Nunca*."

Solly reached into his pocket and pulled out a couple of five-dollar bills. "Really?"

"*Okay, sí, uno.*"

Solly handed him a bill, waving the other.

"With a gringo, white as an egg, had to stay out of the sun."

Solly still waved the bill. "Name?"

"Drayton. Some gringo name like that. Drayton Scott."

Bingo, Solly thought and handed him the other bill. "*Gracias, camarada.* There's more like that for every bit of information you can give me."

"*Hay que ganarse la vida, no?*" A man's got to earn a living. "*Claro que sí.*" Adrian laughed, then pointed out the window. "*Tierra a la vista.*" Land ahoy.

Solly squinted at the western horizon to see a rough blur of palm trees on a strip of white beach. He was taking everything Smith and Grace had told him as fact, wasn't he? What if there was no one to meet him, no Monsieur Jean-Pierre Cordier? What if the Germans had already gotten wind of Solly's arrival and were waiting with their own special welcoming committee? He rattled the pill in the bottle. There was always that.

At least he wouldn't be transmitting, *not at first anyway*. A dangerous job, transmitting. It would only take the Germans a couple of days to locate the transmission site and only one day more to torture everyone into selling Solly out, so it was a good thing he was only intercepting messages *at first*. No need for the cyanide yet, that he could see. All he had to do was transcribe the numbers, fit the transcribed message, as Smith had shown him last night, into a hidden compartment in his elegant cigarette case, and then ask for *el Cubano* at the swanky tobacco shop on Calle 55, three blocks from the plaza. This *el Cubano* guy would keep the transcribed numbers in a safe place. Once Solly located the code and converted the numbers into letters and words, things got tricky. He would have to find a remote place to transmit from. Then, when Smith and the others had what they needed, *el Cubano* would inform Solly he could no longer supply his specialty cigarettes. Adrian would be summoned, and he would be on a boat back to Cuba. Or, if he was unlucky, he'd be six feet under.

He pulled the case out from his shirt pocket, stuck a cigarette between his lips, cupped his hand around his lighter, and flicked. Okay, he thought. I didn't die in Spain, so let's see if I'm just a lucky son of a bitch one more time.

When the *Orquidea* docked and Rogelio and Hector tied the boat to the pilings, Solly had just finished splashing water on his face and brushing his hair. He'd strapped on his gun holster and donned the tropical guayabera shirt someone—Grace?—had packed in his new brown leather suitcase last night, one large enough to hold the radio spy set but not so large as to call attention. The tuxedo was folded at the bottom, the cuff links with their chloral hydrate tucked into the pockets of the khakis Solly had been given. If they didn't work to knock out a would-be assailant, there was always the gun he'd brought hidden in the lining. He felt in his pocket for the Swiss Army knife he'd brought with him, something he'd won in a poker game and had named after Estelle in her memory, a talisman he'd carried in the hopes it would give him luck and bring her back. Maybe he'd give it to her when they met up again and let her use it on the damn German. That would bring the whole deal full circle, wouldn't it?

In the bright light of day, *too bright*, Solly thought, the whole setup struck him as overly dramatic, and he started to doubt Smith's expertise in these matters. For all Solly knew, Smith had just walked off a Hollywood set with Grace, and the newly created COI, desperate for recruiters, hired anyone who could play the part. Stupid, Solly realized, not to have grilled him, but seeing his name on an FBI dossier had a way of answering a lot of questions. Seeing Estelle with a Nazi raised even more.

What Smith and Grace probably didn't know was that war, and possibly spying, was unbearably boring most of the time. A lot of waiting around with nothing to do until pandemonium hits and you're terrified. A revolver? Slipping someone a Mickey? That was out of some James Cagney movie Smith probably saw in a theater on the Cape or on Hollywood Boulevard. Still, Solly checked the cylinder for bullets, fit the gun into the shoulder holster, buttoned his shirt, and headed up the stairs from the galley to find Adrian pacing the flybridge, motioning for him to come up.

"*Problemas*," he said.

"What kind of *problemas*?"

Adrian sat on a bench and rubbed his hands over his face. "The name of the man who was supposed to meet you? What was it?"

"Cordier."

"Well, Cordier's not out there. It's some *polaco*. The guy just kept shaking his head, his eyes as big as plates. I don't know what happened to him, but he looked like he'd seen a ghost. All he could say in Spanish was," Adrian paused, picked up the binoculars still hanging around his neck, and peered through them toward the shore where the car and the *polaco* were waiting. "*Escúchame bien, camarada. Muerto.* Dead. Somebody's dead, and it's not going to be us. We're heading back. Rogelio says the water is still cool, and the wind smells like earth, not like chemicals or electricity." Adrian rolled his eyes. "*De todos modos,* no hurricane. We'll go to Rio Lagartos near here for gasoline, *y ya.* All these changes? It could be a trap."

"You got something against Poles?"

"No, I got something against Poles that keep saying '*muerto, muerto, muerto.*'"

"Give me those," Solly reached for the binoculars, lifted them to his eyes, and focused on a skinny, dark-haired man, about thirty or so years old, wearing an old-fashioned linen suit, a straw hat, and a pair of round glasses. The man stared back at the boat, and it hit Solly with a bang. If Solly had been a betting man, and he was, the *polaco* was as Jewish as he was. "You're right, *amigo,* he's seen a ghost." He handed the binoculars back to Adrian. Solly knew what ghosts the Pole had seen: the ghosts of Warsaw, of Europe, and if Solly and the COI failed to stop the Germans this time, his parents' days of relaxing in their backyard in Cleveland would be over. They'd be ghosts too.

He lifted his suitcase—Christ it was heavy—and raised his fist. "*No pasarán, camarada!*"

Adrian shook his head. "I hope you're right."

Solly walked down the gangplank and across a shell-strewn lot to where the Pole was waiting, leaning against a five-seater Packard sedan, its once shiny paint job peeling off in sheets, its hood ornament missing. Solly figured it was a late twenties model, probably bought before the crash and then left to rot in the jungle. He was surprised it even ran. Solly set down his suitcase, reached into his pocket for his cigarettes, and extended the open case to the Pole. "*Papiros*," he said in Yiddish. Cigarettes. "*Amerikaner.*"

The Polish man said nothing, just stared as Adrian had said he'd stared—like he'd seen a ghost. And then he burst into tears.

6

Estelle

Villa Balaam, Mexico
*Diary entry written on September 6
in the year of our Lord 1941*

I will somehow find a way to get you this notebook as I now have my new life arranged. Hopefully, I will be successful in this endeavor, and you will read this one day when I am no longer here. It is my fervent hope that, before the jungle devours me like it has those ruins I am determined to lose myself in, if you survived (also my fervent hope, though you may not believe me), you should have my account of all of the events that occurred which led me to take the drastic actions I did. It is only fair to both of us. We can then leave it to others to judge, though I am most assuredly well past judgment and can only hope that Our Lady will intervene on my behalf.

I was the only daughter of older Victorian parents who had already spawned three boys and had no more interest in children, especially female ones, and so novels were my true friends. Those classic characters and stories were the voices I heard resounding in my ears as comfort for my loneliness—*Middlemarch* most of all. (Have you read it? Poor Dorothea Brooke trapped in a loveless marriage, one for which she had such high hopes, to a mediocre man with a mediocre mind.) When you read it, imagine me—will you?—married off to a minor royal, a dullard, and at the ripe old age of eighteen, doomed to endless rounds of teas and luncheons with other young matrons of my age only to watch them wither from oppressive boredom or swell into overripe plumpness, stuffed with cream teas to the gills. It was a fate I was determined to avoid. I just didn't know how.

And then suddenly, praise be, like rays of sunlight piercing through the clouds after weeks of winter gray, I met a man at a dreadful dinner, most of the conversation heavy, dull, and weighed down even further by the rich courses being served, one after the other. He was blond and vibrant, and the men gathered around the table (all fervent Mosley followers) called him Eton because of where he went to school, he told me later, and because of his impeccable pedigree as an English lord. Later in Spain, the Nationalists fell all over themselves for that sort of thing, not to mention the Germans. They loved it. So much so that they couldn't see it was all false. And neither did I. That is, until it was too late and I had made all the thrilling choices (at least they seemed thrilling at the time) that led me to the jungle where I am now and to whatever lies ahead. It will involve more sins to commit. Of that I am certain.

Dickens once began a very long novel with the words, "To begin my life with the beginning of my life. . ." Well, I won't do that to you. I will only begin at the beginning of us. Or perhaps the middle. And now that I think of it, aren't I really beginning at the end of us? An end that started one sweltering afternoon just a few short weeks ago.

My lover, yes, I think we can use that word, Gunther had sent the servants away, so now we were able to swim naked in the pool all the insufferably hot afternoon. At intervals, we climbed the metal ladder up to the deck and walked dripping into the salon just to stand in front of the Carrier air conditioning machine, which *Oberstleutnant*

Gunther Brandt had shipped for an exorbitant sum from the United States, until gooseflesh appeared all over our bodies, and we ran back into the tropical heat, jumping and shrieking like children into the tepid pool water.

After a while, Gunther climbed out, walked to the ice bucket on a table on the porch, and poured more champagne. He sat on a deck chair and sipped from a crystal flute.

"My dear," he said in his throaty accent, "I swear to you, when this fucking war is over, I will never spend another summer away from the Alps."

I remember swimming toward Gunther's deck chair, Gunther handing me his glass.

"*Köstlich.*" Delicious, I said in German. Gunther thought all other languages inferior, so I spent most, but not all, of my mornings with a tutor learning proper German and my nights with Gunther learning all the words the tutor didn't teach. At that point, as far as I was concerned, the war could go on forever.

"You'll never guess what information passed my desk yesterday, Estelle. Remember that little Jew, the radio operator from Spain you thought you had fooled? I thought you told me he died in the siege." Gunther reached for the champagne glass.

"I gave the address to the right people, the people Eton told me to give it to. All names, I gather, he'd gotten from you, no? The building was demolished. Kaboom. All gone." Not the entire truth, if you must know.

"Well as it turns out, Jews are like cats or vermin. They have more than one life. He's here, Estelle, alive as day. He's been seen in Mérida."

I laughed. "Gunther, this is one of your games, is it not? The ones where you hurt me just so you can comfort me. Fine. I am defeated. I surrender. Come and capture me." The water around me had suddenly turned cold. This was not a reunion I had ever expected. I would play it off as one of Gunther's jokes.

"A game? Not at all, darling." Gunther walked over to his robe and pulled something out of its pocket, which he clutched in his fist. He slipped into the water and walked toward me. "What is that look on your face, my love? I almost think I see happiness in your eyes. Happiness that the little Jew survived perhaps?"

"Don't be ridiculous." I waved him off as if he were crazy, as if my heart was not pounding in my chest.

He stood behind me then, slipped something around my neck, and pulled tightly, too tightly. I reached up and felt the jewels.

"A down payment, Estelle. Our friend Eton assures me that you'll do what you have to do."

And now Eton knew, so there was really no escaping. Eton wouldn't help me. He'd have to save himself. All's fair, and so forth.

The heat of September these days is so enervating, or maybe memories of my past are as suffocating as the tropical air, and putting pen to paper cataloging my burdensome remembrances has me quite fatigued. Sitting under this cloud of gauze mosquito netting only makes it more unbearable. But I've been warned of yellow fever so often I don't dare go anywhere without a veil of some sort. So many things to fear in the jungle: fevers, snakes, the pitch-black dark. But the one thing I've never feared is that Solly—the magician his comrades called him, always pulling cards out of his sleeves, making things appear and disappear—would burst once again into my life like a rabbit out of a hat. Or a gunshot.

But I have tricks up my sleeve, too, and a few weapons as well. It's clear that I have no choice. I'm going to have to use the tricks, the weapons, and whatever else is at my disposal. All's fair, is it not?

7

Solly

Puerto Chichan, Mexico
August 1941

S olly lit the cigarette he'd just offered to the Polish man. *Papiros,*
amerikaner, he'd said, trying to coax him out of his crying jag.
And now, straining for the few Yiddish words he could still remember,
he muttered, "*Filn beser.*" Feel better. It was something his mother
used to say as she fed him spoonfuls of brandy-soaked rock candy, a
concoction she kept in a jar out of his reach and saved for colds and
sore throats. The Pole shook his head and continued crying.

Taking a drag on the cigarette the Pole had just refused, Solly
turned to see Adrian still standing on the boat deck, probably waiting for some sign. He knew the sane thing to do would be to take his
suitcase, head back to the boat, and return to Cuba. Hoover could do
what he wanted with him. But standing on the beach near the sweltering jungle, birds whistling and geckos vibrating like tambourines
in the tangled, green foliage, he breathed in the smell of river mud,
rotting vegetation, briny inlet, and dead fish and knew more with
each passing minute the world was already well past sanity—Franco,
Hitler, Mussolini, Hoover, and even Mr. Jim Crow himself. The world,
all of it was rotten, all of it was crazy. Yet he, the ex-*brigadista*, was
the one being asked to atone for his sins, for having been on the

losing side. Hoover was letting the Klan and the American Bund off scot-free, but not old Solly. Well, to hell with them. To hell with the unfairness of it all. When had life ever been fair? Besides, he had scores of his own to settle, leftover business from Spain, and he was going to damn well do it. It didn't take Hoover breathing down his neck to stiffen his spine.

Maybe it was the heat or the screeching sounds of tropical insects, or maybe it was the thought of being too close to Estelle to give up now, too filled with the hope of beginning where they'd left off, that pushed him on like a shove in the back. And if their reunion failed, if he found out she really had betrayed him, he knew he'd want revenge and he knew he'd take it. Whatever was about to happen, it would put an end to his miserable regrets one way or another, which sure beat the hell out of mulling them over at the Rexall drugs lunch counter while scanning the *Pennington Gazette* and was certainly better than seeing his name printed there with a big headline, "Lawyer on Trial for Subversive Activities," which seemed to be the only other option. He cleared his throat, reverted to English, and asked the Pole, "Do you have the keys?" He made a motion of inserting a key that seemed incomprehensible to his companion, so he walked to the driver's side and opened the door, ready to point to the ignition switch when he saw the keys dangling there. That was a start. At least this jalopy had an electric starter, not a crank. But even more encouraging, a road map lay open on the worn, upholstered seat, its once claret-colored velvet faded to a dull, stained rose. Solly lifted the map of *carreteras y autopistas nacionales de Mexico* and traced the line someone had drawn in red pencil with his finger ten kilometers down something that must be a dirt road if the dashes that indicated its location meant what they usually meant. Then they connected with Federal Highway 176, which connected with Mérida a hundred kilometers later. After that, the red line jogged to the south and then east to an *X*, which must be their final destination. More or less thirty more kilometers. They'd be there in four hours, Solly guessed. He walked back around to the front of the car, put his hand on the Pole's shoulder and tapped his own chest. "I'm Solomon Meisner." He pointed to the Pole. "*Du? Nomen?*"

"Yakov." The man's voice was hoarse from weeping. "Yakov Oberstein."

Solly tossed his cigarette on the ground, stomped the butt with his heel, and wondered why this wreck of a human being had been sent to pick him up and what Jean-Pierre Cordier's plan was now that there was a death on his hands to deal with. Was there no one else up to the job—perhaps someone who spoke English and wasn't bawling his eyes out?

Solly walked Yakov to the passenger side, helped him into the seat—the guy was nothing but a bag of bones—and shut the door. He figured if the car actually started, his fate was sealed, and when it did, Solly stuck his arm out the window and waved to Adrian.

In the rearview mirror, he saw the Mexican lift his arm and circle the air above his head with his red *brigadista* scarf. Solly couldn't hear him but was certain he was yelling, "*No pasarán, cabrón*" and "*buena suerte*"—good luck. Solly would need it, and with that send-off, he stepped on the gas, steering the ancient Packard down the shell-strewn road under a tunnel of palms with only a thin red line drawn on a map like a trail of blood to guide him the rest of the way.

By the time they reached Mérida, it was afternoon and huge purple storm clouds had formed in the south, the direction they were heading. Solly glanced at his watch. He figured they were at least another hour from Cordier's hacienda, which actually had a name on the map—Hacienda Ah Kin. He wanted to ask his silent companion if he was right about the timing but figured it would hardly be worth the effort. Yakov had said a total of five words the whole trip.

A few kilometers past Puerto Chichan, Solly had gotten the Packard up to what appeared to be its maximum speed of seventy kilometers an hour, shifted into fourth gear, and rolled down the window, hoping for some air, when suddenly his companion began shrieking in Yiddish, "*Neyn, moski'ts. Aroyf!*" and spinning his fists in circles, frantically miming rolling up the window. No, mosquitos. Stop.

Solly had pulled off to the side of the road, hopped out of the car, and retrieved his Dopp kit from the trunk, producing a brown glass bottle of 6-2-2 repellent, which he carried back to the car. Once inside, his attempts to explain the magical mosquito-killing properties of dimethyl-phthalate and indalone to Yakov failed terribly. He found himself shouting, "US Army, GIs, the Yanks, your friends use this. *Moski'ts toyt.* Mosquitos dead, buddy. *Toyt.*" Solly doused himself with the oily substance while Yakov recoiled, refusing to touch the stuff. "Too bad, because the windows stay open," Solly snarled before rolling down the passenger window and slamming the door. Yakov pulled his jacket sleeves over his hands and sank down into his collar, curled up like a beaten dog. "This is no joyride for me either, pal," Solly growled as he started the car up again. "Toughen up."

Three words. Solly counted them as he drove farther south past the large billboards propped up on the outskirts of Mérida, huge garish signs advertising Coca-Cola, Pemex gasoline, and *dentista* Jorge Ramirez's alarmingly white smile. The other two words Yakov had cried out almost in desperation were *vaser, bite.* Water, please.

About twenty kilometers away from Puerto Chichan, past weathered signs for some place called Progreso, Solly had spotted a rusted green and white gasoline pump standing sentry next to a shack, its thatched palm roof perched on stilts above a dirt floor. There were a few metal tables under the roof's shade where someone behind a curtain in a makeshift kitchen seared meat in a cloud of smoke. On top of the gas pump, a sun-bleached metal disk bore the faded words PETRÓLEO MEXICANO. Solly pulled up next to it and noticed the hose, cracked from the heat, was wrapped in a couple of places in green tape. All he could do was hope for the best. Yakov jumped out of the car and headed for the tables, calling out "*Vaser, bite*," and miming drinking from a bottle, calling attention to the two of them like they weren't already a couple of sore thumbs.

After the sweaty and rather dour owner finished filling the tank and swabbing the windows with a soiled rag, he motioned to Solly to park a few meters away from the shack next to a red, flowering tree, which he did. He locked the doors, pocketed the key, and joined Yakov under the shade of the palm roof, not that it was much cooler, just darker. Solly would have taken off immediately just to get the air moving around him, but Yakov was already seated at one of the metal tables, swilling a bottle of mineral water. Solly pulled out a chair next to him and motioned for one more bottle. No sooner had he sat down than Yakov jumped up and started wandering around until the owner figured out what he wanted and mumbled "*baños*," pointing to a pile of sheet metal and leaking bags of concrete with fancy labels behind the kitchen.

Solly glanced around, and in the gloom, his eyes fell on three *federales* at a table in the back, their pistols attached to their belts, black and menacing as their glares. He didn't let his gaze linger.

"Hey! Mister," one of them yelled. "Hey, gringo, my friend."

Solly turned around, wondering what the hell was taking Yakov so long. He waved to the men and was about to go back to his drink when the older of the group called out, "Hey, mister, is your car? American car, yes? You sell?"

"A friend's car. *Es viejo.* The car, very old. No sell."

"Old car, *carro viejo. Amigo viejo.*" The older guy, the big cheese of the group, laughed at some inside joke and continued staring at Solly.

Yakov finally returned, and Solly was about to make a witty remark, ask if he'd fallen in, but then remembered the Pole wouldn't understand, and besides, the atmosphere was getting tense, the heat, the *federales*, the menacing laughter. "Time to scram, Yakov," he said instead, standing up and calling for the bill. "*La cuenta.*" He mimed writing on a piece of paper.

"*Mer,*" Yakov said, almost in a whisper, holding up two fingers. "*Mer vaser, bite.*" More water.

Solly had paid for the water and the bottle deposit and was now putt-putting in the old Packard down the Federal Highway on the southeastern outskirts of Mérida, creeping behind a smoke-belching bus and a flatbed truck full of rope, a rainstorm headed their way. Over on the passenger side, clinging to his two water bottles like a man about to crawl through the desert, Yakov stared out of the window, again saying nothing. Whatever had happened to Yakov, Solly had already figured it out—the camps, the summary executions. Better he couldn't really carry on a conversation. Solly had enough bad memories of his own. Hopefully he wasn't driving straight into more of them, even though the odds were that he was.

Then there was Estelle. He let himself imagine her here in the tropics, some light-colored dress floating around her in the breeze. Maybe Smith was wrong about her—she couldn't have been a Falangist. She was too filled with high spirits to be drawn to those rigid army men, wasn't she? Maybe she'd just got swept up after Madrid fell, got lost in the crowd, and never made it to Lisbon. The aftermath of the war was chaotic and terrifying. Maybe, just maybe, she would be overjoyed to see him and they could start over. Like his aunt used to tell his mother, who was always a worrier, "You act like nothing can ever turn out right. Maybe this time it will." Maybe this time. Hope made him catch his breath.

Past the congestion of Mérida, the traffic petered out and the jungle swallowed them up again. Solly stared warily out the front window as the sky turned increasingly dark and rolls of thunder bellowed in the distance.

Yakov turned from his side and, unwinding out of his fetal position, faced Solly and coughed into his fist. "*Hoyz. Tsen minut,*" he said, his voice hoarse and raspy. House. Ten minutes. He pointed to his wrist as if there were a watch there, but there wasn't. It was probably gracing the thick wrist of some Nazi guard now.

Solly listened to Yakov cough again, like his lungs were being scraped out. All he could think of was whether he might catch the illness Yakov seemed to have picked up in whatever camp they'd thrown him into: TB, pneumonia, rheumatic fever. Poor guy. Europe had turned into a nightmare, and the last thing Solly should be thinking about was himself. Still, he sure wouldn't do Smith and Grace any good if he ended up in some jungle hospital in the middle of Mexico, would he? Then all bets would be off with Hoover's boys, and Solly would be back to square one, going nowhere fast. He rolled the window down a bit more in hopes of blowing away any germs.

Down a strip of gray road bordered by thick greenery, Solly spotted a group of locals squatting on their haunches by the side of a clearing, dressed in what looked like white pajamas.

"*Hoyz,*" Yakov yelled, pointing excitedly to the left past the group. Solly steered the Packard onto the dirt clearing and stopped in front of a pair of huge wooden gates, battered, worm-eaten, and as old as dirt, older maybe. Yakov reached over and leaned on the horn. Solly could hear the Mexicans laughing at the noise. A few minutes later, two different local guys pulled open the gates and motioned for Solly to enter. A yellow stucco building rose up at the end of the drive, appearing larger and more impressive the farther he maneuvered the Packard up the long, rutted lane toward it. Vines crept across the road, palms lined either side, and the underbrush exploded under the trees, having at some point in history been abandoned to nature, the gardeners long gone. But Solly didn't have time to linger and take in the view of his new environs. The skies, which had been only threatening before, opened up. Rivers of water poured over the Packard and down the windshield, blurring the distant building and turning the road to thick mud.

"*Bienvenido,*" Yakov groaned in between the thunder's rumbles. "*Gehinnom. Das zenen mir.*" Hell. Here we are.

The hacienda, which had appeared almost golden when seen from a distance, was decidedly less so as Solly approached it. By the time he'd pulled up in front of the wide, marble stairs that led to a sweeping veranda, he was amazed the chipped yellow walls hadn't crumbled and the roof hadn't collapsed. Huge chunks of stucco were missing, red roof tiles had fallen on the ground, and the veranda's columns were pocked with exposed laths. "You're right, Yakov, buddy. Not exactly the Ritz, is it?" But the Pole, ignoring the comment, opened the car door and bolted up the rain-slick stairs, still carrying the bottles of water. Solly saw two men in rocking chairs stand up, and he witnessed a brief, and what seemed to be agitated, conversation between the three of them with lots of headshaking and waving of hands before Yakov took off.

One of the men, bespectacled, his suit hanging off him, was as skinny as Yakov. What lent him the aspect of health that Yakov lacked was his darker complexion and a five o'clock shadow that rendered him almost dangerous, like a gangster who'd been in a holding cell for a few days. Solly watched as he opened a ripped umbrella, a metal rib dangling like a spear under the canopy, held it above his head, and made his way tentatively, not like a gangster at all, down the slippery stone. He knocked on the window and motioned for Solly to exit.

Once up the stairs, he collapsed the dilapidated umbrella and reached out his hand. "Enjoy the rain, Mr. Meisner, otherwise it's an oven here. I am Professor Herschel Birnbaum and this is my friend in exile, Dr. Bernard Gottman. I'm German; Dr. Gottman is French. I taught physics at the university; he was a psychiatrist. I study the real world; he studies what we think of the world and what we make up, and we spend countless hours debating the validity of each other's field. There is little else to do. Welcome. Please sit. I apologize for Yakov. He is very disturbed but also the only one who can drive."

"*Pas du tout*," the Frenchman said. "Not disturbed at all. He is experiencing dissociation from prolonged trauma. I am trying to help. Of course, this tragedy with the recent death will only intensify the psychological complex." Gottman shook his head, a lock of gray hair falling free over his broad forehead in spite of a heavy layer of Brylcreem. He lifted his pocket watch from his vest pocket, glanced at the time, put it back, and fiddled with the gold chain that dangled from a button. "The rains are now with us. Every day the same time. At least there are some things you can depend on. Do you speak French, Mr. Meisner? German perhaps? My English is limited."

"Sorry." Solly shook his head and sank into one of the shabby rockers.

"But you speak Yiddish. That's what Yakov told us." Birnbaum pulled out a pipe and tried to light it with a soggy match. "Everything here is damp like an old washrag." He gave up. "Yakov apologizes for crying. He hadn't heard Yiddish since his family was . . ." Birnbaum's voice trailed off and all Solly heard for a while were the rockers creaking and rainwater pelting the roof, dripping from the broken gutters. Then just as suddenly as the rain had started, it ceased, and the noise overhead was replaced by the roar of frogs from the ground.

"It's really a shock about what happened, about the death. The whole thing has cast a bit of a pall on us. Tell me, did you notice anything?" Professor Birnbaum asked.

"I'm sorry. What should I have noticed? Where?" Solly said.

Gottman looked at the German and raised his eyebrows.

"Yakov told us you stopped for petrol along the way." Birnbaum aimed his still unlit pipe in the direction of the road. "Well, that's where they found Cordier's body just yesterday at that, what do they call it, a *lonchería*. You didn't know?"

Solly stopped rocking and tried to pick his jaw up from the floor, his mind filling with images from a few hours ago—the *federales*, the grim owner, the miserable cooking area. "Cordier? Dead? What happened?" Solly conjured up an unsavory picture of that filthy kitchen, the greasy plates on the *federales'* tables. "Heart attack? Poison? He choke on something he ate? The place wasn't exactly kosher." It was a pathetic attempt at gallows humor.

Solly thought of the menacing *federales'* question about the car, Yakov's long trip to the facilities. He ran over in his mind the things he might have missed, wondering how close he and Yakov had been to getting picked off. Did the Pole know that? Why had he let Solly stop there? Was he on some suicide mission? What had Smith said about the exiles here? *We don't believe all of them are who they say they are.* Could he risk a telegram to Smith? Probably not. He'd have to send messages through the tobacco shop, and who knew how long that would take. Solly felt dizzy from exhaustion, heat, and now this. Birnbaum had finally gotten his pipe lit and the sweet-smelling smoke wafted like funeral incense in Solly's direction.

Dr. Gottman reached for a cane that was leaning on a column, started to stand, and then appeared to change his mind. "He was murdered. As to what he ate, a bullet, it appears. He was shot dead."

Solly lifted his cigarette case from his pocket. The secret compartment would come in handy after all, but now, he just needed a smoke. He flicked his lighter, heard the tobacco sizzle. "Either one of you gentlemen know who might have wanted to murder Mr. Cordier?"

"Who wouldn't have wanted to murder him?" A woman said, emerging from one of the large doors that led from the veranda to the house.

Solly jumped at the sound of the woman's voice, sharp and full of venom. He expected some harpy, but when he turned in his seat and faced her, he found he was looking at the kind of girl you see on billboards: slender, with sleek, dark hair, bright-red lipstick, and eyelids darkened like Cleopatra. She looked to be about thirty, quite tall, and was dressed in some kind of local Indigenous garb—a white kaftan and sandals. Apparently she'd gone native except for the makeup.

"Even I could have killed him," she sneered, walking the length of the veranda toward the men. "I'm Madame Cordier, Mr. Meisner. And I should have saved the pistoleros the trouble. Please join me in my office after you have settled in and have had the evening meal. I've sent the staff for your valises. *Bon séjour.*" And with that short introduction she turned on her heel, retraced her steps to the large door, and disappeared.

"Whew! Some dame," Solly whistled softly. He waited for the typical male banter to start up, something to break the ice that had formed around them after the widow's freezing-cold response to her husband's death, but the men on the veranda were silent. Solly watched as they stared at each other like they were sending telepathic messages. They seemed to have forgotten him.

Birnbaum finally broke the spell. "Staff," he rolled his eyes. "Hardly trained at the Hotel Adlon, not that they let Jews in there now." He puffed on his pipe, shaking his head. "Madame Cordier." He sighed. "A bitter woman is a terrible thing to behold. Even a very young one."

At this, the Frenchman stood, leaned on his cane, and looked at Birnbaum, once again ignoring Solly. "Or a dangerous one, my friend, a very dangerous one." He walked toward the doors, tapping his way across the veranda with his cane, but before entering the house, he turned back and said, "*Penses-y, mon ami,* just think, Professor Birnbaum, we are now totally in her power. *Bon séjour,* indeed. *Quelle horreur.*"

He passed Solly, pausing a moment to say, "*Très mal, très mal.* This is all very bad. You have arrived, it would appear, at *un moment de crise.*"

"A moment of crisis, Mr. Meisner," the German translated. Not that Solly really needed him to. He'd heard the word "horror" a few sentences back, and that pretty much confirmed what he'd already figured out.

8

Grace

Havana, Cuba
August 1941

Grace stretched out on the bed in her stateroom and listened to the SS *Evangeline*'s engines rumble deep in the bowels of the ship. They had departed Havana at eight in the evening and sometime after dawn would disembark in Miami. After that, she knew Smith expected her to go on with her life and forget she had ever met him or ever encountered Solly. She knew this because Smith had said as much. Her little spoke in the wheel of intelligence gathering was being severed. If they had need of her again, she would be contacted, but Smith told her he certainly hoped that would not be the case. Standing in the ship's narrow hallway next to her room, he'd thanked her for "aiding her country" and said goodbye, disappearing down the corridor into a crowd of boisterous tourists looking for their quarters.

Her shoulders burned from a day wandering around Havana's old city. Stupid to wear a sleeveless dress, but it had been so hot and she'd been distracted thinking about Solly, about the danger he would find himself in, that she had helped put him in.

She got up and ran some cold water over a washcloth and, after placing the damp cloth over her shoulder, pushed open the door of her room and stepped onto the balcony. The cold sea breeze soothed the burning on her skin but not in her heart. *Her heart*, she chuckled, shaking her head. She'd never been corny like that, in spite of doctoring up dozens of weepy love story scripts each year. Maybe that was why she was so cynical. All the stories seemed so boringly the same. Solly, and whatever had passed between them, if only briefly—his arm around her waist, his voice whispering in her ear, *tell me you'll miss me*—felt different, which was why she had kissed him. She'd felt an urgency that had made her eyes water and her chest tighten as if she couldn't breathe unless she pressed herself as close to him as possible.

After the kiss, the red smear of her lipstick still on his lips, she'd turned away and bolted off the boat without looking back. He'd once said he liked her moxie. She wondered if he still did or if he found her forward and trampy. Such stupid rules girls had to play by, and she'd never been good at playing by them—even less so with Solly Meisner.

She switched the cloth to the other shoulder and noticed her hand was shaking. Her arm felt weak. Maybe it was the adrenaline running through her veins, the memory of the gun she'd seen packed in Solly's suitcase, the rising fear that he would have to use it. And what if it failed to do the job against the German? He was the enemy, she had always assumed, but now that she thought about it, the enemy could be the girl or the Brit. Anyone, really. Each day the world became more dangerous, its inhabitants more unhinged.

The stars over the open water flew above her like sparkling confetti tossed into the black sky. She looked up, searching for her constellation, Scorpio. Not that she believed in astrology, but her ward over the past week, Mattie Pennington, did, and so Grace had heard all about her celestial strengths and weaknesses.

Just above Scorpio, with its tail of stars, was an obscure constellation with a strange name—Ophiuchus, the Serpent Bearer—which you could see in only the darkest night. And wasn't that what they were in now? The darkest nights of history?

She'd dated a med student once who'd told her about the Greco-Roman myth of Ophiuchus in which a serpent cured another wounded serpent with healing herbs. The future doctor told her that he only knew about the myth because it explained why the symbol for a physician was a pole with intertwining snakes, depicting the ancient belief that serpents could bring the dead back to life. Solly was with serpents now, and a hopeful myth was what she found herself clinging to, as she supposed the ill did—the belief that some strange turn of events, no matter how painful or even poisonous, would make it all come out right.

She found herself shivering as the wind picked up over the open sea, so she stepped back into her room and closed the door. She needed some reassurance from Smith that the endeavor he'd sent Solly on would yield results, that he was more or less safe. While it was true that he was in Mexico and not behind enemy lines, it was also true that there were no lines in the world anymore, not really. The enemy was all over the place. Hadn't the US instituted the Good Neighbor Policy for that reason? To keep the Germans from gaining a grip on the southern US border?

The American Embassy wouldn't be any help to Solly either. Announcing himself to them or asking for assistance would just lead to more people in Washington finding out about his activities, something the COI didn't want. She needed to ask Smith about all of this and wondered if the steward could take a message saying that she needed to see him. She had no idea where the steward was, but maybe someone in the bar would know. Tossing her sweater over her burned shoulders, she grabbed her purse and key, stepped into the hall, and headed toward the stairs.

* * *

As luck would have it, the minute she pushed open the doors to the ship's bar and left behind the roar of the wind and slap of the waves, she saw Smith seated alone at a table, staring out the blackened windows. The bright light of the chandeliers rocked slightly with the ship's movements and had turned the window glass into wavering mirrors. She knew that Smith could see her approach his table in the reflection as clearly as she could, but he did not turn around to welcome her.

Invited or not, she walked to his table, sat down, and said, "I need to have a word with you." She waved the waiter over and ordered a bourbon with a water back.

Smith turned from the window, looking tired and tight-lipped. He took a sip of his rum and Coke and said, "You order drinks like a man."

She didn't know why he was trying to insult her, but neither did she care. Being called mannish was the least of the invectives she'd had hurled her way in Hollywood, most of which started with the letters B, C, or D. Any time you crossed a member of the XY chromosome club, that was what happened, and she was used to it. That Smith was pissed off was strange, but again, she didn't care. Her drink arrived, and she took a sip. "Why me?" she asked. "Why Solly Meisner?"

Smith took a pack of Lucky Strikes from his pocket, stuck a cigarette in his mouth, flipped a lighter, and inhaled. "Ask Moses Blumberg. Your uncle, right?" he said, exhaling smoke from the left side of his mouth. He rested his cigarette on the ashtray, took a sip of his drink, and shook his head. "Forget I said that. Don't ask him. He won't tell you anyway. At least, he's not supposed to."

Grace's neck stiffened, and her head jerked back. "Uncle Mo?" What could mild-mannered Uncle Mo have to do with this? "He's the least politically involved person I know. He goes along to get along, as they say."

"Maybe you don't know him as well as you think you do. At any rate, this war has changed us all, hasn't it? Ever heard the expression 'gentlemen do not read each other's mail'? No. I suppose not. It's a bit of agency inside baseball. Henry Stimson said it when he shut down the US's first spy agency, the Cipher Bureau, back in '29 when he was Secretary of State. Now that he's Roosevelt's Secretary of War, he's changed his mind. We do read gentlemen's mail, it turns out, and listen to whatever gossip William Donovan's COI operatives can gather from all the movie stars, society ladies, and, yes, Jews like your uncle, who he has on the payroll."

Grace's drink began to slide along the table to the left. The waves underneath the *Evangeline* had gotten choppier and larger, and the boat was shifting from side to side, as was her understanding of the events of the last day. Her mind was shifting and twisting around almost as if she were in a carnival ride, taking the rises and dips and all the curves too fast. "My uncle knows about all of this?"

"Grace, you look like a smart woman. Think about it. How do you think your uncle came to hire Mr. Meisner? How did Miss Pennington get involved? A certain amount of serendipity was involved, I'll grant you, but then sometimes the dots just connect and bingo! A plan is conceived. We got some useful information from your uncle, who had gotten it from someone else. He did the right thing, got in touch with someone he knew in Washington, and well, here we are. The dots connected to Pennington, to Mexico, to Mr. Meisner, and to Miss Pennington, Mrs. Scott, I believe now. You just happened to be one of those convenient dots as well. It really was rather amazing. None of us could believe our luck as dominos with all their dots fell, one after the other, into place, but that's all I can tell you. I've really said

more than I should have. Spying is hardly a gentleman's business, nor
a gentlewoman's either. I'd put it all in the back of my mind if I were
you." He stubbed out his cigarette and stood up to leave. But Grace,
in a definitely ungentlewomanlike manner, grabbed him by the arm.

"Not so fast, Smith. How safe is Mr. Meisner? How likely is he to
succeed?"

Smith pulled his arm away and leaned toward her. "Not that safe,
but who of us will be if we go to war, or even if we don't? Do you realize the Nazis are this close to us?" He pinched his thumb and forefinger almost together. "I've even heard, through the channels open
to us, that they have a plan to publicly execute Jews in Hollywood if
England falls and they can cross our borders. I'm afraid our days of
believing we are safe are over. As far as being successful goes, that
will be up to Mr. Meisner's own ingenuity. He is a stone we have
thrown at the bushes to see what buzzards fly up from the branches
and what rats climb out from underneath. Depending on the outcome, we'll take it from there. Like I said, we'll be in touch with you
if there's anything you need to know. Now good night."

After Smith had been gone for several minutes and Grace had gathered her thoughts as best she could, she waved over the waiter and
ordered another drink. She would need something strong to block
out the image Smith had put in her head. Scaffolds on the streets of
Los Angeles, bodies hanging, many of them people she knew, one of
them maybe even her own corpse.

Swirling the bourbon around in her glass, Grace tried to read
some meaning into the whiskey, the way the girls in the tacky cos-
tumes at the Egyptian Tea Room across from Bullocks had read her
friends' fortunes in the soggy tea leaves when they'd stopped in after
shopping. She hadn't forgotten what the fake gypsies had said, ludi-
crous clichés Grace had committed to memory in order to use them

in some noir script she might find herself rewriting. *You will go on an ocean voyage. You will meet a mysterious man.* It had seemed like laughable hooey at the time. Laughable and sad.

That was the thing people never admitted about Los Angeles. They never talked about how the sunlight blended like Renaissance landscapes painted with sfumato into desperation and disappointment. All the beautiful boys on muscle beach lifting dumbbells, oiling their bodies, hoping to be noticed; all the girls like the fake gypsies in the tearoom praying for a break, struggling to make the rent, older versions of them already defeated, camped out in cheap resident hotels, eating canned soup warmed on a hot plate. What had Grace answered that Shabbos evening when Solly had asked, "What's California like?" "Sunny," she'd said.

But her future really wasn't all that sunny there, was it? A few more years and she'd be just another invisible typist for the studio, wearing her glasses around a chain on her neck, dying her hair so they'd still call her one of the girls. Maybe her mother had been right and she should have been more amenable to the med student's attentions. Here she was thirty-one years old and already on a downhill slide. Now if the war came, it would take all the eligible men with it.

Smith was right. The war could very well come to the States, and all they could do now was smoke out the rats on this side of the Atlantic. "From my lips to God's ears," she whispered. "Let Solly trap these vermin and then come back alive." No sooner had she said these words than it hit her—and it really shouldn't have been a shock, should it? Solly was a man she could admire, someone extraordinary, not some striving med student imagining movie star clients and the money that would come with them, not the cynical film attorneys or, God forbid, the very nice assistant rabbi her mother thought had promise. Solly had been a hero in Spain. He would be a hero again, and she would have played her part in something brave and daring because of him. And while it wasn't fair that women had to latch themselves on to men in order to do something, almost anything really, her other attempts to rebel against the constraints placed on her sex hadn't changed the world.

You will take an ocean voyage; you will meet a mysterious stranger, the tearoom gypsy had crooned. Grace burst out laughing and then shook herself once she noticed the bartender giving her an alarmed glance—a woman alone in a bar laughing like a lunatic, not a respectable sight. He couldn't have known that the fortune teller had been right after all. How strange the world was.

Admit it, she told herself, swallowing her bourbon and standing to leave, not wanting to call more attention to herself. What she really meant was *Solly, come back alive to me.*

9

Solly

Mérida, Mexico
August 1941

One of the staff, a barefoot local, had shown Solly to his quarters, down one wing of the U-shaped hacienda, past a drained pool, and through doors flanked by a couple of rockers and some large pots, which were stuffed years ago with tropical plants that were now choking on their confinement. He closed his shutters, drained the toilet cistern (one of those old Victorian jobs on the wall), and hid his spy set in the tank, where it just fit. When the time came, he figured he'd run the antenna out of the bathroom window, where it would be held up by vines—the best he could do. He'd washed his face and gone to the dining salon, where he'd been served a rather strange evening meal of a spicy bean soup and rolls. Then, as he'd been commanded, he wandered to Madame Cordier's office, where he found himself sitting in front of what must have been the old owner's ornate desk.

The place looked like it had not been touched since the turn of the century, except by whatever creatures had gnawed through the woven cane of the rocking chairs and whoever had recently run a mop over the painted floor tiles, smearing years of dirt as they did. The last few rays of a red sunset caught on the cobwebs in the high rafters. When this ragtag group of European exiles staggered in, dazed from war, they must have been horrified. Well, the Nazi camps would have been worse. Someone must have said that to Yakov, obviously, to no avail. But, as Solly's mother used to say, countering his pop's optimism, *It's never so bad it can't get worse.* Solly figured he was about to find out if that were true as he faced the young and bitter Mrs. Cordier seated behind the ancient carved desk rifling through a file.

Whatever Cordier's widow was looking for, she was having a hard time locating it and paid no attention to Solly, which left him to his own devices. He managed to get a pretty good look at her, and she sure checked all the boxes, everything about her glossy as a glazed donut and reeking of glamour.

"Your accommodations, they are acceptable, yes?" She had found whatever it was she was looking for and now eyeballed Solly like she was looking at an adding machine, sizing him up.

"Better than a tent in a battlefield, Mrs. Cordier."

"Madame, *s'il vous plaît.* In English, which I was forced to learn in a beastly British boarding school, the word *missus* makes me sound like an old housewife. Bad enough that I am a film star—you didn't know that, did you, Monsieur Meisner? Or was. Now my career is kaput, and I am a widow. Or maybe it's better that way. He was a bastard, you know?" Madame Cordier fitted a cigarette into an opera-length ivory cigarette holder. "Do you have a light?"

Solly stood and walked to the desk, behind which Madame Cordier waited like a child-queen perched on an antique rococo throne. "*Aussi,*" she warned once her cigarette was lit. "Also, use the mosquito netting over the bed. I don't need a tenant with malaria. The netting is everywhere in this house. You'd think they'd never heard of screens." She waved her arm at the huge doors where gauze curtains sagged in the damp heat and let barely enough pale twilight in to see. "We have no electricity this evening, Mr. Meisner. It's all quite primitive, and I don't dare light the candles. The light attracts the bugs, the bugs the frogs, the frogs the snakes. A veritable biblical plague." She leaned her head back, exhaled smoke, and then waved the holder in Solly's general vicinity, its mouthpiece now smeared with red. "I got this in a quaint shop in Venice when we were there in '32," she sighed. "It was the Biennale. The very first *Esposizione Internazionale d'Arte Cinematografica*. We practically drowned in champagne and that glorious Italian light that shone on the terrace at the Lido. It was my first public outing with Cordier after his divorce. I was barely eighteen, wearing the most gorgeous silver gown, and Capra—you know, Frank Capra—said I looked like a crescent moon. I'm afraid all that went to my head. I thought those beautiful days would last forever. Cordier told Capra he'd discovered me, his own *croissant de lune*. But it was I who made sure he did, throwing myself at a married man—they really are the easiest prey to fell, *tu sais*—so I have no one to blame but myself. I guess you and I have that in common. Fatal errors." She tapped the file on the desk with a painted nail. "You got yourself in a mess with the communists. Cordier has it all written here. He was particular that way."

Solly didn't like the way this was going and was glad he'd thought to hide the radio in the toilet cistern, which he'd just drained and disabled. He'd have to use the waste can filled with bathwater for flushing. He was pretty sure the staff would have been told to search his room. Her next words made him certain. "So, you are here to spy. For whom, Mr. Meisner? Your friends the communists or your enemy Mr. Hoover? Bah! I don't care. American politics. Too boring." She slammed the file closed. "I am just relieved the Americans will be paying your rent. Cordier got all he could out of the rest of the inmates here before we left. Convinced them he had a genius plan to start up a rope factory and sell it to the world's armies. Ah, but now we have a real communist here. Maybe you can come up with a five-year plan. Actually, more like five months. Well?"

"I don't know anything about plans, Madame Cordier. And I don't know where your husband got his information about the spying," Solly lied. "Must have made it up for one of his movies. I'm here to buy up rope for the Department of Defense. They must figure they'll be using it. I'll just try to make some money down here until they need me to enlist. The way things are going, it shouldn't be long."

All the while he was blowing smoke up the widow's nose, he was starting to think he might take a look at the rope. Blumberg had a friend he always talked about who bought up odd lots of anything—socks, hair curlers. Mo said he learned from him you could sell anything if you bought it cheap enough, even half-rotted peaches. Maybe Mo's friend would be interested in the rope, in the sheet metal, the bags of concrete Solly saw down at the petrol shack. With a war, those things would be hard to come by. The widow and her inmates sure seemed desperate enough for cash. Solly figured he could ask Grace to ask Mo. It was worth a try. He wasn't going to get rich on what Smith was doling out by the week into his bank account at the Banco de México. The more he thought about it, the better the idea seemed. Why not?

The room had grown dark, the only light coming from the veranda where maids scuffled around lighting lanterns. Madame Cordier walked to the curtain and called out to one of them in Spanish before turning back to Solly. "The electricity is hopeless. Sometimes it works, sometimes it doesn't. The natives think it is a gift from God, like sunlight. We have gone so far back in time we live like cavemen some days. I'll get one of the maids to lead you to your rooms." She opened the file once again and handed him an envelope. "You don't

need to read it. Cordier already did. He told me you have a friend at
the British Embassy. He made sure to get in touch with him, this Mr.,"
she glanced at the envelope. "Cecil Phillips-Boyle."

Eton—Solly recognized the royal-sounding name. *So, he knows
I'm here.* He tried to figure out whether to be relieved to have leaped
over one hurdle or to panic.

"You are being invited to lunch." Madame Cordier interrupted
Solly's thoughts. "Try to sell the British navy our rope, please. I want
to get out of this shithole."

Solly followed the maid and the wobbling light of her lantern as she
led him back to his quarters. The jungle night was gloomy, turbid
with humidity, and filled with the sounds of monkeys screeching
from the trees and bats flying about. And the letter from Eton was
practically burning a hole through Solly's palm. He wished that the
maid would speed it up a bit. He didn't need a candlelight procession.
But as they approached his room, he was dismayed to see that he had
company. The two exiles were seated in front of his door.

"*Je suis désolé*, Monsieur Meisner." Gottman stood using his cane
and bowed. "We are sorry to disturb your evening, but my friend and
I were wondering if Cordier's widow talked to you about the plans,
the money? This is of the utmost urgency. Everything depends on it."

Solly unlocked his door with a rusty key, a medieval-looking thing
that had been weighing down his pocket all evening. The two men
entered his room, and he passed his hand over the switch plate on the
wall, hoping for some light. No luck. He flicked his cigarette lighter
so they could find their way to the seating area near the window, and
when they'd settled in, he practically collapsed in a wicker rocker in
the corner. He was beat.

If there was anything Solly wanted to be doing less than listening to another desperate tale of woe, he would be hard-pressed to say what it was. Eton's letter remained unopened, and right now its contents were all Solly could think about. Well, except for his radio hidden in the toilet's tank, his bone-weary exhaustion, and, as always, Estelle. He was that much closer to her now. Maybe he could postpone the gabfest for tonight. "Gentlemen, I've had a long day. Can this wait? Where's Yakov anyway? Isn't he in on this? What's his game?" He started to stand, but his visitors didn't seem to get the hint.

"Alas, poor Yorick, or in this case Yakov, I knew him: 'a man of infinite talent' . . . to paraphrase the great Shakespeare. A part of Yakov does seem to have died," Birnbaum sighed, reaching into his pocket for his pipe. "Can I borrow that?" He pointed to Solly's lighter.

It was going to be a long night.

Solly pulled out the silver cigarette case that Smith had tricked out for him to carry concealed messages back and forth to the tobacconist, took out a smoke, lit it, and passed the lighter to the German. The professor flicked it and began sucking the flame into his pipe bowl like a man gasping for his last breath. As the fragrant smoke clouded Solly's room, he continued. "Yakov was a prodigy, you know. Mozart. No one before had ever played the pieces with such perfection. When he was only nineteen, he performed with the Berlin Philharmonic. I heard him in concert there in 1931 before the world went mad. Jews were allowed to go everywhere then, free as birds. Hard to believe now."

No wonder Yakov was such a wreck, Solly realized. How was a man supposed to cope with all the losses, having fallen from the heights of concerts with the Berlin Philharmonic to losing everyone and everything and finally ending up here like some castaway?

"How could I have imagined this then?" Birnbaum continued his story. "That I would meet the maestro Yakov Oberstein under such dreadful conditions? But anyway, enough with the reminiscences of happier times. You have had a long day. All our days are long and tedious it seems, and that is for the lucky ones, like us, who got out."

"Please, Birnbaum, explain to the man, *vite, vite.*" Quickly, quickly. Gottman passed his hands over his slicked-back hair, ran them over his face, and shook his head.

"Of course, *bien sûr*, of course. Dr. Gottman and I met Cordier in Sanary-sur-Mer in Feuchtwanger's Villa Valmer. Cordier was very well-known, you know, even then, and he seemed to enjoy filming famous exiles like us picking figs from the garden trees, like we were all on a lark. One afternoon, Cordier showed up with an American diplomat, a friend of Vice Consul Harry Bingham. That was to prove fateful. For you see, it was Cordier who secured Bingham's help to get us—Birnbaum, Yakov, and me—to Spain over the Pyrenees and then here to Mexico. Who knew Birnbaum and I were such mountaineers? Well, we weren't such good ones. That's how Gottman got his limp."

"We would have preferred New York, but Bingham's friend showed Cordier a letter from the American State Department's office. Some official had written to him, chastising him for his rescue activities. Not that Cordier's rescue efforts were on par with Bingham's. Just the three of us, I'm afraid, so no need for the State Department to worry. Do you know what the letter said, Mr. Meisner? Jews didn't need to be protected because history showed that our race can survive suffering. Have you found that to be true in your experience? I'm sure our psychiatrist friend here will have an explanation." He turned to the Frenchman.

"Anti-Semitism is a cactus with a thousand thorns. You can never remove them all. As to why they think these things?" Gottman left the answer to that question to our imaginations, turning away to stare out the dark window.

"Besides, the same official was concerned about allowing Jews of childbearing age to enter your country. Didn't want to pollute the bloodstream, he said. So here we are."

Gottman seemed to snap out of whatever reverie he'd been in and reached out to grab Birnbaum's arm. "My friend, you have forgotten the most important part. *L'argent*." The money.

"Ah yes. Ah yes." Birnbaum sagged into his chair and stared at his hands. Cordier, he told Solly, had charged quite a large sum for his services, for exit visas and the like, and promised the men they would get free room and board on his plantation, as he called it, which conjured up more elegant accommodations, and that they would get at least three-fourths of the money back after his rope factory sold the product—rope for ships anchors, or something like that. "For that we have been waiting, you see. Cordier told us you were arranging the sales. Is this true? When can we expect to be reimbursed, if you please?"

Solly had barely been listening, but this question snapped him to attention. Somehow the widow and these refugees all thought he was going to save them. Who had given them that idea? Cordier? The whole rope purchase was a ruse. The men looked at Solly for an answer, hope seeming to make them sit up straighter. Solly didn't have it in him to tell them the truth. He hadn't the foggiest idea when they'd get money, if they'd get money, or how they were ever going to get out of here.

Solly stood and walked to the door and opened it. "Fellas, believe me, as soon as I know, I will tell you." What else could he say? "Things will look better in the morning."

Gottman and Birnbaum stood, scraping the bentwood chairs

against the tile. "We are extremely desperate, Mr. Meisner," Gottman said. "We are begging you for help."

Solly closed the door behind them and waited until he heard the rattling of their keys and the creaking of their old doors, their murmured goodnights, before he tore into Eton's letter, setting the thick white paper on his bureau and holding his lighter above it to read the words. Underneath the official engraved letterhead, Eton had scrawled, "Blimey, comrade. How did you end up here in *el quinto coño*, as we used to say? Lunch whenever you can, my digs, which are rather grand. Call," and a number followed. Solly read the letter again looking for any nuance, any sliver of concern that might have revealed itself in the handwriting, but he was no mind reader.

It was somewhere during his third perusal of the letter that he became aware of a soft tapping on his door. It was Gottman, the head doctor, who said in halting English that if Solly ever wanted to go into the city, Yakov drove in two days a week.

This got Solly's attention. "Why does he do that?" *Not all living there are who they seem.* Solly heard Smith's warning and started to wonder what the recruiter had held back, what his shtick really was.

"Yakov plays the piano at the fancy hotel in town and gives piano lessons to French-speaking rich ladies and their daughters at the University." Gottman chuckled. "Maybe one of them will fall in love with him, and Yakov can save us with their money and connections." He leaned against one of the porch columns, jumping back when a bat flew past. "*Je suis certain* Dr. Jung would find all these—how do you say?—*mystères* very illuminating. I, myself, do not. But it hasn't escaped me, with my training, that the situation *est très mythique.* One could make quite a dream analysis if this were *un vrai rêve,* a real dream, and not a living nightmare."

Solly didn't know much about the head-doctoring business, not exactly his area of expertise, though God knows he might need one after he left this place. However, he got the drift about the nightmare. Europe, the apex of civilization, was now in tatters, so much so that the safest place for a bunch of Jewish professors and a famous goddamn pianist for Christ's sake was in the middle of the jungle.

The monkeys in the trees started up their shrieking again, and when they quieted down, Gottman continued. "And in this nightmare, all we have to save us from *les Enfers*—how you say 'underworld,' *oui?*—is a man named after the wise king Solomon—you—and some piano student named *pour une étoile*, for a star. Estelle, *je crois*. What would you make of such a nightmare, Monsieur Wise King? Are we not truly back in prehistory with only hope and omens to guide us? Some girl named for a star to help us and Yakov?"

Solly froze. If he'd wanted to tell Gottman the truth, he wouldn't have been able to. He just said good night, closed the door, and leaned on it, his heart racing. A piano student named for a star. What would he make of such a nightmare? Well, he was about to find out.

10

Estelle

Villa Balaam, Mexico
*Diary entry written on September 7
in the year of our Lord 1941*

I will never know why a parent's life is so fascinating to children. When you are young, the adult world seems so mysterious, and one's mother, in particular, seems the embodiment of that mystery. Imagine my dismay when I found out that my own mother's life consisted of myriad tedious tasks, dogs, horses, and dress fittings. I was determined not to fall into that trap and instead fell into something even deeper, as deep as the Yucatán cenotes, the ones in which they sacrificed maidens to bring rain or fertility. However, I was determined to fight my way out of the depths. I was determined to not have you drown with me. My darling, we are almost there.

I want to tell you the steps I took. They might be like fairytale breadcrumbs for you to follow, so I will start with the quotidian. Every week I followed a certain routine. Monday, I studied Maya archaeology with a French-speaking tutor at the Universidad de Yucatán on Parque Santa Lucia. As a young girl I'd studied French enough to get by, and Gunther approved of my bettering myself. Speaking French was one way to do that. He had visions, or so he claimed, of settling me in Paris once the Nazis won the war, and he was not impressed with my academic lapses. You have to understand my education had been abysmal—governesses who swilled cough syrups laced with narcotics, tutors from upper-class families now down on their heels after World War I. It's amazing that I'm not completely illiterate, really.

Wednesday, I had piano lessons with that anemic Polish man who fell in love with me. Even though he was a Jew, he was some sort of Mozart prodigy, so Gunther tolerated my lessons. Mozart was good, and did I know the Germans were so enlightened that they let Jews form orchestras in the camps? He'd heard them perform once.

On Tuesdays I went to the shore. No point in living so close to the sea and not bathing in it was what I told anyone who asked. The Tuesday I write about in this entry was no different from any other save for the fact that my whole world—our world, if you must know—had changed after Gunther's revelations.

At nine in the morning, I packed my bathing costume and cap into a straw bag, put several hundred pesos in an envelope wrapped in a towel, and then asked the butler to summon the driver. It was all perfectly planned to look as though I had nothing to hide. I had much to hide, as you are finding out, diary by diary.

As soon as the car was on the road, I leaned back against the upholstery and slipped my sunglasses on. They were so dark that through them the world looked like an old sepia-stained photograph, almost as if I were already in the past. My departure from the villa had all gone smoothly. Nothing had stopped this excursion, and I looked forward to the hour's drive through the scrubby landscape to my secret place, a beach resort called Hotel y Club del Caribe. When you read this, I wonder if you will be curious enough to go there, to remember me, what little you knew of me that is. I would like to think of you sitting on the sand, staring out to sea, imagining me floating out there somewhere. It's a way for me to return once again.

I mentioned the place to Gunther months ago, casually of course, telling him I liked to swim in the sea. "Real ocean," I told him. "Not a little puddle of a pool." He never let on that he didn't believe me. I would have had no reason to think that he paid much attention at all to my daily comings and goings. I should not have been such a fool. I put you in such danger yet again.

Gunther hated the ocean. For someone as fearless as he when it came to the brutalities of his intelligence work, he hated the thought of being in the water with things, *die dinge*, like jellyfish and sea worms. Plus, he was certain the salt water was unclean and the lukewarm temperature bred disease. He had a list. It was just as well— otherwise I would have never had the privacy I, or rather we, needed. And besides, I love the sea. I love swimming, reaching my arms in front of me, taking long strokes, feeling my legs kicking hard with nothing to stop me, as if I could reach the horizon, go over the edge, and disappear.

The driver turned from the paved road onto the familiar drive lined with palms and hibiscus, slowing in front of the resort and pulling up under the pink colonnade. Of course the driver didn't believe I was going to a hotel just to rent a room to swim. No Mexican man in his right mind would allow such a thing. And of course I knew that he lurked about the place, ready to report any strange men coming and going to my cabana, so I had taken precautions. Still, I remained cool as a cucumber, simply saying *gracias* and telling him that I would be ready to leave around three in the afternoon. That's when the summer monsoons erupted with thunder and rain. I'd be done by then anyway.

The receptionist at the desk handed me the key to my usual cabana, the one at the far end with the screened porch whose door I always left open as I swam. That was the plan we'd devised. Gunther's little spy would not have been allowed on the beach. You had to be a guest. I had no reason to think any change of policy had been arranged.

My visitor was already there, sitting in a chair in the corner when I returned from swimming, wet and covered with sand. I knelt in front of the chair, lifted my visitor's hand, and kissed it. "*Gracias por venir, Hermana*," I said. Thank you for coming, Sister. And I was grateful, beyond grateful, for everything she had done.

"I go where I'm needed, daughter. Now change, you'll catch the grippe."

I pulled off the suit. It was only in front of Sister Immaculata that I felt relaxed about my body. After the degradations of pregnancy and birth, the probing and pain, the chloroform rag over my face, you would think I would be inured to bodily shame, but the opposite was true. Even at the most intimate moments, I felt disgust. Fortunately, Gunther couldn't discern anything unusual about my feigned pleasure. I think that is the root of the Nazi mentality. They cannot imagine anything but their own needs, which of course are paramount. Even with you I was awkward, but you didn't notice. You were so attached to me, so unaccustomed to anyone else, really. What did you know?

Maybe as a very young child I felt my body a natural, uncomplicated thing, but from as far back as I can remember, being female was a source of disturbance and irritation. Should I reveal more or less of my assets, as my mother called them? When would it be to my advantage or not? And once I learned how to use those female assets as a weapon to get what I wanted or thought I wanted, I did just that. Look where my seductive ways have gotten both of us now.

I showered off with the room's lukewarm water, wrapped myself in the hotel bathrobe, and sat on the bed facing the warm sun coming through the shutters and wondered if anyone had ever looked at

me with the kind of love Sister Immaculata did: a calm, benevo-
lent, maternal gaze, which must be the face of our Lord's love. Well,
maybe you did. But that was just need, wasn't it? Any willing body
would have sufficed.

"Let us resume where we left off, Estelle."

Where was that? I tried to remember. Of course it was about the
war and what I had done. Hadn't the priest said it was a crusade
against the Reds, who would destroy Christianity? Hadn't Eton said
the communists were thugs and brutes who would destroy art, literature, everything that made life worth living? And now what was
I about to do? Whatever Gunther demanded. How was that God's
work?

"What you must know is there is nothing you can tell me that
will shock me," Sister Immaculata told me, much as she did every
week. "Why is this? Because our Lord and Savior already knows you,
has seen you. Who am I in comparison? No. Jesus is always looking
down at you. Always."

"That's horrifying."

"Not at all, *mi hija*. Your shame, your guilt, your sins, your vanity
are like yesterday's newspaper, nothing new. All our Savior wants is
for you to look up at Him as He looks down upon you. Can you do
that?"

I noticed my red-painted toenails, my vanity for our Lord to see in
full display. Who would want that to be observed? I looked at Sister
Immaculata and shook my head. "No."

"Not yet," the nun said. "One day you will."

Not ever, I feared, but I tried to mimic a hopeful smile. It seemed
that everything I did and had done for some time was a kind of mim-
icry: of love, of commitment, of passion. Pretending to be in love
with that filmmaker Cordier, and even now pretending to that Polish

pianist that I loved Mozart, anything to lure him in. He might be needed, I'd been told. Not by Gunther but by Eton, who wanted to keep tabs on the rope production, especially if anything happened to Cordier. And it had. I took it as a kind of warning for myself. Be useful or else.

What I did know at that moment, as the slats of sunlight fell on the floor, as the whoosh and slap of waves hit the shore, was that I loved the nun's gentle voice and just wanted to listen to her words like a lullaby. I leaned over and took her hands in my own, a liberty I would never have been permitted in England or Spain, but here I called the shots. I was English and wealthy. It was a kind of power I'd never had before, as these attributes were a dime a dozen in my old world. I closed my eyes as the sister recounted the familiar story of Saint Paul on the road to Damascus. I was momentarily soothed by the tale of this transformation, Paul's pride turning into a surrender to God.

"Open your eyes, Estelle," the nun said. "Look around you. God is infinitely merciful." She tugged on my hands, pulling me closer. "He knows your failings. He died for them. Seeking guidance is the first step. The rest will come." Eventually, she stood and smoothed the front of her blue smock, straightened the heavy wood cross hanging around her neck, and waited.

As I always did, I pulled the envelope from where it was hidden in my beach towel. "I'm sure this will help you and the other sisters."

After Sister Immaculata left, I felt my sins settle on my soul again like dust on an ancient, dark cabinet shoved into an attic corner. I stood, pulled on my suit, and headed back to the beach, past the lounge chairs full of sunbathers, aware that the men's eyes were upon me as always, my body and blond hair a magnet. If Gunther were here, I would have slowed down, let the men ogle me, reminded him that

I was a catch he didn't want to lose. But he was not, so I ran toward the surf's edge and dove through the first row of waves coming to the shore. Perhaps this time there would be an undertow, a riptide, and would that be any worse than what I had to face on shore? There are, I have discovered, many ways to get pulled under.

11

Solly

Mérida, Mexico
August 1941

"How very strange." Jean-Pierre Cordier's widow lowered her sunglasses and stared past the rough trunks of palm trees toward the sea. "This has never happened before. I have to say it is something of a shock." She and Solly were seated at a table on a beachside resort's patio, a bottle of the local anise liquor between them, their glasses half full. She pulled off the top of the bottle, swatted at a fly, and refreshed the drinks while Solly squinted at the bathers splashing in the shimmering water, focusing on one in particular. The widow leaned to the right to get a better look. "Ah yes," she said. "That one."

A couple of hours earlier, before the drive to the beach that Madame Cordier had insisted upon, before drinks at the seaside, Solly had been in the hacienda's kitchen entertaining the help with his cooking skills. He'd waved a spatula around, making what he called *huevos americanos*, and cracking dirty jokes about eggs—Mexican slang for testicles, something he had learned from the Mexican *brigadistas* in Spain—much to the delight of the two young women and to the horror of the older one in charge, the scowling majordomo of the household.

After yesterday's breakfast in the hacienda, which had consisted of perfectly good fried eggs drowned in a fiery sauce, he knew that he needed to take matters into his own hands. The problem confronting him at the moment was toast. "*Pan tostada?*" he asked, which caused a bit of consternation until eventually one of the young women procured a roll from a sack, cut it in half, and placed it on top of a gas flame. "*Gracias, señorita.*" Solly bent to place a chivalrous kiss on her hand, which was a step too far for the older woman, who grabbed the spatula, pushed Solly out of the way, and commanded him to sit down, shoving him to a table next to the big windows overlooking the courtyard. In the corner of the kitchen, an old Zenith radio played Mexican music, electricity having, for the moment, at least, reached the hacienda from the poles and lines that ran through the scrub jungle from Mérida. The overall feeling in the blue-tiled room was cheery, unlike the rest of the gloomy, funereal joint.

Outside, several birdcages hung from the wrought iron bars covering the windows, and Solly watched brightly colored parakeets flutter inside them, chirping and pecking at seed. From a giant wire-covered tree house on the veranda, a parrot shrieked "*buenos dias*" every now and then to a gardener sweeping the tile floor. The gardener called back, "*Cállate pendejo,*" shut up, asshole. When the parrot screamed, "*No, pendejo, tu cállate,*" Solly and the girls convulsed in laughter. But the revelry came to a halt when the cook placed Solly's eggs in front of him, handed him a fork, and shooed the girls out of the room, where he watched them collide with Madame Cordier in the doorway. One look at her put the final damper on the festivities. The older woman focused on swabbing the counters as Madame waltzed over to Solly. "When you're quite through chatting up the young ladies, I need to speak to you in my office."

"Sure thing," Solly said, scraping up egg with his toast. "Will do."

"By the way," she said, turning on her heel. "I hear you don't like hot sauce. Well, get used to it. The Mayans say salsa is what cools you down in the heat. You should eat what you're served."

"Really?" Solly asked. "Is that a fact?" He lifted his hand to his forehead and saluted, but by then she was out of the room.

Solly knocked on Madame Cordier's office door about a half an hour later and heard her shout something in French that he figured was "come in," so he pushed against the heavy wood, walked a few paces into the room, and bowed slightly at the widow. "Here I am, at your service."

"Well, you took your sweet time, didn't you?" the widow Cordier said.

And it was true. He had indeed taken his sweet time. Something about being ordered around did that to him, so he'd meandered back to his room by way of the drained swimming pool on the south side of the building. Well, not completely drained. A layer of green algae and rotting leaves coated the bottom along with a few inches of watery sludge. The pool was a malaria factory. He'd see if something could be done. Maybe a swim would be just the ticket for someone like Yakov, make him less pasty-looking and build up some biceps doing laps. Anyway, Solly would like it.

After he'd brushed his teeth and put on a fresh shirt, after he'd slicked back his hair with a dab of brilliantine, and after he'd smoked a cigarette on the chair in front of his room, only then did he figure it was time to mosey on over to see what Madame Cordier required.

"Finally," she sighed dramatically, looking up from a stack of papers on the desk. "*Tu es arrivé.* Sit." She waved her hand like the Queen Mother in the direction of a chair. "And you may call me Veronique. I'm finding Madame tedious now."

"Well, Veronique"—Solly stretched his legs out in front of him and locked his hands behind his head, a man totally at his leisure—"you should get that pool fixed."

"Tell him that." She waved her arm toward a small galvanized pail on her desk. "Jean-Pierre's ashes. I need your help disposing of them."

Solly dropped his arms, straightened up, and said, "I'm not here to run a funeral parlor, Veronique."

"No, you seem to think you are on a tropical vacation with room service and pools. I hate to disabuse you of your illusions. I am disposing of them"—she pointed to the ashes—"in the sea, and I need you to drive me. Yakov seems to have stayed in town last night, the other two are useless, and the man who usually drives is needed at the *fábrica,* where they are processing the henequen fibers you intend to buy. Something has gone wrong with one of those blasted machines."

"Any idea what it is since I have a vested interest?" Solly figured he should play the part of a concerned rope fiber merchant. "Wouldn't a better use of my time be to go down there and take a look?" He pointed to the bucket on the desk. "Your husband probably isn't in too big of a hurry."

"No, but I am. I want his ghost out of my life. There are too many ghosts in this place as it is." She grabbed her purse and a big straw hat. "*Allons-y, s'il vous plaît.*" She pointed to the bucket on the desk. "And take him with you, will you?"

The ancient Packard was waiting in the drive, but no one was around to witness Cordier's final procession to the grave except the gardener, a guy who, from what Solly had observed, seemed to spend his life sweeping up palm branches and dead flowers around the place in a kind of eternal damnation. Solly nodded to the gardener, opened the car door, and set the bucket of Jean-Pierre Cordier's remains on the seat beside him. He was surprised at how heavy a man's dust-to-dust weight could feel. His widow glanced at the bucket with nary a tear in her eye, Solly observed, before pushing it closer to his side. If that gesture had seemed rather unceremonious of her, and indeed that thought had occurred to Solly, it didn't bode well for the poor guy's final internment.

About forty minutes outside of Mérida, they approached the coast. Solly could smell the sea air through the open windows and was looking forward to saying farewell to Jean-Pierre Cordier if only to have this errand over with. Cordier, a man he'd never met, wasn't exactly Mr. Popularity around here, so it was hard to come up with tender feelings for his demise. Solly had the Packard humming along at a good clip when Veronique Cordier called out something in French. "*Arrête*," she shouted. "Stop. Pull off the road there." She aimed her hand toward a clearing just past a small bridge that spanned a muddy, vine-covered river, its banks splattered with bits of garbage.

He did as she asked, not that he had much choice, but kept the car running, a hint that she should make it speedy. Veronique opened the door, reached for the bucket of her husband's remains, walked to the bridge, and heaved the whole thing over the side. Solly watched her light a cigarette and lean against the railing, where she lingered for a while as if deep in thought. For his money, he figured she wasn't praying.

"That was a touching ceremony," Solly quipped when she finally climbed back into the car.

"*Oui*, it was quite moving, wasn't it?"

"I thought we were scattering his ashes in the ocean."

"They'll get there eventually, no? All rivers lead to the sea." She reached into her bag for her compact, dabbed her nose, and reapplied her lipstick. "Now, I need you to buy me a drink for my nerves, something strong and sweet. There's a resort with a bar, just go straight."

Sure enough, a few miles down the road there was a sign for the Hotel y Club del Caribe. Solly pulled into the drive and parked where the doorman pointed. So while Cordier's ashes made their slow, torturous way to the ocean, Solly and his widow ordered drinks, relaxing in the shade on the beachside resort's sandy patio, a fancy bottle of the local liquor on the table in front of them, some brew with an unpronounceable Mayan name.

"We ought to drink to my dead husband, don't you think?" Veronique lifted tongs out of a sweating ice bucket, dropped a couple of cubes in each glass, and grabbed the bottle to turn it around, pointing to the gaudy label. "*Xtabentún*. It's pronounced ish-ta-ben-TOON. Lovely sound, like wind in the palms."

Solly actually wished there was some wind. In the still afternoon air, the place was a steam bath even under the shade trees. He glanced at his watch, remembering the other days' downpours. They seemed like a regular occurrence around these parts, like the safety valve on a pressure cooker, something to keep the place from exploding from the heat. He figured he'd give Veronique about fifteen minutes to hold this little wake for poor Cordier and then tell her the party was over, time to shove off. He wanted to get back to the hacienda before the deluge.

Veronique lifted her glass, swirled the ice cubes, and sipped. "The locals distill this from white flowers that grow all over the jungle. Apparently, the ancient Maya claimed they grew from some goddess's corpse. Maybe it was just her grave. I can't remember, but they are very fragrant, like tuberose." She swirled the contents of her glass again, breathing in the bouquet. "They used the liquor for ceremonies. Anyway, the drink tastes like Pastis, so it reminds me of Sanary-sur-Mer in happier days." She added more ice, lifted her glass, and said, "*Sant*é. To happier days."

To a bourbon on the rocks, Solly thought, but aimed his glass in her direction as a toast to happier days in general. The liquor was thick and sweet. Not his poison, but then she hadn't asked him to pick it.

In the background, over the lapping waves and the clatter of glasses, over the sound of flies buzzing in the sand, Veronique continued her tale of the dead goddess, a story that, with the heat, began to lull Solly into drowsiness. He swiveled around and stared enviously at the bathers, wishing he had brought a suit, making a mental note to buy one in town. Watching the swimmers bobbing in the waves, he was suddenly overcome with a searing memory, as if being stabbed in the heart by *happier times*. He was, for a moment, back in those times, and once again it was that day Estelle had borrowed Eton's car and driven Solly to Playa de Ocata a half an hour or so from Barcelona with the sole intention of seducing him. Solly winced at his loss.

Veronique interrupted his thoughts, her voice a sort of salt in the wound. "There were two women. Are you listening?" She waited for a response, and when Solly nodded without looking at her, she resumed the lesson. "This one"—she clinked her spoon on the bottle—"Xtabay, a whore with a heart of gold, and another one whose name I can't recall, a chaste woman with a heart of stone, *une salope*, a bitch in other words. There are always two women, aren't there, in the stories that men tell themselves? We women, on the other hand, notice all the varieties of men's behavior—the bully, the egomaniac, the would-be hero."

Solly had no interest in discussing the war between the sexes. He was still watching the swimmers, one tourist in particular, blond, shapely, wishing she would turn into Estelle like a genie out of a lamp, and he remained only vaguely aware of Veronique's voice in the background murmuring, "How very strange. This has never happened before. It's something of a shock."

He glanced at her as she lowered her sunglasses and directed her gaze to the swimmer Solly had been watching. "It is usually me that men are staring at," she said and laughed.

Just then, the blond swimmer walked from the sea to her beach chair and called out in English for a rum and Coke, shattering Solly's vision of Estelle, and one of the waiters scurried in the direction of the bar to comply.

"*Ah oui*," Veronique hissed, "*Une touriste américain.* They are the only ones in the world still dumb enough to be having a good time. Anyway, she's not the one we should be looking for."

"Who's that? Who should we be looking for?" Solly reached down to brush away the sand gnats that were swarming around his ankles. He was getting impatient to leave and started to scan the premises for the waiter. Veronique's theatrical shenanigans were getting to be too much.

"Who indeed? Remember what I told you? There are always two women. *Regarde!*" She waved her arm toward the beach chairs. "There is your sweet, little, blond American sipping a tropical cocktail and thinking she is in paradise. Yes, but paradise always has more demons than you might imagine, mostly in the shape of stinging bugs and reptiles. The blonde I am looking for is not your American. She is of the German reptilian variety, or at least she lives with one, some Abwehr monster named Brandt. Jean-Pierre told me she was a collaborator. It didn't stop him from screwing her, however."

Solly felt a distinct chill, strange in this heat. It was crawling up the back of his neck, connecting with the part of his brain that could still think in this humidity and after downing the native hooch. She's talking about Estelle, he thought, and sat up straighter, suddenly more interested in Veronique Cordier.

"I feel I owe the bitch the courtesy of informing her of Jean-Pierre's death. She comes here every Tuesday. I had her followed because I thought this was their trysting spot. I was going to sue him for adultery. But he bit the dust first. *Quel dommage.*"

Every Tuesday. Every Tuesday. Solly's brain pistons finally started to fire. He was that close to her.

"But I have another plan." Veronique reached into her bag and pulled out a letter. "Voilà! A love letter." She handed it to Solly. "'Your star,' she signed it. *Mon Dieu*, the arrogance of the little slut."

Even though the body of the letter, written in French on pale-blue onionskin, was indecipherable to him, and his eyes blurred with jealous rage, he could see the closing lines well enough to know a love letter when he saw it. *Estelle*, she had written in her spindly script. *Je suis ton* étoile. His star. Jean-Pierre Cordier's. Not Solly's. He shoved the letter back toward Veronique and shrugged, hoping Cordier's ashes got stuck in the mud and vines and never reached the pearly gates.

"Good for blackmail, don't you think?" Veronique chuckled. "I show this to her Nazi, and she's a dead woman. I need five thousand pesos to get to Mexico City. Her life ought to be worth that to her, no? Always two women, don't you see? Now, it's between her and me. Shall we go?"

12

Solly

Mérida, Mexico
August 1941

S tatic was all he heard as he waited for the broadcasted numbers to come through the earphones. Endless, headache-inducing static. He'd set up the Whaddon spy set he'd pulled down from the toilet tank on the bathroom floor, and next to it, his third cigarette glowed in the ashtray. The cold from the hard floor tiles crawled up his backbone as he sat there staring at the radio, bored, tired, but jumpy with impatience.

Smith had told him the broadcasts occurred, when they occurred, at 11:45 p.m., well past sundown, so the shortwaves could bounce off the ionosphere and broadcast without interference from the sun. Clever, Solly thought, the radio technology that let spies all over the world receive messages. Now all he needed was the code, wherever it was written. Who would have the one-time pad, the rice paper, the gum wrapper that would give the numbers meaning? He'd have to get lucky to find it. For all he knew, those papers had been burned to ashes a while ago and were buried with Cordier, never to be seen again. Wouldn't that be just ducky? That's when he heard the eerie music box chime that always preceded a transmission. He grabbed his pen, and the broadcast began with a singsong girlish voice repeating the numbers—five, seven, nine, one, five, seven, nine, one—several times before changing to another series of four different numbers. Solly had no trouble writing them down. When the maniacal, tinny music box chime sounded again, indicating the end of the broadcast, Solly opened his silver cigarette case and copied the numbers onto the rice paper inserted in the hidden compartment. Then he flicked his lighter and burned the paper he'd written the first broadcasted numbers on, put the ashes in the sink, and ran the water. He hid the radio in the tank again, opened the small bathroom window wider to pull in the antenna, and turned on the light. Glancing in the mirror, he noticed a fine sheen of sweat covering his face. He ran a washcloth under the tap and swabbed himself with cold water. Had he really been that nervous, or was it just the swamp-like heat? Hard to tell. He switched off the light, walked to the door, and went outside, where he sagged into one of the chairs in front of his door just to cool off. It had been a long day.

After a while, with nothing but the din of frogs and occasional shriek of a monkey, Solly heard a car engine approaching, the noise growing louder as it got closer. At midnight? What was that about? He stood and locked his door, trying to avoid making noise as he did, and headed along the covered walkway to find out who had arrived in the middle of the night.

The light was on in Cordier's old study, and from the shadows where he stood, Solly could see Veronique and Yakov arguing. Too bad everything they said was in French, but it was definitely a spat, which was broken up only by a knock on the door. He got a glimpse of a native worker and the older maid as well. "*Dígame,*" he heard Veronique shout. "*Qué tipo de catástrofe*? Tell me, what kind of catastrophe?" Solly heard more mumbled conversation, heard Veronique's heels clicking on the floor, and for a minute, as she stood at the window, he watched her run her hands over her face before pulling the shutters closed.

Tell me, what kind of catastrophe? Solly would sure as hell like to know the answer to that question himself. He slipped into the large hallway that connected the main rooms of the building to the courtyard. There was an urn on a big table against the wall filled with purified water, or so they said. He could always grab a glass and say he'd neglected to fill the pitcher in his room. What could they say to that?

After what seemed like an eternity of silence—the walls were too thick to allow any sound to be heard—a door opened, and within a minute Solly saw the four of them, Yakov, Veronique, the worker, and the maid, pass through the front salon and out to the eastern veranda where he'd first met Birnbaum and Gottman. Solly grabbed a glass as a prop, filled it with water, and entered the salon. Through the floor-to-ceiling windows he could see a black Ford Standard idling in the drive. The worker walked to the passenger side and opened the door for Veronique before he and Yakov piled into the back.

The interior light was on for probably less than a minute, but Solly saw all he needed to see. The refined profile that only years of English upper-class breeding could produce was unmistakable, a profile that had been burned into his memory since that summer evening in Barcelona and brought back to the present day in the dossier Smith had pushed toward him in Pearson's office.

What catastrophe? Solly still didn't have the answer. But he knew one thing. Eton was driving the car, and since Solly was a gambling man, he'd bet his last nickel that whatever the catastrophe was, Eton was up to his neck in it.

He walked out onto the veranda and lowered himself into one of the rockers, sipped his water, and tried to take it all in. He reminded himself that his only job was to find the code. Now, it turned out,

Eton was one more piece of straw on the haystack he had to hunt through.

"Curiosity killed the cat." A man approached from the salon.

Solly jumped and turned to see Gottman standing in the salon door. "Jesus, you scared me."

"Mr. Meisner, you should be scared," he said as he walked over to Solly's rocker. "It's not a good idea to see what you shouldn't see." He patted Solly's shoulder. "But don't worry. Your secret is safe with me."

When Solly showed up for breakfast the next morning, his was the only place setting still left untouched. True, he was on the late side. He'd had a long night. After finally catching an earful of the numbers code, after watching suspicious activities going on with Veronique and Yakov, after running into Gottman on the veranda, he'd waited up in the dark for over an hour, peering out of his window until, sure enough, what he suspected would happen did happen. Bingo! Yakov showed up, knocked on the professor's door, and Birnbaum, still dressed—had he been waiting up to let him in—answered the door. What had Solly said when Gottman told him his secret was safe? Oh yes, he remembered. "What secret, buddy?" Now he wanted to know what Birnbaum and Yakov's little secret was, what they knew about the nocturnal activities going on around here.

"*Dónde están?*" Solly asked the girl who brought him his eggs. Where is everybody?

"*La biblioteca.*" She pointed down the hall. "*Periódicos.*" Newspapers.

Once Solly finished up his second cup of coffee, he figured he'd mosey on down to the library and see if he could rustle up some interest in a reconnoiter of the factory, get the gang to show him the ropes, so to speak. After which he intended to make a call to Smith. This whole setup reeked of malfeasance. Finding the code in this nuthouse was Smith's pipe dream, and Solly would be damned if he'd go up in smoke with it. He needed some guidance, and if he didn't get some, he had every intention of cashing out his account at the Banco de México, hopping the next train out of Mérida to Matamoros, and trying his luck walking across the border. A bribe would probably go a long way to forgiving his unstamped passport. What had Grace said at that Shabbos dinner at Mo Blumberg's? *You're a hero, you know.* Well, she was about to find out he wasn't. He did, however, have other fine attributes, and one of them was that he wasn't some stupid schmuck.

Solly found the *biblioteca*, a small dark room lined with glass-fronted bookcases. Gottman and Yakov were seated in a couple of armchairs, reading ancient-looking books by the light of floor lamps, their moth-eaten, fringed shades drooping above the two men. Birnbaum sat at a table in the middle of the room, a banker's lamp casting light on the gray newspaper spread out in front of him. Overhead, a revolving fan rattled the newspapers' pages as it turned.

"*Buenos dias,*" Birnbaum looked up from his paper. "We have news of the world here finally." He waved his hand at the stack of *London Times* on the table. "Of course, they are two months old, but at least we will be somewhat more up-to-date. It appears the Germans have invaded the Soviet Union in Bialystock and that they have bombed Minsk. Did you know that?"

Solly glanced at the *Times*. They smelled damp and musty as an old basement, and he noticed their sad, out-of-date headlines. "A lot has happened since then, Birnbaum. For starters, just a little more than a week ago, Churchill and Roosevelt met on a boat in the middle of a bay in Canada and signed the Atlantic Charter, for all the good it will do. Don't get too excited. The Americans aren't entering the fight anytime soon."

Birnbaum turned to the two other men and spoke in French, and Solly assumed by their grim-faced reception of the words that Birnbaum was translating what he'd told him. They stared at Solly for a while and then returned to their books. "Better Dr. Gottman and Maestro Yakov should return to the study of the Mayan kings. Who knows? They may become archaeology experts, an unusual benefit of our exile."

Solly pulled up a chair. "Look, Professor Birnbaum, how about you and me take a little walk over to the rope factory. See what's going on. Maybe you can explain things to me since you're one of Cordier's investors, right?"

"You can't go there."

"Why not?

"I completely forgot. I was lost for a moment with these papers, back in Europe. I was supposed to tell you the Englishman's driver, the one who brought the papers, is waiting for you. Come, come."

A polished Aston Martin Roadster was parked in the shade, its ginger-haired, uniformed driver with it, catching a snooze. When Solly and Birnbaum approached, he jumped up and opened the passenger door, motioning for Solly to get in. "Mr. Phillips-Boyle is waiting for you. He hopes to have the pleasure of your company at luncheon," he said.

The driver, it turned out, was Irish, had lived in India, and had been brought over by the consul when his post transferred to Mérida. Solly, being the suspicious type, figured there was more to the story, but since it wasn't his story, he decided to put it out of his mind and nodded along agreeably as the driver told him in great and boring detail how Mr. Phillips-Boyle—a.k.a. Eton—had the British car reconfigured so that the steering was on the left.

But underneath Solly's agreeable manner, he was a million miles away, wondering what Eton wanted and how he should respond. He had to admit he was in over his head. His assignment to find out what he could about these people and to get the code seemed further and further out of reach. And what about Estelle? Was she really some sort of Mata Hari, cozying up to the enemy? That just didn't fit with what he knew of her. Then again, what did he really know? To reassure himself, he ran over in his mind the few things he actually was certain of. One, something funny was going on at the hacienda. Two, the expats there were in on it. And three, Cordier, the guy who'd gotten this whole ball rolling, was dead. It hit him. Cordier was the key to all this, and who was his only real link to Cordier besides his bitter widow? Estelle. Eton had to know where she was. Solly had to arrange a meeting. Chalk it up to true love and let Eton think he was still a heartbroken kid.

Before Solly knew it, he was driving down a wide tree-lined avenue, ornate pastel mansions on either side. His anxiety had abated, and he was actually looking forward to the little charade he was about to play with Eton. He would not fool Solly twice. Of that Solly would make damn sure.

"Paseo de Montejo." The driver interrupted Solly's thoughts. "Where all the consulates are and all the rich people. Very fine street, very posh."

Just like the fine apartment Eton had inhabited in Barcelona, on whose terrace Solly had first met Estelle. He'd just been too dumb back then to have seen that as a red flag, that Eton had just been playing at war, only too happy to drink at the popular watering holes, feed off the pumped-up adrenaline from war reports. Now Eton's family connections must have ended him up here in the lap of luxury instead of behind a machine gun in some pillbox on the damp coast

of England. Just another rich boy's scam. This place was full of scam-
mers. Maybe war just brought that out in people, so easy to hide in
the chaos and panic, so easy to make a buck.

"Here we are." The driver pulled into a driveway, turned to Solly,
and beamed as if he were the owner of this palatial building, as
embellished with architectural furbelows as a wedding cake with
icing. "Mr. Phillips-Boyle is very happy to see you." He jumped out
of the car, ran to Solly's side, opened the door, and pointed to Eton
bounding down the marble stairs in front of the villa, just as blond
and handsome as ever, as if Spain hadn't broken him, as if the war
were just one big carnival ride. Maybe for him, it had been. And why
was that? Solly was now dying to know.

"Blimey, mate. You are a sight for sore eyes." Eton grabbed Solly by
the shoulders. "How the hell did you wash up here? Look, let's talk
over a proper G and T, shall we? No more of this wretched cactus
juice. It's up to me, I fear, to uphold the standards of the realm in
these backwaters."

Once inside the high-ceilinged mansion the air turned dark and
cool. The hall was filled with tall palms like some British conser-
vatory Solly might have seen in a film. The tile floors were almost
Moorish, like Spain, and Solly felt a stab of pain like an unhealed
wound. He'd thought he'd gotten used to the loss of Spain. But here
it was just as raw and new as ever.

Eton told the butler to bring in the drinks, lots of ice, cheese and
chutney sandwiches. "That one is a fantastic cook, fabulous chutneys
and curries, which the consul is addicted to. He's teaching the local
help how to prepare them. I suppose India does that to people. Either
you run screaming from the place or it's in your blood. The consul
falls into the latter category." He turned serious for a minute. "Look,
Solly, if you need a better place to kip, I can make arrangements here.

You're out there in the bush. I'm afraid you'll go stark raving mad, screaming monkeys and all that. Why don't you bunk here for a bit?"

Now why would Eton want him away from the hacienda? Not because he was concerned for Solly's mental health. All the more reason to stay. "I'll think about it, Eton. Right now, I've got my eye on the widow. She's a looker, isn't she?" This seemed like a good enough excuse, man to man, something Eton might fall for.

"She's a hothead and a lunatic. Watch out, Solly. All the more reason you should stay here."

"Let me try my luck first, and then we'll talk about it. How's that?"

"We've got a deal then. But say, Solly, there's someone who wants to see you. This way." Eton aimed his arm down the hall, indicating Solly should proceed.

Estelle. Solly felt his legs turn to rubber.

Eton opened the door, waving the doorman away, and stepped out onto a deep, covered veranda where two men were lounging in wicker chairs, both vaguely familiar. One was sandy-haired with chiseled features and clear blue eyes, the other large and florid with a mane of white, close-cropped hair, a drink in one hand, a cigar in the other. Still, there was something menacing in the air, something grim and determined about these men he knew he'd seen somewhere before.

"Solly, I'd like you to meet the committee, as we call ourselves. Senator Clay Wright is from your neck of the woods these days, he tells me. South Carolina."

Of course, now Solly knew where he'd seen him—the Pennington wedding. He was head of one of the isolationist groups, the Silver Wings, one step away from the Klan, if at all. The locals called him Red Clay Wright. They liked to say he was "one of them." Something Solly sure wasn't. The senator nodded. He didn't look too pleased to be here or to see Solly. He took a deep drag on his cigar and blew smoke in Solly's direction.

And where had Solly seen the other man who was now standing, giving Solly a curt nod?

Eton answered that question. He'd been in the picture Smith had shown him, decked out in his Nazi uniform, Estelle by his side. "I'd like you to meet Lieutenant Gunther Brandt, Solly. You don't mind having a little chat with the enemy, do you? It's all a bit of the Wild West down here in Mexico. We're far from the flagpole, and we pretty much run our own ship. We'd like to make you an offer." He motioned for Solly to sit. It wasn't like he had any choice.

Later that night, Solly watched the ribbon of smoke from his cigarette drift toward the ceiling. Twenty to eleven and he was back at his post, sitting on the hard floor of the bathroom, waiting to hear the numbers pierce through the relentless static. The floor was still as cold as yesterday, but even colder was the chill up his spine that he got from remembering the offer given to him by the committee: basically, get out, forget about buying rope from Cordier's factory, and go home, or else. Not that they specifically said the *or else* part, and Eton had tried to sweeten the deal with a payoff. The committee members had each taken pains to remind Solly of poor Cordier's unfortunate death, what happened when you stepped on the wrong toes, when you didn't know the way things were done.

Solly closed his eyes, listening to an annoying drip from the leaking faucet. He could still see Red Clay's glare clear as day and Estelle's Nazi friend giving him the deadeye. None of these men were stupid; neither was Eton. All Solly had going for him was to play the dumb rube from the Midwest, gee-whiz card, saying, "I had no idea buying rope was top secret. Nope, can't remember who told me about it. I just heard it from someone in the rag trade on the Southern circuit. Gossip really. Looked like a quick way to make some money for the company. Thought I'd look into it." He'd known he could rely on old Red Clay's deeply held belief about the avariciousness of Jews, views that he published in local papers and spoke about at Chamber of Commerce breakfasts with increasing frequency as war with Germany loomed. According to Red Clay, all Jews cared about was money. That, and bringing Communism to America, which was sort of the opposite. Solly had figured the contradiction was above old Red Clay's IQ level.

It should have been no surprise Red Clay would be sipping cocktails and smoking Cuban cigars with a Nazi. He took enough money from the Germans to spread his anti-war and anti-Jew ideas all around South Carolina. Once the Americans entered the war, that golden goose would be illegal. Whenever someone like the senator accused a Jew of being Shylock, it was a dead giveaway he had his hand in someone's pockets, the deeper the better.

Sitting in the dark bathroom, Solly would have given a lot for a bourbon, something to tamp down the anger he felt. Anger and Solly mixed together made a potent explosive. He could still hear old Red Clay's Southern drawl as he lectured Solly about Roosevelt's Good Neighbor Policy with the Mexicans. If there was one thing Clay Wright hated more than the food down here, it was the people who made it. Still, he was on a Senate committee that had to deal with Roosevelt's foolishness, and here he was. He wanted Solly to know he should mind his own business and that he was in over his head and other such pompous baloney.

The more he remembered the sneering faces of the committee, the more he knew he was not going to rest until he got to the bottom of their swindle. If Hoover wanted to investigate someone and build up a fat dossier, he could start with South Carolina's esteemed senator, and Solly would be more than happy to help.

Added to the things that clouded his thinking was his beef with the Nazi, Estelle leaning close to him in that photo like he was a knight in shining armor. Solly had every intention of bringing the Nazi to his knees. Just how, he hadn't a clue, but something would come to him. He remembered the gun, the powder in the cuff links.

And just then, he remembered the girl who'd put the shirt in his suitcase next to the gun—Grace—and had a sudden urge to talk to her, spill all the beans of the day's activities to someone who would feel the same fury he felt. For a brief minute, the candle he'd been holding for Estelle flickered. It was a strange feeling, almost sad. One woman was trouble enough. No reason to complicate matters with another, least of all his employer's niece. He put both women out of his mind.

While the static spat and crackled through his earphones, he returned to thinking about what had happened with Eton after the other men had left. Solly had brought up the subject of Estelle, saying that Veronique had told him she was in Mérida and had been having an affair with Cordier, that Solly wanted to see her again. He couldn't very well tell the truth about Smith and the photo, so he was grateful to Veronique for the gossip, which he repeated and which certainly got Eton's attention. He'd rung a servant for another round of drinks. "Do tell us more, Solly."

Solly shrugged, saying that was all he knew.

After a few sips of his gin and tonic, Eton put his glass down and told Solly in no uncertain terms he should stay away from Estelle. "Yes, she is here. Yes, she is living with Gunther Brandt." And did Solly know why? "Well. I'll tell you, mate," he continued. "Gunther pulled her out of one of Franco's detention camps. He saved her life.

That's why she didn't follow you to Lisbon. She couldn't. She'd been rounded up once Franco entered Madrid. Don't interfere now. What happened between you two was a wartime romance. Believe it or not, she's safe with Brandt. War makes strange bedfellows. I should know." He stood, as did Solly, and walked him to the door. Just before he opened it to lead Solly to the waiting car, he turned. "And by the way"—he laughed—"as far as Veronique goes, I'd stay away from her too. She's completely off the trolley."

The static was starting to get to Solly, and everything that Eton had told him that afternoon hissed in his head as well. Eton practically said outright that Brandt was a war profiteer or, at the very least, was hedging his bets. If he helped His Majesty's navy get rope for ship hawsers and the Germans lost, he'd cash in his chips. If the Germans won, well, even Eton had to admit obtaining rope wasn't much of a service. The war was going to be an air war, even if there were U-boats. Rope for anchors was neither here nor there. And the American? "He's actually the true believer, Solly old man. More of a Nazi than Brandt. The fact that he's in on this only proves my point. He doesn't care how the rope matters in the scope of things as long as the war profits go right into his bank account. You Yanks are all business all the time, aren't you?"

Solly stared up through the bathroom window at a little square of cloudy night sky. Brandt had saved Estelle's life. Not him, not Solly. There was the answer to the question that had been burning inside him for the past two years. It was all so simple. She wasn't a Nazi spy—she was trapped by indebtedness. What Brandt's motives were remained pretty obvious. Estelle was a beauty, though already damaged goods in the eyes of someone like Brandt. He could discard her at will. At any rate, that made a good story, and maybe that's all it was.

Horseshit. There was a good chance of that, and if that was so, Solly's questions about Estelle and Eton remained. He was back at square one.

It was just then that the static ended and the music began. Then came the singsong numbers. Same as last night, whatever that meant. Solly wrote them down to be transferred later to the sheet of paper in his cigarette case. Tomorrow he'd pay a visit to the tobacco store, hail a cab, and stake out the German consulate, see who came and went. He closed his eyes and tried to think of things to say to Estelle once he saw her again, words that made him seem more of a hero than Brandt, ones that would make her think he could save her now, take care of her. He had no intention of heeding Eton's advice to stay away. He'd find out where Brandt was settled down and go from there, lying in wait until he could get to Estelle.

He was lost in his daydream when the static changed abruptly to words, plain code the cryptologists called it, startling him into the very real present, the one where the Nazis could set up camp in Mexico and be a mere two hours from an American city. Wasn't that what Roosevelt had been warning about in his fireside chats? Hadn't he told Americans that we now had to protect the whole hemisphere? We were that close to losing this thing, just like Spain. Solly grabbed the pencil and wrote the German words, or what they sounded like—someone else could figure them out—as fast as he could. It would be something Smith could give the cryptologists. He knew enough from manning a radio in Spain during a war that a different message meant something was very likely about to happen soon. Whatever it was, Solly was determined to put himself right in the middle of it. It didn't take a Roosevelt to know that the same fascists he fought in Spain were right here on this side of the Atlantic. "*No pasarán,*" Solly whispered in the dark. He'd never run like a yellowbelly ever again. They'd have to crawl over his dead body this time.

13

Solly

Mérida, Mexico
August 1941

The next morning, after a rough, sleepless night, all that adrenaline running through him like a freight train, Solly found himself sharing a taxi, or what passed for a taxi out in the jungle, with a grim-faced Yakov. As Solly settled himself in the back seat, he started counting up the days he'd been out here away from civilization. Only a week. God, it seemed like an eternity, but it really was only the third week in August. Ten days ago, he was having Shabbos dinner with Mo, looking forward to a little postprandial game of pinochle and not much else, frankly. Now, here he was on some movie set for Tarzan. That is if it were set in an asylum, because only a lunatic, or maybe a man running from his past like Solly, would find himself here, sweltering in the heat and drowning in the monsoon rains. Still, and maybe this was proof that he, too, was losing his marbles, he had adapted to his bizarre surroundings. Even this cab, festooned with tinsel, religious medallions, and a big rosary and cross dangling from the rearview mirror, was starting to seem totally normal. He supposed all the religious paraphernalia meant he was in good hands. Either that or the driver, who had managed to acquire a dilapidated yellow cab and keep it running down here a million miles from auto parts, needed divine help. Anyway, the driver was in better spirits than Yakov, who was sulking in the front seat.

Solly was not certain whether the vehicle was more or less reliable than the beat-up Packard, but Veronique had needed the automobile last night and hadn't returned, so there wasn't much choice. He was stuck with Yakov, who spent the drive staring out of the open passenger window, clinging to his sheet music flapping in the breeze, and saying nothing during the ride into town. Fine with Solly. He had his own thoughts to mull over, thoughts that even the soggy heat couldn't wilt. They all concerned one thing: springing Estelle from the clutches of Brandt and then ratting out the three men in the "committee" to Smith. But not Estelle. Never her. Solly mentally brushed his hands off, imagining a job well done. He'd be a free man, Smith had said, and so he would.

Solly told the cab driver to drop him off at the post office, a faded pink neoclassical building badly in need of a new paint job. He'd go in, wander around, and once he was sure the coast was clear, he'd head to the tobacconist, a store called Los Cubanos, to hand over his notes. The cab pulled over on the corner of Calle 65. Solly hopped out and stood on the steps in the bright and boiling sun as the taxi bearing Yakov and his sheet music pulled into the traffic and disappeared behind a smoke-belching bus, heading off to the Gran Hotel de Mérida, where his talents were wasted every Thursday playing light classical music and show tunes to tea-drinking ladies. No wonder the guy was so glum. He was alive though, Solly kept wanting to remind him, not that Yakov seemed to care. That started to gnaw at him. A guy who didn't care if he lived or died could do anything. Solly climbed the stairs and lingered in the dark hallway of the post office, glancing at his watch, waiting for the appropriate number of minutes to pass, and wondering if he should be more worried about

Yakov's state of mind than he had been, which was to say not at all, and decided he should pay a little more attention to the pianist.

After a third glance at his watch, Solly stepped into the line leading to the cashiers, bought a sheet of stamps, just in case anyone asked, and headed to the doors and back into the noise and heat of Mérida. Turning left down Calle 65 and then north on Calle 62 to the tobacco store on Calle 55, he hoped the directions he'd been given were right. As light as the sheets of paper were where he'd written the numbers, they were starting to feel like lead weights in his cigarette case. The text of the plain code was a ton of bricks. If any of Brandt's minions caught him with them, he was a goner. They could use the stamps he just bought to inform his mother of his death, not that Solly thought they'd bother.

Señor Echeverria, the proprietor of Los Cubanos, motioned Solly to sit in one of the wicker chairs under a couple of lazily moving ceiling fans. They were in the humidor room in the middle of Los Cubanos, and Solly was anxious to unload his cargo, so to speak, and escape, but Echeverria seemed to want to drag the whole thing out. He called for *dos cafecitos Cubanos*, and soon a lovely young woman brought in small white cups of black coffee and little shooters of rum. A nice touch, but Solly thought time was wasting here.

"We should at least attempt to be civilized, no? War or no war," Echeverria said in perfect English, explaining that he had lived in Miami half his life but had a taste for gambling, went to Havana often, and won this little enterprise from a rich Mexican in a private craps game. He also won the rich Mexican's daughter's hand in marriage, all this before being told they were Jewish. Not that he cared, Echeverria said, but Solly figured it was an explanation of sorts, that his wife's religion could be seen as a reason for Echeverria to trust him.

Echeverria continued chatting about tobacco, describing the different types and sizes of cigars. He cut and lit a Corona Puro, passed it to Solly, and repeated the action on another cigar for himself. The wicker chair creaked as he leaned back, puffed on the Corona, and exhaled. He turned, glancing through the glass walls as he leaned toward Solly. "The wonderful thing about a humidor is that it is completely sealed from drafts to keep the temperature and humidity perfect." He spoke softly, not a whisper exactly, but close to it. "It's also soundproofed, not that I'd divulge anything, but privacy is nice, no? Drink your coffee with your cigar, Mr. Meisner. It's a perfect combination. Both come from the golden zone between the Tropic of Cancer and the Tropic of Capricorn, that bit of paradise where coffee, chocolate, and tobacco grow. It would be a terrible idea to have that fall into enemy hands, don't you think? First Paris, then the Caribbean. Not good at all. Tell me, Mr. Meisner, what is your smoking pleasure? Cigarettes, I suppose, like in the American detective movies. If so, let me offer you some of our specially blended Cherokee tobacco." He reached out his hand. "Your case please."

Feeling a hundred pounds lighter without the numbers and the plain code words stuck in his cigarette case, and with a slight buzz from the Cuban rum and cigars, Solly decided to wander over to the Gran Hotel de Mérida. Maybe he'd buy Yakov a meal. The kid could use a sixteen-ounce porterhouse to put some meat on his bones. The hotel dining room would be just the place to get a slab of beef in this town. While Yakov dug into his lunch, Solly would try to dig for more information, find out what was going on the other night when they all piled into that waiting black car. Something was up.

Solly wandered under the trees in the plaza across from the Gran Hotel de Mérida, watching the street urchins beg or, like the girl with the tangled hair who grabbed his knee, try to sell some murky-looking potion. "*Huérfanos*," the man at the kiosk laden with lurid tabloids and movie magazines told him. "Orphans. Don't let them bother you." He shook his head and handed Solly the English-language newspaper he'd bought.

Solly tried not to think of the orphans—he had enough problems already—and hopped into a chair for a shoe shine. Might as well be civilized. Isn't that what Echeverria had said, war or no? Solly nodded at the man in the next chair, who interrupted his work on a crossword puzzle to nod and say, "*Buenos dias.*"

Solly folded his paper so that the article on America's Good Neighbor Policy was prominent and glanced over at the hotel, where a large crowd had gathered, before he turned back to the news. Much of it gossip. The American ambassador had arrived, which probably accounted for the crowd. Some muckety-muck from the State Department had written a piece on the virtues of the Lend-Lease Act and another about how America was decking out its ships in Long Beach with the latest armaments, accompanied by pictures of healthy-looking, corn-fed American sailors in bright white uniforms, as if the USS *whatchamacallit* was a ship full of angels in white robes.

Solly glanced over at the hotel, where the crowd was getting even larger and noisier. He turned in his seat to see that the side street running next to the hotel had been cordoned off, police standing shoulder to shoulder to keep the crowd from entering. Solly pulled up a few more words of Spanish from the back corners of his memory. "*Qué pasa?*" he asked the shoeshine boy.

The kid kept flapping his blackened rag over Solly's shoes, babbling excitedly. All of which went over Solly's head. That was when the man in the next chair put down his puzzle and said in English. "Someone fell from a balcony at the Gran Hotel a couple of hours ago.

That is what the *muchacho* is telling you. A foreigner, a woman it seems. An accident, I gather. Drink was involved. At least, that's what they are saying. No one you know, I hope. Are you staying there?"

Solly shook his head. "Nah, I was going to meet a friend for lunch. Not a woman friend, so no one I know." He hoped he was more convincing than he felt, because his blood had turned suddenly cold with the chilling question—Estelle? Could she have fallen?

"Well," the man interrupted Solly's thoughts, "I would suggest another place to dine this afternoon." He paid for his shoeshine, nodded, and headed off in the opposite direction from the hotel.

Solly, on the other hand, couldn't get there soon enough.

He held up his US driver's license, waving it at the cop standing in front of the hotel, the only ID he had as the trip over from Cuba meant no stamped passport, no tourist visa, but it seemed to be sufficient to the distracted police officer. Solly slipped in under the covered stained-glass portico and aimed straight for one of the wingback chairs in the courtyard, one that gave him a view of all the comings and goings along the hallways that opened onto the lobby and restaurant. He scanned the guests for Yakov, but he was nowhere to be seen, and no piano music drifted down from the mezzanine. Solly figured he'd probably hotfooted it once there was a problem, but where did he go? They'd arranged for the cabbie to meet them at 4:00 p.m. in front of the hotel to take them back to the asylum, as Solly was now calling it. He flagged a waiter and ordered a sandwich, a *limonada*, and a shot of tequila to make it look like he was doing something besides snooping.

After he gave up on finding Yakov, he turned his gaze to the reception desk. It didn't take him long to figure out who the manager was—an overweight, middle-aged man with thinning hair who looked harried, probably had a wife and a bunch of kids to support.

And now this problem to deal with—an accident. And on his watch. Enough to make you worry about your job, enough to make you need a little extra cash. Solly figured he'd make what he was about to ask worth the manager's time and effort.

He finished picking at his chicken sandwich, downed his tequila, dabbed his lips, and called for the check. As soon as he saw the manager slip behind the door with the word *Gerente* written on it in gold paint, he decided to make his move. He wandered over, knocked on the office door, and didn't bother to wait to be told to come in.

"You speak English, I assume." Solly shut the door behind him, pulling out his wallet. "I need to look at the registration book. Just a quick look." He put a twenty peso note on the desk. Enough to feed a family for a week.

When the manager returned with the book and set it on the desk, it only took Solly a few minutes to find what he wanted. He pointed to the name, the person who signed into room 311. Even he was shocked to see it there. "Is this where the accident occurred? In this guest's room? Was she an Englishwoman? The one who died?"

"No. Not English. She was drunk. We can't be responsible for all our guests' bad behavior. Surely you understand."

Solly practically swooned with relief. Not Estelle. He pointed to the name in the register. Drayton Scott III. "His father is a bigwig in the US Navy. Did you know that? Admiral or something. Owns half the state of South Carolina. Could be an unpleasant problem for you."

"Well, his father must be very, very old then, because this man could have been my *bisabuelo*. My great-grandfather."

Solly reached into his wallet again for a few more pesos. "Tell me why you say that? What did he look like?"

As he took the money, the manager gave a perfect description of Senator Clay Wright. Not Drayton Scott III at all. Old Red Clay himself. And when Adrian had told Solly he'd smuggled a gringo into Mexico before by the name of Drayton Scott, he most likely meant the senator. *Well, I'll be damned*, Solly thought. *Now we're getting somewhere.* "By the way, who was she? The dead woman?" he asked as he walked to the door.

"French. Madame Cordier. Her husband died. Maybe she couldn't live with the grief."

Solly jerked his head back and stared. Veronique? Jesus. He wanted to tell the manager, *Not grief, bud—more likely murder.* But he didn't speak, just closed the door. They were getting somewhere all right, but just where he really couldn't say.

14
Solly
Mérida, Mexico
August 1941

The taxi that had ferried Solly and Yakov to the city that morning was waiting in its designated spot next to the covered arcade that faced the Parque de los Hidalgos, the driver leaning against the hood, eyeing and catcalling the girls passing by. But once Solly arrived, he stood up, ran to the door, and opened it, motioning for Solly to get in, all business now. An hour later the door was still open and Solly was still in the back seat, hoping for a breeze, hoping Yakov would finally show up, and wondering how he was going to break the news about Veronique to him. Her death did not bode well for their future at the hacienda. Solly and the driver had been waiting for more than an hour and forty-five minutes.

Solly got up, walked back into the Gran Hotel, and asked the man at the reception desk about the pianist. The man told him that they'd not seen Yakov since the afternoon, probably because everyone had been too distracted by the "accident" to listen to music. Perhaps he'd been sent home?

After a while, twilight descended over the city, turning the sky above the palm trees and the cathedral spires a fiery coral. White clouds ballooned on the horizon, and Solly wondered how long it would take for them to turn black and menacing. Would he be driving home in the dark in a downpour? The driver kept giving Solly worried glances, and his only recourse was to open his wallet and pull out a few more pesos. After another half hour of growing increasingly anxious, of getting out of the car a couple of times to walk down the block and peer down the side streets, hoping to see a scrawny, pale European among the crowds of people heading to the center of town for an evening stroll, he gave up. *"Algo de comer?"* he asked the driver. Something to eat?

The man took him to a local dive a few blocks away, a corner taco place with doors open on each side, so the heat was only mildly insufferable, and the smell of heavily spiced, grilled meat drifted out in a cloud of grease. Overhead, the fluorescent lights hummed, and in the back, men gathered at a table around a radio, squinting with concern, swilling beers. From the sound of the announcer, Solly could tell it was a fight, even if he couldn't understand the Spanish words. The driver seemed mesmerized by the sportscaster's voice as well, and Solly was grateful to eat in silence whatever it was they had put in front of him.

What was Yakov up to now? Solly mulled the question over with every bite. Girlfriend? Not likely. Hooker? Even less likely. A friend? Hardly. He didn't seem to have any. Eventually, the driver pointed to his watch and said, *"Casa."* Home. It was not a question. Solly paid, they walked back to the car, and still no Yakov. Solly shrugged. *"Vamos,"* he said, and the driver headed off for the jungle.

It was dark as tar when they pulled up in front of the rambling hacienda, which appeared even more forlorn and empty to Solly now that Veronique was dead. Not that she'd been his favorite girl in the world, but still, she was a life and that life had been extinguished.

On the drive out here, he had gone over his options, or rather, his one option: He would have to leave. Even in the black of night that fact couldn't have been clearer. The police would be swarming around here like ants because of Veronique, and by now, if they'd gotten the news, the staff would have surely taken off, knowing their chances of getting paid were nil. He would have to convey this message to Smith as soon as possible, have him round up Adrian and his boat for a trip back to Cuba. But the thing that kept gnawing at Solly was the question of what to do about the three abandoned exiles: Gottman, Birnbaum, and Yakov, wherever the hell he was. Solly couldn't just leave them. Grace would understand, and again, Solly wished he had her phone number, address, something so he could just get in touch, but he didn't. He was pretty sure that Smith would not approve of Solly's bringing in more exiled Jews, and he looked like he was the boss. Well, he who saves a life saves the world. Wasn't that what his old rabbi used to say? Not that Solly had ever paid much attention to religious instruction, but those words had certainly gotten drilled into him. Now with a war that Solly could barely get his thoughts around, he wished the teaching were more than a metaphor. But maybe a metaphor was the best he could do.

And then there was Estelle. He'd come down here to find her, and from what Eton had told him, she'd been pretty much blackmailed into living with Brandt. The thought of what that entailed made him sick to his stomach. How could he leave without her? He'd done it once but couldn't do that again. This time he'd get her to safety and see what happened after that.

The cab's headlights swiped the hacienda's gates and the driver jumped out to open them, the iron chain knocking against the ancient wood, the hinges creaking. Solly could still hear Yakov's words, *Gehinnom, das zenen mir*—here we are in hell—as clear as the day he'd first arrived, only a short time ago and also a lifetime ago. Maybe Yakov had been right. Since Solly had been here, he had witnessed the following demonstrations of misery: Veronique throwing her husband's ashes into a murky, garbage-strewn creek, her threatening Estelle's life by blackmail as well as sneaking around in the dead of night, and now, Veronique was dead and Yakov was worryingly missing. *Not exactly a fun time at Coney Island,* Solly thought as the car bounced up the drive.

He paid the driver and waited until he had driven away before he climbed the stairs, the racket of croaking frogs pounding in his ears. Halfway up, he saw Birnbaum and Gottman sitting in the rockers on the veranda, concealed from sight of the drive by heavy vines. He sat down next to them, prepared to tell them about Veronique and about Yakov's strange disappearance. When his eyes finally adjusted to the dark and a slice of moonlight appeared from behind the clouds, illuminating the porch, he turned to face them, about to deliver the blow. And he would have if he hadn't been stopped in his tracks.

Gottman was holding a German Luger in his hands, and he was aiming it right at Solly.

"Dr. Gottman, please," Birnbaum shouted. "Put the gun down. Don't aim it at him."

Gottman's hands shook as he lowered the gun to his lap, where he stared at it for a moment before looking up, blinking, as if he'd just emerged from underwater. *"Mon Dieu. Je suis très, très désolé."* He shuddered, gripping the rocker's arms.

Only after Gottman was no longer pointing the gun at Solly did Birnbaum face him. "Mr. Meisner, you know the Hebrew words *Nes Gadol Haya Sham*, like on the dreidel? A great miracle happened there? Well, my head"—he turned to Gottman—"*our* heads, they are spinning like a dreidel." He slurred his words. "A very great miracle has just happened. You can't imagine."

Solly got the picture. They were several sheets to the wind, happy as clams. "You gentlemen have been drinking, and I hate to spoil the party, but our landlady is dead. Fell from a balcony."

"Yes, yes, Mr. Meisner. We know," Birnbaum hastened to say.

Solly sat up straight.

"But first, we must tell you something." Birnbaum shook his head. "Something very sad, very shameful, and then very happy. Let me explain." He turned to Gottman, spoke rapidly in French, and after the Frenchman nodded, he swiveled in his seat and began. "This morning, Yakov called us, extremely upset, telling us that Madame Cordier had fallen to her death, that he believed that she'd been murdered like her husband, and here he became almost hysterical. 'What will we do,' he kept asking. Mr. Meisner, explain to me how he thought I should know what to do?"

"Yakov said they will come after us and we had to leave. But to go where, Mr. Meisner? First, I run from Germany and Gottman from Paris. For a while, we think we are safe in the south of France, and then we must run again, this time to the jungle, where we were foolish enough to once again hope we could be saved. When I asked Yakov who *they* were, he told me the Germans, the Nazis. 'They are every-where,' he said. At first, I thought this was Yakov imagining things, that he had finally broken down completely, but he swore that he knew what he was talking about and that we must listen to him and leave."

"So, I go to Gottman and tell him what Yakov has said, and at that moment, we decided it was time to realize there were no safe places. The Americans are not letting Jews in, and the Mexicans have no need for a French psychiatrist and a German professor. We have lost most of our families, and now should we end up as beggars in the street too? No. It would be better to die by our own hands than let the Nazis have the satisfaction. Can you see our reasoning?"

Birnbaum continued, telling Solly that Gottman knew that Cordier kept a weapon in his night table, and just as he had said, they found it in a drawer by the bed. They decided to take the gun into the office, where a large window looked over the courtyard, a nice view to see before one died, they agreed.

They planned to flip a coin to see who would go first. However, before they took their lives, they decided to fortify their resolve with a few bottles of Cordier's brandy, which he kept in a closet in his office. "And that is where we found it."

"Found what?" Solly asked, growing worried.

"The safe, Mr. Meisner. We found the safe with all our money in it." The professor jumped up and slapped his forehead with his hand. "Such a miracle."

"You're telling me the safe was open?" Solly knew that if that were the case, whoever opened it was very likely still around and was probably dangerous to boot. Two drunk professors and an old Luger were more of a liability than a help. This could end very badly.

"No, no, we decided to shoot the safe open like we see in your American movies. Always the cowboys go boom, boom, and the safe opens."

"It doesn't work that way, Birnbaum, not in real life."

"So we discovered. The first bullet ricocheted, and I said, 'Dr. Gottman, we must be careful of the ricochets.'" Birnbaum turned to Gottman and said something in French. Both men began to laugh. "Can you imagine? Here we were going to kill ourselves, and I am worrying about a ricocheting bullet. As my friend told me, the bullet would save us the trouble of pulling the trigger. Now, we should show you what we did. Come." They all trooped through the empty salon to the office. Birnbaum closed the door behind them, took the gun from Gottman, and gave it to Solly. "Better you should have it," he said, flipping on a desk lamp.

The dented and mangled safe, which had been previously hidden from view behind a paneled door on the bookcase, gaped open, the door hanging off broken hinges. Solly pointed to a crowbar on the floor next to the safe. "Where'd that come from?"

Gottman finally spoke. "The kitchen. The cook used it to lift the hot burner lids." He tapped his head. "I noticed once when I was in the kitchen, because my mother had one." He reached for the lid lifter and demonstrated how, after the hinges were damaged by the gunshots, they had pried the door off with the iron bar. "We took the money, Mr. Meisner, and hid it. There are some loose tiles in my bath. Six thousand American dollars. Enough to get us to Los Angeles, all of us, to start a new life. We can walk across the border and maybe they don't ask where we are from or if we are Jews." He sat down in Cordier's desk chair, looked at Solly with the same glazed expression he'd had when he pointed the gun at him, and then he began to weep. "*Mon Dieu, mon Dieu*, we are saved."

Solly wanted to say, *Not so fast*, but he didn't have the heart. He could almost feel himself tearing up, too, and that was the last thing they all needed now. No. What they needed was to face facts, as others would come looking for whatever the Cordiers had squirreled away. Solly was just surprised they weren't here already. How would they get away? Veronique had taken the car, but he still had the number the cab driver had given him. Apparently, the idea was to call a local cantina and the owner would send a family member over to the cabbie. If he was there—one could hope, right?—he would show up.

"Mr. Meisner." Birnbaum interrupted Solly's getaway planning. "There is more." He lifted the lamp from the desk, set it on the floor in front of the safe, and knelt, motioning for Solly to do the same. "What do you see?"

Kneeling beside Birnbaum, Solly reached inside the safe and pulled out something cold and heavy, the size of a large wallet. Silver. There must have been twenty bars in there. A fortune.

"You are thinking we have discovered a pirate's chest of silver." Birnbaum was almost whispering. "But we have not. No, it is much more valuable. Look." Dr. Birnbaum drew the lamp close to the bar and pointed out the insignia: PLAT 999. "Platinum is worth nearly as much as gold, almost one hundred times the price of silver. But its value is much more than monetary. Platinum is used for bombers, and the Germans are desperate for it."

Solly was starting to get the picture. Platinum could withstand the heat of the bombers' engines. What had Eton said? *It's going to be an air war.* Good old Senator Red Clay stood to make a fortune selling out his country.

Birnbaum continued his lecture. "The strange thing is they have very little platinum in Mexico. Most comes from South America, Colombia, if I remember my studies from university, and the Germans, I'm afraid, control the mining of it in that country. So you have to ask what is going on here, do you not?"

Dr. Gottman rubbed his face with his hands, wiping his tears, and began a frantic monologue all in French, none of which Solly could understand. He turned to Dr. Birnbaum and said, "Explain."

"Ah yes, the night you came to the hallway to get water and Gottman saw you. I will explain." He launched into a story about a drill bit that was always getting broken when the workers were sealing up the crates of rope to be shipped. One day, they were working late because the crates had to be trucked to Puerto Progreso the next day. The drill broke again, and they decided to open the crate up to see what hard object they kept hitting with the bit. That is when they thought they had discovered silver ingots and the foreman came to tell Madame Cordier. "I suppose she took some of the platinum and hid it here. Apparently she told the workers to seal everything up. She called the man at the British consulate, told him to send someone to get the crates loaded onto trucks, and she asked Yakov to witness the transfer with her, which my friend here," he pointed to Gottman, "thinks was some kind of trap. Anyway, her British partner came in a black car."

Solly figured he meant Eton. "Okay," he said. "Go on."

"Gottman says the trucks came within the hour, they loaded them up, and they were gone. So whatever trap it was, it appears Madame Cordier has fallen into it. Don't you agree? Although Dr. Gottman thinks the Germans here will think we are the thieves, Jewish thieves. So maybe Yakov was right. They will be coming for us."

The three men sat silently for a few minutes. Outside, an owl called, a monkey shrieked, heat lightning flashed, and thunder rumbled in the distance.

"Yes," Solly agreed. "Be ready to leave in an hour." He had no idea how they would get out of there, but they'd better be ready just in case a great miracle happened here.

Once the men had gone to their rooms to pack, Solly shut off the desk lamp and sat in the dark, trying not to panic. The same closed-in feeling he'd had in Spain in that basement when he'd run up the stairs, abandoning the men to their fate and saving himself like a coward, was beginning to overwhelm him. He needed to get ahold of himself, to move, to do something. He could not let that weakness overtake him again.

He lifted the Luger and checked the magazine cartridge. No bullets, just as he figured. They'd shot them all at the safe. An empty

Luger was not the solution to his problems, and even though the suffocating feeling of being trapped made him sick to his stomach, he knew he needed to hunt for bullets, maybe an already loaded magazine. He and the two expats were sitting ducks armed with just the pistol he had packed in his suitcase. They were probably sitting ducks even with a loaded Luger.

Feeling his way down the hallway in the dark to the Cordier's bedroom, he found the door, went in, and sat on the bed. The room smelled vaguely feminine, perfume and something heavier, like sweat and hair, a bit of Veronique still lingering. When he switched on the light, he knocked a piece of flowered silk to the floor. It seemed the bedside lamp had been covered with a silk scarf, now a bit of unnecessary romance, he thought. Lifting the scarf to replace it, his hand bumped the hard cover of a book that must have dropped beside the bed. *All This, and Heaven Too*, a popular novel about a governess accused of murder. He flipped through the pages, remembering taking his mother to the movie they'd made of the book when it came out, a real tearjerker starring Bette Davis. He'd just gotten the job in Pennington and he'd asked his mother out to celebrate. Her relief that he'd landed on his feet after Spain had been sharp enough to cut through the steak he'd ordered for dinner. She should see him now. More like he'd landed on his face.

He pulled open the nightstand drawer—no bullets. Then he got up, walked to the other nightstand, opened the drawer, and fished around—aspirin, a few pens, nothing of interest. There was a notepad beside the phone, but the pages were blank. He looked at the phone, wondering how early he could call a cantina, or how late for that matter. He looked at his watch. Only eleven o'clock. He would give it a try. He fished in his pocket for the card the cabbie had given him, and just as he found it, the phone began to ring, piercing the silence of the empty house in the middle of the jungle as if it had read his mind.

Solly grabbed the receiver. Maybe it was Yakov. Who else would call? Before he could speak, he realized his mistake. There were others—Brandt, for one—who would be interested in finding out if the house was still occupied and who might be checking to see who would answer. Solly put his hand over the mouthpiece so no one could hear him breathe. There was no sound coming from the other end. They'd clearly got the answer they were looking for—he was here, or at least someone was. He waited for the caller to hang up, his heart pounding so hard he was sure they could hear it over the line, but there was no click, no sound of the receiver being placed into the carriage, ending the call. Solly didn't move; he was hardly breathing. Then almost out of nowhere on the other end of the line, he heard a voice that was almost a whisper.

"Solly, if that's you, I need to see you. It's me. Estelle."

15

Izzy

UCLA Conference Center, Los Angeles
September 2008

Postpresentation bar meetups like this one used to be my favorite part of academic conferences. Well, at least in the later years of my career they had been, after I'd already made a name for myself and grad students would swarm around me, begging to hear, once again, about the discovery of the sarcophagus of the Red Queen at Palenque, whom my colleagues and I had unearthed. It was the stuff of archaeology legends. Now I was just a legend, an old one. Almost seventy, swilling my second martini, reveling in my memories of past celebrations like the one in Mexico City (complete with mariachis) after my paper "Sisters of the Red Queen: How Many More Will We Find?" had been called a game changer. That paper had eventually earned me an endowed chair and a huge amount of grant money that I could bestow like, well, like royalty. To tell you the truth, I was amused, to say the least, that the archaeology world had been so surprised about the discovery of a powerful Mayan queen, a warrior at that. There have always been powerful women everywhere, many of them warriors after a fashion. One just needs to know where to look.

My other favorite part was another kind of meetup, a run-in with

Cameron Wilson, whose photo you will have seen in many *National Geographics*, waist deep in a dig, looking sunburned and rugged in a way I think of as particularly British. These conferences were our trysting places, what two professors might consider romantic. At least now I had a companion in my dotage here in LA, the city of the young and beautiful, and in this bar, which was not dark and moody at all, on a sun-filled, open terrace, the air all balmy. It hardly felt like a place for drowning one's sorrows. What sorrows could someone possibly have in such golden light?

"So, how's the old man?" Cameron interrupted my self-pity. He always called my father, Solly, the old man, not that Cam and I weren't getting up there ourselves.

"Old, and a man. So, a toxic combination." I sipped my martini, feeling a pang of guilt about my father. I felt pity for his recent lapses. Flights of fancy? I hardly knew what to call them. "He's taken to wearing an old Panama hat around the house like a riverboat gambler."

"Not the worst I've ever heard. My father was drooling and pissing himself in a care home by the end. Sad, really, the Greatest Generation and all."

"Tell me we've got a few years before those indignities descend, Cam." Here she was, feeling sorry for herself because she hadn't been asked to serve on any panels. They'd only given her the keynote address slot. Basically being put out to academic pasture. It could be worse. It could always be worse.

"Don't brood, Izzy. We've had a good run. Speaking of which . . ." He reached for my hand under the table and held it, always careful not to let people know we were an item, as if people didn't already know and hadn't known for years. "Why did we never marry?"

"Oh God, not that again, Cam. I believe it was because you wouldn't leave the UK."

"No, it was because you wouldn't move to Britain, to Cambridge, no less."

"And be what? In your shadow day and night. No. Besides, didn't we have this discussion a decade ago?"

"I have a theory."

"I'm sure I'm about to hear all about it. If it's some therapeutic malarkey, spare me."

"You couldn't leave your parents. That's my theory. And now look at you, hovering over the old man like a nanny, so QED."

"You think I'm too attached?"

"I think that, yes, but here's where the therapeutic malarkey, as you call it, comes in. Have you heard of attachment theory?"

I rolled my eyes.

"Well, my sister is giving me an earful. She's a new grandmother. Attachment theory is all the rage."

"Cam, I'm perfectly attached to you in my own way."

"See, that's it. Your own way, as you call it, is what the psychiatrists call 'avoidant attachment.'" He raised his free hand and made an air quote. "As opposed to secure attachment, which is what parents of newborns should strive for."

"If it wasn't in Dr. Spock at the time, I'm quite certain my mother didn't think about it. She thought security was a roof, food, and two parents. Oh and no war. God, we are becoming soft." I thought of my mother. She was the opposite of soft. A queen. A warrior. That's what she was. "Honestly, this is ridiculous, Cam. I simply didn't want to be a housewife. I wanted my own life, and now some psychiatrist is going to lump that in with a bevy of women's disorders like hysteria? Can you imagine a whole lifetime of dinner table arguments like this? You would have gone batty, as you say."

I know I would have, I thought, glancing at the tables filling up with clusters of conference attendees, all young, talking a mile a minute, excited as gamboling foals. I couldn't help remembering when they clustered like that at my door during office hours, just dying to tell me about their *amazing* insights into whatever and the direction their theses were going, each one staring at me smitten and wide-eyed as if I were a rock star, so in love with life, the beginning of it, at least. The ending was starting to look like a slog to me.

Cam tugged at my hand. "Don't look now but we are about to have company."

I turned my head and saw her, a girl with long dark hair, and Cam tugged my hand harder. "I said, don't look. Oh God, now we are doomed." That didn't stop him from grinning in the girl's direction as she approached. Pretty girls, one of his weaknesses. Another reason we didn't marry. But why bring that up now? It was all water under an old bridge. We'd made it through that period. Meanwhile, the girl was on a definite trajectory to our table. I turned back to my drink, ready to order another. Let Cameron chat her up.

"Oh, wait, Izzy, she's the girl who worked with Dolin at Naranjo. Lady Six Sky, stela 29. You remember." He was already standing, pulling out a chair, ever the English gentleman.

I have to say this got my interest. Lady Six Sky, another Mayan queen, another warrior. I swiveled in my seat just as the girl reached the table. Cam was already waving the waiter over, asking the girl what she would like.

She nodded briefly at Cam and turned back to face me. "Please sit," I said. "You are with Dolin's team, right? Exciting time, yes?" I pointed to my glass when the waiter arrived and asked for another, but the girl just shook her head.

By now she had almost turned her back on Cam, something he was not used to. She placed her hands on the table and took a deep breath. . . . *Here comes the request for a recommendation.* I knew the signs.

"Dr. Meisner," she said, leaning forward, blushing just a bit. Her seeming awe of my reputation shouldn't have been so flattering to my old ego, but, alas, it was. I was already trying to scheme how this conversation could get me back on the excavation site at Naranjo. Now that would be a thrill, so I almost missed what she was saying. "Excuse me, could you repeat that?"

"Yes, of course. I'm Marissa Birnbaum, and there's the most amazing coincidence. I was talking to my grandfather about the conference, telling him who was speaking. He had his caregiver look you up on his computer." She waved her phone. "The caregiver just emailed me the most incredible thing. She says my grandfather is insisting he knew your father and that your father saved his life."

16

Estelle

Villa Balaam, Mexico
*Diary entry written on September 8
in the year of our Lord 1941*

Had the accident, or rather what they called the accident, not happened, perhaps I would never have encountered Solly Meisner again, at least not in this life, and Gunther would have forgotten his order that I dispense with him. However, the accident did indeed happen: the person fell, I was informed, from the third-floor balcony of the Gran Hotel across from the Parque. Drunk. At least that's what Gunther told me, saying it was nothing to concern ourselves with, though he seemed highly aggravated over an accidental death, especially that of someone he claimed was a stranger. So of course I knew he was lying. At any rate, I already knew about the supposed accident. I had been there at the scene of the crime so to speak. Well, the scene of my crime, my most recent.

I knew because my piano teacher, Yakov Oberstein, one of those pathetic refugees who had straggled onto the shore here, played the piano on the second-floor mezzanine of the Gran Hotel. He saw the body sprawled on Calle 60 beneath the balcony and called me, rather breathless, to tell me about it, to tell me that I should meet him, that there was more, that it was most urgent. I should never have given him my number. On the other hand, where would we be, you and I, if I hadn't?

By the time I arrived, the authorities had carried the body away. I flashed my English passport at the police officer holding back the crowd in front of the hotel entrance, told him I was meeting a friend, concerned that she would be in a state of shock, and he let me pass.

The first-floor patio was abuzz with chatter, a flurry of waiters running around like mad, supplying distraught guests with mineral water or spirits. I looked up and saw Yakov leaning against the iron railing that surrounded the open second-floor mezzanine. I nodded in his general direction and mounted the stairs.

I found him huddled in a corner sitting area, hunched on a pink brocade settee next to an abundant palm, peering about anxiously as if he'd just fought his way out of the jungle. I sat in a wing chair next to the palm, close enough to hear what he had to say but not so close as to cause comment should anyone have been watching me, which I assumed they were most of the time. In the end, I was not proven wrong, was I? I pulled out a cigarette and asked for a light.

He reached into a pocket for a box of hotel matches, struck the match head against the phosphorus strip, his hands shaking so he could hardly perform the task, and stood in front of my chair as my cigarette caught the flame. "*Une femme a* été *assassinée,*" he whispered. A woman has been murdered. "They say she fell, but I saw your husband leave through the kitchen soon after it must have happened. You must no longer live with this monster, Estelle."

Of course Yakov had obviously hoped the news that Gunther was somehow involved in the woman's death would horrify me and further endear me to the pianist, that I would recoil in terror at the thought of Gunther's dastardly dealings. But did this poor, skeletal musician really think I was so fond of him that I would run off with

him? God, men are romantic fools, aren't they? I wonder if you have
learned this by now.

I finished my cigarette, crushed it in the sand in the ashtray,
and told him he must be mistaken, that just because Gunther was
German didn't mean he was a murderer. "Not all Germans are, you
know," I said.

Yakov leaned closer. "She was Cordier's wife. First Cordier, then
her. Who is next? I need your help. I have to get out of this miserable
place."

He couldn't be serious, thinking that I could or would help him.
I was still trying to get my bearings. Veronique, Cordier's wife. The
noose around me was tightening. Veronique must have no longer
been useful to them, as I could very well be useless one day. And
then what? Well the answer was obvious, wasn't it? I shook off the
thought and returned to Yakov's request. "I am totally powerless
in this, maestro. You would have to ask my husband, and he would
require something from you in return." I continued with the charade
that I was married to Gunther.

It was then that Yakov recoiled, horrified, turning an uneven
shade of red, splotchy as a pox, as if I were the murderess, which I
wasn't. At least Gunther had not turned me into one yet.

"*Tu me dégoûtes*," Yakov hissed. You disgust me. He stood, turned
on his heel, thought better of it, returned to the settee, and buried his
face in his hands. When he looked up, he seemed resigned to begging.
"What would he need me to do? Your husband. Ask him."

"I have absolutely no idea," I lied. Gunther had been agitated ever
since his meeting with Solly and Eton, telling me I needed to arrange
a rendezvous and help him dispense with Solly once and for all. He
knew he wasn't here to buy sisal rope, because there really wasn't
any—he had to be here to spy. It was the only logical conclusion, and

Gunther was nothing if not logical, cold-bloodedly so. And Yakov had knowledge of Solly Meisner's activities since he lived with him, which could be of interest to Gunther, maybe of such interest that it would keep Solly alive a little longer. I could use that interval to buy myself some more time and find a way to get out of my dilemma.

What dilemma, you ask? This one: I despised Gunther Brandt with every fiber of my body. Therefore, I did feel a pang of guilt for Yakov. I'm not completely inhumane. I knew as well as the sun rises that once Yakov's usefulness had been exhausted, his days would be numbered. However, it was he who volunteered that he had information he could offer, that he knew the "secrets of the hacienda," as he'd called them. He'd told me there were many and that the Germans might like to know what they were. He'd made his choice and had to live or die with it, just as I'd made mine. So I sent him to seek out a hotel notepad and pen, and when he returned, I gave him the German consulate address with Gunther's name and phone extension and told Yakov to say I'd sent him.

After he retreated, I stayed where I was, half hidden by the palm, and waited until I heard the mournful notes of "Für Elise," which meant Yakov was back at work. I had to hope now that he would indeed be useful, and because I'd sent him Gunther's way, remind the German that I was still useful as well. Because with Gunther, I had three choices: be amusing, useful, or dead.

I searched for my cigarette case in my purse, asking myself what difference Yakov's betrayal of his comrades really made in the whole scheme of things. Small potatoes in the face of the war.

I finished my cigarette, touched up my makeup, and wandered down to the lobby, where I encountered a bellboy on the landing. "*Joven*," I called to him and stepped back into a corner, reaching for my wallet from my purse. First, I showed him the photo of Gunther, then pulled out a ten peso coin, a small fortune. Was he here? I asked. Did you see him? He eyed the coin hungrily but remained silent. "Look, you don't have to say anything, just nod yes or no." He nodded yes. "Which room?" I asked as I extended the coin closer, then closer until he finally told me, and I dropped it in his palm.

My hairdresser was around the corner. I called from the reception desk phone and made an appointment for a shampoo, set, and manicure. That should take about an hour and a half. By then the commotion would have died down. I had a plan.

17

Solly

Mérida, Mexico
August 1941

Solly shook himself, knowing he'd lost precious time sitting in the Cordiers' dark bedroom, hand on the phone out of which Estelle's voice, the voice he had longed to hear for over two years, had just floated like a butterfly or a genie from a bottle, like magic.

How long had he held on to this dream of her, of them? It was as if during the years they had been apart, his life's clock had stopped. Now with one call, the gears had been wound and were pulsing once again, the clock's hand moving forward finally.

Her British voice, how he had longed for the sound of it. That accent—Eton had called it posh pronunciation—where a cat was a *ket*, a hat was a *het*. To Solly, back in Spain, it had sounded lazy and breathless and postcoital, which must not have been what the royals intended, but now that voice rang in his ears and filled his head. No, his heart.

"Solly," she'd said, her voice scarcely more than a whisper. "Have you got a moment? Perhaps we could have a chat? I'm finding myself all rather desperate." Those last words had been mumbled, as if she'd just sipped a martini at some terribly tedious party. But there was a tell. Solly noticed it right away, good gambler that he was. Her voice was shaking. Not that Solly was surprised by that. He'd figured she was in trouble, that she had to be if she were with some German, regardless of what Eton had said about strange bedfellows and all that. He'd wanted to save her since the minute Smith had shoved Hoover's dossier his direction. Now was his chance. He closed his eyes and remembered her lifting her gold hair, spritzing that scent—Shalimar, she'd told him—on her neck before going out into the heat of Barcelona. All the sun- and blood-soaked memories of Spain came back. That's what she'd called them, saying they'd never forget. And they wouldn't.

"Meisner! Meisner!" Someone was shouting his name, and he heard footsteps racing down the long hallway to the bedroom. "Meisner!" Birnbaum called again, snapping Solly out of his reveries. "Is here. The car you called. We can go."

"What car?" Solly shouted. He hadn't called the cantina, hadn't contacted the cabbie. He'd been swooning over Estelle's call. Jesus. "What car?" he shouted again. "Where's Gottman? Get down, Professor Birnbaum, and stay down."

All Solly had was a dead Luger and the Swiss Army knife that he'd put in his pocket on the boat and had never taken out and that he now flipped open so that the blade was gleaming in front of him. Whoever walked up those stairs, well, Solly would be waiting for him. He would bring the gun down as hard as he could on the intruder. Knock the guy out, use the knife to take care of the rest, get in his car, and go. If there was more than one intruder, if there were both Brandt and Eton, then Solly and the other two were goners. He left the Cordier's bedroom, walked down the hall, crouched, and hurried to the door at the top of the stairs. Plastering himself against the wall next to it, he lifted the gun and held his breath.

Someone outside was yelling. Not Eton. Not Brandt. Not a

language he could understand. Solly slid down the wall, crawled to the window, and peered above the sill. There it was. The old Packard parked in front of the house, and Yakov climbing the porch stairs in a rage. "Birnbaum," Solly called out. "It's Yakov."

"Ah, Jacob returning from his journey," Birnbaum cried out, rushing down the stairs. He flipped on the light switch and brightness exploded in the room. Yakov was still shouting when he pushed through the door.

"What's he saying?" Solly demanded.

Birnbaum shrugged. "The Polish, I don't know. The German, yes. He wants to know why we were all standing around in the fucking dark."

Solly pushed the blade of his knife into its cover, shoved it in his pocket, went through the door to the stairs, and sank down on the landing, staring at the useless gun. They weren't out of the woods yet, but they had a car. They were no longer trapped here, and he wouldn't have to call some jungle cantina and pray someone arrived to rescue them. As dilapidated as the Packard was, it would get them where they needed to go, to Puerto Chichan, to Adrian's boat, which would ferry them to Cuba. "Explain to Yakov," he told Birnbaum, "that he needs to pack. Explain the whole goddamn megillah. Make sure you pack up as much of the platinum as you can. We leave in an hour. And keep the lights off. We don't want to give ourselves away."

Solly figured an hour would afford him enough time to pack up his radio and rummage around Cordier's closet for clothes these guys would need in order to look like vacationing Americans. He'd check them into the beach resort Veronique had taken him to. They could hide out there for a few days while he got in touch with Smith, who could call Adrian to bring the boat. He headed back to the bedroom, pulled a suitcase from a shelf in Cordier's closet, and went to work opening drawers, pulling out linen shirts.

He rummaged through Cordier's clothes for swimsuits, sandals, anything the men could wear so they didn't immediately give themselves away as Jewish refugees in their dark clothes and brown fedoras. He unclasped the suitcase, opened it up on the bed, and then remembered something a Russian spy in Spain had told him on those long, boring nights waiting for a radio communication, how a suitcase could be outfitted to carry contraband, that it happened all the time.

He pulled his knife out of his pocket, sliced into the side of the lining, and peeled it aside, revealing a leather-covered false bottom. Slicing down the sides again, he pulled off the false bottom to see a pile of hidden papers filling the space. He didn't have the time to sort through the documents carefully, but he got a good enough look to tell that he'd hit the jackpot. He rifled through the pages, Spanish bank statements, shipping inventories, papers from a Danish company in a language impossible for him to decipher but that repeated the word *cement* several times. If *cement* in Danish meant what it meant in English, he might be onto something. He remembered those piles of cement bags he'd seen at the roadside cantina where Cordier's body was found. He had a strong feeling there was a connection that Cordier had known about.

Pushing those papers aside, he opened a folder holding receipts for wire transfers from the Banco de Portugal to the Banco Alemán Transatlántico and records from a Colombian merchant. "Holy moly," Solly mumbled to himself.

He'd heard rumors from the *brigadistas* that banks in Spain and Portugal laundered money for the Nazis. Solly would bet the farm that was what he was looking at here. The way he figured it was this:

the platinum got shipped with the cement bags and the sisal rope, whatever would look like normal business. Then the Germans purchased it with dirty money stolen from all the confiscated Jewish accounts and property, money that had been warehoused in accounts in Portugal before being sent to untouchable accounts in Switzerland. It was a nice living if you were a Nazi and things like stealing from innocent people and then murdering them didn't bother you.

Then Solly pulled out a photograph of Senator Clay Wright on a dock, a freighter's hull looming up the side of the picture. So not just German Nazis were involved in this scammeroo. Hoo boy, Solly was definitely in the money. On the back of the photo someone had written *Campeche—the Montevideo*. Solly would find out where Campeche was, what the *Montevideo* carried, and prove what he already knew: an American senator was in the employ of Nazis, shipping platinum and hiding the payments. Money laundering, at the very least. Not quite trading with the enemy yet since the US was not at war, but still, it would be a savory morsel for the Pennington newspaper to get ahold of, wouldn't it?

Wait up, he told himself. What was that story Mo's friend Hurwitz had told him? About the loan officer, about things being put into a safe-deposit box in Pennington? Drayton Scott complaining about how heavy they were? About a German voice? Maybe the loan officer's death in Pennington hadn't been a suicide at all, and everyone there was a lot closer to the enemy than they knew. Solly's thoughts froze.

Unless Mo knew or suspected. Hadn't he hinted at that? *A terrible thing for a man to end his life. Even worse if someone else wants to help him do it.* That's what he'd said.

Jesus. Solly sucked in his breath, gasping, almost dizzy. The way he saw it, Cordier had been planning to blackmail his business partners.

Why else were these papers hidden in a false compartment of a valise? Cordier wasn't just keeping a record of standard transactions.

Well, Solly had the documents now, and all he would have to do was have a nice little chat with the American ambassador. Clay Wright's career would be toast, Eton would be hung for treason, and the German? President Camacho's hired guns would take care of him.

Cordier was dead, ditto Veronique, the poor sap of a loan officer, too. They had been murdered for a reason.

He put the documents back, checked his watch, and carried the suitcase to the waiting Packard. He wondered how long he had before Eton and the German came after him like they had come for Cordier. Not long, he thought, heading to his room. He called out to the men to be ready in half an hour. They had to get moving.

He stood in his cleaned-out quarters and felt around for his cigarette case, realizing there was no way he could explain all this on a small piece of paper delivered to the tobacco store. No, he would have to call Smith. But whatever Smith's reaction was, Solly knew he was going for broke. He would get to the bottom of this. Southern Mexico was hiding Nazis and traitors—that was the only word for Wright—behind palm trees and candy-colored, pastel buildings, and whatever they were plotting in the unbearable heat of August, they were a mere two hours by ship or U-boat to New Orleans. The Nazis were damn well nipping at the States' heels. Hard to really believe, and too dangerous not to. He lifted the suitcase and closed the door behind him, hoping to never see the place again.

Over and over again as he drove the three men down the dark roads of the jungle, he asked himself where he would be now if he hadn't felt around the lining of the suitcase, used his knife to cut through the false bottom. But he had, and there, hidden by the lining, was everything he would need to give to Smith, to make him honor his word about his FBI dossier, make his past all go away. Solly didn't have much love lost for the Russians in Spain—they had been pretty horrible—but he did have to thank that NKVD spy for the lesson in subterfuge. A little knowledge and a Swiss Army knife could get you far, he thought, realizing he'd be telling himself that for the rest of his life. It would be his motto. He should live so long.

Solly leaned over a bit to look at himself in the rearview mirror, wanting to tip the classy Panama hat he'd grabbed from Cordier's hat rack at the last minute. Cordier wouldn't be using it anymore, would he? But just as Solly pulled the brim down, something metallic and sharp scraped his forehead.

"Hold the wheel," he told Birnbaum. It would take only a minute to turn the hat over and check to see what was hidden—another clue, no doubt. He pulled the sweatband away from the straw and poked around with his thumb. A wire, razor thin. He had an idea of what that could be used for. Had Cordier known? Too late for him now, as it turned out. Solly put the hat back on and took the wheel from Birnbaum. He was getting to the bottom of something, a lot of things, and when he did—what had Smith said?—he'd be a free man. Yes, indeed, he would. They all would be.

18

Grace

Los Angeles, California
August 1941

Grace had gotten Smith's telegram around seven thirty in the morning. She was still in her bathrobe standing in the kitchen when the doorbell rang, the chime filling her with dread. Knowing her crowd, people who slept until noon unless they were working on the set, the chances of this being a friendly visit were slim to none. She tightened the tie on her robe and rushed to the door, where a Western Union messenger handed her a beige-colored envelope, hopped on his bike, and pedaled away, not waiting around to see her reaction to the news. She ripped open the envelope and stared at the blocks of type pasted on strips of white tape: *PLEASE CALL COLUMBUS 4786. STOP. URGENT. JOHN SMITH.*

It had taken at least two hours for Smith to pick up the phone, and even then, he had told her he would have to call her back. After she had spent another forty-five minutes pacing back and forth in front of the telephone, he rang her from some drugstore phone booth, coins jingling as they dropped in the slot. While the lunch counter's malt machines whirred in the background, he told her Solly had gone off in his own direction according to the tobacconist, which was unfortunate, dangerous even. It seemed they might need her help once again. He'd be in touch with more.

Wasn't that what he had said on the ship crossing from Havana to Miami? *We'll be in touch if we need you.* Now several hours after the call, which had rattled her, she hadn't heard anything else and was trying to play it cool in front of her guests as she lounged by her pool in the last scorching days of August, a cold gin and tonic sweating in her hand.

Her coworkers—Mort, one of the makeup guys, and Sam, his longtime friend, as he called him—had no idea of her clandestine activities and were at this moment regaling her with the stories of Mattie Pennington's drunken husband's recent escapade at a wrap party. Grace nodded and said the appropriate words when necessary, but her mind was a million miles away. Closer than that actually, but she didn't really know the distance from LA to the east coast of Mexico, so a million miles would have to cover it.

Sam was operating the cocktail shaker at the swim-up bar, and to the sound of ice rattling in the background, he said, "You missed a real wingding last night, Gracie, baby. First, Drayson—"

"Drayton," Mort corrected him, drawling out the words "Drayton Scott the Third. Rhymes with 'turd,' darling."

"Call him Rhett Butler, for all I care," Sam laughed. "Anyway, he was several sheets to the wind when he began holding forth, a little too loudly, on how Los Angeles was a city of mongrels. Don't you love it?"

Mort rolled his eyes. "These rubes. Where did Mattie Pennington find him?"

Sam poured a couple of martinis. "Well first, Drayton the Turd started in on the, let's see, what did he call them? Ah yes, first the hebes, then the beaners, next the niggers, and—a new one for him—the nips. He said he had never really seen any of those slanty-eyed bastards before. Please, God, let the navy send him to the Pacific."

Mort took the drink Sam handed him, sat down on the chaise next to Grace, and continued the tale of the disastrous party. "At some point, Gracie, I lost count of how many times he said the word *hebes*, but Jim Walter, the writer—he's not even Jewish—walks over to him and says, 'You say that word one more time, and I'll knock your teeth so far down your gullet you'll have to see a proctologist for your dental work.'"

Grace set her drink down and threw an arm over her eyes, feeling weary to her bones with one more story of Hollywood shenanigans—one too many, frankly—one more rendition of what passed as revelry here in the City of Angels. She longed for that quiet evening at her uncle's, for the sound of the crickets at night, for another meeting with Solly Meisner, who was operating on his own, it seemed, no longer following orders, off on a wild hair Smith had said.

Solly had gone to Spain to be a hero once. Who was to say he wasn't trying to be one again? But heroes did more than just ignore protocols. They didn't ride off tilting at ancient windmills anymore. What if Solly was trying to be some shining knight, only now the enemies of this twentieth-century world were far from Siglo de Oro giants or a romantic nobleman's imaginings? Nazis and fascists were true looming terrors in the distance, hiding behind their slogans, slogans that promised jobs, order, and prosperity, but only if the fanatics were allowed to rule unobstructed, only if society cast out the degenerates. And who were those degenerates? Everyone Grace knew. All her kind, all her funny friends and family—artists, writers, homosexuals, Jews, liberals, her sweet Uncle Mo. Grace sighed. It would be wonderful if there were more Quixotes than Hitlers these days, but there weren't. Smith was right: Solly was in danger.

But just as worrisome to Grace was Smith's sudden desire to rein Solly in. He hadn't seemed so concerned on the boat, had said Solly's job was to rout out the rats, and had implied Solly's death would just be collateral damage. So what had caused Smith to change his mind?

"Yoo-hoo! Penny for your thoughts?" Mort dipped his hand in the pool and sprinkled her with water. "This story isn't over yet, doll. So, after Walter tells Drayton he's going to shove his teeth out his ass, Mattie starts laughing, and I do mean *laughing*."

"Hysterically," Sam said. "Like she was high on something. So Drayton walks over to her and shuts her up." Sam made a fist and punched the air. "Pow! He belts her right in the kisser. The party ended then. Drayton the Turd stormed off, and we've been waiting to hear if there has been a police report of a car wrapped around a telephone pole somewhere off Mulholland. Alas, not yet."

"Anyway"—Mort sipped his drink—"Sam and I were left with Mattie, who is going to have a shiner the size of Texas. Good thing the movie wrapped. No makeup person, not even me, darling, would be able to cover that up." Mort sighed. "She hates him you know. Any idea why?"

"No idea," Grace said, sipping her gin and tonic and squinting at the sunlight reflecting off the pool. "Well, I can think of a million reasons, but what hers are specifically, no. Furthermore, I don't care."

"I had no idea you were so heartless, darling."

"I'm not. I'm just bored to smithereens by all the drama." She set her drink down, swung her legs off the lounge chair, slipped into the pool, and swam a lap to cool off. The heat was fierce and so were her thoughts. She shouldn't dismiss Mattie so quickly, she realized. If Smith never got back to her, Grace, too, could go off on her own, find Solly, and perhaps aid him in some way. Mattie knew where Adrian, that man with the boat, could be located. She was the one who led

Solly to the *Orquidea,* after all. It wouldn't be hard to get her to spill the beans. She would tell Mattie that she heard about the fight and that she could find a private eye to catch Drayton in flagrante delicto. He'd be too stupid to know how those things work in Hollywood. A quickie Mexican divorce would follow. If that promise didn't work, she could always threaten to tell the studio about Dr. Boyle and the happy pills Mattie got from his sleazy office out in the Valley. Mattie must know how the studio felt about dope fiends, and Mattie must also know something about Solly's whereabouts. They'd make a trade. Her silence for Mattie's information.

"Well, there's a little more drama," Sam said. "Mort and I have to take a trip to TJ in a few days. Want to join us? We could go to Caesars, have one of those special salads, the"—he batted his lashes—"'gastronomic invention of our generation,' as *Vogue* magazine called it. Do a little shopping, take in some shows in the clubs on Avenida Revolución, absorb the faded glory."

"Who is she?"

"The supporting." Sam shook his head. "The lead knocked her up. That's why the studio keeps a Tijuana doctor on the payroll to take care of these little problems. The actress keeps her mouth shut and gets a big payoff."

"If she lives."

"Yeah, I know. Seems like a rum deal to me, being a girl."

Or what had Drayton called them? Grace counted the slurs. Hard to be anybody except a leading man or Drayton the Turd. Well, she would like to make it a little harder for the leading men of the world. Do her bit to even things out. What had she said to Solly when she left him on the boat? *The last thing the world needs is another dead Jew. Be careful.* Looked like he wasn't taking her advice.

"Sorry, Sam. I have other plans." Then she remembered the gullible supporting actress, the poor kid. The last thing the world needed, too, was another knocked up girl dead from a botched job. "Promise me you won't let her bleed to death. But I can't go."

She thought of the TWA Stratoliner ticket she would purchase at the travel agency whether or not Smith called. The suitcase she had to pack. The little chat she would have with Mattie Pennington. She would find Solly, be a heroine in her own right, and ride off on her own horse to slay monsters no matter how quixotic it seemed to others. What did she have to lose, really, given where the world was headed, where her life was headed? She and Solly might have a lot to gain. Anyway, that was her hope, something in very short supply these days. A little hope wouldn't hurt either of them, would it?

19

Solly

Progreso, Mexico
August 1941

Solly leaned forward over the hotel bar's second-floor balcony, clutching the rickety iron railing and squinting over the roofs of shabby buildings past drooping electrical wires toward the Gulf of Mexico, its brackish, green water blindingly bright and waveless in the hot, still afternoon. He felt feverish from heat and from nerves, as well, he had to admit. *Why here?* he wondered. There were certainly higher-class establishments around, ones that were not occupying the floors above a ground-level tortilla shop and a pungent-smelling butcher, places more up Estelle's alley. So why had she specifically named this hotel, the Playa Blanca, at this time, three o'clock? The summer afternoon's most suffocating hour. She must have had a reason.

Just the jitters talking to him, he told himself. Who wouldn't have them? He was about to see the woman he'd loved and thought he'd lost after a harrowing past twenty-four hours. Going over the recent episodes, Veronique's death, the gun in Gottman's hand, their wild tales, and finally the money, the platinum, he felt as if he'd landed in a comic book world, explosions going off right and left—*KAPOW,*

BOOM—colored lightning bolts shooting from the villain's fist aimed right for his jaw.

As if that weren't enough, he'd just parked three lost Jews at a beachside resort with a promise to return, and the anxiety of what blunders they could commit during the day was weighing on him too. He hadn't signed up to babysit refugees. But that was the way life was. Who signed up for any of this? You just did the best you could.

"Looking for someone?" a voice called from inside the bar. "I wouldn't lean too heavily on that railing, by the way. Not sure it's up to code if they have such a thing down here."

Solly turned, took off his sunglasses, and peered past the jalousie door into the barroom's shadows where, under the twirling overhead fan, a blond man was seated at a table with a bottle of Coca-Cola and a couple of now empty shot glasses, cards lined up in front of him. Solly recognized the spread. Solitaire.

"An old friend," Solly answered and turned back to the street, hoping the stranger would take the hint and leave him alone. He didn't.

"More unsolicited advice: I'd get out of the afternoon sun if I were you." He placed another card on the table, looked up, and laughed. "Do you think anyone ever wins this?"

Solly glanced briefly at the cards before checking his watch: 3:15. "Not my game, sorry." He wiped his sweaty hands on his slacks and gave up staring at the street. Gave up trying to get a glimpse of Estelle before she saw him. He walked into the bar, grabbed a couple of paper napkins from a dispenser on an empty table, and mopped his face and neck, reminding himself Estelle was never prompt.

"Not mine either, apparently. I'm on my third game and have lost every one. Care to join me?" He waved at a seat next to him. "Rum and Coke? It's the mineral water of the Yucatán."

Solly shook his head. "A little early, I'm afraid. You Swedish or something? It's the accent."

"Danish actually. Frans Pedersen." He stood and walked toward Solly, leaned on the door next to the balcony, and lit a cigarette.

He looked to be around six foot two, Solly figured, and since he was only five-ten, it was like standing next to a Viking, one who must have navigated far off course. "What brings you down here?"

"Same as you, I suppose. Work. Money. Certainly not the malaria. What do you do, anyway?" the Dane asked. "Not much down here but rope and mineral smuggling—tungsten, mercury—and you don't look like a smuggler. What's your line?"

"Sisal." Solly hoped he wouldn't ask more, because that was the sum total of his guidance from Smith and the COI.

Pedersen stepped out onto the balcony and pointed over a row of buildings to a long pier, where trucks and burro carts carrying crates of sisal and bags of cement, and Solly could just imagine what else, maneuvered their way around dockworkers. "See that? All the lorries? My company. Well, not mine. The one I work for, overseeing this endeavor." He pulled out a card and handed it to Solly. "The water depth here is too shallow for large ships, so the idea is to extend the pier about three kilometers into the gulf. We'll have to see if we're building it for Nazi ships or for the Yanks, won't we? We could use your country's help, frankly."

"Building the pier? Or in Denmark?" Solly took off his Panama hat and fanned himself with it. "Anyway, your country will have to get in line after the Brits."

"Actually here in Progreso and not with the pier." Pedersen nodded toward the north. "Pretty much a free-for-all sixteen kilometers out there in international waters. We've had all types of vessels come in, steal things, drop off contraband, pick up contraband, or worse. The local police force is not much help. One worries about getting shang-haied onto an Axis boat. Do you think the Americans will get into the war?"

"Roosevelt doesn't confide in me, so I can't exactly say." Solly glanced at his watch again. 3:30. He turned to face the street, but the Danish man didn't leave.

"Well, I'll confide something. You should stay out of the sun." Pedersen walked to the bar, ordered a bottle of cola, and beckoned to Solly. "You're perspiring like a fire hose. Eat some of these." He pushed a dish of peanuts toward the empty seat at his table, set the cola bottle next to it, sat down, and resumed his futile solitaire hand. "Salt. You need it. You can get lightheaded and not think straight. Not a good idea here in Mexico."

Solly sat down across from the Dane, turned the chair so he had a good view of the door, and swilled some of the soda pop, all the while watching, listening for footsteps outside, but the whole street below was deadly quiet.

Estelle had stood him up once before, made a fool of him. Why wouldn't she do it again? Or worse, maybe the damsel in distress act was a setup. What was Smith's warning? *They tried to kill you once before. Who's to say they won't try again?* Maybe the Nazi would appear instead of Estelle, and Solly would be a sitting duck, wait-ing for his girlfriend on the second floor of a fleabag hotel bar with no way out. This wasn't some kid's Action Comics issue at all, and he was no Superman able to leap from the balcony and swing on the electrical wires. He eyed the Panama hat he'd set on the table, remembering the thin sliver of wire he'd found in the lining. Too bad Cordier hadn't been wearing it when they came for him. Good thing Solly had checked once more when he got to the resort. A gar-rote, that's what it was. And he remembered another little morsel, one he'd learned from the Russian spy in Spain. *Get behind the guy, wrap the wire around his neck, ram your kneecap behind the guy's knee. He'll lose his balance. Then, pull as hard as you can.* These were the things you learned in a war's quiet moments, what passed for a friendly chitchat.

Solly grabbed another napkin, wiped his face, and swilled some of his drink. Maybe a shot of rum wouldn't hurt. He raised his arm at the bartender and pointed to Pedersen's shot glass. "*Uno más, por favor.*"

"That's the spirit," Pedersen said, placing a spade on a row of the same suit. He leaned back in his chair and shook his head. "Good thing I'm a better blackjack player. After this blasted war is over, I'm going to hit the tables at Monte Carlo. That is, if there's even a casino left or a bank with my money in it. I thought my cash would be safe in that little principality— nothing to spend it on here—and Monaco has declared itself neutral. Old Prince Louis seems to be working the room, so to speak, so maybe I've nothing to worry about. He just turned over all the Jews to Vichy France, so he'll probably be getting something in return." Pedersen turned over a diamond and placed it under a jack.

The bartender pushed a glass of rum across the counter. "*Señor,*" he called out. "*Su ron.*" Solly got up, using all the energy he had that hadn't been sapped out of him by the humidity, by his thoughts of Estelle, and by restraining himself from saying to Pedersen, "Nothing to worry about if you're not Jewish." He couldn't battle every callous remark. He'd have a heart attack, be dead before Estelle's German could get to him. Solly grabbed the shot glass and took a swig. "*Es Cubano,*" the bartender said. "*Lo mejor.*" The best. "You drink slow. Okay, gringo?" Solly nodded, sat down, and took another sip of rum. All he wanted was to belt it back, to numb his rising despair at being stood up again. But that would give away his game, wouldn't it? Not that his game was very good at this point.

"She'll be here," Pedersen said, sweeping up his cards, not looking at him. "Actually, she is here, the woman you're waiting for. Been here for about an hour, I'd say." He reached into his pocket and pulled out a key. "Room twenty. Mine." He pushed the key across the table.

"How the hell?" Solly sputtered.

Pedersen coughed into his fist, covering up the sound of Solly's words. "Don't look surprised. Don't say anything. Just take the key. I'll settle up with the bar. Walk down the hall, turn left, and then up another flight of stairs. Oh, one more thing." He pulled out a deck of cards from his pocket. "Always good to have one of these. Helps while away the long hours and then some. Don't open it now. Goodbye, Mr. Meisner. I'm sure we'll meet again." He turned to the bar. "*Joven*," he called out.

Solly reached out his hand for the cards, wanting to slug the Dane for leading him on, for having Estelle in his room all the while, but the minute he had his hand around the pack, he knew it wasn't cards. A camera he guessed. Maybe Frans was a spy as well. Maybe his answer, "same as you," meant more than it had seemed at the time.

Nodding to the Dane, Solly walked off, weaker and dizzier than he'd been in Spain with bombs falling all around him, and that scared him. In none of his daydreams about meeting Estelle again was this what he'd pictured—sweating in a run-down hotel in the middle of a dusty Mexican port, a stranger handing him a key to her room. No. He was forever on Eton's balcony in Barcelona overlooking Las Ramblas, and she was always standing in that golden light, young and beautiful.

Walking down the dark, narrow hall to the stairs, he sensed that image was about to be shattered forever, and he hesitated before bounding up the stairs, filled with more dread than delight but still doing his best to play the part of a man overjoyed to have found his true love after so many years, grinning like some sap on a movie screen.

Stopping for a minute, he leaned against the wall to catch his breath, to still his heartbeat, and saw his hands were shaking. He pressed them flat behind his back, and when he felt the tremors stop, he reached for the key, turned it in the lock, and opened the door.

It took him a minute to get his bearings. "I'm sorry," he said, stepping back into the hall to look at the number by the door, but it was room twenty, all right. If so, who was the elderly woman sitting in a chair facing him, a small child at her feet, clinging to a rag doll? "I must have the wrong room."

"No." The woman stood, walked to the bathroom, and tapped on the door. "*Está bien. Es él*," she said. And then she turned to Solly, saying in English, "You have the right room. I'm Sister Immaculata. The child and I are going for a walk. We'll leave you alone. "*Ven, mi hija*," she said, lifting the dark-haired girl. "Say bye-bye."

"Bye-bye, bye-bye," the child chirped, blowing kisses from both tiny hands.

The sister made the sign of the cross on Solly's forehead. "Remember that God gives us no burden he cannot help us bear. *Dios le bendiga, señor.*"

Solly waited until they had closed the door, not knowing whether he'd been blessed or cursed, wondering whether he should stand, sit, knock on the door, or call out her name when, finally, the bathroom door opened.

"Well," Estelle said. "Look what the cat dragged in. Have you a cigarette? I'm a bloody nervous wreck."

Solly's sight blurred, and with it, Estelle's face. To his shame, he realized he was weeping. "Jesus, Estelle," he said, reaching into his shirt pocket and pulling out the silver case. "Long time, no see." He wiped his face with the back of his hand.

She hadn't changed that much, if at all, and now the faded memory of her turned into a flesh and blood woman, not quite as tall as he remembered, her features not as symmetric. Still beautiful, but something was off. A certain sparkle was gone, but why wouldn't it be? They were no longer in Spain, in that beautiful country before everything went bad, before they lost the war, their dreams, each other. Even a phoenix rising from ashes was probably more bedraggled than the Greek myths had let on. He reached for his lighter, flicked it, and lit her cigarette. She inhaled, leaned forward, snapped the lighter shut, and moved into his arms.

"When is the nun coming back?" he asked, his voice breaking like a teenager's.

"She's not."

"Who's the kid?"

"An orphan. The sisters run an orphanage."

"So, it's just you and me?"

"For now, yes. And really, Solly, that's all that should matter."

Solly unbuttoned his shirt, threw it on the chair, pulled the gun from his shoulder holster, and unsnapped the lock. "In case your Nazi boyfriend shows up." He walked to the bed and set the pistol on the nightstand.

"He won't." Estelle followed, sat on the bed, and set her cigarette in the ashtray.

"You sound sure of that." Solly unbuckled the shoulder holster and tossed it on the chair on top of his shirt. "Why not?"

"Because he knows I'm here. He sent me to—how did he put it?— dispose of you," she said, taking off her heels. Waving her shoes, she added, "I'm not carrying, so you know. Care to pat me down?" She threw her shoes on the floor, stood, and wrapped her arms around Solly's neck, pressing herself against him. "It's been a while, hasn't it?"

Solly reached behind him, grabbed her wrists, and lowered them to her sides. After years of longing, after reliving every moment, every tangled sheet in every hotel bed in Spain where he couldn't quench his thirst for her, couldn't soothe his need, he had never dreamed that when the moment he saw her again finally came, he would feel nothing. No, not nothing. Loss, sorrow, pain, rage—those things he felt, maybe even fear—but as he looked at the gorgeous woman offering herself to him now, the lace of her slip under her blouse, the swell of her breasts, all those other feelings crushed him like an avalanche, suffocating whatever desire he'd thought he would have. She'd put him through so much grief, and right now he hated her for it.

When Smith had pushed his dossier across the desk and he'd seen Estelle with her Nazi lover, he'd wanted to find out all he could. Hadn't that been the goal? Hadn't he thought that would make him free? Well, if freedom were a kind of emptiness, then perhaps he had it. "We have a lot of catching up to do, Estelle." Solly let go of her wrists and sat down on the bed. "For starters, who's the Dane, who's the nun? Why are we here in this dump, and why didn't you come to Lisbon? After we clear up those little items, we can move on to the safe house in Madrid. Who did you tell? Why were we bombed? You know something, *Estrella*, my beautiful, golden star." He jumped up and took her face in his hands. "You broke my goddamned heart."

20

Estelle

Villa Balaam, Mexico
*Diary entry written on September 9
in the year of our Lord 1941*

I was supposed to "dispose" of Solly Meisner with strychnine, a substance more suited to a British mystery novel than an actual wartime murder, but most Nazis, and Brandt was no exception, were not readers of popular fiction. That is if you didn't count the absurdly maudlin tome *All This, and Heaven Too*, which they used as a code book for cryptic messages. Gunther had an English copy in his drawer, random words underlined in pencil. Once when I asked him about it, he told me he'd meant to look up the words in a dictionary. Not believable, but I played dumb and never saw the book again. It was Cordier who told me it was a code book. He talked too much, that one, trying to impress me, something Solly Meisner did not, upon the occasion of our first meeting in years, attempt to do in the least.

Why had I told him to meet me at a port hotel of questionable reputation? Very well, I will begin there. It was disreputable, I'll give Solly that, just a step up from a place rented by the hour, but the sheets were clean, I'd been told by Frans Pedersen, a Danish engineer who was rather fond of the place. As he liked to say, the rum was good, the tacos weren't made of bush meat, and the whores that hung around were young, pretty, and creative.

I'd met Frans at some soiree or another at Eton's. He knew I was off-limits, so we struck up a friendship. One afternoon, he brought a stunning couple, friends of his, to the library at the local university where I used to retreat. They were Mayanists, Danish like Frans, and lived the most adventurous lives, digging up ancient pyramids and floating in canoes on jungle rivers with Indians that even Cortez never discovered. I was smitten. Wherever they were going, I wanted to come along. Like most bohemians, they had more wild ideas than they had money, and that's how I could be of service, having recently come into a rather large inheritance from a Bloomsbury aunt, money that my family couldn't touch. It was a secret I'd kept from Gunther as well. I no longer needed him to support me financially, and his knowledge of that would have only put me in danger.

It was then and there, at that library, that I began to plan my escape, pouring over Catherwood's books and reading Bernal Castillo de Diaz's *True History of the Conquest of New Spain*. I learned the Indigenous Mexicans called chocolate *comida de los dioses*, food of the gods, and that the nobility drank cups of it in their honor. What else, what other knowledge, I wondered, was buried out in those jungles?

For the first time since Spain, I had direction, and that path was about to lead me to a jungle paradise at the edge of a broad savanna where the trees were full of quetzal birds and butterflies that swarmed in such numbers the Danes said it was like walking through a storm of blue wings, an exotic place called Palenque. There, I could enter another world, another century, and I vowed to myself nothing would keep me away.

Not even you.

But back to that afternoon in the Playa Blanca.

Almost all of my answers to Solly's questions were true, but with gaping holes. I told him Gunther Brandt demanded that I "dispense" with him using strychnine—a terrible way to die. "Shooting you," I told Solly, "would have been kinder, but it was really Gunther's decision. He was not about to give me a gun."

I explained that I had told Gunther that I would arrange a tryst, so the Playa Blanca seemed like a good cover. It was also next to the pier and near Frans Pedersen's office. I told Gunther I would arrange passage on a ferry to Veracruz, where I would administer the strychnine. But, unbeknownst to Gunther, we would not be on the ferry when it arrived in Veracruz. I would go off with the Danish couple who, delighted with my offer of support for their work, would meet me at the Port of Campeche and take me overland to Palenque. Whereupon I would disappear into the jungle and be gone forever. What Solly did once he got to Campeche was up to him, at any rate. "Why look so glum?" I asked him. "I'm saving your life now."

I should have left Mérida sooner, but then who was to know that Cordier's wife would be assassinated and that Gunther would suddenly demand my services, or . . . well, or else? Like a fool, the Frenchwoman must have revealed that she knew about the platinum smuggling, leaving Gunther worried that Solly knew as well. She should have kept her mouth shut, as I have. She was beautiful but dumb as a post. What did she think spilling the tea would get her? The American senator was up to his neck in financial problems, Eton needed a nest egg to bolt back to India where he could carry on with his houseboys as in the past, and Gunther wanted to rise up in the Reich. They called themselves the committee, and Veronique Cordier was certainly not a member. Whatever she had told them had got her killed. *Et voilà*, as they say in France, I was the one having to deal with the wreckage she left behind. Of course Gunther would insist that I do the dastardly deed and eliminate Solly. He couldn't get his hands dirty.

But someone else knew about the smuggling as well: Frans, who'd seen it before his very eyes at Puerto Progreso. It had been careless of Eton and Gunther, but they'd been confident that the Danish company was on their side, that it was all just business. The fact that Frans cared at all about what Gunther was up to made me suspect he was in the employ of more than just the Danish engineering company. Very likely the British spy agency had him on their payroll as well. That suspicion was more or less confirmed when he suggested that we pull Solly in at about the same time Gunther said it was my turn to honor our bargain. I can still see Gunther lifting a vial, raising it to my face, and asking, "Do you know what this is, Estelle?"

So, I picked up the phone, called Solly, and pretended to be desperate. Perhaps not such a pretense after all.

Solly's question about the nun and the orphan was more complicated. That's when the gaps in the story became giant craters. I told him that helping at the orphanage was a cover. It allowed me to get out from under Gunther's grasp by visiting. His men couldn't follow me into a convent. The church had been desperately poor since the revolution, Sister Immaculata and I needed each other, and for my meager financial support, which I mostly stole from my allowance from Gunther until my recent inheritance, she had been helpful in orchestrating my escape. Did that satisfy his question? I didn't tell Solly about my need to save my soul. That was between our Lord and me. There was more, one last secret to reveal, but I would save it for later.

By now, Solly had gotten up, had grabbed a wet washcloth, and was swabbing himself off, looking at me like I was Lucrezia Borgia or something, so I lowered the boom, no longer needing to be careful with his feelings. His for me were disappearing before my very eyes. "About the bombing of the specific villa off Retiro Park. How did you escape anyway, Solly? You're accusing me. How do we know it wasn't you who sold them all out?"

I will never forget the look of hatred on his face. He threw the rag on the bed and grabbed the gun off the nightstand. I thought he might shoot me, and I was truly terrified. That possibility had never occurred to me. I'd been certain that I could woo him back as easily as I had seduced him the first time, but I was wrong. I breathed a great sigh of relief when he shoved his gun into his shoulder holster and said, "Take my word for it. I didn't."

No woman likes to be scorned, and while I never loved Solly—I'm not sure I believe I'm capable—I was attracted to him, to his good looks, his liveliness, and to his fascination with me. So to bolster my own esteem, I went in for the kill. "Ah, but you did." I almost laughed in his face. "That room where we stayed? There was an air vent. Eton heard everything." I let that sink in before I finished with the coup de grâce and said, "Remember how you wanted me to know where to find you? Remember? How many times did you give me the address? That was all the information Eton needed to supply to the Falangists. You told them, Solly, because you were a lovesick fool."

Perhaps I was being too cruel, but I couldn't stop myself. That look of contemptuous judgment on his face about my decisions goaded me on. What do men know of the terrible challenges women face? Nothing. Anyway, I was on a tear, so I continued.

"Have you figured it out yet, Solly?" I asked him. "That Eton and I were never on the Republican side? Russian thugs and peasants and disheveled intellectuals in moth-eaten jackets, communist writers, and, well, Mosley's least favorite people—Jews—were not our type of crowd." I let that sink in. "Yes. We had been Mosley supporters all the time." I must have been sneering by then. I could tell because my voice had got that pinched sound it gets, as if it had to squeeze itself past a gullet full of disgust. "Don't think your side didn't commit atrocities, because you did. At least we wanted to save all the beauty, all the art you barbarians were destroying with every church burning, every castle you ransacked. Half the Spaniards fighting with you couldn't even read." I was standing by then, full of umbrage, righteous in my fury against the masses. "For God's sake, what have the masses ever created of value?"

"Spoken like a true member of the nobility," Solly spat back. "It's the backs of the masses that have raised you so high." He looked sick, so I let that jab at my being a member of royalty status pass.

As far as why I didn't go to Lisbon? "Female trouble," I told him. "We should have been more careful. Eton got me some help. It was brutal, but you don't need to know the details." And he didn't, at least not yet.

But as for you who are now reading this, know that you are descended from that nobility Solly so disparaged. However far back in our history, it is still in your blood.

I'm usually known for calculating self-control, so what got into me, I don't know. I told him even more than I had intended just to watch him suffer. Why should he, a man, get to escape the pain of the decision I, a woman, was forced to make simply to live a life I desired? "I was pregnant. I had a baby, you bastard. Her name is Isabella." It was done, the last secret divulged. No going back or hiding you now. "She's with the nun."

21

Solly

Campeche, Mexico
August 1941

"The Mexicans have a saying," Frans told Solly just as the lights of Puerto Campeche came into view. The two men were stretched out on deck chairs on the first-class level of the Progreso–Veracruz ferry, the one that made a stop in Campeche, where Estelle, Frans, and Solly would get off.

Estelle had bought tickets all the way to Veracruz, one for Solly and one for herself, just in case any inquiries were made about the two *gringos* and their whereabouts. Estelle had insisted on the full passage, telling Frans it could buy her some time if someone—Brandt?—had to waste a few hours checking to see if she had purchased train tickets from Veracruz to Mexico City instead of returning to him on the next boat. None of this was exactly safe, but then it seemed none of them was in the business of safety. Not anymore, that much was certain. Solly, least of all.

Another ship, the SS *Bolivar*, was due into Campeche's port at noon, several hours after their ferry docked, and Frans had told him that among the passengers who would disembark were two America First politicians, isolationists who ranted to one and all that the Jews were profiting off this war and that was reason enough for America to remain neutral, and a handful of Germans, one named Bachmann, were naturalized American citizens, all spies for the Nazis. Their staterooms were pretty much Nazi Party headquarters.

When Solly asked him how he knew all this, he shrugged and told him he could probably figure it out. "Your British girlfriend," he said, "is pretty good at finding out this kind of thing."

What she and Frans didn't know was that Solly already had the goods on these guys—the papers, the photograph. Frans went on to inform him that the men he'd just mentioned were planning on hunkering down at the only decent hotel in town for a few days until the transfer of platinum and funds was complete. After that, they would pick up the SS *Montevideo* and head for Florida. *Bingo*, Solly thought. The same ship as in the photo with Senator Red Clay. He was getting closer and closer. Estelle, Frans continued, had eavesdropped on everything and had ratted them out as her final act of revenge on Brandt. Frans wanted Solly to document these men's activities. *Not a problem, pal*, Solly thought. Consider it done.

"By now, you might want to have a look at that deck of cards I gave you. Not cards. A Minox Riga, the best little spy camera in the world. Pictures of all this could sway Roosevelt or, at the very least, expose these isolationists for what they really are: traitors and war profiteers. People like them always accuse the Jews of doing exactly what they themselves intend to do. Are you willing to do this job?"

And what else could Solly say but yes? Because saying no was not an option, not when people, whole countries, in fact, were willing to follow a madman.

"They will kill you if they find out, you know."

"I know," Solly said. If his family had stayed in the old country, as so many had, he would have been dead already. Being an American had already bought him a few more years. He was grateful enough for that to do what needed to be done.

"Good. Well then, so, about the women in our lives, the Mexican saying goes like this: There are three women in every man's life," Frans continued, lifting a bottle of rum and taking a swig while ticking the numbers off on the digits of his left hand. "There's the woman he wanted to marry but couldn't; the woman he should have married but didn't; and the woman he did marry but never should have." He sat up, reached over, and shook Solly's shoulder. "So, which one is she? The mysterious Estelle?"

The truth was she was none of the above, even though after he had learned of their daughter back in the Playa Blanca hotel, Solly had pleaded with her to marry him, even dropped to one knee, held her hand, and begged, swearing that he would be honored and so on, to which she had only laughed, saying, "I'm not the marrying kind, Solly." He had been raised to think all women were the marrying kind, especially women who'd found themselves pregnant out of wedlock.

"Don't think you're doing me any favors by asking for this fallen woman's hand in marriage. I'm beyond being shamed on that account, and I don't need your help." She'd rubbed her rejection deeper into the wound in his heart.

He'd jumped up, donned his holster, gun, and shirt, turned on his heel, and without so much as a farewell, stormed out of the hotel room, slamming the door behind him, filled up to his throat with rage and shame. If Frans hadn't been waiting for him, leaning on the Packard, saying it stuck out like a sore thumb so you couldn't miss it, and if he hadn't convinced him to go to Campeche with the lure of getting a firsthand glimpse of the platinum transfer, Solly would have been back at the beach resort by now, finding his daughter. It was still a bit of a vertigo-inducing shock to know he was a father, and God, he wished he'd gotten more than a glimpse of his child, his own flesh and blood. He should be contacting Adrian at this moment and getting them both the hell out of Mexico, not lying on a deck chair, listening to the waves slap against the sides of the boat and eyeing the lights of Campeche as if they were torch-bearing warriors amassed along the horizon.

"Did she tell you where your daughter is?" Frans asked.

And that was the sticking point. She hadn't.

Soon after they'd left the port of Progreso, Solly had knocked on Estelle's cabin door, wanting the answer to just that question. He was actually surprised that she'd opened it and that she had left it open, inviting him in. But no sooner had he entered the cabin than he'd felt the old claustrophobia starting to strangle him and had asked if they could talk on the deck.

"Good idea," she'd said. "That means you won't be badgering me to marry you since we'll be in public." She grabbed a wrap and locked her door.

They'd found a sheltered spot behind the lifeboats, lit a couple of cigarettes, ducking under the tarps out of the wind when Solly realized he didn't know where to begin. He muttered the expected words, that he was sorry she'd had to face such a terrible experience alone, that he could understand why she was angry, he hadn't meant to abandon her.

"Bloody hell, Solly, stop," Estelle demanded, exhaling cigarette smoke from the side of her mouth, holding her hair back with her hand and shaking her head. "We both know that isn't what happened. I abandoned you. And in the end, I experienced only a few months of discomfort, and it was over. The nun at the hospital, Sister Immaculata, had a cousin who had gone to save the souls of heathens in Mexico, and she intended to go there herself. Eton was being sent there, or had arranged it. You never know with him. He lured Brandt into my orbit, and I did the rest. Anyway, I believe in destiny, so here we all are, even little Isabella. It's all God's plan."

"I think God has his hands full these days, and he's doing a pretty piss-poor job of managing the business."

Estelle's face hardened into disdain. "Don't say things like that. Showing contempt for God is blasphemy."

"Blasphemy? God? What about our daughter? Because you see, I think showing contempt for human beings is the real sin here." Solly had to shout over the ship's motor and the rushing wind. "You intend to let Isabella grow up on the streets of Mexico, selling those nostrums the nuns make for cough syrup in the plazas? Being pushed away like a stray dog? Have you seen those urchins? Who's to say those nuns will use the money for Isabella?" Solly grabbed Estelle's arm. "Tell me where this nun is, and I will bring our daughter to my parents. They will love her, a surprise grandchild, a *mameleh*." He could just see his mother sewing party dresses with ribbons and tulle, his father in his shop building dollhouses. This little girl would be cherished.

But Estelle had other plans. "Of course not, Solly," she said, yanking her arm away. "I will pay to keep her here at the convent until after the war and then send her to board in England when she is seven. Don't interfere." With that, she stubbed her cigarette out under her shoe and walked away.

"And what if there isn't an after the war?" Solly shouted after her. "What if Hitler wins that war? What happens to our little *mischling* then? She could grow up in a world where the storefronts have signs that say 'No dogs, no Jews.' That is if your new boyfriend Brandt has his way." He only had to think of the despair in Yakov's eyes, of the beaten spirits of Gottman and Birnbaum, their wasted genius and talents. These were not things his daughter would ever experience or know. Not if he could help it. "Wait until your daughter finds out you were a Nazi collaborator. She'll love that about her mother."

Estelle turned around, rushed back to Solly, and shouted in his face, "Who are you to judge me? Men have all the choices in the world, and each little act of theirs is deemed remarkable. And women? We can choose the kitchen or the convent, motherhood, monotony, or madness. I'm no saint, and I'm not maternal in the least. Think what you like if it seems I've chosen the latter. It was the only thing left, and madness, at least, is interesting."

Solly could see she was shaking and went to embrace her, his instinct to keep her from the cold, or from her despair, or her mania.

Estelle pushed him away. "Don't worry. No one will know she's Jewish. I'll tell everyone there was a handsome Spanish *marqués* who seduced me, that she'll carry on the royal line. You've been erased from the picture." She walked away, this time without looking back.

Solly gripped the lifeboat, dizzy with horror, the blood pounding in his ears. The woman he had loved so desperately was making up some fairy tale about their child. He threw his cigarette overboard, his mood as dark and roiling as the night-black sea. He decided to play his last card, to see where it got them, and ran toward her, pulling her around to face him. "Did you ever love me, Estelle?"

It had taken only a minute to realize she had no intention of answering him, and in that brief interim, as the whitecaps rose and crashed around the boat, Solly knew he would never see her again. Once she marched down the gangplank and rode off to the ancient ruins with the mysterious Danes, whatever had occurred between them would be over.

Except for the child. He could still hear her little singsong *bye-bye* in his ears, see her mass of black curls. He only had three clues to Isabella's whereabouts that Estelle had let slip—*Sister Immaculata, here,* and *convent.* Well, if he had to search every convent in the Yucatán jungle, he would find her. If it was the last thing he ever did, he would find her.

"Well did she?" Frans interrupted Solly's thoughts. "Did she tell you where your daughter is?"

"Why wouldn't she?" he answered, not wanting to spill his guts.

"Well, first of all she's hidden the child from Brandt, and from what I understand, Brandt wants you gone, so he's keeping an eye on you. Speaking as an engineer, someone whose job it is to make things fit together, I'd say she doesn't want you leading Brandt to the child. And if she didn't tell you, then I suspect I am right. What are you going to do?"

"Why do you want to know, Frans? What's it to you anyway?" But he had to admit it had never occurred to him that he could bring even more danger to Isabella.

"I owe you something for the work you're about to do. I could ask around and look for the child. I could help."

A Danish engineer with a rum bottle in his hand didn't look like too promising an accomplice to Solly, but it was all he had. "Thanks, *amigo.* I'm usually a bit of a lone wolf, but I don't have much choice, do I?"

"No," Frans said. "You don't."

22

Solly

Campeche, Mexico
August 1941

I n the sweltering noon heat, Solly sat at a rickety table by the window of the Bar Rincón across from the terminal at Puerto Campeche, from which he had a perfect view of arriving passengers as they lugged their baggage out of the customs terminal past clusters of beggars, hailed fly-swarmed, horse-drawn taxis, sweat stains under every raised arm, and haggled with the drivers over fares under the blistering sun. He'd passed the Rincón on his way to the *zócalo* after getting off the ferry and had noticed its prime location, good for capturing pictures of the Nazi-loving suspects he was looking for from the SS *Bolivar.*

Once he'd checked into the only decent hotel in town, where Frans had assured him they would be staying, and had taken a room with doors opening onto a second-floor veranda with a good view of the church and the people milling about, perhaps even the men he was looking for, he'd returned to the bar, first stopping to buy a pair of cheap binoculars in the hotel's gift shop. He'd positioned himself by the large, arched window next to the bar's swinging doors, and feeling around in his pocket for the Minox camera, reassured it would only take a second to pull out and shoot a photo, he waved the bartender over. "*Ron? Tequila?*" he asked, and, pointing to the menu painted on the wall, he mimed eating. "*Comida?*" He would need some food to sop up the alcohol he intended to drink in order to drown his sorrows. They were many, starting with Estelle and ending with his daughter, who was somewhere in the jungle.

When he'd gone to fight the fascists in Spain, he'd had no idea he would return with new enemies, demons created by his cowardice, his stupid lovesickness, and that he would be left with a whole new war to fight, one that would require a different strategy: that he put his grief for Estelle aside, expose the traitors, find his daughter (and then what, exactly?), and get Birnbaum and the others to safety. He was starting to understand that a large part of being a mythic hero was simply showing up and completing the required tasks, and that from where he sat, Hercules had gotten off easy. What was slaying a lion or the Hydra compared to fighting Hitler and Franco?

After the ferry from Progreso had docked in Campeche, Solly had completed his first task, heroically willing himself to stay in his cabin, to not watch Estelle get off the boat, to not attempt to catch one last glimpse of her. What difference would it have made? Frans had continued on to Veracruz, but Solly had his card in his wallet and would see him back in Progreso. He could always find out from him where Estelle was then and follow her, couldn't he? Sure, hope springs eternal, but who was he kidding? She'd made it clear they were finished.

The bartender, mumbling the word "*botanas*," interrupted Solly's daydreams and placed a plate of *panuchos* on the greasy oilcloth-covered table in front of him. "*Cuál? Ron o tequila?*" Which one? the bartender asked, bringing Solly back to his sad, lonely reality.

He understood why they called it heartbreak. The pain in his chest was like a just-forged nail burning into his sternum. He could hardly breathe and almost panted the word *tequila*, wanting something strong and bitter to wrestle his grief to the ground. The bartender nodded and brought a shot glass and a bottle to his table, marking the height of the liquor with a stub of charcoal. Solly figured you paid by the inch.

"*Camarada*," a woman's voice called out from the corner of the dark bar. "*Más vino tinto, por favor, más vino para la gitana.*"

The woman's staccato Castilian accent pulled him right back to the streets of Spain. More wine for the gypsy, she called out, but when he turned around, he found himself looking at a very pale blond woman hiding in a shadowy corner, hardly anyone's idea of a gypsy, hardly a maja flamenco dancer. No, from what he'd seen in Spain, she was clearly from the upper classes, so why was she here?

"*Ya basta, borracha*," the bartender shouted back. You've had enough. The few men leaning on the bar swilling the local *micheladas* laughed, shrugging off the woman with scorn.

"*Cobardes*," she yelled at them. "Cowards, all of you." And with that, she began to pound the table in a rhythmic beat and to sing words Solly would never forget. "*Viva la Quince Brigada, rumba la, rumba la, rumba la.* They will cover us with glory, ay Carmela," she continued singing. "But bombs can do nothing when the heart is strong. *Pero nada puedan bombas, donde sobra corazón.*"

"Is your heart strong, *gabacho*?" she shouted. "*Oye, gabacho, te hablo.*"

Solly realized she meant him—he was the reviled foreigner—and he glanced at the bartender, who looked down, absorbed in washing glasses. Clearly he wasn't going to intervene. He'd just let the *extranjeros* work it out.

"What does a girl have to do to get a drink in this place?" the *gitana* asked, walking over to Solly's table, pulling out the chair opposite him, and straddling it like a film star gun moll, raising her chin, daring Solly to ignore her.

She was surprisingly well dressed for a drunk woman in a seamy bar at noon and beautiful in that European way—the high cheek-bones, the aquiline nose, all the hauteur of a Greta Garbo etched on her face. Leaning forward so that Solly could smell the sour wine and cigarettes on her breath, she whispered, "Do you know what I am?" she asked. "A whore." With that she burst out laughing, a rasping laughter that quickly turned to sobs.

The last thing Solly needed was a barroom scene, but instead of throwing the drunk woman out, the bartender brought a coffee to the table and pushed it toward the Spanish woman, who grabbed the tequila bottle before he could get his hands on it and swilled. "*Sol*," she said, after knocking back the tequila. "*Y sombra*"—she pointed to the black coffee. "*Lo que construye la vida.* What life is made of, sun and shadow, sweet and bitter, rich and poor, fascists and *la gente buena.* Are you one of the good people, *gabacho*?"

Solly stood, trying to attract the bartender's attention, pay his bill, and leave, but as he stepped away from the table, the *gitana*—he couldn't think what else to call her—grabbed his arm.

"How much will you pay, *gringo*? How much an hour? You owe me. The Americans could have stopped Franco, you bastards. He killed my husband and my son. I took the first ship out of Barcelona and washed up here. *Destruida*." Destroyed.

He breathed in hard and wondered if she noticed, if she would recognize that reaction and understand that he knew and might have been there. How could she? Still, he wanted her to know, wanted to say something, have her understand that he was one of the fighters, the ones *La Pasionaria* called "history, legend," but he was in too much danger now as it was, and others—his daughter for one—depended

on his cool head. If word got around that some American who'd
been in Spain was singing *brigadista* marching songs in a bar, well,
he worried the information could find its way back to Eton and to
the murderous Clay Wright. Solly uttered something stupid about
how well she spoke English, just to cover his tracks if he'd revealed
himself in any way.

The woman straightened up. "I was a professor. English literature,
the modernists. Hemingway, Orwell, they all came to my home." And
with that information, as if it had taken the last bit of strength she
had, she placed her arms on the table, put down her head, and wept.

Solly leaned against the old fort's walls in the shade, swatting mosquitos, and lifted his binoculars, scanning the horizon for the *Bolivar*,
which was scheduled to dock in an hour, trying to get the image of
the weeping Spanish woman out of his mind. *Destruida*, she had said.
Destroyed. *How many of us were among them?* he wondered. All of
Europe, if you looked at it a certain way. Solly had got off easy. He just
had a broken heart, a broken spirit, not a completely destroyed life.

In the distance, several ships floated in the water's haze. Any of
them could be the one he was looking for. He watched the brown
pelicans through the circles of his binoculars as they settled like bar-
nacles on the fishing boats, waiting for bait to be thrown, for prey,
and reviewed his plans, all the while hearing his father's voice, *Man
plans, God laughs.* When the pelicans suddenly lifted, taking flight,
squawking like geese, flapping their huge wings as they flew toward
him, he jumped back. Were they an omen? Was he starting to believe
goofball stuff? He shook himself, turned from the old fort's walls,
and walked toward the marina, steering himself through the suffocating heat.

By the time he reached the terminal, his shirt was limp with sweat.

He pushed past the usual phalanx of beggars, dropping a few coins in the nearest outstretched, gnarled hands, headed over to the bar, ordered a Coca-Cola, and studied his surroundings.

The arrivals entered the terminal on the right-hand side. Between the archways that said *llegadas* and *salidas* stood a large round kiosk, now ringed with customers. Solly figured he could wait, hanging around the kiosk. He could buy a paper and a pack of cigarettes, a roll of Life Savers, get the first glimpse of the war-profiteering Nazi bastards. He would be just any inconspicuous customer, and he did rather blend in, his Semitic coloring and black hair an asset under the circumstances. With the tropical shirt Grace had packed in his valise and his newly acquired straw hat, pilfered from Cordier's closet, he could pass for Mexican or some version of a Caribbean native. What had Mattie Pennington said? He looked like a rich Cuban. Let's hope she was right.

Solly walked toward the kiosk, dodging a man on a ladder adjusting the letters and numbers on the board that announced the shipping schedules. When he got past him and looked up, he saw that the *Bolivar* had been delayed and would now dock an hour later. With time to kill, Solly bought a copy of the *Excélsior* newspaper, not that he could understand the articles, but it made him look like even more of a local, and grabbing a seat on one of the waiting room benches, he opened his paper and pretended to read, waving away Chiclets sellers, girls selling melting popsicles dotted with flies, another kid hawking a pamphlet, shouting, "*Horario. Horario de buques semanal.*" Ship schedules for the week.

The man across from Solly called the boy over, bought the pamphlet, glanced at it, and threw it down, disgusted. As he rose from his seat, he looked at Solly, raised his eyebrows, sneered, and said, "*Tarde como siempre,*" before storming off. Late as usual. Even Solly understood that. He grabbed the *horario* off the seat, scanned it, and muttered, "Jesus." There it was. All the information he needed.

The *Montevideo*, the ship in the photo Cordier had stashed away, would arrive tomorrow at three. Another look at the columns told him she would leave at eight in the morning the following day. He walked to the ticket counter, looked at the brochure displaying the fares, and for thirty bucks bought a ticket for steerage to Portugal. Cheap, and—who knew—it might come in handy. He passed a five hundred peso note under the grille and waited for his ticket and change.

The large clock on the south wall of the terminal read 4:30 when some functionary finally rang a bell and announced the *Bolivar*'s arrival over a bullhorn, more than two hours late. Solly was dead on his feet from fatigue. He'd already frequented the bar countless times for shots of café Cubano, thick black sludge, sweet enough to make his teeth ache, anything to help him stay awake in the miserable heat of the terminal. He was tired to the bone but so close to getting what he needed. He couldn't tell if that thought made him jittery or if it was the combination of coffee and Coca-Cola, but he could feel his heart skip every so often. When he held his hand out in front of him, it shook like a flimsy kite in the wind. *Calm down*, he told himself. *You can't spoil this now.*

Pandemonium ensued as porters ran every which way, pushing their luggage carts, scrambling to be the closest to the gangplank when the first-class passengers strode down in their white linen suits and summer dresses. A great deal of shouting echoed in the terminal, the noise amplified by the hard, concrete walls. *Rapido, rapido*, the porters cried out, but they were soon drowned out by the bleating of the ship's horns and the motors of the tugs. *This is it*, Solly thought, reaching in his pocket for the camera. He walked to the kiosk and leaned on the counter, scanning the gates for arriving passengers, not exactly sure who he was looking for. He'd only been given the name Bachmann by Frans. He would have to rely on hearing them speak. German-accented English and Southern drawls would be his only clues.

There was, however, one familiar face in the crowd. *La gitana*, the woman from the bar. Of course she would be here. A port terminal might as well be a prostitute's office. Why hadn't he thought of that? Because he hadn't taken her seriously when she had said she was a whore. He'd seen whores in Spain. They were all over soldiers like lice. None of them were this fragile, so he'd ignored that bit of information. However, now that he watched her in action, her skills could be useful.

She eyed the *Bolivar*'s passengers like a housewife searching for a butcher shop bargain as they dragged themselves into the terminal, wobbly-legged after a long sea voyage, and struggled to keep up with their racing porters who had dashed off with their luggage to the immigration office for customs processing. She only approached the single men, especially those with small valises, possibly businessmen away from home and its moral constraints. Most of them shoved her aside. How could one person endure so many curdled glares, so many shoves? Solly lit a cigarette, inserted himself in the crowd, and wandered over to her. "How much for the whole night?" he asked.

She jumped back and then squinted, drawing closer, "Ah *sí, el gabacho*. I remember you. You apparently have more energy than I realized," she said, regarding him with contempt. "I wouldn't have thought you had it in you. I had you pegged as *muy flojo* in the bar."

"I can imagine what you're thinking," Solly said, noticing that she hardly seemed thrilled with the prospect of hours of work feigning pleasure, providing it. He leaned in close and whispered in her ear, trying to make it look like a normal hooker-john transaction. "But that's not what I have in mind."

"When men say things like that, it's usually worse than I've imagined."

"Not this time," he said. "Maybe we can help each other."

"Give me a cigarette," she demanded, stepping back and looking him up and down. "Not bad," she purred, looking at him as he lit her cigarette, acting the part of the whore now. "Why would you want to help me?"

"Because," Solly grabbed her arm, whispering as softly as he could, "I was in Spain, *mujer*," he told her, throwing down the best card he had. "A *brigadista*, the Lincoln Brigade, and I'm still fighting now."

She jumped back, eyes wide. "*No me mientes, cabrón*," she hissed. Don't lie to me.

"Never," he said, slipping her fifty pesos, watching as she regarded it hungrily before shoving it into her purse. "*Camarada*," he said, "here's what I need you to do."

Solly stepped closer to the arrival door, leaned against the wall, and watched her work her magic. She should have been on the stage, not selling her wares in a pestilent little port town in the tropics. "*Sprechen sie Deutsch? Hallo, schöner Mann*," she called out, waving, wiggling her hips, offering herself just as Solly had asked her to do, using the little German he'd taught her. Hello, handsome man. *Sprechen sie Deutsch?*

He'd learned those phrases from the giggling German nurses in Spain, the ones who always brightened the surgery tents, teasing their wards, batting their eyelashes. *Hallo, schöner Mann*. It was a surprise what information could come in handy later in your life. "Hello, handsome" was about the sum total of Solly's German, and now he was having a hooker use it as a trap.

After an hour passed, only a few stragglers wandered in from the dock. The crowd had thinned considerably, and the porters had returned to their stations and were sitting on their luggage carts, joking around. Solly was about to give up, wondering how he'd missed the men he'd been sent to find. He'd been too focused on the Spanish woman's antics, certain they would work. He glanced briefly at three uniformed crew members as they walked by the *gitana*—he would have to learn her name—and who burst out laughing when she called out, "*Hallo, sprechen sie Deutsch.*"

"*Ja, ja,*" they shouted, surrounding her, leering, joking lewdly, Solly guessed. When one of them put his arm around her and said, "*Ich heiße Herr Bachmann, Fräulein. Ich liebe dich.*" Solly jerked to attention, reached for his camera, and began to click away. Bachmann, the German that Frans had told him to be on the lookout for. But just then Senator Clay Wright stepped out of a door to the left of the ticket counter, the one with the words *Agentes de Estibadores* written in black letters on its pebbled glass window. He beckoned to a couple of porters, their carts loaded with fifteen or twenty wooden crates, all leaking straw and covered with official-looking stamps that should get them through customs, no questions asked. Solly figured out what *estibadores* meant—the stevedore office, the agency that would load the crates, also no questions asked. He aimed the camera right at old Red Clay Wright and snapped. Ain't we got fun, Senator? Solly knew damn well what the porters were pushing into that office and why. *America First baloney*, he thought. *Got you dead to rights, Senator, selling platinum to the Nazis.* J. Edgar Hoover was going to have other fish than Solly to fry. The thought of his FBI dossier being tossed into the waste can made him feel as lighthearted as if he had sprouted wings. He would no longer have to rely on Mo Blumberg looking the other way, ignoring his commie past, and hiring him. He could go someplace glamorous, to New York or to Hollywood, where Grace Weintraub lived, where it was always sunny. Hell, he felt free enough to fly to the moon.

It had been a long time since he'd felt this unburdened and dizzy with . . . what? Was it relief? His vision blurred and he hardly knew where he was or how he'd gotten there. But the search was over. He'd done his job. What had Grace called him? A hero. This time maybe he damn well was.

After the terminal had cleared out, and Bachmann and the rest of the crew had followed the senator into the *oficina de estibadores*, Solly motioned the *gitana* out to the street and told her to follow him to a little straw-roofed fish shack he saw down the road by the beach.

"Buy me dinner," she told Solly when she joined him at a rough-hewn table placed in the sand near the water's edge. "And while we're at it, you owe me for the whole night. Fifty more pesos," she said. With that, she turned her face from him, watching the seagulls fly up into the sunset-colored sky.

Under normal circumstances, the setting would have been beautiful, even romantic. But these were not normal circumstances, were they? He looked at the ripple of waves on the gulf, heard the calling of gulls heading for nighttime shelter, and thought of the menacing pounds of platinum waiting to be sent to Germany, waiting to go into bombers that would blow up normal circumstances for a long time to come. He waved over the cook, who was sporting a greasy apron, and asked *la gitana* to order some cold beers and to ask if he could make them a large plate of shrimp and rice. "It won't be paella," he said, "and this isn't Spain, but it will have to do."

"Speaking of Spain," she said, "prove to me you were a *brigadista*."

He told her about being a radio operator, about friends who had died on the banks of the Ebro River, about how he survived the siege of Madrid, though he left out his great shame about the bombing of the villa, the men he'd left dead. He told her how he'd fled to Portugal at the end and was now being investigated by the FBI in his own country for being a communist.

She reached her hand across the table to grab his and held it for a long time, not letting go until the meal came, and, even then, doing so reluctantly.

After they finished the *arroz con camarones*, the papery pink shrimp shells lined up on their plates, they ordered coffee and drank it in silence, lost in their memories of Spain. When they were done, he fished the fifty pesos out of his wallet, handed her the money, and then reached into his pocket for the ticket. "It's steerage," he told her. "Not very elegant, but it will get you close to home. Go home," he said. "Franco won't live forever."

After she left, he ordered another beer, smoked another cigarette, and listened to the waves lapping against the rocks and pilings, wondering if she would go back to Europe or if she'd go to Veracruz and ply her trade there, certainly more lucrative hunting grounds than this small port. He felt himself heave a sigh, something he thought they only did in novels. The fact was he'd done all he could for her, which was more than most people had.

He paid for the meal, walked back through the entrance in the fortress wall, a cool tunnel of stone, and headed up the narrow cobblestone street in the night's hot summer air, past the cantina where he'd met the *gitana*—he never had found out her name—which was lit up and hopping with men. He strolled up the few blocks to the plaza and into his hotel, which was empty, as far as he could tell.

The man at the reception desk handed him his key, and once Solly climbed the stairs to his room, he turned on the light and the fan, peeled off his sweaty shirt—it was stuck to his skin like a stamp to a letter—draped it over a chair to dry off, and stood for a while under the turning blades of the ceiling fan, taking deep breaths, trying to cool off. He needed to come up with a serious plan to find his daughter, but his brain seemed to have short-circuited from the events of the past twenty-four hours. He was too exhausted to think, and nothing really brilliant popped into his mind.

He smelled like an army barrack's latrine, and even in the heat, he would have given anything for a steaming-hot shower and some decent soap, something that would make him feel sanitary, at the very least. But the chances of hot water were nil, and tepid water just as unlikely, so maybe the cold water would revive him. He pulled off the rest of his clothes, hanging his filthy trousers on the corner of a creaking armoire, and walked into the bath where the shower head simply protruded from the wall, the drain in the middle of the floor, no extra frills like a shower stall or a WC. Even the fanciest hotel in a decrepit jungle port town on the curve of the Gulf of Mexico was a bare-bones establishment. He turned on the tap, stood under the stream of cool water, grabbed the sliver of soap left on the sink, and lathered up.

After drying off with the one limp towel provided by the hotel, he stretched out on the bed, hoping for no bed bugs or fleas, and let evaporation do the rest of the job. When he'd reached a state somewhere between damp from the shower and damp from sweat, he put his clothes back on, grabbed a cigarette, and opened the doors that led to a broad veranda.

It was dark now, and below him the plaza was lit with yellow sodium lamps. Couples paraded around under them with children running this way and that, while the elderly parked themselves on the benches and fanned themselves with Panama hats, enjoying a band that had set up in the gazebo. It was all very festive unless you looked closer. The beggars seemed to have come out from the shadows, grime-covered children selling whatever there was to sell—chewing gum, little bags of stale popcorn. They were mostly ignored, and on a few occasions that he observed, they were roughly shooed away. Solly's heart fell into his stomach. He would never forgive himself if his daughter—Isabella, right?—ended up like that. Would he keep that name? By tradition, her name should start with the letter of a dead relative, but he was hardly observant or traditional. The girl's name was the only thing her mother left her. Let her keep it. He just had to find her.

Solly lit another cigarette, inhaled, and noticed that the arcade surrounding the municipal building across the plaza had suddenly lit up with bright fluorescent lights, like a splash of white paint had spilled on a black canvas. Two men stepped out of a heavy wooden door that had probably been there since Sir Francis Drake roamed these waters. They were soon joined by a third man. Solly watched as the three men stood around chatting until finally they shook hands, and the third man stepped back into the door, closing it behind him. Twentieth-century pirates, Solly thought, robbing and pillaging. He watched Senator Clay Wright and Gunther Brandt walk across the plaza, head toward the hotel, and disappear under its columns. He went back into his room, dropped his cigarette in the john to stifle the smell of smoke, drew the curtains, locked the doors, and cut off the light. Crouching by the wall next to the veranda's doors, he waited.

Maybe the darkness, maybe fear, who knew what amplified the sound, but as clearly as if he were standing in the room next door, Solly heard the door open and close, a man's heavy footsteps, the toilet flush, and the tap water run. He listened with a pounding heart as the veranda doors opened and as a man walked out a few feet and coughed. Solly realized it could be anybody, some traveling salesman—what kind of wood did they export from the jungles of Campeche? But since the guy at reception had told him they only had four rooms (they were fumigating the others for *escorpiones*), odds were on his side that his neighbor was the German or Red Clay, and when there was a soft knock on the door, and his neighbor walked over to open it, those odds proved to have been pretty good. The senator was bunking down next door, his headboard mere inches from Solly's.

"What do you want, Brandt?" Wright said.

Brandt was a little harder to hear, but Solly could tell from his tone things were not going well, and he wondered if he had been at the port. If so, why hadn't Solly seen him? What had the German been up to? Nothing good, that was for certain.

"I said I'm done. Now get out of my room. I'm going out to the porch to smoke a fine Havana cigar and relax. I want you out of here, understand?"

Obviously, Brandt did not understand because the argument continued. Sotto voce on Brandt's part, but Wright was nothing if not a big mouth, and he was shooting it off right now.

"I don't have a dog in your race, Brandt. I don't care if the Krauts bomb Europe into the ground and round up every Jew they can find. No sweat off my brow. I helped y'all out because it helped me. Now, it doesn't. So I'm done. I'm gonna buy myself a big ol' horse farm and a low-country plantation near the beach with my earnings. Bribe someone so my grandkids get nice desk jobs in Washington where they can sit out the war if Roosevelt and Churchill get their way, which I suspect they will. I want my daughter's sons to stay alive and help me raise a bunch of Derby-worthy breeds. Do you *comprende* what I'm telling you?"

Brandt said something about listening to reason, to which Wright just laughed. "I think you Nazis let the reason ship sail a while ago."

Solly's blood was pounding in his ears, and he was afraid he was breathing so hard they'd be able to hear him out on the porch.

"Besides Brandt, I got a little phone call tip-off from a man in Hoover's outfit, what we call the Federal Bureau of Investigation, the other day. Roosevelt, that commie, has set up some kind of spook shop to spy on folks like me. They sicced one of their fellas on my ass. The guy calls himself John Smith, if that ain't a joke. Who'd believe that was his real name? It's one you use in a no-tell hotel when you register for a night with a hooker. My boy over at the FBI says that the Jew we met over at our British friend's is onto us. If I know how these government spooks operate, they're going to rat out the Brit. He'll be swinging from the end of a rope in a month or so, convicted of treason. You? They'll get one of *el presidente* Camacho's thugs down here to blow your butt to the great beyond. You've got bigger problems than me, and one of them is this Jew named Meisner. If I was you and the little Brit fairy, I'd get the bastard."

Solly saw his gun hanging from its shoulder holster over the chair, crawled over to it—slid, really, he was so covered with sweat—and lifted it out as slowly as possible, afraid the sound of the gun sliding against the leather could be heard next door. He moved to the far side of the bed from the door, where he stretched out on the tile floor, waiting.

23

Grace

Mérida, Mexico
August 1941

"I'm very sorry, Miss Weintraub," Mr. Echeverria, the proprietor of Los Cubanos cigar store, said, "but I can't help you. I'm afraid I haven't seen Mr. Meisner for several days."

It was the worst possible news, and Grace kicked herself for not expecting it. She leaned on the counter, feeling nauseated. She'd come straight here after a horribly turbulent plane ride, and she must have looked pretty raw. Mr. Echeverria came around from the counter, took her arm, and escorted her to a private humidor room, which was blissfully cool, and asked his assistant to bring her an *agua mineral*.

He guided her to the wicker rockers, and she sank into one of the chairs, extremely grateful for the cold glass of water the assistant handed her. She drank several sips, realizing she hardly knew what to do next. Smith had tried to warn her off this trip, but she hadn't listened. Now, she had only herself to blame.

She'd landed in Mérida a mere two hours ago after a layover in Mexico City, where she'd stayed up all night in the airport, not willing to risk missing her early morning flight. Well, here she was, and

Solly had gone off without communicating at all with his contact. Jesus, he could be anywhere. He could be dead.

"Mr. Meisner came to us for fine cigarette tobacco, not our excellent cigars," Echeverria explained, waving his arm at the boxes displayed against the wall. "I'm afraid I was never able to convert him."

Grace realized that he didn't really trust her or believe her story that she was working with Mr. Meisner and the COI and that he was pretending that Solly was merely a customer, that he hadn't passed messages to him. Well, she'd been prepared for that, at least, and reached into her bag, pulling out the original telegram from Mr. John Smith, which she hoped would be enough to verify her identity. She passed it to Echeverria and watched as he read it.

"I see," he said, handing it to her. "How long will you be here, Miss—"

"Grace," she interrupted. "As long as it takes to find him."

"*Muy bien*," he said, reaching for a cigar in one of the containers on the table. "Here." He handed her a cigar. "This makes our conversation look like a normal transaction if anyone were to look in. We can say you are buying them for your father, some man in your life. That is the usual reason women come into the store. Although seldom . . . well, never . . ." He stopped himself.

Grace finished his sentence for him. "Never alone, am I right?"

"Yes," he said. "It is unusual."

Grace stared at the cigar like it was a missile in her hands. "The whole situation is unusual, Mr. Echeverria. And then there's the little matter of the war in Europe and the United States being worried about Mexico's loyalties, shall we say?"

Echeverria nodded, saying nothing. After a while, he reached for the cigar in her hand and returned it to the container. Standing, he turned and peered through the glass to the inside of the store before walking to the display cases and pulling out another box of cigars. He set it on the table between them, looking at it as if he were worried it was poison or that it would explode.

"I will of course have to confirm all this with Mr. Smith," he told her in a tone of voice that betrayed his concern. I imagine that should take a day. Can you come back tomorrow? At noon, perhaps?"

A whole day to do nothing but worry about what Smith would or wouldn't say was the last thing Grace wanted, but it was what she had. She walked past a pharmacy a few blocks from the tobacco shop and remembered what her friend Mort had told her about food poisoning in Mexico. Whenever he went to Tijuana, he always took Pepto-Bismol. "Two tablespoons, whether you need it or not, and you probably will. It's supposed to treat cholera, God forbid." God forbid was right. She pushed open the door and walked to the counter.

After she paid for her purchase, she headed to the Plaza Principal and sat under the heavy shade of the laurel trees. But when the unwanted advances of men sitting down uninvited and too close to her on the bench, hissing the words "*hola, mamacita*," hello, beautiful lady, became too annoying to tolerate, she headed for the protection of the cathedral on the east side of the plaza. Walking into the church's cool gloom, she sat on a hard, wobbly pew as a priest droned the mass to a handful of old people. At least she wouldn't be bothered by insistent lotharios.

Honestly, what had she been hoping to accomplish here? Solly had gone off on his own, Smith had said, but he didn't say why. When she'd asked for more information in their second call, he'd told her that it was privileged and that they were cutting Solly loose. It turned out they would not be needing her help after all, as it was too dangerous. He'd advised her to forget about the whole enterprise, advice which, obviously, she told him she was going to ignore. Once he had realized her determination, he'd relinquished a bit and told her to have Echeverria call him. "Against my better judgment," he'd said. Maybe no one, not Solly, not Smith, and not Grace herself, was using good judgment. War had a funny way of causing you to go off the rails. Now, here she was, sitting in a sixteenth-century cathedral built from the stones of Mayan pyramids, with all the time in the world to be a curious tourist and no inclination whatsoever to be one.

She got up and stepped out into the hot sun and oppressive humidity, wondering how any civilization in the world could have developed in this heat. If it had been up to her, she would have passed her life lying in some hammock drinking from coconuts, no stone temples, no churches, *nada*.

By the time she was back in her room at the Gran Hotel, she was soggy with perspiration and had to shower for the second time that day. After that, she swallowed what she assumed were roughly two table-spoons of Pepto-Bismol and went downstairs to face lunch and possible food poisoning. Never had she been more grateful for her high school Spanish, because she managed to order poached eggs on unbuttered toast and black coffee. Who could die from that combination? Anyway, she was weak from hunger, so she didn't have the choice not to eat.

It was only after her plate had been taken away and she had been offered more coffee that she looked around long enough to notice that she was the only single woman at any table and that people were staring. She felt like she'd stepped back into another century, that she should have been accompanied by some matronly chaperone. Didn't a war change all these ridiculous rules? And what was so scandalous about lunch, for God's sake? She was hardly swilling martinis and throwing herself at men. Or was she? Maybe not men plural, but she was certainly throwing herself pretty hard at Solly Meisner, wasn't she?

The last man before Solly in whom she'd had any interest was the med student, and that hadn't worked out. He had been foolish enough to remark, after meeting one of her married friends who worked at the studio, that he would never allow his wife to work. His words: "allow" and "never." Her parents had been devasted that the relationship hadn't survived—her mother had already picked out flowers for the chuppah and had decided what color blue was most becoming for a mother-of-the-bride gown.

When Grace told her why she'd ended it, her mother had been incredulous. "Oh, men say these things. There's always a way around them. You can't take them so seriously." But Grace had wanted a man she could take seriously, and Solly Meisner sure fit the ticket.

Just as she was thinking it would be so much easier to be married, hearing her mother saying she wasn't getting any younger, as if she were curdling like milk before everyone's eyes, an American couple next to her, young enough to be honeymooners, began to argue. "I don't know, Margaret," the man sniped in a bullying voice. "This was all your idea." At which point, Margaret grabbed her purse and stormed off, her heels clicking against the marble stairs as she ran up to the mezzanine floor. The husband waved the waiter over, ordered a whiskey, and continued to sulk.

Solly did not look like a sulker, nor could she ever imagine him being a bully. If the stars did align and they managed to survive this endeavor long enough to fall in love, Margaret's fate would not befall her. And with that thought, she realized she could not care less what tourists and locals thought about her morals. She called one of the waiters over and, just like the bully husband, ordered a whiskey. "*Un doble, por favor*," she added, going for broke.

After tossing and turning all night with the heat and with her mounting anxiety, Grace showered yet again, donned a nice dress, a pair of heels, and a stylish straw cartwheel hat, attempting to look as respectable as any single American woman could look in this city, and walked the two blocks to the tobacco store. Mr. Echeverria was alone when she arrived, a worried scowl lining his face.

He stepped outside onto the sidewalk and rolled down the aluminum shade, indicating he was closed. In the now-darkened shop, he escorted Grace into the humidor room, turned on a low table lamp, and ducked his head for a moment before sitting up, squaring his shoulders, and speaking. "Mr. Meisner came to see me one morning about three days ago. He first asked about my wife's involvement in the Israelite Committee. She is Jewish, you see, and is involved in resettling refugees. The committee is located in Mexico City, but there are a few Jews who manage to get here from Cuba and need help. As it turned out, Mr. Meisner was trying to secure contacts in Mexico City for three refugees who had been living in the Cordier's hacienda. I only wish we had known sooner. Mr. Cordier was something of *un estafador*, a confidence man, I believe you say. Well, at any rate, we didn't. What's done is done. Mr. Meisner has hidden these men, who he believes are in danger from some unsavory German elements who are unfortunately infiltrating Mexico now, desperate to see that my country does not side with your country should the United States go to war. They are residing in a small beach resort east of the Puerto Progreso. I am able to tell you where that is." He handed her a piece of paper with an address and a phone number. "Unfortunately for Mr. Meisner, Mr. Smith wants nothing to do with this problem and will be unwilling to secure any sort of visa for them."

"As far as where Mr. Meisner is," Echeverria winced at this point. "He was going to meet a woman, someone he knew from Spain. I'm sorry if that is unwelcome information for you."

"My being here has nothing to do with my feelings for Mr. Meisner."

Grace tried to convince herself as much as Echeverria. "I helped get him into a dangerous situation, and I need to help get him out of it. I'm atoning for my misdeeds."

"Well, I'm glad he will have some help because Mr. Smith wants no more communication with him. My wife and I will be leaving Mérida tomorrow—the hot weather is not healthy for the children. I can also give you the name and address of the Israelite Committee should the Jewish gentlemen be inclined to go to Mexico City." He pulled out a business card from his shirt pocket, wrote down the address, and pushed it across the table toward Grace. "As far as where Mr. Meisner is now, I can't tell you. I have no idea."

Now what? Grace asked herself as she walked away from the tobacco store, listening to the door close behind her, sealing her off once and for all from any assistance. She would call Smith herself. He couldn't just abandon someone he sent to operate on behalf of the US Government, could he? What if she threatened to go to the consulate and blow the cover off this whole covert adventure? What if Smith and this new outfit had no idea what they were doing and were just grossly incompetent? What if the men at the embassy, and they would all be men, just thought she was off her rocker, a kook?

When she reached the hotel lobby, she stopped at the reception desk and asked if she could place a long-distance call, but the man at the desk said it was not possible. Mérida had only telegraph service for long distance, and for that she would have to go to the international telegraph office. He wrote down the address, told her it was about four blocks, and asked if he should call a taxi, mentioning it might take an hour for one to arrive. "No," Grace said. She would walk.

She had no address for John Smith, only the phone number he'd asked her to call when he sent the telegram saying Solly had gone off script. She would have to send a wire to her Uncle Mo. She hated to worry him, but it was the only thing she could think of, and besides, according to Smith, he was already involved in this subterfuge. She would ask him to get an address for Smith; she would tell him where she was staying and that Solly was in trouble.

A man brushed past her on the sidewalk, too close, an attempted robbery, perhaps. Mort had warned her about that, too. She clutched her purse in front of her, stopped, and let the man go ahead.

He didn't look Mexican or Mayan. In fact, with his white skin and red hair, he must have been as much of a tourist as she was. Didn't mean he couldn't be a pickpocket though.

She turned away from the park, and as soon as she headed south to the telegraph office, she was aware of him again. Was he following her? Was she losing her mind in the heat? Some spy she would make. And Solly? What had they both been thinking?

The redheaded man was still following her and only stopped when she pushed open the door to the telegraph office. Past the office's grimy windows, she watched him cross the street, walk half a block, stop, and lean against the wall, watching the building. There was a long line of people queued up to send telegrams, and Grace actually felt relieved that she would be forced to spend time waiting. Maybe the man would be gone by then.

Eventually, she was called to the desk, given a stubby pencil and a piece of paper, and asked to write her message. *Need address for Smith, Solly in danger,* Grace wrote, adding the following: *Send to Grace Weintraub, Gran Hotel, Parque de los Hidalgo, Mérida.*

The telegram cost a small fortune, and as she paid the bill, she turned to look out the window once more, just in time to see a black sedan pull over to the curb. The redhead got in. Maybe she was making up things about his following her. Maybe she was just running on nerves.

Back in the hotel restaurant, she sank into one of the chairs by the splashing fountain facing the lobby desk, just in case the man should reappear, and ordered poached eggs and a *limonada* made with *agua purificada*. There was nothing to do but wait for Uncle Mo's telegram—*Please, God, make it come*. If she were being honest, there was really nothing to do at all. She had made an absolute fool of herself, charging off into the wild blue without the foggiest idea of what she was doing.

An afternoon of waiting loomed in front of her, so she ordered another *limonada* just to kill time. No scandalous bourbon today. Glancing around the room, wondering what had happened to Margaret and her grumpy husband, her eyes fell on a familiar figure leaning over the mezzanine balustrade, staring right at her. Familiar from where?

She pulled her compact out of her purse and pretended to attend to her powder and lipstick, all the while staring over the gold-rimmed mirror. The man was blond and slight in build. It hit her why she remembered him. His face had been in a photo in Solly's dossier, something Smith had only given her a quick glimpse of. Was he one of the boys from Spain? Although most of them were dead, weren't they? Ah yes. She snapped her compact shut. It was coming back to her. He was one of the men she'd seen standing on the stairs in the photograph of the beautiful woman Solly had been so in love with, the woman he must have run off with, if Echeverria had been right. Her competition.

She put her compact back in her purse and stared at the inside of her bag, hoping when she looked up that he would be gone. This man must have been the one they called Eton, one of the Fascists, someone who was now lurking around Mérida at the British consulate. No friend of Solly's so no friend of hers. She waved at the waiter, indicating she wanted to pay, and by the time he brought the check and she had signed, the man called Eton was gone.

Grace locked her hotel room door with a dead bolt, closed the dark wooden shutters, and stretched out on the bed. Only when the phone rang did she realize she must have dozed. Mo, she thought, relieved at first, and then dreading the conversation they would have to have.

She swung her legs around the side of the bed, awake now and realizing it couldn't be Mo. There was no long-distance service. So who then? Echeverria, maybe? The phone screamed like a fire alarm. Grace shook herself. Maybe it was just the reception desk. Maybe they wanted to ask if she needed a towel or soap.

"Hello," she answered, holding the receiver with both hands to keep them from trembling.

"*Señora*, this is reception. You have a visitor." He hesitated like he was reading the name. "A Mr. Meisner."

Grace bolted out of bed and checked that her door was locked. She didn't believe for a minute the person claiming to be Solly was indeed Solly. "I'm sorry," she told the man at the reception desk. "I think you have the wrong room. I don't know a Mr. Meisner. Did you say that was his name?"

"*Disculpe, señora.* I am very sorry to have disturbed you."

If it were Solly, he would leave a note and try again, and if it weren't, she should get away from whoever was pretending to be him. She grabbed her purse and key, and, remembering the many signs on the hotel walls that said *Ruta de Evacuación*, she decided to follow them, find a back way out of the hotel, and figure out what to do next.

The emergency exit door let her out onto the crowded street, fortunately without a bleating alarm, and she hurried to blend in with the throng of people heading toward the Plaza Principal for a nightly stroll in the cool evening air. Once she reached the plaza she darted into the church and hid in the shadows, having absolutely no idea what to do next. Find another hotel, find a taxi that would take her to the beach resort—she reached in her purse for the address—if she could trust the driver not to rob and murder her on the way. Another one of Mort's stories.

A nun, or at least Grace assumed she was a nun, with her plain navy shift and white blouse, was leading a tour group up the nave to the chancel and around the small chapels of the cathedral, the wooden cross hanging from her neck almost as large as the original. The odd thing was that she was speaking English, and Grace was so relieved to find an English-speaking woman that she entertained a moment of believing in divine intervention. She had a plan. After the tour, she would approach the nun and ask for help.

They did that sort of thing, nuns. She knew this from her girlfriend at the studio, the girl who was shockingly, at least to Grace's med student ex-beau, still working even though she was married. The friend had gone all over Europe, staying at convents, she had told Grace, because they have to take you in if you asked. Sometimes they made you go to prayers or work in the kitchen. It all sounded very medieval to Grace at the time, but a cloister, medieval or not, was exactly what she needed at the moment. Grace got up and joined the tour.

The nun made sure the tour group all bought candles for a few pesos each and lit them before dismissing them. Grace lingered behind, and when the nun turned at the transept and walked toward the northern door, she approached her. "You speak English, yes? I need your help."

"What kind of help?"

"A man. I think I am in danger. I've heard that nuns take in women in trouble. Is that true?"

The nun walked to one of the pews, scooted over, and patted the space next to her, indicating Grace should sit. When she did, the nun, who had a kindly face that Grace knew she would never forget, turned and said. "I am Sister Immaculata. Who might you be?"

24
Solly
Campeche, Mexico
August 1941

Solly had paid extra for a cabin in primera clase on the 8:00 p.m. Campeche–Progreso ferry, one that was a half meter, at most, larger than second class, but it had a window that could open. Still, even with an ocean breeze blowing over the bunk, he felt his skin crawl as it always did in any enclosed space. Outside his little porthole, the dark sky and dark water felt like just another wall holding him in. He sat cross-legged next to the window and gulped air just to reassure himself that there was enough oxygen for him.

He should have been knocked out in bed he was so exhausted, but he sat there wide awake, still feeling the ache in his hip from the cold tiles he'd slept on last night, hiding behind the bed, the gun in his hand—if you could call that sleep.

But he must have slept because around seven in the morning he was startled awake by a loud bang next door. Someone had knocked over a chair on the veranda outside his room. Solly sat up, blinking from a dozing kind of dream, and focusing as quickly as he could, he aimed the gun at the door. Pretty soon he heard two girls laughing, the sound of a broom's bristles against the tile floor, and the thwap of a rag dusting the porch furniture. All the while, the girls kept chattering.

Solly sat up, leaning against the side of the mattress, and when he heard the door close next to him, he jumped up, stuck his head out his door, and called, "*Señorita*?" He motioned to the maid carrying a mop and bucket from the next room. She stepped forward, standing a good three feet outside the doorway, and stared at him until Solly said, "*Ingles*?" She shook her head no and started to walk away.

"*El hombre*?" Solly called after her, nodding at the next room where Clay Wright had slept. "*Está*?" he asked. He pointed to the door, hoping that better communicated his question: Was the man still here?

The maid turned and scowled, shrugging her shoulders and stepping back as someone might if they thought the person they were talking to had lost his marbles. Then something dawned on her. She raised her eyebrows, aimed her mop at Clay Wright's room, and mumbled the words "*se fue, se fue*."

"*No comprendo*." Solly kicked himself for not having learned more words when he was in Spain.

The maid walked back to the senator's door, mimed carrying a suitcase, and said, "*El gringo, adiós*. Goodbye," she waved.

Solly exhaled, his chest relaxing finally as if he'd been holding his breath underwater for a very long time. "*Sí, gracias*," he said. For now, the danger had passed.

"You only gringo at hotel," the maid added.

Solly reached into his pocket and pulled out a couple of coins, handed them to her, and once he closed his door, fell on the bed and was out like a light for several hours. He woke around three in the afternoon, sticky with sweat and starving. He pulled a cord hanging by the door, one that summoned maids, and when one came, he pointed to the room service menu that he'd pulled off the desk in the corner, ordering a sandwich and coffee.

Once he'd eaten, he took the ferry schedule from his shirt pocket, the one-page *horario* he'd grabbed at the terminal and looked at the departures. A large ferry had left for Veracruz at nine o'clock that morning, and Solly was pretty sure Wright would have taken that one. Considering the conversation Solly had overheard last night, Brandt was unlikely to have continued accompanying him, as their business seemed to have been concluded. Solly glanced at the rest of the departures and noticed that another local ferry had left at eight that morning, an hour before the ferry to Veracruz departed, and was scheduled to arrive in Progreso at eight that night. Dollars to donuts said Brandt was on that one. He'd probably hotfoot it back to Mérida to come up with plans to cover his and Eton's tracks, plans that included getting rid of Solly.

Not all of them are who they say they are. Solly could still hear the recruiter John Smith's words ringing in his ears, see the narrow-eyed, downturned look on his face, as if he'd just revealed to Solly some profound secret. Who is? Solly thought at the time. Even you, pal. But back then, a mere few weeks ago in Pearson's office, he'd been more fixated on Smith's promise: *You'll be a free man.*

Well he wasn't free yet, not with Brandt and Eton after him, and the sooner he got out of Mexico, the better.

They tried to kill you once; they may try again. Solly replayed Smith's words in his mind over and over, realizing now just how seriously he should have taken them. He'd been so cavalier, so full of strutting bravado, thinking *what the hell, Solly—go to Mexico, have a look around, listen in on some radio communications, report back, win Estelle's hand in marriage, and come home, victorious, free. A hero.* What a fool.

Now he figured Smith must have known more than he was letting on at the time, and Solly had been easy pickings, desperate enough to escape the threat of Hoover's goons to be led into danger.

The boat's engine droned, pushing the night ferry eastward, and the vessel rocked back and forth ever so slightly, just enough to make Solly sick to his stomach and dizzy, but he didn't dare go out. Brandt, if he were on the boat, might be out now for a stroll on the deck, and Solly couldn't take a chance that he'd not taken the later ferry like he had. If Solly encountered him, the German would think nothing of throwing him overboard. Solly would be wise to be ready for him.

Now locked in this cubicle, hiding from the threat of the German, he couldn't help but remember that basement in Madrid when the panic of being trapped got ahold of him and he'd felt like he was suffocating. He couldn't forget gasping for breath, certain he would pass out, and how he had fled like a lousy coward. He should have been dead like the others. But he'd been given a second chance. Maybe Isabella, his daughter, was the reason. No way was he leaving Mexico without her. He had to find her.

He reached for Cordier's Panama hat and felt around the hat band for the thin line of wire no bigger than a thread. No bigger, but much more deadly. Pulled tightly enough around an assailant's neck, and here Solly imagined Brandt, it would slit his throat. That is, if he could get the right angle on him, which would require some luck. He lifted the wire from the hat band, rolled it into a small circle, and stuck it in his pocket. He'd have some kind of weapon, at least, just in case he got a bad case of nerves and bolted from his cabin, just in case the German was up and about on the boat if he did.

He grabbed a cigarette from a pack he'd tossed on his bunk, lit one, and, crouching on his knees, exhaled out the small window. The ship's lights illuminated the sea, its black, watery surface corrugated with ripples. Solly shuddered, still imagining an encounter with Brandt, imagining flailing hopelessly in the sea's cold, dark vastness. He shook himself, trying to banish the image, and glanced at his watch. Midnight. He had eight more hours to go before they docked in Progreso. He really should try to sleep.

Getting up from the bunk, he took the gun out of its holster and put a glass of water in front of the door. If anyone broke in, they would knock over the glass, maybe trip. It was the only thing Solly could think of that would buy him time if the worst-case scenario came to pass. Then he lay on the bunk, placed the gun on the foot of the bed so he didn't accidentally blow his brains out in the middle of the night, and closed his eyes.

Sharp blasts from the ship's horn jolted Solly awake after a few undisturbed hours. When he sat up and peered out of the porthole, he could see the low-slung concrete buildings that lined Progreso's shore.

He grabbed the gun from the foot of the bed and glanced at the glass, which had turned over with the rocking of the ship, spilling its contents on the floor. He felt foolish, got up, took the hand towel from the rack, and mopped up the water. It was only after brushing his teeth and splashing water on his face that he realized he should have felt relieved. Better a live fool than a dead hero. Why were men always taught to believe the opposite? It was a good question, but he didn't have the time to be a philosopher. He had to find Frans and enlist his help to find the girl.

The ferry was pretty much empty by the time Solly walked down the ship's half-rotten wooden gangplank. He scanned the crowd for Brandt, who would be taller, whiter, and blonder than the locals, and from what Solly could see, no one standing around the docks jumped out fitting that description. He could only hope the coast was clear. He felt around in his pocket for the wire. It was still there, along with the gold cufflinks filled with chloral hydrate, the cyanide suicide pill, if it came to that, and a few large Mexican coins. His thumb flipped one over. Heads or tails. Heroes or fools. He was on track to be one or the other.

Solly crossed the sandy avenue that ran along the gulf and headed a block off the main drag. He reached into his shirt pocket for Frans's business card, figuring he could find someone in a local shop who could point him in the right direction. The whole town seemed to die out into scrub jungle after about five blocks each way.

The sky was leaden with an oncoming storm, and without sunshine, the colorful gaiety of the tropical town disappeared. The dull concrete buildings and the beach's dun-colored sand seemed even more dreary than a November day in Ohio. The heavy air only made the heat more oppressive, and walking one block was like trudging through a bog. He was dripping sweat when he noticed that the cross street at the corner was exactly the street printed on Frans's card. A quick glance at the numbers on the buildings told him he was only a couple more blocks away. He felt instantly lighter and less clammy at the thought of encountering Frans, maybe in a quiet office with a fan blowing cooler air. Two more blocks, and he'd have an ally who knew the whole story and could help him out.

Solly walked past the small, nondescript building without even noticing it before he looked at the card again, realized his error, and turned around. The office was as unimposing as a local vet clinic, and the only indication that it was a business at all was the handwritten sign taped on the door reading C and N *Compania de Ingeniería*. He checked the card again, finding it hard to believe that such a massive undertaking as the world's largest pier was being run out of a two-room storefront, but it appeared that it was. He tried the doorknob, but it was locked.

Pressing his face against the door's glass window, he could see a sandy-haired girl at a desk, her back to him. He tapped on the glass a few times, and she finally turned around, walked to the door, unlatched a dead bolt, and fiddled with the doorknob. "*Sí? En qué puedo servirle?*" she said, peering out from a narrow opening in the door. She appeared to be ready to slam it in Solly's face.

"*Ingles?*" Solly asked, using one word in his fifty-word Spanish vocabulary. He noticed that she seemed to relax once she heard his American accent and opened the door a bit more. He wondered why she would be afraid of the locals but then realized that wasn't his big problem at the moment. He held up Frans's business card, and she nodded, opened the door enough for him to pass, and then locked it after him.

"Yes, I speak English," the girl said. "Are you here for the delivery? If so, I'm afraid Mr. Pedersen is not in." She glanced at the half-open office door next to the waiting room. "I have not seen him since yesterday."

"Do you know where I might find him?"

"Well normally I would say check the office on the pier, but I wouldn't bother. We just had a call from one of the foremen asking where Mr. Pedersen is. I'm sorry I can't help you."

Dead end. Solly felt as dizzy as he had on the rocking ferry, and the face of the girl wobbled in front of him as he stared at her. Now what? He wondered. "Thanks anyway," he said, lifting his chin and straightening his shoulders so he didn't appear as washed-up, defeated, and out of ideas as he actually was.

He turned around, and the girl scurried to unlatch the door's locks with a bunch of keys. *Pretty high security for such a small construction office*, Solly thought. He then asked, "Did Mr. Pedersen say anything about his plans the other day, the last day you saw him?"

"No, not really," the girl said, opening the door, seeming to want to hurry him on his way.

"Miss," Solly tried his best smile, his best puppy dog look. "I could use a little help."

She leaned back on her heels, looking once again at the adjacent office. "Mérida," she whispered. "He said he was meeting a friend."

Back out on the street, Solly decided to head to Frans's hotel first. Maybe the bartender knew the friend, the place in Mérida Frans intended to go. It was a long shot, he knew, and he pushed himself several blocks against the thick, damp heat, thinking, *Mérida, friend. What friend?* What if Frans wasn't as trustworthy as he seemed? Always a possibility here. What if his offer to help find Isabella had been a trap? Another possibility. But the truth was Solly didn't have many options left.

He turned east up the street toward the Playa Blanca. There, looking even worse for wear, was the old Packard just where he'd left it, and he was more than grateful it hadn't been stolen or cannibalized for parts. It seemed like a good sign.

He climbed the stairs to the second story of the hotel and stuck his head into the bar. No bartender, no customers. That seemed strange, or maybe not. It was about ten in the morning, and even alcoholics would probably still be sleeping it off. Maybe the cash register was empty. Not Solly's problem.

As he continued up to the third floor, his chest clenched. The last time he'd climbed these stairs, he'd been full of love, full of hope and nerves. Estelle had been waiting for him. Just three days ago he'd had no idea what he was about to find out, what was about to hit him. And now? He was a father, and he was a man hunted by a Nazi. Solly felt like a billiard ball hit by an expert's cue, ricocheting wildly against the rails, landing in a pocket. And some pocket it was—a lost love, a new child. Well, he was in it now.

He reached Frans's room and knocked on the door. No one

answered. He knocked again, tried the doorknob, and when it turned in his hand, he pushed open the door. The balcony doors had been left open, but since there was no wind, the stench, something like a mixture of shit and sulfur, filled the room. The smell of death. They say you never forget it.

The drawers were upended on the floor, the contents of the closet dumped in a pile, and Frans was sprawled on the bed, fully clothed. The blowflies had already gotten to him and laid their eggs, and maggots, like squirming grains of rice, filled the cavity in his head where the gun had blown off part of his skull. They crawled out of his nose, his eyes, and the gaping hole of his mouth. Solly gagged and then vomited all over the floor.

It wasn't until he was a few miles outside of Progreso, and he hardly remembered running down the stairs to the car or praying to God the damn thing started, that he pulled the car over on the sand next to a tangle of scrubby trumpet trees and tried to catch his breath. His mouth was sour and his ribs and stomach muscles ached from heaving. He would have given anything for some water. Dragging himself out of the car and opening the trunk, he hoped to find a forgotten bottle or a metal canister tucked away next to the spare tire in case the radiator overheated, anything at all, even a hidden flask of tequila. But there was nothing.

He walked around to the passenger side, squatted, and felt under the seat. Again, he was out of luck, so he tried the driver's side, not that he'd ever put anything there. When his hand bumped against something hard, he got his hopes up for a second before he realized it was a book, its paper cover torn and strings from the binding dangling from the ends. He sat on the seat and stared at the novel, the same one he'd seen on the floor by the Cordier's bed—*All This, and Heaven Too*. It had to be more than a coincidence. He flipped through the pages and saw several underlined words. No way to know if they were the same underlined words in Cordier's book, but if they were, and Solly was willing to bet that was the case, he was looking at the code book. And if he was, Frans must have hidden it there the day Solly found him sitting in the Packard before they left for Campeche. He must have had a reason. Whoever blew Frans's brains out and ransacked the room must have been looking for it too. He'd never thought that when Smith had tasked him with finding the code there was even the remotest possibility of that happening. Now he had good reason to think he had got ahold of it, it was practically burning a hole in his hand.

Solly started up the car. He was about twenty minutes south from the beach resort where he'd left Birnbaum and the others. He'd check in with them, take a shower, eat something, grab his radio, and head back to the hacienda. If the book were still there next to the bed, he'd compare the two texts, get the message about the code book to Smith, and then get the hell out of there. It was a risk, but one that wrapped up his job here. He felt certain that after all he'd done, Smith would have the decency to get the embassy to find his daughter. He had a lot to do and little time to do it before he ended up like Frans.

No one was in the room when Solly made it back to the resort. In fact, the place was weirdly empty and neat for a bunch of guys on their own. Solly's heart raced. Were they even still there? Had something happened? He reached under the bed, relieved to see his Whaddon radio was still there. If the German or Eton had rounded up the men, they would have certainly taken that. He sat on the bed, a bit calmer now, and looked around, reassured when he saw a few articles of clothing hanging in the open armoire, a comb and brush on the bureau next to a bottle of aspirin, and a carafe filled with water, a glass perched on top. He got up, grabbed the tumbler, poured the water, and drank like a man who had just crossed the Sahara.

As he collapsed back on the bed in the quiet, the full impact of what he'd just been through, losing Estelle, finding out he had a child, seeing Frans dead—his skull shattered, maggots crawling out where his brains should have been—spilled over him, and he couldn't fight his way out from under the avalanche of all that pain. He buried his face in the pillow, and without warning, he began to sob into the floral bedspread, his body shaking as violently as it had when he'd vomited at the sight of Frans dead in his hotel room. When the tears stopped coming and he was no longer trembling, he realized that his romantic dreams of Estelle had been as much a part of him as a limb, had kept him upright and moving, and now that they weren't there, he was completely on his own.

He hauled himself off the bed, knowing he had to get moving, that he couldn't curl up like a baby and cry. Pulling his suitcase out from under the bed, he rummaged around until he found a clean pair of boxers, a shirt, and a less filthy pair of pants, all of which he tossed on the chair. Hardly sartorial splendor, but they would have to do. He stared out of the window screens, scanning the beach for the men he'd left behind. Strange that they hadn't turned up. He'd check the restaurant or bar after a shower. Right now, he looked like a hobo and they probably wouldn't even serve him.

He stripped out of his grubby clothing, walked into the bathroom, and flipped on the light. The men's razors and toothbrushes were there. Another good sign. He pulled open the shower curtain, jumped back, and screamed, "What the hell?"

"You wouldn't have a light, would you, mate?" Eton asked, slurring his words and waving an unlit cigarette back and forth. "I'm dying for a smoke."

25

Izzy

Los Angeles, California
September 2008

I probably shouldn't have changed my airline ticket after the conference, shouldn't have agreed to meet Professor Birnbaum, and certainly shouldn't have let curiosity about my father's early years, years that had always been shrouded in mystery, get the best of me. But I had, and now here I was, pulling into a parking space at the Vista Las Palmas Living Center, a sprawling collection of pastel bungalows built to kennel the elderly. Jesus, irony must have been in short supply when they were passing around names for an old age home in Pasadena, but what would have been better? Vista Pearly Gates? The Dying Center?

I should turn around, cancel the appointment with Marissa Birnbaum and her grandfather, not poke this hornet's nest. However, I'd come this far, and Marissa's revelation that my father *might*—and that was the operative word here—have saved her grandfather's life in Mexico had exploded in front of me like a grenade. Fate seemed to have lobbed it into all the doubts I'd had as a child, blowing them up anew. And now on top of that, I had to contend with Solly's new, strange behavior—that weird trip to his "office," Linda's reports of him asking her to get into his safe and then locking himself in his room, that vintage Panama hat he never took off, and, worst of all, the gun Linda had found in the back of the safe. "An old one with no bullets, praise Jesus," she'd told me.

She had called her father, who'd been in the marines in World War II and during the Korean War, someone my father knew from back in the day, to come over and take a look. Good God, I was relying on the extremely elderly to take care of the totally ancient. They should both be here at the Vista Las Palmas Living Center. Except that Solly would kill me if I even mentioned it. He assured me every chance he got that he was as good as he'd ever been. Better, in fact. There was no reasoning with him.

I pulled a mirror out of my bag, checked my lipstick, and ran a small brush through my hair, gearing up for my meeting. I could feel myself getting sweaty, and while the car was already baking in the sun and would reach pizza oven temps by the time I returned, it wasn't just that. I was anxious, homesick, tired of the unfamiliar glare, the brilliant California sunshine unmitigated by humidity. Was there some law in this state that prohibited the planting of shade trees in parking lots?

Trees. My mother always said trees and sky, that the absence of trees was why she and my father never lived in some glamorous place like California or New York. "Your father," my mother said when I'd asked why we didn't live in California or Manhattan, "told me he had to have trees and sky around him, not palm trees, not gray buildings, but big maples and sycamores that turned colors in the fall."

Even when I was young, their reasoning seemed to be just one more way to evade the past. Who, I used to wonder when I was a teen, would choose to live in the Carolinas in the 1940s and '50s? California was booming and New York had Broadway, while the South had the GDP of a Banana Republic, plus Jim Crow and no real love for Jews,

either, while we were at it. I always thought their decision had to do
with some arrangement with the owner of Pennington Mills—but I
could never figure it out and I never asked. Children learn to do that,
avoid their parents' third rail, so no sparks would go flying and no
one burned by hidden secrets.

Until now.

I hauled myself out of my rental car, clicked the lock shut with
the key, and headed to the Vista Las Palmas reception office. The
office was up a couple of wooden stairs and had a wheelchair ramp
off one side, which led to a faux-homey front porch with rockers, as
if neighbors might come over for iced tea. And do what? Stare at a
parking lot full of Toyotas?

Pushing through the door with its fake leaded glass window, I
found myself in an empty air-conditioned room ringed with chairs
and side tables laden with magazines like *AARP* and *Golden Age
Cruises*. Surely no one here was cruising over anything except the
River Styx. These were for family members, relatives my age, who,
now having deposited their elders in the care of Vista Las Palmas,
were planning to live it up.

No one was standing behind the curved reception desk to check
me in, no Marissa there to meet me either, so I tried the handle of
a door on a far wall, which didn't move. It was locked, and judging
from a keypad on the right-hand wall, the polished brass doorknob
was probably another one of those just-for-appearances, home-sweet-
home objects like the empty rockers.

Shoot me, please, before I end up here, I thought, lifting a
copy of a cruise magazine and flipping through page after page of
photos of svelte silver-haired models holding hands on deck as the
Mediterranean sun, sparkling off an azure sea, set behind them.
Aging—isn't it glamorous?

The door opened, and just as I looked up, a harsh screech bleated from small speakers in the corners of the room near the ceiling.

"Oh no, no, no," a woman in a flowered lab coat, reading glasses dangling from pop beads around her neck, sputtered as she hurried in. "I've set off the darn alarm again." She began poking at numbers on the keypad, which, after what seemed an eternity, finally worked. "Thank God," she said, sinking into the chair next to me. "You can't imagine what happens in there"—she lifted her chin and nodded to the door—"when the alarms go off. Total hysteria."

In there did not sound like a place I wanted to venture into or an environment conducive to a meeting. If Marissa didn't show up soon, I would bolt.

I was about to pull my phone out of my bag and contact her when the woman in the flowered lab coat turned and gushed, "So, you must be Marissa's friend. Isabella Meisner, right? She's already in there with her grandfather, Professor Birnbaum. I'm Shelly Klein, resident activities coordinator." She folded her hands, pressed them between her knees, and leaned toward me conspiratorially, a worried frown forming on her brow. "Let me tell you a little about our residents before I buzz you in."

It was quite a spiel.

They can get agitated easily, she told me. *Let them guide the conversation. Try to do what they want, even if it seems ridiculous. Oh, about that. Don't have judgments. Did I say they get anxious? Sometimes, forgetting is a blessing from God. Holy anesthesia, am I right? Don't push them to remember. If they start to rock back and forth, bang on the table, or demand something, usually cookies or ice cream—yes, they can be like children—try to distract them. Or ask a nurse. We have sugar-free ice cream—so many are diabetic—maybe the nurse can get some,* and so on and so on until I was exhausted and dizzy, more certain than ever that I'd made a huge mistake in coming, and even wondering why Marissa had suggested it. What question did she want answered for herself? The same, of course, could be asked of me. Did I really want to know my father's secrets? Yes, actually. Because, in a way, they were mine, answers to questions I could never quite form.

Once the resident activities coordinator wound up her dire warnings, she jumped up, smiling, and chirped, "Ready to go in?" It was the kind of question orderlies ask before they wheel you on your gurney into open-heart surgery. What are you supposed to say other than sure?

Which was what I said, though I wasn't sure at all. As Shelly punched the numbers on the alarm keypad, I couldn't help but notice that in spite of her cheery smile, that frown was still etched above her eyebrows. "Why don't I walk you in there? Make sure we all get off on the right foot." It wasn't really a question but an order, a dead giveaway she thought this visit was a bad idea.

Professor Birnbaum was seated in his wheelchair, his back to me, a white kippah with a blue Star of David on his balding head. He was facing a window where a cluster of hummingbirds swarmed around a few feeders dangling just outside the glass. Marissa, all long, shiny hair and dressed in flowing linen, the epitome of LA chic, saw me and walked to the door, her finger to her lips, indicating we shouldn't speak. Shelly Klein and I stepped into the hall, and Marissa followed.

"They're called a charm," she said, leaning back and peering through the door. "The flock of hummingbirds, I mean, though they do seem to charm him. So, has Shelly given you the rundown?"

"Yes, I have." Shelly nodded. "I'll leave you to it, Marissa." She handed her some sort of device. "Buzz if you need anyone. Good luck."

We were going to need luck?

Marissa leaned against the wall and sighed. "Thank you so much for coming. He's been telling these wild stories, and no one in the family believes him but me. My mother just says these old survivors," she hesitated and looked questioningly at me. "The Holocaust, survivors, you know?"

"Yes, I know."

"Well, everyone says they don't remember things as they really were. The trauma and everything. He lost his family to the Nazis, and now recently since he moved here," she waved her arm down the bleak hallway, painted a dusty beige as if the ashes of time had been descending on it for years. "He's been talking about Mexico, and bars of platinum that he found hidden in some safe, someone named Cordier, and a whole cast of characters, including of all people, your father, who he said saved his life. My mother thinks these are delusions, but now here you are. Do you think you can clear some of this up?"

Marissa's explanation was interrupted by a loud scream from Professor Birnbaum's room. "They need more food," Marissa's grandfather shouted from what I thought of as his cell. "They need more food."

"We have to go," Marissa said, turning and walking into the room where an old, clearly demented man was shouting because his birds had flown off and, most likely, because he was alone.

"*Zayde*?" Marissa sat on a chair next to her grandfather and raised her voice in that way people do with the elderly, a tone that always drove Solly nuts, and motioned me to take the other seat, a towel-draped La-Z-Boy recliner. "This is Solomon Meisner's daughter. Remember?"

"Who?" Professor Birnbaum shouted.

"Solly Meisner. That man from Mexico?" Marissa shouted louder. "Remember you were talking about him?"

Professor Birnbaum waved his hand, irritated, as if swatting flies. "The birds need food," he wailed. "Where are my birds?"

"We can't feed them any more food, *Zayde*, or they'll get too fat to fly."

Birnbaum chuckled. "Like Mrs. Feldman next door."

"Right, *Zayde*. She's not flying anywhere, is she?"

"Not flying this coop anytime soon." Professor Birnbaum laughed, delighted with this banter.

If they get agitated, distract them. Marissa was doing a good job.

She turned her grandfather's wheelchair away from the window so he could face me. "*Zayde*," she said. "This is Mr. Meisner's daughter."

"Isabella," I said, extending my hand where it hung in the air, unaccepted. Professor Birnbaum's face had frozen into a blank stare. Was he looking at me? The wall? This was going nowhere. Down the hallway I heard someone yell, "Hi, Mom, it's me." That loud voice again, like trying to reach the dead.

Professor Birnbaum leaned forward—he wasn't having a stroke, was he? Apparently not, because he lifted his head, stared at me like a man coming to, and finally grabbed my hand, saying, "You are a very lucky girl. You should be dead."

I jerked back, noticing Marissa's alarmed face over her grandfather's shoulder. "Excuse me?" I said. "Dead?"

Marissa hurried to interject. "*Zayde*, tell us how Isabella's father saved your life in Mexico, okay? Remember how you told Mom and me that story? About the hacienda? The French movie star who was murdered?"

"He saved your life too," he said, nodding at me, holding my hand tighter, his bony grasp dry and papery. He smiled briefly, looking right into my eyes, seeming to focus on me like he knew me. But that interlude lasted only a few seconds before a distant gaze came over him, vague and questioning, and he turned his head away, like someone listening to music coming from another room. "Izzy," he said as if to someone in that room, someone not with us. "That's what Mr. Meisner called you." He looked up at his granddaughter. "Yes, Izzy."

My name. An electric jolt ran down my arm, and after a few seconds, I realized that I was holding my breath, my chest tight. How could he have known? Had my father been in some kind of contact with this man? I made myself exhale, telling myself my nickname was obvious, the name Isabella being a bit ornate for Americans. There must be countless Izzys.

But I was wrong.

Memories seemed to come to him like Scrabble tiles falling, the words clattering like wooden bits, tumbling all around him. "The Nazi, he would have killed you first. Just for fun because he hated your mother and because Meisner was a Jew. And me? It goes without saying." He patted his kippah. "And Dr. Gottman, Yakov. All of us. And if he hadn't, the other one would have. But that was later."

Marissa rushed to ask a question, trying to catch all the words while this moment lasted. "How did Mr. Meisner save you, *Zayde*?

"How?" He sounded indignant like it should have been obvious. "He cut the Nazi's head off. It hung like this." He tilted his head to left, his tongue hanging out. "We all shouted bravo and applauded." He grinned almost crazily.

Okay, now we were totally off the rails, and Marissa looked stricken. I would have stood up and left, but the old man was still clinging to my hand. "I'm sorry, but my father never told me about any of this," I said, hoping he would go off into space again and that I could end this interview.

"Of course not." Birnbaum looked at me like I was an idiot. "No one wanted to talk about the horrors. He was like us, your father, like the survivors, because of Spain."

Wait. Spain? "What about Spain?" I asked. Another thing I'd never heard about.

"We all kept things to ourselves. For your father, it was Spain, where he'd been a *brigadista*. For the rest of us, it was Germany, Poland. Why remember the past? We were in America now. The land of the free." He sighed like someone catching his first glimpse of the Statue of Liberty, understanding all that it promised. "Mr. Meisner, Mr. Meisner," he dropped my hand finally, mumbling my father's name over and over. "Ask him about the safe. He'll tell you. I was the one." He pointed to his chest. "I knew it was platinum. I was the scientist."

Now I did stand, desperate to leave, wondering who I could call and ask about all this. Who was still alive from that time? I wasn't blurting all this out to Solly without my ducks lined up. "Thank you so much, Professor Birnbaum," I said, trying to sound calm and pleasant, as if I were thanking a docent for giving me a tour of a museum. "I certainly will. I'm sure he will be happy to know I met you."

"No, no," the old man began to pound on his chair. "I forgot. Don't say a word. No one must know he was there. It was top secret. He was a spy," Birnbaum whispered in a raspy manner. "Yes, a spy."

Spain, a spy, my father decapitating someone? If he hadn't known my nickname, I could forget this ever happened, and maybe I should anyway. Maybe he'd confused his own story with a bunch of other people's memories, with movies he'd seen and books he'd read. God, was old age just one garbled collection of images that made no sense? As my eyes passed around the room at the photographs on the wall and the picture frames clustered on the bureau, I was relieved that Jews didn't dwell much on heaven or hell. Maybe death would be just one infinitely long, good night's sleep, full of more pleasant images than those the old had to cling to. That was a comforting thought.

I stood to go, and if I hadn't just quite accidentally glanced at one framed photograph among the many clustered on the bureau as I walked to the door, I would have never given this encounter another thought. But there it was, a photograph gone yellow with age, a group of people on a boat, my mother unmistakable, and next to her, in the Panama hat I had been seeing constantly this past month, was my father.

"Professor Birnbaum?" I walked to the bureau, the room around me spinning. "Can I ask you about this?" I said, my voice pinched in my dry throat. I handed the photograph to Marissa.

She showed it to the old man. "This one, *Zayde*, that you said was taken in Cuba when you were deep sea fishing."

Birnbaum shrugged. "Cuba, Mexico, who cares?"

I took the photograph and sat down next to him again. I could tell he was beginning to drift away, so I hurried. "This is my father, Professor Birnbaum," I said, pointing to Solly in his Panama hat.

"Yes, I know that."

"And, look." I pointed to the stunning black-haired woman next to him. "My mother, Grace."

"No," he shouted and began to bang his fists on his chair. "Not your mother. She was the other one."

"I don't understand," I said, not knowing whether I, too, was shouting or whispering. There was such a ringing in my ears. "But this is my mother." I pointed at Grace several times.

"No buts," Dr. Birnbaum yelled in my face. "Your mother was the other one. Estelle. *Une collaboratrice.* He never would have come to Mexico if it hadn't been for her. He never would have found you. And you wouldn't be here today. You would have been dead."

26

Grace

Mérida, Mexico
August 1941

Sister Immaculata stood up from the church pew and motioned for Grace to move to the aisle. "Six o'clock Mass will start in a bit," she said, nodding toward the cathedral's stark apse where an enormous crucifix several meters high loomed from the white-washed wall over the priest and altar boys. Shafts of evening light fell from the dome's skylight high above the altar, and Grace knew she had to enlist the nun's help now or she would be forced back to the hotel where the stranger could still be lurking. And what then? She was running out of time.

The nun took her hand and led her to a chapel on the shadowy northwest side, stopping before a chipped, gold-painted statue, its dusty velvet and lace robes frayed and worn. She lifted a candle from a pile next to the saint and lit the wick. "Throw a peso in the box," she told Grace, still keeping her back to the people wandering down the nave, assembling for Mass. "Tell me whatever you have to say."

There in the flickering candlelight with the smell of smoke and melting wax all around, Grace mumbled the reasons she needed a place to hide, her voice gaining urgency as she told the nun that she was being followed, that she had come to Mérida searching for a man who had gone missing, someone who had been staying on a plantation owned by a French filmmaker. She continued giving what details she had, that the filmmaker had died, how he had been housing refugees, Jews from Europe. It was then that the nun turned and, placing her fingers over Grace's lips, shook her head.

"You've told me enough." She glanced around the church, looking for something or someone, but it was not clear to Grace what or who, and then said, "Follow me. We need to get you out of here."

The sister hurried out of the cathedral, hailed one of the cabs idling in front of the church, and told Grace to get in. The nun climbed in next to her and, after a quick conversation with the driver, settled back in her seat. "We'll talk more later," she said, and turned away.

As the taxi bounced over the narrow, half-paved road, Grace gripped the seat, wondering if the solution she'd imagined for her predicament, escaping the hotel for a convent, wasn't worse than the problem, a feeling that only intensified when the taxi deposited them in a clearing in the middle of a forlorn jungle, the tangled trees around them filled with ominous croaking and shrieking sounds, the still air suffocatingly hot. She watched as the taxi drove off, belching exhaust from a rattling tailpipe, leaving them alone as night started to fall, knowing it was too late to change course now. It probably had been too late since the day she'd met Solly and the wheel of fate had started turning.

"We have to hurry," the sister said, tugging Grace's hand, leading her down a rutted dirt road, more of a path, really. "It gets dark quickly here."

By the time they reached the convent, a sprawling, low-slung building, its walls an impossible wash of white against the dark night, the only other light to be had shone from a milky-colored waning moon, veiled by the humid air.

Sister Immaculata placed two fingers between her teeth and whistled like a drill sergeant, and soon several lanterns flickered on the veranda. The nuns carrying them appeared to be eerie shadows behind the candlelight until one sister set the lantern on the table and her face glowed above it like a fortune teller's in a carnival séance. The sisters with the lamps left them alone again, and in the glowing candlelight, the place seemed almost homey, safe enough from jaguars, snakes, and shrieking night creatures, whatever they were, and Grace felt her chest ease.

"Sit." Sister Immaculata pointed to a chair on the veranda beside her and pulled out a pack of cigarettes from the pocket of the blue shift she wore, waving them in Grace's direction. "Do you smoke?"

"Yes, please," Grace said, reaching for one as the nun pushed a small box of matches in her direction. "So, Grace, can you do anything?"

"What do you mean?"

"Anything useful. Are you a nurse? Can you teach English or cook? Something? Everyone here has to earn her keep."

"Nothing, I'm afraid." Her life in Los Angeles suddenly seemed hopelessly unnecessary, pointless, which is why she'd gotten herself into this mess, wasn't it? She wanted to matter. Then, it occurred to her she earned money. That's what she did. "I can pay," she said, thinking of the elegant letter of credit folded in her purse. She unfastened the clasp, reached inside, pulled out the envelope from the California Bank and Trust, and handed it to the sister. "I can pay quite a bit," she said.

Sister Immaculata read the letter, folded it, and handed the envelope back to Grace. "Good," she said. "We could use the cash. Although the accommodations are not so luxurious as your previous lodging, we need money more than that fancy hotel. Finish your cigarette, and I'll show you your room."

"How will I get my things from the fancy hotel?"

"A novice here has a cousin or some such relative. They have so many, too many, frankly. That's why we have an orphanage." She shrugged her shoulders and shook her head. "You can explain the rhythm method until you're blue in the face, but it doesn't matter. The men here, like men everywhere, do what they want, when they want." She shuddered and wrapped her arms around her chest as if to ward off a chill. "Anyway, this relative works as a custodian at the hotel where you were staying." The nun rose. "You will have your things tomorrow. It's already late; let's go. Morning prayers are at dawn."

Sister Immaculata led Grace down a narrow corridor, pushed open a creaking door, and switched on a light. "The guest suite," she said, waving her arm in the direction of the one bare bulb that hung from the ceiling on a fraying wire. "One of the few rooms with electricity, although it goes out frequently."

Grace glanced around what could only be called a cell furnished simply with a desk below a wooden crucifix on the wall, a chair, an armoire, and a small table with a pitcher of water and a bowl, a washcloth folded next to it. In the corner was a bucket with a wooden cover, the toilet facilities, such as they were. It was as if she had walked back into the mid-nineteenth century. "There's no bed," she blurted out, startled by its absence.

"It's the Yucatán. We don't use beds." Sister Immaculata pulled the handle of a hammock from the wall, extending its intricate web of strings, and attached it to a hook on the opposite side of the room. "Cooler this way, and it keeps the scorpions from climbing into the bed. Don't forget this." She unfurled a gauze canopy from the ceiling, letting it fall over the hammock. "Mosquito netting. Don't open the windows until you are ready to sleep, and then duck under the net as quickly as possible. Oh, and in the morning, shake your shoes before you put your feet in them. A few survival tips before I leave you." She made the sign of the cross in Grace's general vicinity and told her God would watch over her. She walked to the door but then hesitated. Turning around, she stared at Grace. "This man you are looking for. His name is Solomon Meisner, am I correct?"

Grace jerked her head back. "How did you know?"

"The world is a small place and danger large. I know more than you can imagine. However, I do not know where Mr. Meisner is at this moment as much as I might like to."

And with that, she closed the door behind her.

"Wait," Grace called out, running to the door and opening it, but the hallway was completely dark now. All she could hear were the nun's footsteps retreating, and she knew she couldn't just shout out her name in a convent full of sleeping nuns whose days began before dawn.

She went back in the room and collapsed onto the lone, hard chair. The nun knew Solly, or knew of him, and was interested in finding him. Why? Because he was in danger? Equally likely, Grace thought, she or someone she knew was, and Solly had something to do with it. The world was small, the danger large. No sooner had that thought crossed her mind than the room's one electric bulb snapped off and the room went pitch black, just one more of the day's disturbing events.

Thin lines of moonlight peeked through the cracks in the closed shutters. Air would be good, Grace realized, and would clear her thoughts. She shuffled across the tile floor, felt for the latch, lifted it, and pushed the shutters open. A bird, startled awake, flapped and flew off in a whoosh. Pushing aside the mosquito netting, she sagged into the flimsy hammock, letting the net fall around her. She slipped her shoes off and stretched out, feeling tangled in a web, which she was, wasn't she? Whatever was holding her up seemed so fragile, so insubstantial. She closed her eyes, hoping she didn't fall during the night any farther than she already had.

By morning the sun shone through her window, a bright, hot square, and its light must have woken her. She lay there in the rocking hammock, blinking and stunned, trying to remember where she was and how she'd got there, surprised that she'd slept at all, surprised she wasn't waking up in her hotel or in Los Angeles, surprised that any of this was real. Finally, after realizing this was indeed the situation she found herself in now, she flung her legs over the side of the hammock and reached for her shoes, remembering to shake them as she'd been told. When she looked up, she saw a cluster of girls peering at her. "*Buenos dias*," she said, nodding their direction just as a harsh voice called out in Spanish and the girls scattered. Soon, Sister Immaculata appeared in the window they'd vacated. "You missed breakfast," she said. "We don't have room service. Come with me, and I'll see you get some coffee and a roll. Afterward, there's something I need to show you."

The cenote, a large azure pool hidden in the jungle, was the communal bathing spot for the convent, and Grace was curious why the nun wanted her to witness this. It was a beautiful spot, but there had to be more to it than that, more than its exoticness. Orchids wrapped around brilliantly green, broad-leafed plants, hung over the water, over a wooden ladder that descended from the rocky ledge into the pool, and over the bench where Grace and Sister Immaculata sat. Below them in the cenote, the nuns and novices cavorted naked in the water, soaping each other's shorn hair, dousing themselves with bowls full of water that seeped up clear and fresh through the limestone. Gauguin, Rousseau, only they could have imagined such a paradise, or maybe Hollywood with its new Technicolor film. But frankly, if such a movie script had ever crossed Grace's desk reading: EXTERIOR. MEXICAN JUNGLE CENOTE—DAY, she wouldn't have got past the first scene of nuns leaping into the water naked like nymphs before crossing it out with a big red pencil, writing the words *Hays Code* in the margin. It would never get past the censors.

"Can you swim?" the sister asked. "Of course you can. You're American, from California you said, didn't you? I imagine swimming is de rigueur there."

"Yes, I swim," Grace nodded, and before she knew it, the nun was unbuttoning her blue shift, the garment nuns wore instead of the black habits that the government had forbidden. In no time, the sister was standing in front of her wearing nothing more than white cotton underpants; no need for lingerie to accentuate breasts that would never be admired by men.

"Let's get in before the mosquitos have us for lunch," Sister Immaculata said before turning and climbing down the ladder to the pool.

Grace undressed and was in the pool in a matter of minutes. She had to admit that the cool water was heaven, and when the older nun dove under the surface, emerging with her cropped hair slick and wet, Grace followed suit.

"We are going to the cave," the nun said. "You'll see why when we get there." She flipped over and began swimming with strong, smooth strokes toward the far side of the cenote.

Closer to the limestone walls bordering the pool, Grace could see that there was indeed an opening, the mouth of a cave. Sister Immaculata stood by the wall. Grace swam up to her.

The nun felt around on the wall, removed a rock, and reached for two flashlights. "We have to hope the batteries still work." She waded over to the mouth of the cave and pushed the switch on one. The dripping rock walls lit up. "Good. Let's try the other one." That flashlight worked as well. "You have to keep pushing the button down or the light goes out," the sister told Grace. "Follow me. There are fish and turtles in the water, but no snakes. The boas are up on land, so if you feel anything, don't be afraid. There are several different caverns, so stay close to me. It will take about ten minutes of wading to get to what I have to show you. Until then, no talking. Our voices can carry. Only a few people know about this place. I'm showing you because if you ever find Mr. Meisner, he needs to know where we have put his platinum bars."

"His what?" Grace shouted, just as she had been told not to.

Sister Immaculata shushed her, turned, and continued wading forward. The water that had seemed pleasantly cool in the hot sun had now turned frigid once they were deeper inside the cave. The dark walls narrowed, closing in around them, and when Grace's shoulders brushed the slimy sides, she had to fight every urge to turn back, to get out of the tunnel where the nun was leading her. And she would have, except for the platinum bars, whatever they were. Maybe they were a clue to Solly's actions, his disappearance, his current location.

The nun stopped and aimed her flashlight at an opening along the left wall, indicating that they should follow the cave in that direction. Soon, much to Grace's relief, the cave widened into a large circle. Against one of the walls, a rock ledge about six feet wide jutted out over the water. Grace aimed her flashlight at some makeshift stone steps and followed behind Sister Immaculata as she climbed them.

Once above the water level, the nun aimed her flashlight at a large trunk. *Something out of a pirate movie,* Grace thought.

"We can talk now," the nun said. "No one can hear us. The platinum bars are in the bottom of the trunk. During the War of Independence, the peasants ransacked the haciendas and the churches," the sister told her. "The nuns living here found this place to hide what few valuables this poor church had. The Yucatán was not rich in silver or gold like other parts of Mexico. Still, the priests had some items for the sacraments that were made of precious metals and stone, also gold coins, money to pay bills. Well, here it all went. And now, Mr. Meisner's platinum bars. If you find him, tell him they are here." She stood up, opened the trunk, and sure enough, several silver bars lay in the bottom. "Actually, I was told the Germans are involved in smuggling them." She closed the trunk and stood, saying, "There's another way out."

Grace followed the sister to an opening in the limestone wall on the opposite end of the bowl-shaped pool. They continued wading down another tunnel until they emerged into the light, which streamed from a hole in the ground above them, huge columns of sunshine pouring from the opening, turning the water a shimmering turquoise.

"Beautiful, isn't it?" The sister smiled at Grace. "I imagine arriving at heaven to be like this. It makes me unafraid of death. A good thing these days, don't you think?"

Grace didn't agree. She much preferred life with all its problems and with Solly in it somewhere walking about on terra firma. But she didn't say so. Sister Immaculata seemed certain heaven would be her reward. Why challenge such a comforting belief? "There's the ladder, right?" Grace pointed to a rope contraption hanging from above, lifted her flashlight over her head, and swam toward it.

"There." The nun aimed her finger toward a stick ramada once they had climbed out of the deep pool and pointed to large sheets of fabric hanging on nails. "Towels, of sorts," she said, grabbing one and wrapping it around her. "We'll dry off here."

Sister Immaculata lifted one of the wooden crates strewn about. "*Gracias a Dios*," she said, retrieving a couple of pairs of men's woven sandals. "There's a roadside cantina down that path. The owner gets paid to keep these things here for us and to keep the path cleared through the forest back to the convent."

"Aren't you worried he'll get the platinum?" Grace asked, rubbing herself with the rough cloth.

"Not at all. The man who runs the cantina is Mayan. He's terrified of Xibalba, the god of the underworld. He wouldn't go near it. He's also afraid of going to hell if he lies to a nun. So, the bars are doubly protected," the nun laughed. "Let's head back."

"How did you get the platinum in the first place? Grace asked, wrapping the towel tighter around herself and following the nun along the rocky path. "I mean if Mr. Meisner didn't give it to you . . ."

"Then who did?" The nun pushed a vine away with her hand. "We have other guests besides you. They, too, would like to find Mr. Meisner. I'm sure they will want to meet you. Although one hardly talks at all, he tunes our old piano and can play Ave Maria, though he winces when he hits some of the untuned keys. One is French but doesn't speak much to us. But the German is quite talkative. I'm sure you will have a lot to say to each other. Now, watch for snakes. The fer-de-lance is deadly."

27

Solly

Waxhaw, North Carolina
September 2008

Solly sighed loudly, just to let everyone know that he could barely contain his irritation, that he was on what Linda called his last nerve. Here he was, ninety-five years old, comfortably ensconced on his sofa, watching the most exciting US Open tennis match he'd ever seen, and at his age, who knew how many more he'd get to watch? Andy Murray had just won the first two sets, beating the top seed Rafael Nadal, and what did Izzy do? She brought up the name Birnbaum.

One word, one name, was all it took, and Solly's past came back, circling, hunting like a hawk, ready to pick him off the sofa and devour him. All these years he'd believed he'd outrun what had happened in Mexico, outlived most of the people involved, at least with one notable exception: the daughter who was pestering him with questions. Now what was he supposed to do?

Jesus, he hadn't thought about Birnbaum in sixty years, not since the day they last shook hands, saying their goodbyes. It had been the end of August in 1941, and they'd both thought, or at least Solly had, that the worst was over. Neither of them had known then, but they should have guessed, that in a mere four months the worst would come gunning for them—Pearl Harbor, all the carnage that followed, Iwo Jima, D-Day, the death camps full of starving Jews—and those were the lucky ones who'd survived—revealing the Nazi's depravity for all the world to see. Who had time in those years to think about Birnbaum? And now Izzy had met him in a memory care home, in Los Angeles of all places, and wanted to know if her father had been a spy. This, it seemed, old Birnbaum could remember. Well, Izzy, your father was much worse, and he had no intention of telling her the truth now. Better she not know any of it, or she'd have to know all of it.

Solly pointed to his hearing aids, an excuse that often came in handy, and said they weren't working. "Too much background noise," he told his daughter, pointing to the TV. But did that stop her? No.

She grabbed the remote and hit mute. Well, let her. *Who needs the sound anyway?* Solly thought, turning back to the TV. *Just look at the way Murray curves his arm.*

"Dad, you're not even listening. He said you were a spy or something in Mexico."

Birnbaum. The big mouth. Still a talker even now. "What's to tell? This *alter kaker*"—Solly made sure he rolled his eyes like a Grossinger's comedian—"is off his rocker. He's talking about another Solomon Meisner. Do I look like James Bond Mr. Secret Agent to you?"

"What are the chances that he could make up something like that? He was so specific." Izzy wouldn't let up.

"What are the chances?" Solly grabbed the remote back, raising his voice, "Have you looked in the Los Angeles phone book? There must be a million Solomon Meisners. Probably, the geezer in the room next to him at the Alzheimer's home is named Solomon Meisner. How old was this guy? A guy with dementia, and you're taking his word over mine?"

"He's the same age as you, Dad, more or less."

This was too much. The beautiful Grace Weintraub had once called him a hero, and now his own daughter was comparing him to a man in an old age facility? She should only know. Still, he'd made a promise once that she wouldn't, and he had no intention of breaking that promise now. "There's a big difference between me and this Los Angeles Birnbaum," he said. "For one, I'm not in an old age home, wandering around in a *schmata* of a bathrobe, my dentures in a glass." He turned back to the tennis match and tried to ignore her.

She didn't think he knew what it took, how much work, how much money was required to keep him out of one of those places, but he did. For one, he still paid those bills every month, writing his name on the checks with a monogrammed Mont Blanc pen his wife had given him. She grew up rich, so she knew about that sort of thing. A drugstore ballpoint would have been fine by him, but whatever pen he used, he was still the one paying his live-in caregiver Linda's salary, not to mention helping out her mother, Miss Alma, who was no spring chicken herself, eighty-five years old more or less, and could use the money. Eighty-five years old. How did that happen? Well, the same way it happened to him. They both got old. He could still remember her standing in front of his office door that night after he'd been at the Cardinal Club, holding a basket of peaches that covered Professor Pearson's legal documents, asking him if he worked for "coloreds." She'd probably strangle anyone who used that word now.

Izzy knew that she and Solly went way back, but that was all she knew. Solly knew she had no idea why every August Alma brought him a basket of peaches, just that it was a little in-joke between them, a little in-joke about something that was no laughing matter. Alma would never say a word—she'd told him that was his business.

And for another thing, he had Izzy. Solly was no dummy. He knew she spent hours organizing the housekeepers, doing the grocery shopping. He would watch her from behind his newspaper sorting out all his pills, putting them into marked, plastic containers, though she didn't know he was paying attention. He was painfully aware that she had to organize her week around driving him to the doctors. God, being old was a full-time job, what with one appointment after another, cardiologists, neurologists, so many *ists* it would drive you crazy. Still, the nurses made a big fuss over him, refusing to believe he was ninety-five, told him he looked like Clark Gable, that he was as fashionable as a movie star. They'd ask him his secret, and he'd say, "Poker and bourbon." He could still make the girls laugh.

But in August he'd had that lapse where he thought he had people to meet at his old office, one person in particular. He'd made Linda swear she wouldn't call Izzy if he pulled some cockamamie stunt like that again. "Call 911," he'd told her, "but don't call my daughter." Now here comes Professor Birnbaum with everything he knew like so many pins to stick in the balloon of Solly's secrets. No, his life hadn't been all jokes and laughs, all bourbon and poker. Far from it. Birnbaum, even with his brain scrambled with Alzheimer's, apparently could still remember what happened in Mexico almost seventy years ago, and now he'd told Izzy about everything and everyone, maybe even about herself.

He looked back at the game. The underdog, Andy Murray, was turning out to be a real contender, and as everyone knew, Solly was nothing if not a champion of underdogs. Now Nadal, after an incredible volley, had the serve, and Solly wanted nothing more than to lose himself in the match. The thud of the balls and the sneakers squeaking on the court were music to his ears, or at least to his hearing aids, but when he looked up from the screen, Izzy hadn't moved. She was still sitting in the wing chair next to him, her arms crossed, a stern look on her face. Solly had to get her off the scent. "The one thing Murray has going for him is that Nadal can't play on hard courts," Solly said, trying to distract his daughter. Then he looked at what she was holding. She had his Panama hat in one hand and, in the other, the thin wire he'd kept hidden in the hat band all these years.

"Can you explain this?"

"Easily," Solly shrugged. "That hat was made before there was AAA. No one was going to come if you locked yourself out of your car, so just to be on the safe side," he shrugged again. What was one more lie? He turned back to the TV. "Oh great," he said, hoping Izzy would drop the whole thing. "Now, there's a hurricane. This could get rained out, for Christ's sake."

"Look at me, Dad." Izzy leaned in close. "Professor Birnbaum said you killed a Nazi."

Solly aimed his forefinger at his temple, making little circles, indicating the guy was nuts. "If I get dementia like this Birnbaum, I give you permission. You can shoot me. Forget about this *meshugas*." He watched as Izzy fit the wire back into the hatband, walked to the hall console, and set it there by the lamp.

"Linda's making your favorite. Baked cod for dinner," she said, heading into the kitchen.

"With steamed potatoes?"

"Yes, Dad."

"So, tell her a little salt won't kill me."

"That's the problem. It will." Izzy leaned against the living room wall. "Birnbaum had pictures of you and Mom with him on some beach. I didn't believe him until I saw that."

"Oy, Izzy. Stop with this. Some picture from a million years ago? How could you even be sure it was me and your mom? Oh, I know.

Because I looked like Clark Gable, right? He cut that picture out of some magazine."

"You know what else he told me?"

Solly steeled himself.

"He said Mom wasn't my mom."

Solly caught his breath, lifted his hands in the air, and said nothing. Let her think it was exasperation. "This kibitzer clearly talks too much about nothing."

"You know what else? He said you saved his life."

"Too bad," Solly said. "Another big mouth loose in the world. At least they've got him in a locked facility. Anyway, so now I'm Superman. *Gey vays*. Go know."

28

Grace

Mérida, Mexico
August 1941

"**M**y friend here says there has been news of Mr. Meisner's most recent location," one of the convent's guests, Professor Birnbaum, told Grace as he pulled out her chair before lunch. "I'm sure this will come as good news," he continued in heavily accented English, patting her hand in an attempt to be reassuring. The friend, a skinny young man seated next to Grace, said nothing as the professor spoke to him in German. "Yakov Oberstein." The professor introduced him, and the young man nodded briefly in Grace's direction before slumping into his seat and staring glumly at the empty plate in front of him. "And Dr. Gottman," the professor said, walking around the table and resting his hand on the doctor's shoulder a moment before sitting down next to him. "We are very indebted to Mr. Meisner."

They were all assembled at a table on the convent's veranda away from the nuns' and novices' dining hall so that the brides of Christ would not be corrupted by their guests' worldly behavior, Grace assumed. Only Sister Immaculata had joined them and now sat at the head of the table serving up plates of tamales and beans. "No pork in any of this, I can assure you," she told her guests. "The cook was delighted. It means the meat we have can stretch for another meal. A vow of poverty is one thing. Starvation, quite another." She briefly said a prayer, not one familiar to any of the Jews seated there, but the idea of a meal being holy, even if it was wrapped in banana leaves, was not foreign to them. That she knew. "Tell him he can use his fingers to untie the tamales." The nun nudged Dr. Gottman and pointed to Yakov, who was attempting to cut through the leaves with a knife.

A few scrawny cats sidled up to the table, and a nun, who must have been standing in the hall next to the door should she be needed to help serve, rushed out with a broom. The cats scampered off, causing a cluster of bobwhites pecking in the grass to take off with a great flapping sound. *Under other circumstances*, Grace thought, *this would be a travel story, an adventure*, but in spite of what the professor had just told her, that there was news of Solly, she was not feeling a tourist's curiosity. She was feeling a cold, gnawing cramp in her gut, something she could only call dread.

"Excuse me, but you said you'd heard something about Solly, about Mr. Meisner?" Grace leaned across the table, directing her question to the professor.

"Well, Yakov overheard someone in a beach restaurant where we were staying prior to coming here for more safety. They were speaking Danish, you see, and Mr. Oberstein used to travel in that country to perform, so he speaks a little. He tells me that he overheard someone saying that he saw Mr. Meisner having a drink with a Danish engineer in a beach town near here where the Danes have been hired to build a long pier. So, good news, yes?"

"Maybe. Maybe not. When was Mr. Meisner seen? Who were these people who saw him?" Grace peppered the man with questions.

Birnbaum turned to Yakov and, speaking in German, appeared to be trying to coax more information out of him, more than Yakov had or was willing to offer. His answers were curt. Anyway, Grace wasn't sure she would have believed him even if he'd been speaking English. He seemed shifty to her.

"Almost five days ago, I'm afraid. This is the first we have heard of Mr. Meisner since he left us, saying he had a meeting and would be back soon. So perhaps there is cause for worry after all."

"There is always cause for worry and always cause for hope," Sister Immaculata said, crossing herself.

"Has anyone tried to contact this Danish man?"

"Which Danish man?" Birnbaum shook his head. "They are all Danish. It's a Danish company."

"Well, does he"—Grace pointed to Yakov—"know where the Dane and Solly were seen? Were they in a hotel, in a cantina?"

"I'm afraid that's all he knows. We have decided that one of us should go back to the resort where we were staying to wait for Mr. Meisner."

"You were staying at a resort?"

"Yes, Mr. Meisner thought it would be safe, but Yakov believes it is not."

And you believed him, Grace wanted to blurt out but didn't. She kept silent as Dr. Birnbaum told her how Yakov tuned the piano here, how he had made arrangements for them to hide here, as he felt they'd been discovered in the resort.

"I should complain? It is better than Dachau." Birnbaum attempted a weak smile.

Gallows humor. Jews were famous for it. She used it herself all the time. But none of this was humorous. It was just hard to grasp the horror far away while in the tropics with plates of food in front of them and birds chirping in the background.

"They needed to hide the platinum they'd found in the hacienda," the nun explained to Grace. She turned to Birnbaum and said, "She knows. I showed her the water cave."

Dr. Gottman, who had been mostly silent this whole time, dabbed his lips with his napkin and spoke. "*Bien. Parfait,*" he said, good. "Because none of us can swim, only the nuns. *Nous vous sommes redevables.*" We are in your debt. Gottman bowed his head in the nun's direction.

"And we are in yours, *monsieur.* You are all paying guests, and we are rather desperate for money."

Everyone seemed desperate to Grace. Where did that leave her, or Solly, for that matter?

Siesta was a word Grace now realized sounded more romantic than the experience actually was. Here in the jungle, it was a survival skill, like learning to drop and roll on a battlefield, not something sensual and relaxing. She balanced herself in the hammock, waiting for the assigned period of time to elapse until the convent woke from its self-imposed stupor until she could get more information about Solly from Sister Immaculata. Grace had a feeling she knew more than she was letting on.

She got up and pulled the shutters tight against the suffocating heat, grabbed a pen and the notepad she always carried in her purse, sat at the desk, and began to sketch out a timeline of Solly's last few days.

Number one, she wrote. *Solly, platinum, hacienda.*

Solly and the other men had found the platinum at the hacienda where John Smith had arranged for Solly to stay. Did Smith know about the metal?

Smith? she wrote.

Number two, Solly, beach resort.

So, he knew of a resort where they and the contraband would be safe. How? Grace gnawed on her pen, thinking.

Next, Solly left the men, claiming to have a meeting, saying he would return in a day. He didn't return. *Who was he meeting? The British woman?* Grace wrote. She had to find him.

She pushed her bare feet down on the cold tile, hoping the cool sensation would move upward to her sweaty face. Solly, she figured, had been missing from about the time she had arrived. Had he told Smith whom he was meeting? Why had Smith declined her calls? She was completely out of her depth.

There was a knock at the door. Grace folded her scribblings in half and shoved them in her purse just before Sister Immaculata stuck her head in the door.

"Come with me," she said. "There's one more thing I have to show you."

Grace followed Sister Immaculata down a chipped flagstone path overgrown with palms and giant hibiscus until they reached a white-washed, tile-roofed building.

"I'm very proud of that roof. One of our benefactors paid for it, a woman who owes me a great deal. Tile is less likely than palm thatch to house scorpions, which, of course, would be bad for the children."

"Children?" Grace asked, and then she remembered the nun saying something about an orphanage.

"Only girls. The priest and brothers take the boys. We have about fifteen with us now. Many of them are over five years old, old enough to work."

"Work?"

"Shocked like a true American. What choice do we have? Dickens would have written about this if he could have survived the fevers and the snakes, the scorpions and the dysentery. But he couldn't have survived. It's one thing to write about the workhouses from the comfort of your own Victorian drawing room. Quite another to live here and have to feed hungry mouths. As soon as our girls are old enough, we send them to the cathedral to sell our cough syrups to the faithful." She opened the door. "They are very beneficial, our *jarabes*. People swear by them."

A few small children were still asleep in their hammocks. "They must be in the kitchen," the nun whispered. "Come this way."

They exited another door at the end of the long hammock-strung hall and walked down another flagstone path to a small outbuilding—the kitchen—where a nun was warming milk in an enameled pan over a primitive open-fire stove. A small black-haired toddler was bouncing in another nun's arms, singing the sounds *ba-ba, ba-ba*.

"It's universal, isn't it? That baby word for 'bottle.'" The baby looked at Grace and reached out her arms, saying, "Mama, mama."

"You can hold her," Sister Immaculata said. She turned to the nun, spoke a few words in Spanish, and the girl quickly put the baby in Grace's arms.

"Mama," the baby said, patting Grace's face with her tiny hand. Grace froze, afraid to move, afraid she would drop the baby or break her.

"You'll get the hang of it," Sister Immaculata told her. "Here." She handed Grace a bottle. "Feed her. There's a place to sit over there." She led Grace to a wooden bench, propped the baby in her arms, and handed Grace the bottle, showing her how to hold it at the right angle. The baby grabbed it with both hands and went to work.

Grace stared at the baby's beautiful face, her wide black eyes now shut with bliss as she sucked in the warm milk. "Where are her parents?" Grace asked.

"Gone, as are the parents of the others. This one has it a little better. Once the war is over, I'm to send her to Europe to be with the mother's family. Meanwhile, I'm being paid to house her. I don't think it will be a happy reunion. A bastard offspring is never welcome. She will be something to hide away in a miserable boarding school. Talk about Dickens." She paused for a minute before adding, "Unless something else happens to her."

Grace tightened her arms around the girl's little body, and the terror of all the things—disease, fever, death—that could befall the baby here filled her with horror. How common the death of children was to most of the world, something she had never faced in her Hollywood, make-believe life—at least, not until now. The baby leaned into her, pushing her mop of curly hair against her breast, so trusting. Oh God. Grace wanted to weep.

"What do you mean, 'unless something else happens to her'?" Grace wanted reassurance that her worst imaginings wouldn't come to pass.

"You could take her."

Grace jerked back, startled, and the baby popped off her bottle, staring at Grace with alarm before squinching her face and starting to bawl. "No, no," Grace hummed, aiming the nipple at the girl's perfect little mouth and crooning some long-remembered lullaby. After the baby settled down, Grace spoke as calmly as she could. "I don't know the first thing about babies. I'm not married. I couldn't. Why can't she be adopted?"

"Well, there's the problem of her father." The nun sat next to Grace.

"What problem is that?"

"He's a Jew. People have prejudices."

"Yes, I'm aware." Grace shook her head. "How on earth did a

Jewish baby end up here?" Grace asked, and then it all dawned on her before the nun could even speak.

"Because her father is Solly Meisner." Sister Immaculata seemed to wait for that to sink in, for Grace to speak, and then when Grace, who had no words, said nothing, she continued. "Which is, of course, why the Lord sent you to me."

29

Solly

Progreso, Mexico
August 1941

Solly stared at Eton, who was crouched in the corner of the shower, grinning up at him in that sneering, bemused way he always affected, a bottle of tequila resting on the moldy tiles next to him.

"I just asked for a light, mate. How long does it take, for bloody Christ's sake?"

"You're drunk," Solly said, trying to sound tougher than he felt. He leaned against the sink to steady himself and stop his thoughts from racing in a dangerous direction. What if it had been Brandt hiding in the shower instead of Eton slumped on the floor with a bottle of booze? That would have been the end of him. He would have been left for the cleaning lady to find, dead in a shoddy Mexican hotel bathroom. Hadn't the senator given the German those instructions? *I'd get rid of the bastard if I were you.*

"Stating the obvious about my condition, don't you think?" Eton said. "While you, my friend, are bloody naked. We're a pair, aren't we?"

Solly yanked a towel off a hook, wrapped it around his waist, reached down, and grabbed the tequila bottle, placing it on the side of the sink. "Get out of my shower, Eton. That is if you can walk." He turned, headed into the bedroom, taking the tequila with him, and lit a cigarette for himself, waiting until Eton finally staggered out of the bathroom and collapsed on a chair by the window. "You smell like a goddamn distillery. How the hell did you get here?" Solly picked up his watch, which read one thirty. It had been a long morning. It was starting to look like an even longer afternoon.

"Yes, well, you know what they call the local brew?" He didn't answer Solly's question, just pointed at the tequila bottle. "To kill you, or me, rather, as the case seems to be. Give me a ciggie, please. Mine seem to be all wet." Eton reached out his hand. It was shaking like he'd come down with St. Vitus dance. Solly stubbed his cigarette out into the ashtray, pulled out another from the pack, lit it, and handed it to him.

The Brit inhaled deeply, closed his eyes, and leaned back, gazing up at the ceiling. "Amazing, all the things you appreciate, all the simple pleasure of life, just before they are about to be snuffed out. What about you? I heard you in here bawling like a baby."

Solly's face burned, the heat rising from his neck like fire. "None of your business. Not that you care, Eton, so let's cut the baloney."

"The girl, Estelle, right? That's how I found out you were here, not that she told me. I followed her on occasion, and what do you know? A few days ago, my driver saw your little band of refugees wandering around here like the Marx Brothers, obviously out of place, I'm afraid." Eton dragged on his cigarette again and blew smoke rings above his head. "Well, from what I gather about where your girlfriend is headed, she'll probably die of malaria anyway. A few preemptive tears will save you from having to shed them later. She did do you one favor though before she left."

Solly grabbed his boxers and slacks, stepped into them, and yanked his tee shirt over his head. Parading around like Tarzan in a loincloth made him feel a little too vulnerable, which was not a good thing to be under the circumstances. "Eton, I doubt seriously that's the case, and anyway, how the hell would you know?"

Eton propped his feet on the bedside table next to the chair and smirked in his know-it-all way. "I had a little visit the other day from the assistant to the ambassador, no less, all the way from Mexico City. Silly me. I thought he was going to promote me, get me out of this bug-infested hellhole, but I couldn't have been more wrong. You can't imagine what he told me."

"Eton, I'm too tired for this little chat." Solly squinted past Eton's head and stared out the window at the flat, green water of the Gulf and the hot, white sand. He was tired of the tropics, tired of the rattling palm fronds scraping the walls as if they were sabers. It was all starting to seem sinister to him now, rats in the palm trees, alligators lumbering across the roads, Nazis and profiteers like Eton swanning around like they owned the place, and maybe they did. If so, it was time to get out, clearly. "Get to the point."

"The point. Ah yes. The point would be that I'm being investigated for aiding the enemy—treason, if you will, some such nonsense," he said, watching the tip of his cigarette burn, gazing at the coil of ash forming there as if reading it for some meaning. "They'd had a little tip-off from a German officer's former girlfriend. He thought I'd like to explain myself, one gentleman to another, that sort of thing." More smoke rings floated above him as he exhaled. "Now, who do you think that little bird could've been?"

Solly watched the ash of Eton's cigarette collapse on the floor. Who indeed? He sagged onto the bed. "Why would she do that? I thought you two were pals."

"She had her reasons."

"Because you gave Franco's pilots the information they needed to bomb the villa back in Madrid?"

"Perhaps. She thought that was a bit excessive, if I remember. I was surprised at the time. I thought ice water ran through her veins. Turns out she must have known she was preggers with your little brat."

"So it was you."

"I suppose. Rather unsporting of me. I mean, how were you to know we were listening from the next room with a stethoscope pressed to the wall? A little advice. Next time you're fighting a war, don't confide your secrets in bed. Loose lips and all that."

"What do you want from me, Eton? Not that I'm inclined to help."

"You've read my mind, chap. Help. Yes. That would be the ticket." Eton pulled himself up from his slouch, planted his feet on the floor, and squared his shoulders. "I mean, look what happened to Cordier when he tried to abscond with the platinum. Death sentence." Eton raised his trigger finger to his temple and mimed pulling it. "Boom. All over. And then there's the dead Dane. Nice fellow but a bit too earnest, as it turned out. Cynics are so much better prepared to skim riches off war."

"Like you, right, Eton? Cynics and rats."

"Indeed. A much-maligned creature, the rat." Eton dropped his cigarette butt on the floor and twisted the sole of his shoe on top of it before staggering to the bureau and grabbing another one from the pack. It took several strikes from Solly's lighter in Eton's trembling hand to ignite the flame. "All in all, Cordier and the Dane had it good, a much easier way to go than what the British do to traitors. They string them up like pigs in a slaughterhouse." Eton walked to the screen door, holding onto the wall as he went, as if his knees were about to give out, and leaned against the doorjamb until he was more or less steady on his feet before heading back to the bureau where Solly had set the tequila bottle. Lifting it, he took a long swig and then turned. "They'll hang me, you know." He swilled more booze, wiping his mouth with the back of his hand. "Rather undignified way to go, don't you think? Twisting in the wind, shitting all over yourself after the trap door goes *thunk*." He slammed the bottle on the bureau. "Help me, Solly," he said, his voice almost a whisper.

Solly laughed, and as he did, he could feel the bitterness come out of him, the cold rage. "Surely you jest. Why the hell would I help you, you treasonous, Nazi-collaborating swine? I'm taking a shower, and when I get out, I want you gone." Solly got up from the bed and was halfway to the bathroom door before Eton spoke up.

"I can give you a bit of information. You have a daughter, and I know where Estelle stashed her away. Interested in finding out?"

Solly turned.

"For a price," Eton said. "Believe it or not, I'm dead broke. If I try to withdraw from my account, the Royal Military Police will be all over me. They've staked out my bank by now, I'm sure. That's sort of how they operate."

"And why should I believe anything you say?" Solly hoped he'd managed to conceal the fact that he cared about what Eton could tell him, because he did. He cared a great deal.

"Because even if the bloom is off the rose and you're well past true love and all that..." Eton placed his hand on his heart like a vaudeville comedian. "Funny, I always thought you *brigadistas* were the romantic sort. Well, here's throwing a little cold water on your torrid affair. It resulted in an unfortunate illegitimate offspring that Estelle wanted to be rid of, and I—for a price—can tell you where she dumped the girl, if that matters to you, having the spare before the heir."

Solly pulled out his wallet and grabbed a hundred peso note, trying to keep a poker face. "Just give me the facts," he said, throwing the money on the tiles. "Where's Estelle?"

Eton dropped to the floor and grabbed the bill. "Palenque, in an old hacienda on the way to Agua Azul, where the archaeologists bolt to this time of year. It's called Villa Balaam, somewhere in the god-forsaken bush."

"Okay. That's a start. Now, who killed the Dane?" Solly pulled out another bill and dangled it from his fingers, waving it at Eton.

"I did," Eton said.

"I should have figured as much. Any reason why?" Solly threw the bill on the floor just far enough away that Eton had to crawl to get it. "And Cordier. Who knocked him off, Eton?"

"That would be me as well. Same reason as the Dane. I was told to. Otherwise they said they would go to the embassy. I thought Brandt and I had a deal, that he'd get me to Berlin. Instead, blackmail was his game all along."

"Gee, Eton, who would have thought the Nazis could be so cold-hearted?" Solly threw another bill on the ground. "What about the wife, Veronique?"

"Sorry, can't help you there. Wasn't me. I think it was that fat rube of an American, or so Brandt said. It could have been Brandt. I don't know anymore." Eton began to sob. "I don't know anything anymore."

"Yeah, you do. Let's get to the important part." Solly waved another bill. "Where's my daughter, Eton?" He leaned down and held the note in front of Eton's face. "Before I kick your teeth in."

"With nuns at a convent. Who knew Estelle was such a goddamn religious fanatic?"

"What convent? Where?"

Eton shrugged. "She never said."

Solly tossed the bill to the ground, stepping on it before Eton could grab it. "Not good enough, buddy. You said you used to follow her."

"It's around here somewhere, if I remember correctly. Estelle used to visit, but I don't remember the name. Ask one of the priests in the big church in town."

Solly lifted his foot off the bill. "There's enough to get you to Rio. Get the hell out of here. The sight of you makes me sick."

"Why not call the police on me now? They'll bring in Camacho's pistoleros and shoot me on the spot."

"You know why? You're not worth it. I've got enough dead bodies on my conscience. I'm not going to bother getting my hands dirty with you. I'll let the British government hunt you down and hang you like you said they would." Solly walked back to the bathroom and slammed the door, hoping with luck and the money he threw Eton's way that he'd never see the bastard again.

He let the lukewarm water wash over him, trying to add up how much money he had thrown Eton's way. He'd have to cash one of his few remaining traveler's checks. Maybe he'd just wasted his reserves. Maybe everything Eton had told him had been just a pack of lies. Maybe he'd been played for a fool. But closing his eyes as the water ran over his face, he could still see the haunted look on Eton's face, like those Goya paintings he'd seen in the Prado, men staring at the guns of the firing squad, back when the war in Spain had seemed glamorous, before he'd seen that look in the eyes of living, breathing men the minute before they were no longer.

Eton's tears were more than the booze crying. What the hell had he expected? Kid gloves? A pass because of his royal family connections, handed down from some low-level nineteenth Earl of Shitshire who was somewhere still lording it over people as his family had done since the fifteenth century? Solly twisted the faucet and the water stopped running. He listened in the silence and heard nothing. No Eton staggering around sniveling. Good.

He leaned back against the wall, trying to come up with a plan.

He was now that much closer to finding his child, thanks to Eton's desperation. He'd go to the bank and then to the big cathedral in town to get a list of convents. He'd find his girl, fly to Mexico City, and who cared what top-secret mission John Smith and the rest of them thought they'd signed him up for. He'd head to the embassy and spill the beans. He was a civilian. He wasn't a spy. He'd found out enough to get Hoover off his back. The Germans were smuggling platinum for bombers from Colombia through Mexico. That ought to set Roosevelt's hair on fire. No one wanted the German's airpower to outdo the Brits'. The code book for the operations was some sappy novel. He had a copy of it with the words underlined. A quick look through it told him they were sending messages about boats, refueling ships they called "milk cows" on the radio transmissions. There had to be U-boats in the Gulf, or at least plans to put them there. The Germans in Mexico could be our worst nightmare, and good old boys like Red Clay Wright were more than happy to let them have their way.

Yes, Solly had done enough. He would get his daughter, and he would get out. He lathered up his face with shaving cream and lifted a razor one of the men had left behind. Where the hell were they anyway? A shadow passed over Solly's newly improved mood, but he scraped it away like he did the soap with the razor blade. He'd worry about them later. He slipped on his boxers, his slacks, and his shirt. Now, with a shave and his hair clean and combed, he was ready to go. All he needed was some aftershave, and he'd be a brand-new man.

The bedroom was indeed empty when he got out of the shower. That was a relief. Eton wasn't mulling around getting in his way or luring the dangerous Brandt or his henchmen to Solly's hotel room. He reached into his suitcase for some clean socks, an item he would never take for granted again, and that's when it jumped out at him. His clothes had been rifled through, and in the place of the pistol—he'd been an idiot not to take it into the bathroom with him—was a sheet of hotel stationery folded in half, a note in Eton's drunken scrawl. *Try the Convento del Rosario on the carretera federal. Get there before Brandt. He's livid as hell at your old paramour. Nazis use Jewish babies for skeet shooting practice in the camps, he used to say. Here's your chance to be the hero you always wanted to be, camarada.*

Solly slammed the suitcase closed, grabbed his hat and the keys to the dilapidated Packard, and transferred the contents of his filthy slacks pockets into his clean ones. He'd ask at the desk for a phone book to look up the convent. If that didn't work, he'd try a gas station. Best not to give the hotel staff any idea where he was going in case Brandt came calling. He had just closed the clasp on his suitcase when something caught his eye out the window—Eton on the beach, staggering around in looping figure eights, waving his arm in the air, Solly's gun in his hand, while terrified, sunburned tourists jumped off their canvas beach loungers and ran for the hotel as fast as they could.

Solly stepped out onto the screen porch to get a better view, not that there was much he could do but watch, the same way you'd watch a rabid dog walk down the street, foaming at the mouth. No point in getting out in front of him. And just as Solly was questioning that line of reasoning, he saw Eton turn and walk into the sea. Soon he was knee-deep, struggling to lift his legs against the waves, probably pushing against the weight of his waterlogged pants and shoes. Then he was waist-deep, then neck-deep, and then he was gone.

30

Grace

Mérida, Mexico
August 1941

Sister Immaculata spread several documents across her desk, all typed on heavy bond paper, stamped with numerous ornate bureaucratic seals. The Spanish flag's red and gold stripes with the image of a filigreed crown gleamed in the upper margin. The pages looked like medieval illuminations, and Grace half expected to see thick circles of sealing wax imprinted with a king's coat of arms.

The nun waved her arm over the pages. "Adoption papers, birth certificate, everything you need is here. Mother's name, hospital. The *lugar de nacimiento* was Úbeda, Spain, as you can see."

Grace saw Estelle's full name written in elegant script and did not want the nun to know she recognized it. Better to keep some things to herself. Changing the subject, she asked, "Where is Úbeda?" It was an exotic word, like the name of a faraway planet, as if the baby had been born in outer space. This whole scene could have been something she might read in a bizarre movie script.

"A decimated village in the south of Spain where I was trying to keep a hospital running and where the mother's British friend dropped her off just in time. Here . . ." Sister Immaculata pointed to thin, flowery script. "The mother has signed her relinquishment of maternal rights, as they were called in Spain, giving them to the church. She did all this before we sailed for Mexico in case she didn't survive and left the daughter orphaned. Pretty much her intent all along, it seems."

Grace leaned over the desk and shuffled the papers in front of her, looking for Solly's name. It was nowhere to be found. "How do you know the child is Solly's?"

"Because the mother told me."

"Any reason to believe her?" The nun had cut off the fan to keep the documents from blowing around, and the room's heat pressed in on Grace, who was sweaty and lightheaded, trying to figure some way to get out of this predicament. She knew there was no reason to believe this woman Estelle.

"Yes. She was screaming his name with every contraction, and not lovingly. Poor thing. There was very little chloroform left to knock her out. We had to save what we could for the soldiers." She pushed one of the pages toward Grace, one that had a passport-size picture of an infant stapled at the bottom. "All you have to do is look at the girl. The mother didn't want it known that the father was a Jew, so she didn't list his name. Obvious reasons, I suppose."

"Less desirable? Is that it?"

"Unfortunately, the way of the world, it seems."

Because of the Church, Grace wanted to snap back, but she was wilting from the heat and was too sodden with perspiration to fight that battle now. Frankly, Grace thought the baby in the picture looked like no one, just a black-haired, red-faced blur. She pushed the pages back across the desk. Was she really as disinterested as she was trying to appear? No. She was terrified, afraid she was getting swallowed up in some kind of scheme. Did this qualify as kidnapping? She turned away from the nun and looked out the window, where scratchy guitar music wafted in from a radio in the kitchen. "Is that allowed?" she asked.

The nun shrugged. "We're not Cistercians, after all, not monastic. Sometimes I wonder what we are if you must know the truth. We serve the poor, and even they have radios, so I see no harm." She tapped her fingers on the papers. "You have a decision to make."

"I'm sorry. I'm feeling a bit trapped. I'm a single woman with no ability to take care of a child. You've picked the wrong person for this job."

Sister Immaculata leaned forward. "How old are you, Grace?"

This was a sore subject. Too old to be single. Her mother's admonitions about rotting on the shelf rang in her ears. She was almost thirty-two, not that she would admit to it.

"I'd say you're over thirty. I'd say your chances of having a child are slim. The Lord is offering you this chance."

"I'm sorry. I came here to help Mr. Meisner, not to adopt orphans."

"And so you will be helping Mr. Meisner."

The room was so quiet Grace could hear the nun's watch tick. She looked at her own. Two thirty. She could be back in Mérida before dark she realized. "I'm afraid if you agreed to help me because you thought I would adopt one of your orphans, you've misjudged me." She stood up. "If you can find me transportation back to town, I'll be going."

Sister Immaculata walked to the door and blocked Grace's exit. "Listen to me. Have you seen all the urchins out in the streets, starving, only to turn later to crime and prostitution just to eat? If the mother's family refuses to take the child, that, my dear, is her future. No law says they have to take her, you know. Is this what you want for the child of the man you love?"

Grace jerked her head back. "I never said anything about love."

"You didn't have to. You're here, aren't you? Trying to find him. Sign the papers and take the child to Mr. Meisner's family. Let them decide."

Grace reached around Sister Immaculata, pushing the nun aside. "How do I know Solly won't come looking for her? I should just wait and see. Wouldn't you agree? And more importantly, how do I know the mother won't come looking for her child and drag us all into court?" Grace demanded, holding onto the door latch.

"Because she signed the relinquishment and because I know." The nun sighed, shaking her head. "She is not interested in the girl, believe me, and she would never tell Solly where the child is. She plans to send her to some needy relative in England who will take her in for money as soon as the war is over. Send her to boarding school and have her raised as a proper little Anglican."

"She could change her mind," Grace said, as the latch suddenly pushed up against her fingers and the door burst open, knocking against her. A breathless, wide-eyed novice stood there, shaking and babbling rapidly to Sister Immaculata in Spanish. The nun slammed the door and pushed the novice against it. Outside, a man's shouts echoed up and down the convent halls. Even Grace could understand the words—*Dónde están los judíos? Dígame ahora o los mato.* Where are the Jews? Tell me now, or I will kill you all.

Sister Immaculata grabbed Grace's arm and pulled her to another door down the hall off the office. "The German is here. Hurry, run. Get the baby. Go. Hide her."

"Hide her? Where?"

"The cave, you idiot. Why do you think I showed it to you? It wasn't just for the platinum. I've been afraid of this ever since Estelle ran off. She knew too much and is now a danger to him. Move. He will kill the baby just for revenge if he finds her. And you too. Go."

* * *

Grace ran down the convent's veranda, the German's shouts getting louder, and ducked under a tunnel of hibiscus bushes, following a worn path she hoped led to the kitchen and orphans' dormitory. She slipped off her shoes to run faster, ignoring the pebbles and stickers that jabbed at the soles of her feet. Even so, it seemed that she would never get away, that the buildings had vanished. She didn't remember the distance being this long, and it didn't help that she tripped on one of the tree roots, falling and skinning her knee.

When the stucco walls of the orphanage dorm emerged in a clearing, she cut across the grass to the doorway, but when she pushed the door open, only a few children were there, sitting on the floor, playing jacks. They stared back at her, looking like they would get up and bolt any minute. *"Dónde?"* she asked them and cradled her arms as if holding a baby. They said nothing, just continued staring at her, and every minute they hesitated felt like one of her last minutes on earth.

She gave up and ran through the dorm to the kitchen, which was empty, the only noise a dripping faucet, water plunking into an empty coffee can in the sink. Panic started to take over her thinking. She ran back to the dorm, but the children had fled. Then back to the kitchen she went, darting like a trapped animal. Still no one there, empty as a gourd. From the window above the sink, she glimpsed what she realized was the little toddler tied to a tree with a long rope leash like a dog, a nun nearby hanging clothes on a line. She ran to the tree, yelling to the nun, "Help me," but the nun, of course, understood nothing and just stared at her as dumbfounded as the children.

The baby toddled toward her, the rope dragging behind, circling around Grace's legs as she got close. "Oh, sweetheart, not the rope," she said, stumbling while trying to untangle her feet.

The baby sat down hard on the ground, screwed up her face, and started to cry.

"Oh God." Grace felt sick, dizzy. She ran back to the kitchen. Maybe someone was there by now. Again, the room was empty, but this time she glimpsed a cleaver on the counter next to the baby's unfinished bottle, the nipple swarming with flies. She grabbed the knife, ran back to the tree, and hacked at the rope until it split.

Lifting the baby, she tried to remember the way through the forest to the cenote, the one she had walked just yesterday, but she got lost in the dense scrub and could barely find the worn line of dirt amid the trees and creeping ground cover. *Watch for the fer-de-lance*, the nun had told her. They hung in trees and were the deadliest snakes in the jungle. Still, she had no choice but to keep moving. It was that, or she and the baby would die at the hands of the German. Almost as if the baby had read her mind, she started to scream. What if the German heard? Grace cooed *shhh*, but the baby leaned her head back and bawled. Grace did the only thing she could: she ran, holding on to the baby and the cleaver for dear life, ready to lunge at the German and hack the bastard to death if she had to.

31

Solly

Waxhaw, North Carolina
September 2008

Solly hated rainstorms. Ever since that night in Mexico so many years ago, he had developed some kind of phobia—at least that's what the doctor had called it. He got a bad case of nerves whenever it started pouring outside. Not that he had needed anyone to tell him why the sound of rushing water filled him with dread, but his internist, the one who had reluctantly written him a prescription for Seconal back around the time hurricane Hazel hit in '54, suggested he consult an analyst, saying it just wasn't normal for a grown man to be scared of thunder and rain. "It was a hurricane, Doc," Solly had said, trying to salvage his dignity.

On the night Hazel's outer bands had swept through the Carolina Piedmont, thirteen years after the whole Mexican ordeal, Solly experienced some kind of attack. Even though the radio had been warning all day about flooding, and businesses and schools had closed early, he hadn't really been prepared for what losing power felt like, for staggering around the house, trying to find his way with a flashlight, the trees groaning over the roof, the wind howling like a murderous demon.

What had the nun in Mexico called a flashlight? A torch, that's

right. *Look for the torch behind a rock,* she'd said, and that memory
had hit him like a sock in the gut. He'd looked out the window as
Hazel lashed at the house, sheets of water rushing down the blackened plate glass in front of him, no longer knowing where he was.
The cave walls pressed in around him, close and suffocating. He'd
never get out, not even with the circle of light cast by the flashlight,
the torch.

He'd started to scream, and the next thing he knew, Izzy was in
the living room—it must have been two in the morning—staring at
her father like he was a crazy man. He'd gone to the doctor as soon
as the roads were cleared of downed trees, told him he needed some
kind of pill.

Now they were expecting Hanna to hit. Every year the storms
seemed to be getting worse. What could you expect with that two-bit
Texas oil baron in the White House? Like he cared about climate
change as long as the fossil fuel profits kept rolling in. But who had
the money to buy gas these days with the subprime mortgage crash
and people out of work like in the Great Depression? Solly felt like
his life was passing before his eyes, and he was back at the beginning,
back when he thought he could change the world. Only this time he
knew he couldn't.

"You changed enough. You saved a life," Grace would tell him
when he got in these moods, during McCarthy, or when the little
girls in Birmingham were murdered and he looked at all those sneering, white faces on the television, wondering if any of them were the
offspring of Senator Clay Wright, wondering if Red Clay had ever
been found. God, if he were young again, he'd be trying to track him
down, maybe in Rio with Eton, if he hadn't drowned that day at the
beach, maybe playing polo in Argentina with a bunch of Nazis, all of
them thinking they could just get off scot-free.

But he wasn't young again. He was just hoping to live long enough to vote for the Black man with the big ears. Good luck to him. He was inheriting a mess.

Solly pushed himself up from his chair and switched on the light next to the old hi-fi that looked like someone's china cabinet. Izzy thought it was hysterical that he still had it, but looking at that machine brought back so many good memories: sitting on the sofa with Grace, listening to Toscanini conducting on the radio, or both of them singing "Venga Jaleo" along with the Weavers, shouting *bajo con el fascismo* to the tune of Seeger's banjo in the heady days after the death of McCarthy, remembering Izzy coming home from college with a recording of a folksinger named Bob Dylan whom she'd seen at the Village Vanguard with some boyfriend back in her beatnik days. How he and Grace had laughed at his voice. "You call that music?" Grace had shaken her head, but she got won over once he started protesting civil rights abuses and the war.

Grace, who by some miracle had lived to be his wife, had been guided all of her days by one saying taken from the Talmud: "He who saves a life, saves the world." She would say it when she froze chicken soup to take to sick neighbors or made sugar-free brownies for the diabetics at Oneg after Shabbos services, to which she had often dragged Solly. And on those dark nights when the weather report called for rain, she would save him, too, from his terrors. She would close the curtains and put several LPs on the hi-fi, show tunes like *South Pacific* that she would sing along with, trying to shut out the sound of water pouring from the gutters so he wouldn't feel like he was drowning. To this day, he could close his eyes and still see her singing along with the sailors "There Is Nothing Like a Dame" or crooning with that Italian heartthrob who sang "Some Enchanted Evening." God, he missed her.

"Some Enchanted Evening." Did they still have that record? He got up and shuffled across the carpet; the last thing he needed was a fall. Leaning with difficulty—what wasn't difficult at his age?—he opened the hi-fi cabinet door and squinted at the records.

When did the weather report say that Hanna was supposed to reach them? Midnight? Was it that late? He flipped through the albums until he found the record jacket, "Rodgers and Hammerstein" written in big letters next to the words *South Pacific* and Mitzi Gaynor and the heartthrob actor staring into each other eyes. He pulled out the record—Christ, why did his hands shake so much?—set it on the metal rod, and turned on the record player, watching the arm drop the needle onto the disc. The room filled with the swelling music of the overture. Solly closed his eyes.

"Tell me what in the name of sweet baby Jesus you are doing up at this hour of the night dancing around the room?" Linda stood in front of him in her bathrobe, her hair covered in some kind of night-cap, glaring. He'd forgotten all about her, that she lived here now and had lived here ever since he'd moved into this reservation for old people that Izzy had found in case he had an accident, an event. They had all kinds of names for things that could happen to him.

"And with that hat on your head like you're in something out of *Gone With the Damn Wind*?"

Solly took off the hat and waved it in circles around his head. "Miss Linda, did you know that I once killed a man with this hat?"

"No, I did not, but what I do know is that you have lost your mind. We need to get you to bed before you kill me. You can listen to your records tomorrow."

A feeling swelled up in his chest like the string section of the musical's orchestra on the hi-fi. He wanted to shout. He wanted Linda, someone, anyone, to know that he hadn't always been helpless, that once he had been someone his wife had called a hero. He pulled the wire from the hat band and waved it in the air. That wire, something so thin, so seemingly useless and fragile, had saved them all. It would have been hard to believe if you hadn't been there. But Solly had been there. They had all been there and had never forgotten. Even old Birnbaum, who probably couldn't remember if he'd had Cheerios for breakfast, remembered that day.

After he'd watched Eton float off in the waves, Solly had loaded up the Packard with his suitcase and his radio, hopped in, and checked the gas gauge. Not good. Somewhere down the road toward Mérida he remembered that roadside stand where he'd stopped on his first day in Mexico, the place where Birnbaum and Gottman had told him Cordier's body had been dumped. It was then that he recalled the rusty Pemex gas pump next to the palm-covered shack where they had parked in the shade of a red-flowering tree. He hoped the pump had been filled since then. It wasn't until he'd driven a few kilometers down the road that he remembered something else—all those cement bags lined up on the way to the primitive toilets, the ones with the fancy labels, FEUILLE D'OR, something like that, and a stamp of a henequen plant.

Wait a minute, Solly thought, slowing down, looking for a place to pull over. He hadn't paid much attention to the label on the bags at the time. Who would have? But now that he thought about it, hadn't he seen that name someplace else?

Right. It hit him. Yes, indeed. On a bookplate in the library at the Cordier's hacienda. He was sure of it. Maybe it was on his copy of that cornball novel, the code book, as it turned out, hiding in plain sight. Solly found a place by the side of the road, went to the trunk, grabbed the book, and bingo! There it was: FEUILLE D'OR. Jesus H. Christ. The bags probably hid a lot more than cement.

He closed the trunk, leaned against it, sweating like a dog in the late-afternoon heat, and considered his options. Probably better not to go to the roadside shack. The owner might remember him, and the *federales* could be there once again, swilling Coca-Colas. They could recognize him too. Could even let Brandt know he was still alive if that's what they were being paid to do. A big if, but not worth the risk. Solly might have felt as though he'd been in Mexico for an eternity, but when he added up the days, they amounted to only ten. His face could be fresh in their memories.

Ten days. Jesus. And his whole life had changed. He now had a child who was in danger, an ex-lover who hadn't bumped him off as she'd been told to do—nice of her—and, because of that, a bull's-eye on his back made for a German officer's gun. He reached into his pocket to grab a coin to flip—tails he risked running out of gas, heads he risked going to the roadside shack and being found out.

A truck passed him, slowed down, and then backed up. A man in the passenger seat leaned out the window, calling to Solly. "Hello, *gringo*," he said. "You okay? Got a problem?"

"*Gasolina*," Solly said, thinking on his feet. They might have a couple of liters in a can, enough to get him to Mérida.

The passenger flashed a smile full of silver fillings. "No *problema*," he said.

Both men hopped out of the truck. Turned out they'd been in Florida, picking oranges. They planned to go back and become Americans. They liked hamburgers. Did Solly like hamburgers? They liked America, and, lucky for Solly, they seemed to like Americans. He pulled out enough pesos to cover what a gallon of gas would cost in the States. It seemed to be enough from the smiles he got from the driver and his pal.

One problem solved, but Solly had another. "You guys wouldn't know where the *Convento del Rosario* is, would you?"

"A convent," the driver laughed. "We take you to a *burdel*. Is more fun. Better looking women."

Solly laughed, too, trying to play along, hoping not to seem too anxious, to not to give them a whiff that something was wrong. "Nah, I'm supposed to meet someone there."

They said it was just a few more kilometers, that they would lead him as they were going past it. And so he followed the truck to a small side road. The man in the passenger seat waved his arm and pointed. Solly looked up at a sign on the gate's concrete pillars—*Convento del Rosario*. The driver beeped his horn, and off his two saviors went, leaving Solly alone in the jungle.

He'd taken the drunken Brit's word for it that his daughter was here in the middle of nowhere, and it was too late to start wondering if this was a mistake, which was exactly what he was doing, wasn't it? He checked his pants pockets for the wire he'd pulled from the hat band on the ship last night. A thin wire garrote and his Swiss Army knife, its longest blade extended, were all the weapons he had on him if things didn't go well now that Eton had taken off with his pistol. He didn't count the cyanide pill. What had Grace said? The last thing the world needed was another dead Jew. He wouldn't want to have to use it and let her down, would he?

By now Linda had gotten him into bed and helped him like a baby with his pajamas. Christ, did he have any of his manliness left? She'd turned on a night-light in case he needed to get up, propped his cane beside his bedside table, and set his hearing aids in a small bowl on top. The sound of rain hitting the roof was no longer a problem for him. He couldn't hear much of anything now except the voices in his head, most of them from years ago, and if he closed his eyes, the pictures that popped up were just as vivid as the sounds.

In this dark bedroom near the end of his life—*Let's not kid anybody*, Solly thought—the bright sun of that long ago late afternoon exploded in front of him like a fireball, and the German's sneering voice greeted him all over again.

"Just the man I was looking for." Brandt was standing once again on the convent's porch, shouting, "*Komm her, Jude*," waving his arm at a chair next to him, trapping Solly, leaving him only one way out.

Solly had driven up the road to the convent, dodging ruts and stones, and at first had felt relieved when he had reached the building. He cut the Packard's engine and got out, catching an eyeful of the black Ford sedan with diplomatic plates parked under a tree. And then he saw the three Jews from the hacienda sweltering inside behind the closed windows. Brandt and the nun who'd been with his daughter and Estelle in Progreso were sitting at a table on the veranda. His previous feeling of relief evaporated.

Come here, Jew, the German had commanded, and then pointed to Birnbaum and the others. "Sorry, there won't be enough room for you in the car." Brandt attempted a laugh, if that's what you could call it, if a laugh were filled with hate and fury. "But you probably won't be going anywhere, will you?" he asked, certainly not laughing now.

"I guess we'll have to see, won't we?" Solly replied, walking around the side of the Packard, opening the door, and pulling out the pack of cigarettes he'd thrown on the passenger side of the car next to his open Swiss Army knife. He reached into his pocket for his lighter and made a big show of lighting his smoke before he grabbed his knife and shoved it and the pack of cigarettes back in the pocket next to the wire, hoping he'd distracted the German enough with his movements that he wouldn't notice the knife, that it had been hidden by his pack of Pall Malls.

He walked to the veranda, glancing at the men in the German's car as he passed, getting a good enough look to see the terror in their eyes, and sat down at the table next to his would-be assassin. "My friends don't look too happy. Maybe you should let them take the bus."

In '50s Hollywood movies about World War II, the Germans always stormed into a scene dressed to the nines in their military regalia and knee-high boots, swastikas and gold medals dripping off them. The truth was that when they went to their offices to facilitate the bureaucracy of slaughter, most of them dressed in perfectly ordinary clothes like Brandt had done that August afternoon. He sported an open-collared, loose-fitting, white linen shirt and khaki slacks, not looking like a movie enemy at all. The Nazi could have been any man from any European country, or even an America for that matter, relaxing on vacation. That made him all the more deadly.

When Solly told Grace the whole story later, she acted like he was some kind of daredevil, like he was Errol Flynn in one of his swash-buckling roles, but how much of what happened on the veranda that day was just dumb luck? After all, all war victories had a bit of luck and magic going for the winners. Everyone said D-Day succeeded because the Germans were sure that the Allies wouldn't attack. A huge storm was expected to whip up the English Channel. It was said that Hitler drank a glass of beer and went to sleep, thinking he had nothing to worry about. Who would cross the channel in that mess? Apparently, his generals had agreed and headed off to their mistresses' beds, certain they had the whole thing under control. And in August 1941, Brandt was as confident as the rest of them. The world would belong to the Germans. It was with that arrogance and swagger that he pushed his chair back and stood, leaning over Solly, demanding, "Where is the rest of the platinum? You have one minute to answer."

"Or what?" Solly couldn't help himself. Always the joker. He corrected course. "It's a rhetorical question. You don't have to answer."

"Then I won't," the German hissed, putting both hands on the sides of Solly's chair, leaning even closer, spittle flying when he spoke. "Don't waste any more of my time."

"I have no idea where the platinum is," Solly said, noticing that the German's blue eyes had flecks of brown, thinking, *This is what eyeball to eyeball means.* It was a stupid thing to think at that moment, he knew, but when you are a thin wire away from death, even the most ordinary clichés seemed remarkable.

"You have no idea. Let me help refresh your memory." He turned his head toward the nun. "Explain to him what will happen to his girl if he doesn't tell me."

"I'm afraid, Mr. Meisner, he will kill her," the nun said. "It would be better if you spoke up. Better for all of us." She nodded toward the men in the car.

What had the nun told him that afternoon in Frans's hotel room in Progreso? That the Lord doesn't give you more than you can bear. Solly hoped to live long enough to discuss that with her. Over the past few days, the Lord—let's just say for a minute He existed—had given Solly quite a bit. On the other hand, here he was, so point taken.

"You are wasting the one minute I have given you, Meisner." Out from under his perfectly normal white shirt, the German pulled a pistol from a shoulder holster.

"Okay, okay, you've convinced me." Solly lifted his hands. "It's in the Packard. You can look for yourself." He shrugged and leaned his head toward the car.

"Get up," the German yelled. "Come with me."

"Sure thing," Solly said, pushing the palms of his hands against the seat, rising.

* * *

Solly glanced at the alarm clock, the one Izzy had found with the extra-large glow-in-the-dark numbers. It beamed 4:30. He had no idea how long he'd been in bed. With his fading hearing, he couldn't recognize the thwap of the newspaper hitting the driveway, the grinding machinery of the garbage truck, the sounds that tell you it's almost time to get up. But lying in the dark, he could still hear the sound of those Mexican blackbirds, shrieking like rusty gates, swooping and careening in the trees above him. For how many hours had he been walking over and over again in his mind's eye from the convent's veranda to the Packard to open the trunk, where he would reveal to the German his radio equipment and the code book, wondering what the hell he would do then?

Grackles, they were called, those blackbirds. He'd learned that from Grace, who said she had asked the nun about the birds at some point. Grace was curious about nature: noisy blackbirds, plants, trees. It was why their yard looked like a park, with azaleas and camellias, a yellow rose climbing up the trunk of a longleaf pine in the front yard. He had been happy with his girls, as he called Izzy and Grace, his evening bourbon, the daily paper. He was a suburban dad, something he was surprised to have lived to be, with a barbecue grill and a pool in the backyard. He thought the peace would go undisturbed forever.

That is until one day when his secretary buzzed his phone and said there was some English lady who wanted to talk to him, and that peace shattered. He'd stared at the phone for a long time, wondering whether to pick it up, but he did. Estelle had just shown up, she'd said, in the garage next to his old office, the only address she had for him. The garage owner had given her Solly's number.

Solly had canceled his appointments, had driven back to

Pennington, had told her that no way could she see Izzy. But later he'd relented. He wasn't a complete bastard after all.

It was summer, and Izzy was home from college, working as a lifeguard at the Jewish country club. Solly took Estelle to lunch there, and they sat at a window with a view of the pool. She had left her sandwich almost untouched, her iced tea as well, and had stared out the window, watching her daughter, tan, healthy, flirting with boys, until Solly paid the bill, stood, and said, "Time's up."

He drove her back to the garage and had the owner call her a cab. Waiting around without much to say, he'd tried to remember that young guy who'd been so in love with her on the balcony overlooking Las Ramblas. He was gone; it turned out he'd simply evaporated as if he'd been no more substantial than haze.

The cab came, and he opened the door. "Don't do this again, Estelle."

"Don't worry. I won't," she said, handing him a box. "I did what I came here to do."

And now that box was in his safe, holding pages that began with *Villa Balaam. Diary entry written on September 6 in the year of our Lord 1941. I will somehow find a way to get you this notebook as I now have my new life arranged. Hopefully, I will be successful in this endeavor, and you will read this one day when I am no longer here. It is my fervent hope . . .*

Her fervent hope, and now that hope was in Solly's hands. He could do what he wanted, let Izzy know or not. Solly felt his heart race and turned on the light to make sure his bottle of nitroglycerin was there. That a box of letters should make him feel like he was having a heart attack was another cruel joke of age. He'd been in worse jams, hadn't he? Like the one back in Mexico in '41, when he sure hadn't had time to pop a heart pill. What had it taken? Five minutes, all of five minutes, and the German was dead. Five minutes, and Solly had lived. They'd all lived.

After Brandt had barked his order to go with him to the car, Solly stepped off the porch. The German shoved him in the back. "Walk in front, *Jude*," he yelled.

"You're the boss," Solly said, as if this were a friendly little walk in the park, as if it wasn't really a death march. He kept his hand in his pocket, the wire closed in his fist, and went over in his mind what the Russian spy had told him in Spain—*get behind your victim, throw the wire around his neck, jam your knee behind his, and he will fall. He will lean into the wire and sever the veins in his neck.*

"Open the trunk," the German demanded once they were standing in front of the Packard.

Solly reached into the other pocket with his left hand, pulled out the key chain, and pretended to struggle inserting the key into the cylinder, letting his hand shake. "Sorry, I must be nervous. What do you think?"

The German grabbed the key and stepped right in front of Solly, who had no time to think, to pray. As the German leaned into the trunk, and just as he was saying, "What have we here? A radio, our code book . . .," Solly threw the wire over the German's head, looping it around his neck, and rammed the back of his knees as hard as he could, pulling the wire toward him with all his might, like he was holding onto the ropes of a sail in a storm, like he would die if he didn't pull even harder.

When the guttural sounds the German made finally stopped and his head dangled to the left, hanging limp on his neck like a rose wilted on a stalk, Solly still couldn't let go of the wire, still he kept pulling. The Nazi's blood was everywhere. Solly felt faint and staggered from the body, but the sudden sound of a gunshot snapped him out of it. Yakov, who must have jumped out of the car and grabbed the gun when the German, desperate and struggling to breathe, had dropped it, now stood over Brandt and pulled the trigger again. The German's skull shattered, bits of bone flying like pebbles.

Solly watched, lightheaded, reeling as Yakov shot again and again until there were no more bullets, until there was only silence. Not even the grackles in the trees made noise. The only sound to be heard was the sound of Solly and Yakov breathing hard, gasping for air.

32

Solly

Mérida, Mexico
August 1941

Solly backed away from the body of the dead German, from his bloody, half-severed neck, his shattered head, his limbs splayed on the dirt, and staggered along the side of the Packard, where he collapsed next to the front bumper. Dizzy and breathing like a man saved from drowning, gulping as much air into his chest as he could, the echo of gunshots still exploding in his ears, Solly found that the front of the car was as far as his legs would carry him. He sank to the ground where at least he could look up at trees and flowering vines, blurry and looming over him, instead of at the sickening carnage by the back of the car, at a corpse that could have easily been his own. Too weak to hold up his head for long, he dropped his forehead to his knees, closed his eyes, and for a while saw nothing but the black and orange glow behind his lids, colors that looked like a world on fire.

The birds had started shrieking again, and from somewhere nearby he heard raised voices, some kind of argument, a woman and a man shouting in French. Solly rallied a bit, realizing it must be Yakov arguing with the nun. *About what?* he wondered and opened his eyes just as the nun rushed past him, speaking in Spanish now to a group of girls, nuns, too, he supposed, who disappeared into the house.

Solly clenched his bloody hands, torn from the wire he'd used to kill the German, unclenched them, clenched them again, a movement he couldn't stop repeating over and over. His arms shook, his shoulders, too, he realized. In fact, his whole body was shaking uncontrollably. All he wanted was to run somewhere—but where? He felt too weak to get up, and when he lifted his head, everything began spinning around him. He dropped his forehead onto his knees again, feeling as if his heart were a racing engine ready to explode.

"Get up," the nun barked, leaning over him, grabbing his shoulder and shaking him. "We have to get the German out of here now. Get up."

Solly leaned his head back on the car's front grill and whispered, "Can't. Can't do it."

"Mr. Birnbaum," the nun yelled. "Help me." She leaned down, shouting in Solly's ear. "You have no choice. If Camacho's pistoleros find the Nazi here, they will shoot you, Birnbaum, and the other one, Gottman, too. Execution by firing squad without a trial. *El presidente* wants no trouble from foreigners here in Mexico. It's all guitar music and cocktails for the tourists. Get up." She kicked his leg.

Solly felt Birnbaum's hands reach under one of his armpits and the nun's forearm under the other one. It wasn't an even match. The nun appeared to be the stronger of the two. Solly swayed as they pulled him to a standing position, and then he leaned over the car, pushing his sliced-up hands against the hood for support. "What do you want me to do?"

"Get the German into the boot of his car," the nun said. "And then drive him to the shack where they found Cordier. It will look like he was in cahoots or something, which he was," she said, grabbing two cigarettes out of her pocket, placing them between her lips, and lighting them both. She handed one to Solly. "Take this. It will give you some energy, and then just get him out of here."

Solly took a drag on the cigarette, hoping she was right.

A young nun, pale and wide-eyed, stepped up to Sister Immaculata and held out a dark, amber-colored bottle. The older nun took it, twisted its rusty cap, and shoved the bottle at Solly. "Drink," she said. "It's the local brew. It will revive the dead. At least the ones that still have their heads attached." She tilted her head toward the German and sneered. "Not him, obviously."

Solly swilled from the bottle and coughed, choking on what tasted like licorice, embers, and gasoline, a liquid that burned all the way down his gullet. "Jesus. What the hell is that?"

"Don't ask," the nun said. "Could be petrol and snake venom for all I know, but the girls seem to think it will cure anything from boils to the grippe." She tugged Solly's arm. "We need to get moving. Stop that," she shouted at Yakov as they rounded the side of the Packard. He was kicking the dead German violently. "Do something useful. Help us."

She got on the ground and rifled through the German's pockets, all the while rattling off in French to Yakov and the other two, Gottman and Birnbaum, who had gathered around, and shouting at the nuns in Spanish. A couple of them came back with a flour sack, a sheet, and rope. The nun found what she was looking for, the German's car keys, jogged over to his car, and opened the trunk. Then she went to work, issuing orders. "*Docteur* Gottman!" She called him over, but Solly couldn't understand the rest, except the arm waving and eye-rolling. Whatever she said resulted in Gottman tying the sack around the German's lopsided, bloody head with the rope.

Solly, still reeling from the homemade brew, felt as if he might pass out and grabbed onto the Packard's door handle to steady himself.

"Roll him onto this," the nun shouted at Solly before yelling some-thing in French to Gottman and Birnbaum and stretching the sheet on the ground beside the German. "We have to do this before he goes rigid."

"Do what?" Solly asked.

"Get him into the boot of his car with what is left of his head still stuck to him, even if it is by a thread. If we lift him by his limbs, it could just fall off from the weight. Maybe not, but why risk it? Hold the end tight." She yanked her side and issued more orders in French to the two other men. Gottman held onto the head in the sack while Birnbaum got on his knees and pushed the body onto the sheet. Soon they'd rolled the German into the middle, and each of them lifted a side, carrying the dead weight of the Nazi to his car, where they dumped him into the trunk.

When the nun told them to pull the sheet out from under him and remove the sack, Birnbaum asked, "Why do that? Maybe even a Nazi should have a shroud, no?"

The nun shook her head. "Give me strength, Lord," she said, look-ing heavenward. "Because the sheet could lead to us. Everyone here in the Yucatán sleeps on hammocks. Only hotels, the rich, foreigners, and priests have European sheets. The Germans will be up in arms when this one's body is discovered, and *los federales* will descend on us like a plague of locusts." She whistled, and the girls came run-ning. The nun handed them the sheet and sack, speaking quickly and waving her arms.

"What are they going to do with those?" Solly asked

"Burn them," the nun answered, handing him the car keys. "Can you drive a Ford sedan?"

"Why me?"

"I don't have time for endless questions like you are a child. Just do what I say." She slammed the trunk shut, climbed into the passenger seat, and sighed. "Because in a *machista* country like Mexico, the men drive. That's why. I don't want anything to look unusual."

Solly turned the key in the ignition, checked the rearview mirror, and backed up. "How are you planning to get us back here? Call a cab?"

"There's a path back here through the jungle from the shack," the nun told him. Then she shrieked, "Wait. Oh my God, wait."

Solly slammed on the brakes. "Wait? Why? What's going on?"

"You can't go. I almost forgot." She crossed herself. "You have to go get her." The nun jumped out of the car, ran to Yakov, and pulled him by the arm to the driver's side. "Birnbaum, go with Meisner," she yelled.

"Get who?" Solly was shouting now. "Who?"

"Who do you think, *idiota*," the nun shrieked louder this time, opening the car door. "That woman Grace. Get out of the car."

"What woman Grace?" Solly hauled himself off the driver's seat, and then, of course, he remembered—the boat, the suicide pill, the kiss. "Grace Weintraub? How the hell did she get here?"

"Yes. That's it. Grace Weintraub. You have to hurry. It will be dark. There's a torch behind a rock. I've explained it all to him." She pointed to Birnbaum. "They can't stay there all night."

"They? Who's they?"

"Grace has your daughter, Mr. Meisner. She kept her from Brandt, saved her life. Go get them before anything worse happens in this godforsaken place."

Solly gripped the open door and leaned into the car. "Tell me this is the truth. Swear to me that my daughter is safe."

"I can't swear anything now. It's up to you to find out. Just go."

* * *

Solly, Birnbaum, and Gottman followed one of the nuns Sister Immaculata had pressed into service down a wide path under the branches of enormous trees. Soon they reached a large, round pool surrounded by the jungle, a circle of twilight reflecting the blue sky above.

"*El cenote*," the nun said, pointing to the pond sunk deep into limestone walls, the water dark gray in the evening light. In the distance, a howler monkey shrieked, and the nun turned and ran back toward the convent, leaving Solly and his companions staring at the water, which was darkening by the minute. Mosquitos swarmed Solly's head and buzzed in his ears. It took all his strength to swat them away.

"The whole place," Dr. Gottman waved his arm in a circle, "is connected by underground rivers. An amazing geology."

"Dr. Gottman." Birnbaum shook his head. "Now, I think, is not the best time for a lecture on geology. Hurry," he said, tugging at Solly's sleeve. "You have to swim through a tunnel to the cave. I'll show you the opening. *Mein Gott*—" he slapped his forehead. "—you can swim, can't you?"

"Wait. You're coming with me, Birnbaum. I thought you were the one who knew the way. Isn't that what the sister told me?" Solly was beginning to feel desperate. He had to get his child. He couldn't afford to chicken out. He needed someone with him to keep the panic at bay, even if it was some befuddled professor.

"I'm scared of water. I don't even fill the bathtub all the way. I can't swim."

A prickly feeling of terror crawled over Solly. "What about you, Gottman? There should be two of us."

"I come from Alsace, not the sea. My parents thought recreation was frivolous, so, no. *Je suis désolé.*" He placed his hand on his heart, bowed slightly, and when he straightened up, pointed to Solly's trousers. "You'll have to take those off to swim. Your clothes, yes?"

The monkey screamed again.

"So, I'm on my own, huh?" Solly sat on the ground, beginning to sweat from fear, and leaned against one of the huge trees whose roots seemed to stretch toward Mérida. He closed his eyes, tried to not think about the cave, his worst nightmare of being alone, suffocating in an enclosed place. He tried to think only of his child, a girl he had only seen briefly, who was now in some cave with Grace, a woman who needed him, a woman who had once called him a hero. Well, he didn't have much choice except to be one now. And how did he think he was going to pull that off? Hadn't he told Blumberg that he wasn't religious? Well, like someone once said, *There are no atheists in foxholes.*

Solly opened his eyes, untied his shoes, and yanked off his socks, stuffing them into the toes of his shoes. He kept hearing Grace's voice, trying to let it guide him. *You were a hero,* she had said to him the first time they'd met. But he hadn't been, not really. He'd been a chickenshit coward. Men had died. And the excuse of being young and stupid, the one he'd fallen back on in his darkest guilt-ridden moments? Well, he'd used up that defense—it was only good once, if at all. He didn't have that card to play again. He thought of the things that could happen if he didn't hurry. Grace could pass out from hypothermia. She could let go of the little girl, who could wander off, who could drown.

He stood, his hands shaking as he fiddled with his belt and his zipper, and his legs almost buckled from the jitters when he stepped out of his slacks. There was no running this time. There was no escape.

He folded the slacks, felt the pill bottle in his pocket, and remembered the cyanide pills at the bottom of the left one. If he failed, if he didn't reach Grace and the child in time, there was always that. Not a great way to end up, but at least he hadn't given the Nazi the pleasure of murdering a few more Jews. It was some consolation.

Consolation. He needed it at the moment, standing in the middle of the jungle wearing nothing but his boxer shorts, his bare limbs like a banquet for mosquitos. And for some reason he remembered his mother, trying to impress upon her young son that he should always wear clean underwear. *Every day,* she'd said. *And a new pair when you go out to Aunt Sylvia's for dinner.*

Why? he'd asked.

Because what if you get hit by a bus? His mother's answer to any question. *You want to be in the hospital and all the pretty nurses should think you are a schlub?*

What if I get hit by the bus and die? He'd always been a smart-ass.

So, you would just be a dead schlub, which would be worse.

Solly started to laugh.

"Mr. Meisner, this is no time for laughing," Birnbaum said. "You must go."

Had he been laughing? Had he gone nuts? "My mother," he said. "She used to worry about me getting hit by a bus in dirty underwear."

The two men exchanged glances. "There is no bus here, Mr. Meisner," Birnbaum said. "I don't understand."

Solly took a deep breath and waved his hand toward the pond. "What do I do now, gentlemen?"

"There," Gottman said. "You go down the ladder."

Solly walked to the edge of the grass clearing where the rocks jutted up above the pool, turned, and stepped down the wooden rungs. The water came up to his waist, cool and heavy, like weights ready to pull him away from the ladder and into something dangerous and unknown. He felt the urge to leap out, but his daughter's life was at stake. Fleeing was not on the table. So he slipped farther down into the pond until his feet touched the slimy rocks on the side of the pool. "Where do I go now?" he called up to the two men.

Birnbaum walked around the edge of the pool and Solly followed, dog-paddling to keep his head above water, finally seeing what Birnbaum was pointing at—an opening in the rocks, covered in vines, and behind the vines, more rocks.

"In the middle somewhere," Birnbaum shouted, "there are loose rocks. Behind one of them, somewhere, is a torch. And also, Mr. Meisner, this is important," Birnbaum yelled even louder. "The cave divides into two. You must remember to go to the left. Take the left tunnel."

"There's more than one damn tunnel in here?" Solly's voice shook as he called up to Birnbaum.

"I'm afraid so," the professor said. "At least, that is what Sister Immaculata told me. She was quite insistent."

The water was shallower here. Solly could stand and keep his balance as he tugged on the rocks above the cavern's opening. After his third try, he found the loose rock and, behind it, a flashlight, which he stuck under his arm before shoving the rock back in its place. He flipped the switch and aimed the light into the opening of the narrow cave, swiping the light along the slimy walls. Beyond the flashlight's reach he could see nothing, just a black cave with rocks hanging from above. It was something from a horror movie. What had Yakov said that first day as they drove up to the hacienda? *Welcome to hell.* "That was nothing, buddy," Solly muttered as he stepped into the cave, feeling like he was about to be swallowed up.

After Solly had pushed his way about ten yards through the icy water, far enough that he could no longer see the cave's opening behind him, the nerves hit even harder, squeezing his chest like a vise. He began to pant, and that racing feeling in his heart revved up again. *Don't faint*, he told himself. *You faint, and you'll die here.*

Beyond the reach of the flashlight he could see nothing but a dark, dank hole, and if the flashlight went dead? Jesus. Who knew if the nun had bothered to check the batteries.

"Grace," he called out, probably sounding terrified. Wasn't he supposed to be rescuing her? Rescuing his child? What kind of coward was he? "Grace," he shouted again, the sound of his voice bouncing off the black stone walls. No answer. He waded farther, pushing against the weight of the water. Where the hell was he going? Wasn't there supposed to be some kind of left turn? And if he'd missed it? Solly began to shake. "Grace," he screamed. Nothing.

Wouldn't a small child be crying? Wouldn't he hear them? Solly forced himself to keep going. Had he already taken the wrong turn? Had there been someone else with Brandt? Could that person have known about the cave, found them, and be waiting for Solly?

The bottom of the canal he was wading through plunged away, and he was suddenly neck-deep in water. He lifted the flashlight above his head just as he slammed his right foot against a rock. "Shit," he muttered, pain stabbing his toes. What if he fell and broke something? Stretching his throbbing foot forward, he bumped into a rock slab, swore again, and stepped up onto what seemed like a ledge, the water only up to his thighs here. "Grace," he shouted once more. No response. By now he was shivering and weak with fear and exhaustion. There hardly seemed to be a point in calling out again. What if they were gone? What if they'd been met with a horrible fate? He couldn't bear thinking about that, couldn't bear thinking at all, and trudged forward.

He swiped the flashlight this way and that in front of him as if he were painting a wall and saw that the cave was narrowing even more. Soon he would have to crouch. Why the hell didn't he get more information from the nun? Why did he go off with just Birnbaum to guide him? The blind leading the blind, except that Birnbaum was safely aboveground, and Solly was in a watery hellhole. He swiped the flashlight up and down, then sideways, and he noticed the tunnel seemed to widen and then divide. Solly veered to the left down a grim underworld tube, but then he saw it—an opening to the sky. There was still a faint circle of blue above it, a few lingering rays of evening sun shining on a small pool below. He blinked, wanting to reach his arms upward to heaven, to that small blue circle of light and air that would save him, save them, lead them all out of this black hell.

But his joy was immediately snuffed out. There was another problem. Where was the cave? He didn't see it, and panic returned again, freezing his limbs like it would paralyze him. Where was Grace? Where was his daughter? Solly tried to jog, to get there—wherever "there" was—faster, but the stones underneath his feet were too uneven and he had to give that up. He waved the flashlight against the walls. No cave, no hiding place. Nothing but what felt like a grim tomb.

Just as a sinking despair had overtaken him, he aimed the flashlight once more at the right side of the tunnel and blinked. Was he really seeing an opening in the cavern's walls, like the edge of a bowl turned on its side? He was. Solly pushed his body hard against the water, trying to reach the cave. It had to be the one. "Grace," he screamed as he got close. "Grace." He shone the flashlight at the opening, a round ledge above the water.

The nun had been right. And even better, there was a rope ladder next to the wall by the pool. He would get out of here. He would get them all out of here. They would survive, and just as relief filled him with something like ecstasy, he turned and saw her.

He saw her and began to scream.

A wild-eyed woman rose up from the water where she must have been crouching and lunged toward him, the knife in her hand aimed straight at his chest.

33

Solly

Havana, Cuba
End of August 1941

I
t wasn't much of a wedding reception, but it was the best he could
do: daiquiris at the Floridita bar on swanky Obispo Street. The
place had been packed, no free tables anywhere, when he, Grace, Izzy,
and their friends had wandered in. But then Adrian, the boat captain
who'd gotten them out of Mexico as he'd promised, explained to the
bartender that his friends were newlyweds, that they'd just tied the
knot at the US Embassy up the block. Tables were vacated, chairs
were pulled together, and there were toasts and cheers all around
from the patrons—in Spanish, of course. Solly had to take it on faith
that they were good wishes. He, Grace, and Izzy had been through
enough. They'd used up all the luck they'd been allotted and needed
to stockpile as many good thoughts as could be found.

The bartender had produced a dish of ice cream for Izzy, along with
drinks for Solly's wedding party—Yakov, Birnbaum, and Gottman—
and Solly almost wept when he saw his daughter's face light up, her
eyes growing wide as Grace spooned the first bite of ice cream into
her mouth. He realized she'd never had ice cream before, or much of
anything, for that matter. All he could think was, *What if I hadn't
found her? What if Grace hadn't been there?* He lifted Grace's hand to

his lips and kissed the spot next to the diamond ring he'd placed on it an hour ago, the biggest he could find at the Palais Royal jewelry store, a place he'd been told all the gangsters shopped at. After all he'd done, he was practically a gangster himself.

"Better this on your hand than a dagger in it, Lady Macbeth," he had whispered in her ear when she'd tried it on.

She'd told him she'd heard someone yelling in the cave. Well, "told" wasn't the right verb. Whatever she was saying down in that dark, watery, underground world had come out in screams and tears, a garble of words and sobs, as she shook violently in his arms, trying to explain.

Later, back at the convent, after they were warm and dry, sitting together in her hammock, rocking little Isabella, Grace had started to wonder aloud why she hadn't recognized Solly's voice, how she had convinced herself the voices were the Germans, that they knew where she was. She'd made the thing she was most terrified of come true. She told Solly that she had put the child in one of the trunks, as if that would have protected her. She was so terrified, she'd told Solly, she couldn't think.

"I know the feeling," he said, taking her hand.

Solly had followed Grace up onto the dry rocks of the cave and over to the trunk where she had hidden Izzy. He had picked up his daughter, who was limp and silent, and grasped her small hands, looked at her perfect nails, like those tiny shells on the beach, the color of pearls. Had those hands really come from him? Those perfect arms? The long, black lashes, the rosebud mouth? Could he have had anything to do with making something so perfect, something so completely his own? He could have stared at her for hours, but Grace was tugging at him, saying they had to hurry.

Maybe the girl was in a state of shock since she wasn't crying. Her silence frightened him. In spite of her perfection, it was so strange. How had he not noticed that? He had been so concerned and so mesmerized by the sight of his own flesh and blood, a child who could have died or starved if fate had not conspired to bring him here, that he had failed to notice the other contents of the trunk—the platinum. Grace had to show him, had to tell him what the nun had said.

Well, he would have time later to explain all that he knew about the platinum, about Eton, about the esteemed Senator Clay Wright from South Carolina—a louse, a murderer, and a traitor—to the men who were gathered right now at the embassy to debrief him. But for now, he was a newly married man, and he planned to enjoy the event, however brief the celebration would have to be.

By four in the afternoon, he and the refugees were due back at the embassy. That gave them two hours in the heat of the day to drink icy rum cocktails under the swirling ceiling fans while a radio played jazzy Cuban songs and sunlight poured into the bar through the long green shutters, light that seemed as bright to Solly as Roman candles exploding in the sky.

"*Mazel tov,*" Birnbaum called out, lifting his glass to Solly and Grace. "*L'chaim.*"

"To life." How many times had Solly heard that expression and not thought of its meaning? But now, as he sat in a cluttered embassy office while a dull-witted American official tried to explain how entrance visas for the three Jews would be impossible, life was the only thing that mattered to Solly, his life and the lives of all the others.

"We have a quota on the number of Jews we can admit," the embassy functionary said, like it was a fact of nature, something that could not be altered.

"Okay, I'll make this easy," Solly said. "Don't say they are Jews. Dr.

Gottman here is French, Mr. Oberstein is Polish, Professor Birnbaum is German. Oh, and by the way, I'm an American, same as you, pal."

He stood and turned, grinning at the startled functionary like he didn't have a care in the world. He told him that he and his friends were staying at the Hotel Nacional and that he should call him when he changed his mind. If President Roosevelt wanted to know how to save the US Navy in the Gulf, if he wanted to protect the Army Air Corps pilots, and Solly was fairly certain that was the case, they might want to reconsider. Otherwise, his secrets would remain with him. "There are worse fates than staying in Cuba, smoking cigars, and gambling for a living." He lifted his Panama hat, waved it at the bureaucrat, and put it on his head. He was gambling, he knew, but the whole enterprise had been a gamble. He sure as hell wasn't about to stop now.

When the rather sheepish bureaucrat showed up at the hotel a few hours later with entrance visas and the adoption papers Solly had demanded as well, Solly knew he was holding the winning hand.

Two winning hands, really. One of them was Grace's, the one she'd slipped into his that night on the deck of Adrian's boat as they crossed the sea to Cuba. "Little Izzy is finally asleep," she'd told Solly. Little Izzy. It was a nickname that stuck, like everything else between them. "Yakov was singing Brahms's 'Lullaby' to her, and she just conked out. He's going to stay there with her. He says she reminds him of his little sister."

Solly remembered how Grace had shivered then, how he'd taken his hand out of hers and wrapped his arm around her shoulders, pulling her to him.

"Who knows where she is now. The sister," Graced had sighed.

"I think we do know. That's the terrible thing, isn't it?" Solly had wanted to tell her how Yakov had cried when he'd first met him, weeping at the sound of Yiddish, which he hadn't heard since he'd been with his family, and how Solly had thought he was a weakling. He'd been wrong. After all that Yakov had endured, he was probably the strongest man Solly knew. Maybe even the bravest.

He and Grace were staring out at the black sea, the black sky, the wind blowing. She'd turned, leaned her back against the railing, holding her dark hair in her fist, and Solly thought he'd never seen a more beautiful face, even weary as she was after all the exhausting days waiting to get out of Mexico with the constant fear the Germans would find them, even with no golden Spanish light on a balcony overlooking Las Ramblas, even though she was not Estelle. And that's when he turned briefly toward the east, toward what he'd left behind, and realized he was glad to have left it in the past now, his broken heart. And grateful, all of a sudden, to the same woman who'd broken it, because she'd given him this moment, this woman, this child, this life he was about to embark upon. What a gift, and he wished her well wherever she was in the jungle.

"It's up there somewhere." Grace had interrupted his thoughts. "The constellation of the Serpent Bearer, the god that brings the dead back to life. I wish we could do that, don't you?"

Ah, but they had, in a way, Solly thought, wrapping both his arms around her. It had taken courage, and it had taken love, but they'd done it. Then with all the desire he had stored up in him for life, for love, he'd kissed her. "All we can do is what we've done, Grace," he whispered. "Bring souls back from the brink of death like those refugees, like—" he hesitated, getting used to the sound of his daughter's name. "Like Izzy."

They held on to each other for a long time, saying nothing, listening to the drone of the boat's engine, to the slap of the waves against the starboard side.

Finally, Grace whispered, "What do we do now, Solly? I think you'll have a hard time prying Izzy away from me."

He'd pulled her as close as he could, thinking of what to say, how to propose to this beautiful woman, and then he remembered that afternoon in Spain a long time ago, another gift he'd been given. "Well," he said, holding her face in his hands, staring into her dark eyes, suddenly terrified he'd misunderstood what she'd said, that if he asked, she would say no. But he charged ahead, saying words he would never forget. "There's a war going on, and we're young. I think we should fall in love."

Izzy would hear a version of that story her whole life, a version that was not the complete truth she would find out later. But every anniversary, every Passover when the *slivovitz* had been drunk, someone, Uncle Mo or her mother, would tell the story of how you could put Solly Meisner in a glued-together Soviet bomber, dodging Franco's anti-aircraft guns, but the thing that had scared him the most was that her mother wouldn't marry him. And Grace would always laugh, her cheeks flushed with holiday wine. "What else was there to do?" she would say. "There was a war, we were young. Loving one another was all we had left."

Acknowledgments

Thank you to the wonderful, supportive team of women at She Writes Press: Brooke Warner, Shannon Green, Lauren Wise, Cait Levin, Krissa Lagos, my fabulous copyeditor Michelle Lippold, and proofreader Stephanie Clarke. I will be eternally grateful to you all for the care and support you gave me and my book. Thank you for your wisdom, insight, and grace and for all you do to support women authors.

I feel incredibly lucky to have had such an amazing and talented cover designer as Julie Metz, who captured the feeling of my novel with just the perfect image. Thank you, Julie. You are a genius.

I don't know how to begin to thank Crystal Patriarche, Leilani Ftzpatrick, and Hanna Lindsley, my talented and hardworking publicity team at BookSparks, for helping *The Serpent Bearer* reach its audience and for guiding me through the daunting publicity process. A million thanks, sisters.

Also, a huge thanks has to go to Michael and Tara at Caroff Communications for designing and maintaining my beautiful website JaneRosenthal.com and keeping me afloat on social media. Thank you.

A big gracias to the travel company Journey Mexico and to the team of Zaira and Carolina, who helped me arrange travel and hotels all over the Yucatan and Campeche, to places actually in this book or places (run down haciendas) that were very similar. Thank you to Russell for doing all the driving and schlepping of bags and for all your knowledge of the history of the Yucatan and Campeche, places central to this book. Also, thanks for showing me the best place to buy my own Panama hat.

My gratitude and heartfelt thanks must go to my gifted and brilliant editor Annie Tucker. I could not have told this story, which is so close to my heart, without your patient reading of draft after draft and all your insightful and wise comments, my dear friend.

I am so lucky to have such supportive friends and family who encouraged me to put myself and my stories out into the world. I hold you all in my heart. Thank you for being beside me for so, so many years. What would I have done without you?

I will always be grateful to have grown up in Charlotte, North Carolina's vibrant, generous and welcoming Jewish community. Thank you for being such a wonderful influence on me and on the city of Charlotte as well. Also, I am thankful to have found an equally warm and wonderful community here at Temple Beth Shalom in Santa Fe, New Mexico. Thank you, TBS, for being an important part of my life here.

This book is dedicated to my parents, who exposed me to a fascinating and complicated world full of books, travel, and artistic and intellectual pursuits. My gratitude has no bounds. May your memories be for a blessing.

A day does not go by that I don't consider how lucky I am to be the mother of my brilliant, talented, and lovely daughter. Anna, you are as compassionate as you are beautiful and wise. My life is overflowing because of you.

Finally, to my beloved husband, David, the light of my life. You are my everything. You always will be.

About the Author

photo credit: Gabriella Marks

Jane Rosenthal studied creative writing at San Francisco State University. She worked for NPR and California Public Radio before teaching English in public high schools in Oakland, California. She grew up Jewish and southern in Charlotte, North Carolina, and now resides in Santa Fe, New Mexico, with her husband, astrophysicist David Hollenbach.

Looking for your next great read?

We can help!

Visit www.shewritespress.com/next-read
or scan the QR code below for a list
of our recommended titles.

She Writes Press is an award-winning
independent publishing company founded to
serve women writers everywhere.

BAYESIAN
POPULATION
ANALYSIS
USING WinBUGS

A HIERARCHICAL PERSPECTIVE

MARC KÉRY AND MICHAEL SCHAUB

Swiss Ornithological Institute
6204 Sempach
Switzerland

Foreword by

STEVEN R. BEISSINGER

AMSTERDAM • BOSTON • HEIDELBERG • LONDON
NEW YORK • OXFORD • PARIS • SAN DIEGO
SAN FRANCISCO • SINGAPORE • SYDNEY • TOKYO

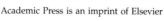

Academic Press is an imprint of Elsevier

Academic Press is an imprint of Elsevier
225 Wyman Street, Waltham, MA 02451, USA
525 B Street, Suite 1900, San Diego, CA 92101-4495, USA
The Boulevard, Langford Lane, Kidlington, Oxford, OX51GB, UK
Radarweg 29, PO Box 211, 1000 AE Amsterdam, The Netherlands

First edition 2012

Notice
No responsibility is assumed by the publisher for any injury and/or damage to persons or
property as a matter of products liability, negligence, or otherwise or from any use or
operation of any methods, products, instructions, or ideas contained in the material herein.
Because of rapid advances in the medical sciences, in particular, independent verification of
diagnoses and drug dosages should be made.

Library of Congress Cataloging-in-Publication Data
Kéry, Marc
    Bayesian population analysis using WinBUGS : a hierarchical perspective / Marc Kery and
    Michael Schaub. – 1st ed.
        p. cm.
Includes bibliographical references and index.
ISBN 978-0-12-387020-9 (alk. paper)
    1. Population biology–Data processing. 2. WinBUGS. I. Schaub, Michael. II. Title.
QH352.K47 2011
577.8'80285–dc23
                                    2011029641

British Library Cataloguing in Publication Data
A catalogue record for this book is available from the British Library.

For information on all Academic Press publications
visit our Web site at *www.elsevierdirect.com*

Typeset by: diacriTech, Chennai, India

Transferred to Digital Printing in 2012

Working together to grow
libraries in developing countries

www.elsevier.com | www.bookaid.org | www.sabre.org

ELSEVIER   BOOK AID
            International   Sabre Foundation

We dedicate this book to our children Gabriel, and Lilly and Lukas.

Contents

4. Introduction to Random Effects: Conventional Poisson GLMM for Count Data

5. State-Space Models for Population Counts

6. Estimation of the Size of a Closed Population from Capture–Recapture Data

7. Estimation of Survival from Capture–Recapture Data Using the Cormack–Jolly–Seber Model

8. Estimation of Survival Using Mark-Recovery Data

9. Estimation of Survival and Movement from Capture–Recapture Data Using Multistate Models

10. Estimation of Survival, Recruitment, and Population Size from Capture–Recapture Data Using the Jolly–Seber Model

11. Estimation of Demographic Rates, Population Size, and Projection Matrices from Multiple Data Types Using Integrated Population Models

12. Estimation of Abundance from Counts in Metapopulation Designs Using the Binomial Mixture Model

13. Estimation of Occupancy and Species Distributions from Detection/Nondetection Data in Metapopulation Designs Using Site-Occupancy Models

14. Concluding Remarks

Foreword

Scientific disciplines are often judged by their success in translating ideas and principles into outcomes under future conditions. One of the greatest challenges faced by ecologists and conservation biologists of our time is to use our knowledge to understand how species, populations, and communities will behave, persist, and evolve in the future in a world with more people and a changing climate. Models are central to this undertaking.

Models have become an important tool for conservation planning and managing natural resources. In ecology and conservation biology as in other sciences, models have always driven the development of certain concepts and served a useful role in synthesizing knowledge and guiding research. Computer models also provided ways to gain new insights into modeled systems by running "virtual experiments." But now more than ever, mathematical and simulation models are being used to project future outcomes based on past, current, or projected conditions. Over the past 30 years, models have grown in use, prominence, and complexity with the advent of desktop computers that have become both more affordable and more powerful to run them and with the growth of specialized software to enable users to implement them.

Models are both familiar to us and scary. We unconsciously use models everyday in making life choices. For example, we often use simple "rule of thumb" models when we dress to determine which color combinations are complementary and which are clashing, and we take projections from complex weather models into consideration when choosing whether to wear a warm or cool fabric. Scientists have routinely used conventional statistical models or "frequentist models" when determining whether relationships differ by testing a null hypothesis to a specified confidence level (e.g., $p < 0.05$). Yet, models are not a panacea. Many ecologists, conservation biologists, and resource managers distrust models because they can be overly complex, use mathematical methods, and contain computer code that they do not understand, or they are based on uncertain relationships and parameter estimates. The accepted convention of a p value of 0.05 (or a 5% chance of wrongly rejecting the null hypothesis of no difference when it is true) is an artificial construct and perhaps too restrictive for gleaning useful information from nature to use in management.

Bayesian methods can address some of these concerns. They use data or hypothesized relationships about data to make inferences about ecological systems. Bayesian models have the advantage of making probabilistic statements about the veracity of hypotheses or relationships, given the data. They can explicitly incorporate uncertainty in model structure and parameter estimates through both prior knowledge and expectations about data into models that produce posterior distributions of outcomes. Bayesian methods depend on resampling distributions, and their recent growth is a result of both their utility and the ease with which computers can implement numerical recipes using Markov Chain Monte Carlo (MCMC) sampling.

This book provides an accessible introduction to Bayesian methods as applied to analyzing populations. It covers a breadth of applications that are widely used in ecology and population management, from analysis of count data and demographic rates for understanding the fluctuations of single populations to estimation of patch occupancy, and metapopulation dynamics that characterize more widely distributed species. Moreover, it uses a practical approach to model building that recognizes most data obtained in field studies of population ecology will have associated sampling uncertainties that arise from hidden processes, so-called hierarchical models. These models account for both the ecological processes of interest and the additional uncertainty caused by unobserved processes that always accompany field sampling, such as variation in the detectability of individuals. The book also makes extensive use of the free and widely used computer programs R and WinBUGS to implement these models. It is the ideal combination for both beginning students and beginning modelers to learn these methods. Advanced users will find plenty of wisdom in these pages to gain new skills, as I have.

Wise use of a model to make decisions that prevent extinction and recover populations requires understanding the unique attributes of a model, determining whether the assumptions that underlie the model's structure are valid and testing the ability of the model to predict the future correctly. This book goes a long way toward building models that can address the first two goals. Ecologists and conservation biologists will still have much work to do to determine how well their models perform. Although the future remains unpredictable as always, there will undoubtedly be a great need to manage wildlife and plant populations by applying the kinds of models presented in this book and by conducting field studies to improve their performance, if the looming extinctions that are projected to be associated with growing human populations and a warming climate are to be prevented.

Steven R. Beissinger
Berkeley, California

Preface

You are looking at a gentle introduction for ecologists to Bayesian population analysis using the BUGS software. We emphasize learning by doing and leisurely walk you through a wide range of statistical methods for a broad array of model classes that are relevant for population ecologists. We focus on hierarchical models for estimation and modeling of quantities such as population size or survival probability, while accounting for imperfect detection probability. The reading is intended to be light and engaging, while at the same time, we hope that the content is represented accurately.

This book has been written by ecologists for ecologists. For this project, two experienced population ecologists have teamed up in a complementary way. Marc has been working chiefly in projects involving the estimation and modeling of population size and occurrence and the simplest description of population dynamics, population trends. The work of Michael has focused on teasing apart the demographic rates that underlie the observed dynamics (i.e. trends) of a population. In this way, we neatly combine our strengths and experience. We have published papers that use WinBUGS to fit almost all model classes described in this book and have experience in their frequentist analysis as well.

Both in content and in style, this book is a sequel to a similar book written by Marc (Kéry, 2010). In content, the latter is more introductory and directed to the general ecologist or indeed to anybody interested in regression modeling in WinBUGS. In Kéry (2010), most of the typical ecological statistics examples, such as estimation of population size and demographic rates, that is, our Chapters 6–11, are lacking conspicuously. In addition, in Chapters 12 and 13, we now extend the binomial mixture and the site-occupancy model to multiple "seasons" and the single-state site-occupancy model to multiple states. These important generalizations are lacking in Kéry (2010). We make occasional reference to Kéry (2010), but our current book is independent from the earlier one. Nevertheless, should you find some material in here difficult to follow, we suggest to use Kéry (2010) for learning about ecological modeling in WinBUGS at a more introductory level.

In style, the key concepts of Kéry (2010) have been retained for this book:

1. We provide a large number of richly commented worked examples to illustrate a wide range of statistical models that are relevant to

the research of a population ecologist and to the analyses of wildlife or fisheries managers or analysts in more applied branches of ecology.

2. We have written the book using WinBUGS, but most of the code should run fine with OpenBUGS and JAGS as well.

3. All WinBUGS analyses are run from within software R; hence, this is also an R book.

4. We provide a complete documentation of *all* R and WinBUGS code required to conduct *all* our analyses and show *all* the necessary steps from having the data in some sort of text file to interpreting and processing the output from WinBUGS in R. Thus, you are almost *guaranteed* to be able to replicate our analyses for your own data sets.

5. We make extensive use of the simulation of data sets and their analysis. We believe that simulating data sets can be crucial to your understanding of the models. However, we also provide 1–2 analyses of real-life data in each chapter.

6. We have a clear and consistent layout for all computer code.

7. We aim at a light and engaging language.

8. Each chapter has a set of exercises with solutions for all of them provided on the book website (**www.vogelwarte.ch/bpa**).

In scope and in style, our book intends to build a bridge between introductory texts by McCarthy (2007) or Kéry (2010) and three more advanced texts on the analysis of populations, metapopulations, and communities, which have recently been published and which all use WinBUGS as their primary software: Royle and Dorazio (2008), King et al. (2010), and Link and Barker (2010). If your primary research topic is population ecology as covered in our book, you should consider buying some or all of these books as well.

Our book is based on a one-week course for graduate students and postdoctoral researchers that we teach at universities and research institutes. For this course, we require participants to have some basic knowledge of program R or other programming languages as well as of basic statistical methods such as regression and ANOVA. It helps a lot if they have also had some exposure to generalized linear models (GLMs) and random-effects models and know what the design matrix of a linear model is. These requirements fairly accurately describe the intended audience of our book. We believe that our book is well suited for a one-semester course in modern population analysis for subjects such as quantitative conservation biology, resource management, fisheries, wildlife management, or general population ecology. In addition, our book is perfect for self-study, owing to its gentle style and because the complete code is shown and is amply documented. Our book website contains a text file with all R-WinBUGS code, data sets, solutions to all exercises, our utility functions, additional bonus material, a list of Errata plus some other information, such as about upcoming workshops.

Recently, the active software development of the BUGS project has moved over from WinBUGS to OpenBUGS (Lunn et al., 2009 see www.openbugs.info). As of early 2011, the syntax of the two BUGS sisters has remained virtually identical. We have written and tested our code in WinBUGS 1.4. (and with R 2.12.), but we have checked a sample in OpenBUGS also and most ran fine. The latest release of OpenBUGS contains a series of ecological examples that are all of relevance for the readers of this book. The JAGS software (see www-fis.iarc.fr/~martyn/software/jags) is another MCMC engine that uses the BUGS language, as do WinBUGS and OpenBUGS. Hence, most code in our book should run in JAGS as well. In contrast to Win- and OpenBUGS, JAGS also runs on Macs.

Here are a few tips on how to use this book. We strongly suggest you first read Chapters 1–4 because they contain important introductory material that you will need to know in later chapters. Only then should you pick chapters according to your interests. Evidently, before starting to work through this book, you need to have installed the necessary software: R, with some packages (especially R2WinBUGS, but also lme4) and WinBUGS, with both the upgrade patch and the immortality key decoded, or else have OpenBUGS or JAGS functional. When using Win-BUGS from R, you need to always first load the R2WinBUGS package (Sturtz et al., 2005). We do not usually say this, but simply assume that you issue the command `library(R2WinBUGS)` at the start of every R session. In addition, you need to tell R where the WinBUGS executable is residing on your computer. For that, we define an object that contains this address (`bugs.dir <- "c:/Program Files/WinBUGS14/"`; this is the default) and refer to it when calling WinBUGS with function `bugs()`. If WinBUGS is placed in another folder on your computer, the path information needs to be modified accordingly. Such information can also be written into the text file `Rsite.profile`, which sits in the R folder `etc` and contains global R settings (see Kéry, 2010, p. 32). Several models in the book take a long time to fit, hence, we give approximate bugs run times (BRT) for each. We use the R function `sink()` to write into the R working directory (which you can set yourself using `setwd()`), a text file containing the model description in the BUGS language. We find it useful to have all our code in a single document. You have to be totally clear about which part of the code is in the BUGS language and which is in the R language. This may be a little confusing at first, especially, because the two languages are quite similar (R is a dialect of S, and BUGS is strongly inspired by S). See the WinBUGS tips in Appendix 1 for more explanation. Finally, an important tip for when you cannot follow an analysis in this book is to execute code line by line (if possible) and inspect all objects generated until you understand what they represent and how they fit together.

We truly hope that you find our book useful, whether you do population analysis for your research or for more applied goals, such as management or conservation biology. We even hope that you actually *enjoy* reading and working through it for its content, its style, and its presentation. In reality, we have written a book that we would have liked to have when we started our statistical population modeling in WinBUGS some years ago. If you have comments or find errors, please drop us an email at marc.kery@vogelwarte.ch or michael.schaub@vogelwarte.ch. We hope that WinBUGS frees the creative population modeler in you, as it has done for us.

Marc and Michael,
April 2011

Acknowledgments

We are indebted to three of our colleagues with whom we have collaborated for many years and who have directly or indirectly contributed much of the code, and more, documented in this book: Andy Royle, Olivier Gimenez, and Bob Dorazio. Over the years, they have been extremely generous in helping us to learn how to use WinBUGS efficiently and correctly. We thank the following people who have read and commented on parts or the book or helped otherwise: Andy Royle, Fitsum Abadi, Raphaël Arlettaz, Florent Bled, Richard Chandler, David Fletcher, Beth Gardner, Olivier Gimenez, Vidar Grøtan, Jérôme Guélat, Ali Johnston, Fränzi Korner Nievergelt, Bill Link, Mike Meredith, Jim Nichols, Marco Perrig, Tobias Roth, Beni Schmidt, and Giacomo Tavecchia. We are grateful to Steven Beissinger for writing an inspiring foreword. We furthermore thank the people who provided data sets, as well as the photographers who gave us their great shots of some of the organisms behind the numbers we crunch. The participants at our workshops (Sempach 2010 and 2011; Patuxent 2010) have been extremely important to try out what works and what does not and for honing our book, which is meant to be a gentle introduction to Bayesian statistical population modeling for exactly this kind of audience. Specifically, we are indebted to Andy Royle and his colleagues at Patuxent for hosting the BPA workshop in November 2011. We also thank our employers, the Swiss Ornithological Institute (www.vogelwarte.ch) and the Laboratory of Conservation Biology (www.cb.iee.unibe.ch) at the University of Berne, for giving us creative time for research and writing. Finally, we feel a deep gratitude to our families, especially our wives Susana and Christine, for their love and patience and for granting us the freedom required to write this book.

Introduction

1.1 ECOLOGY: THE STUDY OF DISTRIBUTION AND ABUNDANCE AND OF THE MECHANISMS DRIVING THEIR CHANGE

Ecology is concerned with the number (abundance, N) of living things—how many individuals there are and how their number evolves over time, where they are and where they go to. Important questions concern their interactions with the abiotic and biotic environment, including each other, and what mechanisms drive these numbers and their dynamics. This classic view of ecology is reflected by the titles of two seminal textbooks: *The Distribution and Abundance of Animals* (Andrewartha and Birch,

1954) and *Ecology: The Experimental Analysis of Distribution and Abundance* (Krebs, 2001).

More generally, ecology can be described as the science that studies how states of biological systems interact with their environment and how this results in the temporal dynamics and spatial patterns of organisms that we observe. Figure 1.1 shows how state S evolves over time. The arrows connecting states between successive time periods denote the rate parameters that govern changes of state. State S may denote an individual state such as "alive" or the state of a collection of individuals, that is, population, such as "occurrence" or "local abundance, N". For the individual state "alive", the arrows may represent the coin-flip-like survival process. For the abundance state (N), the arrows may represent the demographic rates of survival, fecundity, immigration, and emigration. It is those rates on which the ecological mechanisms act to determine how a population is distributed in space or evolves over time.

A pervasive theme in ecology is that of hierarchical scales of organization—genes are nested within individuals, individuals within populations, populations within metapopulations or communities, and communities within metacommunities. Interestingly, this view of ecology is again reflected by the title of an influential ecology textbook: *Ecology: Individuals, Populations, and Communities* (Begon et al., 1986). These scales have biologically quite different meanings, and the practitioners of the associated branches of ecology often have very little in common with one another. And yet, it is fascinating to recognize that we can move among these scales simply by a redefinition of counted units (i.e., what we call an "individual") and that they can be characterized by what is essentially the same set of quantitative demographic descriptors (Table 1.1).

At Scale 1, the unit is the classical individual living in a population (Table 1.1). It can move between states such as "alive" and "dead" or "newly recruited" and "not newly recruited", thereby defining demographic rates such as survival and recruitment, respectively. Scale 1 represents the classic population concept. The interest is usually in understanding how biotic and abiotic factors impact vital rates (e.g., Newton, 1998) and

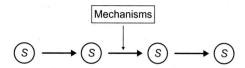

FIGURE 1.1 The classic view of ecology as the science dealing with how the state S (for instance, local population size N) of a living system evolves over time. These changes are governed by rate parameters (e.g., survival, fecundity, and dispersal in case of the abundance state). The interactions between the living system and its environment represent the ecological mechanisms that create the temporal dynamics we observe. An analogous scheme could be drawn also for spatial patterns.

TABLE 1.1 Four Ecological Scales of Organization; the First Three of which Are Dealt with in This Book (see Royle and Dorazio, 2008, for the Fourth)

Scale of Organization = Type of Population	Description	
	Static (State Variable)	Dynamic (Vital Rates)
(1) One Site, One Species: Classic Population = Population of Individuals	Abundance N	Survival Probability (ϕ) Recruitment Rate (γ)
(2) Multiple Sites, One Species: Metapopulation = Population of (Local) Populations	N_s z_s Occupancy $\psi (= \Pr(N > 0))$	Extinction Probability $(1 - \phi_s)$ Colonization Rate (γ_s) Dispersal Rates
(3) One Site, Multiple Species: Community = Population of Species	N_k z_k Species Richness	Extinction Probability $(1 - \phi_k)$ Colonization Rate (γ_k),
(4) Multiple Sites, Multiple Species: Metacommunity = Population of Communities	$N_{k,s}$ $z_{k,s}$ Species Richness	Extinction Probability $(1 - \phi_{k,s})$ Colonization Rate ($\gamma_{k,s}$) Dispersal Rates

Notes: All four can be represented as "populations" by simply redefining what represents an "individual" making up that population. These scales are hierarchical in the sense that each lower scale is included in a higher one. This means, for instance, that the quantitative descriptors of a classic population (Scale 1) may also be applied to the components of a metapopulation (Scale 2). N, abundance; z, presence/absence indicator; k, index for species; s, index for site.

how changes in vital rates translate into changes in numbers, that is, of population size (e.g., Sibly and Hone, 2002). Moving up one level, but still considering the individual unit, we have a collection of sites in which individuals can live. The movement probability among the associated populations (dispersal) is now an additional vital rate. The state variable is the size of the different populations.

At Scale 2, we view a single local population (or more generally, an occupied spatial unit) among a collection of potentially occupied spatial units as the item, and thereby obtain a metapopulation (Hanski, 1998). The basic, static descriptor of a metapopulation is the set of N_s values, that is, classic abundance at each spatial unit s. A less information rich, yet easier to measure version is the occupancy state $z = I(N > 0)$, where $I()$ denotes the indicator function that evaluates to 1 for an occupied unit and zero for an unoccupied one. The population average of z_s is called "incidence" in the metapopulation literature (e.g., Hanski, 1994, 1998) or occupancy probability, ψ (e.g., MacKenzie, 2006). Occupancy and abundance are directly related to each other via $\psi = \Pr(N_s > 0)$, that is, occupancy probability is simply the probability that abundance at a site is greater than zero (Royle and Nichols, 2003). So, clearly, there is a sense in which "distribution and abundance" in the book titles cited above is redundant; the characterization of a metapopulation by local abundance is fully sufficient and directly yields a description in terms of occupancy (Royle et al., 2005, 2007b).

Metapopulation ecology has been a part of ecology's mainstream for several decades now (Levins, 1969; Hanski, 1994, 1998; Hanski and Gaggiotti, 2004) and has been extremely influential in conservation biology, for instance, by highlighting the importance of random extinctions of local populations even at sites with suitable habitat, and consequently, by stressing the importance of connectivity among subpopulations as a means of avoiding permanent extinction of patches. In a similar vein, metapopulation biology provides the understanding for why currently unoccupied habitat patches may be as important for the long-term survival of a species as currently occupied ones (Talley et al., 2007). The dynamic descriptors of a metapopulation are analogous to those of a classic population, except that "individuals" (=occupied sites, local populations) can be reborn, that is, go extinct and yet later the site may be recolonized. Metapopulation-like dynamic models of occurrence proved insightful in epidemiology and disease ecology and have been used to model the spread of a disease (e.g., West Nile virus, Marra et al., 2004) or invasive species (Wikle, 2003; Hooten et al., 2007; Bled et al., 2011b).

An alternative way to quantify the total occurrence of an organism in some area is simply the sum of occurrences (i.e., $\sum_s z_s$); this represents a "population size" of occupied spatial units. Both the ratio ψ and the sum of z_s characterize the *range* or *distribution* of an organism. Ranges are the focus of macroecology and biogeography (Brown and Maurer, 1989; Gaston and Blackburn, 2000). Many ecological studies aim to predict species occurrence (i.e., z_s) from habitat or other local site attributes (e.g., Scott et al., 2002), either for fundamental reasons, for example, to study a species' niche (Guisan and Thuiller, 2005), or for applied reasons, for example, to predict the location of previously undetected occurrences, or to determine the most suitable sites for reintroduction projects. In essence, these models focus on the extent of a metapopulation, and the latest of them try to incorporate biological interactions (such as the possibility for an unoccupied site to become recolonized from an occupied site nearby; Guisan and Thuiller, 2005), thus bringing them increasingly closer to a classical and more mechanistic, metapopulation model of a species distribution.

Another increasingly common example of an occupancy study is a distribution atlas (Hagemeijer and Blair, 1998; Schmid et al., 1998; see review in Gibbons et al., 2007) that documents distribution ranges, for instance, by the presence or absence of a species in each cell of a grid. The data collected during such atlas studies, when repeated over time in the same area, have become an important raw material for studies documenting effects of climate change on species ranges (Thomas and Lennon, 1999; Huntley et al., 2007). Finally, occupancy is an important state variable for biodiversity monitoring, for example, in the Swiss biodiversity monitoring program BDM (Weber et al., 2004, also see www.biodiversitymonitoring.ch), in amphibian monitoring (Pellet and Schmidt, 2005), and as one of the important and most widely used criteria by which the IUCN Red list status of a species is assessed (www.iucnredlist.org/about/red-list-overview#redlist_criteria).

Moving up another level among the ecological scales of organization, a community can be conceived of as a "population" of species at a single site (Table 1.1, Scale 3). A community can be described at a point in time by the species–abundance distribution, N_k (Engen et al., 2008). A simpler community description is the sum of individual species' occurrences, that is, species richness ($\sum_k z_k$). Species richness and its dynamic components are the central focus of research in many branches of ecology such as biogeography (Jetz and Rahbek, 2002), as well as conservation science, for instance, when looking for hotspots of species richness to direct conservation funds (Orme et al., 2005). Indeed, species richness is the most widely used measure of biodiversity (Purvis and Hector, 2000) and is frequently used in monitoring programs (e.g., Weber et al., 2004; Pearman and Weber, 2007).

At the highest level of ecological scales of organization (Table 1.1, Scale 4), a metacommunity is a set of population of multiple species at many sites. Metacommunities have recently taken center stage in ecology with the neutral theory of biodiversity (Hubbell, 2001; Gotelli and McGill, 2006). In terms of its quantitative description, a metacommunity can be dealt with fairly analogously to a community (Table 1.1).

Of course, not every ecologist focuses directly on the population descriptors of Table 1.1. For instance, evolutionary, behavioral, or physiological ecologists deal with the interactions among individuals and with the environment that may become the mechanisms determining the size (N) and dynamics of a population (Sibly and Calow, 1986; Stearns, 1992; Krebs and Davies, 1993; Sutherland and Dolman, 1994). However, N remains important implicitly: because in order to be ecologically relevant, any evolutionary, behavioral, or physiological mechanism must ultimately have at least the potential to affect N.

The modeling of these hierarchical scales may be conducted very naturally in a hierarchical manner, that is, a metapopulation can be modeled in terms of patch occupancy z_s or in terms of the local population size N_s. Similarly, its dynamics can be expressed by the survival and colonization probabilities of patches or by the survival and recruitment probabilities of the individuals occupying these patches and by their dispersal among the patches. Analogous alternative descriptions in terms of the state and the dynamics are possible for communities and metacommunities. One important descriptor of the dynamics of all four levels is the sustained rate of change of the system, or trend. Trend is a consequence of survival, recruitment, and dispersal probabilities and thus a derived quantity rather than a driver of the system. Nevertheless, it is the simplest and most parsimonious description of system dynamics and of tremendous practical importance in many applications of population ecology, such as conservation biology and wildlife management (Balmford et al., 2003).

In summary, the three key state variables used to describe populations, metapopulations, communities, and metacommunities are abundance, occurrence (distribution), and species richness (Royle and Dorazio, 2008). From a pure modeling point of view, all three simply represent variants of a "population" that can be described by its size. In addition, there are the parameters that govern the dynamics of these state variables: survival/extinction, fecundity, colonization, and dispersal (immigration and emigration). Collectively, we call the study of these demographic quantities *population analysis*. Population analysis permeates a large part of ecology and of its applications such as conservation biology or fisheries and wildlife management. Indeed, it could be argued that population ecology, which we see as somewhat synonymous with population analysis, is a central pillar of the entire discipline of ecology.

1.2 GENESIS OF ECOLOGICAL OBSERVATIONS

A widely ignored consideration regarding all these varieties of the state variable, along with their dynamic rates, is that they are usually not directly observable; rather, "individuals" of all kinds can be overlooked; their *detection probability* is not perfect (i.e., $p < 1$; Schmidt, 2005). Therefore, a more accurate view of ecology is depicted in Fig. 1.2. This *hierarchical* view considers all observations in ecology as a result of two coupled processes: an ecological process, which usually is the focus of our interest, and an observation process, which is conditional on (i.e., whose result depends on) the result of the ecological process (Royle and Dorazio, 2006, 2008). In most ecological studies, the state of the system and its dynamics are latent. Therefore, they must be inferred from the observations O by modeling the main features of the observation process.

The ecological process itself is influenced by mechanisms that may be deterministic (e.g., habitat) or stochastic (e.g., demographic or environmental stochasticity) and that together determine the state of a system, for example, the population size, N. However, our observations of the system are also the result of an observation process, which may again be influenced by a variety of factors, among them deterministic (e.g., habitat-dependent observation errors) and stochastic mechanisms. Our observations in ecology are thus always a combination resulting from ecological *and* observation mechanisms.

For instance, assume that more birds are counted (i.e., *observed*) in habitat A than B. This can mean that there really *are* more birds in A than B, but

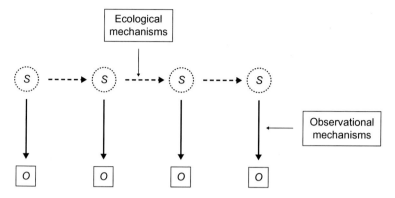

FIGURE 1.2   A hierarchical view of ecology that acknowledges the fact that state S is fully or partly unobservable (latent). Ecological mechanisms (representing the ecological process) affect the dynamics of the latent state, while observational mechanisms constitute the observation process. The observation process maps the latent state S (for instance, local population size N) on the observation O (for instance, a count). To emphasize the latent nature of the state process, arrows connecting states and circles around S are dashed.

it can also mean that birds are simply more *visible* in A than B or indeed any combination of the two. Similarly, not only the mean but also the variability of the observations is made up of these two components: one coming from the ecological process and the other from the observation process (e.g., nondetection error, sampling error; Royle and Dorazio, 2008, pp. 11–13). In most branches of ecology, we are thus faced with a situation where we have incomplete knowledge about an ecological system under study, and we must use error-prone observations to infer its characteristics, such as state variables or dynamic rates and the kind and strength of their interactions with the environment. In short, in the study of ecological systems, we must account for the fact that detection probability (p) of all three kinds of "individuals" shown in Table 1.1 is usually less than 1.

   Direct inference based on the raw observations in ecology, and disregard of the observation process, may be risky. If nondetection error (rather than, say, false positives or double counting) represents the main feature of the observation process (i.e., $p < 1$), population size, distribution, or species richness will all be underestimated (Schmidt, 2005). Similarly, estimates of dynamic population descriptors will be biased. For instance, survival probabilities will be underestimated (Nichols and Pollock, 1983; Martin et al., 1995; Gimenez et al., 2008); extinction and turnover rates in metapopulations, communities, and metacommunities will be overestimated (Nichols et al., 1998b; Moilanen, 2002); and the perceived strength of a relationship between survival, abundance, or occurrence and environmental covariates will be underestimated (Tyre et al., 2003; MacKenzie et al., 2006); also see Section 13.2. It has not been sufficiently widely recognized that what is typically called a distribution map in ecology (see, e.g., Scott et al., 2002), may in fact simply be a map of the difficulty with which an organism is found (Kéry et al., 2010; Kéry, 2011b). For instance, any spatially varying mechanism such as local density that causes a species to be more likely to be detected at some sites than at others will leave its imprint on a map of putative species distribution.

When imperfect detection is not accounted for in the modeling of ecological systems, the observed variation in the system (e.g., variance in population size) will typically be greater than the true variation in the ecological system (e.g., Link and Nichols, 1994). Some sort of variance decomposition must then be employed to separate true system variability from variability that is due to observation error (Franklin et al., 2000; De Valpine and Hastings, 2002). Such a partitioning of the observed variance is particularly important for population viability analyses (Lindley, 2003), investigations of density dependence (Dennis et al., 2006; Lebreton, 2009), and the setting of harvest regulations (Williams et al., 2002).

Consequently, we think that it is important in population analysis to include the essential features of the observation process when making inferences from imperfect observations about the underlying ecological process, for example, about the quantitative descriptors of all ecological scales of organization depicted in Table 1.1. Otherwise, we risk describing features of the observation process rather than of the ecological process we are really interested in. We need special data collection designs and methods of interpretation of the resulting data (i.e., models) that take explicitly into account the observation process to tease apart the genuine patterns in the ecological states from those induced in the observations by the observation process (MacKenzie et al., 2006). That is, when the quantities in Table 1.1 need to be studied directly, they must be *estimated* from, and cannot usually be equated with, the observed data.

To explicitly accommodate both the ecological and the observation process, an emerging and very powerful paradigm for population analysis is that of hierarchical models (Link and Sauer, 2002; Royle and Dorazio, 2006, 2008), sometimes also called state-space models (Buckland et al., 2004). One reason why these models are so useful for population analysis is that they simply replicate the hierarchical genesis of ecological data on animals and plants depicted in Fig. 1.2: one level in the model is the un- or only partially observed true latent state (e.g., being alive, abundance, or occurrence) and another level is the observation process, typically represented by detection probability p. Among the several advantages of hierarchical models is that they achieve a clear segregation of the observations into their two (or more) components. Thus, these models greatly foster intellectual clarity.

In this book, we follow Royle and Dorazio (2008) in emphasizing the distinction between the true state of an individual, a population, or a community, and their observed state, and that the two are linked by an observation process, which imperfectly maps the former onto the latter. An explicit modeling of the observation process is thus essential to our approach of population analysis. Because we are convinced that most ecologists learn best by seeing examples, we next provide a brief numerical illustration for the observation process that shows why it is so important to consider it when making an inference in population ecology.

1.3 THE BINOMIAL DISTRIBUTION AS A CANONICAL DESCRIPTION OF THE OBSERVATION PROCESS

To better understand the key features of the observation process behind most ecological field observations, let us assume 16 sparrows live in our yard and that their population size was constant over a few weeks during which we make some observations (i.e., count them) to find out how many there are. Let us assume that there are no false-positive errors, only false-negative errors. This means that one sparrow cannot be counted for another and that another species cannot erroneously be identified as a sparrow. Let us further assume that each sparrow is independently observed or heard with a constant detection probability of 0.4. This means that if we step out into our yard 10 times, we will expect to see or hear (i.e., detect) that particular sparrow about 4 times. Of course, these are all abstractions of the real-world observation process, but they are very often plausible and adequate assumptions.

When we are interested in the total count of sparrows in our yard, then we have just defined a binomial random variable with sample or trial size $N = 16$ and so-called success probability $p = 0.4$. The binomial distribution is the mathematical abstraction of situations akin to coin flipping, where an event can either happen with a certain probability (p) or not (with $1 - p$), and we watch a number of times (N), all assumed independent, and count how many times (C) that event happens. The event here is the detection of an individual sparrow, and N is the latent state of the local population size of sparrows in the yard. Since detection is a chance process, we will typically not wind up with the same count all the time when we repeat the exercise. We can use a physical model, for example, the flipping of one or several coins, or a computer model to study the features of the observation process.

As we will see throughout the book, program R (R Development Core Team, 2004) is great for conducting quick and simple simulations to better understand a system. We first define the constants in the system:

```
N <- 16      # Population size of sparrows in the yard
p <- 0.4     # Individual detection probability
```

To simulate a single count, we simply draw a binomial random number with sample size N and success probability p (of course, most of you will get different simulated counts from those shown here).

```
rbinom(n = 1, size = N, prob = p)
 [1] 11
```

So the first time, we count 11 sparrows. The next time we go out into the yard, we count again:

```
rbinom(n = 1, size = N, prob = p)
 [1] 4
```

Now only four! This is a large difference to the previous count, so we count again a little later.

```
rbinom(n = 1, size = N, prob = p)
 [1] 9
```

This count is more similar to the first one. But perhaps we are a little worried about the variability in these counts. Were the lower counts made under somewhat inferior conditions? Or did we not pay so much attention to the counting then?

We can very simply use R to study the long-term behavior of the assumed observation process in our example: we simply draw a large number n of samples from the binomial random variable defined by N and p and summarize that sample. Let us draw one million then, since this does not cost us anything and R is free.

```
C <- rbinom(n = 10^6, size = N, prob = p)
```

Next, we describe that big sample in a graph (Fig. 1.3) and numerically to better understand some of the essential features of the counting process, that is, of the observation process behind our counts of a sparrow population of size 16.

```
mean(C)
 [1] 6.404259
var(C)
 [1] 3.842064
sd(C)
 [1] 1.960118
hist(C, breaks = 50, col = "gray", main = "", xlab = "Sparrow count",
   las = 1, freq = FALSE)
```

This simple example illustrates several features about an observation process that is dominated by nondetection error (i.e., where misclassification and double counts are absent):

1. The typical count C is smaller than the actual population size N. Indeed, the mean of a binomial random variable and hence the expected count

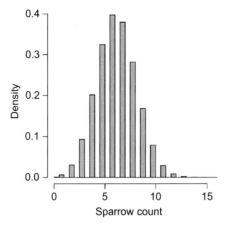

FIGURE 1.3   Frequency distribution of the observations, when 16 sparrows are counted repeatedly and each has independently a detectability of 0.4. The binomial distribution is our canonical model for the observation process involving detections of plant or animal "individuals", where "individual" can mean many different things (see Table 1.1).

of sparrows, equals the product of N and p. This should be 6.4 in the sparrow example and in our sample we get pretty close to that.

2. However, the counts vary quite a lot, *even under totally identical conditions*. Indeed, some of the counts in our sample were 0 and one was 16, meaning that sometimes not a single sparrow was detected but another time, all 16 of them were. Hence, there is nothing intrinsically wrong or inferior with smaller counts. Smaller counts may simply result from the random nature of the counting process in the presence of imperfect detection. Thus, any count with $p < 1$ will automatically tend to vary from trial to trial. Unless $p = 0$ or $p = 1$, it is impossible to eliminate that variation by the sampling design or standardization (though other components of variation may be eliminated).

3. Actually, not only the mean count but also the magnitude of the variation of counts is known from statistical theory. The variance is equal to the product of N, p, and $1 - p$ and thus should be around 3.84. Up to sampling variation, the observed variance of the 1 million counts of sparrows is identical to that.

False negatives will not only affect population counts and thus estimates of population size but also parameter estimates derived from the counts, such as survival or state-transition probabilities. In addition, the observation process will often be affected by explanatory variables and perhaps even by the exact same ones in which we are interested for the ecological process (see Figures 12.3. and 13.2.). Unless detection probability p is estimated then, any patterns in p will be perceived in the apparent state of the ecological process. For instance, one can often read that state-space models (Chapter 5) correct for observation error. In truth, they only do so in a rather vague way. They only account for the binomial sampling variation around a mean count (i.e., Np), but cannot correct for the general bias in the counts relative to true population size, nor any patterns (e.g., over time) induced in counts by patterns in p (see Section 5.3). These latter two kinds of observation error (detection bias and patterns in detection) cannot be corrected for by the methods in Chapter 5 unless one has extra information about the detection process and uses the methods in Chapters 6, 10, 12, and 13.

We have claimed that the binomial distribution is the canonical description of the observation process. This is true in the sense that it underlies the vast majority of statistical methods that correct for imperfect detection in population analysis (Buckland et al., 2001; Borchers et al., 2002; Williams et al., 2002; Royle and Dorazio, 2008). However, other statistical distributions may be adopted as a description of the observation process in some cases, for instance, a beta-binomial distribution to account for nonindependent detections (Martin et al., 2011). The Poisson distribution is an appropriate description of the observation process if encounter frequencies rather than simply detection events are observed, for example, when we know that y_1 animals were observed once, y_2 twice, and so forth. In fact, there is a natural relationship between a Poisson and a binomial model of detection because the binomial detection probability may be expressed as the probability of observing Poisson counts greater or equal to one (Royle and Gardner, 2011). Finally, the negative binomial distribution may be adopted to model over-dispersed encounter frequencies, such as arise from nonindependent detections of individuals, for instance, animals in groups (Boyce et al., 2001).

The binomial distribution is a useful starting point for modeling an observation process that is dominated by false-negative errors, that is, where false-positive errors are rare or absent. False-positive errors arise when one "individual" in Table 1.1 is mistakenly identified as another one. Variants of this kind of error include unoccupied sites being identified as occupied when modeling species distributions or mistakenly identifying one species for another when modeling communities.

In the fields of statistics covered in this book, almost all methodological development over the last decades has dealt with false-negative errors; false-positive errors were essentially assumed away. There are two reasons for this. First, false-negative errors are ubiquitous in ecology and probably much more widespread than false positives. Moreover, false positives can more easily be eliminated by the design of a study, by good training of a field crew or adequate calibration of a measuring device. For instance, any doubtful records, for example, detections of a species when estimating the size of a community (see Section 6.3) may simply be eliminated (J. D. Nichols, personal communication). This will weed out false positives at the risk of losing some valid detections of species. The latter will simply lower detection probability but obviously not bias estimators from models that account for false-negative errors.

However, a second reason for why false positives have received much less attention than false negatives is that they are harder to deal with mathematically. Although on the whole, false positives may have less biasing effects in population analyses than false negatives, they are nevertheless important to account for in some situations. It has been shown that even relatively rare false-positive events may induce strong biases in site-occupancy models (Royle and Link, 2006). Interestingly, the effects of false positives often become stronger with larger sample sizes, for instance, when more surveys are conducted at each site in the context of site-occupancy sampling (see Chapter 13). Thus, it is important to watch out for this kind of error and if necessary account for it in population analyses. Therefore, it is encouraging that during the last decades a steadily increasing number of papers has dealt with false-positive errors, including Kendall et al. (2003), Nichols et al. (2004), Lukacs and Burnham (2005), Pradel (2005), Royle and Link (2006), Nichols et al. (2007), Conn and Cooch (2009), MacKenzie et al. (2009), Wright et al. (2009), Yoshizaki et al. (2009), Link et al. (2010), McClintock et al. (2010), and Miller et al. (2011). It is likely that we will see much more developments in this important topic in the near future.

In summary, we believe that it is important to account for the observation process when making an inference about any quantity in Table 1.1 for populations of animals or plants in population ecology, management, and conservation.

1.4 STRUCTURE AND OVERVIEW OF THE CONTENTS OF THIS BOOK

In this book, we deal with populations of the first three kinds in Table 1.1 and most intensively with classical population size and the demographic processes underlying its change (survival, fecundity, and dispersal or movement) and with the "population size" of occupied patches, that is, species distributions or occupancy, and its dynamic rates. We also see a little bit of species richness, that is, the size of the third kind of "population" (Section 6.3). The structure of this book is summarized in Table 1.2. We present this overview by distinguishing population studies at single sites from those at multiple sites, which we call studies with a metapopulation design (Royle, 2004c; Kéry and Royle, 2010). The scheme in Table 1.2 covers a fairly large part of the questions and models that ecologists might want to consider when analyzing populations of plants and animals.

We start with simple models for counts in Chapter 3 and then introduce more complexity via random effects in Chapters 4 and 5; it is the presence of

TABLE 1.2   Structure of This Book and Loose Chapter Overview

Quantity Modeled	Single Site	Multiple Sites
Distribution		
Apparent Distribution	–	Logistic Regression (Chapter 3)
True Distribution	–	Site-Occupancy Model (Chapter 13)
Abundance		
Apparent Abundance	Poisson GLM (Chapter 3)	
	Poisson GLMM (Chapter 4)	
	State-space Model (Chapter 5)	
	Integrated Population Model (Chapter 11)	
True Abundance	Closed Population Capture–recapture Model (Chapter 6)	Binomial mix Model (Chapter 12)
	Jolly–Seber Model (Chapter 10)	
	Integrated Population Model (Chapter 11)	
Vital Rates		
Survival Probability	Cormack–Jolly–Seber model (Chapter 7)	
	Ring-recovery Model (Chapter 8)	
	Multistate Model (Chapter 9)	
	Jolly–Seber Model (Chapter 10)	
	Integrated Population Model (Chapter 11)	
Fecundity/Recruitment	Poisson GLM (Chapter 3)	
	Jolly–Seber Model (Chapter 10)	
	Multistate Model (Chapter 9)	
	Integrated Population Model (Chapter 11)	
Movement Probability	–	Multistate Model (Chapter 9)
Leslie-Matrix Modeling	Integrated Population Model (Chapter 11)	

Notes: A distinction is made between models that can be applied to data from a single study site and those that require data from multiple sites. All former can also be applied to data from multiple sites.

these random effects, which converts the models in Chapter 3 to hierarchical models. The so-called state-space models of Chapter 5 attempt a partitioning of the total variation in the observations into one portion due to the ecological system and another portion due to observation error. We have claimed previously that the only accounting possible in this kind of model is for the random sampling variation (due to imperfect detection) in the counts, but not for detection probability proper. Hence, all models in Chapters 3–5 deal with apparent, not true abundance, where "true" to us means "corrected for imperfect detection". In Chapter 6, we encounter for the first-time models that achieve a comprehensive accounting for detection error: these are the classical capture–recapture models for closed populations.

In Chapters 7–11, we move on to the quantities driving the changes in population size: demographic or vital rates. We note in passing that vital rates that represent probabilities such as survival are still often called rates, but this is not completely correct: a rate, unlike a probability, is not bounded by 0 and 1. We model survival probabilities based on two kinds of data, resighting and dead recoveries, respectively, as well as movement probabilities between states. These models again fully account for detection error. As an aside, in Chapter 3, we show a simple example of the modeling of another important dynamic rate: fecundity. Chapter 10 introduces the Jolly–Seber model, where inferences about abundance, survival, and recruitment from capture–recapture data can be made. In Chapter 11, we introduce a sort of synthesis of several models in preceding chapters and fit simple population models of the Leslie-matrix type. One important feature of these integrated population models is that by the joint modeling of several data sets and data types, parameters can often be estimated that are not identifiable with each data set alone.

Most methods for population analysis at single sites (in the left column in the body of Table 1.2) can also be used for populations at multiple sites. In the last two main chapters of the book, we present two classes of models that explicitly focus on distribution and abundance in a metapopulation setting: the binomial (or N-)mixture model for abundance (Chapter 12) and the site-occupancy model for species distributions (Chapter 13).

There are several important, recurring themes throughout our book. The three most essential ones are actually recurrent themes in much of applied statistical modeling:

1. Linear models
2. Generalized linear models
3. Random effects, or more generally, hierarchical modeling

First, in linear models, the mean of a response is thought to be made up of additive effects of covariates. This is one of the most widespread manner in which relationships between a response and explanatory variables are modeled. If you understand how to build a linear model using a design matrix (Chapter 3), you will achieve an extraordinary flexibility in your modeling. Second, generalized linear models (GLMs) use the same concept of linear models and the design matrix and carry that over to nonnormal responses, such as Poisson or binomial random variables. A Poisson or binomial response may also be the components in a larger model, for instance, to model survival events over a number of years. We may then encounter a GLM as part of a larger model. We will meet GLMs all over in this book and give a concise introduction to them in Chapter 3. Finally, random effects are another key concept in applied statistical modeling and are introduced in Chapter 4. They give considerable flexibility to our modeling of variation and of correlations. Like GLMs, random effects, or hierarchical models, permeate this entire book. A GLM containing random effects is typically called a generalized linear mixed model (GLMM). We believe that if you understand linear models, GLMs, and random effects, then you understand a large part of applied statistical modeling. You then achieve an organic understanding of many of your models and will be able to build your custom models in a modular, creative, and efficient way (Kéry, 2010). In particular, you may then start to see hierarchical models as a natural way of describing complex stochastic systems by a nested sequence of component GLMs.

Other important concepts or techniques that you may be particularly interested in include the following:

- The distinction between an implicit and an explicit hierarchical model (Chapters 4–6, also see Royle and Dorazio, 2008)
- Data augmentation (Chapters 6 and 10)
- Posterior predictive checking of model adequacy (Chapters 7 and 12)
- The assessment of parameter estimability (Chapter 7)

We emphasize that by combining these basic concepts in a creative way, you will be able to create a large variety of statistical models that will help to obtain better inference from your data.

You will see plenty of WinBUGS and R code in this book. We use Courier font to highlight code. We comment our code quite extensively to make it easier to understand. In both R and WinBUGS, comments are flagged with a hash (#) sign, which means that the line following the hash is ignored.

1.5 BENEFITS OF ANALYZING SIMULATED DATA SETS: AN EXAMPLE OF BIAS AND PRECISION

One key feature of this book is that we work a lot with simulated data sets. There are tremendous benefits in doing so. As argued elsewhere (Kéry, 2010), the advantages of simulating (=assembling) data sets and then analyzing (=disassembling or breaking apart) them again are manifold:

1. Truth is known, so we know what to expect from the analysis.
2. We get a check for whether we have coded things correctly.
3. We can experience sampling error, that is, the variation in results. For instance, we may study long-run characteristics of estimators such as bias or precision (see example below).

4. In particular, repeatedly simulating data under some conditions and analyzing them provides an extremely flexible way of conducting power analyses.
5. We can check the effects of assumption violations: simulate data under a different model than that which is used to analyze a data set.
6. Finally, we can prove to ourselves that we understand an analysis: when you can assemble, that is, generate a data set under a model, you can also disassemble it, that is, break it down again in the analysis of that model.

As we will see many times in this book, we simulate data "from the inside out", that is, we first decide on values for any covariates and on coefficients that relate these covariates to the mean response, and then we add residual variation by drawing random variables with a given expectation and possibly a specified variance. When we disassemble the data set, we go the opposite way and break apart the full response into its ingredients, that is, covariate effects, random effects, etc. Arguably, you will only be able to simulate data under a model if you have really understood that model!

As an illustration, let us look at the concepts of bias and of the precision of an estimator. Both are often misunderstood by ecologists. One can often read an *unbiased estimate*. Strictly, this is wrong because estimates cannot be unbiased, only *estimators* can (Link and Barker, 2010). Estimators are the procedures that produce a particular estimate and if the estimates they produce are right on target, on average, an estimator is said to be unbiased. Right on target means that the mean of all estimates an estimator produces is the same as the population quantity (the parameter) estimated by that estimator. This may sound like counting green peas, and perhaps in ecological writings one could accept *unbiased estimate* as synonymous with the more accurate *unbiased estimator*. However, we must be able to make a clear distinction between a population quantity (a parameter), an estimator (a procedure), and a particular estimate of the population quantity produced by that procedure. Each individual estimate can be far off the target (the parameter), meaning the precision of the estimator is low, and yet the average of all estimates produced by the same procedure may be right on the mark, meaning the estimator is unbiased. Thus, the precision of an estimator expresses the similarity of repeated estimates produced by an estimator. Bias and precision are different aspects of the quality of an estimator: an estimator can be biased but precise, unbiased but imprecise (MacKenzie et al., 2006), or any other combination of these terms.

We next illustrate bias and precision by simulation: we simulate data from a large population, for which we want to estimate the population mean. We assume that we estimate body size of adult asp vipers (Fig. 1.4) by taking a sample of 10 snakes, measuring them, and calculating the mean

FIGURE 1.4   Asp viper (*Vipera aspis*), Germany, 2009 (Photograph by T. Ott).

length. We will see that the mean from one individual sample of 10 will hardly ever be right on target; rather, due to sampling variation (individuals in the population differ and we only sample 10 of them), the mean of 10 will be lower or higher than the true population parameter. However, *repeatedly* sampling that population, by measuring the length of 10 snakes, and producing a histogram of these means of 10 will show that the sample mean is an unbiased estimator of the population mean. Moreover, from statistical theory we know by how much, on average, means of 10 vary around the true population mean: this is given by the standard error of the mean.

So here we go: we assume that full-grown asp vipers in the Jura mountains average 65 cm with a standard deviation of 5. We sample 10 snakes, measure their length and use that sample to say something about the population mean.

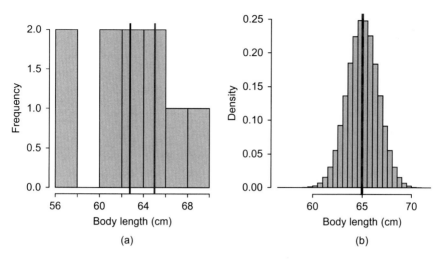

FIGURE 1.5   Histogram of body length of 10 asp vipers (a) and histogram of 1 million sample means of the body length of 10 asp vipers (b). Red line: population mean, blue line: mean of sample (means).

```
# Population values for mean and standard deviation of individual
lengths
mu <- 65        # Population mean
sigma <- 5      # Population SD

# Draw a single sample of 10 and summarize it
x <- rnorm(n = 10, mean = mu, sd = sigma)
```

Figure 1.5a shows one data set; do not forget that yours will be different. The red line indicates the population mean (i.e., the value of the parameter that we want to estimate when calculating the sample mean), and the blue line is the mean for our particular sample of 10 snakes. We see that here the sample mean is too small relative to the population mean.

To see whether the difference between the blue line and the red line is simply sampling variation, we can repeatedly draw such samples and plot the means. Hence, let us use R and draw 1 million samples of 10 snakes and plot their means (Fig. 1.5b).

```
reps <- 10^6
sample.means <- rep(NA, reps)
for (i in 1:reps) {
    sample.means[i] <- mean(rnorm(n = 10, mean = mu, sd = sigma))
    }

# Produce figure
par(mfrow = c(1, 2), las = 1)
hist(x, col = "gray", main = "", xlab = "Body length (cm)", las = 1)
abline(v = mu, lwd = 3, col = "red")
abline(v = mean(x), lwd = 3, col = "blue")
```

```
hist(sample.means, col = "gray", main = "", xlab = "Body length (cm)",
nclass = 50, freq = FALSE, las = 1)
abline(v = mu, lwd = 5, col = "red")
abline(v = mean(sample.means), lwd = 5, col = "blue", lty = 2)
```

We see that the distribution of the sample means in Fig. 1.5b is much more narrowly centered on the true population value. Moreover, from theory we know the spread of the distribution of sample means, that is, we know the precision of the mean as an estimator of the population mean: this is given by the standard error of the mean, that is, by $sd(x)/\sqrt{n} = 5/\sqrt{10} = 1.58$. Let us see how closely we get to that in our simulation. Remember, the standard error of our parameter estimator (here, the sample mean as an estimator of the population mean) is the standard deviation of the distribution of the estimates.

```
sd(sample.means)
[1] 1.581443
```

This is pretty close. You can make your estimate of the standard error of the mean arbitrarily exact by increasing your simulation sample size (n).

We always need to clearly distinguish between sample and population quantities. A parameter is a feature of the population and we want to estimate it based on some sample statistic (something that can be measured in the sample), such as the sample mean. Sample statistics, and therefore our parameter estimates, are affected by sampling variation: not all individuals are identical and we only measure a sample, not the entire population. Sampling variation may be quantified by the standard error of our estimator; this quantifies the precision of an estimator. The standard error of the sample mean as an estimator of the population mean can be estimated by the population standard deviation divided by square root of the sample size. Here, the standard error is the standard deviation of a hypothetical distribution of parameter estimates (means) from a sample size of 10. It may be confusing that the standard error is in fact a standard deviation, but one characterizing the variability in a collection of *parameter estimates*, rather than the variability among individual *measurements*.

1.6 SUMMARY AND OUTLOOK

Distribution and abundance, along with their dynamic rates of change such as survival or extinction probability, and the factors that affect them, lie at the heart of the science of ecology. Alas, almost universally, neither state nor rate parameters in natural populations of animals and plants can ever be observed without error. In particular, detection error (manifest in the presence of false-negative observations) is a hallmark of ecological observations of populations. We have seen that the binomial distribution is the typical description of an observation process that is dominated by false-negative errors, but that other statistical distributions may sometimes be appropriate, for example, the beta-binomial, Poisson, and negative binomial. We have seen that the opposite type of error, false positives, has received far less attention in the literature so far, but that it is the focus of much recent work. We think that the observation process should be accounted for as much and as often as possible in the analysis of wild populations. Therefore, much of this book covers methods that attempt a clean partitioning of the ecological and the observation processes that underlie ecological observations. This partitioning is often achieved using hierarchical models, where separate model components describe the latent ecological process and the observation process. We are big fans of analyzing simulated data sets; perhaps the single biggest advantage of using simulated data sets is that the mere act of simulating data enforces an almost complete understanding of a model. Next, after having motivated the population analysis part in the book title, we give a very brief review of the other half of our book's title, namely "Bayesian" and "WinBUGS".

1.7 EXERCISES

1. Detection probability: convince yourself that very few quantities in nature are ever perfectly detectable. Stand at the window for 1 min and make a list of all the bird species that you see. Repeat this once or twice, then compare the lists among times and observers. If detection were really perfect (for all species, at all times, for all observers, etc.), then all the lists would be the same for all observers and it would not matter for how long you watched. Essentially, you would detect all species instantaneously.

   You may conduct that exercise with a quantity of your choice: for example, the number (or identity) of people in your office hall, and the number of people in your bus. Alternatively, you could also count the brands of cars that pass in front of you.

2. Intrinsic variability of counts: it is our experience that ecologists often do not realize that counts vary intrinsically as soon as detection is imperfect. Moreover, counts that vary more are sometimes viewed as being of inferior quality than counts that vary less, or, that the observers producing these counts are better or worse. It is true that, everything else equal, sloppy counts will usually be more variable than those made by a more dedicated observer. However, owing to the mean–variance relationship in binomial counts, two of the most important factors affecting the variability of counts is (1) the number of things available for counting (i.e., N) and (2) detection probability, p. Produce a plot or a table that makes you better understand these relationships.

Brief Introduction to Bayesian Statistical Modeling

2.1 INTRODUCTION

In this chapter, we attempt to give a brief overview of the following topics: (1) role of models in science, (2) statistical models, (3) Bayesian and frequentist analysis of statistical models, (4) Bayesian computation, (5) WinBUGS, (6) advantages and disadvantages of Bayesian analysis by posterior sampling, and (7) hierarchical models. This list of topics is vast and it would be impossible to give them extensive coverage even in a whole book. For topics 3–7, unless you understand the theory of frequentist and Bayesian inference fairly well, we would expect you to also read some books or parts of books that delve more deeply in that, for instance, Gelman et al. (2004), McCarthy (2007), chapter 2 of Royle and Dorazio (2008), Carlin and Louis (2009), Ntzoufras (2009), or the introductory chapters in Link and Barker (2010). There are also useful introductory articles, such as Ellison (2004) or Clark (2005).

2.2 ROLE OF MODELS IN SCIENCE

Science is about rationally explaining nature by obtaining mechanistic or other explanations for the workings of a system and/or being able to predict the results of the system. However, most observable phenomena in nature are too complex for us to understand directly by simply staring at them, or rather, the system that has generated them is too complex, that is, affected by too many factors, too variable over space or time, and so on. So, explaining always requires simplifying things. Broadly, a model is nothing but a formal simplification of a complex system that we would like to explain or whose behavior we would like to predict. Indeed, at the start of this book, we have claimed that *every* interpretation of *any* observation *always* requires a model, that is, a simplification of the system, so that everybody who offers an explanation of anything has in fact a model, whether he or she knows it or not. It could also be said that explanation is impossible without a model.

So, an explanation or a more formal model is an abstraction of nature, that is, a rendition of nature with much reduced complexity. The crucial point is that we should use a good model, that is, one in which we retain the important features of the system in nature that we want to explain and only ignore the less important features. Then, by looking at this greatly simplified toy version of nature, we hopefully get a better understanding of nature herself and also can use our toy to make predictions of future or unobserved things in nature.

There are many famous sayings about models, some of which follow here. We think that they express nicely some key features of models, statistical or not:

Modeling is as much art as it is science (McCullagh and Nelder, 1989): this statement expresses the fact that there are not, nor can ever be, automatic, brain-free rules for building a model (although in some disciplines much effort is spent in this pursuit).

All models are wrong, but some are useful (Box): this is perhaps the most famous saying about models. It emphasizes that one must not look for an exact rendering of nature in a model; it is in this sense that every model is wrong. However, by simplifying, we should get some use out of a model.

Another meaning, which is perhaps not so widely appreciated, is that not all models are useful, so we should try and find the useful ones. Of course, it also begs the question of how wrong a model can be to still be useful.

There has never been a straight line nor a Normal distribution in history, and yet, using assumptions of linearity and normality allows, to a good approximation, to understand and predict a huge number of observations (Youden): This statement again expresses the fact that models are mere approximations, but that they can be hugely successful.

Everything should be a simple as possible, but not simpler (Einstein): this statement is related to the principle of parsimony and is an important guide for creating models. Very similar is the "Occam's razor" attributed to the English logician William of Ockham, which states that the explanation of any phenomenon should make as few assumptions as possible, eliminating (or *shaving off*) those that make no difference in the observable predictions.

Nothing is gained if you replace a world that you don't understand with a model that you don't understand (we heard Maynard Smith quote this one, but he may have had it from somebody else): we like this statement because it reminds us of the importance of the principle of parsimony in modeling—"*Keep it as simple as possible*". It also expresses the notion that we must replace a world that we *do not* understand by a model that we *do* understand, that is, typically something simpler. Of course, we could also understand this statement as a call for becoming a better modeler.

Finally, here is a claim we have made elsewhere (Kéry, 2010): *It is difficult to imagine another method that so effectively fosters clear thinking about a system than the use of a model written in the language of algebra.* There are various ways to express a model; words (language), graphs, and equations are some of them. Unfortunately, the human language is often very inadequate to express the subtle details of the multitude of potential explanations (= "models") for a given system. Trying to put down on paper all the elements of an explanation in the language of algebra has the big advantage that it forces us to think much more clearly about the system we want to understand. One of the things we like most about the WinBUGS software (Section 2.5) is the BUGS language (Gilks et al., 1994). Describing a model in BUGS comes very close to describing it in simple algebra. So to us, describing a model in the BUGS language is one of the most transparent ways of building a model.

Conceptually, and written in algebra, a model looks something like the following:

$$y = f(x, \theta)$$

Here, y is a response, something that our study system has produced and whose genesis we would like to understand. Often, we are interested in predicting future responses produced by the study system or responses for particular values of one or several explanatory variables x. The response is a function f of one or several explanatory variables x and of some system descriptors, or parameters, θ. Here, f would include the particular parametric form of the relationship between y and x. In essence, then, modeling means to replace a complicated reality of very large dimension with a much smaller set of system descriptors called parameters (θ). An explicit simplified system description in algebra is called a mathematical model.

There are broadly two different objectives of modeling, and they may lead to two different modes of building a model: explanation and prediction. Explanation means understanding and will typically require simpler models than prediction (Caswell, 1988). The explanatory mode of modeling focuses on the actual model structure. It is hoped that the kind of parameters and their values have some relevance for how nature generated the observed output. The focus is more on the parameters θ. In contrast, prediction focuses on the system output, the response y, and thus aims at predicting the response as well as possible either within the sample studied or for the entire statistical population that is represented by the sample. Common to both modes of modeling is that we must first build a model and estimate its parameters θ.

There is an important distinction between what might be called implicit and explicit models. We have claimed before that any interpretation of nature requires a model, but we believe that many people are not aware of this. When we talk to somebody in the general public or to not-so-modeler-types of ecologists, we often sense a certain distrust in formal, explicit modeling explanations of nature. Also, folks often have a strong feeling that the observed data are somehow superior to an inference made from these same data under a formal model. We often hear exclamations like the following: "oh yes, but this is only a model and we all know models are wrong; better stick to the data—there at least we *know* where we're at". On the whole, we think that the reasoning behind this feeling is flawed in the sense that *any attempt at explanation requires a model.*

Of course, it is possible to build models that have little to do with reality and are useless to understand or to predict a particular system. However, there cannot ever be a conclusion, deduction, or inference from any observation alone. Data need models, simply some people have explicit models and others have only implicit models. Implicit modelers frequently do not know that they are modelers, too, and that their conclusions are always contingent upon a certain set of assumptions.

These assumptions are usually unstated and may or may not be appropriate for any particular case. But just because you do not describe assumptions explicitly does not mean that these assumptions do not exist. Worse yet, if assumptions are not made explicit, they cannot be scrutinized. Just go and ask an implicit modeler about the goodness-of-fit of his or her explanation, that is, implicit model! So, again, everybody is a modeler, but some recognize this and some do not.

2.3 STATISTICAL MODELS

Almost anything in nature is affected by such a large number of factors that we could never measure or even identify them all. The result is that virtually any system that we encounter in nature will be stochastic, that is, its outcome is to some degree unpredictable. This means that a response is best thought of as the realization of a random variable. In colloquial language, we might say that chance is involved in the generation of our observations. Chance does not mean that something has no reason for happening, in the sense that there is no cause for it: there is always a cause, simply we do not know it and therefore cannot understand it completely or predict an observation perfectly.

In our models for explaining or predicting nature, we then need a description of the combined effects of all unknown and un- or mismeasured factors. A convenient mathematical description is by use of the concept of a random variable with a probability distribution function (pdf). For a random variable, this function assigns a probability of occurring to each element of a set of outcomes that are possible. To account for the unpredictable element in our observations, a model must incorporate a stochastic component and then a mathematical model becomes a statistical model. Our sketch of a model might then become:

$$y = f(x, \theta) + \varepsilon \quad \text{with} \quad \varepsilon \sim g(\phi)$$

Here, ε is the part of the response that is not explained by the functional form of the model f, the explanatory variable(s) x, and the parameter θ, and g is a function describing that unexplained part using parameter ϕ. A statistical model is often paraphrased as

$$\text{response} = \text{systematic} + \text{stochastic}$$

That is, we imagine that our response consists of a systematic and a stochastic part. Other pairs of terms for the same idea are deterministic + random and signal + noise. We will see later (Chapter 3) that this concept must be extended in so-called hierarchical models, where it applies separately to each component model, that is, level in a hierarchy.

2.4 FREQUENTIST AND BAYESIAN ANALYSIS OF STATISTICAL MODELS

One often hears the phrase *"we analyzed the data"*. We believe that data analysis should be seen as consisting of two fairly distinct activities: first, to construct a plausible model of the processes that could have produced the data we observe and second, to analyze that model, for example, to find values for its parameters or to predict what the observed data might be under specific circumstances. Of course, the two activities are intertwined, but nevertheless we think that it is useful to distinguish them conceptually. One example of where this helps is by recognizing that in a sense, there is no "Bayesian so-and-so model". Rather, we first build a model and then, we may decide to analyze it in a Bayesian or in a classical framework. So what is the difference between a Bayesian and a classical (or frequentist) analysis?

The difference between classical and Bayesian statistics really starts with the analysis of a model, if one forgets for a moment the obvious difference that any model analyzed in a Bayesian mode of inference must contain prior distributions (see below). Frequentists and Bayesians differ in the way they treat the uncertainty about what is unknown in a model, especially the uncertainty about a parameter θ.

For a frequentist, parameters are fixed and unknown quantities and uncertainty about them is expressed in terms of the variability of hypothetical replicate data sets produced by them. Uncertainty is evaluated over these hypothetical replicates, even if the only thing we ever have is a single data set. Probability is defined as the long-run frequency of events in such hypothetical replicates; therefore, classical statistics is often called frequentist statistics. Frequentists only make probability statements about the data, given fixed parameter values, but never about the parameters themselves, as one might want to. In other words, frequentists do not assign a probability to a parameter; rather, they ask about the probability of observing certain kinds of data given certain values of the unknown parameters. Probability statements such as standard errors refer to hypothetical replicate data that would be expected if certain parameter values hold; they are never directly about these parameters. In the frequentist world, it is impossible in principle to make a statement such as "I am 95% certain that this population is declining".

Bayesians define probability in a fundamentally different way. Their probability is the individual belief that an event happens or that a parameter takes a specific value. No hypothetical replicates are required in Bayesian inference (though they are useful for instance in model checking; see posterior predictive checks; Gelman et al., 1996). For a Bayesian, probability is the sole measure of uncertainty about all unknown quantities: parameters, unobservables, missing or mismeasured values, or future or unobserved responses (predictions). Bayesians use probability as their unified measure of uncertainty. This allows them to apply the mathematical laws of probability for parameter estimation and all their statistical inference. Therefore, it is possible to make probability statements about the unknown quantities, given the data, by simple use of conditional probability.

One often reads that in frequentist statistics, a parameter is a fixed and unknown quantity, while in Bayesian statistics it is a random variable. This is misleading. Rather, also for Bayesians, parameters may represent fixed and unknown quantities, but because Bayesians describe their uncertainty, or their imperfect knowledge, about the unknown parameter in terms of probability, they are *treating* parameters as random variables (Link and Barker, 2010).

So how do frequentists and Bayesians go about parameter estimation and inference? Both usually start with the sampling distribution of the data, also called the data distribution. This is the statistical description of the mechanism that could have produced the observed data, that is, the statistical model. The sampling distribution of the data y is a function of a possibly vector-valued parameter θ. It is denoted $p(y \mid \theta)$ and read "the probability of y, conditional on (given) θ". An example might be that conditional on θ, a set of counts y has a Poisson distribution: $p(y \mid \theta) \sim \text{Pois}(\theta)$. This is often abbreviated to $y \mid \theta \sim \text{Pois}(\theta)$ or even $y \sim \text{Pois}(\theta)$.

In frequentist statistics, the likelihood function plays a central role for inference about parameters. The likelihood function is the same as the sampling distribution, but "read in reverse": we interpret the sampling distribution of the observed data as a function of the unknown parameters θ, with the data y fixed . This is denoted $L(\theta \mid y)$ and read as "the likelihood of parameter θ, given the data y". We choose as our best guess of θ that parameter value which leads to the maximum function value when plugged into the sampling distribution function for the observed data y. The likelihood is not a probability because it does not integrate to 1, and the maximum function value may be greater than 1. Frequentists estimate a single point of the likelihood function and call the value which maximizes that function the *maximum likelihood estimate* or *MLE*. In other words, the MLE represents parameter value(s) which maximize the probability of getting the data actually observed. Any other value gives a lower probability of getting one's data.

Here is an example for a simple maximum likelihood analysis. Let us assume we wanted to empirically determine the detection probability of tadpoles by releasing some in a small artificial pond and counting them later. Say, we released $n = 50$ tadpoles and then count $y = 20$ of them and we want to estimate the probability that a tadpole is seen (θ). The typical sampling distribution assumed for this scenario is a binomial, that is,

$$p(y \mid \theta) = \frac{n!}{y!(n-y)!} \theta^y (1 - \theta)^{n-y}.$$

The method of maximum likelihood takes as the best estimate that value of θ, which, when plugged into this sampling function along with the data (y), yields the highest function value, that is, the highest likelihood $L(\theta \mid y)$, where $L(\theta \mid y) \propto p(y \mid \theta)$. Thus, we can plug in different possible values of θ (we know that the value must be in the range from 0 to 1), compute the value of the likelihood function, and take that values of θ for which the likelihood is maximal (Fig. 2.1). We see that the likelihood function reaches a maximum for $\theta = 0.4$, so this is the maximum likelihood estimate (MLE) of θ, often denoted $\hat{\theta}$, and written as $\hat{\theta} = 0.4$.

In this simple case, it is possible to obtain the MLE analytically. This requires that we calculate the first derivative of the likelihood function, set it to zero, and solve the equation with respect to θ. Since the binomial coefficient (the ratio of factorials just after the equal sign above) is a constant, we do not need to include it in this calculation. Thus, we have

$$L(\theta \mid y) \propto \theta^{y}(1-\theta)^{n-y}$$

$$L(\theta \mid y)\partial\theta = \theta^{y}(1-\theta)^{n-y}\left(\frac{y}{\theta} - \frac{n-y}{1-\theta}\right)$$

$$\theta^{y}(1-\theta)^{n-y}\left(\frac{y}{\theta} - \frac{n-y}{1-\theta}\right) = 0$$

$$\hat{\theta} = \frac{y}{n}$$

We see that the ratio 20/50 is the MLE of θ, which is what we have expected.

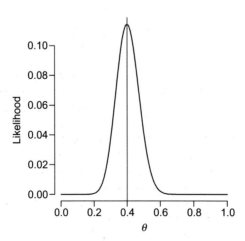

FIGURE 2.1   Binomial likelihood function for detection probability (θ) in the tadpole example, where 20 of 50 released tadpoles were seen. The MLE of θ is 0.4.

MLEs have several desirable features, such as asymptotic unbiasedness, consistency, and invariance to transformation (see, e.g., chapter 2 in Royle and Dorazio, 2008, or any book about mathematical statistics). However, the method of maximum likelihood is based on asymptotic approximations; for instance, MLEs are only unbiased and associated standard error estimates valid when sample size goes to infinity. Every ecologist knows that we rather rarely have infinite samples in ecology. How well MLEs and their standard errors perform in the typical small sample size situations in ecology is an open question in any actual application (Le Cam, 1990).

In contrast, the basis for Bayesian inference is the so-called Bayes rule. Bayes rule is attributed to the seventeenth century English minister and mathematician Thomas Bayes (Bayes, 1763). It is an undisputed mathematical fact which is easily proven from the rules of probability. Consequently, not every application of Bayes rule makes an analysis Bayesian: the application of Bayes rule to observables is undisputed. However, what Bayesians do is to apply Bayes rule also to unobservable quantities, such as, most importantly, the parameters in a statistical model. As Lindley (1983, p. 2) put it so succinctly, the recipe for every Bayesian analysis about any uncertain quantity is quite simple and mechanical:

- *What is uncertain and of interest to you? Call it θ.*
- *What do you do know? Call it D [...].*
- *Then calculate $p(\theta \mid D)$.*
- *How? Using the rules of probability, nothing more, nothing less.*

To describe how Bayesians learn from data using the rules of probability, we will introduce Bayes rule in the context of two sets of mutually excluding, *observable* events, A and B. Remember that a vertical bar ($\mid$) means "conditional on" and is read as "given".

$$p(A \mid B) = \frac{p(B \mid A)p(A)}{p(B)}$$

This says that the conditional probability of observing A, given that B has happened or is true, $p(A \mid B)$, is equal to the conditional probability of observing B given A, $p(B \mid A)$, times the marginal probability of A, $p(A)$, divided by the marginal probability of B, $p(B)$. To better see how Bayes rule works for statistical learning from data, consider the following example which is inspired by a similar example in Pigliucci (2002). Assume that our activity after work consists of bird watching (B) or watching football on TV (F) and that this depends on whether the weather is good (g) or bad (b) on a particular night. Let us assume that you knew the following: the joint probability of good weather and us watching birds is 0.5, the marginal probability of good weather is 0.6 and the marginal probability of us watching birds is 0.7. Now if you are told that we were watching football on a particular night, what is your best guess about the weather that night?

For illustration, we present all involved probabilities in a two-by-two table with margins added (Table 2.1). In this example, we deal with mutually exclusive events (e.g., the weather cannot simultaneously be good and bad); hence, probabilities must add up within the same rows and columns, respectively. We also know that the four main cells must sum to 1, so we can fill in all cells in the table from the information just given.

Note that $p(A, B) = p(A \mid B)p(B) = p(B \mid A)p(A)$: the joint probability that A and B both occur is equal to the product of the probabilities that A occurs given that B has occurred and that B occurs, and vice versa. We had asked for your best guess about the weather on a night we were watching football. As a response, we can compute $p(b \mid F)$, the conditional probability of bad weather, given that we were watching football:

$$p(b \mid F) = \frac{p(b, F)}{p(F)} = \frac{0.2}{0.3} \approx 0.66$$

So at the outset, without any additional information, your best guess of the probability of bad weather that night would simply have been the marginal probability $p(b) = 0.4$. However, given that we watch football more frequently when the weather is bad, the knowledge that on that particular night we were watching football has increased your best guess at the probability of bad weather from 0.4 to 0.66.

This example illustrates how the information about our postwork activity (D in Lindley's recipe) influences our knowledge about the weather on a given night. In other words, it shows how our prior knowledge about the weather, $p(\theta)$, was updated by the observed data D to become $p(\theta \mid D)$. This example deals with observable events of a binary nature and nicely illustrates the use of conditional probability for learning from data, which is the basis for using Bayes rule for statistical inference about unknown quantities. In Bayesian inference, parameters take the place of the weather in our example and the data correspond to the knowledge about our

TABLE 2.1   Joint and Marginal Probabilities of Events for Two Sets of Mutually Exclusive Events, Bird Watching/Watching Football and Good/Bad Weather

	Good Weather (*g*)	Bad Weather (*b*)	
Go Bird Watching (*B*)	**0.5**	0.2	**0.7**
Watch Football (*F*)	0.1	0.2	0.3
	0.6	0.4	1.0

Note: The probabilities given in the text are printed in bold face and the remainder can be obtained by simple addition and subtraction.

postwork activity. In addition, we use Bayes rule to assess the uncertainty about both discrete events and continuous quantities.

When Bayes rule is applied to statistical inference about parameter θ based on the information in the data D, the probability $p(\theta|D)$ is called the posterior distribution of θ: it is the conditional probability of parameter θ, given the (known) data D, the prior and the model:

$$p(\theta|D) = \frac{p(D|\theta)p(\theta)}{p(D)}$$

There are three further quantities in Bayes rule, apart from the posterior distribution $p(\theta|D)$. In some ways, $p(D|\theta)$ is the opposite of the posterior: it is the probability of the data, given the parameters, or, as used here, the likelihood function. It may appear confusing that the likelihood in Bayes rule is traditionally written as $p(D|\theta)$, that is, in the same way as the sampling distribution of the data. Quantity $p(\theta)$ is the probability of the parameters, that is, the prior distribution. Finally, $p(D)$ is the marginal probability of the data and is defined as the integral of the numerator over θ. This is a constant used to normalize the right-hand side of Bayes rule so that the result integrates to one and becomes interpretable as a probability. As an aside, we note that it would be wrong to say that Bayesian inference is not likelihood based. Obviously, the likelihood function is a central part of Bayesian inference.

Following up the tadpole example from above, how would we estimate the unknown parameter θ in the Bayesian framework? Well, we have already defined the likelihood function. We now need to define a prior distribution of θ, that is, specify what we know *a priori* about θ and express this knowledge in a probability distribution. We know that θ must lie between 0 and 1. A useful probability distribution defined on the interval $(0, 1)$ is the beta distribution with parameters α and β. By specifying values of α and β, we can express our knowledge about θ. Generally, we have

$$p(\theta) \propto \theta^{\alpha-1}(1-\theta)^{\beta-1}.$$

Note that we have excluded a constant of the beta distribution as it has no relevance for estimating θ. Having chosen likelihood and prior, we can analytically obtain the posterior distribution:

$$p(\theta|y) \propto p(y|\theta)p(\theta)$$

$$p(\theta|y) \propto \theta^y(1-\theta)^{n-y}\theta^{\alpha-1}(1-\theta)^{\beta-1}$$

$$p(\theta|y) \propto \theta^{y+\alpha-1}(1-\theta)^{n-y+\beta-1}$$

We see that this posterior distribution is also a beta distribution, with mean $\frac{y+\alpha}{n+\alpha+\beta}$ and mode $\frac{y+\alpha-1}{n+\alpha+\beta-2}$.

Absent any prior knowledge about θ, we would specify $\alpha = 1$ and $\beta = 1$ because this would result in a uniform prior distribution for θ, representing a belief that any value of θ between 0 and 1 is equally likely. A prior which says that we do not know anything about the parameter (or do not care about what might be likely values) is called noninformative, vague, flat, or diffuse prior. In the tadpole example, the resulting posterior mean is 0.404 and the mode is 0.400. The posterior mean is very close to the MLE and the mode is exactly the MLE, as we would expect—with a noninformative prior, the posterior mode of a parameter in a Bayesian analysis corresponds to the MLE of that parameter in a frequentist analysis. We notice that the impact of the prior (the values of α and β) on the posterior distribution diminishes with larger sample size (n). The posterior distribution can also be plotted and functionals (e.g., probability that $\theta > 0.5$) may be computed (see later).

So Bayesian statistical analysis is conceptually very simple: probability (via Bayes rule) is the basis for all inference about parameters and any other unknown quantities in a system analyzed. Bayesian statistics has great philosophical appeal (Link and Barker, 2010) since it is conceptually so simple (all inference is based on Bayes rule), exact (e.g., standard errors are those for your actual data set and not for some infinite version of it), and coherent (logically consistent).

Bayes rule is often paraphrased like the following:

$$\text{posterior} \propto \text{likelihood} \times \text{prior}$$

that is, the posterior distribution is proportional to the product of the likelihood and the prior. This makes it clear that in a Bayesian analysis, one's conclusion, that is, the posterior distribution, is very openly *always* a result of both the information contained in the data (as embodied in the likelihood function) *and* of our prior knowledge (our assumptions) about the unknowns in the model. We cannot conduct a Bayesian analysis without formally expressing our *a priori* uncertainty/knowledge about the parameters in the form of a probability distribution.

Several other points are noteworthy about Bayes rule as a basis for inference. First, Bayes rule formalizes the way in which humans learn. Learning always consists of updating what we knew before with what we see now. Bayes rule is thus a mathematical formalization of how we deal with new information: we always weigh the information of any new observation with the knowledge, or prior experience base, that we possessed before making that observation. The result, our conclusion, is then affected by both, and the relative importance of one or the other can vary. For instance, if we know something for almost certain, we would require large quantities of data to overthrow that prior belief. In contrast, if we do not know anything at all about a system, we might be happy to draw a conclusion based on very little data. This conclusion would then be the result almost entirely of the new data. In Bayes rule, this weighting of information happens in a formal and mathematically rigorous way.

As another illustration of this point, note that in virtually every analysis in ecology we know something about the system analyzed and we always use that information, even in a frequentist framework. For example, if we get parameter estimates that seem to make no sense when compared with what we think we know about the system ("results do not make sense biologically"), many of us are prepared to dismiss these results in an act of *ad hoc* Bayesianism. In contrast, in a proper Bayesian analysis, prior expectations about the results could be formally introduced into an analysis. Such expectations really amount to available knowledge that is not formally used otherwise in a frequentist analysis, and this does not seem a very sensible thing to do, if we think about it.

Second, Bayes rule shows us how we can combine several pieces of information in a mathematically rigorous manner. Simply treat one piece of information as prior information and the other piece of information as the data, form a likelihood for the latter, apply Bayes rule and out comes your combination of the information in the form of the posterior distribution.

Third, priors can simply be seen as assumptions. Hence, Bayes rule represents an instrument by which we can compare formally the effect of different assumptions about model parameters by repeating the calculations with different priors.

Finally, and fourth, Bayes statistics is normative in the sense that it prescribes a mathematically rigorous way of arriving at a logical conclusion from data, a model, and *a priori* assumptions (Lindley, 2006). A Bayesian will not argue about what prior assumption one should make; this is really in the realm of the subject-matter scientist. However, once people have decided on their priors, then Bayes rule *prescribes* a mathematically rigorous way in which our statistical conclusions ought to be drawn from some observed data, using a model and these prior assumptions.

Hence, one might think that the ability to specify prior distributions was widely regarded as an advantage of the Bayesian approach. However, interestingly, priors are more often viewed as a liability of Bayesian analyses, for several reasons (Dennis, 1996). The first reason is that priors need to be decided upon. This choice is somewhat subjective even if based on past data because whether these data are relevant for the current analysis may be debatable. Hence, Bayesian analysis is intrinsically subjective (but at least explicitly so, one might want to add). Many people feel uneasy at making an explicit decision about what might be plausible values for a parameter and find it difficult to make a choice for the prior distributions.

Second, if two persons use different priors for their analysis of the same data set, they may clearly get different answers because the posterior is always the result of combining the information in the data with that in the prior. Worse yet, even if both agreed to specify vague priors, which does not contain information, they might still end up with different answers under two different such vague priors. So, even vague priors can be challenging because different forms of specifying absence of knowledge about a parameter might not be equal. For instance, for a parameter representing a probability, we might use a uniform distribution on the interval 0–1 to say that any value is equally likely. When we specify that same parameter on the logit scale as we often do (see Chapter 3), then something analogous would be to use a uniform distribution with a large range, for example, from -1000 to 1000. Although the two prior distributions are both vague on their scales, the posterior distributions will not be exactly the same.

In spite of all this, it must be said that it is easy to exaggerate prior-related difficulties with the Bayesian approach. For once, and perhaps to console some doubters, typically parameter estimates from the Bayesian analysis of a model with vague priors numerically match pretty closely the MLEs from a frequentist analysis of the model. Second, with reasonable sample sizes, the data overwhelm the prior in their influence on the posterior distribution because the effect of the prior diminishes as sample size increases. Data cloning, a method to use Markov chain Monte Carlo simulation (see Section 2.5) to obtain MLEs without effects of priors, is based on this fact (Lele et al., 2007). Third, in any Bayesian analysis, it is customary to report the priors used. If an analyst disagrees with the choice, he or she could—at least in principle—repeat the analysis with his or her favorite prior. Finally, it is a good practice (though far from always done) to try out several priors and see what their effect on the inference is, that is, do a prior sensitivity analysis and report its results.

In this book, we follow Royle and Dorazio (2008), and indeed most applied Bayesian analysts, and specify vague priors for a natural parameterization of a model. For a parameter representing a probability, we often use a uniform(0, 1) or beta(1, 1) distribution or adopt a uniform distribution with a suitably wide range (e.g., -10, 10) for the same parameter on the logit scale. Alternatively, we often specify a flat normal distribution, that is, a normal distribution with suitably large standard deviation. What represents a suitably wide range or large standard deviation depends on the support of the likelihood function. If the likelihood of a parameter is essentially zero outside of, say, 0.4–0.6, then a uniform prior with a range between 0 and 1 may be sufficient to not affect the posterior distribution. On the other hand, if the likelihood function has nonnegligible support over a larger range, a uniform prior intended to be vague must also have a wider range. Whether a prior is sufficiently vague may be easily ascertained by repeating an analysis with narrower or wider priors and seeing whether the posterior is affected or not. In the case of a uniform prior, a posterior distribution that is truncated by either or both limits shows that the analyst has not succeeded in choosing a vague prior. Consequently, a wider range must be chosen.

For variance parameters, the typical prior chosen used to be an inverse gamma distribution for a long time. However, currently, the preferred choice of many Bayesian analysts seems to be a suitably wide uniform for the variance parameter on the scale of the standard deviation (Gelman, 2006). This is our typical choice. We do not usually adopt explicitly informative priors. However, when the Markov chains (see Section 2.5) for a parameter fail to converge, we may narrow the range of a uniform prior or reduce the standard deviation of a flat normal prior to achieve convergence.

We saw that the basis of all Bayesian inference was the posterior probability distribution of the parameters. So once we have that, what should we do with it?

In special cases, we might choose to plot the posterior distribution for an important parameter. However, in most cases, it will be enough to summarize the posterior distribution for some or all model parameters by reporting its central tendency and its spread. Typically, for a point estimate, the posterior mean, median, or mode is used. With vague priors, the posterior distribution reflects the likelihood function directly; hence, the posterior mode is equivalent to the MLE of a corresponding frequentist analysis. The standard deviation of the posterior distribution is analogous to the standard error of a parameter estimate in a frequentist analysis. Any interval which contains 95% of the posterior mass is a Bayesian analogue to the frequentist confidence interval (CI) and is usually called a credible interval (CRI), or sometimes also a Bayesian confidence interval. Often the 2.5th and 97.5th percentiles of the posterior samples are taken as a 95% CRI; this is what we do in this book.

At this stage, and especially because posterior-based Bayesian parameter estimates often very closely match their MLE analogs numerically, it is important not to forget the exact meaning of these quantities. This has to do with the different definitions of probability. For instance, a 95% frequentist CI does *not* contain the target parameter with probability 0.95. In frequentist statistics, probability statements are about the data, or in this case, about the method, and never about the parameters. Hence, the 95% refer to the reliability of the method of constructing a 95% CI. If we sampled data from the same population 100 times and for each formed a 95% CI for a certain parameter, then about 95 intervals would indeed contain the population value and another 5 would not.

In contrast, a Bayesian 95% CRI *does* contain the parameter with probability 0.95. Also, we can make other probability statements about parameters, for instance, of the kind "I am 92% sure that this population is declining", by looking at the proportion of the mass $r < 1$ of the posterior distribution for a population growth rate r. Or else, "I am 50% sure that the growth rate lies between 0.5 and 0.8". This is a great asset of a Bayesian analysis, especially when describing the results to the public or resource managers. The Bayesian definition of probability (and especially of uncertainty intervals) conforms much more closely to the human concept of probability than the repeated-sample definition in frequentist statistics.

2.5 BAYESIAN COMPUTATION

To analytically evaluate the posterior distribution, solving Bayes rule for all but the simplest models involves high-dimensional integrations, which can be very difficult or actually impossible to solve in most cases. The tadpole example above (Fig. 2.1) is a fairly simple example which is not difficult analytically. Most posterior distributions are, however, much more complicated, and no closed-form formulas exist. Hence, up to about 20 years ago, Bayesian analysis of a more complex model was typically not really an option. However, at the beginning of the 1990s, some statisticians rediscovered pioneering work done by physicists back in the 1950s (Smith and Gelfand, 1993). This work showed that simulation techniques could be used to draw samples from the posterior distribution instead of solving the equations. Specifically, Metropolis et al. (1953) and Hastings (1970) developed so-called Markov chain Monte Carlo (MCMC) algorithms. MCMC yields samples of arbitrary size of dependent (i.e., autocorrelated) draws from a distribution and can be constructed so that this distribution approximates the desired posterior distribution. Hence, these samples can be summarized for inference about the posterior distribution; for instance, mean and standard deviation of the samples can be interpreted as the posterior mean and posterior standard deviation, that is, as a Bayesian point and interval estimate of a parameter. Samples can also be plotted, in a raw or a smoothed histogram, for a picture of the posterior distribution.

The rediscovery and successive refinement of MCMC algorithms, along with the ever-increasing power of personal computers, sparked a revolution in statistics and also in the empirical sciences such as ecology (McCarthy, 2007). This revolution is still going on and has catapulted Bayesian methods to the center of the ecological data analysis scene (Brooks, 2003). However, for most ecologists, constructing their own MCMC algorithms would be prohibitively difficult. Hence, the Bayesian revolution has only recently reached ecology.

2.6 WinBUGS

What has brought the Bayesian revolution to ecology has a name: WinBUGS (Gilks et al., 1994; Lunn et al., 2000, 2009). WinBUGS is the Windows version of a free computer program developed as part of the

BUGS project, which means *Bayesian inference using Gibbs sampling*; see www.mrc-bsu.cam.ac.uk/bugs. WinBUGS originally used a particular variant of MCMC called Gibbs sampling (Geman and Geman, 1984), but now uses a variety of other MCMC sampling techniques. For a history of the BUGS project, an appreciation and outlook, see Lunn et al. (2009). The active development in the BUGS project now takes place with Open-BUGS; see www.openbugs.info. At the time of writing, the two BUGS sisters are nearly identical in practice and will run most code from one another fine. The same goes for a BUGS clone called JAGS (*Just another Gibbs sampler*, see www-fis.iarc.fr/~martyn/software/jags). JAGS is another MCMC engine that uses the BUGS language; hence, most BUGS code should run also in JAGS.

For most ecologists, WinBUGS is simply an ingenious MCMC black-box. The analyst communicates with the MCMC engine by providing a data set and describing a statistical model for it using a simple and effective model definition language, the BUGS language (Gilks et al., 1994). In our opinion, the BUGS language can claim a large part of the value for ecologists of the WinBUGS software. All statistical models that we have had to do with are specified more simply and—to us—in a *much* more transparent way in the BUGS language than when using custom code for maximum likelihood estimation. For the latter, one needs to define the likelihood for a model explicitly and then use some function optimizer (for instance, `nlm` or `optim` in R) to find the MLEs (Bolker, 2008). Alternatively, one uses software that shields us from most of the complexity but makes it easy to fit models that one does not understand or that may not make sense. In contrast, BUGS code often looks trivially simple and concise. In the BUGS language, all stochastic models are described by specifying local stochastic or deterministic relationships between quantities such as parameters and data. By breaking apart an entire model into its smaller component parts, understanding is greatly enhanced for an ecologist. Moreover, the construction of even very complex models becomes relatively feasible and transparent. BUGS model descriptions are naturally hierarchical, and indeed, WinBUGS is ideal for fitting hierarchical models (see Section 2.9). We will see many examples for this later in the book. Indeed, we have found that WinBUGS frees the creative modeler in many ecologists.

Once the model is specified, WinBUGS constructs an MCMC algorithm in perfect blackbox manner and runs that for the required length. Its primary product is a long stream of numbers, one for each model parameter that we choose to estimate. If the MCMC algorithm has been constructed adequately and the chains have converged to the desired posterior distribution, then these numbers represent a random sample from these posterior distributions. There is an autocorrelation built into these numbers, since they form a Markov chain. This means that the first part of the chains, where the effect of the arbitrarily chosen starting values will still be felt, must be discarded as a so-called burnin. Whether the burnin period is over or not can be judged by visual means, that is, by inspecting a time-series plot of the sampled values for each parameter. The plot should now randomly jump up and down around a constant mean. There are formal criteria to decide whether convergence has been reached. For instance, the Brooks–Gelman–Rubin statistic (Brooks and Gelman, 1998) is often used. It requires two or more chains for each parameter and compares the between-chain with the within-chain variance in an ANOVA fashion. At convergence, the value of this test statistic, sometimes called Rhat, is 1. After a chain has converged onto the desired target distribution, to save computer space and reduce autocorrelation, one may thin it by k, that is, keep every kth value only. Thus, one gets a smaller, but more information-dense (because less autocorrelated) sample from the posterior distribution.

WinBUGS can be used as standalone software, see McCarthy (2007), Ntzoufras (2009) or chapter 4 in Kéry (2010). However, we find it more efficient to harness it to R via the communicator package R2WinBUGS (Sturtz et al., 2005). This is how we use WinBUGS throughout this book.

There are many Bayesian statistics books that explain MCMC algorithms and give examples (e.g., McCarthy, 2007; Ntzoufras, 2009; Link and Barker, 2010; King et al., 2010); therefore, we skip this here. We feel that the importance of being able to code one's own MCMC algorithm may easily be overstated. After all, hardly any ecologist would nowadays be able to code a Newton–Raphson algorithm for fitting a GLM or a Laplace approximation for the integrals that need to be solved for obtaining mixed-model estimates. And yet, many of us routinely use these methods for our research.

Admittedly, MCMC may be somewhat more difficult than these techniques and may fail in perhaps more ways than other computing algorithms commonly used for a frequentist analysis. We do not doubt that it can be a great advantage to actually *know* how to code MCMC algorithms, not least because custom-written MCMC code often runs much faster than WinBUGS. Nevertheless, a simple intuitive understanding of the nature of MCMC techniques will often be enough for ecologists. Such an understanding may be obtained by simply using an MCMC blackbox, such as WinBUGS and experiencing the behavior of the chains in many situations for many different models. This is what we do in this book.

WinBUGS is a fantastic program, but may exhibit a fair dose of pretty idiosyncratic behavior. There are many things that one just must know in order to succeed. A collection of survival tips can be found in Appendix 1.

2.7 ADVANTAGES AND DISADVANTAGES OF BAYESIAN ANALYSES BY POSTERIOR SAMPLING

There are many advantages of the Bayesian analysis of a model by posterior simulation via MCMC techniques (Kéry, 2010). Some of them which are particularly relevant for an ecologist include the following:

- Even difficult models can be fit, including some which cannot be fitted in the classical framework.
- Derived quantities may be computed trivially easily, with full propagation of the uncertainty in the components that make up the derived quantity. This can be a very hard problem in the classical framework.
- All results are exact; there are no asymptotics involved in the estimates as for MLEs, which may be of questionable value in small-data situations so typical of ecological studies.
- The BUGS language allows the typical quantitative ecologist to actually understand the construction of even complex models so that the code can be modified to fit one's own purposes.

On the other hand, there are also challenges with the Bayesian approach. At first sight, like any new theory or method, Bayesian statistics may appear difficult. Then, the choice of priors and the sensitivity of the estimates to that choice need some thinking. MCMC engines such as WinBUGS are blackboxes and are hard to understand, leaving a certain uneasiness with people who like to understand most of what they do, and convergence of the Markov chains may be difficult to assess.

MCMC-based analyses in general can be slow compared to other ways of model fitting (see, e.g., the comparisons in Kéry, 2010). Just because WinBUGS is an extremely flexible, generic MCMC engine, it is a rather slow software when compared with custom-written MCMC algorithms. For complex models applied to large data sets, WinBUGS may become too slow to be of practical value. Novel algorithmic techniques that provide approximate analytical solutions to the integrations involved in Bayesian analysis (e.g., AD model builder; see http://admb-foundation.org/ or R-INLA, Rue et al., 2009) may then be exciting new avenues for the fitting of some classes of hierarchical models.

Some other difficult topics include the detection of parameter identifiability and model selection. Lunn et al. (2009) say that the flexibility of WinBUGS to specify even very complex models may let the user fit models that do not make sense, for instance, models with parameters that are not identifiable, that is, for which the data do not contain any information. Nonidentifiability of a parameter is often difficult to diagnose in complex models, but perhaps harder still in a Bayesian than in a frequentist analysis.

This is due in part because in a sense, the problem does not really exist in the Bayesian mode of analysis: if there is no information about a parameter in the data (the likelihood), then there is always information coming from the prior, and we still technically get a posterior distribution for that parameter. Hence, one way of checking whether a parameter is indeed identified is by comparing the prior with the posterior and seeing whether changing the prior induces large changes in the posterior (Gimenez et al., 2009b; see Section 7.9). Simulating a data set and seeing whether the analysis is able to recover estimates that resemble the known input values is perhaps one of the best ways for an ecologist to check for nonidentifiability of a parameter (e.g., Schaub, 2009).

Another big topic is model and variable selection. In the frequentist world, many ecologists use model selection criteria such as Akaike's information criterion (AIC; see review by Burnham and Anderson, 2002). Yet, it appears sometimes as if a bunch of models is thrown up into the air in the hope that AIC will do all the work of sorting through them. That such a view is overly simplistic becomes clear when reading through a review paper on model selection in the primary statistical literature (e.g., Kadane and Lazar, 2004). Model and variable selection are deep waters and even among statisticians there is no consensus view on what is the best—and practically feasible—approach. Furthermore, model selection using the AIC is an unsolved problem for mixed models due to the challenge of counting the effective number of parameters (Link and Barker, 2010). Hence, for mixed models even in the classical arena, there does not seem to be a simple approach available.

These challenges appear, if anything, even more acute when one moves to a Bayesian analysis. There is an AIC-analogue called deviance information criterion or DIC (Spiegelhalter et al., 2002), but again, its standard version computed by WinBUGS appears to be problematic for hierarchical models—and most models that ecologists nowadays want to fit have more than one random component and therefore are mixed, or hierarchical, models (see Chapter 4). The DIC can be computed for such hierarchical models (see Millar, 2009, which includes R code), but the required computations are involved and computationally very demanding. Hence, in spite of long-standing criticisms of stepwise model selection and model selection by significance tests, one may effectively be back at one of those. We can look at the significance of a parameter by checking whether its 95% CRI covers zero and based on that decide whether it is warranted in a model or not. This is what we sometimes do. Other times, we simply fit one model that is biologically plausible to us and stick to that. There are yet other approaches, for instance, Bayes factors and reversible jump Markov chain Monte Carlo (RJMCMC); see for instance, King et al. (2010) and Link and Barker (2010). But be warned, Link and Barker's chapter 7 on Bayesian multimodel selection is not easy reading. Also see the overview by O'Hara and Sillanpää (2009). It is likely that we will see more work in the future on Bayesian model selection and hypothesis testing.

2.8 HIERARCHICAL MODELS

In hierarchical models, complex stochastic systems are decomposed into a dependent sequence of simpler submodels. This partitioning is beneficial for a better understanding of a system, for an honest accounting for all levels of uncertainty or for computational ease. A model can be hierarchical in two ways, statistically and conceptually.

In a purely statistical sense, a hierarchical model is composed of a sequence of random variables, with the realization of the random variable at one level being a parameter of the random variable at the next level down. For instance, a hierarchical model with two levels is (dropping indices):

1. $x \sim f(\omega)$
2. $y \sim g(x, \theta)$

That is, at level 1 of the hierarchy, x is a realization of a random variable described by probability distribution f with parameter ω. At level 2, y is a realization of another random variable described by probability distribution g, which depends on the realization of the first random variable, x, and on another parameter, θ. Of course, there may be more than two levels in a hierarchical model. Hierarchical models abound in ecology. For instance, a nested ANOVA model (Kéry, 2010) is an example of a hierarchical model with two levels, with f and g being a normal distribution, such that $x \sim N(\mu, \sigma_x^2)$ and $y \sim N(x, \sigma^2)$, where μ is the grand mean, σ_x^2 the variance among group means x, and σ^2 the residual variance of measurements y around the group means (note indices have been omitted for clarity).

In the context of hierarchical models for population analysis, Royle and Dorazio (2008) make the important distinction between *implicit* and *explicit hierarchical models*. Explicit hierarchical models have random variables or parameters with an explicit ecological interpretation, while implicit hierarchical models do not. As an example of an implicit hierarchical model, the Poisson GLMMs in Chapter 4 have a quantity called the expected count (λ). This is not a real ecological parameter because it is the product of population size and detection probability. In contrast, in the hierarchical models in Chapter 6, N is the sum of the latent indicator variables z and corresponds exactly to the local population size. In explicit hierarchical models, the lowest level in the hierarchy typically represents an explicit description of the binomial observation process. As a result, the ecological parameters in the model become directly interpretable and do have an ecological meaning. In addition, inference from explicit hierarchical models is protected against possible misinterpretations due to a confounding of the ecological and the observation processes in implicit hierarchical models. All else equal, we prefer explicit over implicit hierarchical models.

There is another, conceptual sense in which a model can be hierarchical, and this has to do with exactly this accounting for the observation process. For example, the CJS model fitted via the m-array (Section 7.10) is not a hierarchical model in the statistical sense of the term, but the state-space version of the model (Section 7.2) is. With the m-array, the hierarchical genesis of the observed data is lost by aggregation when creating the m-array. Nevertheless, this model is still an explicit hierarchical model in a conceptual sense because its parameters have an explicit ecological meaning owing to the explicit modeling of the observation process. Similarly, the N-mixture model (Chapter 12) is intrinsically hierarchical, even when fit in a frequentist framework, where the latent abundance states are integrated out from the likelihood and thus the hierarchy is collapsed (Royle, 2004c).

2.9 SUMMARY AND OUTLOOK

In this chapter, we have briefly reviewed statistical models and their analysis in WinBUGS. We have claimed that any interpretation of data requires a model, either an implicit or an explicit one. Then, we briefly reviewed two philosophies for formal learning from data, with their associated methods for fitting models to data and making inferences about their parameters, that is, of obtaining estimates of the parameters and of the uncertainty around these estimates. One is maximum likelihood and the other is Bayesian inference. Bayesian inference is based on the posterior distribution, which is a product of the likelihood (representing the information contained in the data) and the prior distribution (representing what is known about the parameters beforehand). Bayesian inference uses a fact of conditional probability, Bayes rule, to let the data update our prior state of knowledge to posterior state of knowledge. In this way, what we learn from data, the posterior distribution, is a weighted average of the prior distribution and the information of the data at hand.

We have seen that priors can be regarded both as an asset and as a liability in Bayesian inference (of course, we believe that the former outweigh the latter). We have also seen that the results of a Bayesian analysis based on the posterior distribution are much more easily explained to the public owing to the more intuitive Bayesian definition of probability. Bayesian analysis in practice nowadays means obtaining samples from the posterior distribution by simulation techniques such as Markov chain Monte Carlo (MCMC). The free WinBUGS software (along with its "sisters", OpenBUGS and JAGS) is the most widely used MCMC engine currently available.

It allows us to specify almost arbitrarily complex models using an ingenious and simple model definition language. It then constructs an MCMC algorithm, runs it for the requested length, and produces a stream of numbers which, if all went well, represents a sample from the posterior distribution of interest. These samples can be summarized for inference, for instance, posterior means and standard deviations are customarily treated as Bayesian point and interval estimates. Important advantages of the Bayesian model fitting by posterior sampling include the numerical tractability of even very complex models, exact rather than asymptotic inference, and the ease with which derived parameters can be estimated with full propagation of all uncertainty. Some disadvantages are that it may be difficult at first, it may be slow, and parameter nonidentifiability and model selection may be even harder challenges than in the frequentist framework.

We are now armed with the motivation for population analysis and have a basic understanding for how estimation and inference about model parameters is achieved in the Bayesian framework of statistics. Hence, we are ready to move on to see our first population models. In the next two chapters, we will deal with simple models for time series of counts. Importantly, these chapters will also provide an introduction to what may be the three most essential topics of applied statistical modeling: linear and generalized linear models in Chapter 3 and random effects in Chapter 4. You will meet these concepts over and over again in your statistical modeling. If you understand them in a simple model, your understanding for more complex models will be greatly enhanced.

Introduction to the Generalized Linear Model: The Simplest Model for Count Data

3.1 INTRODUCTION

The generalized linear model (GLM) extends the concept of a linear model from normal response models, such as analysis of variance and regression, to many other response distributions, including the Poisson and the binomial. The GLM is a crucial piece in our lego collection of modeling parts, and perhaps *the* crucial piece. Described synthetically in 1972 by Nelder and Wedderburn (also see McCullagh and Nelder, 1989; Dobson and Barnett, 2008), the GLM unifies a huge number of superficially different analytical techniques, such as regression, analysis of variance, log-linear models, and logistic regression, among many others. We believe that a solid practical understanding of the GLM is essential for the work of every serious ecologist. To understand the GLM, you must know how to build a design matrix, what a link function is and how to choose a statistical distribution for an observed response. WinBUGS, with its lucid and elegant BUGS language, is perhaps the best software available to make one really understand the GLM. Useful introductions to the GLM with WinBUGS include Gelman and Hill (2007), Ntzoufras (2009), and Kéry (2010). In this chapter, we introduce two common GLMs for count data: Poisson and binomial GLMs. The essential difference between the two is that in the Poisson GLM, counts are unbounded in principle, whereas in a binomial GLM, counts are bounded by the so-called binomial totals. The GLM is the quintessential statistical model, so we first review the concept of a statistical model as a response being composed of signal plus noise.

3.2 STATISTICAL MODELS: RESPONSE = SIGNAL + NOISE

The basic form of a statistical model is such that we imagine a response as being composed of two components: signal and noise. The main difference between a statistical model and a purely mathematical one is that the statistical model contains a description of the random variability in an observed response, the noise. Alternative names of the signal–noise distinction are random and fixed part of a model, stochastic and systematic part, and mean and variance, or dispersion, structure of a model.

3.2.1 The Noise Component

The defining feature of a statistical model is that it accommodates the randomness and unpredictability that is the hallmark of all empirical data, even those in physics, chemistry, or molecular biology labs. To describe this noise, we use statistical distributions. Our quantitative descriptors of the random part of a model, the noise component, are the parameters of these distributions and of course their identity. Some of the most frequently used distributions in population ecology are Poisson, binomial, normal, multinomial, and exponential. For an ecological modeler, it is important to get a feel for which statistical distribution is suitable as a description of the randomness in the data for a particular sampling situation, feature of the data collection protocol or measured trait. Experienced modelers therefore have a bestiary of distributions (Bolker, 2008) at their disposal, and they may well try out more than one for the same response to see which is most appropriate. Here, we do not describe these distributions but rather point to other books where some of the key distributions are described in more detail. Examples include Bolker (2008), Royle and Dorazio (2008), Kéry (2010), or Link and Barker (2010).

Program R has a large catalog of distributions that one can use and study to see how each one looks. Check out ?ddist, and replace dist by any of the following: pois, binom, norm, multinom, exp, and unif. Changing the first letter of the function name from d to p, q, or r allows one to get the density, the distribution function, the percentiles, and random numbers from these distributions. For instance, to see how a beta distribution with parameters 2 and 4 looks like, you could execute either of the following R commands. Both generate a random sample of size n from the specified beta distribution and produce a plot. Remember that to know how an R function works you can type a question mark and its name (e.g., ?density).

```
plot(density(rbeta(n = 10^6, shape1 = 2, shape2 = 4)))
hist(rbeta(10^6, 2, 4), nclass = 100, col = "gray")
```

The GLM in a strict sense has only a single noise component. Often, however, we need several noise components in a statistical model. Such models are introduced in Chapter 4. They include random- or mixed-effects models, hierarchical models, multilevel models, state-space models, or latent-component models. In a sense, they are all fairly similar, although there is a tremendous variety of them. In this book, we usually speak of random-effects or hierarchical models when there is more than a single noise component, except where there is a strong historic precedent favoring one term over the other, such as the state-space models in Chapter 5. In hierarchical models, the definition of a statistical model as being composed of a systematic and a random part must be made separately for each level of the model and what is the random part at one level becomes a component of the systematic part in the next level of the hierarchy.

3.2.2 The Signal Component

The signal component of the model contains the predictable parts of a response or the mean structure of a model. One of the most widely used descriptions of the mean structure is by a linear model, although nonlinear models can be adopted as well (Seber and Wild, 2003). The linear model is one particular way to describe how we imagine that explanatory variables, such as indicators for group memberships or measured covariates, affect an observed response. A linear model is linear in the parameters and does not need to represent a straight line when plotted; most often it does not. This means that the parameters affect the mean response in an additive way, such as α and β in $y = \alpha^*x_1 + \beta^*x_2$, but not as in $y = (x_1^\alpha)/(\beta + x_2)$, where x_1 and x_2 are variables. Most models that ecologists use in their daily work can be represented as linear models: for example, the t-test, simple and multiple linear regressions, ANOVA, ANCOVA, and mixed models.

All these models can be described in several ways, for example, with a plot, in words or in maths. To be able to code a model in the BUGS language, we need to know how to write it mathematically. Therefore, we need to learn how to describe each model by way of matrices and vectors and, in particular, how to build the so-called design matrix of a model. We briefly illustrate these topics with an ANCOVA linear model for a toy data set of nine data points. We assume that y is a response, A is a factor with three levels (i.e., a categorical covariate), and X is a continuous covariate. Here, they are ready to be defined in R:

```
# Define and plot data
y <- c(25, 14, 68, 79, 64, 139, 49, 119, 111)
A <- factor(c(1, 1, 1, 2, 2, 2, 3, 3, 3))
X <- c(1, 14, 22, 2, 9, 20, 2, 13, 22)
plot(X, y, col = c(rep("red", 3), rep("blue", 3), rep("green", 3)),
    xlim = c(-1, 25), ylim = c(0, 140))
```

In R, we can fit an ANCOVA with parallel slopes by issuing the following command:

```
summary(fm <- lm(y ~ A-1 + X))
[...]
Coefficients:
    Estimate Std. Error t value Pr(>|t|)
A1    1.315    19.260    0.068   0.9482
A2   65.218    17.965    3.630   0.0151 *
A3   58.648    19.260    3.045   0.0286 *
X     2.785     1.031    2.701   0.0427 *
[...]
Residual standard error: 25.05 on 5 degrees of freedom
Multiple R-squared: 0.951,    Adjusted R-squared: 0.9117
F-statistic: 24.24 on 4 and 5 DF, p-value: 0.001798
```

This formula language for defining the linear model underlying the ANCOVA or any other linear model is ingenious because it is quick and error-free *if you know how to specify your model*. The downside is that you must know what this statement actually causes R to do. So, let us look under the hood and see what R does when we tell it y ~ A-1 + X. When fitting this model, we are in effect fitting the following linear models:

$$y_i = \alpha_{j(i)} + \beta^*X_i + \varepsilon_i \quad \text{and} \quad \varepsilon_i \sim \text{Normal}(0, \sigma^2)$$

Here, y_i is the response of unit (data point, individual, row) i, and X_i is the value of the continuous explanatory variable x for unit i. Factor A codes for the group membership of each unit (for the meaning of the -1, see below). We have three groups; therefore, the index j is 1, 2, or 3, and we may write $j = A_i$. This means that units with a value $A_i = 1$ have $j = 1$ and α_1 and so forth. There are two parameters in the model, which describe the mean structure of the model, α and β, of which the first is a vector and the second is a scalar. The vector α has three elements, corresponding to the effects of the three levels of factor A. The part $\alpha_{j(i)} + \beta^* X_i$ represents the expected response for unit i, that is, the value expected to be observed in the absence of any noise in the system. Thus, this is the signal part of the response. The noise part consists of that part of the response, which we cannot explain by our linear combination of the explanatory variables: it is represented by the residuals ε_i. Since we know a little bit about these noise terms, we claim that they come from a normal distribution with mean equal to zero and common variance σ^2. In all, the model has five parameters: α_1, α_2, α_3, β, and σ^2. A little confusingly, we may also say that the model has three parameters: the vector α and the scalars β and σ^2.

Other algebraic ways of writing this model clarify perhaps even more the structure of a statistical model as being made up of a signal or systematic part and a noise or random part. The following shows clearly that the response is normally distributed around the values of the linear predictor, $\alpha_{j(i)} + \beta^* X_i$. Now, residuals ε_i are defined only implicitly.

$$y_i \sim \text{Normal}(\alpha_{j(i)} + \beta^* X_i, \sigma^2).$$

A further possibility is to express μ_i as the expected response of unit i in the absence of any random noise. It is the same as the value of the linear predictor:

$$y_i \sim \text{Normal}(\mu_i, \sigma^2), \text{ with } \mu_i = \alpha_{j(i)} + \beta^* X_i$$

Being able to write a linear model in algebra greatly simplifies the coding of a model in WinBUGS. Most models, when written in the BUGS language, in fact very much resemble their algebraic description.

Yet another way to write this model for our data set is by way of matrices and vectors:

$$
\begin{pmatrix} 25 \\ 14 \\ 68 \\ 79 \\ 64 \\ 139 \\ 49 \\ 119 \\ 111 \end{pmatrix}
=
\begin{pmatrix}
1 & 0 & 0 & 1 \\
1 & 0 & 0 & 14 \\
1 & 0 & 0 & 22 \\
0 & 1 & 0 & 2 \\
0 & 1 & 0 & 9 \\
0 & 1 & 0 & 20 \\
0 & 0 & 1 & 2 \\
0 & 0 & 1 & 13 \\
0 & 0 & 1 & 22
\end{pmatrix}
\times
\begin{pmatrix} \alpha_1 \\ \alpha_2 \\ \alpha_3 \\ \beta \end{pmatrix}
+
\begin{pmatrix} \varepsilon_1 \\ \varepsilon_2 \\ \varepsilon_3 \\ \varepsilon_4 \\ \varepsilon_5 \\ \varepsilon_6 \\ \varepsilon_7 \\ \varepsilon_8 \\ \varepsilon_9 \end{pmatrix}
, \text{ with } \varepsilon_i \sim \text{Normal}(0, \sigma^2)
$$

From left to right, we have response vector, design matrix, parameter vector, and residual vector. The design matrix (also called model matrix or X matrix) multiplied with the parameter vector produces another vector, which is the expected value of the response for each unit. This expected value is also called the linear predictor and is the same as μ_i above. For example, the value of the linear predictor for the first data point is given by $1^*\alpha_1 + 0^*\alpha_2 + 0^*\alpha_3 + 1^*\beta$.

It is useful to practice so that you can jump back and forth between different ways of describing the same model: the R formula language, in algebra, and using matrices and vectors. We need this clear understanding of the linear model if we want to succeed in our modeling with WinBUGS. This may be awkward at first, but a tremendous benefit is that this finally forces on us what we may not have achieved before: a clear understanding of linear models.

The interpretation of the elements of the vector of the mean parameters $(\alpha_1, \alpha_2, \alpha_3, \beta)$ depends on the way the design matrix is structured, and there are different ways for doing this. These variations are called para-meterizations of a model; they are equivalent ways of writing what is effectively the same model. Sometimes one parameterization may be more convenient and sometimes another. WinBUGS can be very sensitive to the choice of parameterization of a model; sometimes one will not work at all, for example, the chains would not mix, but another will result in beautiful mixing. Hence, it is important that we know how to specify different parameterizations of the same model.

One clever trick when trying to understand the design matrix of a model is the use of the R function model.matrix(), especially for those of you who have some experience in fitting linear models with a model-definition language such as that in R. We have had cases in which we did not quite understand the structure of a complicated linear model that we wanted to fit in WinBUGS. To understand the design matrix of the model and, therefore, to be able to specify the model in WinBUGS, we went into R and used model.matrix() to find out how the design matrix of the model we wanted to specify in WinBUGS looked like.

As an example, two possible parameterizations of our ANCOVA model are those which we specify by the following R commands:

```
# Effects or treatment contrast parameterization
model.matrix(~ A + X)
  (Intercept) A2 A3  X
1           1  0  0  1
2           1  0  0 14
3           1  0  0 22
4           1  1  0  2
5           1  1  0  9
6           1  1  0 20
7           1  0  1  2
```

```
8                1   0   1   13
9                1   0   1   22
[ ... ]

# Means parameterization
model.matrix(~ A-1 + X)
  A1 A2 A3    X
1  1  0  0    1
2  1  0  0   14
3  1  0  0   22
4  0  1  0    2
5  0  1  0    9
6  0  1  0   20
7  0  0  1    2
8  0  0  1   13
9  0  0  1   22
[ ... ]
```

The former is the R default called the effects or treatment contrast parameterization. It specifies the linear model in terms of a baseline response, which here is that for the first level of factor A, plus effects of the other levels of A relative to the first level and effects of each unit change in the covariate X. Hence, the intercept is the mean response of units with level 1 of factor A at $X = 0$, and the parameters corresponding to the design matrix columns A_2 and A_3 quantify the *difference* in the mean response in levels 2 and 3, relative to that of level 1, for a given value of X. The parameter representing column X in the design matrix is the common slope of the regression of y on X, regardless of which group a unit belongs to. In contrast, in the means parameterization, the first three parameters directly represent the mean response for each level of factor A at $X = 0$, while the meaning of the parameter represented by the column X is the same as before.

The overly simple setting chosen here allows one to see the main features of these topics very clearly, and in real-world modeling, where one typically has many explanatory variables, one must strive for an understanding of the linear model by breaking down the problem into its smallest understandable parts. In reality, there may be main effects and interaction effects and perhaps aliasing between columns of the design matrix, meaning some parameters cannot be estimated independently. This complicates the construction of the design matrix even more (although most problems are really ones of bookkeeping). We will not go further into these topics, but refer you to any of a huge number of books that explain the linear model, such as Kéry (2010) or chapter 6 in E. Cooch and G. White's free *Gentle Introduction to Program MARK* (www.phidot.org/software/mark/docs/book).

This concludes our very brief description of how the signal component of a linear statistical model is built using the design matrix, which, when matrix multiplied with the parameter vector, yields the value of the linear predictor or the expected or "typical" response, μ_i, which is also what you get in R by typing `model.matrix(~A+X) %*% fm$coef`.

3.2.3 Bringing the Noise and the Signal Components Together: The Link Function

In the linear models mentioned so far in this chapter, we assumed a normal distribution for the random part of the response. Thus, we directly wrote the response y_i as a simple additive combination of the signal μ_i and the noise ε_i. For responses that cannot be modeled with a normal distribution, this direct combination is no longer possible. For instance, directly adding noise from a Poisson or a binomial distribution to the value of a linear predictor would typically result in inadmissible values for the response, for example, fractional or negative counts.

The big advantage of generalized linear models (GLMs) is that we can apply a linear model to the response indirectly: namely, to a transformation of the mean response. The function that transforms the expected response is called the *link function*. The reason for that name should now be clear: the link function allows us to link the noise component and the signal components in a model. In this way, the useful concepts of linear models can be carried over to a vastly larger class of models.

The classical way to describe a GLM is by three components: a random part (noise), a systematic part (signal), and a link function. More generally, for response y_i, we can write the following:

1. Random part of the response (the noise)—a statistical distribution f with mean response μ_i:

$$y_i \sim f(\mu_i)$$

2. A link function g, which is applied to the mean response μ_i:

$$g(\mu_i) = \eta_i$$

3. Systematic part of the response (the signal)—a linear predictor (η_i), for example, for a simple linear regression–type of GLM:

$$\eta_i = \alpha + \beta^* x_i$$

We can describe a GLM succinctly in only two lines:

$$y_i \sim f(\mu_i)$$

$$g(\mu_i) = \alpha + \beta^* x_i$$

This is exactly the way in which GLMs are specified in the BUGS language, and this is the reason why BUGS is so great if you want to really understand ,GLMs. The GLM concept gives you considerable creative freedom to combine the three components of a GLM, but there are typically pairs of response distributions and link functions that go together particularly well. These link functions are called canonical link functions and are the identity link for normal responses ($\eta_i = \mu_i$), the log link for Poisson responses ($\eta_i = \log(\mu_i)$), and the logit link for binomial responses ($\eta_i = \log(\mu_i)/\log(1 - \mu_i)$). Together, these three standard GLMs make up a vast number of statistical methods used in population ecology and elsewhere; for an overview, see Kéry (2010).

The broad scope of the GLM is one reason for the great importance of the GLM for you. The other one, which we will see many times later in the book, is that the GLM represents the main building block for many more complicated models, especially hierarchical models. Many of the most exciting ecological models for inference about populations can be viewed simply as a sequence of coupled GLMs (Royle and Dorazio, 2008).

3.3 POISSON GLM IN R AND WinBUGS FOR MODELING TIME SERIES OF COUNTS

The Poisson distribution is defined for positive integers at 0, 1, 2, … and hence is a suitable model for counts under the assumption of independence and spatial or other randomness. It describes the "residual variation" (noise), after any kinds of systematic effects (signal) in the Poisson mean have been taken account of, for example, in the form of covariate effects.

The Poisson distribution has a single parameter, the intensity or rate parameter λ representing the expected count. The variance of a Poisson random variable is not a free parameter, rather it is identical to the mean (expected) count. In practice, this strong assumption about the mean–variance relationship is frequently violated and the variance of counts is larger than their mean. There are various ways to take account of this. The conceptually easiest is perhaps the introduction of data-level random effects to take account of such overdispersion (Section 4.2).

For an example of a Poisson GLM, let us assume we model counts C_i from a number of years i. Here is the algebraic description of the Poisson GLM for count C_i in year i with a single covariate X:

1. Random part of the response (statistical distribution):

$$C_i \sim \text{Poisson}(\lambda_i)$$

2. Link of random and systematic part (log link function):

$$\log(\lambda_i) = \eta_i$$

3. Systematic part of the response (linear predictor η_i):

$$\eta_i = \alpha + \beta^* X_i$$

Here, λ_i is the expected count (the mean response) in year i on the arithmetic scale, η_i is the expected count in year i on the link scale (i.e., the linear predictor), X_i is the value of covariate X in year i, and α and β are the two parameters of the log-linear regression of these counts on the covariate. We will next look at the generation and analysis of Poisson GLM data for a simulated and also for a real data set.

3.3.1 Generation and Analysis of Simulated Data

We define a function that generates Poisson counts of peregrine falcons (Fig. 3.1) for one population over n years. The parameter values are inspired by actual data from the French Jura mountains (Monneret, 2006), see Section 3.3.2. In this example, the linear predictor will be a cubic polynomial function of time, $\eta_i = \alpha + \beta_1^* X_i + \beta_2^* X_i^2 + \beta_3^* X_i^3$. In this section, we will, first, show how a GLM is analyzed in the frequentist framework in R and in the Bayesian framework using WinBUGS and illustrate how similar numerically the resulting estimates are. Second, as this is the first time we run WinBUGS, we explain each step of the analysis in more detail than later in this book.

FIGURE 3.1   Peregrine falcon (*Falco peregrinus*), Switzerland (Photograph by B. Renevey).

```
data.fn <- function(n = 40, alpha = 3.5576, beta1 = -0.0912,
    beta2 = 0.0091, beta3 = -0.00014){
    # n: Number of years
    # alpha, beta1, beta2, beta3: coefficients of a
    #    cubic polynomial of count on year

    # Generate values of time covariate
    year <- 1:n

    # Signal: Build up systematic part of the GLM
    log.expected.count <- alpha + beta1 * year + beta2 * year^2 + beta3 *
        year^3
    expected.count <- exp(log.expected.count)

    # Noise: generate random part of the GLM: Poisson noise around
    expected counts
    C <- rpois(n = n, lambda = expected.count)

    # Plot simulated data
    plot(year, C, type = "b", lwd = 2, col = "black", main = "", las = 1,
        ylab = "Population size", xlab = "Year", cex.lab = 1.2,
        cex.axis = 1.2)
    lines(year, expected.count, type = "l", lwd = 3, col = "red")

    return(list(n = n, alpha = alpha, beta1 = beta1, beta2 = beta2,
        beta3 = beta3, year = year, expected.count = expected.count, C = C))
    }
```

We obtain one realization of the stochastic process, that is, population counts over 40 years, and plot the population trajectory over time (Fig. 3.2a)

```
data <- data.fn()
```

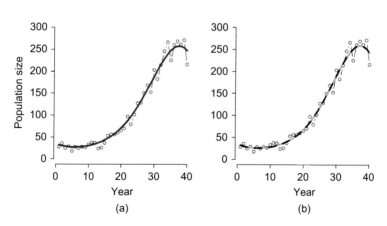

FIGURE 3.2   Simulated population size of peregrines in the French Jura over 40 years. (a) Expected population size (red) and the observed data, the realized population size (black). (b) Observed data (black) and estimated population trajectories from a frequentist (green) and a Bayesian analysis (blue) of a Poisson regression with cubic polynomial effects of year. The R code to produce this figure slightly differs from the one shown in this book.

Next, we analyze this data set in R and in WinBUGS. Fitting a GLM in the frequentist mode of analysis, using the method of maximum likelihood, is trivially easy in statistical software like R that have canned functions such as glm(). Here is the analysis using R; one or two lines of code suffice. Up to Poisson sampling error, this will recover parameter estimates that resemble the values of the input.

```
fm <- glm(C ~ year + I(year^2) + I(year^3), family = poisson, data = data)
summary(fm)

Call:
glm(formula = C ~ year + I(year^2) + I(year^3), family = poisson,
    data = data)

Deviance Residuals:
    Min       1Q    Median        3Q       Max
-1.9036  -0.5815    0.2250    0.8888    1.4972

Coefficients:
                Estimate Std. Error z value Pr(>|z|)
(Intercept)    3.570e+00  1.159e-01  30.797  < 2e-16 ***
year          -1.099e-01  2.023e-02  -5.431 5.61e-08 ***
I(year^2)      1.026e-02  1.005e-03  10.204  < 2e-16 ***
I(year^3)     -1.578e-04  1.467e-05 -10.756  < 2e-16 ***
—

Signif. codes: 0 '***' 0.001 '**' 0.01 '*' 0.05 '.' 0.1 ' ' 1

(Dispersion parameter for poisson family taken to be 1)

    Null deviance: 2771.076  on 39  degrees of freedom
Residual deviance:   42.729  on 36  degrees of freedom
AIC: 297.77

Number of Fisher Scoring iterations: 4
```

We note in passing that in order to arrive at this solution, R had to turn the handle on a blackbox called "Fisher Scoring" four times.

In contrast, the code for fitting the same model in WinBUGS is less succinct: about 20 lines compared with 1–2 for the same analysis in R. And this is only for the description of the model in the BUGS language; more lines of code are required to actually conduct the analysis of that model with WinBUGS from R.

```
# Specify model in BUGS language
sink("GLM_Poisson.txt")
cat("
model {

# Priors
alpha ~ dunif(-20, 20)
beta1 ~ dunif(-10, 10)
```

```
beta2 ~ dunif(-10, 10)
beta3 ~ dunif(-10, 10)

# Likelihood: Note key components of a GLM on one line each
for (i in 1:n){
    C[i] ~ dpois(lambda[i])              # 1. Distribution for random part
    log(lambda[i]) <- log.lambda[i]      # 2. Link function
    log.lambda[i] <- alpha + beta1 * year[i] + beta2 * pow(year[i],2) +
        beta3 * pow(year[i],3)           # 3. Linear predictor
    } # i
}
",fill = TRUE)
sink()
```

In this book, we present each WinBUGS analysis in a common lay-out, by first writing a text file with the model definition in the BUGS language, followed by all the other ingredients that the function bugs() in the R2WinBUGS package (Sturtz et al., 2005) requires to instruct Win-BUGS from R. Remember that before executing the following code, you must define an R object called bugs.dir that contains the address of WinBUGS. For a Swiss-German locale, this might be

```
bugs.dir <- "c:/Programme/WinBUGS14/"
```

Next, we bundle into an R list the data needed for the analysis by WinBUGS.

```
# Bundle data
win.data <- list(C = data$C, n = length(data$C), year = data$year)
```

The next step is to define initial values for the estimated quantities. WinBUGS can generate initial values by drawing them from their priors, so it is not necessary to give inits for all estimands. Nevertheless, when running WinBUGS by calling it from R, we need to define inits for at least one quantity. For complex models, it is often vital to choose good initial values because otherwise WinBUGS may crash. It is useful to define a function to define inits. This function is then executed once for each Markov chain run in the analysis.

```
# Initial values
inits <- function() list(alpha = runif(1, -2, 2), beta1 = runif(1, -3, 3))
```

Next, we write a list with the quantities we want to estimate ("monitor" as WinBUGS calls it), that is, for which we want WinBUGS to save the draws from the joint posterior distribution. This includes derived quanti-ties such as lambda here.

```
# Parameters monitored
params <- c("alpha", "beta1", "beta2", "beta3", "lambda")
```

Before running the analysis, we set the MCMC characteristics: the number of draws per chain, thinning rate, burnin length, and the number of chains. The burnin should be long enough to discard the initial part of the Markov chains that have not yet converged to the stationary distribution. We typically determine the required burnin in initial trials. Thinning is useful to save computer disk space. We run multiple chains to check for convergence.

```
# MCMC settings
ni <- 2000
nt <- 2
nb <- 1000
nc <- 3
```

Now, we have defined all R objects that we need as arguments for our call to R function bugs(). When calling WinBUGS from R, we usually set the argument debug = TRUE. WinBUGS then remains open after the requested number of iterations has been produced, and we can visually inspect whether the chains have converged, or in the case of an error, directly read the log file.

```
# Call WinBUGS from R
out <- bugs(data = win.data, inits = inits, parameters.to.save = params,
    model.file = "GLM_Poisson.txt", n.chains = nc, n.thin = nt,
    n.iter = ni, n.burnin = nb, debug = TRUE, bugs.directory = bugs.dir,
    working.directory = getwd())
```

Most shockingly, WinBUGS almost immediately crashes, claiming that there was an "undefined real result" trap. Why on Earth should you continue with this book (or even buy the book!) when GLMs can be fitted so very much more easily using functions in software such as R? There are at least three reasons for why you should continue:

1. You can use the same kind of analysis for *much* more complex models, models that you will hardly or not at all be able to fit with R. So, understanding how to fit the simpler models in WinBUGS rather than in R is an essential preparation for that.
2. You conduct a Bayesian analysis instead of a frequentist one. The Bayesian view of statistics has several advantages as argued by many (e.g., McCarthy, 2007; Link and Barker, 2010; also see Chapter 2).
3. The model that you fit is more transparent when using the BUGS language to describe it than when describing it in R. So, there is a huge heuristic benefit of statistical modeling in WinBUGS: that of actually understanding the model you are fitting.

But back to our Bayesian analysis of that really simple model, our Poisson GLM: why was WinBUGS not able to get a solution in this simple case? The answer is that we need to ensure that covariate values are not too far away from zero, that is, that they have neither too large negative nor too large positive values. Note that $year^3$ goes up to $40^3 = 64,000$, and this causes numerical overflow (covariate values in the 10s or even in the 100s should not be a problem). To avoid this problem, we usually center or standardize our covariates. We could use the usual standardization by subtracting the mean and dividing by the standard deviation; this results in transformed covariates with approximately zero mean and unit standard deviation. However, any other transformation usually also works, provided that the range of the transformed covariate does not extend to far on either side of 0. Here, we subtract 20 and divide 10. This is easy and the only cost is when we want to present the results and when we want to compare the input values with our parameter estimates. We will graph the results of the model fitted in WinBUGS with the standardized year covariate. This will convince you that we have actually fitted the equivalent model. So next we repeat the analysis using the standardized covariate values. We can do this simply by adapting the statement in which we package the data and then recycle the rest of the code.

```
# Bundle data
mean.year <- mean(data$year)          # Mean of year covariate
sd.year <- sd(data$year)              # SD of year covariate
win.data <- list(C = data$C, n = length(data$C),
   year = (data$year - mean.year) / sd.year)

# Call WinBUGS from R (BRT < 1 min)
out <- bugs(data = win.data, inits = inits, parameters.to.save = params,
   model.file = "GLM_Poisson.txt", n.chains = nc, n.thin = nt,
   n.iter = ni, n.burnin = nb, debug = TRUE, bugs.directory = bugs.dir,
   working.directory = getwd())
```

This works smoothly and produces a nice first bit of output from our first Bayesian analysis; how reassuring! To return the data into R, you have to manually exit WinBUGS and can then obtain a numerical summary of the Bayesian analysis.

```
# Summarize posteriors
print(out, dig = 3)
Inference for Bugs model at "GLM_Poisson.txt", fit using WinBUGS,
3 chains, each with 2000 iterations (first 1000 discarded), n.thin = 2
n.sims = 1500 iterations saved
              mean     sd    2.5%     25%     50%     75%   97.5%  Rhat n.eff
alpha        4.268  0.030   4.208   4.248   4.268   4.288   4.324 1.005   410
beta1        1.308  0.042   1.230   1.277   1.307   1.338   1.391 1.003   590
beta2        0.076  0.024   0.031   0.060   0.076   0.093   0.122 1.013   480
beta3       -0.253  0.022  -0.297  -0.268  -0.253  -0.237  -0.212 1.006   340
```

```
lambda[1]    32.367 3.243  26.579 30.000 32.340 34.492 38.965 1.007   340
lambda[2]    29.815 2.562  25.184 27.997 29.850 31.490 35.057 1.006   390
lambda[3]    27.993 2.068  24.229 26.550 27.995 29.402 32.111 1.005   480
   [ ... ]
lambda[38]  257.081 6.451 245.100 252.600 256.900 261.500 269.800 1.001  1500
lambda[39]  251.555 7.723 237.442 246.000 251.300 256.700 267.252 1.000  1500
lambda[40]  242.160 9.271 225.147 235.700 241.900 248.325 261.400 1.000  1500
deviance    293.695 2.622 290.300 291.800 293.200 295.000 300.700 1.001  1500
```

For each parameter, n.eff is a crude measure of effective sample size, and Rhat is
    the potential scale reduction factor (at convergence, Rhat=1).

DIC info (using the rule, pD = Dbar-Dhat)
pD = 3.9 and DIC = 297.6
DIC is an estimate of expected predictive error (lower deviance is better).

We note that there is a plot function for R objects of the bugs class. Typing plot(out) will produce a useful graphical summary of the Bayesian analysis, but we do not show this plot here.

Now, before we even inspect the parameter estimates, we should make sure that their Markov chains have converged. Only then are the random draws produced a valid sample from the desired target distribution, which is the posterior distribution of these parameters. Convergence can never be proven; what *looks* like convergence may indeed sometimes represent chains that have definitely not reached their stationary distribution (see Kéry, 2010, for some nice examples of this). However, in many cases, visual and numerical checks are adequate, and this is what we do in this book: we always inspect the time-series plots in the WinBUGS log file and the values of the Rhat statistics in the table of posterior summaries produced by the function bugs(). Rhat is a formal convergence test criterion comparing the among- and the within-chain variance in an ANOVA fashion; values around 1 suggest the absence of a "chain effect" and therefore convergence (Brooks and Gelman, 1998). Often, 1.1 or 1.2 is taken as an Rhat-value that indicates convergence (Gelman and Hill, 2007).

The eye is quite good at picking up a pattern in a graph, and this visual assessment of the likely convergence of chains will complement the numerical assessment by the Rhat values (Fig. 3.3). With experience, you will get a trained eye because you will have seen so many plots of chains that have converged (based on Rhat) and so many others that have not. With debug = TRUE as an argument of the function bugs(), WinBUGS stays open after execution of the desired number of iterations, and the full Win-BUGS functionality can be used for further analyses. For instance, additional iterations could be asked for and numerical summaries produced. However, one may also simply skim over the time-series plots of all monitored parameters to see whether any of them looks like they have not converged (yet). At convergence, the chains should oscillate randomly around a horizontal level and (when three parallel chains are run) should look "grassy" (Link and Barker, 2010). There should not be a sustained trend.

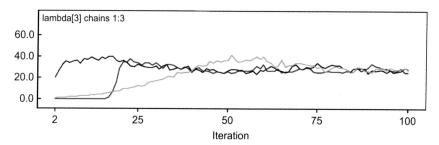

FIGURE 3.3 Example of a time-series plot with three chains for one parameter (the expected count in year 3). The chains have converged after around 75 iterations and show good mixing. Thus we would repeat the analysis and might set the burnin to at least 75, but probably even to several 100 to be on the safe side.

Furthermore, the lines representing the different chains (usually, 2 or 3) should be strongly interspersed: if this is the case, one says that the chains mix well. In our simple model, we can inspect the time-series plots and see that after the burnin of length 200, the chains of all parameters have indeed converged. We arrive at the same conclusion based on the Rhat values.

To see what initial nonconvergence looks like, you may repeat the analysis with the below MCMC settings. Looking at the plots in WinBUGS shows that convergence is generally achieved after some 75 iterations (Fig. 3.3).

```
# New MCMC settings with essentially no burnin
ni <- 100
nt <- 1
nb <- 1

# Call WinBUGS from R (BRT <1 min)
tmp <- bugs(data = win.data, inits = inits, parameters.to.save = params,
    model.file = "GLM_Poisson.txt", n.chains = nc, n.thin = nt,
    n.iter = ni, n.burnin = nb, debug = TRUE, bugs.directory = bugs.dir,
    working.directory = getwd())
```

Once we are satisfied with the convergence of the chains, we can see what we learn from the analysis of the model. For instance, we can plot the Poisson means (the `lambda` parameters) for each year; these represent the expected peregrine counts in each year. We plot them in the same figure as the predicted values from the analysis of the same model using the R function `glm()`, and we will see that our inference is virtually identical (Fig. 3.2b).

```
plot(1:40, data$C, type = "b", lwd = 2, col = "black", main = "", las = 1,
    ylab = "Population size", xlab = "Year")
R.predictions <- predict(glm(C ~ year + I(year^2) + I(year^3),
    family = poisson, data = data), type = "response")
lines(1:40, R.predictions, type = "l", lwd = 3, col = "green")
WinBUGS.predictions <- out$mean$lambda
lines(1:40, WinBUGS.predictions, type = "l", lwd = 3, col = "blue", lty = 2)
```

We see that the predicted population sizes are so similar from R and WinBUGS that we can hardly see both lines. This is a very common observation: typically, inference from a frequentist and a Bayesian analysis of a statistical model is numerically almost identical when noninformative priors are used. Let us plot the two predictions side by side to convince us that they are indeed so similar:

```
cbind(R.predictions, WinBUGS.predictions)
   R.predictions WinBUGS.predictions
1       32.14482           32.36720
2       29.66780           29.81523
3       27.89637           27.99280
   [ .... ]
38     256.76388          257.08067
39     251.21847          251.55480
40     241.79082          242.16020
```

R was able to recover parameter estimates that were very similar to those that we input when assembling the data set. Now we see that the predicted population trajectory from the frequentist analysis in R, using untransformed covariate values, and from the Bayesian analysis in WinBUGS, using transformed covariate values, are virtually identical.

There is always a trade-off between simplicity of model fitting and flexibility: R functions such as glm() are very handy, but they can only fit a relatively limited array of models. In addition, and perhaps more importantly, the model fitted with a function like glm() is much less transparent than when the same model is fit in WinBUGS. We will see this in the random-effects extension to GLMs in Chapter 4; in WinBUGS, it is conceptually trivial to go from the pure Poisson GLM to the Poisson-lognormal mixed-effects GLM or Poisson generalized linear mixed model (GLMM). In contrast, in R we would have to use a different setting of the same function (glm(, family=quasipoisson)) or use an altogether different function, such as lmer().

3.3.2 Analysis of Real Data Set

We will repeat this analysis now using actual data by analyzing the trajectory of the peregrine population breeding in the French Jura from 1964 to 2003 (R.-J.Monneret, personal communication). Note that by merely conducting this analysis, we implicitly make the assumption that the survey coverage and detection probability of peregrine pairs in the French Jura have not changed in a sustained way over time, otherwise our perceived trends will be distorted (see, e.g., Nichols et al., 2009; Kéry, 2010; Chapter 5). If we have doubts about this important assumption, then a survey design should be used that allows detection probability to be estimated and therefore corrected for. The metapopulation estimation methods in Chapters 12 and 13 illustrate ways this could be done in the context of population studies of raptors such as the peregrine. Another feature that our model does not address either is possible temporal auto-correlation. To add this, we could use models developed in Chapter 5.

```
# Read data
peregrine <- read.table("falcons.txt", header = TRUE)
```

We attach the data set to be able to directly write the variable names when addressing them.

```
attach(peregrine)
```

The data set contains the counts of adult pairs (Pairs), reproductive pairs (R.Pairs), and fledged young (Eyasses) for each of 40 years. We plot variable Pairs (Fig. 3.4a).

```
plot(Year, Pairs, type = "b", lwd = 2, main = "", las = 1, ylab = "Pair
    count", xlab = "Year", ylim = c(0, 200), pch = 16)
```

We fit the model in WinBUGS and plot the predictions, vector lambda, into the same plot (Fig. 3.4a, blue line). We will use the same R/WinBUGS code as before.

```
# Bundle data
mean.year <- mean(1:length(Year))       # Mean of year covariate
sd.year <- sd(1:length(Year))           # SD of year covariate
win.data <- list(C = Pairs, n = length(Pairs), year = (1: length(Year) -
    mean.year) / sd.year)

# Initial values
inits <- function() list(alpha = runif(1, -2, 2), beta1 = runif(1, -3, 3))
```

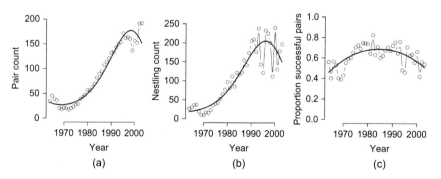

(a)   (b)   (c)

FIGURE 3.4 Analysis of (a) population size (number of territorial pairs), (b) fecundity (total number of fledged young), and (c) proportion of successful pairs in the peregrine population of the French Jura from 1964 to 2003 (data courtesy of R.-J. Monneret). Observed data are in black and Bayesian posterior means from WinBUGS in blue. The R code to produce this figure slightly differs from the one shown in this book.

```
# Parameters monitored
params <- c("alpha", "beta1", "beta2", "beta3", "lambda")

# MCMC settings
ni <- 2500
nt <- 2
nb <- 500
nc <- 3

# Call WinBUGS from R (BRT < 1 min)
out1 <- bugs(data = win.data, inits = inits, parameters.to.save = params,
    model.file = "GLM_Poisson.txt", n.chains = nc, n.thin = nt,
    n.iter = ni, n.burnin = nb, debug = TRUE, bugs.directory = bugs.dir,
    working.directory = getwd())

# Summarize posteriors
print(out1, dig = 3)
               mean     sd    2.5%      25%      50%      75%    97.5%  Rhat n.eff
alpha         4.234  0.030   4.176    4.214    4.234    4.254    4.293 1.006   400
beta1         1.115  0.047   1.022    1.082    1.116    1.147    1.204 1.009   250
beta2         0.005  0.024  -0.040   -0.012    0.005    0.021    0.052 1.006   350
beta3        -0.233  0.025  -0.280   -0.250   -0.234   -0.215   -0.183 1.010   220
lambda[1]    32.258  3.231  26.499   29.880   32.160   34.450   38.980 1.005   450
lambda[2]    30.221  2.572  25.600   28.367   30.155   31.942   35.550 1.004   570
lambda[3]    28.787  2.088  25.020   27.310   28.710   30.150   33.060 1.003   830
[ ... ]
lambda[38] 169.689  5.294 159.700  166.100  169.700  173.300  179.900 1.001  2800
lambda[39] 162.276  6.248 150.397  158.000  162.200  166.500  174.700 1.002  1500
lambda[40] 152.733  7.347 138.797  147.700  152.600  157.600  167.202 1.003   920
deviance   322.348  2.785 318.900  320.300  321.700  323.600  329.400 1.004   590
[ ... ]
DIC info (using the rule, pD = Dbar-Dhat)
pD = 4.0 and DIC = 326.3
```

Convergence of all chains looks decent; the values of Rhat in the summary are close to 1, and the plots of the chains in WinBUGS look nice. Therefore, we now plot the predicted population trajectory into the previous plot (Fig. 3.4a).

```
WinBUGS.predictions <- out1$mean$lambda
lines(Year, WinBUGS.predictions, type = "l", lwd = 3, col = "blue", lty = 2)
```

3.4 POISSON GLM FOR MODELING FECUNDITY

The Poisson distribution is the standard model for any kind of unbounded count data. Counts could be alleles, individuals, family or other groups, or species. To make this very clear, we will swiftly conduct an analogous analysis for the counts of fledged young, that is, for fecundity, in this same peregrine population (Monneret, 2006). We will use the same model and code and directly plot a Bayesian analysis of a cubic polynomial of the number of fledged young on year (Fig. 3.4b).

```
plot(Year, Eyasses, type = "b", lwd = 2, main = "", las = 1,
    ylab = "Nestling count", xlab = "Year", ylim = c(0, 260), pch = 16)

# Bundle data
mean.year <- mean(1:length(Year))      # Mean of year covariate
sd.year <- sd(1:length(Year))          # SD of year covariate
win.data <- list(C = Eyasses, n = length(Eyasses), year =
    (1: length(Year) – mean.year) / sd.year)

# Call WinBUGS from R (BRT < 1 min)
out2 <- bugs(data = win.data, inits = inits, parameters.to.save =
    params, model.file = "GLM_Poisson.txt", n.chains = nc, n.thin = nt,
    n.iter = ni, n.burnin = nb, debug = TRUE, bugs.directory = bugs.dir,
    working.directory = getwd())
```

Skimming over the plots of the Markov chains in WinBUGS and inspecting the values of Rhat in the summary (not shown) suggest that convergence has been reached. Therefore, we are satisfied to plot the estimates under the model (Fig. 3.4b).

```
# Plot predictions
WinBUGS.predictions <- out2$mean$lambda
lines(Year, WinBUGS.predictions, type = "l", lwd = 3, col = "blue")
```

3.5 BINOMIAL GLM FOR MODELING BOUNDED COUNTS OR PROPORTIONS

We saw that the Poisson distribution is the standard model for unbounded count data. However, frequently we have counts that are bounded by some upper limit. For instance, when modeling the number of females in a brood, counts of female nestlings cannot exceed the size of a brood. Similarly, when modeling the number of successful broods, counts cannot exceed the total number of broods monitored. As a special case, when modeling the number of survival events for an individual over a single time step, the count cannot exceed 1. The standard model for all these kinds of counts is the binomial distribution. It arises when N independent individuals all have the same probability p of experiencing some event (for instance, being female, successful or a survivor). The number of events counted (C) will follow a binomial distribution. A special case with $N = 1$ is called a Bernoulli distribution.

As our example for a binomial GLM, we will model the number of successful pairs (C_i) among all monitored pairs (N_i) in year i for a total of 40 years. We will treat year as a continuous covariate and fit a quadratic polynomial. That model can be written like the following:

1. Random part of the response (statistical distribution):

$$C_i \sim \text{Binomial}(N_i, p_i)$$

2. Link of random and systematic part (logit link function):

$$\text{logit}(p_i) = \log\left(\frac{p_i}{1 - p_i}\right) = \eta_i$$

3. Systematic part of the response (linear predictor η_i):

$$\eta_i = \alpha + \beta_1{}^* X_i + \beta_2{}^* X_i^2$$

Here, p_i is the expected proportion of successful pairs on the arithmetic scale. It is the mean response for each of the N_i trials. η_i is that same proportion on the (logit) link scale. The primary parameter of the binomial distribution is p_i. It is often called the success probability because there are two events: the one of focal interest termed a success and the other a failure. In contrast, the binomial total, or trial or sample size N_i is not normally a parameter; rather, it is typically observed or a fixed element of the design.

The usual link function adopted for a binomial GLM is the logit. It maps the probability scale (i.e., the range from 0 to 1) onto the entire real line (i.e., from $-\infty$ to ∞) and ensures that a linear model does not result in probabilities outside of that admissible range, that is, below 0 or above 1. The rest of the model (the linear predictor η_i) is up to your data, your questions, and your imagination. Here, α, β_1, and β_2 are simply the three parameters of the logit-linear regression of the unobserved proportions on covariate *Year*. Next, we simulate binomial data for the proportion of successful peregrine pairs and analyze them with WinBUGS.

3.5.1 Generation and Analysis of Simulated Data

We write a function that simulates data from this simple setting that typically leads to the adoption of a binomial GLM.

```
data.fn <- function(nyears = 40, alpha = 0, beta1 = -0.1, beta2 = -0.9){
    # nyears: Number of years
    # alpha, beta1, beta2: coefficients

    # Generate untransformed and transformed values of time covariate
    year <- 1:nyears
    YR <- (year-round(nyears/2)) / (nyears / 2)
```

```
# Generate values of binomial totals (N)
N <- round(runif(nyears, min = 20, max = 100))

# Signal: build up systematic part of the GLM
exp.p <- plogis(alpha + beta1 * YR + beta2 * (YR^2))

# Noise: generate random part of the GLM: Binomial noise around
expected counts (which is N)
C <- rbinom(n = nyears, size = N, prob = exp.p)

# Plot simulated data
plot(year, C/N, type = "b", lwd = 2, col = "black", main = "", las = 1,
    ylab = "Proportion successful pairs", xlab = "Year", ylim = c(0, 1))
points(year, exp.p, type = "l", lwd = 3, col = "red")

return(list(nyears = nyears, alpha = alpha, beta1 = beta1,
    beta2 = beta2, year = year, YR = YR, exp.p = exp.p, C = C, N = N))
}
```

We create one data set, which is inspired by the data in Section 3.5.2.

```
data <- data.fn(nyears = 40, alpha = 1, beta1 = -0.03, beta2 = -0.9)
```

The model as written in the BUGS language is a trivial variant of the Poisson GLM encountered earlier; the key word for the binomial distribution is dbin(). Remember that the binomial distribution in WinBUGS is specified with the success parameter (p) *before* the binomial total (N).

```
# Specify model in BUGS language
sink("GLM_Binomial.txt")
cat("
model {

# Priors
alpha ~ dnorm(0, 0.001)
beta1 ~ dnorm(0, 0.001)
beta2 ~ dnorm(0, 0.001)

# Likelihood
for (i in 1:nyears){
    C[i] ~ dbin(p[i], N[i])        # 1. Distribution for random part
    logit(p[i]) <- alpha + beta1 * year[i] + beta2 * pow(year[i],2) # Link
        function and linear predictor
    }
}
", fill = TRUE)
sink()
```

We choose a different scaling of year this time and simply subtract 20 and divide the result by 20. This leads to values of the covariate that range from about −1 to 1.

```
# Bundle data
win.data <- list(C = data$C, N = data$N, nyears = length(data$C),
    year = data$YR)
```

```
# Initial values
inits <- function() list(alpha = runif(1, -1, 1), beta1 =
    runif(1, -1, 1), beta2 = runif(1, -1, 1))
```

```
# Parameters monitored
params <- c("alpha", "beta1", "beta2", "p")
```

```
# MCMC settings
ni <- 2500
nt <- 2
nb <- 500
nc <- 3
```

```
# Call WinBUGS from R (BRT < 1 min)
out <- bugs(data = win.data, inits = inits, parameters.to.save = params,
    model.file = "GLM_Binomial.txt", n.chains = nc, n.thin = nt,
    n.iter = ni, n.burnin = nb, debug = TRUE, bugs.directory = bugs.dir,
    working.directory = getwd())
```

We first check convergence by looking at the plots in WinBUGS and skimming over the values in the column entitled Rhat in the summary of the analysis in R (not shown). Both tests look very satisfactory, so we add a plot of the predicted proportion of successful pairs.

```
# Plot predictions
WinBUGS.predictions <- out$mean$p
lines(1:length(data$C), WinBUGS.predictions, type = "l", lwd = 3,
    col = "blue", lty = 2)
```

3.5.2 Analysis of Real Data Set

We fit the same model to the proportion of successful peregrine pairs in the French Jura. We do not need to define the model again, since we did this in the previous section already.

```
# Read data and attach them
peregrine <- read.table("falcons.txt", header = TRUE)
    attach(peregrine)
```

```
# Bundle data (note yet another standardization for year)
win.data <- list(C = R.Pairs, N = Pairs, nyears = length(Pairs),
    year = (Year-1985) / 20)
```

```
# Initial values
inits <- function() list(alpha = runif(1, -1, 1), beta1 = runif(1, -1, 1),
    beta2 = runif(1, -1, 1))
```

```
# Parameters monitored
params <- c("alpha", "beta1", "beta2", "p")
```

```
# MCMC settings
ni <- 2500
nt <- 2
nb <- 500
nc <- 3

# Call WinBUGS from R (BRT < 1 min)
out3 <- bugs(data = win.data, inits = inits, parameters.to.save =
    params, model.file = "GLM_Binomial.txt", n.chains = nc, n.thin = nt,
    n.iter = ni, n.burnin = nb, debug = TRUE, bugs.directory = bugs.dir,
    working.directory = getwd())

# Summarize posteriors and plot estimates
print(out3, dig = 3)
plot(Year, R.Pairs/Pairs, type = "b", lwd = 2, col = "black", main = "",
    las = 1, ylab = "Proportion successful pairs", xlab = "Year",
    ylim = c(0,1))
lines(Year, out3$mean$p, type = "l", lwd = 3, col = "blue")
```

Convergence looks wonderful: the plots in WinBUGS look "grassy" (Link and Barker, 2010) and all Rhat values are close to 1. The proportion of successful pairs increased and then declined again over the years (Fig. 3.4c). The initial increase may be due to the recovery from pesticide effects and the decline to density dependence and the spread of a predator, the eagle owl.

3.6 SUMMARY AND OUTLOOK

In this chapter, we have covered much and important ground. We have illustrated the concept of a statistical model as being composed of a statistical distribution, to account of the noise, and a linear predictor for the signal. We have also introduced generalized linear models (GLMs); they allow distributions other than the normal to model the noise in a response. GLMs do so by using a link function, a transformation of the mean response that linearizes the relationship between the transformed mean response and covariates. We examined two common GLMs: Poisson and binomial. With the Poisson GLM, we saw how a classical analysis using maximum likelihood typically yields estimates that numerically closely match those from a Bayesian analysis with vague priors. In every example, we have illustrated convergence assessment of Markov chains by visual and formal means. We have modeled the temporal variation in counts exclusively, but the Poisson and binomial distributions may also be used to describe spatial variation of counts. We expect that much of this is a repetition for you rather than the first time you encounter the concept of a GLM. Otherwise it will be beneficial to first read more specific references that deal with this essential topic of applied statistical modeling, for example, Crawley (2005), Dobson and Barnett (2008), and Kéry (2010). In the next chapter, we will generalize the GLM to include so-called random effects and to become a generalized linear mixed model (GLMM), an example of a hierarchical model. One other interesting extension of the GLM, to include nonlinear, "wiggly" terms to become a generalized additive model (GAM; Hastie and Tibshirani, 1990), is not dealt with in this book. However, such spline models can be implemented in WinBUGS as sort of random-effects model. For code examples, see Gimenez et al. (2006a, b) and Grosbois et al. (2009).

3.7 EXERCISES

1. Adapt the first data-generation function in this chapter to generate the data using coefficients that refer to the values of standardized covariate values and repeat the analysis in R and in WinBUGS.
2. Take the following toy data set and fit a logistic regression of the number of successes r among n trials as a function of covariate X. Also write out the GLM for this data set.

   ```
   n <- c(22, 8, 10, 7, 10, 6, 11)
   r <- c(20, 7, 10, 6, 0, 1, 2)
   X <- c(0, 3, 1, 4, 5, 8, 10)
   ```

3. The Bernoulli distribution is a special case of the binomial with trial size equal to 1. It has only one parameter, the success probability p. The Bernoulli distribution is a conventional model for species distributions, where observed detection or nondetection data are related to explanatory (e.g., habitat) variables in a linear or other fashion with a logit link. Write an R function to assemble "presence or absence" data collected at 200 sites, where the success probability (i.e., occurrence probability) is related to habitat variable X (ranging from -1 to 1) on the logit-linear scale with intercept -2 and slope 5. Then write a WinBUGS program to "break down" the simulated data (i.e., analyze them) and thus recover these parameter values.
4. In Section 3.5.2, we used a binomial GLM to describe the proportion of successful peregrine pairs per year in the French Jura mountains. To see the connections between three important types of GLMs, first use a Poisson GLM to model the number of successful pairs (thus disregarding the fact that the binomial total varies by year), and second, use a normal GLM to do the same. In the same graph, compare the predicted numbers of successful pairs for every year under all three models (binomial, Poisson, and normal GLMs). Do this in both R and WinBUGS.

Introduction to Random Effects: Conventional Poisson GLMM for Count Data

4.1 INTRODUCTION

In Chapter 3, we have seen that the generalized linear model (GLM) is an extremely flexible and useful model and that much of applied statistics in ecology is based on GLMs. Now, we introduce perhaps the most important extension of the GLM: random effects. A GLM with fixed and random effects is also called a generalized linear mixed model (GLMM; Bolker, 2008). In this section, we explain what random effects are and describe the reasons for wanting to describe, and the consequences of declaring, a set of effects as random. After that, we look at a simple example of a Poisson GLMM, where random year effects are used to account for overdispersion in a time series of counts (Section 4.2). The resulting Poisson–log-normal model may not be the most familiar application of random effects, but it builds directly on the peregrine GLM example in Chapter 3. Furthermore, it illustrates the important topic of accounting for overdispersion in nonnormal GLMs for count data (Lee and Nelder, 2000; Millar, 2009). In Section 4.3, we fit more complex GLMMs with multiple sets of random effects. This is the kind of random effects that you may be more familiar with: latent, that is, unobserved, effects that are shared by all members of a group and that induce a correlated response among members of the same group. We call all models in this chapter "conventional" mixed models because they are not based on any underlying population model such as the mixed models in Chapter 5.

4.1.1 An Example

To illustrate, we revisit the ANCOVA example from Section 3.2.2, simply with changed variable names. We assume that we studied the mass–length relationship in asp vipers (Fig. 1.4) and had examined nine individuals in three populations. Here are the data and code for a plot.

```
# Define and plot data
mass <- c(25, 14, 68, 79, 64, 139, 49, 119, 111)
pop <- factor(c(1, 1, 1, 2, 2, 2, 3, 3, 3))
length <- c(1, 14, 22, 2, 9, 20, 2, 13, 22)
plot(length, mass, col = c(rep("red", 3), rep("blue", 3),
    rep("green", 3)), xlim = c(-1, 25), ylim = c(0, 140), cex = 1.5, lwd = 2,
    frame.plot = FALSE, las = 1, pch = 16, xlab = "Length", ylab = "Mass")
```

The plot suggests a linear relationship between mass and length with a different baseline in each population. A regression model ought to account for population differences. In one of the simplest such models, the mass of snake i depends on length in a linear way, allows populations j to have a different intercept, and has residuals ε_i come from a zero-mean normal distribution with variance σ^2.

$$\text{mass}_i = \alpha_{j(i)} + \beta * \text{length}_i + \varepsilon_i$$

$$\varepsilon_i \sim \text{Normal}(0, \sigma^2)$$

One way to motivate random effects is to recognize that there are two assumptions that one could make about the three asp viper populations studied:

1. They are the only populations that we are interested in.
2. They merely represent a sample from a larger number of populations that we *could* have studied and we would like to generalize our conclusions to this larger statistical population of snake populations.

These assumptions about the populations can be translated into the following assumptions about the population effects α_j:

1. The three α_j are completely independent.
2. The three α_j are not independent; instead, we regard them as a sample from a larger number of effects, which *could* have appeared in our study, and we would like to learn something about that population of effects.

Traditionally, assumption 1 leads one to treat the α_j as fixed effects, while assumption 2 leads to the adoption of a random-effects model for the effects α_j. Algebraically, the *only* difference between the two models is that for the random-effects ANCOVA, we add a distributional assumption about the intercepts of the three regression lines, that is, about the population effects α_j.

$$\text{mass}_i = \alpha_{j(i)} + \beta * \text{length}_i + \varepsilon_i$$

$$\varepsilon_i \sim \text{Normal}(0, \sigma^2)$$

$$\alpha_j \sim \text{Normal}(\mu_\alpha, \sigma_\alpha^2). \quad \text{This line makes } \alpha_j \text{ random!}$$

The third equation is the *only* difference between a model that treats the population effects α_j as fixed and one where α_j are random: without that line, the effects are fixed, and with it, they are random. Line 3 defines α_j as random draws from a normal distribution with mean μ_α and variance σ_α^2. This model is also called a random-intercepts model and is an example of a mixed model, that is, one with both random effects (α_j) and fixed effects (β). See Kéry (2010) for many further examples of fixed-effects models and their random-effects analogues; also see Section 4.3.2.

We use R to fit both models and plot the resulting regression lines (Fig. 4.1). For the random-effects model, we use the REML method, a variant of maximum likelihood that is better suited for mixed models and fit the model with the function `lmer` in the R package lme4, which we need to load first.

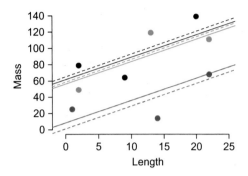

FIGURE 4.1   Relationship between mass and length of asp vipers in three populations (indicated by colors). Circles are the nine measurements. Dashed lines are the estimated regressions for each population under an ANCOVA model with fixed population effects (intercepts). Solid lines are the estimated regressions under a mixed ANCOVA model with random population effects (intercepts). Intercepts under the random-effects ANCOVA are shrunk toward the grand mean, that is, the average intercept.

```
# Fit fixed-effects model, print regression parameter estimates and
    plot regression lines
summary(lm <- lm(mass ~ pop-1 + length))
abline(lm$coef[1], lm$coef[4], col = "red", lwd = 3, lty = 2)
abline(lm$coef[2], lm$coef[4], col = "blue", lwd = 3, lty = 2)
abline(lm$coef[3], lm$coef[4], col = "green", lwd = 3, lty = 2)

# Fit mixed model, print random effects and plot regression lines
summary(lmm <- lmer(mass ~ length + (1|pop)))
ranef(lmm)
abline((lmm@fixef[1]+ranef(lmm)$pop)[1,], lmm@fixef[2], col = "red",
    lwd = 3)
abline((lmm@fixef[1]+ranef(lmm)$pop)[2,], lmm@fixef[2], col = "blue",
    lwd = 3)
abline((lmm@fixef[1]+ranef(lmm)$pop)[3,], lmm@fixef[2], col = "green",
    lwd = 3)
```

Thus, when we describe a model in algebra, the difference between a fixed- and the random-effects version of a model is really trivial. Nevertheless, random effects appear to be a fairly challenging concept for many ecologists. This may have to do with two things. First, random effects are often introduced within the context of ANOVA decompositions of sums of squares. This may simply not be the best setting within which to explain the concepts of the actual models. Second, in almost all software, there is a big divide between procedures that are used to fit the fixed- and the random-effects versions of a model. For instance, in R, there is lm for fixed-effects normal linear models and lmer for random-effects normal linear models. The two have quite a different syntax and lmer cannot even be used to fit fixed-effects models, and vice versa. Hence, the differences rather than the similarities between the two versions of a model are emphasized.

Fortunately, this is different with WinBUGS and the BUGS language; here, we can easily switch between fixed and random effects in a model. We have met quite a few ecologists who have only started to understand random effects after fitting random-effects models in WinBUGS. In the next sections, we try to explain in more detail random effects, the motivation for treating a set of effects as random, and why we will not always treat all effects in a model as random. When possible, we will refer back to the introductory example.

4.1.2 What Are Random Effects?

Put simply, random effects are two or more effects or parameters that "belong together" in some way. Specifically, they are estimated under the constraint of a common distribution. We may imagine that a common stochastic process has generated the effects. Therefore, replication of a study would yield a different set of realizations from that random process, that is, a different sample of effects from the distribution describing the stochastic process. In the Bayesian literature, one often reads that to assume effects as random, they must be exchangeable. Exchangeability implies similar, but not identical effects, and is a judgment, not something that can be tested. We are usually free to choose to treat a factor as fixed or random, but there are cases in which the assumption of exchangeability (treating effects as random) would not be biologically justified. For instance, if two of our snake populations are wild and one living in captivity, we would probably not choose to treat the intercepts as random. Rather, we would do so only after having accounted for another fixed effect coding for life in the wild versus in captivity.

The distribution that collects together a set of random effects is called a prior distribution by Bayesians. This may be slightly confusing, since it is not exactly the same kind of prior distribution as the distribution with which we describe our knowledge about each parameter of a model; this typically has known constants only. Instead, a prior governing a set of random effects itself has parameters that must be estimated and which therefore need priors themselves. Hence, the parameters of the random-effects distribution become hyperparameters and their priors become hyperpriors. Such a hierarchical scheme may include additional levels, so we might have hyper-hyperparameters and so forth. Of course, these names would soon become unwieldy, and indeed, are uninteresting, but it is important to recognize the common principle: as soon as we assume effects are random, we introduce a hierarchy of effects. The parameters at one level of the hierarchy can be seen as the realization of some probability distribution, the parameters of which may themselves be the realization of another probability distribution one level up. Hence, any model with random effects is intrinsically a hierarchical model; see Section 2.8.

Typically in ecology, random effects are continuous, and a normal distribution is assumed for them. However, random effects may also be discrete, for instance, in the state-space representation of survival models (Chapters 7–11), in binomial mixture models (Chapter 12), or in occupancy models (Chapter 13). The prior distribution for these discrete random effects is the Bernoulli and the Poisson.

We find the terminology surrounding random-effects models fairly confusing, so here we try to make some connections:

- Random effects always imply grouped effects; we model grouped parameters, batches, or sets of parameters (Gelman, 2005). We cannot declare a single effect as random.
- The factor that indexes group membership is called a random-effects factor or random factor for short, and the groups of a factor in general (fixed or random) are also called levels.
- The simplest random effects perhaps are intercepts or mean effects, and the associated models are sometimes called random-intercepts or varying-intercepts models (Gelman and Hill, 2007). However, we can just as well assume that a collection of slopes comes from a common distribution, leading to a random-coefficients or varying-slopes model (Gelman and Hill, 2007). Typically, random-coefficients models also contain random intercepts.
- We can also model variance parameters as random (Lee and Nelder, 2006).
- Models with random-effects factors are typically called random-effects models. When they also have fixed effects, they become mixed models or mixed-effects models. The following names are largely synonymous or at least overlap with the term, mixed model: variance-components model, hierarchical model, state-space model, latent-component, and latent-variable model.

4.1.3 Why Do We Treat Batches of Effects as Random?

There are many different motivations for random-effects modeling. This section lists some of them.

Scope of Inference

With random effects, the scope of inference of a study extends beyond the particular levels of a factor that appear in the study. In our snake example, this formally allows us to generalize to a larger number of populations, from which the three population studied were drawn from. Hence, we buy greater generality in treating our populations as representatives of a larger (statistical) population of populations that we *could* have studied and about which we would also like to learn something, for instance about how they vary among each other. In truth, such a population of populations may be fairly hypothetical and hard to define in practice, yet it may be sensible to assume it exists. Of course, we can estimate the effects of the particular populations in our study. In addition, when random, we can also estimate or predict the effects of populations that are *not* in the studied sample but that belong to the same statistical population of populations. This is interesting for predicting a process into the future, for instance, when temporal random effects are included in a model, or for making similar extrapolations over space with spatial random effects.

Assessment of Variability

A random-effects model often focuses on the variability in a process. For instance, in a population viability analysis (Beissinger, 2002), the appropriate way to estimate temporal variance in a quantity like a survival probability is to model annual survival as a random effect (see Chapter 7). Actually, we can then estimate two kinds of variability: first, the variation among the levels in the population, that is, the population standard deviation (or variance); this is the parameter estimated in the model (e.g., σ_α^2 in the snake example). However, we can also estimate the variation among the observed levels in our study, that is, $\mathtt{sd}(\alpha_j)$ in our example. This is called the finite-population (or finite-sample) standard deviation. Gelman (2005) suggests the latter as a unified measure of the importance of a factor.

Partitioning of Variability

A random-effects factor codes for unstructured variability among the units in a group. For instance, it quantifies the variability in some process such as survival over a series of years. We may then be interested to explain that variability by covariates, for instance, a weather covariate measured every year. Covariate effects can be assessed by fitting a model first with a random-effects factor alone, for example, time, and second with a temporally varying covariate included. The proportional reduction in the time variance component is a measure for the proportion of the temporal variance in survival explained by that covariate (e.g., Grosbois et al., 2008; see also Section 7.4.3).

Modeling of Correlations among Parameters

Since we can assess the variation among the levels of one factor using random effects, we can also assess the covariation among pairs of levels of two factors using correlated random effects. For instance, we may model a correlation between intercepts and slopes (see Kéry, 2010) or between pairs of annual values of survival and fecundity (Cam et al., 2002) or juvenile and adult survival (see Section 7.6.2). Similarly, most modeling of spatial or temporal autocorrelation first declares random site or time effects, on which a correlation structure can then be imposed. For instance, a random time effect at $t + 1$ may be assumed to depend on the time effect at t in an autoregressive time series (Chapter 5). Similarly, spatial correlation may be modeled by assuming a correlation matrix for random site effects, with the correlation being a function of the distance between the sites (e.g., Royle et al., 2007b).

Accounting for All Random Processes in a Modeled System

Random-effects modeling results in a more honest accounting for the total uncertainty in a modeled system. Treating some components as random rather than as fixed recognizes the additional variability in, and hence uncertainty stemming from, these components. For instance, in our snake example, a replication of the study might have chosen different populations, with slightly different average mass, and by treating snake populations as random rather than fixed accounts for the fact that this sampling process introduces additional variability in our study, that is, additional uncertainty in our conclusions. If we estimate mass–length regression lines without accounting for this component of variation among populations and implicitly assume that our results are valid for other snake populations as well, our standard error for the regression lines will be too small. Thus, random effects account for the added uncertainty in the form of the sampling error incurred by sampling just some populations in a study, while many other, different, but similar and therefore exchangeable populations could have been selected instead.

Avoiding Pseudoreplication

Historically, one of the first motivations for random-effects modeling was the desire to account for inherent structure in many data sets, that is, to correct for intrinsic correlations and thereby avoid pseudoreplication (Hurlbert, 1984). For instance, in a study where plant height is measured for each of a sample of plants drawn from multiple populations, a random population effect will avoid committing pseudoreplication. The shared population effect in the measurement of two plants in the same population induces a correlation in their height. This correlation coefficient is sometimes called intraclass correlation; it is equal to $\sigma_{pop}^2/(\sigma_{pop}^2 + \sigma_{res}^2)$, where σ_{pop}^2 is the population variance component, and σ_{res}^2 the residual variance component among plants within populations. Similarly, the blocking structure in a designed experiment will be accounted for by random block effects.

Borrowing Strength

Random-effects modeling consists of constraining grouped parameters by a common distribution. Effects are no longer estimated independently from one another; rather, the estimate of each effect is influenced by all members in the group. Thus, the groups share information. One also says that individual estimates "borrow strength from the ensemble". If the assumption of exchangeability holds, individual estimates will be improved (Link and Sauer, 1996; Sauer and Link, 2002; Welham et al., 2004). One consequence is that individual estimates are pulled in (shrunk) toward the grand mean, an effect called shrinkage. Effects that are estimated with less precision or are more extreme are pulled in more than the effects estimated with greater precision and that are more "average". This can be seen in the snake example, where the intercept of the more extreme red population is shrunk most. Shrinkage is greater when group effects (σ^2_{pop}) are smaller relative to the residual variation (σ^2_{res}), that is, when the intraclass correlation is small. With large sample size in each group (i.e., small σ^2_{res}) and highly variable groups (large σ^2_{pop}), hardly any shrinkage takes place. Random-effects estimates then become essentially identical to fixed-effects estimates. In fact, fixed-effects are a special case of random-effects estimates when the group variance component (σ^2_{pop}) is infinite.

Random Effects as a Compromise between Pooling and No Pooling of Batched Effects

Random-effects modeling can also be seen as an alternative to model selection: rather than making a hard decision about whether a factor should be in the model or out, we let the data (and the model) decide and allow a factor to be in the model in a fractional manner. Gelman and Hill (2007) argue that the random-effects assumption represents an intermediate between assuming all groups (levels) of a factor have an effect and assuming that none of them has an effect. Under the first assumption, all effects are independent and not pooled; this results in the classical fixed-effects estimates. Under the second assumption, the effects are absent or pooled, that is, we simply estimate the grand mean. In contrast, the random-effects assumption is equivalent to partial pooling of the effects, with the degree of pooling depending on the relative size of the among-group variation (σ^2_{pop}) and the within-group variation (σ^2_{res}) and on the precision of each individual group mean estimate.

Combining Information

Random-effects modeling is a natural way in which information may be combined over groups. For instance, results from different studies can be combined by assuming study random effects in a meta-analysis. The combined estimate is then automatically weighed by the information content of each study. Similarly, when combining the analysis of multiple data sets, each data set might be considered a sample from some larger hypothetical population of such data sets and modeled as a random effect.

4.1.4 Why Should We Ever Treat a Factor as Fixed?

So why do we not always treat all effects as random? There are several reasons.

First, the assumption of exchangeability may simply not hold and units in a group of effects may differ systematically. The assumption of a common prior distribution is then not sensible. "Borrowing strength" would backfire in these cases, by pulling extreme effects estimates toward the mean of the effects, in spite of them being *really* different and extreme.

Second, treating a factor with very few levels as random will result in very imprecise estimates of the hyperparameter. Hence, when factors have fewer than, say, 5–10 levels, they will rarely be treated as random (but see Gelman, 2005).

Third, random effects are computationally more expensive. We will see this many times with WinBUGS: as soon as we move from a fixed-effects formulation of a model to the corresponding random-effects version of the model, we need to run longer Markov chains to get convergence and run times will be increased, and sometimes greatly so. Similarly, it is often more difficult to get converging Markov chains in the analysis of random-effects versions of a model compared with the grouped effects when they are assumed fixed.

Fourth, another practical reason may be that many ecologists find random-effects models more difficult to understand. We believe that this has to do with the way in which random-effects models are presented in statistics classes at university, that is, within an ANOVA framework. To many, this is challenging and somewhat opaque. In contrast, within a linear model framework, with the models written in algebra, it becomes much more transparent what random effects are, as we have seen above. Another practical reason may be that historically, flexible software for modeling random effects has become widely available much later than software for modeling traditional fixed-effects models.

4.2 ACCOUNTING FOR OVERDISPERSION BY RANDOM EFFECTS-MODELING IN R AND WinBUGS

We introduce random effects in an application that may not be so familiar: as a way of accounting for overdispersion in count data. Overdispersion in Poisson or binomial responses denotes the situation that a response is more variable than prescribed by these two distributions where the variance is a function of the mean and thus not a free parameter. Overdispersion arises when important covariates are not in the model or when units are not independent, such as when nestlings are grouped in the same nests or plants within the same population.

Not accounting for this overdispersion would lead to too liberal tests and too short (e.g., 95% credible) intervals. In our example, we estimate one random effect for each observation. Thus, in a sense, we fit extra residuals in addition to the implicit residuals coming with the Poisson assumption and assume that the extra residuals are normal on the log link scale. More typical applications of random-effects modeling usually have effects that are shared by more than one observation (see Section 4.3 for random site and random year effects).

Overdispersion is very frequent when modeling counts; actually, it is the rule rather than the exception. The variance of counts modeled by a Poisson is not a free parameter, so when fitting a Poisson GLM with a function such as `glm()`, the residual deviance of a model should be about the same as the residual degrees of freedom. For example, look at the analysis of the (real) peregrine counts in Section 3.2.2:

```
[ ... ]
    Null deviance: 1591.395  on 39  degrees of freedom
Residual deviance:   76.448  on 36  degrees of freedom
[ ... ]
```

The residual deviance is more than twice as large as the residual degrees of freedom, a clear indication that the observations (i.e., the counts) are more variable than expected under the Poisson assumption. Since we have one observation per year, we may imagine the presence of unmodeled year effects. These can be modeled as coming from a normal distribution. The resulting model is also called the Poisson–log-normal (or PLN) model; see also chapter 15.1 in Gelman and Hill (2007), or Millar (2009). Other possibilities to account for overdispersion in R would be to use a negative binomial distribution or quasi-likelihood (Lee and Nelder, 2000). For the latter, see the family argument `quasipoisson` in the R function `glm()`.

As usual, it is enlightening to write down the model in algebra. In Section 3.2.2, we had assumed the following GLM for count C_i in year i:

1. Statistical distribution to describe the random part of the response: Poisson

$$C_i \sim \text{Poisson}(\lambda_i)$$

2. Link function to transform the mean of the parameter so that it can be expressed as a linear function of covariates and random effects: the log

$$\log(\lambda_i) = \eta_i$$

3. Linear predictor to describe the systematic part of the response:

$$\eta_i = \alpha + \beta_1 * \text{year}_i + \beta_2 * \text{year}_i^2 + \beta_3 * \text{year}_i^3 \quad \text{(old linear predictor)}$$

So far, the model is the usual Poisson GLM. To convert it into a Poisson GLMM, we simply introduce into the linear predictor random effects ε_i. Hence, we replace component 3 with a new linear predictor:

$$\eta_i = \alpha + \beta_1 * \text{year}_i + \beta_2 * \text{year}_i^2 + \beta_3 * \text{year}_i^3 + \varepsilon_i \quad \text{(new linear predictor)}$$

The fourth component of the model is the distribution of the extra residuals:

4. Distribution of extra residuals (ε_i): Normal

$$\varepsilon_i \sim \text{Normal}(0, \sigma^2)$$

We could have written the same model without the ε terms, but instead making the intercepts year specific and collecting them together in a normal distribution like the following: $\alpha_i \sim \text{Normal}(\mu, \sigma^2)$. This is simply a reparameterization of the same model.

This completes our algebraic description of the model, and we will recognize later how the model description in the BUGS language is almost a direct transcription of this algebraic description. Note that the random effects ε are year specific, so we may call them random year effects, but we should not confuse them with the three polynomial regression effects of year. Also, we may only think of overdispersion here as being caused by unmodeled year effects because we have a single observation per year.

4.2.1 Generation and Analysis of Simulated Data

We will now assemble random-effects counts and then break them down using mixed modeling in R and WinBUGS. This will illustrate again that inference from frequentist and Bayesian analyses will often be numerically very similar. Note that some versions of the lme4 package do not allow the fitting of the PLN model, so you will have to choose a version of the package that does (e.g., 2.8.1 or 2.12.1).

```
data.fn <- function(n = 40, alpha = 3.5576, beta1 = -0.0912, beta2 = 0.0091,
    beta3 = -0.00014, sd = 0.1) {
    # n: Number of years
    # alpha, beta1, beta2, beta3: coefficients of a
    #     cubic polynomial of count on year
    # sd: standard deviation of normal distribution assumed for year
        effects

    # Generate values of time covariate
    year <- 1:n

    # First level of noise: generate random year effects
    eps <- rnorm(n = n, mean = 0, sd = sd)
```

```
# Signal (plus first level of noise): build up systematic part of the
   GLM and add the random year effects
log.expected.count <- alpha + beta1 * year + beta2 * year^2 + beta3 *
   year^3 + eps
expected.count <- exp(log.expected.count)

# Second level of noise: generate random part of the GLM: Poisson
   noise around expected counts
C <- rpois(n = n, lambda = expected.count)

# Plot simulated data
plot(year, C, type = "b", lwd = 2, main = "", las = 1, ylab = "Population
   size", xlab = "Year", ylim = c(0, 1.1*max(C)))
lines(year, expected.count, type = "l", lwd = 3, col = "red")

return(list(n = n, alpha = alpha, beta1 = beta1, beta2 = beta2, beta3 =
   beta3, year = year, sd = sd, expected.count = expected.count, C = C))
}
```

We generate one data set. The expected count now contains a random contribution from each year, so it is no longer a smooth line as in Chapter 3. We can also say that the response contains two random components now: one from the year and the other a common Poisson residual.

```
data <- data.fn()
```

In R, we use the function lmer() in the lme4 package to fit the model.

```
library(lme4)
yr <- factor(data$year)          # Create a factor year
glmm.fit <- lmer(C ~ (1 | yr) + year + I(year^2) + I(year^3), family =
   poisson, data = data)

Warning message:
In mer_finalize(ans) : false convergence (8)
```

We fail to get convergence, so we see that numerical challenges are not restricted to Bayesian computation. We manually standardize the year covariate and see whether this helps—it does:

```
mny <- mean(data$year)
sdy <- sd(data$year)
cov1 <- (data$year - mny) / sdy
cov2 <- cov1 * cov1
cov3 <- cov1 * cov1 * cov1
glmm.fit <- lmer(C ~ (1 | yr) + cov1 + cov2 + cov3, family = poisson, data =
   data)
glmm.fit
Generalized linear mixed model fit by the Laplace approximation
Formula: C ~ (1 | yr) + cov1 + cov2 + cov3
   Data: data
  AIC   BIC  logLik deviance
  63   71.44  -26.5     53
```

```
Random effects:
  Groups Name          Variance      Std.Dev.
yr        (Intercept) 0.0059868 0.077374
Number of obs: 40, groups: yr, 40

Fixed effects:
              Estimate Std. Error  z value  Pr(>|z|)
(Intercept)    4.33482    0.03412   127.05   < 2e-16 ***
cov1           1.22411    0.05627    21.75   < 2e-16 ***
cov2           0.06023    0.02686     2.24    0.0250 *
cov3          -0.23495    0.02934    -8.01  1.17e-15 ***
[ ... ]
```

We form predictions and plot them (Fig. 4.2). If we wish, we can inspect the random-effects estimates by typing `ranef(glmm.fit)`. We could also have formed predictions by typing `fitted(glmm.fit)`, but doing this by hand enhances our understanding.

```
R.predictions <- exp(fixef(glmm.fit)[1] + fixef(glmm.fit)[2]*cov1 +
    fixef(glmm.fit)[3]*cov2 + fixef(glmm.fit)[4]*cov3 +
    unlist(ranef(glmm.fit)))
lines(data$year, R.predictions, col = "green", lwd = 2, type = "l")
```

Here is the WinBUGS solution. Remember that WinBUGS parameterizes the normal distribution in terms of the precision, that is, one over the variance.

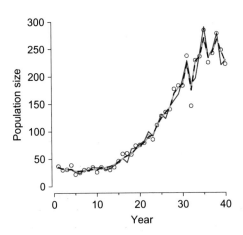

FIGURE 4.2   Simulated population size of peregrines in the French Jura over 40 years: expected population size (red), observed data (pair counts; black), estimated population trajectories from a frequentist (green, using REML in `lmer`), and a Bayesian analysis in WinBUGS (blue; posterior means) of a Poisson regression with cubic polynomial effects of year and year overdispersion. The R code to produce this figure slightly differs from the one shown in the book.

```
# Specify model in BUGS language
sink("GLMM_Poisson.txt")
cat("
model {

# Priors
alpha ~ dunif(-20, 20)
beta1 ~ dunif(-10, 10)
beta2 ~ dunif(-10, 10)
beta3 ~ dunif(-10, 10)
tau <- 1 / (sd*sd)
sd ~ dunif(0, 5)

# Likelihood: note key components of a GLM in one line each
for (i in 1:n) {
    C[i] ~ dpois(lambda[i])            # 1. Distribution for random part
    log(lambda[i]) <- log.lambda[i]    # 2. Link function
    log.lambda[i] <- alpha + beta1 * year[i] + beta2 * pow(year[i],2) +
        beta3 * pow(year[i],3) + eps[i]   # 3. Linear predictor incl.
                                               random year effect
    eps[i] ~ dnorm(0, tau)         # 4. Definition of random effects dist
    }
}
",fill = TRUE)
sink()

# Bundle data
win.data <- list(C = data$C, n = length(data$C), year = cov1)

# Initial values
inits <- function() list(alpha = runif(1, -2, 2), beta1 = runif(1, -3, 3),
    sd = runif(1, 0,1))

# Parameters monitored
params <- c("alpha", "beta1", "beta2", "beta3", "lambda", "sd", "eps")

# MCMC settings
ni <- 30000
nt <- 10
nb <- 20000
nc <- 3

# Call WinBUGS from R (BRT <1 min)
out<- bugs(win.data, inits, params, "GLMM_Poisson.txt", n.chains = nc,
    n.thin = nt, n.iter = ni, n.burnin = nb, debug = TRUE, bugs.directory =
    bugs.dir, working.directory = getwd())
```

Here are two important comments. First, when calling the `bugs()` function, we will from now on use so-called positional matching of the arguments. That is, unlike in Chapter 3, where we wrote `bugs(data = win.data, inits = inits, ...)`, we will now let the position of some arguments determine their identity, so the first argument is data, the second is the inits function, and so on. This achieves more succinct code. Second, we will no longer formally comment on convergence in every example. In reality, we always check for convergence by looking at the plots in WinBUGS and

by inspecting the values of Rhat in the summary produced by the bugs()
function, we just do not say so.

```
# Summarize posteriors
print(out, dig = 2)
```

	mean	sd	2.5%	25%	50%	75%	97.5%	Rhat	n.eff
alpha	4.33	0.04	4.26	4.31	4.33	4.36	4.40	1.00	1800
beta1	1.22	0.06	1.11	1.18	1.22	1.26	1.35	1.00	450
beta2	0.06	0.03	0.01	0.04	0.06	0.08	0.12	1.00	1300
beta3	-0.23	0.03	-0.30	-0.25	-0.23	-0.21	-0.18	1.01	360
lambda[1]	35.51	4.20	28.04	32.55	35.23	38.10	44.84	1.00	1700
lambda[2]	32.02	3.53	25.48	29.49	31.93	34.43	39.20	1.00	1200
lambda[3]	30.86	3.13	25.12	28.75	30.84	32.82	37.37	1.00	2600
[...]									
lambda[38]	267.75	14.22	241.29	257.80	267.30	277.40	296.30	1.00	660
lambda[39]	246.04	13.55	220.20	236.67	245.80	255.22	273.00	1.00	3000
lambda[40]	226.47	13.47	200.90	216.90	226.55	235.30	252.90	1.00	3000
sd	0.09	0.02	0.05	0.07	0.09	0.10	0.14	1.01	340

We get estimates that are fairly similar to those from the frequentist
analysis using maximum likelihood. We plot the predicted population
trajectory into Fig. 4.2.

```
WinBUGS.predictions <- out$mean$lambda
lines(data$year, WinBUGS.predictions, col = "blue", lwd = 2, type = "l",
    lty = 2)
```

Hence, overdispersion in counts can be accounted for by adding ran-
dom effects at the data level (here, random year effects ε_i), assuming a normal distribution on the scale of the linear predictor for them, and
estimating the spread of that normal distribution. Accounting for overdispersion more adequately accounts for the full uncertainty in the modeled
system. We can see this by comparing the standard errors of the regression
estimates under a simple GLM with those obtained under the GLMM. We
quickly fit the respective models in R.

```
glm.fit <- glm(C ~ cov1 + cov2 + cov3, family = poisson, data = data)
summary(glm.fit)
summary(glmm.fit)
```

The uncertainty of all regression estimates is slightly increased under
the GLMM compared with the GLM. Thus, the GLMM propagates the
additional uncertainty in the modeled system into the regression estimates
as it should. See also exercise 1 in Section 4.5.

4.2.2 Analysis of Real Data

Now, let us repeat these analyses for the real data from the French Jura.
We need to standardize year to avoid worries with convergence.

```
# Read data again
peregrine <- read.table("falcons.txt", header = TRUE)

yr <- factor(peregrine$Year)
mny <- mean(peregrine$Year)
sdy <- sd(peregrine$Year)
cov1 <- (peregrine$Year - mny) / sdy
cov2 <- cov1 * cov1
cov3 <- cov1 * cov1 * cov1
glmm <- lmer(peregrine$Pairs ~ (1 | yr) + cov1 + cov2 + cov3, family =
   poisson, data = peregrine)
glmm
Generalized linear mixed model fit by the Laplace approximation
Formula: peregrine$Pairs ~ (1 | yr) + cov1 + cov2 + cov3
   Data: peregrine
   AIC   BIC  logLik deviance
  77.01 85.46 -33.51   67.01
Random effects:
 Groups  Name         Variance   Std.Dev.
 yr      (Intercept)  0.0098814  0.099405
Number of obs: 40, groups: yr, 40

Fixed effects:
              Estimate  Std. Error  z value  Pr(>|z|)
(Intercept)    4.21205    0.03841   109.65   < 2e-16 ***
cov1           1.19085    0.06507    18.30   < 2e-16 ***
cov2           0.01720    0.02980     0.58    0.564
cov3          -0.27162    0.03361    -8.08   6.4e-16 ***
[ ... ]
```

We estimate an overdispersion standard deviation of about 0.1 (R also gives the square of that estimate, that is, the variance).

Next, we conduct the analysis in WinBUGS. We can reuse most ingredients of the analysis from Section 4.2.1. Do not forget to check convergence; if there is trouble, you have to increase the chain length and/or the burnin period.

```
# Bundle data
win.data <- list(C = peregrine$Pairs, n = length(peregrine$Pairs),
   year = cov1)

# MCMC settings (may have to adapt)
ni <- 30000
nt <- 10
nb <- 20000
nc <- 3

# Call WinBUGS from R (BRT < 1 min)
out <- bugs(win.data, inits, params, "GLMM_Poisson.txt", n.chains = nc,
   n.thin = nt, n.iter = ni, n.burnin = nb, debug = TRUE, bugs.directory =
   bugs.dir, working.directory = getwd())
```

```
# Summarize posteriors
print(out, dig = 3)
              mean      sd    2.5%      25%      50%      75%    97.5%  Rhat  n.eff
alpha        4.210   0.043   4.120    4.181    4.211    4.239    4.291 1.002  1700
beta1        1.200   0.078   1.057    1.147    1.197    1.250    1.361 1.005   420
beta2        0.017   0.033  -0.048   -0.004    0.016    0.038    0.083 1.002  1500
beta3       -0.275   0.040  -0.356   -0.302   -0.274   -0.247   -0.200 1.005   440
lambda[1]   34.252   4.364  26.549   31.130   34.010   37.010   43.451 1.002  1400
lambda[2]   35.796   4.640  27.859   32.487   35.510   38.590   46.121 1.001  3000
lambda[3]   32.141   3.800  25.450   29.490   31.850   34.540   40.401 1.001  3000
[ ... ]
lambda[39] 180.358  12.146 157.600  171.775  180.050  188.600  205.100 1.001  3000
lambda[40] 176.702  12.751 152.597  168.100  176.300  185.300  202.402 1.001  3000
sd           0.117   0.032   0.059    0.095    0.116    0.136    0.182 1.002  3000
[ ... ]
```

As usual, we get similar estimates for both mean and variance parameters in R and WinBUGS. It is instructive to compare the posterior summaries from Poisson GLMM with those under the simple Poisson GLM in Section 3.2.2: you will see that the estimates of the mean parameters (alpha, beta1, beta2, and beta3) are not that different under both models. However, the uncertainty around them (posterior sd) is greater under the mixed Poisson model. Similarly, the 95% CRI are wider, and also the uncertainty around the lambda components is larger. Hence, our estimates properly account for the added uncertainty introduced by the second component of variation in the modeled system, the random year effects. Without accounting for the extra-Poisson variability in the counts, we would have underestimated parameter uncertainty.

4.3 MIXED MODELS WITH RANDOM EFFECTS FOR VARIABILITY AMONG GROUPS (SITE AND YEAR EFFECTS)

For the remainder of this chapter, we look at models for population counts that are indexed by both space and time, rather than only by time as in the preceding examples in this chapter. We will model counts $C_{i,j}$ made at time i and site j as a function of cubic polynomials of year and start by assuming a Poisson distribution with expected count $\lambda_{i,j}$:

$$C_{i,j} \sim \text{Poisson}(\lambda_{i,j}).$$

To model spatiotemporal structure in the expected counts, we apply the usual log link function and express the log (expected count) as a function of covariates in a linear way:

$$\log(\lambda_{i,j}) = \alpha_j + \sum_k \beta_p * X_i^p + \varepsilon_i$$

This equation describes a log-linear multiple regression of the expected count on an additive function of $k = 3$ time covariates X, that is, a fixed-effects Poisson GLM, with an added residual term ε_i. Now, look at the indices of the parameters: the slope parameters (betas) do not vary by time or by among sites (they are not indexed by i or by j): we estimate a single set of beta for all sites and times. However, the intercept α is indexed by site (j) and so codes for site effects, and the residual ε is indexed by time (i) and hence codes for time effects in addition to those of the covariate X.

The model, as written so far, is a fixed-effects model. The GLMMs considered in the rest of this chapter extend the fixed-effects Poisson GLM by adding two (or more) distributional assumptions to the equation above, for instance

$$\alpha_j \sim \text{Normal}(\mu, \sigma_\alpha^2) \text{ and}$$

$$\varepsilon_i \sim \text{Normal}(0, \sigma_\varepsilon^2).$$

This allows for stochastic site differences in the level of the population trajectory, that is, in the intercepts α_j, and for stochastic year effects ε_i common to all sites. Note that we could also estimate random year-by-site noise, say $\varepsilon_{i,j}$, but we will assume here that our current model is sufficiently flexible. To describe each set of parameters, α_j and ε_i, we will estimate one (hyper)parameter that expresses the magnitude of the variability among sites (σ_α^2) and another for the variability among years (σ_ε^2).

Note that a simple reparameterization of this model would consist in "pulling out" the mean site effect, μ, into an overall intercept. The site effects would then come from a mean-zero normal distribution rather than one with mean μ.

$$\log(\lambda_{i,j}) = \mu + \sum_k \beta_p * X_i^p + \alpha_j + \varepsilon_i$$

$$\alpha_j \sim \text{Normal}(0, \sigma_\alpha^2)$$

$$\varepsilon_i \sim \text{Normal}(0, \sigma_\varepsilon^2)$$

Models of this kind have become sort of standard for analyzing population counts (Link and Sauer, 2002; Ver Hoef and Jansen, 2007; Cressie et al., 2009, among many others). They are often called hierarchical models, since they contain a hierarchy of effects, and we can think of a nested relationship among the parameters in the model. However, the term, hierarchical model, by itself is about as informative about the actual model used as it would be to say that I am using a four-wheeled vehicle for locomotion; there are golf carts, quads, Smart cars, Volkswagen, and

Mercedes, for instance, and they all have four wheels. Similarly, plenty of statistical models applied in ecology have at least one set of random effects (beyond the residual) and therefore represent a hierarchical model. Hence, the term is not very informative about the particular model adopted for inference about an animal population.

4.3.1 Generation and Analysis of Simulated Data

For data simulation, we adapt the data generation function from Section 4.2.1 to several parallel time series of counts and to allow for random site and random year effects. We assume that there are site effects on the intercept of the trajectory only, not the slope parameters. So, we might think that this function generates replicate trajectories of counts of the peregrine population in the French Jura. We consider balanced data for convenience only; the models work also if there are missing values in the year-by-site data.

```
data.fn <- function(nsite = 5, nyear = 40, alpha = 4.18456, beta1 =
    1.90672, beta2 = 0.10852, beta3 = -1.17121, sd.site = 0.5, sd.year =
    0.2){
    # nsite: Number of populations
    # nyear: Number of years
    # alpha, beta1, beta2, beta3: cubic polynomial coefficients of year
    # sd.site: standard deviation of the normal distribution assumed for
        the population intercepts alpha
    # sd.year: standard deviation of the normal distribution assumed for
        the year effects
    # We standardize the year covariate so that it runs from about -1 to 1

    # Generate data structure to hold counts and log(lambda)
    C <- log.expected.count <- array(NA, dim = c(nyear, nsite))

    # Generate covariate values
    year <- 1:nyear
    yr <- (year-20)/20   # Standardize
    site <- 1:nsite

    # Draw two sets of random effects from their respective distribution
    alpha.site <- rnorm(n = nsite, mean = alpha, sd = sd.site)
    eps.year <- rnorm(n = nyear, mean = 0, sd = sd.year)

    # Loop over populations
    for (j in 1:nsite){

        # Signal (plus first level of noise): build up systematic part of
            the GLM including random site and year effects
        log.expected.count[,j] <- alpha.site[j] + beta1 * yr + beta2 * yr^2
            + beta3 * yr^3 + eps.year
        expected.count <- exp(log.expected.count[,j])
```

```
    # Second level of noise: generate random part of the GLM: Poisson
    noise around expected counts
C[,j] <- rpois(n = nyear, lambda = expected.count)
    }

# Plot simulated data
matplot(year, C, type = "l", lty = 1, lwd = 2, main = "", las = 1, ylab =
    "Population size", xlab = "Year")

return(list(nsite = nsite, nyear = nyear, alpha.site = alpha.site,
    beta1 = beta1, beta2 = beta2, beta3 = beta3, year = year, sd.site = sd.
    site, sd.year = sd.year, expected.count = expected.count, C = C))
    }
```

We generate one very large data set and plot it (Fig. 4.3). Simulating 100 populations will result in a very large BUGS run time, and you may want to choose fewer sites to reduce the run time in your analysis, for example, nsite = 10 will result in a BUGS run time (BRT) of about 12 min.

```
data <- data.fn(nsite = 100, nyear = 40, sd.site = 0.3, sd.year = 0.2)
```

We analyze using BUGS.

```
# Specify model in BUGS language
sink("GLMM_Poisson.txt")
cat("
model {
```

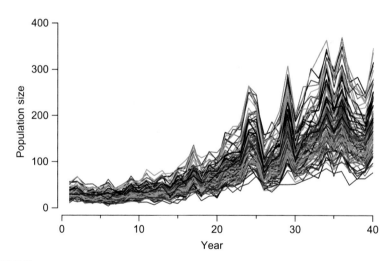

FIGURE 4.3   One hundred replicate population trajectories with additive random site and year effects. We emphasize how a single stochastic process, here, the data.fn() function and in an ecologist's daily life, nature, can produce spectacularly different outcomes. In nature, we typically only ever see a single outcome of the stochastic process from which we want to infer the characteristics of the latter—a difficult challenge.

```
# Priors
for (j in 1:nsite){
    alpha[j] ~ dnorm(mu, tau.alpha)        # 4. Random site effects
    }
mu ~ dnorm(0, 0.01)                        # Hyperparameter 1
tau.alpha <- 1 / (sd.alpha*sd.alpha)       # Hyperparameter 2
sd.alpha ~ dunif(0, 2)
for (p in 1:3){
    beta[p] ~ dnorm(0, 0.01)
    }

tau.year <- 1 / (sd.year*sd.year)
sd.year ~ dunif(0, 1)                      # Hyperparameter 3

# Likelihood
for (i in 1:nyear){
    eps[i] ~ dnorm(0, tau.year)            # 4. Random year effects
    for (j in 1:nsite){
        C[i,j] ~ dpois(lambda[i,j])        # 1. Distribution for random
                                           #    part
        lambda[i,j] <- exp(log.lambda[i,j]) # 2. Link function
        log.lambda[i,j] <- alpha[j] + beta[1] * year[i] + beta[2] *
            pow(year[i],2) + beta[3] * pow(year[i],3) + eps[i] # 3. Linear
            predictor including random site and random year effects
        } #j
    } #i
}
",fill = TRUE)
sink()

# Bundle data
win.data <- list(C = data$C, nsite = ncol(data$C), nyear = nrow(data$C),
    year = (data$year-20) / 20) # Note year standardized

# Initial values
inits <- function() list(mu = runif(1, 0, 2), alpha = runif(data$nsite,
    -1, 1), beta = runif(3, -1, 1), sd.alpha = runif(1, 0, 0.1),
    sd.year = runif(1, 0, 0.1))

# Parameters monitored (may want to add "lambda")
params <- c("mu", "alpha", "beta", "sd.alpha", "sd.year")

# MCMC settings (may have to adapt)
ni <- 100000
nt <- 50
nb <- 50000
nc <- 3

# Call WinBUGS from R (BRT 98 min)
out <- bugs(win.data, inits, params, "GLMM_Poisson.txt", n.chains = nc,
    n.thin = nt, n.iter = ni, n.burnin = nb, debug = TRUE, bugs.directory =
    bugs.dir, working.directory = getwd())

# Summarize posteriors
print(out, dig = 3)
```

Estimation in more complex mixed models can be challenging. Estimating variance parameters is always more difficult than estimating fixed-effects parameters. This is manifest in slower convergence rates of the Markov chains, longer run times or trouble in getting convergence at all. Problems are compounded by small sample sizes. For the estimation of a variance parameter, the relevant sample size is the number of groups among which we want to estimate the variability in some parameter. Estimating variance parameters with fewer than 5–10 groups can be particularly difficult.

4.3.2 Analysis of Real Data Set

We analyze data from the Swiss breeding bird survey MHB ("Monitoring Häufige Brutvögel"; Schmid et al., 2004), a scheme launched in 1999. During each breeding season, a systematic sample of about 300 1-km² quadrats is surveyed 2–3 times using the territory mapping method. This produces a count of putative bird territories at each site and year. We will use a sample of data from 235 sites over 9 years and model the annual territory counts of the coal tit (Fig. 4.4). We are interested in whether there is an overall population trend in Swiss coal tits and in the variation of counts among sites, years, and observers. In addition, we would like to see whether observers count fewer birds during their first year of survey in a particular quadrat.

FIGURE 4.4   Coal tit (*Parus ater*), Finland, 2007. (Photograph by M. Varesvuo.)

Typically, each observer surveys only a small number of quadrats per year, but surveys the same quadrat(s) over a series of years.

We will fit a sequence of models starting with fixed effects only and then move on to including random effects. The comparison of analogous fixed- and random-effects models will be illuminating for your understanding of random effects. The most complex model entertained for count $C_{i,j}$ in year i at site j will be as follows:

$C_{i,j} \sim \text{Poisson}(\lambda_{i,j})$ Data Distribution

$\log(\lambda_{i,j}) = \alpha_j + \beta_1 * \text{year}_i$ Link Function and Linear Predictor
$\qquad + \beta_2 * F_{i,j} + \delta_i + \gamma_{k(i,j)}$

$\alpha_j \sim \text{Normal}(\mu, \sigma_\alpha^2)$ Random Site Effects

$\delta_i \sim \text{Normal}(0, \sigma_\delta^2)$ Random Year Effects

$\gamma_{k(i,j)} \sim \text{Normal}(0, \sigma_\gamma^2)$ Random Observer Effects

Thus, the log expected count, $\log(\lambda_{i,j})$, is a linear function of random site effects α_j, random year effects δ_i, and random observer effects $\gamma_{k(i,j)}$. In addition, there is a slope on year of magnitude β_1 (i.e., a trend) and a change in the expected count of magnitude β_2 if the indicator of first-year-of-service $F_{i,j}$ is equal to 1. The three sets of random effects are assumed to be drawn from independent normal distributions whose variances (or standard deviations) we estimate along with a grand mean μ.

```
# Read in the tit data and have a look at them
tits <- read.table("tits.txt", header = TRUE)
str(tits)
```

We have two environmental covariates (elevation and forest cover), annual territory counts 1999–2007 (y1999, etc.), an observer code (obs1999, etc., scaled to protect true observer ID), and finally a set of indicators for years when an observer surveyed a quadrat for the first time (first1999, etc.). Variable first1999 contains 1's only (except for some NAs), since MHB was launched in 1999. When modeling first-time observer effects, we may want to discard the 1999 data; otherwise the year 1999 effect is confounded with the first-time observer effect.

We collect counts, observer code, and first-time observer indicator variables in separate matrices and then plot the counts (Fig. 4.5; note use of the transposition function t()).

```
C <- as.matrix(tits[5:13])
obs <- as.matrix(tits[14:22])
first <- as.matrix(tits[23:31])
matplot(1999:2007, t(C), type = "l", lty = 1, lwd = 2, main = "",
    las = 1, ylab = "Territory counts", xlab = "Year", ylim = c(0, 80),
    frame = FALSE)
```

From Fig. 4.5, it appears that the Swiss coal tit metapopulation fluctuates around some fairly constant level. We will thus consider only a linear

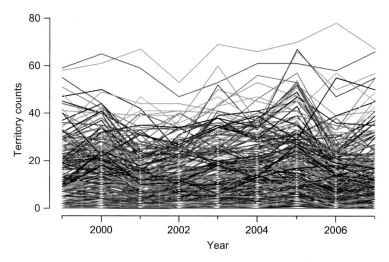

FIGURE 4.5   Territory counts of coal tits in 235-MHB quadrats in the Swiss breeding bird survey.

regression of counts on time rather than a higher order polynomial as for the French peregrines. However, we will try to explain variation among years and among sites by observer identity and first-year observer effects.

```
table(obs)
length(table(obs))
```

A total of 271 observers served from 1999 to 2007 and surveyed a fairly variable number of site years.

```
apply(first, 2, sum, na.rm = TRUE)
first1999 first2000 first2001 first2002 first2003 first2004 first2005
   first2006 first2007
      176        37        22        25        40        31        25        33        24
```

After 1999, about 10%–20% of observers are new on their quadrat each year. To model observer ID as a factor in WinBUGS, we need to recode it to be continuous.

```
a <- as.numeric(levels(factor(obs)))      # All the levels, numeric
newobs <- obs                             # Gets ObsID from 1:271
for (j in 1:length(a)){newobs[which(obs==a[j])] <- j }
table(newobs)
```

We also need to fill up any missing values in the explanatory variates in WinBUGS (or else we have to specify priors for them). Unfortunately, there are two kinds of missing values in the observer ID data: one for site years when a quadrat was not surveyed (these correspond to NAs in the counts matrix C) and another when a quadrat was surveyed, but the observer identity was not recorded. We impute some values in them, for example, 272 for missing observer identity and a zero in the first-year observer indicator variable. When transforming all NAs in the observer ID matrix to 272, we lump all unknown observers into a single observer identity. Given the large number of observers, this should hardly have an effect on the inference.

```
newobs[is.na(newobs)] <- 272
table(newobs)
first[is.na(first)] <- 0
table(first)
```

We are now ready to model these counts. Our strategy will be to start with the simplest possible model, with an intercept only, and then gradually build in more complexity. More specifically, we will first fit some fixed-effects models and only then we add the additional random-effects assumptions about some sets of previous fixed effects. This modification should clarify the exact meaning of the random-effects assumption. We will look at the deviance information criterion (DIC) as long as all effects in the model are fixed, but abandon it when we move to random effects, since the use of the standard DIC seems to be problematic then (Millar, 2009).

Null or Intercept-Only Model

This model has a constant expected count throughout space and time.

```
# Specify model in BUGS language
sink("GLM0.txt")
cat("
model {

# Prior
alpha ~ dnorm(0, 0.01)      # log(mean count)

# Likelihood
for (i in 1:nyear){
   for (j in 1:nsite){
      C[i,j] ~ dpois(lambda[i,j])
      lambda[i,j] <- exp(log.lambda[i,j])
      log.lambda[i,j] <- alpha
      }   #j
   }   #i
}
",fill = TRUE)
sink()

# Bundle data
win.data <- list(C = t(C), nsite = nrow(C), nyear = ncol(C))

# Initial values
inits <- function() list(alpha = runif(1, -10, 10))
```

```
# Parameters monitored
params <- c("alpha")

# MCMC settings
ni <- 1200
nt <- 2
nb <- 200
nc <- 3

# Call WinBUGS from R (BRT < 1 min)
out0 <- bugs(win.data, inits, params, "GLM0.txt", n.chains = nc,
n.thin = nt, n.iter = ni, n.burnin = nb, debug = TRUE, bugs.directory =
   bugs.dir, working.directory = getwd())

# Summarize posteriors
print(out0, dig = 3)
                mean    sd    2.5%      25%      50%      75%    97.5% Rhat n.eff
alpha          2.668 0.006   2.656    2.664    2.667    2.672    2.679    1  1500
deviance   32853.240 4.724 32850.000 32850.000 32850.000 32860.000 32860.000    1  1500
pD = 11.2 and DIC = 32864.4 (using the rule, pD = var(deviance)/2)
DIC is an estimate of expected predictive error (lower deviance is better).
```

This cannot be a very good model, but it's a start. It says that the mean observed density of tits per 1 km^2 is exp(2.67) = 14.4. Next, we add in fixed site effects.

Fixed Site Effects

This model is essentially a one-way ANOVA, except that it is for a Poisson rather than a normal response.

```
# Specify model in BUGS language
sink("GLM1.txt")
cat("
model {

# Priors
for (j in 1:nsite){
   alpha[j] ~ dnorm(0, 0.01)      # Site effects
   }

# Likelihood
for (i in 1:nyear){
   for (j in 1:nsite){
       C[i,j] ~ dpois(lambda[i,j])
       lambda[i,j] <- exp(log.lambda[i,j])
       log.lambda[i,j] <- alpha[j]
       }   #j
   }   #i
}
",fill = TRUE)
sink()

# Bundle data
win.data <- list(C = t(C), nsite = nrow(C), nyear = ncol(C))
```

```
# Initial values (not required for all)
inits <- function() list(alpha = runif(235, -1, 1))

# Parameters monitored
params <- c("alpha")

# MCMC settings
ni <- 1200
nt <- 2
nb <- 200
nc <- 3

# Call WinBUGS from R (BRT < 1 min)
out1 <- bugs(win.data, inits, params, "GLM1.txt", n.chains = nc,
n.thin = nt, n.iter = ni, n.burnin = nb, debug = TRUE, bugs.directory =
    bugs.dir, working.directory = getwd())

# Summarize posteriors
print(out1, dig = 2)
```

	mean	sd	2.5%	25%	50%	75%	97.5%	Rhat	n.eff
alpha[1]	-0.17	0.36	-0.91	-0.40	-0.16	0.08	0.47	1.00	1500
alpha[2]	-0.49	0.41	-1.36	-0.76	-0.45	-0.19	0.22	1.00	1200
alpha[3]	2.46	0.10	2.26	2.40	2.46	2.53	2.65	1.00	980
[...]									
alpha[233]	3.68	0.05	3.57	3.64	3.68	3.71	3.78	1.00	1500
alpha[234]	3.36	0.06	3.24	3.32	3.36	3.40	3.48	1.00	1500
alpha[235]	3.59	0.06	3.48	3.56	3.59	3.63	3.70	1.00	490
deviance	11688.71	21.82	11650.00	11670.00	11690.00	11700.00	11730.00	1.00	1500

```
pD = 238.3 and DIC = 11927 (using the rule, pD = var(deviance)/2)
DIC is an estimate of expected predictive error (lower deviance is better).
```

Fitting site effects has greatly improved the fit of the model; the deviance has come down by half and so has the DIC. Next, we also add fixed year effects.

Fixed Site and Fixed Year Effects

This model is a two-way, main-effects ANOVA for a Poisson response. Note how, in the inits function, we must not give an initial value for the first level of the year effects factor, which we have to set to zero to avoid overparameterization.

```
# Specify model in BUGS language
sink("GLM2.txt")
cat("
model {

# Priors
for (j in 1:nsite){          # Site effects
    alpha[j] ~ dnorm(0, 0.01)
    }
for (i in 2:nyear){          # nyear-1 year effects
    eps[i] ~ dnorm(0, 0.01)
    }
eps[1] <- 0                       # Aliased
```

```
# Likelihood
for (i in 1:nyear){
    for (j in 1:nsite){
        C[i,j] ~ dpois(lambda[i,j])
        lambda[i,j] <- exp(log.lambda[i,j])
        log.lambda[i,j] <- alpha[j] + eps[i]
        } #j
    } #i
}
",fill = TRUE)
sink()

# Bundle data
win.data <- list(C = t(C), nsite = nrow(C), nyear = ncol(C))

# Initial values
inits <- function() list(alpha = runif(235, -1, 1), eps = c(NA, runif(8,
    -1, 1)))

# Parameters monitored
params <- c("alpha", "eps")

# MCMC settings
ni <- 1200
nt <- 2
nb <- 200
nc <- 3

# Call WinBUGS from R (BRT < 1 min)
out2 <- bugs(win.data, inits, params, "GLM2.txt", n.chains = nc,
    n.thin = nt, n.iter = ni, n.burnin = nb, debug = TRUE, bugs.directory =
    bugs.dir, working.directory = getwd())

# Summarize posteriors
print(out2, dig = 2)
```

	mean	sd	2.5%	25%	50%	75%	97.5%	Rhat	n.eff
alpha[1]	-0.18	0.37	-0.96	-0.40	-0.16	0.07	0.49	1.00	1500
alpha[2]	-0.50	0.43	-1.37	-0.78	-0.47	-0.20	0.26	1.00	1500
alpha[3]	2.46	0.10	2.25	2.39	2.46	2.53	2.65	1.00	1000
[...]									
alpha[233]	3.67	0.06	3.56	3.64	3.67	3.71	3.78	1.00	920
alpha[234]	3.36	0.06	3.23	3.32	3.36	3.40	3.48	1.00	460
alpha[235]	3.59	0.06	3.47	3.55	3.59	3.63	3.69	1.00	1500
eps[2]	0.08	0.03	0.03	0.06	0.08	0.09	0.13	1.02	85
eps[3]	-0.16	0.03	-0.21	-0.18	-0.16	-0.14	-0.10	1.03	69
eps[4]	-0.11	0.03	-0.15	-0.12	-0.11	-0.09	-0.05	1.04	59
eps[5]	0.06	0.03	0.01	0.04	0.06	0.07	0.11	1.02	97
eps[6]	0.10	0.02	0.05	0.08	0.10	0.12	0.15	1.03	76
eps[7]	0.22	0.02	0.18	0.21	0.22	0.24	0.27	1.02	110
eps[8]	-0.16	0.03	-0.21	-0.18	-0.16	-0.14	-0.11	1.02	98
eps[9]	-0.07	0.03	-0.12	-0.08	-0.07	-0.05	-0.02	1.02	94
deviance	11237.79	22.12	11200.00	11220.00	11240.00	11250.00	11280.00	1.00	1500

pD = 244.7 and DIC = 11482.4 (using the rule, pD = var(deviance)/2)

DIC is an estimate of expected predictive error (lower deviance is better).

With the introduction of year effects, the deviance and the DIC have gone down quite a bit again, so there seem to be annual population fluctuations. Now, we increase the model complexity by specifying random instead of fixed effects. Watch how simple the move from fixed to random effects is when a model is defined in the BUGS language. Essentially, all that is required is a common distribution to be assumed for a set of grouped effects with hyperparameters that are going to be estimated and that therefore need hyperpriors in turn. We start with the random site model.

Random Site Effects (No Year Effects)

The linear predictor of this model is that of a one-way, random-effects ANOVA.

```
# Specify model in BUGS language
sink("GLMM1.txt")
cat("
model {

# Priors
for (j in 1:nsite){
    alpha[j] ~ dnorm(mu.alpha, tau.alpha)      # Random site effects
    }
mu.alpha ~ dnorm(0, 0.01)
tau.alpha <- 1/ (sd.alpha * sd.alpha)
sd.alpha ~ dunif(0, 5)

# Likelihood
for (i in 1:nyear){
    for (j in 1:nsite){
        C[i,j] ~ dpois(lambda[i,j])
        lambda[i,j] <- exp(log.lambda[i,j])
        log.lambda[i,j] <- alpha[j]
        } #j
    } #i
}
",fill = TRUE)
sink()

# Bundle data
win.data <- list(C = t(C), nsite = nrow(C), nyear = ncol(C))

# Initial values
inits <- function() list(mu.alpha = runif(1, 2, 3))

# Parameters monitored
params <- c("alpha", "mu.alpha", "sd.alpha")

# MCMC settings
ni <- 1200
nt <- 2
nb <- 200
nc <- 3
```

```
# Call WinBUGS from R (BRT < 1 min)
out3 <- bugs(win.data, inits, params, "GLMM1.txt", n.chains = nc,
n.thin = nt, n.iter = ni, n.burnin = nb, debug = TRUE, bugs.directory =
    bugs.dir, working.directory = getwd())

# Summarize posteriors
print(out3, dig = 2)
```

	mean	sd	2.5%	25%	50%	75%	97.5%	Rhat	n.eff
alpha[1]	-0.03	0.33	-0.69	-0.25	-0.02	0.21	0.57	1.00	1500
alpha[2]	-0.26	0.36	-1.03	-0.49	-0.24	0.00	0.40	1.00	1500
alpha[3]	2.46	0.11	2.25	2.39	2.46	2.52	2.67	1.00	1500
[...]									
alpha[233]	3.68	0.05	3.57	3.64	3.67	3.71	3.78	1.00	1500
alpha[234]	3.36	0.06	3.24	3.32	3.36	3.40	3.48	1.00	1500
alpha[235]	3.59	0.06	3.48	3.55	3.59	3.63	3.69	1.00	650
mu.alpha	2.09	0.09	1.93	2.03	2.09	2.15	2.27	1.00	1500
sd.alpha	1.33	0.06	1.21	1.28	1.32	1.37	1.46	1.00	1500
deviance	11692.91	22.38	11650.00	11680.00	11690.00	11710.00	11740.00	1.00	650

The mass of the posterior distribution of the standard deviation of the random site effects is concentrated well away from zero. This confirms our previous conclusion that sites differ substantially in their expected counts of coal tits. We next add a set of random year effects and in addition reparameterize the model to have a single grand mean. Each set of random effects is then centered around that grand mean, which helps convergence.

Random Site and Random Year Effects

This linear model corresponds to a main-effects ANOVA with two random factors. In comparison to the fixed-effects counterpart of this model (GLM 2), we no longer need to constrain one effect of one factor to zero to avoid overparameterization. The borrowing strength among parameters within the same random-effects factor ensures that all can be estimated.

```
# Specify model in BUGS language
sink("GLMM2.txt")
cat("
model {

# Priors
mu ~ dnorm(0, 0.01)                      # Grand mean
for (j in 1:nsite){
    alpha[j] ~ dnorm(0, tau.alpha)       # Random site effects
    }
tau.alpha <- 1/ (sd.alpha * sd.alpha)
sd.alpha ~ dunif(0, 5)

for (i in 1:nyear){
    eps[i] ~ dnorm(0, tau.eps)           # Random year effects
    }
tau.eps <- 1/ (sd.eps * sd.eps)
sd.eps ~ dunif(0, 3)
```

```
# Likelihood
for (i in 1:nyear){
    for (j in 1:nsite){
        C[i,j] ~ dpois(lambda[i,j])
        lambda[i,j] <- exp(log.lambda[i,j])
        log.lambda[i,j] <- mu + alpha[j] + eps[i]
        } #j
    } #i
}
",fill = TRUE)
sink()

# Bundle data
win.data <- list(C = t(C), nsite = nrow(C), nyear = ncol(C))

# Initial values (not required for all)
inits <- function() list(mu = runif(1, 0, 4), alpha = runif(235, -2, 2),
    eps = runif(9, -1, 1))

# Parameters monitored
params <- c("mu", "alpha", "eps", "sd.alpha", "sd.eps")

# MCMC settings
ni <- 6000
nt <- 5
nb <- 1000
nc <- 3

# Call WinBUGS from R (BRT 3 min)
out4 <- bugs(win.data, inits, params, "GLMM2.txt", n.chains = nc,
    n.thin = nt, n.iter = ni, n.burnin = nb, debug = TRUE, bugs.directory =
    bugs.dir, working.directory = getwd())

# Summarize posteriors
print(out4, dig = 2)
```

	mean	sd	2.5%	25%	50%	75%	97.5%	Rhat	n.eff
mu	2.09	0.10	1.89	2.03	2.10	2.16	2.29	1.01	860
alpha[1]	-2.13	0.34	-2.83	-2.35	-2.12	-1.90	-1.51	1.00	3000
alpha[2]	-2.36	0.37	-3.14	-2.60	-2.35	-2.11	-1.68	1.00	2100
alpha[3]	0.36	0.13	0.10	0.27	0.36	0.45	0.62	1.00	590
[...]									
alpha[233]	1.57	0.10	1.38	1.51	1.57	1.64	1.76	1.01	260
alpha[234]	1.26	0.10	1.05	1.19	1.26	1.33	1.46	1.00	770
alpha[235]	1.49	0.10	1.30	1.42	1.49	1.55	1.68	1.01	310
eps[1]	0.00	0.06	-0.12	-0.03	0.00	0.04	0.12	1.03	88
eps[2]	0.08	0.06	-0.04	0.04	0.08	0.11	0.19	1.03	86
eps[3]	-0.16	0.06	-0.27	-0.19	-0.15	-0.12	-0.04	1.03	93
eps[4]	-0.10	0.06	-0.22	-0.14	-0.10	-0.07	0.01	1.04	67
eps[5]	0.06	0.06	-0.06	0.03	0.06	0.10	0.17	1.03	89
eps[6]	0.10	0.06	-0.02	0.06	0.10	0.13	0.21	1.03	89
eps[7]	0.22	0.06	0.11	0.19	0.22	0.26	0.34	1.05	77
eps[8]	-0.16	0.06	-0.28	-0.19	-0.16	-0.12	-0.05	1.03	83
eps[9]	-0.06	0.06	-0.18	-0.10	-0.06	-0.03	0.05	1.03	84
sd.alpha	1.33	0.07	1.21	1.28	1.33	1.37	1.47	1.00	3000
sd.eps	0.15	0.05	0.09	0.12	0.14	0.18	0.28	1.00	1100
deviance	11240.99	22.57	11200.00	11230.00	11240.00	11260.00	11290.00	1.00	3000

The year effects do not seem to be very large; at any rate, they (sd.eps) are much smaller than the variation of counts among sites (sd.alpha). Next, we add a fixed first-year observer effect.

Random Site and Random Year Effects and First-Year Fixed Observer Effect

This model is analogous to a three-way ANOVA with two factors random and one fixed and all of them acting in an additive way.

```
# Specify model in BUGS language
sink("GLMM3.txt")
cat("
model {

# Priors
mu ~ dnorm(0, 0.01)                    # Overall mean
beta2 ~ dnorm(0, 0.01)                 # First-year observer effect

for (j in 1:nsite){
    alpha[j] ~ dnorm(0, tau.alpha)     # Random site effects
    }
tau.alpha <- 1/ (sd.alpha * sd.alpha)
sd.alpha ~ dunif(0, 5)
for (i in 1:nyear){
    eps[i] ~ dnorm(0, tau.eps)         # Random year effects
    }
tau.eps <- 1/ (sd.eps * sd.eps)
sd.eps ~ dunif(0, 5)

# Likelihood
for (i in 1:nyear){
    for (j in 1:nsite){
        C[i,j] ~ dpois(lambda[i,j])
        lambda[i,j] <- exp(log.lambda[i,j])
        log.lambda[i,j] <- mu + beta2 * first[i,j] + alpha[j] + eps[i]
        } #j
    } #i
}
",fill = TRUE)
sink()

# Bundle data
win.data <- list(C = t(C), nsite = nrow(C), nyear = ncol(C), first = t
    (first))

# Initial values
inits <- function() list(mu = runif(1, 0, 4), beta2 = runif(1, -1, 1),
    alpha = runif(235, -2, 2), eps = runif(9, -1, 1))

# Parameters monitored
params <- c("mu", "beta2", "alpha", "eps", "sd.alpha", "sd.eps")

# MCMC settings
ni <- 6000
```

```
nt <- 5
nb <- 1000
nc <- 3
```

```
# Call WinBUGS from R (BRT 3 min)
out5 <- bugs(win.data, inits, params, "GLMM3.txt", n.chains = nc,
    n.thin = nt, n.iter = ni, n.burnin = nb, debug = TRUE, bugs.directory =
    bugs.dir, working.directory = getwd())
```

```
# Summarize posteriors
print(out5, dig = 2)
```

	mean	sd	2.5%	25%	50%	75%	97.5%	Rhat	n.eff
mu	2.09	0.09	1.92	2.02	2.09	2.16	2.27	1.06	37
beta2	0.00	0.02	-0.04	-0.02	0.00	0.01	0.03	1.00	2800
alpha[1]	-2.12	0.33	-2.80	-2.35	-2.11	-1.88	-1.53	1.00	460
alpha[2]	-2.36	0.37	-3.15	-2.59	-2.34	-2.11	-1.69	1.00	1900
alpha[3]	0.36	0.14	0.09	0.27	0.36	0.46	0.62	1.02	140
[...]									
alpha[233]	1.58	0.10	1.38	1.51	1.58	1.65	1.77	1.03	68
alpha[234]	1.26	0.11	1.06	1.19	1.26	1.34	1.47	1.03	81
alpha[235]	1.49	0.10	1.29	1.42	1.50	1.56	1.70	1.03	74
eps[1]	0.01	0.06	-0.10	-0.03	0.00	0.04	0.14	1.05	74
eps[2]	0.08	0.06	-0.02	0.04	0.08	0.11	0.20	1.06	59
eps[3]	-0.15	0.06	-0.26	-0.19	-0.15	-0.12	-0.03	1.05	67
eps[4]	-0.10	0.06	-0.21	-0.14	-0.10	-0.07	0.02	1.05	71
eps[5]	0.06	0.06	-0.04	0.03	0.06	0.09	0.19	1.06	62
eps[6]	0.10	0.06	0.00	0.07	0.10	0.13	0.23	1.06	62
eps[7]	0.22	0.06	0.12	0.19	0.22	0.25	0.35	1.05	66
eps[8]	-0.16	0.06	-0.26	-0.19	-0.16	-0.12	-0.03	1.05	64
eps[9]	-0.06	0.06	-0.17	-0.10	-0.06	-0.03	0.06	1.05	66
sd.alpha	1.33	0.07	1.20	1.28	1.32	1.37	1.47	1.00	3000
sd.eps	0.16	0.05	0.09	0.12	0.14	0.18	0.29	1.00	1100
deviance	11240.86	22.54	11200.00	11230.00	11240.00	11250.00	11280.00	1.00	1100

Beta2 is very nearly zero; hence, there is no evidence for a first-year observer effect. Next, we also add an overall linear time trend.

Random Site and Random Year Effects, First-Year Fixed Observer Effect, and Overall Linear Time Trend

The linear part of this model corresponds to an analysis of covariance (ANCOVA), with, in addition to the three factors of the previous model, an added effect of one continuous covariate.

```
# Specify model in BUGS language
sink("GLMM4.txt")
cat("
model {

# Priors
mu ~ dnorm(0, 0.01)              # Overall intercept
beta1 ~ dnorm(0, 0.01)           # Overall trend
beta2 ~ dnorm(0, 0.01)           # First-year observer effect
```

```
for (j in 1:nsite){
    alpha[j] ~ dnorm(0, tau.alpha)      # Random site effects
    }
tau.alpha <- 1/ (sd.alpha * sd.alpha)
sd.alpha ~ dunif(0, 5)

for (i in 1:nyear){
    eps[i] ~ dnorm(0, tau.eps)          # Random year effects
    }
tau.eps <- 1/ (sd.eps * sd.eps)
sd.eps ~ dunif(0, 3)

# Likelihood
for (i in 1:nyear){
    for (j in 1:nsite){
        C[i,j] ~ dpois(lambda[i,j])
        lambda[i,j] <- exp(log.lambda[i,j])
        log.lambda[i,j] <- mu + beta1 * year[i] + beta2 * first[i,j] +
    alpha[j] + eps[i]
        } #j
    } #i
}
",fill = TRUE)
sink()

# Bundle data
win.data <- list(C = t(C), nsite = nrow(C), nyear = ncol(C), first = t
    (first), year = ((1:9)-5) / 4)

# Initial values
inits <- function() list(mu = runif(1, 0, 4), beta1 = runif(1, -1, 1),
    beta2 = runif(1, -1, 1), alpha = runif(235, -2, 2), eps = runif(9, -1, 1))

# Parameters monitored
params <- c("mu", "beta1", "beta2", "alpha", "eps", "sd.alpha",
    "sd.eps")

# MCMC settings
ni <- 12000
nt <- 6
nb <- 6000
nc <- 3

# Call WinBUGS from R (BRT 7 min)
out6 <- bugs(win.data, inits, params, "GLMM4.txt", n.chains = nc,
    n.thin = nt, n.iter = ni, n.burnin = nb, debug = TRUE, bugs.directory =
    bugs.dir, working.directory = getwd())

# Summarize posteriors
print(out6, dig = 2)
```

	mean	sd	2.5%	25%	50%	75%	97.5%	Rhat	n.eff
mu	2.09	0.10	1.88	2.02	2.10	2.17	2.28	1.06	64
beta1	0.00	0.08	-0.15	-0.06	-0.01	0.04	0.18	1.03	210
beta2	0.00	0.02	-0.04	-0.02	0.00	0.01	0.03	1.00	1500
alpha[1]	-2.12	0.34	-2.82	-2.34	-2.10	-1.88	-1.52	1.00	610
alpha[2]	-2.36	0.37	-3.15	-2.60	-2.34	-2.11	-1.67	1.00	3000
alpha[3]	0.36	0.13	0.10	0.27	0.36	0.45	0.63	1.02	110

[...]

```
alpha[233]     1.58  0.10     1.39     1.51     1.57     1.65     1.78 1.04     67
alpha[234]     1.26  0.11     1.06     1.19     1.26     1.34     1.48 1.03     81
alpha[235]     1.49  0.10     1.30     1.42     1.49     1.57     1.70 1.03     74
eps[1]         0.00  0.10    -0.19    -0.06     0.00     0.07     0.20 1.02    140
eps[2]         0.07  0.08    -0.09     0.02     0.07     0.13     0.24 1.02    150
eps[3]        -0.16  0.07    -0.30    -0.20    -0.16    -0.11    -0.01 1.02    150
eps[4]        -0.10  0.06    -0.23    -0.14    -0.10    -0.07     0.02 1.02    170
eps[5]         0.06  0.06    -0.05     0.02     0.06     0.10     0.17 1.02    170
eps[6]         0.10  0.06    -0.03     0.07     0.10     0.14     0.21 1.01    260
eps[7]         0.22  0.07     0.07     0.18     0.23     0.27     0.35 1.01    270
eps[8]        -0.15  0.08    -0.34    -0.20    -0.15    -0.10    -0.01 1.01    270
eps[9]        -0.06  0.10    -0.29    -0.12    -0.05     0.01     0.12 1.02    290
sd.alpha       1.33  0.07     1.21     1.28     1.33     1.37     1.46 1.00   3000
sd.eps         0.17  0.06     0.09     0.13     0.16     0.19     0.30 1.01    650
deviance   11241.89 22.31 11200.00 11230.00 11240.00 11260.00 11290.00 1.00   3000
```

The Full Model

Finally, we fit the full model with random site effects, an overall linear time trend, random observer effects, random year effects, and a fixed first-year observer effect. Based on the estimates in the previous model, we constrain the random effects standard deviations sufficiently (i.e., specify a smaller range for the uniform prior distributions) so that WinBUGS does not easily get lost numerically. We also increase chain length.

```
# Specify model in BUGS language
sink("GLMM5.txt")
cat("
model {

# Priors
mu ~ dnorm(0, 0.01)                         # Overall intercept
beta1 ~ dnorm(0, 0.01)                      # Overall trend
beta2 ~ dnorm(0, 0.01)                      # First-year observer effect

for (j in 1:nsite){
    alpha[j] ~ dnorm(0, tau.alpha)          # Random site effects
    }
tau.alpha <- 1/ (sd.alpha * sd.alpha)
sd.alpha ~ dunif(0, 3)

for (i in 1:nyear){
    eps[i] ~ dnorm(0, tau.eps)              # Random year effects
    }
tau.eps <- 1/ (sd.eps * sd.eps)
sd.eps ~ dunif(0, 1)

for (k in 1:nobs){
    gamma[k] ~ dnorm(0, tau.gamma)          # Random observer effects
    }
tau.gamma <- 1/ (sd.gamma * sd.gamma)
sd.gamma ~ dunif(0, 1)
```

```
# Likelihood
for (i in 1:nyear){
    for (j in 1:nsite){
        C[i,j] ~ dpois(lambda[i,j])
        lambda[i,j] <- exp(log.lambda[i,j])
        log.lambda[i,j] <- mu + beta1 * year[i] + beta2 * first[i,j] +
    alpha[j] + gamma[newobs[i,j]] + eps[i]
        } #j
    } #i
}
",fill = TRUE)
sink()
```

```
# Bundle data
win.data <- list(C = t(C), nsite = nrow(C), nyear = ncol(C), nobs = 272,
    newobs = t(newobs), first = t(first), year = ((1:9)-5) / 4)
```

```
# Initial values
inits <- function() list(mu = runif(1, 0, 4), beta1 = runif(1, -1, 1),
    beta2 = runif(1, -1, 1), alpha = runif(235, -1, 1), gamma = runif(272,
    -1, 1), eps = runif(9, -1, 1))
```

```
# Parameters monitored
params <- c("mu", "beta1", "beta2", "alpha", "gamma", "eps",
    "sd.alpha", "sd.gamma", "sd.eps")
```

```
# MCMC settings
ni <- 12000
nt <- 6
nb <- 6000
nc <- 3
```

```
# Call WinBUGS from R (BRT 11 min)
out7 <- bugs(win.data, inits, params, "GLMM5.txt", n.chains = nc,
    n.thin = nt, n.iter = ni, n.burnin = nb, debug = TRUE, bugs.directory =
    bugs.dir, working.directory = getwd())
```

```
# Summarize posteriors
print(out7, dig = 2)
```

	mean	sd	2.5%	25%	50%	75%	97.5%	Rhat	n.eff
mu	2.08	0.10	1.87	2.01	2.07	2.14	2.27	1.02	570
beta1	0.02	0.09	-0.16	-0.04	0.01	0.07	0.24	1.04	3000
beta2	0.02	0.02	-0.02	0.01	0.02	0.04	0.07	1.00	3000
alpha[1]	-2.43	0.37	-3.18	-2.66	-2.41	-2.18	-1.75	1.00	790
alpha[2]	-2.10	0.41	-2.92	-2.37	-2.08	-1.81	-1.33	1.01	210
alpha[3]	0.36	0.26	-0.15	0.20	0.36	0.53	0.87	1.01	400
[...]									
alpha[233]	1.63	0.30	1.04	1.43	1.62	1.83	2.25	1.01	300
alpha[234]	1.55	0.20	1.17	1.41	1.54	1.69	1.94	1.04	60
alpha[235]	1.78	0.20	1.41	1.64	1.77	1.92	2.17	1.04	61
gamma[1]	0.06	0.25	-0.44	-0.10	0.06	0.23	0.58	1.00	3000
gamma[2]	-0.01	0.34	-0.70	-0.24	-0.02	0.22	0.65	1.00	610
gamma[3]	-0.50	0.27	-1.05	-0.68	-0.50	-0.32	0.00	1.00	1800
[...]									

gamma[270]	-0.57	0.28	-1.15	-0.75	-0.56	-0.38	-0.03	1.00	1600
gamma[271]	0.02	0.23	-0.44	-0.14	0.02	0.17	0.48	1.00	1300
gamma[272]	-0.27	0.20	-0.66	-0.41	-0.28	-0.13	0.08	1.07	36
eps[1]	0.01	0.10	-0.19	-0.05	0.01	0.07	0.24	1.03	220
eps[2]	0.10	0.09	-0.08	0.04	0.09	0.15	0.28	1.03	130
eps[3]	-0.14	0.07	-0.29	-0.18	-0.14	-0.10	0.01	1.03	75
eps[4]	-0.09	0.06	-0.22	-0.13	-0.10	-0.06	0.02	1.04	55
eps[5]	0.06	0.06	-0.06	0.02	0.06	0.09	0.16	1.05	45
eps[6]	0.09	0.06	-0.04	0.06	0.09	0.13	0.21	1.06	52
eps[7]	0.21	0.08	0.05	0.16	0.21	0.25	0.35	1.06	66
eps[8]	-0.16	0.09	-0.36	-0.22	-0.15	-0.10	0.02	1.06	110
eps[9]	-0.07	0.11	-0.30	-0.14	-0.06	0.00	0.14	1.06	130
sd.alpha	1.31	0.07	1.18	1.26	1.30	1.35	1.45	1.00	3000
sd.gamma	0.34	0.03	0.28	0.32	0.34	0.36	0.40	1.00	640
sd.eps	0.17	0.06	0.09	0.13	0.15	0.19	0.32	1.02	130
deviance	10687.47	30.28	10630.00	10670.00	10690.00	10710.00	10750.00	1.00	2200

It appears that there is much variation in the counts of coal tits due to differences among sites and also due to differences among observers. We note, though, that site and observer effects are confounded to some degree, since only one to a few observers are tested on each site and that observers are not randomly allocated to sites. There is a fairly small variance component due to years. Neither year as a continuous covariate (beta1) nor first-year observer effects (beta2) seem important, since their 95% CRI covers zero by a wide margin. Regarding the latter, we repeat that first-year observer effects are confounded with the effect of the first year. For a more thorough assessment of first-year observer effects, we might want to repeat the analysis for years 2–9 only.

This concludes our overview of different variants of a Poisson GLMM. We hasten to say that the models in this chapter are purely phenomenological and not necessarily the best models for animal counts. For instance, we have not built in any population dynamics: changes from year to year are not autocorrelated as one might expect owing to the effects of density dependence or of the vital rates inducing these changes. For models that include such additional ecological realism, see Chapters 5 and 11.

4.4 SUMMARY AND OUTLOOK

In this chapter, we have introduced another crucial concept (besides the GLM) of applied statistical models: random effects. We have seen that the inclusion of random effects changes the scope of inference in an analysis, allows one to study the variability in parameter sets, accounts for internal structure (correlations) in the data, achieves a more honest accounting for the uncertainties in a modeled system, and may result in improved estimates of each parameter owing to "borrowing strength from the ensemble". We hope that the simulation of data sets and model specification in the BUGS language has enhanced your understanding of the actual meaning of random effects, something which we believe is easily lost when specifying random-effects models in software such as R or GenStat. The setting of all random effects in this chapter was the generalized linear model (GLM); hence, we dealt with GLMMs. Poisson GLMMs now form one of the standard models for counts of animals; see, for example, the papers by Link and Sauer (2002), Sauer and Link (2002), Ver Hoef and Jansen (2007), and Cressie et al. (2009). They are hierarchical models and to some (e.g., Cressie et al., 2009) have become almost synonymous with "the hierarchical model" in ecology. However, there are many different hierarchical models in ecology, and we will encounter a variety of hierarchical or random-effects models in almost every chapter in this book.

The Poisson GLMMs in this chapter are useful, for instance, because they more properly partition the effects of multiple sources of variability in a modeled system. One way how a partitioning of the system variability can be achieved is to separate out variability intrinsic to the studied system and variability associated with the measurement, or the observation, of that system. Hence, Poisson GLMMs achieve a certain degree of partitioning of the data into what may be called the ecological process and the observation process.

However, we believe that these models have important shortcomings as a general framework for inference about animal or plant population sizes. Most of all, they cannot directly account for that hallmark of ecological field data, namely, imperfect detection. Models such as those in this chapter do not contain an explicit description of a meaningful ecological process; they are "implicit" hierarchical models in the sense of Royle and Dorazio (2008). Their state is some sort of "expected count", and it is difficult to attach a clear biological interpretation to that. In other words, the expected count is always a result of a certain observation process and will depend to a large extent on how good a job you do at the counting. This can hardly be claimed to be of ecological interest!

A variant of the implicit hierarchical models in this chapter has come to be called "state-space models" in population dynamics and is the subject of the next chapter. They go one step further in introducing biological realism into the modeling, in that they make a better distinction between what they call process and observation models. Furthermore, their process model usually contains added biological realism in the form of an autoregressive population model and may contain a parameter for density dependence. These are powerful and interesting models, and yet, they fail to explicitly account for imperfect detection and its effects on the inference about the population processes. To make a clear and ecologically meaningful distinction between the ecological and the observation processes, other protocols and models must be chosen, leading to what Royle and Dorazio (2008) called "explicit" hierarchical models. These models exploit explicit information about the observation process, enabling one to explicitly model the observation process by estimating detection probability. In the context of statistical inference about animal numbers, the natural generalization of an implicit Poisson GLMM is the class of binomial mixture models introduced in Chapter 12.

4.5 EXERCISES

1. Overdispersion: Generate a data set using the function in Section 4.2.1 and use WinBUGS to compare the regression estimates under the Poisson GLM and those under the Poisson GLMM. The Bayesian analysis yields better estimates of the uncertainty in the estimates of a random-effects model and lets you see more clearly how the regression estimates have an increased posterior standard deviation when estimated under the model with random year effects.
2. First-year observer effect: We have seen that in the tit data, any first-year observer effect is confounded with the effect of the first year. Repeat the last analysis for a restricted data set without year 1.
3. Reparameterizations: In GLMM 2, put the grand mean of the double random-effects model, mu, into the hyperdistribution of one of the random effects, that is, fit the model like the following:

```
for (j in 1:nsite){
alpha[j] ~ dnorm(mu, tau.alpha)
}
```

You will see that convergence is worse. This is an example of where WinBUGS is very sensitive to how a model is parameterized.
4. Interpretation of random effects: Fit a series of models to the tit data with different random effects:
   - A site random effect: random contributions from each site
   - A year random effect: random contributions from each year
   - A site plus a year random effect
   - A site-by-year random effect: random contributions from each site–year combination

   Compare parameter estimates, explain the difference in the interpretation of those models, and try to make sense of the differences.
5. Fixed and random: Convert these models into fixed-effects models, that is, specify each of the following models without making the assumption that a set of effects come from a common distribution: site, year, site + year, observer, site + observer, year + observer,

site + year + observer, first-year indicator. Comparing the fixed- and the random-effects version of a model as specified in the BUGS language will be very helpful for your understanding of mixed models!

6. Covariates: In the tit model in Section 4.3.2, add the log-linear effects of elevation and forest cover in the linear predictor of abundance. Also add in squared effects of these covariates.

7. Take the model and the data from Section 4.3.1.
   a. Drop the quadratic and the cubic polynomial terms of year.
   b. Next, turn the random-effects Poisson GLM into a fixed- (year and site) effects Poisson GLM, that is, drop the randomness assumption for site and year. Hint: your model will then be a two-way, main-effects ANOVA, so you will have to constrain some parameters to make it identifiable.

8. Take the model and the data from Section 4.3.1 and model the response as coming from a normal distribution. This will clarify some of the differences between a normal and a Poisson GLMM.

State-Space Models for Population Counts

5.1 INTRODUCTION

State-space models are hierarchical models that decompose an observed time series of counts or other observed responses into a process variation and an observation error component. They are suitable for the description of Markovian, that is, autoregressive, processes that are latent or hidden, because they are observed imperfectly (Harvey, 1989). Originally developed in industry (Kalman, 1960), the use of state-space models in population dynamics has only recently begun (De Valpine and Hastings, 2002; Buckland et al., 2004; Clark and Björnstad, 2004). The change in population size over time is a Markovian process because population size in year $t + 1$ depends on population size in year t. Perhaps the simplest population dynamics model is the exponential:

$$N_{t+1} = N_t \lambda_t,$$

where λ_t is the population growth rate, defined for $t = 1, \ldots, T - 1$; T being the number of years with observed counts. A typical goal of a population dynamics analysis is to estimate the population growth rate and to study factors affecting it. This is relatively straightforward if the exact population size in each year is known. Regression-like models can then be used to estimate temporal variability, the strength of density-dependence, and the impact of environmental factors (see, e.g., Dennis et al., 1991; Dennis and Taper, 1994; Lande et al., 2003). However, only in exceptional cases do we know the exact size of a population. More typically, we only have a count with some unknown observation error associated. This observation error must be accounted for when analyzing population dynamics data. Otherwise, the power to detect factors affecting population dynamics is reduced and density-dependence may be detected spuriously (Freckleton et al., 2006).

The state-space models of this chapter allow one to deal with the challenge of observation error in the analysis of population dynamics, at least partially (see Section 5.3). The state-space model adopted here consists of two sets of equations. The state-process equations describe the true, but unknown development of a state, that is, the population dynamics free of observation error. For the dynamics of an exponentially growing population, the unknown state is population size N_t at time t:

$$N_{t+1} = N_t \lambda_t$$

$$\lambda_t \sim \text{Normal}(\bar{\lambda}, \sigma_\lambda^2).$$

In this model, we assume that the growth rates (λ_t) are realizations of a normal random process with mean $\bar{\lambda}$ and variance σ_λ^2. The mean is the long-term growth rate of the population, and the variance is a measure of the environmental variability affecting this growth rate, that is, environmental stochasticity. Note that the population size in the first year is not defined by the equations above. We therefore need to define this initial state by another model. In the Bayesian context, we can either specify a prior distribution for N_1, or fix it to the observed count, making the assumption that the first count is error-free.

The second set of equations maps the true state of the process on the observed data. These observation equations are conditional on the process equations. Assume we have a population count for each of a series of years.

We link these observations (y_t) with the true population size using the following equations:

$$y_t = N_t + \varepsilon_t$$
$$\varepsilon_t \sim \text{Normal}(0, \sigma_y^2).$$

They represent the assumption that in year t, we make an observation error of magnitude ε_t and that these errors in the counts around the true population size can be described by a normal distribution with mean zero and variance σ_y^2; the latter is the observation error. In this model, the true population size is as likely to be over- as it is to be undercounted. For instance, in one year, we may miss more individuals than we double-count, resulting in a negative value of ε_t, and in another year, it may be the other way round. The observation error is, in fact, a residual error and therefore incorporates not only observation errors but also the lack of fit of the state equations. Figure 5.1 represents the model graphically.

The model assumes that the two sets of random terms, λ_t and ε_t, are serially independent, independent from each other and that each set is identically distributed. Formulations of the likelihood of the model can be found, for example, in De Valpine and Hastings (2002). The model likelihood is composed of the likelihoods for the initial state, for the state process, and for the observation process.

The state-space modeling framework is very flexible and can be extended in various ways. We could, of course, define different state-processes (e.g., include survival and fecundity, see Chapter 11, or use a logistic growth model). Also, different descriptions of the observation process are possible, for instance, the assumption of binomial, Poisson, or lognormal errors. As we will see later, state-space models can be used for purposes other than estimating the true trajectories of population size. Examples we will see later include probabilities of survival (Chapters 7, 8, and 10), state-transition (Chapter 9),

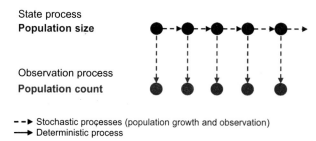

FIGURE 5.1 State process of a population and the conditional observation process. The state process describes the dynamics of population size over time (N_t), whereas the observation process describes the error-prone population counts (y_t). Note that this figure is essentially a version of Fig. 2.1.

and species occurrence and site occupancy (Chapter 12). They are also at the heart of integrated population models (Chapter 11). Because the observation process is conditional on the state process, a state-space model is also a hierarchical model (Royle and Dorazio, 2008).

5.2 A SIMPLE MODEL

We will first simulate and analyze count data in a very simple context. Let's assume that a population of ibex (Fig. 5.2) with initial size of 30 individuals was monitored during 25 years and grew annually by 2% on average. Shortly after the start of snow-melt, ibexes are counted by the aid of a telescope from the slope opposite to the mountain ridge which constitutes the core area of the population. The population survey is not perfect, and we assume that the variance of the observation error is 20. To simulate the data, we first define the underlying parameters.

```
n.years <- 25          # Number of years
N1 <- 30               # Initial population size
mean.lambda <- 1.02    # Mean annual population growth rate
sigma2.lambda <- 0.02  # Process (temporal) variation of the growth rate
sigma2.y <- 20         # Variance of the observation error
```

Next we simulate the population sizes under the assumption of exponential growth.

FIGURE 5.2   Ibexes (*Capra ibex*), Switzerland (Photograph by F. Labhardt).

```
y <- N <- numeric(n.years)
N[1] <- N1
lambda <- rnorm(n.years-1, mean.lambda, sqrt(sigma2.lambda))
for (t in 1:(n.years-1)){
    N[t+1] <- N[t] * lambda[t]
    }
```

Finally, we generate the observed data conditional on the true population sizes.

```
for (t in 1:n.years){
    y[t] <- rnorm(1, N[t], sqrt(sigma2.y))
    }
```

You may have noticed that neither population size nor the counts are integers, as might be expected for a biological population. However, our goal here is to simulate and analyze the data in exactly the same way as the classical state-space models of this chapter are formulated and to explore the performance of state-space models. In Section 5.3, we will simulate a data set under more mechanistic assumptions which lead to integers.

Now, we analyze the simulated data. We first write the model in the BUGS language.

```
# Specify model in BUGS language
sink("ssm.bug")
cat("
model {

# Priors and constraints
N.est[1] ~ dunif(0, 500)          # Prior for initial population size
mean.lambda ~ dunif(0, 10)        # Prior for mean growth rate
sigma.proc ~ dunif(0, 10)         # Prior for sd of state process
sigma2.proc <- pow(sigma.proc, 2)
tau.proc <- pow(sigma.proc, -2)
sigma.obs ~ dunif(0, 100)         # Prior for sd of observation process
sigma2.obs <- pow(sigma.obs, 2)
tau.obs <- pow(sigma.obs, -2)

# Likelihood
# State process
for (t in 1:(T-1)){
    lambda[t] ~ dnorm(mean.lambda, tau.proc)
    N.est[t+1] <- N.est[t] * lambda[t]
    }

# Observation process
for (t in 1:T) {
    y[t] ~ dnorm(N.est[t], tau.obs)
    }
}
",fill = TRUE)
sink()
```

We have chosen uniform priors for the standard deviations of the process and observation errors. This is to be preferred over a gamma prior distribution of the variances because they are less informative (Gelman, 2006). Next, we bundle the data, define initial values and MCMC settings, and analyze the model. The initial value for the population size in the first year needs to be chosen with care; if it is too far from the true value, the model may not run. A practical option is to use a random value close to the population counts. Problems with updating in the MCMC algorithm may also occur if the initial values for the process and observation standard deviations are too large. Again, choosing "good" initial values helps to avoid problems.

```
# Bundle data
bugs.data <- list(y = y, T = n.years)

# Initial values
inits <- function(){list(sigma.proc = runif(1, 0, 5), mean.lambda =
    runif(1, 0.1, 2), sigma.obs = runif(1, 0, 10), N.est = c(runif(1, 20,
    40), rep(NA, (n.years-1))))}

# Parameters monitored
parameters <- c("lambda", "mean.lambda", "sigma2.obs", "sigma2.proc",
    "N.est")

# MCMC settings
ni <- 25000
nt <- 3
nb <- 10000
nc <- 3

# Call WinBUGS from R (BRT <1 min)
ssm <- bugs(bugs.data, inits, parameters, "ssm.bug", n.chains = nc,
    n.thin = nt, n.iter = ni, n.burnin = nb, debug = TRUE, bugs.directory =
    bugs.dir, working.directory = getwd())
```

How quickly the Markov chains converge depends greatly on the data. With some data sets, convergence is obtained much more swiftly than with others. Now we draw a plot (Fig. 5.3) to compare estimated, true, and observed population sizes. We notice that the estimated population sizes are smoothed and closer to the true population sizes than the raw counts.

```
# Define function to draw a graph to summarize results
graph.ssm <- function(ssm, N, y){
    fitted <- lower <- upper <- numeric()
    n.years <- length(y)
    for (i in 1:n.years){
        fitted[i] <- mean(ssm$sims.list$N.est[,i])
        lower[i] <- quantile(ssm$sims.list$N.est[,i], 0.025)
        upper[i] <- quantile(ssm$sims.list$N.est[,i], 0.975)}
```

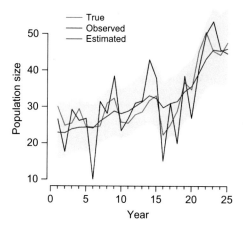

FIGURE 5.3 Analysis of ibex population dynamics: trajectory of true population size (red), observed counts (black), and posterior means of estimated population size (blue; with 95% CRI shaded).

```
m1 <- min(c(y, fitted, N, lower))
m2 <- max(c(y, fitted, N, upper))
par(mar = c(4.5, 4, 1, 1), cex = 1.2)
plot(0, 0, ylim = c(m1, m2), xlim = c(0.5, n.years), ylab = "Population
    size", xlab = "Year", las = 1, col = "black", type = "l", lwd = 2,
    frame = FALSE, axes = FALSE)
axis(2, las = 1)
axis(1, at = seq(0, n.years, 5), labels = seq(0, n.years, 5))
axis(1, at = 0:n.years, labels = rep("", n.years + 1), tcl = -0.25)
polygon(x = c(1:n.years, n.years:1), y = c(lower, upper[n.years:1]),
    col = "gray90", border = "gray90")
points(N, type = "l", col = "red", lwd = 2)
points(y, type = "l", col = "black", lwd = 2)
points(fitted, type = "l", col = "blue", lwd = 2)
legend(x = 1, y = m2, legend = c("True", "Observed", "Estimated"),
    lty = c(1, 1, 1), lwd = c(2, 2, 2), col = c("red", "black", "blue"),
    bty = "n", cex = 1)
}

# Execute function: Produce figure
graph.ssm(ssm, N, y)
```

5.3 SYSTEMATIC BIAS IN THE OBSERVATION PROCESS

In the previous example we have seen that the model performs well in the presence of "random" observation errors. By this we mean that on average, false positives (i.e., double-counting) and false negatives (i.e., nondetection) cancel out. In this sense, the state-space model is able to "correct" noisy counts for observation error. However, the model cannot recover unbiased estimates of true population size, when false negative and positive errors don't cancel out on average. With the data considered in this chapter, there is no direct information about the observation process, that is, about detection probability or double-counting rates. Thus, in the absence of false-positive errors, the "state," modeled in the state-space models of this chapter is the product of population size N and detection probability p, and not population size N, as one might think. We illustrate this next.

We start with a simple example where we assume that the ibex population remains stable at 50 individuals over 25 years. Further, we assume that detection probability is constant at 0.7, thus on average we only count 70% of the population. Each individual can be seen or missed, so the annual count is a binomial random variable, and we write $y_t \sim \text{Bin}(N_t, p)$. We start by defining the true population sizes.

```
n.years <- 25 # Number of years
N <- rep(50, n.years)
```

Then, we simulate the counts using the binomial distribution and inspect the numbers.

```
p <- 0.7
y <- numeric(n.years)
for (t in 1:n.years){
    y[t] <- rbinom(1, N[t], p)
    }
y
[1] 34 34 35 38 29 37 ... 27 35 33 32
```

Clearly, the observed counts are smaller than the true population size (what a surprise!). More importantly, we also notice that the counts vary, although both the true population size and the detection probability were constant across time. As we have seen in Section 1.3, this variation is the binomial sampling variation. The magnitude of this variance is known from statistical theory to be on average $Np(1 - p) = 10.5$.

We next use WinBUGS to fit to these data the same state-space model as in Section 5.2. Thus, we partition the observed variation in the counts into process variation and observation error and use a normal approximation for the latter. In large samples, we would expect the estimate of the process variance to be close to zero and that for the observation error to be close to 10.5.

```
# Bundle data
bugs.data <- list(y = y, T = n.years)
```

```
# Initial values
inits <- function(){list(sigma.proc = runif(1, 0, 5), mean.lambda =
    runif(1, 0.1, 2), sigma.obs = runif(1, 0, 10), N.est = c(runif(1, 30,
    60), rep(NA, (n.years-1))))}
# Parameters monitored
parameters <- c("lambda", "mean.lambda", "sigma2.obs", "sigma2.proc",
    "N.est")
# MCMC settings
ni <- 25000
nt <- 3
nb <- 10000
nc <- 3
# Call WinBUGS from R (BRT <1 min)
ssm <- bugs(bugs.data, inits, parameters, "ssm.bug", n.chains = nc,
    n.thin = nt, n.iter = ni, n.burnin = nb, debug = TRUE, bugs.directory =
    bugs.dir, working.directory = getwd())
# Summarize posteriors
print(ssm, digits = 3)
               mean      sd    2.5%      25%     50%     75%    97.5%  Rhat  n.eff
[...]
mean.lambda  0.999   0.009   0.981    0.994   0.998   1.002   1.020  1.015   4800
sigma2.obs  15.219   5.644   7.157   11.370  14.170  18.020  28.500  1.005    660
sigma2.proc  0.002   0.003   0.000    0.000   0.001   0.002   0.011  1.012    210
[...]
```

As expected, the process variance is estimated to be close to zero and the estimate of the observation variance is large. As a result of sampling variation, the latter estimate is of course not equal to 10.5, although a 95% CRI covers the expected value. With larger population sizes and averaged over many simulation replicates, we would expect to be right on target (see also Section 1.5). The estimate of the average population growth rate is essentially equal to 1, which is also what we would expect from a constant population. Now, let's compare the estimated and true population sizes, as well as the counts (Fig. 5.4).

```
# Produce figure
graph.ssm(ssm, N, y)
```

Figure 5.4 shows that the estimated population sizes are consistently lower than the true sizes, but the temporal pattern of the estimated population sizes matches quite well to that of the true population sizes. Thus, the model is able to correct for the temporal variation of the observation process induced by the binomial nature of the counts. However, the model cannot fully correct for the detection error; the population estimates are all well below the true population size. The mean (over time) of the estimated population sizes is 33.7, which is close to what we would expect, Np ($50*0.7 = 35$). Hence, we obtain an improved estimate of the population index Np with the

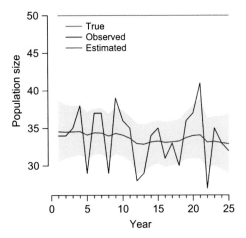

FIGURE 5.4 Effects of systematic observation errors on the state-space model: estimated states represent an unbiased population index. True (red), observed (black), and estimated trajectory of population size (blue; with 95% CRI shaded).

state-space model, by eliminating the effects of annual observation errors, but we are unable to estimate true population size. We feel that the nature of the correction for the observation error in the kind of state-space models considered in this chapter is sometimes misunderstood among ecologists.

Next we conduct a simulation where detection probability is not constant over time, but instead has a positive trend that is linear on the logit scale. What will our simple state-space model tell us about the true trend of the ibex population in this case?

We start by defining the true population sizes.

```
n.years <- 25 # Number of years
N <- rep(50, n.years)
```

Then we simulate the counts using the binomial distribution.

```
lp <- -0.5 + 0.1*(1:n.years)     # Increasing trend of logit p
p <- plogis(lp)
y <- numeric(n.years)
for (t in 1:n.years){
   y[t] <- rbinom(1, N[t], p[t])
   }
```

We analyze the data with the same model as before:

```
# Bundle data
bugs.data <- list(y = y, T = n.years)
```

```
# Call WinBUGS from R (BRT <1 min)
ssm <- bugs(bugs.data, inits, parameters, "ssm.bug", n.chains = nc,
   n.thin = nt, n.iter = ni, n.burnin = nb, debug = TRUE, bugs.directory =
   bugs.dir, working.directory = getwd())
```

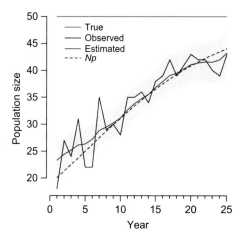

FIGURE 5.5   Effects of temporal change in systematic observation errors on the state-space model: estimated states represent a biased population index. True (red), observed (black), and estimated population size (blue) along with a 95% CRI (shading). The dashed line shows the expectation of the counts under binomial sampling.

The comparison among true, observed, and estimated population size shows that the model succeeds in getting rid of the random sampling variation in the counts that is resulting from binomial sampling (Fig. 5.5). However, the model can't correct the estimated population trajectory for the shift imposed by the deterministic trend in the observation process. To clarify this, we also calculated the expected value of the counts as Np and added this to the plot. Clearly, the estimated population size under the state-space model follows quite closely to this expected value (Np). In other words, our simple state-space model was not able to correct for a systematic pattern in detection, and consequently we would erroneously infer a population increase if we trusted the model result in this case.

```
# Produce figure
graph.ssm(ssm, N, y)
points(N*p, col = "black", type = "l", lwd = 2, lty = 2)
legend(x = 1, y = 45.5, legend = "Np", lwd = 2, col = "black", lty = 2,
    bty = "n")
```

These examples illustrate three important points about the state-space models in this chapter:

1. They yield unbiased estimates of population size only if false-negative (detection probability) and false-positive observations (double-counting) cancel out on average. Counts are then unbiased on average but there is sampling variation, and this is corrected for by the model.
2. They produce unbiased estimates of population indices (i.e., of Np) if detection probability is <1 and has no pattern over time. In that case,

for the example of imperfect detection (and no false positives), the state-space model corrects for binomial sampling variation.

3. They do not yield unbiased estimates of population size nor of indices if there are temporal patterns either in detection probability or in the false-positive rates (unless, of course, the two cancel out).

5.4 REAL EXAMPLE: HOUSE MARTIN POPULATION COUNTS IN THE VILLAGE OF MAGDEN

The population of house martins (Fig. 5.6) in Magden (a small village in Northern Switzerland where MS grew up) has been surveyed by Reto Freuler since 1990. In initial years, Freuler counted all occupied nests himself, but later he sent questionnaires to house owners with known house martin nests asking for the number of occupied nests to be reported to him. The goal of the analysis is to estimate the average stochastic population growth rate, the process variance and to predict population sizes until 2015 with an assessment of uncertainty. Furthermore, we want to estimate the probability that the population size in 2015 is lower than in 2009, the year with the most recent data. In contrast to the earlier examples, we now adopt the exponential growth model on the log scale because it is more appropriate for stochastic environments (Lande et al., 2003).

FIGURE 5.6   House martin (*Delichon urbica*), Finland, 2005 (Photograph by T. Muukkonen).

The state-process model, now, becomes $\log(N_{t+1}) = \log(N_t) + r_t$, with $r_t \sim N(\bar{r}, \sigma_r^2)$; here, r_t is the stochastic population growth rate.

We use a similar state-space model to the one introduced earlier, with the mentioned exception (log scale). We also modify the priors for the initial population size, for the mean growth rate, and for the standard deviation of the state and the observation processes. Sometimes, it can be hard to fit state-space models in WinBUGS, which may fall in a trap or fail to start updating. Often, this has to do with the prior or the initial value for the first-year population size. It is advisable to choose a prior with mean equal to the first-year count and a relatively small variance. The range of the initial value for the first population size should also be relatively small. Although we specifically aim to predict population sizes in the future, the model does not need any changes for this purpose.

```
# Specify model in BUGS language
sink("ssm.bug")
cat("
model {

# Priors and constraints
logN.est[1] ~ dnorm(5.6, 0.01)      # Prior for initial population size
mean.r ~ dnorm(1, 0.001)            # Prior for mean growth rate
sigma.proc ~ dunif(0, 1)            # Prior for sd of state process
sigma2.proc <- pow(sigma.proc, 2)
tau.proc <- pow(sigma.proc, -2)
sigma.obs ~ dunif(0, 1)             # Prior for sd of obs. process
sigma2.obs <- pow(sigma.obs, 2)
tau.obs <- pow(sigma.obs, -2)

# Likelihood
# State process
for (t in 1:(T-1)){
    r[t] ~ dnorm(mean.r, tau.proc)
    logN.est[t+1] <- logN.est[t] + r[t]
    }

# Observation process
for (t in 1:T) {
    y[t] ~ dnorm(logN.est[t], tau.obs)
    }

# Population sizes on real scale
for (t in 1:T) {
    N.est[t] <- exp(logN.est[t])
    }
}
", fill = TRUE)
sink()
```

Next, we load the data. They consist of a vector with the number of observed breeding pairs in each year. Because we want to predict future population sizes, we add NAs in the data. Why? Well, we saw in Chapter 2 that Bayesians treat all types of unknown quantities in the same way, be they predictions, missing values, or parameters. Hence, it is enough to specify some additional years without observations (regardless of whether they occur within the data series, or only at the end) with NA observations, and include them in the loop for calculating the likelihood. They are then updated (estimated) as part of the model fitting. Here, we would like to predict population size in year 2015, and so we need to add six NAs. Another way to achieve the same would be to extend the loop of the state-process to cover the additional years, and to leave the data as they are (i.e., without NAs).

```
# House martin population data from Magden
pyears <- 6 # Number of future years with predictions
hm <- c(271, 261, 309, 318, 231, 216, 208, 226, 195, 226, 233, 209, 226,
    192, 191, 225, 245, 205, 191, 174, rep(NA, pyears))
year <- 1990:(2009 + pyears)
```

We then bundle the data, specify initial values, list parameters to be estimated, determine the MCMC settings, and run the model.

```
# Bundle data
bugs.data <- list(y = log(hm), T = length(year))

# Initial values
inits <- function(){list(sigma.proc = runif(1, 0, 1), mean.r = rnorm(1),
    sigma.obs = runif(1, 0, 1), logN.est = c(rnorm(1, 5.6, 0.1), rep(NA,
    (length(year)-1))))}

# Parameters monitored
parameters <- c("r", "mean.r", "sigma2.obs", "sigma2.proc", "N.est")

# MCMC settings
ni <- 200000
nt <- 6
nb <- 100000
nc <- 3

# Call WinBUGS from R (BRT 3 min)
hm.ssm <- bugs(bugs.data, inits, parameters, "ssm.bug", n.chains = nc,
    n.thin = nt, n.iter = ni, n.burnin = nb, debug = TRUE, bugs.directory =
    bugs.dir, working.directory = getwd())
```

Convergence is satisfactory after 200,000 iterations after a 100,000 burnin. The least well-mixed parameters are, not surprisingly, the two variances. If WinBUGS does not run properly and produces an undefined real result, just start the run again. The inits function will produce a different set of starting values each time it is called.

```
# Summarize posteriors
print(hm.ssm, digits = 2)
```

	mean	sd	2.5%	25%	50%	75%	97.5%	Rhat	n.eff
r[1]	-0.02	0.06	-0.13	-0.05	-0.02	0.01	0.11	1.00	47000
[...]									
r[25]	-0.02	0.11	-0.26	-0.08	-0.02	0.04	0.21	1.00	27000
mean.r	-0.02	0.03	-0.08	-0.04	-0.02	-0.01	0.03	1.00	39000
sigma2.obs	0.01	0.01	0.00	0.00	0.00	0.01	0.02	1.00	870
sigma2.proc	0.01	0.01	0.00	0.00	0.01	0.02	0.03	1.01	770
N.est[1]	274.10	15.88	244.50	265.20	272.30	282.10	310.40	1.00	7100
N.est[2]	269.51	14.50	244.60	260.30	267.20	277.70	302.50	1.00	4500
[...]									
N.est[26]	164.84	54.42	79.43	131.50	159.30	188.60	292.30	1.00	44000

We plot counts and the posterior means of population sizes along with their credible intervals.

```
# Draw figure
fitted <- lower <- upper <- numeric()
year <- 1990:2015
n.years <- length(hm)
for (i in 1:n.years){
    fitted[i] <- mean(hm.ssm$sims.list$N.est[,i])
    lower[i] <- quantile(hm.ssm$sims.list$N.est[,i], 0.025)
    upper[i] <- quantile(hm.ssm$sims.list$N.est[,i], 0.975)}
m1 <- min(c(fitted, hm, lower), na.rm = TRUE)
m2 <- max(c(fitted, hm, upper), na.rm = TRUE)
par(mar = c(4.5, 4, 1, 1))
plot(0, 0, ylim = c(m1, m2), xlim = c(1, n.years), ylab = "Population
    size", xlab = "Year", col = "black", type = "l", lwd = 2, axes = FALSE,
    frame = FALSE)
axis(2, las = 1)
axis(1, at = 1:n.years, labels = year)
polygon(x = c(1:n.years, n.years:1), y = c(lower, upper[n.years:1]),
    col = "gray90", border = "gray90")
points(hm, type = "l", col = "black", lwd = 2)
points(fitted, type = "l", col = "blue", lwd = 2)
legend(x = 1, y = 150, legend = c("Counts", "Estimates"), lty = c(1, 1),
    lwd = c(2, 2), col = c("black", "blue"), bty = "n", cex = 1)
```

Counts and estimated population sizes are quite close (Fig. 5.7), which is reflected in a small estimate of the observation variance. The overall trajectory of the house martin population is negative, but with important annual fluctuations. This can be seen in Fig. 5.7, but is apparently not reflected in the estimate of the process variance, which is only about double of the observation variance. Is there something wrong? No, there is nothing wrong; we just can't compare variances directly if they are measured around different means. A better way to compare variances is to calculate the coefficient of variation (CV), which is the ratio of the

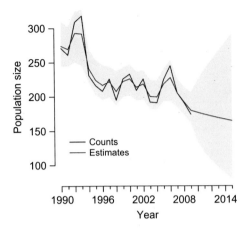

FIGURE 5.7   Counts (black) and estimated population size (blue) of house martins in Magden (with 95% CRI shaded).

standard deviation to the mean. The average population size over the 20 study years is about 230 pairs, thus the CV of the observation error is $\frac{\sqrt{0.006}}{\log(230)} = 0.014$. The CV of the process variation is $\frac{\sqrt{0.012}}{0.022} = 4.98$, and thus about 350 times larger than the CV of the observation error.

The projected population sizes after 2009 are based on the estimates of the population size in 2009, the average growth rate of the population, and the process variance. On average, we predict a steadily declining population, but the uncertainty in the estimated population trajectory is large (as reflected by the wide CRIs). This is mostly because of the large process variance, so it is difficult to make precise predictions. Typically, the uncertainty becomes larger the further we predict into the future. The predicted trajectory is the Bayesian analog of what Lande et al. (2003) call a population prediction interval (PPI). However, it is not based on the bootstrap and the usual approximations involved with maximum likelihood. Such a prediction with full uncertainty assessment is easy to obtain in a Bayesian framework of inference, but is more challenging in the frequentist arena.

We were also asking about the probability that the house martin population in 2015 would be smaller than in 2009. This quantity is again a derived variable and can easily be obtained from the MCMC output. We evaluate the proportion of MCMC samples of the estimated population size in 2015 that is smaller than in 2009. The probability that the population size in 2015 is smaller than in 2009 is 0.689 (code below), the probability that it would be larger is 0.311. Hence, a decline of the house martin population until 2015 is twice as likely as the inverse.

```
# Probability of N(2015) < N(2009)
mean(hm.ssm$sims.list$N.est[,26] < hm.ssm$mean$N.est[20])
```

5.5 SUMMARY AND OUTLOOK

We have introduced classical state-space models of population dynamics, which are used to analyze population counts and to partition the observed variation into a component due to process variation and another due to observation error. We have seen that these models can be useful in some situations, but it must be kept in mind that they usually do not provide an unbiased estimate of the true population size. Instead, they yield a smoothed estimate of a population index (i.e., of Np), which may or may not be unbiased with respect to the true population trajectory. In the absence of temporal patterns in the observation error, the trajectories of the true population sizes and that of the estimated population index will be parallel. The smoothing occurs with respect to the assumed underlying biological processes, and is therefore more mechanistic and perhaps more realistic than the arbitrary smoothing of generalized additive models (GAM; King et al., 2010), which are often used to analyze population counts (Fewster et al., 2000).

We have considered only very simple state-space models to describe state and observation processes. The beauty of these models is that we can readily change them to be more realistic or in a way that specific hypotheses can be tested. An obvious extension is to use a density-dependent model such as the logistic, theta-logistic, or Gompertz model (e.g., Lande et al., 2003; Dennis et al., 2006). However, it appears that models with density-dependence have serious extrinsic identifiability problems. With increasing magnitude of the observation error, the parameters become harder to estimate, especially the parameter which quantifies the strength of density-dependence (Knape, 2008).

If our aim is to get unbiased estimates of the population size, the use of state-space models of the type featured in this chapter is not sufficient. In other words, there is no way around explicitly estimating detection probability. In Chapters 6 (for a single closed population), 10 (for a single open population), and 12 (for metapopulations), we will see how this can be done. This requires additional information to tease apart detection probability and the true levels of the state process (population size). However, when no such additional data are available about the detection process, the state-space models in this chapter represent probably one of the best frameworks for inference about population trajectories. In Chapters 7–10, we will use different, more mechanistic state-space models to estimate survival and other demographic quantities from capture–recapture, mark-recovery, and multistate capture–recapture data, and in Chapter 13 for metapopulation dynamics.

5.6 EXERCISES

1. Random variability in detection probability: quite often we cannot assume that detection probability is constant over time, for example, because of weather factors that affect the counts. Simulate and analyze

data for a population, whose size remains constant at 50 individuals over (a) 25 years and (b) 50 years, but where the annual detection probability varies randomly in the interval between 0.3 and 0.7. Does the state-space model perform well in this situation?

2. Modeling of variance structures: in the house martin data set, we saw that from year $t = 9$ onwards, a different data-collection protocol (questionnaires) was used. Adapt the model to account for possibly different observation errors in the two periods.

3. Unstructured and dynamic hierarchical model for population counts: In Section 3.3.2, we encountered a different two-level hierarchical model for a single time series of population counts. What is the difference to a state-space model in this chapter? Fit the exponential population state-space model to the peregrine data from Section 3.3.2 and compare the inference about the population trajectory under the two models. In addition, construct a model with a linear trend in the population growth rate and another model with a linear trend in the observation error and fit them to the peregrine data.

Estimation of the Size of a Closed Population from Capture–Recapture Data

6.1 INTRODUCTION

In Chapter 5 (and partly in Chapter 4; see Section 4.4), we met models that attempt to distinguish between an ecological process and an observation process. This is important, since it allows for a more proper accounting of the uncertainty in a modeled system (Cressie et al., 2009) and is required to avoid bias in some important system descriptors, such as density dependence (Freckleton et al., 2006). However, at a closer look, these models do not fully deliver what they promise at first sight: after all, they typically do not have parameters with a clear ecological meaning. Or, put in another way, what exactly is the ecological relevance of an "expected count" (Bob Dorazio, pers. comm.)? After all, we would like to describe a population in terms of its size, not in terms of the field method that we apply to produce a count of animals or plants.

In this Chapter, we introduce a different class of models that achieve a proper accounting for the processes that give rise to observed data, in terms of an ecological and of an observation process: closed-population capture–recapture models. Capture–recapture models in general are a very large class of models that have become increasingly used in ecological applications of statistical modeling (Seber, 1982; Borchers et al., 2002; Williams et al., 2002; Royle and Dorazio, 2008; King et al., 2010). In principle, they all boil down to estimation of detection probability, which provides the link between what we observe and the true population parameters, such as population size or survival probability. Detection probability can be estimated from repeated encounters of individually marked animals or plants. Historically, encountering meant capturing an animal and hence, the associated statistical methods have come to be called capture–recapture, or mark-recapture, models. However, the essential feature of these models is that they require as data repeated *observations of individually recognizable units*, such as individuals, occupied sites, or species, to estimate population size, number of occupied patches, or species richness, respectively. Individual recognition may well be possible without physical capture.

Almost all of the remainder of this book will be dedicated to models for inference about populations which contain an explicit parameter representing detection probability. These models describe the observation process explicitly and include capture–recapture models for marked individuals and other methods for unmarked "individuals" as well; see the metapopulation estimation models in Chapters 12 and 13. There is a single exception in Chapter 11, where we partly fall back on the modeling of Chapters 4 and 5. The models in Chapter 6 deal with repeated surveys from a single population. Surveys are conducted over a period that is sufficiently short so that the population can be assumed "closed" to numerical changes, that is, no recruitment, mortality, and dispersal occur. Most of the methods in later chapters relax that assumption, at the expense of not being able to estimate abundance (but see Chapter 10 and also Chapters 12 and 13).

Assessing the size of a closed population (N), or analogously, its density (D), appears simple at first sight; simply tally up all individuals (N) that live on a piece of land (A). However, in reality, assessing N is fairly challenging because of at least two reasons: imperfect detection (p) and the problem of delimiting the size of the study area (A).

First, imperfect detection is a hallmark of all studies of wild organisms, be they plants (Kéry and Gregg, 2003; Kéry, 2004; Kéry et al., 2005a) or animals (Williams et al., 2002; Nichols et al., 2009). In most cases and under most situations, not every individual present in a study area will be seen and hence, counts (C) will typically be an underestimate of true population size (N). Over several decades, a huge number of protocols and associated models have been developed to cope with this challenge and to "correct" the observed counts for detection error induced by $p < 1$. Conceptually, all derive some estimates of the probability to detect a member of N, that is, of detection probability p, and then apply the commonsense or canonical estimator for N, which is $\hat{N} = C/\hat{p}$, where hats denote estimates.

One of the main differences between these methods is in how they derive their estimate of p. Classical capture–recapture models use repeated observations of recognizable individuals and derive information about p from the pattern of detection and nondetection of each marked individual. Capture–recapture methods are huge in scope, and there is a tremendous variety of protocols and associated models (Borchers et al., 2002; Williams et al., 2002; Royle and Dorazio, 2008). Distance sampling methods derive information about p from the distribution of the distances between an observer (or some detection device) and the detected animals or objects sampled (Buckland et al., 2001). Repeated counts methods (Royle, 2004c) do not require individual identification of the objects counted; they are a third and very useful protocol (see Chapter 12).

The second challenge in assessing N is that we need to decide how to delimit the study area or put another way, how should we define the area with which our population is associated or simply, what is A? Obviously, this is trivial for actual islands or islands of habitat such as mountain tops or desert oases. However, in most cases, objectively delimiting the area that is used by a population is difficult or may be downright impossible without making some arbitrary decisions.

One reason it may be difficult to determine the area on which a population lives is movement of animals within their home range. Any defined area will then sometimes contain individuals who have the center of gravity of their entire activity range outside of that perimeter, and who, therefore, in a sense, do not belong to the focal population but can nevertheless be seen within a study area. Similarly, some individuals at the edge of the study area, who do have the majority of their activity range within the nominal area associated with the desired population, may sometimes move beyond that perimeter and therefore be absent and undetectable within the perimeter. But how should an individual at the border of the study area be counted? As a fractional individual only? Or full, if its home-range center is inside and not at all, when it is outside the boundary of the nominal study area? Dealing with this sort of *temporary emigration* (as it is called in the capture–recapture literature; Kendall et al., 1997; Kendall, 1999) is almost always a challenge in population size estimation (although neither in the case of distance sampling nor in spatially explicit capture–recapture models). Conceptually, it is related to the problem of separating permanent emigration from mortality probability in the Cormack–Jolly–Seber model (Chapter 7). Spatially explicit capture–recapture (SECR) models (e.g., Efford, 2004; Borchers and Efford, 2008; Royle and Young, 2008) should be applied in this context because they effectively deal with the challenge of determining the size of A.

In this chapter, we do not describe spatial capture-recapture models but instead assume that we are able to delimit a piece of land with which some unknown number N of animals or plants are associated, and we want to estimate that number N by "correcting" our count by our estimate of detection probability p. One important further assumption is that there are no misclassifications, that is, no individual is mistaken for another. This is the classical setting of a capture–recapture study, where we need repeated surveys to obtain so-called detection histories, strings of ones and zeroes, that denote whether an individual was detected or not during any given repeat survey (also called an occasion). Classical capture–recapture models consist of modeling patterns in p and obtain an estimate of N through the canonical estimator $C/\hat{p}$.

Otis et al. (1978) provided a useful catalog of possible patterns in detection probability in the context of closed-population size estimation. They distinguish between three effects: individual effects, time effects, and behavioral response effects. Individual and time effects are the differences among individuals and those among capture occasions. Behavioral response denotes a situation wherein detection probability at an occasion depends on whether an individual was detected in a previous occasion. The term comes from live trapping of animals, where such a nonindependence of detection probability within an individual detection history is due to the individual changing its behavior in response to a capture event. If trapping leads to an increased detection probability at a later occasion, one talks about "trap-happiness"; the converse is called "trap-shyness". However, patterns akin to a trap response may arise also as a result of quite different mechanisms, for instance, if an observer

TABLE 6.1 Parameters for Detection Probability p_{it} in a Hypothetical Study with Three Individuals and Four Capture Occasions.

Individual	Occasion 1	Occasion 2	Occasion 3	Occasion 4
1	$p_{1,1}$	$p_{1,2}$	$p_{1,3}$	$p_{1,4}$
2	$p_{2,1}$	$p_{2,2}$	$p_{2,3}$	$p_{2,4}$
3	$p_{3,1}$	$p_{3,2}$	$p_{3,3}$	$p_{3,4}$

Note: The models M_0, M_t, M_b, M_h (see text) differ in the assumptions that they make about how cells are related among rows, columns, and within a row.

remembers the location of a species in a study of species richness (e.g., an owl in a hollow tree) and is more likely to detect a species that he/she has detected previously. In addition, individual heterogeneity in detection probability may appear like trap-happiness (Kéry et al., 2006).

The three main classes of models in Otis et al. (1978) are known as models M_h (h for individual heterogeneity), M_t (t for time), and M_b (b for behavioral response). These effects can be visualized in a cross-classification of individuals and occasion such as in Table 6.1 for a toy study of three individuals and four occasions. Model M_h accounts for row effects (i.e., individuals differ), model M_t accounts for column effects (occasions differ), and model M_b accounts for within-row effects, that is, within-individual capture-history dependence.

Otis et al. (1978) defined eight models using these three effects: Model M_0, which assumes that p is constant across all individuals and times; models M_h, M_t, and M_b as defined earlier; and four models with two-way and three-way combinations of effects: M_{th}, M_{bh}, M_{tb}, and M_{tbh}. Estimators for most of these models were implemented in the grandfather of population size estimation software, CAPTURE (Rexstad and Burnham, 1991). Many of these methods have now been superseded by more efficient (e.g., likelihood-based) estimators, and many of those are available in program MARK (White and Burnham, 1999). Indeed, over the last 1–2 decades there has been a proliferation of new methods for population size estimation, see Borchers et al. (2002), Williams et al. (2002) and also Chapter 14 by Paul Lukacs in the *Gentle Introduction to program MARK* (http://www.phidot.org/software/mark/docs/book/). The Otis et al. (1978) catalog of effects remains useful because it clarifies our thinking about possible patterns in such collections of parameters in a cross-classification of individual by time.

Three things must be remembered however. First, what used to be called model t, b, or h is in fact not a single model, but in reality a whole family of models: there are various ways in which temporal, behavioral, or individual effects may be modeled. For instance, we may want to model a permanent trap response, such as is the tradition in population size estimation, or we may want to model an immediate trap response, as is customary in Cormack–Jolly–Seber models (see Section 7.8; Appendix 2.2; Pradel, 1993). Moreover, there are many different ways to model individual heterogeneity, for instance, by finite or continuous mixture distributions, and for continuous mixtures, by different parametric forms (Pledger, 2000; Dorazio and Royle, 2003; Link, 2003). So, it is really not enough to say "we used model M_b" or "we used model M_h"; rather, we need to say (and know) which model M_b or which model M_h we are using.

Second, as there is not a single model M_b for instance, there is not a single model M_{tb} either. When two effects are present in a model, we can combine them in an additive or in an interactive way. So, now that we are not constrained anymore to the rigid set of models for population size estimation from the old CAPTURE days, we must also say (and know) how to combine different effects in a model.

Third, all models in the Otis et al. (1978) classification represent "group" effects, where we batch the parameters in Table 6.1 in some way and estimate differences among these batches. However, once we recognize how these models can be specified as GLMs or GLMMs, we immediately have much more modeling freedom. We can do all this modeling on the scale of the logit-transformed detection probability (p) and then combine group effects and continuous covariate effects in a linear model of the usual form, for instance:

$$\text{logit}(p_{i,j}) = \alpha_i + \beta_j + \delta * F_{i,j} + \gamma * X_{i,j},$$

with $\alpha_i \sim \text{Normal}(\mu_\alpha, \sigma_\alpha^2)$.

For illustration, in this model for detection probability of individual i during occasion j, we specify random individual effects α_i, fixed time effects β_j, an effect δ that depends on whether an animal was captured before or not (this information is contained in the indicator variable F), and an effect γ of another covariate X. In any practical application, we may be far from being able to estimate all these quantities, there may be confounding and not enough data etc. Also, one of the fixed time effects (β_j) would have to be constrained to zero to avoid overparameterization.

So, it is useful to think about all these models in a GLM way. But in addition, we find it useful to be able to relate a model that is written in this way back to the Otis et al. (1978) classification. For instance, our model above would represent a model M_{tbh} with an added covariate X and where all effects are additive rather than interactive (so, we may also want to write that model as $M_{t+b+h+X}$). WinBUGS gives us full modeling freedom to fit such custom models because its model definition language is so apt to free the modeler in us (Kéry, 2010).

It is worth noting that the linear models concept (i.e., the design matrix) underlying capture–recapture models when viewed as GLM are not only important for population size estimation. Far from that: the modeling of time effects (e.g., fixed or random or as a function of covariates), the modeling of "behavioral" effects and the modeling of individual effects are elements that we will see as part of quite different models over and over again. Hence, a full understanding of the material in this chapter will be a great help for your modeling in WinBUGS for a vast range of models. Essentially the same topics arise in other such collections of parameters, for instance, in the modeling of survival probability in a cross-classification of individual and time in the Cormack–Jolly–Seber model (Chapter 7) or of detection probability in a cross-classification of site and time in a metapopulation model for abundance (Chapter 12) or occurrence (Chapter 13). We believe that seeing these connections will be very helpful for obtaining a more synthetic understanding of capture–recapture models. Hence, the way in which we structure such tables of parameters, which is implied by the cross-classification of individuals and time in this chapter is relevant for the modeling of tables of parameters in many other inferential situations as well.

This chapter is the place to describe for the first time data augmentation (Tanner and Wong, 1987), introduced in the context of capture–recapture models by (Royle et al., 2007a); see also Royle and Dorazio (2011) and Section 10.3. Data augmentation greatly simplifies inference for a vast range of models and makes them amenable to simple fitting in WinBUGS. In particular, data augmentation offers an extremely flexible way to model patterns of detection probability in closed populations. We first introduce data augmentation with the simplest possible closed-capture model, M_0. Then, we will look into a few simple examples of closed-capture models with simulated data: M_t, M_b, M_h, and M_{th}. With model M_t, we will see again how one simply changes from fixed effects to random effects, and how transparent this is when the model is described in the BUGS language. Finally, we will analyze a real data set under models M_{tbh} and M_{tbh+X}, where "population size" is represented by species richness. In the latter model, we provide an illustration of individual covariate modeling, which is greatly simplified when using data augmentation (Royle, 2009).

6.2 GENERATION AND ANALYSIS OF SIMULATED DATA WITH DATA AUGMENTATION

6.2.1 Introduction to Data Augmentation for the Simplest Case: Model M_0

The simplest possible model for inference about the size of a single population is model M_0 (Otis et al., 1978), where detection probability is assumed constant over the two dimensions of the detection parameter table, that is, over individuals and over time periods (Table 6.1). First, we write a function that simulates capture data under model M_0. The three arguments are N (population size), p (detection probability), and T (the number of sampling occasions). T is assumed constant for all individuals, but this is for pure convenience. In the analysis of the real data, we will see how we deal with the case where T is not the same across all individuals.

```
# Define function to simulate data under M0
data.fn <- function(N = 100, p = 0.5, T = 3){
    yfull <- yobs <- array(NA, dim = c(N, T))
    for (j in 1:T){
        yfull[,j] <- rbinom(n = N, size = 1, prob = p)
        }
    ever.detected <- apply(yfull, 1, max)
    C <- sum(ever.detected)
    yobs <- yfull[ever.detected == 1,]
    cat(C, "out of", N, "animals present were detected.\n")
    return(list(N = N, p = p, C = C, T = T, yfull = yfull, yobs = yobs))
    }
```

We create one realization of the stochastic process represented by sampling a population of size N. This gives us our data set.

```
data <- data.fn()
```

On execution of that function, we get a list of R objects. We can have a look at them by typing the name of the object, data, or we can get a summary of them by doing this:

```
str(data)
> str(data)
List of 6
 $ N    : num 100
 $ p    : num 0.5
 $ C    : num 87
 $ T    : num 3
 $ yfull: num [1:100, 1:3] 0 0 0 1 1 0 0 1 1 0 ...
 $ yobs : num [1:87, 1:3] 0 0 1 1 0 0 1 1 0 1 ...
```

Here, yfull is the full capture-history matrix of all N animals, including those that were never captured and which have an all-zero capture-history. Evidently, this is not what we ever get to observe. The observed data are called yobs, and they have C rows only ($C \leq N$), corresponding to the observed count of animals. We will apply a model to use these data to make an inference based on the rules of probability, of how great N might likely be.

When modeling population size or other parameters in a model that contains population size using Bayesian MCMC techniques, one formidable technical challenge is that the dimension of the parameter vector for N may change at every iteration of the MCMC algorithm. An ingenious solution is a technique called *data augmentation* (Tanner and Wong, 1987), introduced in the context of capture–recapture models by Royle et al. (2007a); see also Royle and Dorazio (2011) and Section 10.3. Parameter-expanded data augmentation (PX-DA), as it is more accurately called, consists of two things: (1) adding an arbitrary number of zeroes to the data set and (2) analyzing a reparameterized version of the original model. Essentially, it converts the closed-population model into an occupancy model (see Chapter 13) and turns the problem of estimating abundance N into that of estimating occupancy (ψ). Data augmentation may be simple to do in practice, but it has far-reaching consequences: it greatly simplifies the fitting of a large range of capture–recapture type models (Royle et al., 2007b; Royle and Dorazio, 2008).

Data augmentation consists of augmenting a data set by adding a large number of "potential", unobserved individuals, with all zero-only encounter histories. The augmented data set has dimension M by T, where $M \gg N$ (remember, N is the unknown population size, and T is the number of sampling occasions). To this augmented data set we fit a zero-inflated version of the model we would fit if N were known. To do this, we add to the model a binary indicator variable, say z, which is an indicator for whether a row in the augmented data matrix represents a "real" individual, or one that does not exist in practice. These indicators are given a Bernoulli prior distribution, and the parameter of that distribution, say Ω, is estimable from the data. Ω may be called the inclusion probability, since it is the probability with which a member of the augmented data set, M, is included in the population of size N.

Data augmentation translates the problem of estimating N into the equivalent problem of estimating Ω, since the expectation of N is equal to $M\Omega$. Formally, data augmentation induces for N a discrete uniform prior on the interval $(0, M)$. In words, we make our analysis under the formal prior assumption "We do not know how big N is, but it could be any integer number between 0 and M, the size of the augmented data set, with equal probability".

Although simple in reality, our experience suggests that the idea of data augmentation takes some time to sink in. So, here is a numerical example that summarizes what we have just said. Assume that we want to estimate the size of a population with $N = 100$. Of course, that there are 100 individuals is unknown to us because we observe only $C = 87$ of them. So, instead of analyzing the observed data set of size 87 and estimating detection probability p and population size through some variant of the canonical estimator $\hat{N} = C/\hat{p}$, we add to the observed detection history matrix, say, 150 rows consisting of all zeroes. This brings the size of the augmented data set to $M = 237$. This is equivalent to us saying that N could really be anywhere between 0 and 237. We then fit an occupancy model (see Chapter 13) to

MECHANICS OF DATA AUGMENTATION

Fit An Occupancy Model to An Augmented Dataset to estimate the Inclusion Prob. (Ω) and N

How does one augment the CH when there are individual covariates? NA's

these data, where we estimate detection probability p and the inclusion probability Ω and obtain the estimate of N as a derived parameter by summing up the latent indicators z (the expectation of N is $M\Omega$). So, let us see now how this works in practice for the data set previously generated.

```
# Augment data set by 150 potential individuals
nz <- 150
yaug <- rbind(data$yobs, array(0, dim = c(nz, data$T)))

# Specify model in BUGS language
sink("model.txt")
cat("
model {

# Priors
omega ~ dunif(0, 1)
p ~ dunif(0, 1)

# Likelihood
for (i in 1:M){
    z[i] ~ dbern(omega)                    # Inclusion indicators
    for (j in 1:T){                        occupancy model
        yaug[i,j] ~ dbern(p.eff[i,j])
        p.eff[i,j] <- z[i] * p             # Can only be detected if z=1
    } #j
} #i

# Derived quantities
N <- sum(z[])
}
", fill = TRUE)
sink()
```

Data

We started this chapter claiming that capture–recapture models achieve a proper separation of the ecological and the observation process, so where can we see this in the model? In fact, the first Bernoulli distribution governing the inclusion probabilities is equivalent to the ecological process (which creates "real" and nonexisting individuals), whereas the second represents the observation process.

We present the analysis in the usual format by preparing all the ingredients that bugs() require to instruct WinBUGS and then letting Win-BUGS run. We estimate N at 101.8 with 95% CRI of 93–114 (Fig. 6.1), which comfortably includes the truth of 100.

```
# Bundle data
win.data <- list(yaug = yaug, M = nrow(yaug), T = ncol(yaug))

# Initial values
inits <- function() list(z = rep(1, nrow(yaug)), p = runif(1, 0, 1))

# Parameters monitored
params <- c("N", "p", "omega")
```

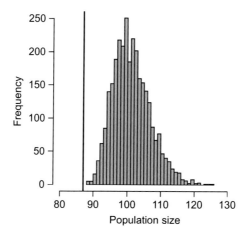

FIGURE 6.1   Posterior distribution of population size N (black line: observed number of animals).

```
# MCMC settings
ni <- 2500
nt <- 2
nb <- 500
nc <- 3

# Call WinBUGS from R (BRT <1 min)
out <- bugs(win.data, inits, params, "model.txt", n.chains = nc,
    n.thin = nt, n.iter = ni, n.burnin = nb, debug = TRUE, bugs.directory =
    bugs.dir, working.directory = getwd())

# Summarize posteriors
print(out, dig = 3)
hist(out$sims.list$N, nclass = 50, col = "gray", main = "", xlab =
    "Population size", las = 1, xlim = c(80, 150))
abline(v = data$C, lwd = 3)
[...]
```

```
            mean     sd   2.5%    25%     50%     75%    97.5%   Rhat n.eff
N        101.803  5.547 93.000 98.000 101.000 105.000 114.000 1.003   940
p          0.479  0.038  0.404  0.453   0.480   0.505   0.555 1.002  1200
omega      0.430  0.039  0.356  0.404   0.428   0.456   0.507 1.001  3000
[...]
```

No doubt some of you will think that data augmentation is some sort of voodoo. Yet, it is not. To convince yourself that the number of zeroes added does not affect the estimates of detection probability (p) and population size (N), we repeat the analysis with the following numbers of all-zero detection histories added (i.e., values of nz): 5, 150, and 1500. For each case, we will inspect the estimates for N, p, and Ω, along with their uncertainty. To help understand data augmentation and this comparison, we also plot the posterior for *N* each time:

```
nz <- 5
yaug <- rbind(data$yobs, array(0, dim = c(nz, data$T)))
win.data <- list(yaug = yaug, M = dim(yaug)[1], T = dim(yaug)[2])
out5 <- bugs(win.data, inits, params, "model.txt", n.chains = nc,
    n.thin = nt, n.iter = ni, n.burnin = nb, debug = FALSE, bugs.directory =
    bugs.dir, working.directory = getwd())
print(out5, dig = 3)
par(mfrow = c(3, 1))
hist(out5$sims.list$N, nclass = 30, col = "gray", main = "Augmentation
    by 5", xlab = "Population size", las = 1, xlim = c(80, 140))
abline(v = data$C, col = "black", lwd = 5)
abline(v = mean(out5$sims.list$N), col = "blue", lwd = 5)

nz <- 150
yaug <- rbind(data$yobs, array(0, dim = c(nz, data$T)))
win.data <- list(yaug = yaug, M = dim(yaug)[1], T = dim(yaug)[2])
out150 <- bugs(win.data, inits, params, "model.txt", n.chains = nc,
    n.thin = nt, n.iter = ni, n.burnin = nb, debug = FALSE, bugs.directory =
    bugs.dir, working.directory = getwd())
print(out150, dig = 3)
hist(out$sims.list$N, nclass = 30, col = "gray", main = "Augmentation by
    150", xlab = "Population size", las = 1, xlim = c(80, 140))
abline(v = data$C, col = "black", lwd = 5)
abline(v = mean(out150$sims.list$N), col = "blue", lwd = 5)

nz <- 1500
yaug <- rbind(data$yobs, array(0, dim = c(nz, data$T)))
win.data <- list(yaug = yaug, M = dim(yaug)[1], T = dim(yaug)[2])
out1500 <- bugs(win.data, inits, params, "model.txt", n.chains = nc,
    n.thin = nt, n.iter = ni, n.burnin = nb, debug = FALSE, bugs.directory =
    bugs.dir, working.directory = getwd())
print(out1500, dig = 3)
hist(out1500$sims.list$N, nclass = 30, col = "gray", main =
    "Augmentation by 1500", xlab = "Population size", las = 1, xlim =
    c(80, 140))
abline(v = data$C, col = "black", lwd = 5)
abline(v = mean(out1500$sims.list$N), col = "blue", lwd = 5)
```

This exercise shows that provided you have augmented the data set enough (Fig. 6.2, central and bottom panels), data augmentation does not have any effect on the estimates, but simply on efficiency: more data augmentation is more costly in terms of computation time. But up to Monte Carlo error, the estimates and their standard errors remain the same (up to Monte Carlo error, as you can see in the posterior summaries). And how do you diagnose not enough data augmentation? Simple: just look at the posterior distribution of *N*: if it is truncated on the right by your choice of *M* (as it is in the top panel), you need to repeat the analysis with more zeroes added, that is, larger *M*.

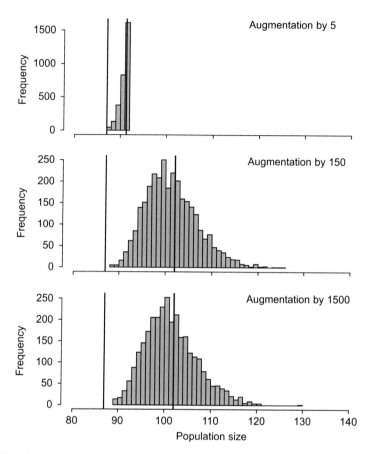

FIGURE 6.2   Posterior distributions of population size N for the same data set but under different degrees of data augmentation (black line: observed number of animals, blue line: posterior mean).

6.2.2 Time Effects: Model M_t

Another model assumes that detection probability p varies by occasion, perhaps because of weather conditions or because different traps or detection devices were used. The simultaneous use of different detection methods (e.g., trap types or observers) during a single occasion can be treated exactly as time effects in capture–recapture modeling. This model is called model M_t by Otis et al. (1978).

```
# Define function to simulate data under Mt
data.fn <- function(N = 100, mean.p = 0.5, T = 3, time.eff = runif(T, -2,
    2)){
    yfull <- yobs <- array(NA, dim = c(N, T) )
    p.vec <- array(NA, dim = T)
```

```
for (j in 1:T) {
    p <- plogis(log(mean.p / (1-mean.p)) + time.eff[j])
    yfull[,j] <- rbinom(n = N, size = 1, prob = p)
    p.vec[j] <- p
    }
ever.detected <- apply(yfull, 1, max)
C <- sum(ever.detected)
yobs <- yfull[ever.detected == 1,]
cat(C, "out of", N, "animals present were detected.\n")
return(list(N = N, p.vec = p.vec, C = C, T = T, yfull = yfull, yobs =
    yobs))
}
```

We create one data set. Again, note that each time you do this you will get a slightly different realization of the same stochastic process. It may even (rarely) happen to have all $N = 100$ individuals captured.

```
data <- data.fn()
```

We do the same kind of analysis as before but just have to add the time effects in the BUGS code.

```
# Augment data set
nz <- 150
yaug <- rbind(data$yobs, array(0, dim = c(nz, data$T)))

# Specify model in BUGS language
sink("model.txt")
cat("
model {

# Priors
omega ~ dunif(0, 1)
for (i in 1:T) {
    p[i] ~ dunif(0, 1)
    }

# Likelihood
for (i in 1:M) {
    z[i] ~ dbern(omega)
    for (j in 1:T) {
        yaug[i,j] ~ dbern(p.eff[i,j])
        p.eff[i,j] <- z[i] * p[j]
        } #j
    } #i

# Derived quantities
N <- sum(z[])
}
", fill = TRUE)
sink()

# Bundle data
win.data <- list(yaug = yaug, M = nrow(yaug), T = ncol(yaug))
```

```
# Initial values
inits <- function() list(z = rep(1, nrow(yaug)), p = runif(data$T, 0, 1))

# Parameters monitored
params <- c("N", "p", "omega")

# MCMC settings
ni <- 2500
nt <- 2
nb <- 500
nc <- 3

# Call WinBUGS from R (BRT <1 min)
out <- bugs(win.data, inits, params, "model.txt", n.chains = nc,
    n.thin = nt, n.iter = ni, n.burnin = nb, debug = TRUE, bugs.directory =
    bugs.dir, working.directory = getwd())

# Summarize posteriors
print(out, dig = 3)
hist(out$sims.list$N, nclass = 40, col = "gray", main = "", xlab =
    "Population size", las = 1, xlim = c(70, 150))
abline(v = data$C, col = "black", lwd = 3)
[...]
```

	mean	sd	2.5%	25%	50%	75%	97.5%	Rhat	n.eff
N	99.854	9.321	85.000	93.000	99.000	105.000	122.000	1.002	1500
p[1]	0.454	0.063	0.333	0.411	0.453	0.497	0.580	1.002	1900
p[2]	0.346	0.055	0.246	0.307	0.343	0.382	0.464	1.001	3000
p[3]	0.326	0.055	0.224	0.288	0.325	0.362	0.439	1.001	3000
omega	0.445	0.052	0.354	0.408	0.441	0.474	0.565	1.001	2000

[...]

The more params. p, the less prec. the estimate of N (handwritten annotation: "needed to describe")

So, all is similar as before. Note that an important contribution to the uncertainty about population size N comes from the uncertainty about detection probability p. The more we need to estimate for p, that is, the more parameters we need to describe the patterns in p, the less precise will be our estimate of N. You can fit the model M_0 to this same data set to confirm this. Therefore, when designing a study, it is always good to try and eliminate as many factors that will introduce variance in p as possible. Of course, we can always model such factors, but we pay with reduced precision.

In the above model, we have assumed that the time effects are fixed (although for convenience we simulated detection probabilities from a uniform random number generator). It would be straightforward to fit random instead of fixed time effects: just add a common prior distribution *(handwritten: random time effect)* to the set of detection probabilities and then estimate the hyperparameters of that prior distribution. It is customary to model detection probabilities on a transformed scale and assume a normal distribution for the random time effects. The usual transformation is the logit, that is, $\log[p/(1-p)]$. We leave this for one of the exercises for you to try out; see also Section 7.4.2.

6.2.3 Behavioral or Memory Effects: Model M$_b$

Another possible effect is within-capture-history dependence of detection probability p. This model is called model M$_b$ by Otis et al. (1978). It fits a different parameter for p depending on whether an animal was caught before or not. We need to distinguish between immediate (or ephemeral) trap response and permanent trap response. We might also envision something in between and make p a function of the number of times that an animal was caught over the last, say, 3 or 5 or 10 occasions. In this example, we model immediate trap response, that is, when an individual is captured, it has a different detection probability only on the immediately following occasion, but not thereafter, unless it is captured again.

In the following function, we simulate trap response on the probability scale. We could also do this on the logit scale, which would be more natural if we were to combine trap response with other effects. We denote the capture probabability as c or p depending on whether an individual has or has not been captured during the preceding occasion.

```
# Define function to simulate data under Mb
data.fn <- function(N = 200, T = 5, p = 0.3, c = 0.4){
    yfull <- yobs <- array(NA, dim = c(N, T) )
    p.eff <- array(NA, dim = N)

    # First capture occasion
    yfull[,1] <- rbinom(n = N, size = 1, prob = p)

    # Later capture occasions
    for (j in 2:T){
        p.eff <- (1 - yfull[, (j-1)]) * p + yfull[, (j-1)] * c
        yfull[,j] <- rbinom(n = N, size = 1, prob = p.eff)
        }

    ever.detected <- apply(yfull, 1, max)
    C <- sum(ever.detected)
    yobs <- yfull[ever.detected == 1,]
    cat(C, "out of", N, "animals present were detected.\n")
    return(list(N = N, p = p, c = c, C = C, T = T, yfull = yfull, yobs = yobs))
    }
```

We create one data set with trap-happiness ($p < c$). You may want to look at the data set created and try to see how trap response induces serial autocorrelation in the individual detection histories. This needs to be accounted for in the analysis.

```
data <- data.fn(N = 200)

# Augment data set
nz <- 150
yaug <- rbind(data$yobs, array(0, dim = c(nz, data$T)))

# Specify model in BUGS language
sink("model.txt")
cat("
model {
```

immediate vs permanent trap response

```
# Priors
omega ~ dunif(0, 1)
p ~ dunif(0, 1)        # Cap prob when not caught at t-1
c ~ dunif(0, 1)        # Cap prob when caught at t-1

# Likelihood
for (i in 1:M){
    z[i] ~ dbern(omega)

    # First occasion
    yaug[i,1] ~ dbern(p.eff[i,1])
    p.eff[i,1] <- z[i] * p

    # All subsequent occasions
    for (j in 2:T){
        yaug[i,j] ~ dbern(p.eff[i,j])
        p.eff[i,j] <- z[i] * ( (1-yaug[i,(j-1)]) * p + yaug[i,(j-1)] * c )
        } #j
    } #i

# Derived quantities
N <- sum(z[])
trap.response <- c - p
}
",fill = TRUE)
sink()

# Bundle data
win.data <- list(yaug = yaug, M = nrow(yaug), T = ncol(yaug))

# Initial values
inits <- function() list(z = rep(1, nrow(yaug)), p = runif(1, 0, 1))

# Parameters monitored
params <- c("N", "p", "c", "trap.response", "omega")

# MCMC settings
ni <- 2500
nt <- 2
nb <- 500
nc <- 3

# Call WinBUGS from R (BRT <1 min)
out <- bugs(win.data, inits, params, "model.txt", n.chains = nc,
    n.thin = nt, n.iter = ni, n.burnin = nb, debug = TRUE, bugs.directory =
    bugs.dir, working.directory = getwd())

# Summarize posteriors
print(out, dig = 3)
[...]
```

	mean	sd	2.5%	25%	50%	75%	97.5%	Rhat	n.eff
N	203.129	11.878	183.000	195.000	202.000	210.000	230.000	1.010	230
p	0.273	0.026	0.223	0.255	0.273	0.291	0.325	1.008	280
c	0.416	0.032	0.356	0.395	0.417	0.438	0.477	1.002	1300
trap.response	0.143	0.041	0.065	0.115	0.144	0.170	0.225	1.003	830
omega	0.652	0.046	0.567	0.620	0.650	0.682	0.745	1.007	350

```
[...]
```

```
hist(out$sims.list$N, nclass = 40, col = "gray", main = "", xlab =
   "Population size", las = 1, xlim = c(150, 300))
abline(v= data$C, col = "black", lwd = 3)
```

6.2.4 Individual (Random) Effects: The Heterogeneity Model M_h

The third model in the Otis et al. (1978) catalog is often called the "heterogeneity model", or M_h for short. This term is misleading, since it suggests a single model. However, a multitude of potential models can all be subsumed under the term M_h. What M_h means is that we assume that each individual has its own detection probability, and that this heterogeneity cannot be described by known and measured covariates; instead, we assume that there are individual latent (random) effects in detection probability.

There are various possible statistical descriptions of this "diffuse" heterogeneity, for instance, finite mixtures (Pledger, 2000) and beta binomial or logistic-normal continuous mixtures (Coull and Agresti, 1999; Dorazio and Royle, 2003). However, Link (2003) has shown that population size N is unfortunately not an identifiable parameter *across different classes of models* for individual heterogeneity in p, such as finite mixtures, beta binomial, or logistic-normal continuous mixtures. This means that models with a different specification of individual heterogeneity may well give very different answers about N, and yet, we have no data-based criterion to choose among them, such as likelihood ratio tests or AIC. However, we believe that simply ignoring individual heterogeneity would mean to throw out the baby with the bathtub, since not specifying effect h would lead to underestimated population size (Williams et al., 2002) and thus probably to worse inference, on average, than specifying the "wrong" mixture distribution (Kéry, 2011a).

Here, we consider one such mixture model, the logistic-normal (Coull and Agresti, 1999), which is a continuous mixture model that allows flexible modeling of individual effects along with others, such as time or behavior effects (see Section 6.3). In this model, individual heterogeneity is modeled as random noise around some mean on a logit-transformed scale, and the model for the noise is the normal distribution. Therefore, it is called logistic normal. OpenBUGS contains another example of model M_h with data augmentation (Examples > Ecology examples > Birds).

In our example, we aggregate the capture-histories to capture frequencies, that is, counts of the number of times each individual was encountered. In the absence of factors that induce time- or trap-dependent effects on detection, we do not need to model the binary detection histories and can parsimoniously model capture frequencies. In our code, mean.p is the average detection probability of individuals in the population studied, and sd is the standard deviation of the normal distribution which describes the heterogeneity in the individual detection probability on the logit scale. That is, we will estimate a normal distribution for individual detection probability with mean equal to `logit(mean.p)` and standard deviation equal to `sd`.

```
# Define function to simulate data under Mh
data.fn <- function(N = 100, mean.p = 0.4, T = 5, sd = 1){
    yfull <- yobs <- array(NA, dim = c(N, T) )
    mean.lp <- log(mean.p / (1-mean.p))
    p.vec <- plogis(mean.lp+ rnorm(N, 0, sd))

    for (i in 1:N){
        yfull[i,] <- rbinom(n = T, size = 1, prob = p.vec[i])
        }

    ever.detected <- apply(yfull, 1, max)
    C <- sum(ever.detected)
    yobs <- yfull[ever.detected == 1,]
    cat(C, "out of", N, "animals present were detected.\n")
    hist(p.vec, xlim = c(0,1), nclass = 20, col = "gray", main = "", xlab =
        "Detection probability", las = 1)
    return(list(N = N, p.vec = p.vec, mean.lp = mean.lp, C = C, T = T, yfull =
        yfull, yobs = yobs))
    }
```

We create one data set and get a summary of how many individuals were ever detected and a histogram of the individual detection probabilities (Fig. 6.3).

```
data <- data.fn()
84 out of 100 animals present were detected.
```

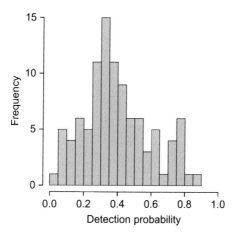

FIGURE 6.3 Distribution of individual detection probability for 100 simulated individuals.

We aggregate the capture-histories to capture frequencies and sort them for convenience. Then, we run WinBUGS on the model. As usual, random-effects models require longer Markov chains to achieve convergence. They also require more data augmentation: the posterior for N is more drawn out (there is more uncertainty about N) and so to avoid truncation of the posterior, we have to allow for more potential individuals by increasing the size of M.

```
# Aggregate capture histories and augment data set
y <- sort(apply(data$yobs, 1, sum), decreasing = TRUE)
nz <- 300
yaug <- c(y, rep(0, nz))
yaug
  [1] 5 5 5 5 5 5 5 4 4 4 4 4 4 4 4 4 4 4 4 3 3 3 3 3 3 3 3 3 3 3
 [32] 3 3 3 3 3 3 3 2 2 2 2 2 2 2 2 2 2 2 2 2 2 2 2 2 2 2 2 2 2 2 2
 [63] 2 2 2 1 1 1 1 1 1 1 1 1 1 1 1 1 1 1 1 1 1 1 0 0 0 0 0 0 0 0 0
[...]
[373] 0 0 0 0 0 0 0 0 0 0 0 0
```

```
# Specify model in BUGS language
sink("model.txt")
cat("
model {

# Priors
omega ~ dunif(0, 1)
mean.lp <- logit(mean.p)
mean.p ~ dunif(0, 1)
tau <- 1 / (sd * sd)
sd ~ dunif(0, 5)

# Likelihood
for (i in 1:M) {
    z[i] ~ dbern(omega)
    logit(p[i]) <- eps[i]
    eps[i] ~ dnorm(mean.lp, tau)I(-16, 16)      # See web appendix A in
                                                 Royle (2009)

    p.eff[i] <- z[i] * p[i]
    y[i] ~ dbin(p.eff[i], T)
    }

# Derived quantities
N <- sum(z[])
}
", fill = TRUE)
sink()
```

```
# Bundle data
win.data <- list(y = yaug, M = length(yaug), T = ncol(data$yobs))
```

```
# Initial values
inits <- function() list(z = rep(1, length(yaug)), sd = runif(1, 0.1, 0.9))
```

```
# Parameters monitored
params <- c("N", "mean.p", "sd", "omega")
```

```
# MCMC settings
ni <- 25000
nt <- 2
nb <- 5000
nc <- 3
```

```
# Call WinBUGS from R (BRT 6 min)
out <- bugs(win.data, inits, params, "model.txt", n.chains = nc,
    n.thin = nt, n.iter = ni, n.burnin = nb, debug = TRUE, bugs.directory =
    bugs.dir, working.directory = getwd())
```

```
# Summarize posteriors
print(out, dig = 3)
hist(out$sims.list$N, nclass = 50, col = "gray", main = "", xlab =
    "Population size", las = 1, xlim = c(80, 250))
abline(v = data$C, col = "black", lwd = 3)
[...]
```

	mean	sd	2.5%	25%	50%	75%	97.5%	Rhat	n.eff
N	101.584	12.927	87.000	93.000	98.000	106.000	134.000	1.015	590
mean.p	0.405	0.074	0.225	0.364	0.416	0.457	0.517	1.023	830
sd	1.091	0.355	0.510	0.845	1.050	1.289	1.904	1.017	260
omega	0.266	0.040	0.205	0.239	0.261	0.286	0.358	1.007	950

[...]

We see that the precision for N is lower compared with that under the previous models. Estimation in individual-effects models is notoriously more challenging than in models without such random effects. We see this in longer run time to get an adequate posterior sample as well as in the drawn-out posterior distribution of the key parameter N (Fig. 6.4).

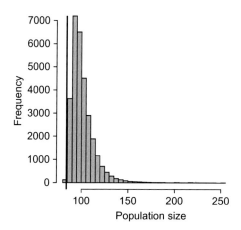

FIGURE 6.4 Posterior distribution of population size N under the heterogeneity model M_h (black line: observed number of individuals). The posterior mass does not extend below the observed number of individuals (84).

6.2.5 Combined Effects: Model M$_{th}$

Time, behavioral, and individual effects may also be combined pairwise or all three, giving rise to what Otis et al. (1978) have called models M$_{th}$ and so forth. Again, this terminology is useful, but may also be misleading, since it may appear as if there was a single such model. Instead, all that a term such as M$_{th}$ means is that a model includes the effects of both time and individual heterogeneity. This term does not tell us about how time and individual heterogeneity is parameterized, for instance, whether time effects are fixed or random or whether a finite or a continuous mixture is assumed for individual latent effects. It also does not specify whether the two effects are assumed to be independent or to act in a combined way (i.e., whether time and heterogeneity act as main effects only or with an interaction).

Here, we give one example of a model M$_{th}$, which may be more precisely described as having additive (i.e., main) fixed effects of time and random (logistic normal) effects of individuals. This is a useful model in many circumstances in the absence of behavioral effects. Now, we consider effects along both dimensions of the capture-history matrix (corresponding to Table 6.1, with columns representing time, and rows representing individuals). so, we model the unaggregated data. Furthermore, we will model all effects on a logistic scale.

```
# Define function to simulate data under Mth
data.fn <- function(N = 100, T = 5, mean.p = 0.4, time.effects = runif(T,
    -1, 1), sd = 1){
    yfull <- yobs <- p <- array(NA, dim = c(N, T) )
    mean.lp <- log(mean.p / (1-mean.p))        # mean p on logit scale
    eps <- rnorm(N, 0, sd)                     # Individual effects

    for (j in 1:T){
        pp <- p[,j] <- plogis(mean.lp + time.effects[j] + eps)
        yfull[,j] <- rbinom(n = N, size = 1, prob = pp)
        }

    ever.detected <- apply(yfull, 1, max)
    C <- sum(ever.detected)
    yobs <- yfull[ever.detected == 1,]
    cat(C, "out of", N, "animals present were detected.\n")
    cat("Mean p per occasion:", round(apply(p, 2, mean), 2), "\n")
    par(mfrow = c(2,1))
    plot(plogis(mean.lp + time.effects), xlab = "Occasion", type = "b",
        main = "Approx. mean p at each occasion", ylim = c(0, 1))
    hist(plogis(mean.lp + eps), xlim = c(0, 1), col = "gray", main =
        "Approx. distribution of p at average occasion")
    return(list(N = N, mean.lp = mean.lp, time.effects = time.effects,
        sd = sd, eps = eps, C = C, T = T, yfull = yfull, yobs = yobs))
    }
```

As shown below, this function can also be used to generate data sets under models M$_0$, M$_t$, and M$_h$ by writing as one or two arguments time.effects = runif(5, 0, 0) and sd = 0 (you have to adjust *T* manually). Here, we create one data set under the model with both effects present and analyze that. We avoid to use the WinBUGS logit function and instead define the logit explicitly, which may sometimes avoid numerical problems.

```
data <- data.fn()
85 out of 100 animals present were detected.
Mean p per occasion: 0.35 0.41 0.47 0.61 0.45

# data<-data.fn(T = 10, mean.p = 0.2, time.effects = runif(10, 0, 0),
    sd = 0) # M0
# data<-data.fn(T = 10, mean.p = 0.5, time.effects = runif(10, 0, 0),
    sd = 1) # Mh
# data <- data.fn(T = 10, sd = 0) # Mt

# Augment data set
nz <- 300
yaug <- rbind(data$yobs, array(0, dim=c(nz, data$T)))

# Specify model in BUGS language
sink("model.txt")
cat("
model {

# Priors
omega ~ dunif(0, 1)
for (j in 1:T){
    mean.lp[j] <- log(mean.p[j] / (1 - mean.p[j]) ) # Define logit
    mean.p[j] ~ dunif(0, 1)
    }
tau <- 1 / (sd * sd)
sd ~ dunif(0,5)

# Likelihood
for (i in 1:M){
    z[i] ~ dbern(omega)
    eps[i] ~ dnorm(0, tau)I(-16, 16) # See web appendix A in Royle (2009)
    for (j in 1:T){
        lp[i,j] <- mean.lp[j] + eps[i]
        p[i,j] <- 1 / (1 + exp(-lp[i,j]))          # Define logit
        p.eff[i,j] <- z[i] * p[i,j]
        y[i,j] ~ dbern(p.eff[i,j])
        } #j
    } #i

# Derived quantities
N <- sum(z[])
}
",fill = TRUE)
sink()

# Bundle data
win.data <- list(y = yaug, M = nrow(yaug), T = ncol(yaug))

# Initial values
inits <- function() list(z = rep(1, nrow(yaug)), sd = runif(1, 0.1, 0.9))
```

```
# Parameters monitored
params <- c("N", "mean.p", "mean.lp", "sd", "omega")

# MCMC settings
ni <- 25000
nt <- 2
nb <- 5000
nc <- 3

# Call WinBUGS from R (BRT 47 min)
out <- bugs(win.data, inits, params, "model.txt", n.chains = nc,
    n.thin = nt, n.iter = ni, n.burnin = nb, debug = TRUE, bugs.directory =
    bugs.dir, working.directory = getwd())

# Summarize posteriors
print(out, dig = 3)
hist(out$sims.list$N, nclass = 50, col = "gray", main = "", xlab =
    "Population size", las = 1, xlim = c(80, 200))
abline(v = data$C, col = "black", lwd = 3)
[...]
```

	mean	sd	2.5%	25%	50%	75%	97.5%	Rhat	n.eff
N	103.665	10.416	89.000	96.000	102.000	109.000	129.000	1.001	6900
mean.p[1]	0.381	0.083	0.214	0.325	0.383	0.439	0.540	1.001	13000
mean.p[2]	0.419	0.085	0.244	0.363	0.422	0.478	0.578	1.001	30000
mean.p[3]	0.419	0.086	0.243	0.361	0.422	0.479	0.578	1.001	12000
mean.p[4]	0.582	0.089	0.388	0.527	0.590	0.645	0.736	1.001	9000
mean.p[5]	0.322	0.078	0.169	0.269	0.322	0.374	0.474	1.001	21000
mean.lp[1]	-0.500	0.371	-1.301	-0.731	-0.476	-0.244	0.162	1.001	10000
mean.lp[2]	-0.338	0.365	-1.132	-0.562	-0.314	-0.086	0.313	1.001	20000
mean.lp[3]	-0.340	0.369	-1.138	-0.570	-0.314	-0.083	0.315	1.001	9200
mean.lp[4]	0.342	0.374	-0.454	0.109	0.362	0.597	1.026	1.001	6600
mean.lp[5]	-0.772	0.376	-1.590	-1.002	-0.746	-0.514	-0.104	1.001	18000
sd	1.411	0.347	0.795	1.173	1.386	1.624	2.173	1.003	2700
omega	0.270	0.035	0.211	0.246	0.267	0.291	0.348	1.001	19000

```
[...]
```

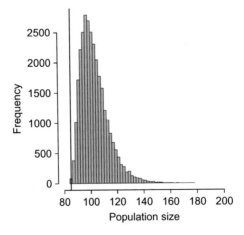

FIGURE 6.5   Posterior distribution of population size N under model M_{th} (black line: observed number of individuals).

We obtain decent parameter estimates (see Fig. 6.5 and preceding posterior summary), judging by their resemblance to the parameter values with which we generated our data set.

6.3 ANALYSIS OF A REAL DATA SET: MODEL M_{tbh} FOR SPECIES RICHNESS ESTIMATION

To illustrate estimation of the size of a real population, we will look at the size of a bird community. It has been pointed out repeatedly that the number of species in a community is analogous to the number of individuals in a population (e.g., Boulinier et al., 1998; Nichols et al., 1998a). Therefore, the same inferential framework, closed-population models (though not, for instance, distance sampling), can be used for both (Kéry, 2011a). One important consideration specific to species richness estimation is that a model that does not allow for individual heterogeneity will probably not be adequate: species in a community usually differ by many factors that determine their detection probability, most of all perhaps in their abundance. Thus, detection probability is likely to vary a great deal more among the species in a community than among the individuals in a population. Since not allowing for heterogeneity in p yields severe underestimates of N, species richness estimation with closed capture–recapture models should always be based on a heterogeneity model.

We will use bird point count data from the Czech republic (data courtesy of Jiri Reif). With some colleagues, Jiri cycled an East–West transect spanning almost the whole country and conducted a 5 min point count after every 500 m in 2004–2005 (768 points in total). They repeated this five times within the same breeding season. A total of 146 species were detected (Reif et al., 2008), among them the wryneck (Fig. 6.6). We will use their data from one such point: point count number 610. For each species and occasion, the data contain the number of individuals counted. For the analysis, we first reduce these data to simple detection/nondetection data.

```
# Read in data and look at them
p610 <- read.table("p610.txt", header = TRUE)
y <- p610[,5:9]                          # Grab counts
y[y > 1] <- 1                            # Counts to det-nondetections
C <- sum(apply(y, 1, max)) ; print(C)    # Number of observed species
table(apply(y, 1, sum))                  # Capture-frequencies
```

The data contain the detection histories not only of the 31 species detected at this particular point but also those of all species detected anywhere along the full national transect. Hence, this data set is "naturally data augmented". We will not add any more zeroes because 115 zeroes corresponding to the species not detected at point 610, but detected somewhere else in the Czech

FIGURE 6.6   Wryneck (*Jynx torquilla*), Latvia, 2004 (Photograph by T. Muukkonen).

Republic, are probably enough. But we can easily check that by inspecting the posterior distribution for N.

All models in this chapter assume closure (here: community closure). In the present context, this means that each species that is part of the sampled community at a given point must be available for detection during all replicate surveys. This may well not be true. For instance, many bird species are migrants, and some may not yet have arrived during early surveys. If typical arrival dates of each migrant species are known, then this problem could be dealt with by simply turning the corresponding data into missing values. Our data set would then no longer be balanced, but this in general poses no problem to the estimation framework, as long as some replicate surveys are available for some species at least.

Here, we will ignore this possibility and assume closure. We adopt a model M_{tbh} which has additive effects of time, behavior, and individual heterogeneity on the detection probability of a species. The test for behavioral effects is particularly interesting, since it has been suggested that in monitoring programs, people may detect species detected previously more or less easily thereafter (Riddle et al., 2010).

```
# Specify model in BUGS language
sink("M_tbh.txt")
cat("
model {
```

```
# Priors
omega ~ dunif(0, 1)
for (j in 1:T){
    alpha[j] <- log(mean.p[j] / (1-mean.p[j])) # Define logit
    mean.p[j] ~ dunif(0, 1) # Detection intercepts
    }
gamma ~ dnorm(0, 0.01)
tau <- 1 / (sd * sd)
sd ~ dunif(0, 3)

# Likelihood
for (i in 1:M){
    z[i] ~ dbern(omega)
    eps[i] ~ dnorm(0, tau)I(-16, 16)

    # First occasion: no term for recapture (gamma)
    y[i,1] ~ dbern(p.eff[i,1])
    p.eff[i,1] <- z[i] * p[i,1]
    p[i,1] <- 1 / (1 + exp(-lp[i,1]))
    lp[i,1] <- alpha[1] + eps[i]

    # All subsequent occasions: includes recapture term (gamma)
    for (j in 2:T){
        y[i,j] ~ dbern(p.eff[i,j])
        p.eff[i,j] <- z[i] * p[i,j]
        p[i,j] <- 1 / (1 + exp(-lp[i,j]))
        lp[i,j] <- alpha[j] + eps[i] + gamma * y[i,(j-1)]
        } #j
    } #i

# Derived quantities
N <- sum(z[])
}
",fill = TRUE)
sink()

# Bundle data
win.data <- list(y = as.matrix(y), M = nrow(y), T = ncol(y))

# Initial values
inits <- function() list(z = rep(1, nrow(y)), sd = runif(1, 0.1, 0.9))

# Parameters monitored
params <- c("N", "mean.p", "gamma", "sd", "omega")

# MCMC settings
ni <- 50000
nt <- 4
nb <- 10000
nc <- 3

# Call WinBUGS from R (BRT 24 min)
out <- bugs(win.data, inits, params, "M_tbh.txt", n.chains = nc,
    n.thin = nt, n.iter = ni, n.burnin = nb, debug = TRUE, bugs.directory =
    bugs.dir, working.directory = getwd())
```

```
# Summarize posteriors and plot posterior for N
print(out, dig = 3)
par(mfrow = c(1,2))
hist(out$sims.list$N, breaks = 35, col = "gray", main = "", xlab =
   "Community size", las = 1, xlim = c(30, 100), freq = FALSE)
abline(v = C, col = "black", lwd = 3)
[...]
```

	mean	sd	2.5%	25%	50%	75%	97.5%	Rhat	n.eff
N	42.050	7.444	33.000	37.000	40.000	45.000	61.000	1.002	2300
mean.p[1]	0.241	0.084	0.096	0.181	0.235	0.294	0.420	1.001	13000
mean.p[2]	0.294	0.096	0.126	0.224	0.288	0.356	0.495	1.002	3100
mean.p[3]	0.295	0.097	0.125	0.225	0.289	0.358	0.502	1.002	2200
mean.p[4]	0.222	0.084	0.083	0.161	0.214	0.274	0.408	1.002	1600
mean.p[5]	0.319	0.099	0.140	0.248	0.315	0.385	0.522	1.002	3200
gamma	-0.080	0.496	-1.062	-0.409	-0.099	0.268	0.892	1.010	300
sd	0.709	0.420	0.044	0.387	0.676	0.983	1.622	1.005	11000
omega	0.291	0.062	0.193	0.248	0.283	0.325	0.435	1.002	3100

```
[...]
```

After 24 min worth of sampling the joint posterior distribution of parameters, estimates look decent, and so we make a first interpretation of these results. With 31 species detected, we estimate there were in fact 42, therefore, only $31/42 = 74\%$ were ever detected (Fig. 6.7a). Given the short survey duration, this appears reasonable. The average detection probability of a species in the community was between 0.22 and 0.32 and did not appear to vary much (in view of the wide uncertainty around these estimates). No behavioral ("memory") effect on detection probability was discernible (95% CRI of gamma: −1.06 to 0.89). Finally, the standard deviation of the heterogeneity distribution was estimated at 0.71, which, not surprisingly, is considerable; species differ greatly.

It appears likely that whether or not "memory" exists should partly be related to scale. If a single person goes out to a small area and surveys on consecutive days then maybe he remembers what he saw. But, over large scales, over long time, and sampling many species, it is probably less important (Royle, pers. comm.). Since behavioral effects appeared to be absent, we might simplify the model and fit a time and heterogeneity model (i.e., M_{th}).

We have mentioned that inference under model M_0 will often lead to a serious negative bias in the estimate of N when there is heterogeneity among species in p. We illustrate this next by fitting model M_0.

```
# Define model
sink("M0.txt")
cat("
model {

# Priors
omega ~ dunif(0, 1)
p ~ dunif(0, 1)
```

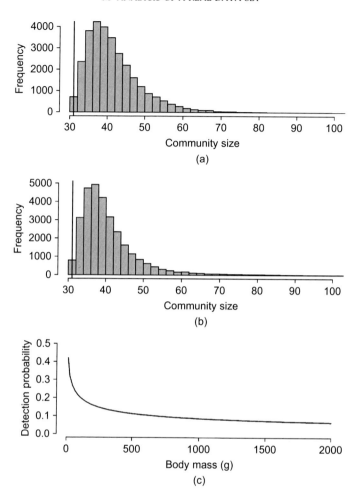

FIGURE 6.7 Analysis of community size (species richness, N) at point 610 in the Czech transect data (courtesy of Jiri Reif). Posterior distribution of N (a) under a model with time, behavioral, and heterogeneity effects (M_{tbh}) and (b) under a model with effects of time and the individual covariate body mass (M_{t+x}). The black line denotes the observed number of species. (c) Effect of body mass (g) on detection probability.

```
# Likelihood
for (i in 1:M) {
    z[i] ~ dbern(omega)
    for (j in 1:T) {
        y[i,j] ~ dbern(p.eff[i,j])
        p.eff[i,j] <- z[i] * p
        } #j
    } #i
```

```
# Derived quantities
N <- sum(z[])
} # end model
",fill = TRUE)
sink()

# Initial values
inits <- function() list(z = rep(1, nrow(y)))

# Define parameters to be monitored
params <- c("N", "p", "omega")

# MCMC settings
ni <- 50000
nt <- 4
nb <- 10000
nc <- 3

# Call WinBUGS from R (BRT 1 min)
out0 <- bugs(win.data, inits, params, "M0.txt", n.chains = nc,
    n.thin = nt, n.iter = ni, n.burnin = nb, debug = FALSE, bugs.directory =
    bugs.dir, working.directory = getwd())

# Inspect output
print(out0, dig = 3)
[...]
```

	mean	sd	2.5%	25%	50%	75%	97.5%	Rhat	n.eff
N	37.877	3.970	32.000	35.000	37.00	40.000	47.000	1.001	21000
p	0.301	0.044	0.216	0.271	0.30	0.331	0.390	1.001	16000
omega	0.263	0.045	0.182	0.231	0.26	0.291	0.358	1.001	30000

```
[...]
```

Under model M_0, we estimate 38 instead of 42 species. This illustrates the point that ignoring individual heterogeneity in detection probability produces underestimates of, and too short standard errors for, population size N.

6.4 CAPTURE–RECAPTURE MODELS WITH INDIVIDUAL COVARIATES: MODEL M_{t+X}

The old classification of Otis et al. (1978) of closed-population models does not include individual covariates. However, continuous detection covariates may often be available, and their effects could be modeled. The challenge is that the covariate values for undetected individuals are not known. Next, we illustrate a model described by Royle (2009), who uses data augmentation to analyze the joint likelihood of the capture-histories and the covariate values. In this model, we describe the distribution of the covariate values in the statistical population in addition to the probabilistic description of the capture-histories. We will give two illustrations for this model: first, in the context of species richness estimation for the Czech transect data and second, in the context of population size estimation in a mussel.

6.4.1 Individual Covariate Model for Species Richness Estimation

In our first example, we model the effect of body mass on detection probability in the Czech bird data. Body mass could affect detection probability p in various ways. First, everything else equal, larger birds are rarer than smaller birds; hence, we would expect p to be lower than for smaller birds. Second, larger birds have larger territories, so their p will contain an important availability component (Kéry and Schmidt, 2008): when they are in a part of their territory that is not sampled, they cannot be detected, and this will lower their p. In contrast, and third, a larger bird may intrinsically be more visible than a smaller bird. Thus, we might expect an effect of body size on p, though its direction may not be obvious.

In the Czech bird example, the total list of species that could occur at point 610 is assumed to be known; it is those 146 species that were ever detected anywhere in the Czech transect study (Reif et al., 2008). Hence, the covariate values for all "individuals" are known, and we could proceed with the modeling without assuming a prior distribution for the covariate. However, more typically, when estimating population size, the covariate values are *not* known for individuals not encountered and hence, to estimate these latent covariate values, we must assume a prior distribution for them and estimate the hyperparameters of the latter. To mimick this situation, we discard all body mass data of the $146 - 31 = 115$ species that were not detected at point 610.

```
p610 <- read.table("p610.txt", header = TRUE)
y <- p610[,5:9]                          # Grab counts
y[y > 1] <- 1                            # Convert to det-nondetections
ever.observed <- apply(y, 1, max)
wt <- p610$bm[ever.observed == 1]        # Body mass
yy <- as.matrix(y[ever.observed == 1,]) # Detection histories
dimnames(yy) <- NULL
```

To determine a distribution suitable to describe the species-specific body mass, we cheat a little and inspect the data for all 146 species. Body mass is expected to be proportional to the cube of length, and length measurements are often approximately normally distributed. Therefore, we take the cubic root of body mass. In addition, we take the log. It is obvious that the lognormal is not a fantastic description of the cubic root of body mass, but here, we assume it is adequate, at least for our illustrative purposes.

```
mlog <- mean(log(p610$bm^(1/3)))
sdlog <- sd(log(p610$bm^(1/3)))
hist(p610$bm^(1/3), xlim = c(0, 30), nclass = 25, freq = FALSE,
    col = "gray")
lines(density(rlnorm(n = 10^6, meanlog = mlog, sdlog = sdlog)),
    col = "blue", lwd = 3)
```

Since we discarded the data on undetected species, we now need to actively augment the data set and add 150 potential species. This yields a detection data set with M = 181 rows. We also need to augment the individual covariate with NAs for individuals 32–181.

```
# Augment both data sets
nz = 150
yaug <- rbind(yy, array(0, dim = c(nz, ncol(yy))))
logwt3 <- c(log(wt^(1/3)), rep(NA, nz))
```

It should in theory be possible to fit the same model as in Section 6.3 with the body mass covariate added. However, trying to squeeze out so many parameter estimates from so little data (31 species) may be asking for too much, and indeed, we failed at getting convergence for this model. Hence, we fit a simpler model with effects of time and the covariate, thus dropping the individual and trap response effects. We center the covariate to facilitate interpretation of the parameters and improve convergence. We also provide part of the prior definition in the BUGS model as data (`prior.sd.upper`), which makes the code more flexible.

```
# Specify model in BUGS language
sink("M_t+X.txt")
cat("
model {

# Priors
omega ~ dunif(0, 1)
for (j in 1:T){
    alpha[j] <- log(mean.p[j] / (1-mean.p[j]))
    mean.p[j] ~ dunif(0, 1)
    }
beta ~ dnorm(0, 0.01)
mu.size ~ dnorm(0, 0.01)
tau.size <- 1 / pow(sd.size, 2)
sd.size ~ dunif(0, prior.sd.upper)        # Provide upper bound as data

# Likelihood
for (i in 1:M){        # Loop over individuals
    z[i] ~ dbern(omega)
    size[i] ~ dnorm(mu.size, tau.size)I(-6, 6)
    for (j in 1:T){ # Loop over occasions
        y[i,j] ~ dbern(p.eff[i,j])
        p.eff[i,j] <- z[i] * p[i,j]
```

```
    p[i,j] <- 1 / (1 + exp(-lp[i,j]))
    lp[i,j] <- alpha[j] + beta * size[i]
    } #j
  } #i
```

```
# Derived quantities
N <- sum(z[])
}
",fill = TRUE)
sink()
```

```
# Bundle data
win.data <- list(y = yaug, size = logwt3 - mean(logwt3, na.rm = TRUE), M =
    nrow(yaug), T = ncol(yaug), prior.sd.upper = 3)
```

```
# Initial values
inits <- function() list(z = rep(1, nrow(yaug)), beta = runif(1, 0, 1),
    mu.size = rnorm(1, 0, 1))
```

```
# Parameters monitored
params <- c("N", "mean.p", "beta", "omega", "mu.size", "sd.size")
```

```
# MCMC settings
ni <- 50000
nt <- 4
nb <- 10000
nc <- 3
```

```
# Call WinBUGS from R (BRT 19 min)
outX <- bugs(win.data, inits, params, "M_t+X.txt", n.chains = nc,
    n.thin = nt, n.iter = ni, n.burnin = nb, debug = TRUE, bugs.directory =
    bugs.dir, working.directory = getwd())
```

```
# Summarize posteriors and plot posterior for N
print(outX, dig = 3)
            mean     sd   2.5%    25%    50%    75%  97.5%   Rhat n.eff
N         41.638 10.384 32.000 36.000 39.000 44.000 68.000 1.099    65
mean.p[1]  0.270  0.075  0.138  0.216  0.264  0.318  0.430 1.003  1100
mean.p[2]  0.320  0.080  0.176  0.263  0.316  0.373  0.488 1.003  1200
mean.p[3]  0.321  0.080  0.175  0.263  0.317  0.374  0.487 1.003  1100
mean.p[4]  0.244  0.072  0.120  0.192  0.239  0.290  0.399 1.003  1200
mean.p[5]  0.345  0.083  0.197  0.287  0.341  0.400  0.518 1.003  1000
beta      -1.313  0.875 -3.143 -1.873 -1.308 -0.725  0.346 1.061    40
omega      0.233  0.064  0.152  0.195  0.222  0.256  0.387 1.049   100
mu.size    0.070  0.111 -0.092  0.002  0.055  0.116  0.342 1.083    63
sd.size    0.366  0.065  0.272  0.323  0.356  0.398  0.520 1.019   230
[...]
```

```
hist(outX$sims.list$N, breaks = 100, col = "gray", main = "", xlab =
    "Community size", las = 1, xlim = c(30, 100), freq = FALSE)
abline(v = 31, col = "black", lwd = 3)
```

We get a very similar estimate of species richness (N) as under model M_{tbh}, though the uncertainty is now greater (Fig. 6.7b). This might suggests that much of the heterogeneity among species in p may be explained by body size and its correlates. What about the relationship between p and body mass? The latter varies about 5–10,500 g, and we produce predictions of *p* in relation to mass (up to 2000 g), averaging over time effects. We find a strong negative effect of body mass on detection probability (Fig. 6.7c).

```
pred.wt <- seq(5, 2000, length.out = 100) # Cov. vals for prediction
pred.wt.st <- log(pred.wt^(1/3)) - mean(logwt3, na.rm = TRUE)
    # Transform them in the same was as in the analysis
pred.p<- plogis(log(mean(outX$mean$mean.p) /
    (1- mean(outX$mean$mean.p))) + outX$mean$beta * pred.wt.st)
    # Compute predicted response
plot(pred.wt, pred.p, type = "l", lwd = 3, col = "blue", las = 1,
    frame.plot = FALSE, ylim = c(0, 0.5))
```

The individual covariate model of Royle (2009) is an interesting and flexible model. As usual, the motivation for the introduction of covariates may be to eliminate unexplained heterogeneity or to explore the covariate relationships. Casting the closed-population model as an occupancy model with or without partly unobserved covariate values gives us much flexibility for either. Of course, the distributional assumption for the covariate is very much part of the model. The dependence of the inference upon this assumption should be tested, as did Royle (2009).

6.4.2 Individual Covariate Model for Population Size Estimation

In our second example, we analyze data from a population study of the pen shell (Fig. 6.8), conducted by Iris Hendriks and her colleagues in the Balearic islands in 2007 and 2010 (Hendriks et al., in preparation). The pen shell is a large bivalve living in *Posidonia* meadows in the Mediterranean. Its habitat is increasingly affected by anchors of leisure boats. Hendriks et al. had two teams of divers who each conducted an independent survey of a number of transects and recorded and measured the size (shell width in cm) of each *Pinna* individual encountered. The resulting data consisted of the detection history of each shell (e.g., 1 0, for a shell detected by the first team and missed by the second) along with its width. We expected a positive effect of mussel size on detection probability. We ignored several other potential covariates, such as site and vegetation density, and restricted our analysis to the 143 shells encountered in 2010.

```
# Read in data and look at shell width distribution
pinna <- read.table("pinna.txt", header = TRUE)
y <- cbind(pinna$d1, pinna$d2)
size <- pinna$width
hist(size, col = "gray", nclass = 50, xlim = c(0, 30), freq = FALSE)
lines(density(rnorm(10^6, mean = mean(size), sd = sd(size))),
    col = "blue", lwd = 3)
```

FIGURE 6.8 Pen shell (*Pinna nobilis*), Spain, 2009 (Photograph by I. Hendriks).

We recycle most code from the Czech bird data analysis in the previous section.

```
# Augment both data sets
nz = 150
yaug <- rbind(y, array(0, dim = c(nz, ncol(y))))
size <- c(size, rep(NA, nz))

# Bundle data
win.data <- list(y = yaug, size = size - mean(size, na.rm = TRUE),
    M = nrow(yaug), T = ncol(yaug), prior.sd.upper = 5)

# MCMC settings
ni <- 2500
nt <- 2
nb <- 500
nc <- 3

# Call WinBUGS from R (BRT 1 min)
outXX <- bugs(win.data, inits, params, "M_t+X.txt", n.chains = nc,
    n.thin = nt, n.iter = ni, n.burnin = nb, debug = TRUE, bugs.directory =
    bugs.dir, working.directory = getwd())

# Summarize posteriors
print(outXX, dig = 2)
```

	mean	sd	2.5%	25%	50%	75%	97.5%	Rhat	n.eff
N	172.04	9.45	156.00	165.00	171.00	178.00	193.00	1.00	450
mean.p[1]	0.67	0.05	0.57	0.64	0.68	0.71	0.77	1.00	1200
mean.p[2]	0.53	0.05	0.43	0.49	0.53	0.56	0.61	1.00	860
beta	0.11	0.04	0.04	0.09	0.11	0.14	0.18	1.09	50
omega	0.59	0.04	0.50	0.56	0.59	0.61	0.68	1.00	570
mu.size	-0.15	0.26	-0.67	-0.33	-0.16	0.02	0.35	1.01	300
sd.size	3.51	0.15	3.22	3.41	3.51	3.61	3.83	1.00	3000

We estimate that 172 instead of 143 pen shells were available for detection along the surveyed transects. This means that 29 (95% CRI 13–50) were missed by both teams of divers. Detection probability was higher for the first teams, and as expected, there was a positive relationship with shell width (Fig. 6.9).

Plot posterior for N and prediction of p
```
par(mfrow = c(1,2), mar = c(4.5, 4, 2, 1))
hist(outXX$sims.list$N, breaks = 30, col = "gray", main = "", xlab =
    "Population size", las = 1, xlim = c(143, 220), freq = FALSE)
abline(v = 143, col = "black", lwd = 3)

pred.size <- seq(0, 30, length.out = 1000)  # Cov. vals for prediction
pred.size.st <- pred.size - mean(size, na.rm = TRUE)  # Transform them
pred.p <- plogis(log(mean(outXX$mean$mean.p) /
    (1- mean(outXX$mean$mean.p))) + outXX$mean$beta * pred.size.st)
    # Compute predicted detection prob.
plot(pred.size, pred.p, type = "l", lwd = 3, col = "blue", las = 1,
    frame.plot = FALSE, ylim = c(0, 1), xlab = "Shell width (cm)", ylab =
    "Predicted detection probability")
```

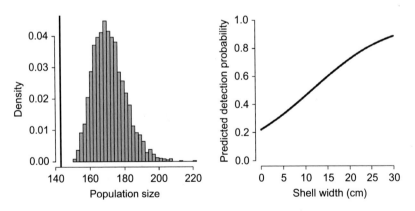

FIGURE 6.9   Analysis of population size (*N*) of pen shells. Left: Posterior distribution of *N* (black line: observed number of individuals); right: predicted detection probability in relation to size.

6.5 SUMMARY AND OUTLOOK

The population is a central concept in ecology and its size N perhaps its key descriptor. Because of detection error, N is usually not directly observable. Capture–recapture methods obtain information about detection probability p from the repeated encounters of uniquely identifiable individuals and from this derive an estimate of N. In practice, estimating N means estimating p and modeling the key patterns in p. The same concepts and methods can be used for vastly different kinds of "populations", including populations of species, that is, communities, where size is equivalent to species richness. In this chapter, we have encountered a catalog of effects (Null, time, behavior, individual heterogeneity) that may be present in p when estimating N, including the effects of individual covariates. These concepts are very general, and we will find them in different situations for parameters other than detection probability later in this book. We have also introduced data augmentation (DA) and fitted all models in this chapter using this ingenious but simple technique. DA is an important concept and helps to unify a vast number of capture–recapture type models, which were hitherto regarded as technically distinct procedures. See Royle and Dorazio (2008) to get a flavor of the power of DA.

Obviously, we have only given a very selective view of the large field of population size estimation, and interested readers will have to refer to the many standard references now available. We also briefly note that we do not deal with one important class of models that also achieve a clean accounting of the ecological and the observation processes in estimating density or abundance: distance sampling (Buckland et al., 2001; Williams et al., 2002; Buckland et al., 2004; Royle and Dorazio, 2008). These models are the focus of an active branch of ecological statistics and have much relevance for the analysis of populations. Distance sampling can be implemented in WinBUGS; see Royle and Dorazio (2008). OpenBUGS contains a distance sampling example (Examples > Ecology examples > Impala).

We have assumed that the area with which a population is associated may be delimited unambiguously. This is often not the case and to solve this problem, spatial capture–recapture methods are required, which represent a merging of the capture–recapture class of models with those of the distance sampling-type (Efford, 2004; Borchers and Efford, 2008; Royle and Young, 2008; Gardner et al., 2009; Efford et al., 2009a, 2009b; Royle et al., 2009a, 2009b). These models are very powerful and flexible. One of their advantages is that they can estimate detection probability, and therefore, can estimate abundance from the spatial pattern of multiple detections of individuals alone (Efford et al., 2009b); no temporal replicate surveys are required. This is a huge design advantage! It seems likely that in the near future we will see much development along this branch of the population assessment tree in ecological statistics. Again, most spatial capture–recapture models can be implemented in WinBUGS in a transparent way. Likelihood inference can be obtained with user-friendly packages such as program Density (www.otago.ac.nz/density/) or the recent R package secr developed by Murray Efford.

All models in the current chapter have assumed closed populations, but we may also want to estimate N in open populations. The Jolly–Seber model (Chapter 10) models population dynamics, that is, survival and recruitment rates and population size, whereas the N-mixture and site-occupancy models (Chapters 12 and 13) may be used to model N in collections of open populations.

6.6 EXERCISES

1. Rewrite the model M_h in Section 6.2.4 for encounter history instead of capture frequency data and fit it. (The response will be Bernoulli instead of Binomial.)
2. Try to fit the model with permanent trap response to the bird survey data. Imagine a biological situation that might represent this model, on the part of the observer? On the part of the animal?
3. Check out the behavior of estimators in small sample situations, example, the heterogeneity model with 20 individuals and heterogeneity. Does this work?
4. Generate data with individual heterogeneity in p and fit model M_0. See how well N is estimated.
5. Find out whether a model with trap response and time effects is estimable with $T = 2$.
6. And what about pure model M_b with $T = 2$?
7. In M_t, adapt both the data generation and the model fitting code to random instead of fixed time effects.
8. Check the effects of assumption violations. Fit a model to a data set that was not generated under the same model. For instance, generate data under model M_t and analyze the resulting data set under M_0 to see what happens to your estimates of N and p when you ignore time variation in p. Do similar things to other pairs of models.
9. Use the Czech point count data and estimate species richness, where detection is a function of body mass, similar as in Section 6.4.1. But this time, include the body mass of all unobserved species. Hint: you then no longer have to give a prior for body mass. Does the estimate of population size and of detection probability become more precise?

Estimation of Survival from Capture–Recapture Data Using the Cormack–Jolly–Seber Model

7.1 INTRODUCTION

The preceding chapters dealt with the modeling and estimation of population size and with the simplest summary of population dynamics: population trend. The following chapters focus on one of the main components of population dynamics: survival probability. Survival probability is a key demographic parameter and can have a strong impact on population dynamics (Clobert and Lebreton, 1991; Saether and Bakke, 2000). Typically, interest focuses on estimation (what is the survival in that population?) as well as on modeling, for example, to test whether survival changes with age or differs between groups of individuals or regions, and to estimate how strongly it varies over time or what proportion of temporal variability can be explained by an external covariate such as weather.

In principle, survival estimation is fairly simple—we just have to count the number of individuals alive at a given time t (C_t), and keep track of how many of them die ($D_{\Delta t}$) during the period Δt for which we wish to estimate survival. Sometimes, it may be easier to count the number of the C_t that are still alive at $t + \Delta t$, that is, the number that survived the period Δt ($L_{\Delta t}$). Then survival probability s_t is

$$s_t = \frac{C_t - D_{\Delta t}}{C_t} = \frac{L_{\Delta t}}{C_t}$$

These numbers may easily be obtained in humans, but they are difficult to get in animal or plant populations. The reason for that is because the detection of individuals is usually far from perfect, so when an individual is not seen, we don't know whether it is dead or still alive. Therefore, such simple calculations cannot often be used, and we need to account for the observation process in our inferences about survival (an exception being data on individuals with radio tags, White and Garrott, 1990). From the number of individuals recorded at t (C_t), we typically detect only a fraction of those still alive at time $t + \Delta t$, which is $p^*L_{\Delta t}$: p is the recapture or resighting probability (depending on the context or study design), which needs to be estimated in order to obtain unbiased estimates of survival. Estimating p becomes possible if we extend the recapture study to at least one further time step ($t + 2\Delta t$). We may then have individuals that are known to have survived until $t + 2\Delta t$, but which have not been seen at time $t + \Delta t$. Intuitively, it is clear that the proportion of these individuals provides information on p.

The most common statistical method to jointly estimate recapture and survival probabilities in animal and plant populations is a class of open population capture–recapture models to which the Cormack–Jolly–Seber (CJS) model belongs (Cormack, 1964; Jolly, 1965; Seber, 1965). Re-encounters may be obtained by different methods (physical capture, sightings, genetic tracking), but the key is that individuals are identified without error. That is, we only have false negatives, but no false positives. The frequentist analysis of the CJS model is described in detail in Lebreton et al. (1992) and Williams et al. (2002). Descriptions and examples of the Bayesian analysis of the CJS model can be found in an increasing number of articles and books (Brooks et al., 2000a; McCarthy and Masters, 2005; Gimenez et al., 2007; McCarthy, 2007; Zheng et al., 2007; Royle, 2008; Royle and Dorazio, 2008; Schofield et al., 2009; Gimenez et al., 2009a; King et al., 2010).

The CJS model can be fitted using either a multinomial (Lebreton et al., 1992) or a state-space likelihood (Gimenez et al., 2007; Royle, 2008). Because these two likelihoods are just different ways of describing what is essentially the same model, they are based on the same sampling design and the same underlying model assumptions. The sampling design is as follows: A random sample of individuals from the study population is captured, all are marked individually, and released into the population again. This is repeated several times. The length of the time intervals between repeated capture occasions depends on the research question, as well as on the life history and population dynamics of the study organism, and capture should be instantaneous or over a short time period. Some marked individuals will be re-encountered, and thus, we obtain capture–recapture data that can be summarized in individual capture-histories.

The CJS model makes a number of assumptions and, as usual, their violation may bias parameter estimators. Some assumptions must be met at the design stage of a study. Tags or other marks must not be lost, otherwise survival is underestimated. If mark loss is suspected, double marking and corresponding model adaptation that account for mark loss are necessary to get unbiased estimates of survival (e.g., Smout et al., 2011).

Ideally, capture should be instantaneous, otherwise the interval between capture occasions may differ among individuals and, consequently, there will be individual heterogeneity in survival. However, simulation studies have suggested that the violation of this last assumption does often not have a strong effect on parameters estimates (Hargrove and Borland, 1994). The CJS model also assumes that the identity of the individuals is always recorded without errors. If this assumption is violated, bias can go in either direction, and there is no means to correct for it. Finally, captured and recaptured individuals are regarded as a random sample from the study population. This sounds easy, but in practice, it can be difficult to achieve. For example, in studies on birds using nest boxes, it is quite typical that adults are only captured after the young have hatched because they are likely to abandon their brood if they are disturbed at an early stage. This results in a sample that is biased toward successfully breeding adults, which may or may not be a random sample from all adults in the population.

Further assumptions of the CJS model cannot be violated or fulfilled by the design of the study, rather they are a consequence of how the model is specified. The basic model assumes that each individual within an age class or group has the same survival and recapture probability. Goodness-of-fit tests help to identify severe violation of these assumptions (e.g., trap-response: Pradel, 1993; transients: Pradel et al., 1997), and modifications to the model allow to account for these violations. Individuals must behave independently from each other in terms of survival and recapture. This may not be the case if members of the same family are included in a sample and especially if they remain in family groups. Violation of this assumption is like pseudo-replication (Hurlbert, 1984). The degree of nonindependence leading to overdispersion can be estimated and the standard errors of the estimates as well as AIC-based model selection can be adjusted accordingly (Anderson et al., 1994).

With CJS models, we estimate recapture probability (p_t; the probability of catching/resighting a marked individual at t that is alive and in the sampling population at t) and apparent (also called "local") survival probability (ϕ_t; the probability that an individual that is alive and in the population at t is still alive and in the population at time $t + 1$). Mortality and permanent emigration are confounded, and therefore apparent survival is always lower than true survival whenever permanent emigration is not zero. The difference between apparent and true survival is a matter of study design. Generally, the larger a study area the closer the match between apparent and true survival because dispersing individuals have a higher probability to remain in the study area (Marshall et al., 2004). Throughout this chapter, we will often just write "survival" for ease of presentation—but it is important to remember that survival in the CJS model always refers to a study area.

In this chapter, we introduce the CJS model and illustrate how it is fitted using the state-space (Sections 7.2–7.8) and the multinomial likelihood (Sections 7.9–7.11). We highlight advantages and disadvantages of each approach. Moreover, we will repeatedly use the generalized linear (mixed) model (GLM and GLMM) formulations to describe structure in the parameters. This allows the modeling of individual and temporal effects, both of which can either be categorical or continuous, as well as fixed or random. We will also see how correlations among parameters can be modeled through correlated random effects, using a multivariate normal distribution. In most examples, we focus on the modeling of survival, yet, clearly, similar modeling can be conducted for the recapture probability, and all these GLM formulations can also be used in other capture–recapture types of models starting with Chapter 6. Finally, in Section 7.10, we introduce posterior predictive model checking (see Gelman et al., 1996, 2004; Kéry, 2010). This provides a very general framework for the assessment of goodness-of-fit of a model to a data set.

7.2 THE CJS MODEL AS A STATE-SPACE MODEL

The state-space formulation of the CJS model has been introduced by Gimenez et al. (2007) and Royle (2008). Let us assume an individual marked at time t. It may survive until time $t + 1$ with probability ϕ_t. Conceptually, we can imagine the individual tossing a coin to determine whether it survives (with probability ϕ_t) or dies (with probability $1 - \phi_t$). Given that the individual is still alive at time $t + 1$, it may again survive until $t + 2$ with probability ϕ_{t+1}. This process is continued until the individual is either dead or the study ends. Clearly, once an individual is dead, its fate is no longer stochastic, and it will remain dead with probability 1. This is the description of the state process, that is, of the states (alive, dead) of an individual over time. We would like to know survival, which requires knowledge of these states of the individuals. Yet, we typically do not have complete information about the true states. A marked individual that is alive at occasion t may be recaptured (or more generally re-encountered) with probability p_t. Again, we can imagine that a coin is tossed, determining whether the individual is recaptured (with probability p_t) or not (with probability $1 - p_t$). Once an individual is dead, it cannot be recaptured anymore. This is the description of the observation process, which is conditional on the state process, and thus there is a hierarchal structure in the state-space model. In Fig. 7.1, the two processes are shown graphically.

The data observed in a capture–recapture study can be summarized in a capture-history matrix (**y**), which has dimension $I \times T$, where I is the total number of marked individuals, and T is the number of capture

State process

Alive

Dead

Observation process

Seen

Not seen

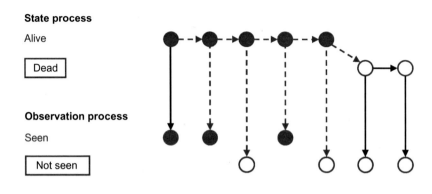

- - ► Stochastic processes (survival and recapture)
——► Deterministic process

FIGURE 7.1   Example of the state and observation process of a marked individual over time for the CJS model. The sequence of true states in this individual is $z = [1, 1, 1, 1, 1, 0, 0]$, and the observed capture-history is $y = [1, 1, 0, 1, 0, 0, 0]$.

occasions. The matrix entries are either a 1 or a 0. A 1 at position i, t indicates that individual i was captured at occasion t, meaning that it was alive for sure; a 0 at position i, t shows that individual i was not captured at t, meaning that it was either dead, or alive but not caught, or not yet marked. ← rather than using NAs

To estimate survival from such data, we define the latent variable $z_{i,t}$, which takes value 1 if individual i is alive at time t, and value 0 if it is dead. Thus, $z_{i,t}$ defines the true state of individual i at time t. We also define vector f_i, which denotes the occasion at which individual i is first captured (i.e., marked) because only events after first capture are modeled in the CJS model. The state of individual i at first capture (z_{i,f_i}) is 1 with probability 1, as the individual is alive for certain. The states on subsequent occasions are modeled as Bernoulli trials. Conditional on being alive at occasion t, individual i may survive until occasion $t + 1$ with probability $\phi_{i,t}$ ($t = 1, \ldots, T - 1$). The following two equations define the state process:

$$z_{i,f_i} = 1$$

$$z_{i,t+1} \mid z_{i,t} \sim \text{Bernoulli}(z_{i,t}\phi_{i,t}).$$

The Bernoulli success parameter is composed of the product of survival and the state variable z. The inclusion of z ensures that a dead individual ($z = 0$) remains dead and has no further impact on the estimation of survival.

If individual i is alive at occasion t, it may be recaptured with probability $p_{i,t}$ ($t = 2, \ldots, T$). This can again be modeled as the realization of a

Bernoulli trial with success probability $p_{i,t}$. The following equation defines the observation process:

$$y_{i,t} \mid z_{i,t} \sim \text{Bernoulli}(z_{i,t} p_{i,t}).$$

The inclusion of the latent variable z in the Bernoulli trial ensures that dead individuals cannot be encountered. The state and the observation process are both defined for $t \geq f_i$. We repeat that the initial capture process is not modeled in the CJS model (see Fig. 7.1) because the initial observation at the time of capture does not contain any information about survival. In contrast, capture-histories at and before initial capture contain information about recruitment, which is a target of estimation of the Jolly–Seber models (see Chapter 10). Because initial capture is not modeled in the CJS model, we say that we condition on first capture.

The implementation of the CJS model in WinBUGS is straightforward. The most general likelihood is based on the above-mentioned three equations and contains different survival and recapture probabilities for each individual at each capture occasion. However, the parameters of this saturated model are not separately estimable (see Section 7.9 for more on this topic), and we need to introduce constraints. These constraints define the structure of the model fitted and may be imposed either along the time or the individual axis of the capture-history matrix, or along both (see Section 6.2). Thus, whatever model we fit, we do not need to change the likelihood, which describes the basic structure of the model, but just these constraints and the corresponding priors. This may not result in code that is the most efficient in terms of computing time and the easiest to read for a beginner. However, with a little practice, it will be seen to be an efficient way of fitting a wide array of models.

7.3 MODELS WITH CONSTANT PARAMETERS

We start with a very simple model, in which survival and recapture, respectively, are identical for all individuals at all occasions. Thus, we impose constraints along both the time and the individual axis of the capture-history matrix. We first simulate the data, and then analyze them. The function to simulate capture–recapture data (`simul.cjs`) is very general and works for all examples in this chapter. We choose the number of individuals released at each occasion. The function then evaluates for each released individual whether it survives, and if so, whether it is recaptured, by two Bernoulli trials governed by individual- and time-specific survival and recapture probabilities that we also provide as input (matrices `PHI` and `P`). Thus, the data-generating function works analogous to the analyzing model.

FIGURE 7.2   Pair of little owls (*Athene noctua*) (Photograph by H. Sylvain).

In the simulation, we will mimic a study on little owls (Fig. 7.2), a small owl species living in semi-open habitats such as orchards, where it likes to occupy nest boxes. Nest boxes in a study area are checked in May in six study years, and breeding adults are ringed. In each of the six study years, 50 unmarked (new) adults are caught, along with a variable number of individuals that are already marked. Survival of adult little owls is typically around 0.65 (Schaub et al., 2006), and we assume a recapture probability of 0.4. The following R code simulates a matrix with capture-histories. We do not consider individuals first captured on the last occasion, because they do not provide information about survival and recapture.

```
# Define parameter values
n.occasions <- 6                    # Number of capture occasions
marked <- rep(50, n.occasions-1)    # Annual number of newly marked
                                       individuals
phi <- rep(0.65, n.occasions-1)
p <- rep(0.4, n.occasions-1)

# Define matrices with survival and recapture probabilities
PHI <- matrix(phi, ncol = n.occasions-1, nrow = sum(marked))
P <- matrix(p, ncol = n.occasions-1, nrow = sum(marked))

# Define function to simulate a capture-history (CH) matrix
simul.cjs <- function(PHI, P, marked){
    n.occasions <- dim(PHI)[2] + 1
```

```
    CH <- matrix(0, ncol = n.occasions, nrow = sum(marked))
    # Define a vector with the occasion of marking
    mark.occ <- rep(1:length(marked), marked[1:length(marked)])
    # Fill the CH matrix
    for (i in 1:sum(marked)){
        CH[i, mark.occ[i]] <- 1        # Write an 1 at the release occasion
        if (mark.occ[i]==n.occasions) next
        for (t in (mark.occ[i]+1):n.occasions){
            # Bernoulli trial: does individual survive occasion?
            sur <- rbinom(1, 1, PHI[i,t-1])
            if (sur==0) break          # If dead, move to next individual
            # Bernoulli trial: is individual recaptured?
            rp <- rbinom(1, 1, P[i,t-1])
            if (rp==1) CH[i,t] <- 1
            } #t
        } #i
    return(CH)
    }

# Execute function
CH <- simul.cjs(PHI, P, marked)
```

Next, we need to create vector *f*, which contains the occasion at which each individual is marked.

```
# Create vector with occasion of marking
get.first <- function(x) min(which(x!=0))
f <- apply(CH, 1, get.first)
```

Finally, we write the BUGS code for a constant model. The two linear models applied are $\phi_{i,t} = \overline{\phi}$ and $p_{i,t} = \overline{p}$. These are in fact the linear predictors (see Chapter 3), but here we call them constraints because we reduce the dimensions of the $\phi_{i,t}$ and $p_{i,t}$, that is, we constrain them. We do not include covariates or random effects, so there is no need for a transformation, and the identity link is applied. The uniform priors ensure that the parameter estimates are in the interval [0, 1]. The specification of noninformative priors is easy because a uniform (U(0, 1)) or a beta distribution (beta(1,1)) can be used. Note that the time indexing in the "Likelihood" part is slightly different to that used in the formulas (see Section 7.2). It avoids the use of separate loops for the state and the observation process.

```
# Specify model in BUGS language
sink("cjs-c-c.bug")
cat("
model {

# Priors and constraints
for (i in 1:nind){
    for (t in f[i]:(n.occasions-1)){
        phi[i,t] <- mean.phi
```

```
        p[i,t] <- mean.p
        } #t
    } #i

mean.phi ~ dunif(0, 1)            # Prior for mean survival
mean.p ~ dunif(0, 1)             # Prior for mean recapture

# Likelihood
for (i in 1:nind){
    # Define latent state at first capture
    z[i,f[i]] <- 1
    for (t in (f[i]+1):n.occasions){
        # State process
        z[i,t] ~ dbern(mu1[i,t])
        mu1[i,t] <- phi[i,t-1] * z[i,t-1]
        # Observation process
        y[i,t] ~ dbern(mu2[i,t])
        mu2[i,t] <- p[i,t-1] * z[i,t]
        } #t
    } #i
}
",fill = TRUE)
sink()

# Bundle data
bugs.data <- list(y = CH, f = f, nind = dim(CH)[1], n.occasions =
    dim(CH)[2])
```

Initial values should be given for the two structural parameters and for the latent variable z. The easiest way for the latter is just to use the observed capture-histories. We have to make sure that initial values for z are provided only after initial capture. The function below creates the required initial values based on the observed capture-histories and the vector with the occasion of first capture.

```
# Function to create a matrix of initial values for latent state z
ch.init <- function(ch, f){
    for (i in 1:dim(ch)[1]){ch[i,1:f[i]] <- NA}
    return(ch)
    }

# Initial values
inits <- function(){list(z = ch.init(CH, f), mean.phi = runif(1, 0, 1),
    mean.p = runif(1, 0, 1))}

# Parameters monitored
parameters <- c("mean.phi", "mean.p")

# MCMC settings
ni <- 10000
nt <- 6
nb <- 5000
nc <- 3
```

```
# Call WinBUGS from R (BRT 1 min)
cjs.c.c <- bugs(bugs.data, inits, parameters, "cjs-c-c.bug", n.chains =
    nc, n.thin = nt, n.iter = ni, n.burnin = nb, debug = TRUE,
    bugs.directory = bugs.dir, working.directory = getwd())
```

The model does not take a long time to run and convergence is reached after just 5000 iterations. The estimates are very close to the values used for the simulations.

```
# Summarize posteriors
print(cjs.c.c, digits = 3)
```

	mean	sd	2.5%	25%	50%	75%	97.5%	Rhat	n.eff
mean.phi	0.679	0.043	0.601	0.649	0.677	0.707	0.767	1.003	980
mean.p	0.370	0.044	0.286	0.340	0.369	0.400	0.458	1.003	1700

Sometimes not all individuals recaptured are released again, for instance, when an individual dies at capture. For these individuals, we know that they have survived from initial capture until the last capture; afterward they are not in the sample anymore. This is easy to model and just requires that we define a vector h which for each individual contains the occasion after which it is not released. For individuals that stay in the sample until the end of the study, the element of vector h is just the last occasion of the study. Then, vector h must become an element of the input data and the loop in the likelihood needs to be changed from `for (t in (f[i]+1):n.occasions){ ...` to `for (t in (f[i]+1):h[i]){...`

7.3.1 Inclusion of Information about Latent State Variable

Written as state-space models, CJS models can take a long time to run because there is a loop over all individuals and occasions. The latent state variable z needs to be updated (estimated) at each MCMC iteration. So far we have treated z as if we had no information about it. The only information that we included are the observed capture-histories (Y), but they are related to z only through the observation process in the state-space model. Therefore, all elements of z (i.e., for all individuals after first capture) must be estimated, even when some of them are known.

To improve computation speed and convergence, we can add what we know about the latent state z, namely, whenever we observe a marked individual we know its latent state is $z = 1$. In addition, we know that $z = 1$ for all occasions between the first and the last observation of an individual, even if it was not seen at all occasions. To include this information in the model (i.e. to prevent estimation of what is not an unknown quantity), we create a matrix that has a value of 1 at all occasions where we know individuals were alive, and NAs elsewhere. The CJS model is conditional on first capture, so the latent state is only defined after first capture, and thus at all first captures, we need NAs as well. The following function creates the required matrix.

```
# Function to create a matrix with information about known latent state z
known.state.cjs <- function(ch){
    state <- ch
    for (i in 1:dim(ch)[1]){
        n1 <- min(which(ch[i,]==1))
        n2 <- max(which(ch[i,]==1))
        state[i,n1:n2] <- 1
        state[i,n1] <- NA
        }
    state[state==0] <- NA
    return(state)
    }
```

This information about z is then given as data as well.

```
# Bundle data
bugs.data <- list(y = CH, f = f, nind = dim(CH)[1], n.occasions = dim(CH)[2],
    z = known.state.cjs(CH))
```

The initial values for z now also require some changes: we should not give initial values for those elements of z whose value is specified in the data; they get an NA.

```
# Function to create a matrix of initial values for latent state z
cjs.init.z <- function(ch,f){
    for (i in 1:dim(ch)[1]){
        if (sum(ch[i,])==1) next
        n2 <- max(which(ch[i,]==1))
        ch[i,f[i]:n2] <- NA
        }
    for (i in 1:dim(ch)[1]){
    ch[i,1:f[i]] <- NA
    }
    return(ch)
    }
```

Now, we give initial values for all the quantities to be estimated and run the model:

```
# Initial values
inits <- function(){list(z = cjs.init.z(CH, f), mean.phi = runif(1, 0, 1),
    mean.p = runif(1, 0, 1))}

# Parameters monitored
parameters <- c("mean.phi", "mean.p")

# MCMC settings
ni <- 10000
nt <- 6
```

```
nb <- 5000
nc <- 3

# Call WinBUGS from R (BRT <1 min)
cjs.c.c <- bugs(bugs.data, inits, parameters, "cjs-c-c.bug", n.chains =
    nc, n.thin = nt, n.iter = ni, n.burnin = nb, debug = TRUE,
    bugs.directory = bugs.dir, working.directory = getwd())

# Summarize posteriors
print(cjs.c.c, digits = 3)
```

	mean	sd	2.5%	25%	50%	75%	97.5%	Rhat	n.eff
mean.phi	0.675	0.040	0.599	0.648	0.675	0.702	0.754	1.003	2500
mean.p	0.372	0.043	0.294	0.342	0.371	0.399	0.461	1.003	2500

The model now runs faster. The difference in run time in this simple case is slight, but time savings can be substantial with more complex models and larger data sets. Therefore, we recommend providing all available information about the latent state in the data. In the following sections of this chapter, we will always, and in most other chapters often, do this. Note that the inclusion of the information about the latent state z has nothing to do with the use of an informative prior, we simply avoid estimation of known quantities to speed up computation.

7.4 MODELS WITH TIME-VARIATION

So far we have fitted the simplest possible model in the CJS family. It assumes that survival and recapture probabilities remain constant over time and are identical for all individuals. In practice, we typically want to relax these strict assumptions. We also may have an interest in fitting models that combine time and individual effects and modeling these effects as additive or interactive. We next consider models with temporal variation, that is, we model the column dimension of the capture-history matrix and constrain the row dimension to be constant (all individuals are treated as identical).

The variation of survival probability from one year to another often has a strong impact on the dynamics of a population. If survival varies much from year to year (i.e., temporal variability is large), population size changes more than when survival probability changes only little over time, all other demographic processes being equal. Thus, there is an interest in measuring temporal variation. Moreover, the annual fluctuations of survival or recapture may be caused by environmental factors that we may have an interest in identifying.

The models to study temporal effects of survival or recapture assume either fixed or random temporal effects, as well as the relationship between focal parameters and temporally varying covariates (e.g., weather).

The fixed-effect time model assumes the parameters to be different at each occasion and independent of each other. This approach is used if there is interest in estimates from particular occasions. By contrast, the model that considers time to be a random effect assumes that time effects are drawn from a statistical distribution, whose parameters we aim to estimate; typically, we will use a normal distribution and estimate a mean and a variance. Therefore, annual estimates are no longer independent from one another. Interest is then not so much in the individual annual effects, but more in an estimation of the mean and the variance of the annual estimates. Fixed- and random-effects models are easily fit within the framework that we have set up (see Chapter 4). The likelihood part of the BUGS code does not need any change at all: all required modifications take place in the "Priors and constraints" section of the BUGS code. In the examples that follow, we will usually model effects on survival only, but of course similar models can be adopted for recapture, too, and any combinations are possible, for example, survival with random time effects and recapture with fixed time effects.

7.4.1 Fixed Time Effects

We now assume that survival and recapture vary independently over time, that is, we regard time as a fixed-effects factor. To implement this model, we impose the following constraints: $\phi_{i,t} = \alpha_t$ and $p_{i,t} = \beta_t$, where α_t and β_t are the time-specific survival and recapture probabilities, respectively. Here is the part of the BUGS model specification that needs to be changed.

```
# Priors and constraints
for (i in 1:nind){
    for (t in f[i]:(n.occasions-1)){
        phi[i,t] <- alpha[t]
        p[i,t] <- beta[t]
        } #t
    } #i
for (t in 1:n.occasions-1)){
    alpha[t] ~ dunif(0, 1)          # Priors for time-spec. survival
    beta[t] ~ dunif(0, 1)           # Priors for time-spec. recapture
    }
```

7.4.2 Random Time Effects

The model just shown treats time as a fixed-effects factor; for every occasion, an independent effect is estimated. To assess the temporal variability, we cannot simply take these fixed-effects estimates and calculate their variance. By doing so, we would ignore the fact that these values are estimates that have an unknown associated error. Thus, we would assume that there is no sampling variance, and this can hardly ever be true (see, e.g., Gould and Nichols, 1998). However, when treating time as a random-effects factor, we can separate sampling (i.e., variance within years) from process variance (i.e., variance between years), exactly as we did in the state-space models in Chapter 5. We model survival or recapture probabilities on the logit scale as a realization of a random process described by a normal distribution with mean μ and variance σ^2. The logit link function ensures that the estimated probabilities remain within the interval between 0 and 1:

[margin handwriting: Treating time as RE allows for the decomp of variance into sampl. and process]

$$\text{logit}(\phi_{i,t}) = \mu + \varepsilon_t$$

$$\varepsilon_t \sim \text{Normal}(0, \sigma^2).$$

ε_t is the deviation from the overall mean survival probability; thus it is a "temporal residual". The temporal variance (σ^2) is on the logit scale; thus, it is the temporal variance of the logit survival. Sometimes, one needs an estimate on the probability scale, for instance, when the temporal variance should be compared with the variance of another demographic rate to decide which parameter is more variable over time. A back-transformation is possible by applying the delta method (Powell, 2007). We use

$$\sigma_\theta^2 \cong \sigma^2 \theta^2 (1 - \theta)^2,$$

where $\theta = \frac{\exp(\mu)}{1 + \exp(\mu)}$ and σ_θ^2 is the variance on the back-transformed scale. It is easy to estimate this quantity directly in BUGS.

To illustrate the approach, we simulate data and analyze them. In the little owl example, we assume a mean survival probability of females of 0.65 and temporal variance of 1 on the logit scale. Reasonable estimates of the temporal variance require a large number of years (>10; Burnham and White, 2002). Here, we simulate data over 20 years.

```
# Define parameter values
n.occasions <- 20                       # Number of capture occasions
marked <- rep(30, n.occasions-1)        # Annual number of newly marked
                                          individuals

mean.phi <- 0.65
var.phi <- 1                            # Temporal variance of survival
p <- rep(0.4, n.occasions-1)

# Determine annual survival probabilities
logit.phi <- rnorm(n.occasions-1, qlogis(mean.phi), var.phi^0.5)
phi <- plogis(logit.phi)

# Define matrices with survival and recapture probabilities
PHI <- matrix(phi, ncol = n.occasions-1, nrow = sum(marked), byrow = TRUE)
P <- matrix(p, ncol = n.occasions-1, nrow = sum(marked))
```

```
# Simulate capture-histories
CH <- simul.cjs(PHI, P, marked)

# Create vector with occasion of marking
get.first <- function(x) min(which(x!=0))
f <- apply(CH, 1, get.first)
```

In the BUGS model description, we only alter parts in the "Priors and constraints" sections; no change is required in the likelihood part. In particular, we have to implement the random-effects formulation (formula above). The prior choices for μ and for σ^2 need some thought. Because μ is the mean survival on the logit scale, a noninformative prior on the logit scale would be a normal distribution with a wide variance. Yet, this prior will not be noninformative on the probability scale. In the code below, we provide two options: first, a normal distribution with a wide variance for μ, and second, a uniform distribution for $logit^{-1}(\mu)$, which is noninformative on the probability scale but informative on the logit scale. A prior is also needed for σ^2. Following Gelman (2006), we use a uniform distribution for the standard deviation because this induces little information. We will fit the same model under which we generated the data, that is, model ϕ_t, p., where by the underlined index for time, we denote random time effects.

```
# Specify model in BUGS language
sink("cjs-temp-raneff.bug")
cat("
model {

# Priors and constraints
for (i in 1:nind){
    for (t in f[i]:(n.occasions-1)){
        logit(phi[i,t]) <- mu + epsilon[t]
        p[i,t] <- mean.p
        } #t
    } #i
for (t in 1:(n.occasions-1)){
    epsilon[t] ~ dnorm(0, tau)
    }

#mu ~ dnorm(0, 0.001)                   # Prior for logit of mean survival
#mean.phi <- 1 / (1+exp(-mu))           # Logit transformation
mean.phi ~ dunif(0, 1)                  # Prior for mean survival
mu <- log(mean.phi / (1-mean.phi))      # Logit transformation
sigma ~ dunif(0, 10)                    # Prior for standard deviation
tau <- pow(sigma, -2)
sigma2 <- pow(sigma, 2)                 # Temporal variance
mean.p ~ dunif(0, 1)                    # Prior for mean recapture

# Likelihood
for (i in 1:nind){
    # Define latent state at first capture
    z[i,f[i]] <- 1
    for (t in (f[i]+1):n.occasions){
```

```
        # State process
        z[i,t] ~ dbern(mu1[i,t])
        mu1[i,t] <- phi[i,t-1] * z[i,t-1]
        # Observation process
        y[i,t] ~ dbern(mu2[i,t])
        mu2[i,t] <- p[i,t-1] * z[i,t]
        } #t
    } #i
}
",fill = TRUE)
sink()

# Bundle data
bugs.data <- list(y = CH, f = f, nind = dim(CH)[1], n.occasions = dim(CH)[2],
    z = known.state.cjs(CH))

# Initial values
inits <- function(){list(z = cjs.init.z(CH, f), mean.phi = runif(1, 0, 1),
    sigma = runif(1, 0, 10), mean.p = runif(1, 0, 1))}

# Parameters monitored
parameters <- c("mean.phi", "mean.p", "sigma2")

# MCMC settings
ni <- 10000
nt <- 6
nb <- 5000
nc <- 3

# Call WinBUGS from R (BRT 17 min)
cjs.ran <- bugs(bugs.data, inits, parameters, "cjs-temp-raneff.bug",
    n.chains = nc, n.thin = nt, n.iter = ni, n.burnin = nb, debug = TRUE,
    bugs.directory = bugs.dir, working.directory = getwd())
```

The chains evolve slowly and convergence is not achieved swiftly. This can be improved if a smaller range is chosen for the prior for the standard deviation of the temporal variance. Here, we used a uniform prior in the interval between 0 and 10, thus the variance could take values between 0 and 100. Had we chosen a higher upper bound, the estimate would probability not change (recall we simulated the data with a variance of 1), but the chains would converge even more slowly. Computation for this model is more efficient for the multinomial formulation of the model (see Section 7.10).

```
# Summarize posteriors
print(cjs.ran, digits = 3)
```

	mean	sd	2.5%	25%	50%	75%	97.5%	Rhat	n.eff
mean.phi	0.634	0.073	0.488	0.590	0.634	0.678	0.787	1.017	120
mean.p	0.394	0.024	0.350	0.378	0.394	0.411	0.441	1.001	2000
sigma2	1.700	1.152	0.548	1.006	1.402	2.005	4.687	1.006	440

```
# Produce histogram
hist(cjs.ran$sims.list$sigma2, col = "gray", nclass = 35, las = 1,
    xlab = expression(sigma^2), main = "")
abline(v = var.phi, col = "red", lwd = 2)
```

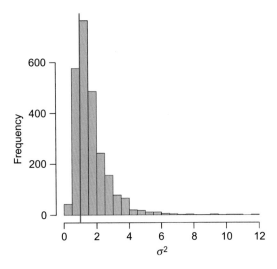

FIGURE 7.3 Posterior distribution of the temporal variance in apparent survival (red: value used for data generation).

The histogram of the posterior samples of the temporal variance for one simulated data set is shown in Fig. 7.3. The point estimate may seem biased; however, recall that this is just a single simulation, and we would need many simulations to check for any bias (see exercise 4 in Section 7.13).

7.4.3 Temporal Covariates

Often we are not only interested in getting a point estimate of survival or of its temporal variability, but also in identifying factors affecting survival. One way to do this is to see whether the observed temporal pattern in survival matches the temporal variation of an environmental factor (e.g., winter severity). From a nonzero correlation we would then infer an effect of that factor on survival. However, regardless of how the model is specified, such evidence is of correlative nature, thus causation cannot be inferred. A properly designed experiment is needed to infer causation, which is not easy in population studies (but see Schwarz, 2002).

Traditionally, so-called ultrastructural modeling has been used to model survival as a function of a covariate (x) (Lebreton et al., 1992; Link, 1999):

$$\text{logit}(\phi_{i,t}) = \mu + \beta x_t.$$

This model assumes that the entire temporal variability of survival could be explained by the covariate x; it is analogous to a linear regression model without residuals. This seems quite unrealistic, but in earlier times, this was the only way that the relationship between survival and a covariate could be modeled. A more realistic approach is to assume that only part of the temporal variability of survival is explained by the covariate, another part being unexplained random variation. Thus, we specify this model:

$$\text{logit}(\phi_{i,t}) = \mu + \beta x_t + \varepsilon_t$$

$$\varepsilon_t \sim \text{Normal}(0, \sigma^2).$$

The residual variance (σ^2) is the unexplained temporal variance. This allows us to estimate the amount of the total temporal variance which is explained by covariate x. We need to fit a model without the covariate to get an estimate of the total temporal variance (σ^2_{total}). The proportion of the variance explained by covariate x is then $(\sigma^2_{\text{total}} - \sigma^2)/\sigma^2_{\text{total}}$ (Grosbois et al., 2008).

To illustrate the model with the little owl example, we assume a mean survival of 0.65 and a negative effect of winter severity with logistic-linear slope of -0.3. The winter severity index is standardized (mean = 0, variance = 1) and the residual temporal variance not explained by winter severity has variance of 0.2.

```
# Define parameter values
n.occasions <- 20                    # Number of capture occasions
marked <- rep(15, n.occasions-1)     # Annual number of newly marked
                                       individuals

mean.phi <- 0.65
p <- rep(0.4, n.occasions-1)
beta <- -0.3                         # Slope of survival-winter
                                       relationship
r.var <- 0.2                         # Residual temporal variance

# Draw annual survival probabilities
winter <- rnorm(n.occasions-1, 0, 1^0.5)
logit.phi <- qlogis(mean.phi) + beta*winter + rnorm(n.occasions-1, 0,
    r.var^0.5)
phi <- plogis(logit.phi)

# Define matrices with survival and recapture probabilities
PHI <- matrix(phi, ncol = n.occasions-1, nrow = sum(marked),
    byrow = TRUE)
P <- matrix(p, ncol = n.occasions-1, nrow = sum(marked))
```

```r
# Simulate capture-histories
CH <- simul.cjs(PHI, P, marked)

# Create vector with occasion of marking
get.first <- function(x) min(which(x!=0))
f <- apply(CH, 1, get.first)

# Specify model in BUGS language
sink("cjs-cov-raneff.bug")
cat("
model {

# Priors and constraints
for (i in 1:nind){
    for (t in f[i]:(n.occasions-1)){
        logit(phi[i,t]) <- mu + beta*x[t] + epsilon[t]
        p[i,t] <- mean.p
        } #t
    } #i
for (t in 1:(n.occasions-1)){
    epsilon[t] ~ dnorm(0, tau)
    phi.est[t] <- 1 / (1+exp(-mu-beta*x[t]-epsilon[t]))  # Yearly
                                                               survival
    }
mu ~ dnorm(0, 0.001)                    # Prior for logit of mean survival
mean.phi <- 1 / (1+exp(-mu))            # Logit transformation
beta ~ dnorm(0, 0.001)I(-10, 10)        # Prior for slope parameter
sigma ~ dunif(0, 10)                    # Prior on standard deviation
tau <- pow(sigma, -2)
sigma2 <- pow(sigma, 2)                 # Residual temporal variance
mean.p ~ dunif(0, 1)                    # Prior for mean recapture

# Likelihood
for (i in 1:nind){
    # Define latent state at first capture
    z[i,f[i]] <- 1
    for (t in (f[i]+1):n.occasions){
        # State process
        z[i,t] ~ dbern(mu1[i,t])
        mu1[i,t] <- phi[i,t-1] * z[i,t-1]
        # Observation process
        y[i,t] ~ dbern(mu2[i,t])
        mu2[i,t] <- p[i,t-1] * z[i,t]
        } #t
    } #i
}
",fill = TRUE)
sink()

# Bundle data
bugs.data <- list(y = CH, f = f, nind = dim(CH)[1], n.occasions = dim(CH)[2],
    z = known.state.cjs(CH), x = winter)
```

```
# Initial values
inits <- function(){list(z = cjs.init.z(CH, f), mu = rnorm(1), sigma =
    runif(1, 0, 5), beta = runif(1, -5, 5), mean.p = runif(1, 0, 1))}
```

```
# Parameters monitored
parameters <- c("mean.phi", "mean.p", "phi.est", "sigma2", "beta")
```

```
# MCMC settings
ni <- 20000
nt <- 6
nb <- 10000
nc <- 3
```

```
# Call WinBUGS from R (BRT 12 min)
cjs.cov <- bugs(bugs.data, inits, parameters, "cjs-cov-raneff.bug",
    n.chains = nc, n.thin = nt, n.iter = ni, n.burnin = nb, debug = TRUE,
    bugs.directory = bugs.dir, working.directory = getwd())
```

In general, models with random effects are more difficult to fit, and we need to run long Markov chains to achieve satisfactory convergence for all parameters. The posterior distributions of the slope and the residual environmental variation (temporal variation not explained by the covariate) are shown in Fig. 7.4.

```
# Summarize posteriors
print(cjs.cov, digits = 3)
```

	mean	sd	2.5%	25%	50%	75%	97.5%	Rhat	n.eff
mean.phi	0.707	0.050	0.611	0.676	0.705	0.736	0.805	1.012	1400
mean.p	0.403	0.032	0.343	0.381	0.403	0.424	0.467	1.002	1800
phi.est[1]	0.686	0.121	0.423	0.610	0.696	0.769	0.902	1.003	1200
[...]

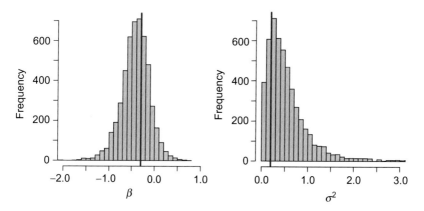

FIGURE 7.4 Posterior distributions of the covariate effect (slope parameter β) and of environmental variability (the residual temporal variance σ^2). Red lines indicate the values used for simulating the data.

```
phi.est[19]   0.681 0.120   0.427   0.603   0.690   0.764 0.902 1.003    950
sigma2        0.566 0.541   0.047   0.234   0.426   0.714 2.012 1.008    390
beta         -0.422 0.308  -1.080  -0.600  -0.410  -0.226 0.160 1.006   1400
```

```
# Produce graph
par(mfrow = c(1, 2), las = 1)
hist(cjs.cov$sims.list$beta, nclass = 25, col = "gray", main = "",
   xlab = expression(beta), ylab = "Frequency")
abline(v = -0.3, col = "red", lwd = 2)
hist(cjs.cov$sims.list$sigma2, nclass = 50, col = "gray", main = "",
   xlab = expression(sigma^2), ylab = "Frequency", xlim=c(0, 3))
abline(v = 0.2, col = "red", lwd = 2)
```

7.5 MODELS WITH INDIVIDUAL VARIATION

So far we have modeled temporal effects, assuming identical survival and recapture for all individuals. Now, we relax this assumption and model individual heterogeneity. Thus, we model effects along the row axis of the capture-history matrix. As with models for time effects, we can model individual effects in different ways—individual effects can be categorical or continuous, fixed or random, or latent or explained by measured covariates (compare with model M_h in Section 6.2). Moreover, individual effects can be constant over time, or they may change over time. Here, we only consider the simpler case, where they are constant over time.

7.5.1 Fixed Group Effects

We may specify fixed effects when we are interested in the estimates of particular groups (e.g., sex) and if the number of groups is low, as it is difficult to estimate the between-group variance with a small number of groups. We define g_i as a categorical variable with G levels (i.e., number of groups) indicating the group membership. The model for survival with a fixed group effect is

$$\phi_{i,t} = \beta_{g(i)},$$

where index $g(i)$ denotes the group g to which individual i belongs and β_g ($g = 1...G$) are the estimated fixed group effects. Because there are no other effects in the model, we can model directly on the probability scale, and the prior distribution ensures that the parameter estimates are between 0 and 1.

We illustrate the model to estimate sex-specific survival and recapture probabilities with simulated data of little owls. We first simulate two separate capture–recapture data sets; one for males and another for females.

Then we create the grouping variable *g* (named "group") and merge the two capture–recapture data sets.

```
# Define parameter values
n.occasions <- 12                    # Number of capture occasions
marked <- rep(30, n.occasions-1)     # Annual number of newly marked
                                       individuals
phi.f <- rep(0.65, n.occasions-1)    # Survival of females
p.f <- rep(0.6, n.occasions-1)       # Recapture prob. of females
phi.m <- rep(0.8, n.occasions-1)     # Survival of males
p.m <- rep(0.3, n.occasions-1)       # Recapture prob. of males

# Define matrices with survival and recapture probabilities
PHI.F <- matrix(phi.f, ncol = n.occasions-1, nrow = sum(marked))
P.F <- matrix(p.f, ncol = n.occasions-1, nrow = sum(marked))
PHI.M <- matrix(phi.m, ncol = n.occasions-1, nrow = sum(marked))
P.M <- matrix(p.m, ncol = n.occasions-1, nrow = sum(marked))

# Simulate capture-histories
CH.F <- simul.cjs(PHI.F, P.F, marked)
CH.M <- simul.cjs(PHI.M, P.M, marked)

# Merge capture-histories by row
CH <- rbind(CH.F, CH.M)

# Create group variable
group <- c(rep(1, dim(CH.F)[1]), rep(2, dim(CH.M)[1]))

# Create vector with occasion of marking
get.first <- function(x) min(which(x!=0))
f <- apply(CH, 1, get.first)
```

Finally, we write the model in BUGS language and fit it to the data.

```
# Specify model in BUGS language
sink("cjs-group.bug")
cat("
model {

# Priors and constraints
for (i in 1:nind){
    for (t in f[i]:(n.occasions-1)){
        phi[i,t] <- phi.g[group[i]]
        p[i,t] <- p.g[group[i]]
        } #t
    } #i
for (u in 1:g){
    phi.g[u] ~ dunif(0, 1)           # Priors for group-specific
                                       survival
    p.g[u] ~ dunif(0, 1)             # Priors for group-specific
                                       recapture
    }

# Likelihood
for (i in 1:nind){
```

```
# Define latent state at first capture
z[i,f[i]] <- 1
for (t in (f[i]+1):n.occasions){
    # State process
    z[i,t] ~ dbern(mu1[i,t])
    mu1[i,t] <- phi[i,t-1] * z[i,t-1]
    # Observation process
    y[i,t] ~ dbern(mu2[i,t])
    mu2[i,t] <- p[i,t-1] * z[i,t]
    } #t
} #i
}
",fill = TRUE)
sink()
```

 # Bundle data
```
bugs.data <- list(y = CH, f = f, nind = dim(CH)[1], n.occasions = dim(CH)[2],
    z = known.state.cjs(CH), g = length(unique(group)), group = group)
```

 # Initial values
```
inits <- function(){list(z = cjs.init.z(CH, f), phi.g = runif(length
    (unique(group)), 0, 1), p.g = runif(length(unique(group)), 0, 1))}
```

 # Parameters monitored
```
parameters <- c("phi.g", "p.g")
```

 # MCMC settings
```
ni <- 5000
nt <- 3
nb <- 2000
nc <- 3
```

 # Call WinBUGS from R (BRT 2 min)
```
cjs.group <- bugs(bugs.data, inits, parameters, "cjs-group.bug",
    n.chains = nc, n.thin = nt, n.iter = ni, n.burnin = nb, debug = TRUE,
    bugs.directory = bugs.dir, working.directory = getwd())
```

The parameter estimates are close to the values used to generate the data.

 # Summarize posteriors
```
print(cjs.group, digits = 3)
```

	mean	sd	2.5%	25%	50%	75%	97.5%	Rhat	n.eff
phi.g[1]	0.656	0.020	0.617	0.642	0.656	0.669	0.694	1.001	3000
phi.g[2]	0.796	0.018	0.760	0.784	0.796	0.808	0.831	1.002	1900
p.g[1]	0.599	0.029	0.541	0.578	0.599	0.619	0.654	1.002	1700
p.g[2]	0.325	0.021	0.285	0.311	0.324	0.339	0.368	1.002	1900

7.5.2 Random Group Effects

We may specify random group effects when we are interested in an overall mean and the variability between groups. A typical example of random group effects is provided by local populations, where we are interested in estimating spatial variation of survival (Grosbois et al., 2009). Survival is then modeled as

$$\text{logit}(\phi_{i,t}) = \beta_{g(i)}$$
$$\beta_g \sim \text{Normal}(\bar{\beta}, \sigma^2),$$

where σ^2 is the variance of logit survival between groups, β_g are the random group effects, and $\bar{\beta}$ is the overall mean. Note that we now use the logit link function to ensure that the realized group-specific survival probabilities ($\text{logit}^{-1}(\beta_g)$) are bound in the interval [0, 1].

Because most BUGS code is identical to that in Section 7.5.1, we just show the part which needs modification:

```
# Priors and constraints
for (i in 1:nind){
    for (t in f[i]:(n.occasions-1)){
        logit(phi[i,t]) <- beta[group[i]]
        p[i,t] <- mean.p
        } #t
    } #i
for (u in 1:g){
    beta[u] ~ dnorm(mean.beta, tau)
    phi.g[u] <- 1 / (1+exp(-beta[u]))  # Back-transformed
                                        group-specific survival
    }
mean.beta ~ dnorm(0, 0.001)        # Prior for logit of mean survival
mean.phi <- 1 / (1+exp(-mean.beta)) # Back-transformed mean survival
sigma ~ dunif(0, 10)               # Prior for sd of logit of survival
                                     variability
tau <- pow(sigma, -2)
mean.p ~ dunif(0, 1)               # Prior for mean recapture
```

7.5.3 Individual Random Effects

As an extreme case of a random group effect, we could also consider each individual as belonging to its own group. This model would not be identifiable when groups are treated as fixed affects, but it is when we treat groups as random effects. Conceptually, we imagine that there is an average survival, around which there is individual-specific noise. To specify individual random effects, we write

$$\text{logit}(\phi_{i,t}) = \mu + \varepsilon_i$$
$$\varepsilon_i \sim \text{Normal}(0, \sigma^2),$$

where σ^2 is the variance of logit survival among individuals, and μ is the overall mean logit survival. The interest of an analysis with individual random effects may be in estimating the mean, the variance, or even the realized survival "residuals" of each individual (sometimes called "frailty"; Cam et al., 2002). Such a model also provides the base for modeling survival as a function of an individual covariate x_i (e.g., size of an individual). This model can be written as

$$\text{logit}(\phi_{i,t}) = \mu + \beta x_i + \varepsilon_i$$
$$\varepsilon_i \sim \text{Normal}(0, \sigma^2),$$

where β is the slope of covariate x on logit survival.

Models with random individual variation in survival are particularly important for the study of senescence (Cam et al., 2002). If individual variation is not included, senescence could easily be overlooked because a decline with age may be offset by increasing proportions of high-quality individuals in the population (Service, 2000; van de Pol and Verhulst, 2006). Sometimes, such a model may also be adopted for recapture probabilities because they are likely to differ among individuals in a similar manner.

Capture–recapture data are often subject to overdispersion, which may be due to a lack of independence among individuals (Lebreton et al., 1992). Overdispersion can be detected with a goodness-of-fit test (Lebreton et al., 1992; Choquet et al., 2001). If overdispersion is not corrected for, parameter estimators tend to be unbiased, but their variances (e.g., standard errors) will be too small (Anderson et al., 1994). The frequentist solution is to calculate a variance inflation factor from the goodness-of-fit test that is called c-hat in the capture–recapture literature, and to compute the true variance of the estimates as the product of the apparent variance and c-hat. An analogous Bayesian solution is to use a model with individual random effects (see also chapter 14 in Kéry 2010 and Section 4.2). The advantage of the Bayesian solution is the flexibility in specifying lack of independence in either survival only, recapture only, or in both parameters.

We now simulate little owl data and analyze them. We assume mean survival of 0.65 and individual variability with a variance of 0.5.

```
# Define parameter values
n.occasions <- 20              # Number of capture occasions
marked <- rep(30, n.occasions-1)  # Annual number of newly marked
                                  #   individuals

mean.phi <- 0.65
p <- rep(0.4, n.occasions-1)
v.ind <- 0.5

# Draw annual survival probabilities
logit.phi <- rnorm(sum(marked), qlogis(mean.phi), v.ind^0.5)
phi <- plogis(logit.phi)

# Define matrices with survival and recapture probabilities
PHI <- matrix(phi, ncol = n.occasions-1, nrow = sum(marked),
    byrow = FALSE)
P <- matrix(p, ncol = n.occasions-1, nrow = sum(marked))
```

(handwritten marginal note:) that ind. survival estimates (p.361) can lead to biased states. This is confounding of C-matrix heterogeneity which

```
# Simulate capture-histories
CH <- simul.cjs(PHI, P, marked)

# Create vector with occasion of marking
get.first <- function(x) min(which(x!=0))
f <- apply(CH, 1, get.first)

# Specify model in BUGS language
sink("cjs-ind-raneff.bug")
cat("
model {

# Priors and constraints
for (i in 1:nind){
    for (t in f[i]:(n.occasions-1)){
        logit(phi[i,t]) <- mu + epsilon[i]
        p[i,t] <- mean.p
        } #t
    } #i
for (i in 1:nind){
    epsilon[i] ~ dnorm(0, tau)
    }
mean.phi ~ dunif(0, 1)              # Prior for mean survival
mu <- log(mean.phi / (1-mean.phi)) # Logit transformation
sigma ~ dunif(0, 5)                # Prior for standard deviation
tau <- pow(sigma, -2)
sigma2 <- pow(sigma, 2)
mean.p ~ dunif(0, 1)               # Prior for mean recapture

# Likelihood
for (i in 1:nind){
    # Define latent state at first capture
    z[i,f[i]] <- 1
    for (t in (f[i]+1):n.occasions){
        # State process
        z[i,t] ~ dbern(mu1[i,t])
        mu1[i,t] <- phi[i,t-1] * z[i,t-1]
        # Observation process
        y[i,t] ~ dbern(mu2[i,t])
        mu2[i,t] <- p[i,t-1] * z[i,t]
        } #t
    } #i
}
",fill = TRUE)
sink()

# Bundle data
bugs.data <- list(y = CH, f = f, nind = dim(CH)[1], n.occasions = dim(CH)[2],
    z = known.state.cjs(CH))

# Initial values
inits <- function(){list(z = cjs.init.z(CH, f), mean.phi = runif(1, 0, 1),
    mean.p = runif(1, 0, 1), sigma = runif(1, 0, 2))}
```

```
# Parameters monitored
parameters <- c("mean.phi", "mean.p", "sigma2")
```

```
# MCMC settings
ni <- 50000
nt <- 6
nb <- 20000
nc <- 3
```

```
# Call WinBUGS from R (BRT 73 min)
cjs.ind <- bugs(bugs.data, inits, parameters, "cjs-ind-raneff.bug",
    n.chains = nc, n.thin = nt, n.iter = ni, n.burnin = nb, debug = TRUE,
    bugs.directory = bugs.dir, working.directory = getwd())
```

We need relatively long runs to reach satisfactory convergence. We note that the random-effects distribution could also be truncated like epsilon[i] ~ dnorm(0, tau)I(-15, 15) to improve mixing of the chains (see Appendix 1, tipp 16). The posterior distributions of the two parameters, mean survival and variability among individuals, show good agreement with the simulated parameters (Fig. 7.5).

```
# Summarize posteriors
print(cjs.ind, digits = 3)

            mean    sd  2.5%   25%   50%   75% 97.5%  Rhat n.eff
mean.phi   0.640 0.026 0.587 0.623 0.641 0.658 0.688 1.001 15000
mean.p     0.410 0.021 0.368 0.396 0.410 0.424 0.451 1.001 13000
sigma2     0.586 0.244 0.176 0.410 0.560 0.739 1.132 1.012  1800
```

```
# Produce graph
par(mfrow = c(1, 2), las = 1)
hist(cjs.ind$sims.list$mean.phi, nclass = 25, col = "gray", main = "",
    xlab = expression(bar(phi)), ylab = "Frequency")
abline(v = mean.phi, col = "red", lwd = 2)
```

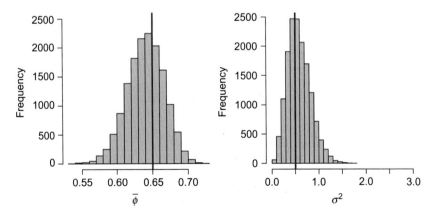

FIGURE 7.5 Posterior distributions of mean survival and of the individual variance in survival. Red lines indicate the values used for data simulation.

```
hist(cjs.ind$sims.list$sigma2, nclass = 15, col = "gray", main = "",
    xlab = expression(sigma^2), ylab = "Frequency", xlim = c(0, 3))
abline(v = v.ind, col = "red", lwd = 2)
```

If we wanted to estimate survival as a function of an individual covariate x, then we just have to adapt a small part in the code:

```
# Priors and constraints
for (i in 1:nind){
    for (t in f[i]:(n.occasions-1)){
        logit(phi[i,t]) <- mu + beta*x[i] + epsilon[i]
        p[i,t] <- mean.p
        } #t
    } #i
for (i in 1:nind){
    epsilon[i] ~ dnorm(0, tau)
    }
mean.phi ~ dunif(0, 1)          # Prior for mean survival
mu <- log(mean.phi / (1-mean.phi))  # Logit transformation
beta ~ dnorm(0, 0.001)          # Prior for covariate slope
sigma ~ dunif(0, 5)             # Prior for standard deviation
tau <- pow(sigma, -2)
sigma2 <- pow(sigma, 2)
mean.p ~ dunif(0, 1)            # Prior for mean recapture
```

Of course, we also have to give initial values for the new stochastic node beta, to include the covariate x in bugs.data, and to monitor beta.

Individual covariates may also change over time, such as, for example, body mass. The difficulty is that the covariate is unknown at occasions when the individual was not captured. Estimating the effects of individual time-varying covariates on survival is a challenge and different approaches have been proposed (Bonner and Schwarz, 2006; Catchpole et al., 2008; King et al., 2010).

7.6 MODELS WITH TIME AND GROUP EFFECTS

7.6.1 Fixed Group and Time Effects

Clearly we can combine the two concepts introduced in Sections 7.4 and 7.5 and model structure both along the time and along the individual axis of the capture-history matrix. The changes needed in the model code are merely an explicit GLM formulation of effects. This offers great flexibility as we can consider interacting or additive time and group effects, and we can treat either or both as random. The different combinations are straightforward and easy to implement, so we now focus in detail on one particular model that is often used, an additive model with fixed time and group effects.

Consider two groups of individuals (e.g., males and females) whose survival varies in parallel over time. Denoting sex by g (for group) and time by t, we can call this model $\{\phi_{g+t}, p_g\}$. Using the GLM formulation, we specify the survival model as

$$\text{logit}(\phi_{i,t}) = \beta_{g(i)} + \gamma_t,$$

where β_g is the effect of the sex g of individual i and γ_t are the fixed time effects. Written in this way, the model is overparameterized. We must either specify the β_g as the survival probabilities of the first year, and thus set $\gamma_1 = 0$, or we specify that γ_t are the survival probabilities of the first group and set $\beta_1 = 0$. Consequently, β_2 is then the difference in survival between the first and the second group. Such constraints must be specified in the BUGS model code, and are usually called corner constraints (Ntzoufras, 2009; Kéry, 2010).

For the simulation example, we assume constant recapture probabilities that are higher for females than for males. We simulate two capture-history data sets, one for males and one for females, merge them, create a group variable, and finally fit the model.

```
# Define parameter values
n.occasions <- 12            # Number of capture occasions
marked <- rep(50, n.occasions-1)   # Annual number of newly marked
                                     individuals
phi.f <- c(0.6, 0.5, 0.55, 0.6, 0.5, 0.4, 0.6, 0.5, 0.55, 0.6, 0.7)
p.f <- rep(0.6, n.occasions-1)
diff <- 0.5      # Difference between male and female survival on logit
                   scale
phi.m <- plogis(qlogis(phi.f) + diff)
p.m <- rep(0.3, n.occasions-1)

# Define matrices with survival and recapture probabilities
PHI.F <- matrix(rep(phi.f, sum(marked)), ncol = n.occasions-1,
    nrow = sum(marked), byrow = TRUE)
P.F <- matrix(rep(p.f, sum(marked)), ncol = n.occasions-1,
    nrow = sum(marked), byrow = TRUE)
PHI.M <- matrix(rep(phi.m, sum(marked)), ncol = n.occasions-1,
    nrow = sum(marked), byrow = TRUE)
P.M <- matrix(rep(p.m, sum(marked)), ncol = n.occasions-1,
    nrow = sum(marked), byrow = TRUE)

# Simulate capture-histories
CH.F <- simul.cjs(PHI.F, P.F, marked)
CH.M <- simul.cjs(PHI.M, P.M, marked)

# Merge capture-histories
CH <- rbind(CH.F, CH.M)

# Create group variable
group <- c(rep(1, dim(CH.F)[1]), rep(2, dim(CH.M)[1]))
```

```
# Create vector with occasion of marking
get.first <- function(x) min(which(x!=0))
f <- apply(CH, 1, get.first)
```

The next piece of code writes the model in BUGS language, and the remaining R code fits the model:

```
# Specify model in BUGS language
sink("cjs-add.bug")
cat("
model {

# Priors and constraints
for (i in 1:nind){
    for (t in f[i]:(n.occasions-1)){
        logit(phi[i,t]) <- beta[group[i]] + gamma[t]
        p[i,t] <- p.g[group[i]]
        } #t
    } #i
# for survival parameters
for (t in 1:(n.occasions-1)){
    gamma[t] ~ dnorm(0, 0.01)I(-10, 10)     # Priors for time
                                              effects
    phi.g1[t] <- 1 / (1+exp(-gamma[t]))     # Back-transformed
                                              survival of males
    phi.g2[t] <- 1 / (1+exp(-gamma[t]-beta[2])) # Back-transformed
                                              survival of females
    }
beta[1] <- 0                                # Corner constraint
beta[2] ~ dnorm(0, 0.01)I(-10, 10)          # Prior for difference in male
                                              and female survival

# for recapture parameters
for (u in 1:g){
    p.g[u] ~ dunif(0, 1)                    # Priors for group-spec.
                                              recapture
    }

# Likelihood
for (i in 1:nind){
    # Define latent state at first capture
    z[i,f[i]] <- 1
    for (t in (f[i]+1):n.occasions){
        # State process
        z[i,t] ~ dbern(mu1[i,t])
        mu1[i,t] <- phi[i,t-1] * z[i,t-1]
        # Observation process
        y[i,t] ~ dbern(mu2[i,t])
        mu2[i,t] <- p[i,t-1] * z[i,t]
        } #t
    } #i
}
```

```
",fill = TRUE)
sink()
```

Bundle data
```
bugs.data <- list(y = CH, f = f, nind = dim(CH)[1], n.occasions = dim(CH)[2],
    z = known.state.cjs(CH), g = length(unique(group)), group = group)
```

Initial values
```
inits <- function(){list(z = cjs.init.z(CH, f), gamma =
    rnorm(n.occasions-1), beta = c(NA, rnorm(1)), p.g = runif(length
    (unique(group)), 0, 1))}
```

Parameters monitored
```
parameters <- c("phi.g1", "phi.g2", "p.g", "beta")
```

MCMC settings
```
ni <- 5000
nt <- 3
nb <- 2000
nc <- 3
```

Call WinBUGS from R (BRT 7 min)
```
cjs.add <- bugs(bugs.data, inits, parameters, "cjs-add.bug",
    n.chains = nc, n.thin = nt, n.iter = ni, n.burnin = nb, debug = TRUE,
    bugs.directory = bugs.dir, working.directory = getwd())
```

Summarize posteriors
```
print(cjs.add, digits = 3)
```

	mean	sd	2.5%	25%	50%	75%	97.5%	Rhat	n.eff
phi.g1[1]	0.614	0.088	0.451	0.554	0.611	0.672	0.789	1.002	2800
phi.g1[2]	0.461	0.065	0.343	0.416	0.459	0.504	0.592	1.001	2800
[...]									
phi.g2[10]	0.752	0.055	0.642	0.716	0.753	0.790	0.859	1.010	260
phi.g2[11]	0.823	0.079	0.683	0.770	0.818	0.868	0.999	1.030	90
p.g[1]	0.567	0.034	0.499	0.545	0.567	0.590	0.633	1.006	350
p.g[2]	0.318	0.022	0.277	0.302	0.317	0.333	0.361	1.005	450
beta[2]	0.603	0.127	0.360	0.515	0.605	0.687	0.848	1.008	300

Figure of male and female survival
```
lower.f <- upper.f <- lower.m <- upper.m <- numeric()
for (t in 1:(n.occasions-1)){
    lower.f[t] <- quantile(cjs.add$sims.list$phi.g1[,t], 0.025)
    upper.f[t] <- quantile(cjs.add$sims.list$phi.g1[,t], 0.975)
    lower.m[t] <- quantile(cjs.add$sims.list$phi.g2[,t], 0.025)
    upper.m[t] <- quantile(cjs.add$sims.list$phi.g2[,t], 0.975)
    }
plot(x=(1:(n.occasions-1))-0.1, y = cjs.add$mean$phi.g1, type = "b",
    pch = 16, ylim = c(0.2, 1), ylab = "Survival probability",
    xlab = "Year", bty = "n", cex = 1.5, axes = FALSE)
axis(1, at = 1:11, labels = rep(NA,11), tcl = -0.25)
axis(1, at = seq(2,10,2), labels = c("2","4","6","8","10"))
axis(2, at = seq(0.2, 1, 0.1), labels = c("0.2", NA, "0.4", NA, "0.6", NA,
    "0.8", NA, "1.0"), las = 1)
segments((1:(n.occasions-1))-0.1, lower.f, (1:(n.occasions-1))-0.1,
    upper.f)
```

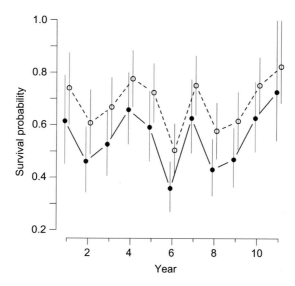

FIGURE 7.6   Posterior means (with 95% CRIs) of male (open circles) and female survival (closed symbols) under the additive model.

```
points(x = (1:(n.occasions-1))+0.1, y = cjs.add$mean$phi.g2,
    type = "b", pch = 1, lty = 2, cex = 1.5)
segments((1:(n.occasions-1))+0.1, lower.m, (1:(n.occasions-1))+0.1,
    upper.m)
```

The posterior means of male and female survival estimated under the additive model are shown in Fig. 7.6. Survival of the two sexes varies in parallel over time, but on the logit scale. Hence, on the probability scale the two curves are not parallel—as the difference becomes smaller the closer the estimates are to 1 or 0.

To fit a model with an interaction between sex and time (i.e., survival of each sex varies independently from each other over time), we would change the "Priors and constraints" part of the model as follows:

```
# Priors and constraints
for (i in 1:nind) {
    for (t in f[i]:(n.occasions-1)) {
        phi[i,t] <- eta.phi[group[i],t]
        p[i,t] <- p.g[group[i]]
        } #t
    } #i
# for survival parameters
for (u in 1:g) {
    for (t in 1:(n.occasions-1)) {
        eta.phi[u,t] ~ dunif(0, 1)    # Prior for time and group-spec.
                                        survival
```

```
        } #t
    } #g
# for recapture parameters
for (u in 1:g) {
    p.g[u] ~ dunif(0, 1)                    # Priors for group-spec. recapture
    }
```

7.6.2 Fixed Group and Random Time Effects

We may combine fixed group and random time effects to estimate temporal variability of survival (or recapture) in each group separately. As for the interacting model before, such a model would assume that the temporal variability of each group is independent of that in the other group(s).

$$\text{logit}(\phi_{i,t}) = \mu_{g(i)} + \varepsilon_{g(i),t}$$
$$\varepsilon_{g,t} \sim \text{Normal}(0, \sigma_g^2),$$

where μ_g are the group-specific means and σ_g^2 the group-specific temporal variances. The model code again only needs changes to the "Priors and constraints" part and looks like:

```
# Priors and constraints
for (i in 1:nind) {
    for (t in f[i]:(n.occasions-1)) {
        logit(phi[i,t]) <- eta.phi[group[i],t]
        p[i,t] <- p.g[group[i]]
        } #t
    } #i
# for survival parameters
for (u in 1:g) {
    for (t in 1:(n.occasions-1)) {
        eta.phi[u,t] <- mu.phi[u] + epsilon[u,t]
        epsilon[u,t] ~ dnorm(0, tau[u])
        } #t
    mean.phi[u] ~ dunif(0, 1)              # Priors on mean group-spec.
                                           #   survival
    mu.phi[u] <- log(mean.phi[u] / (1-mean.phi[u]))
    sigma[u] ~ dunif(0, 10)               # Priors for group-spec. sd
    tau[u] <- pow(sigma[u], -2)
    sigma2[u] <- pow(sigma[u], 2)
    } #g
# for recapture parameters
for (u in 1:g) {
    p.g[u] ~ dunif(0,1)                    # Priors for group-spec.
                                           #   recapture

    }
```

An alternative way to write the same model is to treat the residuals as a realization from a multivariate normal distribution

$$\varepsilon_{g,t} \sim \text{MVN}(0, \Sigma_{g,t}),$$

where $\Sigma_{g,t}$ is the variance–covariance matrix that describes the temporal variance of and the temporal covariance among groups. As we assume independence among groups, the covariance between groups is zero, and the matrix for two groups is as follows:

$$\Sigma_{g,t} = \begin{pmatrix} \sigma_{g1}^2 & 0 \\ 0 & \sigma_{g2}^2 \end{pmatrix}.$$

Temporal variability in survival is usually induced by environmental factors (e.g., weather, food supply). As such, we do not expect survival of groups of individuals from the same population (e.g., sexes or age classes) to vary independently over time. Therefore, we may want to fit a sort of additive model, but where the temporal variance is treated as random. This can be done by considering a correlation of the temporal variability of each group, that is treating two sets of random effects as correleted (Link and Barker, 2005). The advantage of such a model is that (1) the temporal correlation is interpretable as a biological parameter (the extent to which survival varies in common among groups) and (2) the estimates of temporal variability become more precise because information is shared among groups. The temporal correlation of parameters also needs to be included in stochastic population models. Generally, the population growth rate becomes smaller with increasing positive correlation between survival parameters (Caswell, 2001).

With two groups, this model is written as follows:

$$\text{logit}(\phi_{i,t}) = \mu_{g(i)} + \varepsilon_{g(i),t}$$

$$\varepsilon_{g,t} \sim \text{MVN}(0, \Sigma_{g,t})$$

$$\Sigma_{g,t} = \begin{pmatrix} \sigma_{g1}^2 & \rho\sigma_{g1}\sigma_{g2} \\ \rho\sigma_{g1}\sigma_{g2} & \sigma_{g2}^2 \end{pmatrix},$$

where ρ is the temporal correlation coefficient between the two groups. Note that the correlation coefficient between two variables g_1 and g_2 is

$$\rho = \frac{\text{cov}(g1, g2)}{\sqrt{\sigma_{g1}^2 \sigma_{g2}^2}}, \quad \text{and thus } \Sigma_{g,t} \text{ could also be written as}$$

$$\Sigma_{g,t} = \begin{pmatrix} \sigma_{g1}^2 & \text{cov}(g1, g2) \\ \text{cov}(g1, g2) & \sigma_{g2}^2 \end{pmatrix}.$$

Estimating correlation coefficients (or covariances) is challenging, in particular, if there are more than two parameters. This is because several conditions must be met. For example, all correlations must be in the interval -1 and 1, and they are jointly constrained in a complicated way. A standard choice for the prior of the elements of matrix Σ is the inverse

Wishart distribution, which ensures that the estimated parameters have the desired properties.

The inverse Wishart distribution ($IW(R, df)$) has two parameters: the scale matrix (R), with dimension $K \times K$ for K modeled parameters, and the degrees of freedom (df). Depending on the choice of these parameters, we incorporate into the analysis prior information about the correlation coefficients or about the variances (Link and Barker, 2005; Gelman and Hill, 2007). For a uniform prior on the correlation coefficients, we must fix $df = K + 1$. The values of the scale matrix R have an effect on the priors for the variances; large values of R set the prior means of the variances to large values. Because the specification of the priors for matrix Σ is difficult, we recommend conducting sensitivity analyses. The BUGS code to fit this model is as follows:

```
# Specify model in BUGS language
sink("cjs-temp-corr.bug")
cat("
model {

# Priors and constraints
for (i in 1:nind){
    for (t in f[i]:(n.occasions-1)){
        logit(phi[i,t]) <- eta.phi[t,group[i]]
        p[i,t] <- p.g[group[i]]
        } #t
    } #i
# for survival parameters
for (t in 1:(n.occasions-1)){
    eta.phi[t,1:g] ~ dmnorm(mu.phi[], Omega[,])
    } #t
for (u in 1:g){
    mean.phi[u] ~ dunif(0, 1)       # Priors on mean group-spec. survival
    mu.phi[u] <- log(mean.phi[u] / (1-mean.phi[u]))
    } #g
Omega[1:g, 1:g] ~ dwish(R[,], df) # Priors for variance-covariance
                                matrix
Sigma[1:g, 1:g] <- inverse(Omega[,])

# for recapture parameters
for (u in 1:g){
    p.g[u] ~ dunif(0, 1)            # Priors for group-spec. recapture
    }

# Likelihood
for (i in 1:nind){
    # Define latent state at first capture
    z[i,f[i]] <- 1
    for (t in (f[i]+1):n.occasions){
        # State process
        z[i,t] ~ dbern(mu1[i,t])
        mu1[i,t] <- phi[i,t-1] * z[i,t-1]
        # Observation process
        y[i,t] ~ dbern(mu2[i,t])
```

```
         mu2[i,t] <- p[i,t-1] * z[i,t]
      } #t
   } #i
}
",fill = TRUE)
sink()
```

The parameters of the inverse Wishart distribution (R, df) are provided as data. Here, we choose parameters that result in an uninformative prior for the correlation.

```
# Bundle data
bugs.data <- list(y = CH, f = f, nind = dim(CH)[1], n.occasions = dim(CH)[2],
   z = known.state.cjs(CH), g = length(unique(group)), group = group,
   R = matrix(c(5, 0, 0, 1), ncol = 2), df = 3)

# Initial values
inits <- function(){list(z = cjs.init.z(CH, f), p.g = runif(length
   (unique(group)), 0, 1), Omega = matrix(c(1, 0, 0, 1), ncol = 2))}

# Parameters monitored
parameters <- c("eta.phi", "p.g", "Sigma", "mean.phi")

# MCMC settings
ni <- 5000
nt <- 3
nb <- 2000
nc <- 3

# Call WinBUGS from R (BRT 5 min)
cjs.corr <- bugs(bugs.data, inits, parameters, "cjs-temp-corr.bug",
   n.chains = nc, n.thin = nt, n.iter = ni, n.burnin = nb, debug = TRUE,
   bugs.directory = bugs.dir, working.directory = getwd())

# Summarize posteriors
print(cjs.corr, digits = 3)
```

	mean	sd	2.5%	25%	50%	75%	97.5%	Rhat	n.eff
eta.phi[1,1]	0.457	0.391	-0.257	0.190	0.434	0.688	1.304	1.003	870
eta.phi[1,2]	0.794	0.384	0.103	0.537	0.770	1.020	1.605	1.001	3000
[...]									
eta.phi[11,1]	0.945	0.445	0.219	0.647	0.892	1.194	1.995	1.010	420
eta.phi[11,2]	0.800	0.363	0.165	0.554	0.762	1.031	1.546	1.002	1100
p.g[1]	0.572	0.032	0.511	0.550	0.572	0.594	0.636	1.002	1600
p.g[2]	0.327	0.023	0.283	0.311	0.327	0.343	0.375	1.003	970
Sigma[1,1]	0.790	0.391	0.323	0.523	0.704	0.957	1.793	1.001	3000
Sigma[1,2]	0.073	0.156	-0.197	-0.014	0.057	0.146	0.440	1.003	3000
Sigma[2,1]	0.073	0.156	-0.197	-0.014	0.057	0.146	0.440	1.003	3000
Sigma[2,2]	0.243	0.154	0.082	0.144	0.205	0.295	0.631	1.002	1100
mean.phi[1]	0.549	0.067	0.419	0.504	0.549	0.594	0.678	1.002	1400
mean.phi[2]	0.669	0.039	0.593	0.644	0.669	0.694	0.749	1.001	2200

Σ_{11} (note that this is sigma[1,1] in the table above) is the temporal variance of the logit male survival, and Σ_{22} is that for logit female survival.

The elements Σ_{12} and Σ_{21} are the temporal covariances of logit male and logit female survival. This quantity may not be easy to interpret, and we may want to compute the temporal correlation of male and female survival:

```
corr.coef <- cjs.corr$sims.list$Sigma[,1,2] / sqrt(cjs.corr$sims.
    list$Sigma[,1,1] * cjs.corr$sims.list$Sigma[,2,2])
```

The mean and the credible interval of the correlation coefficient (ρ) are 0.16 (−0.43, 0.67), and the probability that $\rho > 0$ is 0.71. As usual these quantities are computed from the posterior distribution of `corr.coef`.

7.7 MODELS WITH AGE EFFECTS

Survival often changes with age. For most species, survival in their first year of life is lower than later. In addition, with senescence, survival may decline in older age classes. Therefore, we might want to estimate different survival parameters for each age class. To model age effects on survival, individuals must be aged when they are first captured, although recently developed models allow relaxing this assumption for some of the individuals (Pledger et al., 2009). We create a matrix $x_{i,t}$, indicating the age at each time t for each individual i. For example, assume a study over 6 years and two individuals that are first captured at the second occasion. The elements of matrix x would then be [NA 1 2 3 4] for the first individual that was born at the second occasion and [NA 2 3 4 5] for the second individual that was 1-year old at the second occasion. We can then model survival as a function of age x as follows:

$$\text{logit}(\phi_{i,t}) = \mu + \beta x_{i,t} + \varepsilon_i$$
$$\varepsilon_i \sim \text{Normal}(0, \sigma^2).$$

This model can be adapted very flexibly. First, we may include an individual random effect (ε_i) as already shown above. Inclusion of individual "frailty" can be important, if we aim at estimating senescence. Second, we may assume that survival changes linearly with age (as in the formula above), that it changes nonlinearly with age (e.g., Gaillard et al., 2004), or that x is a categorical variable. The last is perhaps the most frequent type of model for age effects adopted in practice. If we distinguish only two age classes (i.e., separate survival during the first year of life vs. later), the elements of matrix x would become [NA 1 2 2 2] for the first individual above and [NA 2 2 2 2] for the second individual. Finally, one might include time effects in addition to age effects. A general formation might then be

$$\text{logit}(\phi_{i,t}) = \beta_{x(i,t)} + \varepsilon_i$$
$$\varepsilon_i \sim \text{Normal}(0, \sigma^2),$$

where $\beta_{x(i,t)}$ are the effects of age class x of individual i at time t and ε_i are individual frailty terms. Note that a principal difference between the first and the second model is that the age variable x is continuous in the first but categorical in the second model.

To illustrate the model, we consider a simple example, in which juvenile and adult little owls are marked. We assume that survival in the first year of life (from age 0 to age 1 year) is different from survival in subsequent age classes (from age 1 year onward). Thus, we need a model with two age classes for survival. We simulate data first, by creating two data sets, one for individuals marked as juveniles, and one for individuals marked as adults. We then construct matrix x for each age class and merge the two data sets and matrices (x).

```
# Define parameter values
n.occasions <- 10               # Number of capture occasions
marked.j <- rep(200, n.occasions-1)  # Annual number of newly marked
                                       juveniles
marked.a <- rep(30, n.occasions-1)   # Annual number of newly marked
                                       adults
phi.juv <- 0.3                  # Juvenile annual survival
phi.ad <- 0.65                  # Adult annual survival
p <- rep(0.5, n.occasions-1)    # Recapture
phi.j <- c(phi.juv, rep(phi.ad, n.occasions-2))
phi.a <- rep(phi.ad, n.occasions-1)

# Define matrices with survival and recapture probabilities
PHI.J <- matrix(0, ncol = n.occasions-1, nrow = sum(marked.j))
for (i in 1:length(marked.j)){
    PHI.J[(sum(marked.j[1:i])-marked.j[i]+1):sum(marked.j[1:i]),
       i:(n.occasions-1)] <- matrix(rep(phi.j[1:(n.occasions-i)],
       marked.j[i]), ncol = n.occasions-i, byrow = TRUE)
    }
P.J <- matrix(rep(p, sum(marked.j)), ncol = n.occasions-1,
    nrow = sum(marked.j), byrow = TRUE)
PHI.A <- matrix(rep(phi.a, sum(marked.a)), ncol = n.occasions-1,
    nrow = sum(marked.a), byrow = TRUE)
P.A <- matrix(rep(p, sum(marked.a)), ncol = n.occasions-1,
    nrow = sum(marked.a), byrow = TRUE)

# Apply simulation function
CH.J <- simul.cjs(PHI.J, P.J, marked.j)
CH.A <- simul.cjs(PHI.A, P.A, marked.a)

# Create vector with occasion of marking
get.first <- function(x) min(which(x!=0))
f.j <- apply(CH.J, 1, get.first)
f.a <- apply(CH.A, 1, get.first)

# Create matrices X indicating age classes
x.j <- matrix(NA, ncol = dim(CH.J)[2]-1, nrow = dim(CH.J)[1])
x.a <- matrix(NA, ncol = dim(CH.A)[2]-1, nrow = dim(CH.A)[1])
for (i in 1:dim(CH.J)[1]){
```

```
     for (t in f.j[i]:(dim(CH.J)[2]-1)){
         x.j[i,t] <- 2
         x.j[i,f.j[i]] <- 1
         } #t
     } #i
for (i in 1:dim(CH.A)[1]){
    for (t in f.a[i]:(dim(CH.A)[2]-1)){
        x.a[i,t] <- 2
        } #t
    } #i
```

Next, we combine the two data sets into a common set.

```
CH <- rbind(CH.J, CH.A)
f <- c(f.j, f.a)
x <- rbind(x.j, x.a)
```

Finally, we define the model in BUGS language and fit it to the data. We treat age as a categorical variable, so we use the identity link.

```
# Specify model in BUGS language
sink("cjs-age.bug")
cat("
model {

# Priors and constraints
for (i in 1:nind){
    for (t in f[i]:(n.occasions-1)){
        phi[i,t] <- beta[x[i,t]]
        p[i,t] <- mean.p
        } #t
    } #i
for (u in 1:2){
    beta[u] ~ dunif(0, 1)          # Priors for age-specific survival
    }
mean.p ~ dunif(0, 1)              # Prior for mean recapture

# Likelihood
for (i in 1:nind){
    # Define latent state at first capture
    z[i,f[i]] <- 1
    for (t in (f[i]+1):n.occasions){
        # State process
        z[i,t] ~ dbern(mu1[i,t])
        mu1[i,t] <- phi[i,t-1] * z[i,t-1]
        # Observation process
        y[i,t] ~ dbern(mu2[i,t])
        mu2[i,t] <- p[i,t-1] * z[i,t]
        } #t
    } #i
}
",fill = TRUE)
sink()
```

```
# Bundle data
bugs.data <- list(y = CH, f = f, nind = dim(CH)[1], n.occasions =
dim(CH)[2], z = known.state.cjs(CH), x = x)

# Initial values
inits <- function(){list(z = cjs.init.z(CH, f), beta = runif(2, 0, 1),
mean.p = runif(1, 0, 1))}

# Parameters monitored
parameters <- c("beta", "mean.p")

# MCMC settings
ni <- 2000
nt <- 3
nb <- 1000
nc <- 3

# Call WinBUGS from R (BRT 3 min)
cjs.age <- bugs(bugs.data, inits, parameters, "cjs-age.bug", n.chains =
    nc, n.thin = nt, n.iter = ni, n.burnin = nb, debug = TRUE,
    bugs.directory = bugs.dir, working.directory = getwd())
```

The model runs slowly, but convergence is achieved after only 1000 samples. The parameter estimates are close to the parameters used for the simulations.

```
print(cjs.age, digits = 3)
```

	mean	sd	2.5%	25%	50%	75%	97.5%	Rhat	n.eff
beta[1]	0.317	0.015	0.287	0.306	0.318	0.328	0.347	1.002	880
beta[2]	0.666	0.015	0.638	0.657	0.667	0.676	0.695	1.001	1000
mean.p	0.486	0.019	0.452	0.473	0.486	0.499	0.525	1.005	410

It is straightforward to include other models for the age effect. Depending on the models that we want to fit, matrix x needs to be adapted. If we want to model survival as a linear function of age, x must indicate the true age in each year. If the goal is to treat age as a categorical variable, x must include as many categories as we want to distinguish (e.g., two above). Then the GLM, which relates survival to x, needs to be adapted. For example, if survival is modeled as a linear function of age, we first create x and only include into the analysis individuals marked as juveniles.

```
# Create matrix X indicating age classes
x <- matrix(NA, ncol = dim(CH)[2]-1, nrow = dim(CH)[1])
for (i in 1:dim(CH)[1]){
    for (t in f[i]:(dim(CH)[2]-1)){
        x[i,t] <- t-f[i]+1
        } #t
    } #i
```

As usual, the BUGS model needs a few changes in the "Priors and constraints" part:

```
# Priors and constraints
for (i in 1:nind){
    for (t in f[i]:(n.occasions-1)){
        logit(phi[i,t]) <- mu + beta*x[i,t]
        p[i,t] <- mean.p
        } #t
    } #i
mu ~ dnorm(0, 0.01)              # Prior for mean of logit survival
beta ~ dnorm(0, 0.01)           # Prior for slope parameter
for (i in 1:(n.occasions-1)){
    phi.age[i] <- 1 / (1+exp(-mu -beta*i))   # Logit back-transformation
    }
mean.p ~ dunif(0, 1)                         # Prior for mean recapture
```

Age effects can also be combined with time effects in a very similar way as we have seen with group effects (see Section 7.6). Models can be specified in which survival of the defined age classes vary independently from each other across time, in which the temporal pattern of the age classes is additive, or in which only survival of one age class is time-dependent. Models with random time effects are also useful, allowing the temporal variability of survival of each age class to be modeled independently, or in which the temporal correlation is estimated. It is also possible to consider cohort effects (Reid et al., 2003), that is, the survival of individuals born in one cohort (year) is different from the survival of individuals born in another cohort. This requires that we define a variable indicating the cohort for each individual. In fact, for individuals that are young when marked, our vector f already includes this information. Survival is then modeled as a function of f, we may consider it to be fixed or random, and we can combine it with additional time and/or age effects. Care must be taken with model specification because a model with cohort x time interaction is the same as a model with age x time interaction or one with cohort x age interaction.

7.8 IMMEDIATE TRAP RESPONSE IN RECAPTURE PROBABILITY

One assumption of standard capture–recapture models is that all marked animals alive and available for capture at a given occasion have the same capture probability. Sometimes, this assumption is violated in a very specific way, namely when individuals captured at time $t - 1$ have a different recapture probability at time t than individuals not captured at time $t - 1$. This is called immediate trap response (see also Section 6.2.3).

If recapture probability at time t for individuals captured at $t-1$ is higher than for individuals not captured at $t-1$, this is "trap-happiness" and if recapture probability is lower, then it is called "trap-shyness". Trap-happiness can occur if baited traps are used, and trap-shyness can occur if the interval between capture occasions is short (Pradel, 1993). These effects may also be induced by the sampling method and not reflect a behavioral change of the individuals. However, trap response must be modeled; otherwise, survival estimates will be biased. To account for immediate trap response, a multistate model can be used (Gimenez et al., 2003; Schaub et al., 2009; Appendix 2.2), but here we will use a single-state model and model recapture as a function of whether or not an individual was captured at the preceding occasion. We need, therefore, to construct a matrix m that contains this information. The element of m for individual i at time t takes value 1 if individual i was captured at $t-1$, and value 2 otherwise. The recapture probability is then modeled as

$$p_{i,t} = \beta_{m(i,t)},$$

where β_m takes two values, depending on whether $m_{i,t}$ is 1 or 2. We may also include additive time effects and use the logit link function,

$$\mathrm{logit}(p_{i,t}) = \beta_{m(i,t)} + \gamma_t.$$

The model with interaction between time and behavioral response is parameter-redundant (Gimenez et al., 2003).

Simulating such data is best done with a multistate model (see Appendix 2.2). For illustration, we imagine that we wish to estimate survival of red-backed shrikes (Fig. 7.7), a beautiful bird species of hedgerows. We catch adults during the breeding season, mark them with color rings to facilitate resighting in subsequent years, and survey all potential breeding territories each year. Typically, we focus on breeding territories that were occupied in previous years. If time allows, we search for other, newly established territories. Thus, marked individuals that survive and return to their territory have a higher chance of being resighted, while individuals that establish new territories are less likely to be found. However, once they are found, their chances of being resighted in the next year increase. Such a sampling protocol, which is not uncommon in studies of color-marked birds, induces a "trap-happy effect" which biases survival unless accounted for. For data simulation, we assume survival $\phi = 0.55$ and resighting probabilities $p_{ss} = 0.75$ following a sighting in the preceding year and $p_{ns} = 0.35$ otherwise.

```
# Import data
CH <- as.matrix(read.table(file = "trap.txt", sep = " "))

# Compute vector with occasion of first capture
get.first <- function(x) min(which(x!=0))
f <- apply(CH, 1, get.first)
```

FIGURE 7.7   Male red-backed shrike (*Lanius collurio*) feeding a fledgling (Photograph by D. Studler).

```
# Create matrix m indicating when an individual was captured
m <- CH[,1:(dim(CH)[2]-1)]
u <- which(m==0)
m[u] <- 2
```

The capture-histories of the first four individuals are as follows:

```
1 1 0 0 0 0 0 0
1 0 0 0 0 0 0 0
1 1 0 0 1 1 1 0
1 1 0 1 1 0 1 0
```

and the corresponding matrix *m* for these individuals is

```
1 1 2 2 2 2 2
1 2 2 2 2 2 2
1 1 2 2 1 1 1
1 1 2 1 1 2 1
```

Here a 1 denotes that an individual was captured at the preceding occasion, and a 2 denotes that it was not captured at the preceding occasion. Matrix *m* has as many columns as there are recapture parameters, thus one fewer than the total number of capture occasions.

The BUGS code to fit the trap-response model is as follows:

```
# Specify model in BUGS language
sink("cjs-trap.bug")
cat("
model {

# Priors and constraints
for (i in 1:nind){
    for (t in f[i]:(n.occasions-1)){
        phi[i,t] <- mean.phi
        p[i,t] <- beta[m[i,t]]
        } #t
    } #i
mean.phi ~ dunif(0, 1)              # Prior for mean survival
for (u in 1:2){
    beta[u] ~ dunif(0, 1)          # Priors for recapture
    }

# Likelihood components
for (i in 1:nind){
    # Define latent state at first capture
    z[i,f[i]] <- 1
    for (t in (f[i]+1):n.occasions){
        # State process
        z[i,t] ~ dbern(mu1[i,t])
        mu1[i,t] <- phi[i,t-1] * z[i,t-1]
        # Observation process
        y[i,t] ~ dbern(mu2[i,t])
        mu2[i,t] <- p[i,t-1] * z[i,t]
        } #t
    } #i
}
",fill = TRUE)
sink()

# Bundle data
bugs.data <- list(y = CH, f = f, nind = dim(CH)[1], n.occasions =
    dim(CH)[2], z = known.state.cjs(CH), m = m)

# Initial values
inits <- function(){list(z = cjs.init.z(CH, f), mean.phi = runif(1, 0,
    1), beta = runif(2, 0, 1))}

# Parameters monitored
parameters <- c("mean.phi", "beta")

# MCMC settings
ni <- 20000
nt <- 3
nb <- 10000
nc <- 3
```

```
# Call WinBUGS from R (BRT 1 min)
cjs.trap <- bugs(bugs.data, inits, parameters, "cjs-trap.bug",
    n.chains = nc, n.thin = nt, n.iter = ni, n.burnin = nb, debug = TRUE,
    bugs.directory = bugs.dir, working.directory = getwd())
```

The estimated parameters are close to the parameters used for the simulation.

```
print(cjs.trap, digits = 3)
          mean    sd   2.5%   25%   50%   75% 97.5%  Rhat  n.eff
mean.phi 0.567 0.076 0.462 0.515 0.552 0.602 0.763 1.006   2400
beta[1]  0.756 0.091 0.547 0.701 0.770 0.823 0.897 1.006   2700
beta[2]  0.379 0.207 0.063 0.210 0.359 0.527 0.814 1.003   4500
```

This approach is again very flexible and can be extended easily. For example, if an individual may be captured more than once during an occasion, those captured more may have a higher capture probability. By including the information about how many times an individual was captured, we can adjust for this sort of capture heterogeneity (Fletcher, 1994). The matrix m then contains the number of times an individual is caught at an occasion, and recapture is modeled as a function of m.

7.9 PARAMETER IDENTIFIABILITY

In principle, we are quite free to specify any among a large number of models, especially when using BUGS. However, there is no guarantee that all parameters in a fitted model are indeed identified, that is, can be estimated. In fact, it is common that some parameters are not identifiable. There are two kinds of nonidentifiability: intrinsic and extrinsic. A model has intrinsically identifiable parameters if the same likelihood for the data cannot be obtained by a smaller number of parameters, while parameter-redundant models (those with at least one unidentified parameter) can be expressed in terms of fewer than the original number of parameters (Catchpole and Morgan, 1997). Extrinsic nonidentifiability refers to the situation where a parameter should be identifiable given the structure of a model but is not because the particular data set is insufficient in some regard. Thus, intrinsic nonidentifiability is a feature of a model while extrinsic nonidentifiability is a feature of a data set. Intrinsic nonidentifiability of models can be studied without data using symbolic algebra (Catchpole and Morgan, 1997; Catchpole et al., 2001; Gimenez et al., 2003, 2004) or the analysis of "perfect" data (analytic-numeric method; Burnham et al., 1987), while extrinsic nonidentifiability is best studied using simulation (e.g., Schaub et al., 2004a; Schaub, 2009; Bailey et al., 2010). Of course, intrinsic and extrinsic nonidentifiability may occur together for a particular model and data set.

In the Bayesian framework, the topic of nonidentifiability is slightly different. Because the posterior is a combination of the likelihood and the prior, the posterior is defined (provided that the prior is proper; Gelman et al., 2004). However, if the information in the data is very low for a particular parameter (i.e., there is extrinsic nonidentifiability) or if the likelihood surface is completely flat for a parameter (intrinsic nonidentifiability), then the posterior will simply reflect the prior for that parameter. Therefore, a prior sensitivity analysis can give insights into the identifiability of a parameter. Gimenez et al. (2009b) developed an approach to assess parameter identifiability based on this idea. Using flat priors for parameters, they compared the overlap between the prior and the posterior. If the overlap between the two distributions is large, a parameter is weakly identifiable.

Here, we illustrate this with a well-known example. In the classical, fully time-dependent CJS model $\{\phi_t, p_t\}$, the last survival and the last recapture probability are not identifiable—it is only possible to estimate the product of the two (Lebreton et al., 1992). Thus, this is an intrinsic identifiability problem. In the following example, we fit the model $\{\phi_t, p_t\}$ to the data and use flat priors for all parameters. We then inspect the posterior and the prior of some survival and recapture parameters.

```
# Define parameter values
n.occasions <- 12                    # Number of capture occasions
marked <- rep(30, n.occasions-1)     # Annual number of newly marked
                                       individuals
phi <- c(0.6, 0.5, 0.55, 0.6, 0.5, 0.4, 0.6, 0.5, 0.55, 0.6, 0.7)
p <- c(0.4, 0.65, 0.4, 0.45, 0.55, 0.68, 0.66, 0.28, 0.55, 0.45, 0.35)

# Define matrices with survival and recapture probabilities
PHI <- matrix(phi, ncol = n.occasions-1, nrow = sum(marked), byrow = TRUE)
P <- matrix(p, ncol = n.occasions-1, nrow = sum(marked), byrow = TRUE)

# Simulate capture-histories
CH <- simul.cjs(PHI, P, marked)

# Create vector with occasion of marking
get.first <- function(x) min(which(x!=0))
f <- apply(CH, 1, get.first)

# Specify model in BUGS language
sink("cjs-t-t.bug")
cat("
model {

# Priors and constraints
for (i in 1:nind){
    for (t in f[i]:(n.occasions-1)){
        phi[i,t] <- phi.t[t]
        p[i,t] <- p.t[t]
        } #t
    } #i
```

```
for (t in 1:(n.occasions-1)){
    phi.t[t] ~ dunif(0, 1)                # Priors for time-spec. survival
    p.t[t] ~ dunif(0, 1)                  # Priors for time-spec. recapture
    }

# Likelihood
for (i in 1:nind){
    # Define latent state at first capture
    z[i,f[i]] <- 1
    for (t in (f[i]+1):n.occasions){
        # State process
        z[i,t] ~ dbern(mu1[i,t])
        mu1[i,t] <- phi[i,t-1] * z[i,t-1]
        # Observation process
        y[i,t] ~ dbern(mu2[i,t])
        mu2[i,t] <- p[i,t-1] * z[i,t]
        } #t
    } #i
}
",fill = TRUE)
sink()

# Bundle data
bugs.data <- list(y = CH, f = f, nind = dim(CH)[1], n.occasions = dim(CH)[2],
    z = known.state.cjs(CH))

# Initial values
inits <- function(){list(z = cjs.init.z(CH, f), phi.t = runif((dim(CH)
    [2]-1), 0, 1), p.t = runif((dim(CH)[2]-1), 0, 1))}

# Parameters monitored
parameters <- c("phi.t", "p.t")

# MCMC settings
ni <- 25000
nt <- 3
nb <- 20000
nc <- 3

# Call WinBUGS from R (BRT 7 min)
cjs.t.t <- bugs(bugs.data, inits, parameters, "cjs-t-t.bug", n.chains =
    nc, n.thin = nt, n.iter = ni, n.burnin = nb, debug = TRUE,
    bugs.directory = bugs.dir, working.directory = getwd())

# Plot posterior distributions of some phi and p
par(mfrow = c(2, 2), cex = 1.2, las = 1, mar=c(5, 4, 2, 1))
plot(density(cjs.t.t$sims.list$phi.t[,6]), xlim = c(0, 1), ylim = c(0, 5),
    main = "", xlab = expression(phi[6]), ylab = "Density", frame = FALSE,
    lwd = 2)
abline(h = 1, lty = 2, lwd = 2)
par(mar=c(5, 3, 2, 2))
plot(density(cjs.t.t$sims.list$phi.t[,11]), xlim = c(0, 1),
    ylim =c(0, 5), main = "", xlab = expression(phi[11]), ylab ="",
    frame = FALSE, lwd = 2)
abline(h = 1, lty = 2, lwd = 2)
par(mar=c(5, 4, 2, 1))
```

```
plot(density(cjs.t.t$sims.list$p.t[,6]), xlim = c(0, 1), ylim = c(0, 5),
    main = "", xlab = expression(p[6]), ylab = "Density", frame = FALSE,
    lwd = 2)
abline(h = 1, lty = 2, lwd = 2)
par(mar=c(5, 3, 2, 2))
plot(density(cjs.t.t$sims.list$p.t[,11]), xlim = c(0, 1), ylim =
    c(0, 5), main = "", xlab = expression(p[11]), ylab ="", frame = FALSE,
    lwd = 2)
abline(h = 1, lty = 2, lwd = 2)
```

To inspect the result, we plot the posterior and prior densities of some parameters (Fig. 7.8). It is obvious that ϕ_6 and p_6 are identifiable: their posterior is nicely peaked and does not overlap much with the prior distribution. By contrast, the posterior distributions of ϕ_{11} and p_{11} do not have a clear peak and the overlap with the prior is large. These

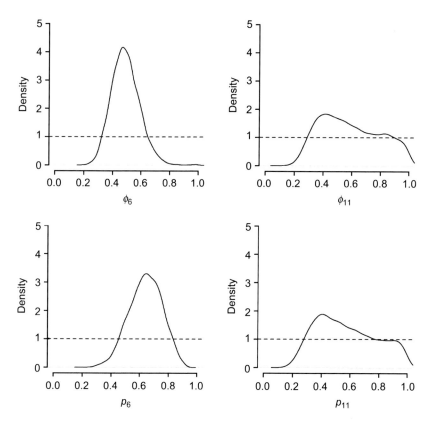

FIGURE 7.8 Posterior density plots of the sixth and the last survival and recapture probabilities. The dotted line shows the prior density. The last parameters (ϕ_{11} and p_{11}) are not separately identifiable.

parameters are not identifiable. Gimenez et al. (2009b) developed a quantitative guideline based on the degree of overlap between posterior and prior to decide when a parameter is identifiable. Note that when the year effects are not fixed as above, but random, the problem of nonidentifiability disappears because information from survival and recapture from the complete data set is used to estimate the last parameters. You may want to try this!

In any analysis of capture–recapture models (or actually, of *any* model), you should be aware that some parameters might not be estimable, although WinBUGS (or another software) may give you estimates for all parameters (Lunn et al., 2010). Obviously, no inference can be made about nonidentifiable parameters. This challenge is even greater for multistate capture–recapture models (see Chapter 9).

7.10 FITTING THE CJS TO DATA IN THE M-ARRAY FORMAT: THE MULTINOMIAL LIKELIHOOD

7.10.1 Introduction

So far we have analyzed the individual capture-histories using a state-space formulation of the CJS model. This is a very general framework within which a multitude of different kinds of models can be formulated, but it comes at a computational cost. As all capture-histories are analyzed individually, a loop over all individuals is necessary. In addition, every unknown latent state (e.g., individual survival) needs to be estimated. Capture–recapture data can, however, also be summarized in the so-called m-array (Burnham et al., 1987). The CJS model is then fitted using a multinomial likelihood. This has the advantage of much faster computation, but the disadvantage of reduced flexibility in the modeling. In particular, models with individual effects can no longer be fitted.

We first introduce the m-array format, by considering the following example—we have capture-histories of seven individuals:

```
1 0 1 0
1 1 0 0
1 1 0 0
1 0 0 0
0 1 1 1
0 1 0 0
0 0 1 0
```

The m-array tabulates the number of individuals released at one occasion that are next recaptured on each subsequent occasion. It is a triangular matrix, in which rows refer to release occasions and columns refer to recapture occasions. An additional column tallies up the individuals that are not recaptured. To create the m-array, the capture-histories of all individuals are broken into fragments. The number of captures equals the number of fragments. Each fragment considers the last release occasion and the next recapture occasion. For example, the capture-history [1 0 1 0] is broken into the two fragments [1 0 1 0] and [0 0 1 0]. The first fragment shows that the individual was released at occasion 1 and first recaptured at occasion 3. The second fragment shows that the individual was released on occasion 3 and was never recaptured. The m-array for the seven capture-histories above is:

	Recapture Occasion			
Release Occasion	2	3	4	Never Recaptured
1	2	1	0	1
2	–	1	0	3
3	–	–	1	2

Fitting the CJS model to the data using the m-array implicitly assumes the absence of any individual effects on survival and recapture probabilities. By summarizing the data in this form, it is evident that effects of individual covariates cannot be fitted because the capture-histories of the individuals are broken up. Age as a special class of individual covariate can be considered but requires a different format of the m-array (see Section 7.10.3). Otherwise, all the information that originally was included in the individual capture-histories is kept; it is just summarized in the form of minimal sufficient statistics.

The following R function converts capture-histories into the m-array format.

```
# Function to create a m-array based on capture-histories (CH)
marray <- function(CH) {
    nind <- dim(CH)[1]
    n.occasions <- dim(CH)[2]
    m.array <- matrix(data = 0, ncol = n.occasions+1, nrow =
      n.occasions)

    # Calculate the number of released individuals at each time period
    for (t in 1:n.occasions) {
        m.array[t,1] <- sum(CH[,t])
        }
    for (i in 1:nind) {
        pos <- which(CH[i,] != 0)
        g <- length(pos)
```

```
        for (z in 1:(g-1)){
            m.array[pos[z],pos[z+1]] <- m.array[pos[z],pos[z+1]] + 1
            } #z
        } #i

    # Calculate the number of individuals that is never recaptured
    for (t in 1:n.occasions){
        m.array[t,n.occasions+1] <- m.array[t,1] -
            sum(m.array[t,2:n.occasions])
        }
    out <- m.array[1:(n.occasions-1),2:(n.occasions+1)]
    return(out)
    }
```

The expected values of the entries of the m-array are given based on the underlying model parameters (ϕ_t and p_t) and the number of released individuals. These define the cell probabilities of the multinomial distributions for each release occasion.

Release Occasion	Recaptured at Occasion			Never Recaptured
	2	3	4	
1	$\phi_1 p_1$	$\phi_1(1-p_1)$ $\phi_2 p_2$	$\phi_1(1-p_1)$ $\phi_2(1-p_2)$ $\phi_3 p_3$	$1 - \phi_1 p_1 - \phi_1(1-p_1)\phi_2 p_2 - \phi_1(1-p_1)$ $\phi_2(1-p_2)\phi_3 p_3 = 1 - \Sigma(\text{rel. occ } 1)$
2	0	$\phi_2 p_2$	$\phi_2(1-p_2)$ $\phi_3 p_3$	$1 - \phi_2 p_2 - \phi_2(1-p_2)\phi_3 p_3 = 1 - \Sigma(\text{rel. occ } 2)$
3	0	0	$\phi_3 p_3$	$1 - \phi_3 p_3 = 1 - \Sigma(\text{rel. occ } 3)$

Note: The entry in cell (1,3) is the product $\phi_1(1 - p_1)\phi_2 p_2$ (and likewise for the other cells).

7.10.2 Time-Dependent Models

The rows of the observed m-array data follow a multinomial distribution with index equal to the number of released individuals at each occasion and the cell probabilities that are functions of survival and recapture parameters, as shown in the table above. Fitting this model in BUGS is straightforward: essentially, we only need to define the cell probabilities of the m-array.

Using the m-array formulation of the CJS model, it is also quite easy to assess the fit of the model, that is, to compute a Bayesian p-value based on the posterior predictive distribution of a goodness-of-fit (GOF) statistic (see Gelman et al., 1996, 2004; Section 12.3). This technique for GOF assessment is also called posterior predictive checking because its rationale is based on a comparison of data simulated (predicted) under the model, and the actual data set that is analyzed using that model. Simulated data sets under a model are obtained easily as part of the MCMC updating from the posterior predictive distribution of the data. Usually, some discrepancy measure is calculated that measures how "far apart" the data are from their expected values under the model. Often, omnibus test statistics such as chi-squared are used as a discrepancy measure, but other statistics may be chosen to specifically highlight how well a model fits the data in some particular manner, for instance, how well it describes extreme values (Gelman et al., 1996). This discrepancy measure is calculated for both the simulated and the actual data set. The values of both discrepancy measures change at each iteration of the MCMC simulation algorithm because the parameter values change with each iteration as well and they are used both to generate a replicate data set and to compute the expected values for the data. At the end of the posterior sampling, one has as many draws from the posterior distribution of the chosen discrepancy measure for the simulated (perfect) data sets as for the actual data sets. The simulated data sets are "perfect" in the sense that they were generated under exactly the same model that is used for parameter estimation in the observed data and using the exact parameter values obtained in that analysis. The posterior draws of the discrepancy measure for the replicate data, therefore, provide the reference distribution for the discrepancy measure under the null hypothesis that the model fits our data. The proportion of times that the discrepancy measure for the simulated data sets is more extreme than that for the actual data set is called a Bayesian p-value. Under the null hypothesis that the model in question is the data-generating model, this should happen about 50% of times; hence, Bayesian p-values close to 0 or 1 are suspicious. A graph of the values of the discrepancy measure from the replicate data sets plotted against those for the actual data sets may be even more informative than the scalar Bayesian p-value to point out ways how a model may not fit. The value of the p-value represents the proportion of points that lie above the 1:1 line of equality.

Bayesian p-values have been criticized for several reasons. First, they use the data twice (once, to generate replicate data sets and then to compute the expected data and compare that with both the replicate and the actual data sets). They may thus not be strict enough and not reject often enough the hypothesis of a fitting model. Second, it is unclear what value of a Bayesian p-value represents a good fit. For instance, there would be no objective way of saying that values outside of the interval (0.05, 0.95) represent models that do not fit the data. Thus, Bayesian p-values are a descriptive technique only. And finally, the rationale underlying a Bayesian p-value is intrinsically frequentist: Learning from the data is not limited to the information content in the actual data set but instead based on hypothetical replicate data sets as well. This may be offensive to hardcore Bayesians who adhere to the so-called likelihood principle (Lindley, 2006), which says that all information about a data set is contained in the likelihood function. Our own position in this respect is pragmatic: We like Bayesian p-values as a simple and very flexible way of pointing out ways in which a model may not fit a data set.

In the current example of a survival analysis, we could not test the GOF of a state-space model for binary responses (observed vs. not observed). The reason for this is that discrepancy measures such as the deviance are uninformative about model fit for binary responses (McCullagh and Nelder, 1989). GOF can, however, be assessed for some summary of binary responses and the m-array represents just one such summary. So here now, we create replicate data (i.e., m-arrays, e_{ij}), and compare the observed (x_{ij}) and the expected m-arrays using a discrepancy measure. We could use the χ^2-dispcrepancy as in Chapter 12, but instead follow Brooks et al. (2000b) and use the Freeman-Tukey statistic ($D = \Sigma(x_{ij}^{1/2} - e_{ij}^{1/2})^2$). It makes unnecessary to pool cells with small expected values. The Freeman–Tukey statistic is computed for the observed and simulated data.

We use the data as created in Section 7.9 to illustrate the use of the model. The following code fits the CJS model using the multinomial likelihood and includes the posterior predictive check.

```
# Specify model in BUGS language
sink("cjs-mnl.bug")
cat("
model {

# Priors and constraints
for (t in 1:(n.occasions-1)){
    phi[t] ~ dunif(0, 1)           # Priors for survival
    p[t] ~ dunif(0, 1)             # Priors for recapture
    }

# Define the multinomial likelihood
for (t in 1:(n.occasions-1)){
    marr[t,1:n.occasions] ~ dmulti(pr[t, ], r[t])
    }

# Calculate the number of birds released each year
for (t in 1:(n.occasions-1)){
    r[t] <- sum(marr[t, ])
    }

# Define the cell probabilities of the m-array
# Main diagonal
for (t in 1:(n.occasions-1)){
    q[t] <- 1-p[t]                 # Probability of non-recapture
    pr[t,t] <- phi[t]*p[t]
    # Above main diagonal
    for (j in (t+1):(n.occasions-1)){
        pr[t,j] <- prod(phi[t:j])*prod(q[t:(j-1)])*p[j]
        } #j
```

```
# Below main diagonal
for (j in 1:(t-1)){
    pr[t,j] <- 0
    } #j
} #t
# Last column: probability of non-recapture
for (t in 1:(n.occasions-1)){
    pr[t,n.occasions] <- 1-sum(pr[t,1:(n.occasions-1)])
    } #t

# Assess model fit using Freeman-Tukey statistic
# Compute fit statistics for observed data
for (t in 1:(n.occasions-1)){
    for (j in 1:n.occasions){
        expmarr[t,j] <- r[t]*pr[t,j]
        E.org[t,j] <- pow((pow(marr[t,j], 0.5)-pow(expmarr[t,j],
            0.5)), 2)
        } #j
    } #t

# Generate replicate data and compute fit stats from them
for (t in 1:(n.occasions-1)){
    marr.new[t,1:n.occasions] ~ dmulti(pr[t, ], r[t])
    for (j in 1:n.occasions){
        E.new[t,j] <- pow((pow(marr.new[t,j], 0.5)-pow(expmarr[t,j],
            0.5)), 2)
        } #j
    } #t
fit <- sum(E.org[,])
fit.new <- sum(E.new[,])
}
",fill = TRUE)
sink()

# Create the m-array from the capture-histories
marr <- marray(CH)

# Bundle data
bugs.data <- list(marr = marr, n.occasions = dim(marr)[2])

# Initial values
inits <- function(){list(phi = runif(dim(marr)[2]-1, 0, 1),
  p = runif(dim(marr)[2]-1, 0, 1))}

# Parameters monitored
parameters <- c("phi", "p", "fit", "fit.new")

# MCMC settings
ni <- 10000
nt <- 3
nb <- 5000
nc <- 3

# Call WinBUGS from R (BRT 1 min)
cjs <- bugs(bugs.data, inits, parameters, "cjs-mnl.bug", n.chains =
    nc, n.thin = nt, n.iter = ni, n.burnin = nb, debug = TRUE,
    bugs.directory = bugs.dir, working.directory = getwd())
```

```
print(cjs, digits = 3)

           mean    sd   2.5%    25%    50%     75%   97.5%  Rhat n.eff
phi[1]    0.632 0.167  0.331  0.505  0.621   0.754  0.960 1.001  5000
[ ... ]
p[11]     0.577 0.206  0.261  0.406  0.547   0.742  0.968 1.006   380
fit      10.563 1.674  7.773  9.378 10.400  11.570 14.320 1.001  5000
fit.new  12.671 2.744  8.095 10.720 12.420  14.330 18.830 1.002  2400
```

The model converges quickly and the MCMC samples are obtained in a short time (to compare, you may use the same data and run the corresponding state-space model of Section 7.3). The comparison of the discrepancy between the observed and the simulated data (Fig. 7.9) shows that they are similar, suggesting that the model is adequate for the data set. This is confirmed by a Bayesian *p*-value of 0.75. For more discussion about checking of capture–recapture models, see Brooks et al. (2000a, 2000b) and King et al. (2010).

```
# Evaluation of fit
plot(cjs$sims.list$fit, cjs$sims.list$fit.new, xlab = "Discrepancy
    actual data", ylab = "Discrepancy replicate data", las = 1,
ylim = c(5, 25), xlim = c(5, 25), bty ="n")
abline(0, 1, col = "black", lwd = 2)
mean(cjs$sims.list$fit.new > cjs$sims.list$fit)
```

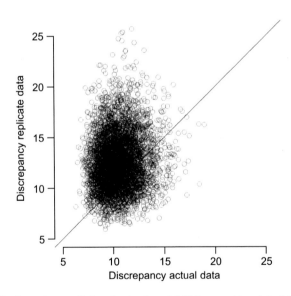

FIGURE 7.9 Posterior predictive check of model fit by a scatter plot of the discrepancy measure for replicate (simulated) versus actual (observed) data in a CJS model. The Bayesian *p*-value is the proportion of points above the 1:1 line.

Construction of models with time effects (fixed or random) using the multinomial likelihood requires changes in the "Priors and constraints" part of the model code, in exactly the same way as we have introduced for the state-space formulation. However, the formulation of models with groups is slightly different. We need to create an m-array for each group and to write a separate likelihood (with different parameters) for each data set. Once this is done, we can constrain the group-specific parameters in the same way as with models using the state-space formulation (i.e., we can regard groups as fixed or as random, and we can combine them with time effects). See exercise 2 in Section 7.13 for an example.

7.10.3 Age-Dependent Models

Models with age-dependent survival fitted with the multinomial likelihood need some adaptations (m-array, analyzing code), and we show this in detail using an example. We look at the situation in which young and adult little owls are marked and assume that survival in the first year of life (from age 0 to age 1 year) is different from survival in subsequent age classes (from age 1 onward). We first start with the simulation of the data. We will create two data sets, one for individuals marked as juveniles, and another for individuals marked as adults.

```
# Define parameter values
n.occasions <- 12                    # Number of capture occasions
marked.j <- rep(200, n.occasions-1)  # Annual number of newly marked
                                       juveniles
marked.a <- rep(30, n.occasions-1)   # Annual number of newly marked
                                       adults
phi.juv <- 0.3                       # Juvenile annual survival
phi.ad <- 0.65                       # Adult annual survival
p <- rep(0.5, n.occasions-1)         # Recapture
phi.j <- c(phi.juv, rep(phi.ad,n.occasions-2))
phi.a <- rep(phi.ad, n.occasions-1)

# Define matrices with survival and recapture probabilities
PHI.J <- matrix(0, ncol = n.occasions-1, nrow = sum(marked.j))
for (i in 1:(length(marked.j)-1)){
    PHI.J[(sum(marked.j[1:i])-
    marked.j[i]+1):sum(marked.j[1:i]),i:(n.occasions-1)] <-
    matrix(rep(phi.j[1:(n.occasions-i)], marked.j[i]),
    ncol = n.occasions-i, byrow = TRUE)
    }
P.J <- matrix(rep(p, n.occasions*sum(marked.j)), ncol =
    n.occasions-1, nrow = sum(marked.j), byrow = TRUE)
PHI.A <- matrix(rep(phi.a, sum(marked.a)), ncol = n.occasions-1,
    nrow = sum(marked.a), byrow = TRUE)
P.A <- matrix(rep(p, sum(marked.a)), ncol = n.occasions-1,
    nrow = sum(marked.a), byrow = TRUE)
```

```
# Apply simulation function
CH.J <- simul.cjs(PHI.J, P.J, marked.j)
CH.A <- simul.cjs(PHI.A, P.A, marked.a)
```

Next, we create two m-arrays, one for juveniles and another for adults. The difficulty is that whenever an individual initially marked as a juvenile is recaptured, it has become an adult. Thus, it must be "released" in the m-array of the individuals initially marked as adults. To achieve this goal, we first split the capture-histories of individuals marked as juveniles based on whether or not they were ever recaptured (recaptured at least once: CH.J.R, never recaptured: CH.J.N). The first capture of CH.J.R is then removed, the resulting capture-histories added to the capture-histories of the individuals marked as adults and the m-array computed. Next, all recaptures after the first recapture of the original CH.J.R matrix are removed and the m-array computed. Because all these individuals are released as adults, the last columns of the m-array summarizing the number of individuals never recaptured have to be set to zero. Finally, we create the m-array for CH.J.N and add it to the previous m-array. The following code performs these data manipulations.

```
cap <- apply(CH.J, 1, sum)
ind <- which(cap >= 2)
CH.J.R <- CH.J[ind,]        # Juvenile CH recaptured at least once
CH.J.N <- CH.J[-ind,]       # Juvenile CH never recaptured

# Remove first capture
first <- numeric()
for (i in 1:dim(CH.J.R)[1]){
    first[i] <- min(which(CH.J.R[i,]==1))
    }
CH.J.R1 <- CH.J.R
for (i in 1:dim(CH.J.R)[1]){
    CH.J.R1[i,first[i]] <- 0
    }

# Add grown-up juveniles to adults and create m-array
CH.A.m <- rbind(CH.A, CH.J.R1)
CH.A.marray <- marray(CH.A.m)

# Create CH matrix for juveniles, ignoring subsequent recaptures
second <- numeric()
for (i in 1:dim(CH.J.R1)[1]){
    second[i] <- min(which(CH.J.R1[i,]==1))
    }
CH.J.R2 <- matrix(0, nrow = dim(CH.J.R)[1], ncol = dim(CH.J.R)[2])
for (i in 1:dim(CH.J.R)[1]){
    CH.J.R2[i,first[i]] <- 1
    CH.J.R2[i,second[i]] <- 1
    }

# Create m-array for these
CH.J.R.marray <- marray(CH.J.R2)
```

```
# The last column ought to show the number of juveniles not recaptured
  again and should all be zeros, since all of them are released as adults
CH.J.R.marray[,dim(CH.J)[2]] <- 0

# Create the m-array for juveniles never recaptured and add it to the
  previous m-array
CH.J.N.marray <- marray(CH.J.N)
CH.J.marray <- CH.J.R.marray + CH.J.N.marray
```

Now we write the BUGS code for the age-dependent model. We specify two component likelihoods, one for the m-array of adults and another for the m-array of juveniles. The code for adults is exactly the same as before (Section 7.10.2), but the code for juveniles has some twists. Here, the first survival for each release cohort (juvenile survival) is different from subsequent survival (which is that of adults).

```
# Specify model in BUGS language
sink("cjs-mnl-age.bug")
cat("
model {

# Priors and constraints
for (t in 1:(n.occasions-1)){
    phi.juv[t] <- mean.phijuv
    phi.ad[t] <- mean.phiad
    p[t] <- mean.p
    }
mean.phijuv ~ dunif(0, 1)        # Prior for mean juv. survival
mean.phiad ~ dunif(0, 1)         # Prior for mean ad. survival
mean.p ~ dunif(0, 1)             # Prior for mean recapture

# Define the multinomial likelihood
for (t in 1:(n.occasions-1)){
    marr.j[t,1:n.occasions] ~ dmulti(pr.j[t,], r.j[t])
    marr.a[t,1:n.occasions] ~ dmulti(pr.a[t,], r.a[t])
    }

# Calculate the number of birds released each year
for (t in 1:(n.occasions-1)){
    r.j[t] <- sum(marr.j[t,])
    r.a[t] <- sum(marr.a[t,])
    }

# Define the cell probabilities of the m-arrays
# Main diagonal
for (t in 1:(n.occasions-1)){
    q[t] <- 1-p[t]               # Probability of non-recapture
    pr.j[t,t] <- phi.juv[t]*p[t]
    pr.a[t,t] <- phi.ad[t]*p[t]
    # Above main diagonal
    for (j in (t+1):(n.occasions-1)){
        pr.j[t,j] <- phi.juv[t]*prod(phi.ad[(t+1):j])*prod(q[t:
            (j-1)])*p[j]
        pr.a[t,j] <- prod(phi.ad[t:j])*prod(q[t:(j-1)])*p[j]
        } #j
```

```
    # Below main diagonal
    for (j in 1:(t-1)){
        pr.j[t,j] <- 0
        pr.a[t,j] <- 0
        } #j
    } #t
# Last column: probability of non-recapture
for (t in 1:(n.occasions-1)){
    pr.j[t,n.occasions] <- 1-sum(pr.j[t,1:(n.occasions-1)])
    pr.a[t,n.occasions] <- 1-sum(pr.a[t,1:(n.occasions-1)])
    } #t
}
",fill = TRUE)
sink()

# Bundle data
bugs.data <- list(marr.j = CH.J.marray, marr.a = CH.A.marray,
    n.occasions = dim(CH.J.marray)[2])

# Initial values
inits <- function(){list(mean.phijuv = runif(1, 0, 1), mean.phiad =
    runif(1, 0, 1), mean.p = runif(1, 0, 1))}

# Parameters monitored
parameters <- c("mean.phijuv", "mean.phiad", "mean.p")

# MCMC settings
ni <- 3000
nt <- 3
nb <- 1000
nc <- 3

# Call WinBUGS from R (BRT <1 min)
cjs.2 <- bugs(bugs.data, inits, parameters, "cjs-mnl-age.bug",
    n.chains = nc, n.thin = nt, n.iter = ni, n.burnin = nb, debug = TRUE,
    bugs.directory = bugs.dir, working.directory = getwd())
```

Convergence is achieved quickly; 3000 iterations with a burnin of 1000 are sufficient. Plotting the posterior distributions shows parameter estimates that resemble well the values used to simulate the data (Fig. 7.10).

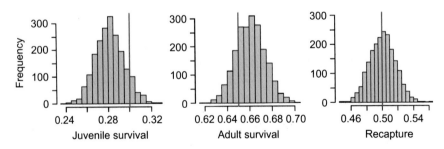

FIGURE 7.10 Posterior distributions of juvenile and adult survival and of recapture probability. Red lines indicate the values used to generate the data set.

```
par(mfrow = c(1, 3), las = 1)
hist(cjs.2$sims.list$mean.phijuv, nclass = 30, col = "gray", main = "",
    xlab = "Juvenile survival", ylab = "Frequency")
abline(v = phi.juv, col = "red", lwd = 2)
hist(cjs.2$sims.list$mean.phiad, nclass = 30, col = "gray", main = "",
    xlab = "Adult survival", ylab = "")
abline(v = phi.ad, col = "red", lwd = 2)
hist(cjs.2$sims.list$mean.p, nclass = 30, col = "gray", main = "",
    xlab = "Recapture", ylab = "")
abline(v = p[1], col = "red", lwd = 2)
```

We assumed that recapture probability was not dependent on age because all birds are >1 year old when they are first recaptured. Sometimes, however, it may be useful to fit age effects for recapture probability. Often, young individuals do not reproduce as successfully as adults. If individuals can only be captured when reproducing, this can result in a lower recapture probability of young individuals.

The model could also be extended to include more age classes. In principle, the number of m-arrays is equal to the number of age classes in the model. However, careful bookkeeping is required to fit these models. The age of each individual at each recapture has to be evaluated, and afterward the individual is "released" in the m-array in the corresponding age class. M-arrays are specified for each age class in the BUGS model code, and all of them have an age structure with the exception of the m-array for the oldest age class. Cell probabilities of the m-array of the second oldest age class have an age structure with two classes, that of the third-oldest age class an age structure with three classes, and so forth.

7.11 ANALYSIS OF A REAL DATA SET: SURVIVAL OF FEMALE LEISLER'S BATS

Leisler's bat (Fig. 7.11) is a medium-sized bat species that forms nursery colonies in cavities in woodlands and is widespread throughout Europe. Northern populations migrate to the Mediterranean in winter. Wigbert Schorcht and his colleagues studied a population of Leisler's bat in Thuringia (Germany) from 1989 to 2008. They placed bat boxes in a forest and regularly captured individuals in them. The capture–recapture data have been extensively analyzed using CJS models fitted in a frequentist framework (Schorcht et al., 2009). Here, we analyze a subset of these data consisting of 181 adult females that were born in the study area. Females are highly philopatric and thus our estimate of apparent survival is likely close to true survival. Some initial modeling suggested that adult survival was subject to strong temporal variation, whereas recapture probabilities were constant over time (Schorcht et al., 2009). Our interest here is to estimate mean annual survival as well as its temporal variance.

FIGURE 7.11   Leisler's bat (*Nyctalus leisleri*) (Photograph D. Nill).

We will therefore fit a model denoted by $(\phi_t, p.)$. We first performed a frequentist GOF test with program U-CARE (Choquet et al., 2001). The test assesses the fit of the time-dependent CJS model (ϕ_t, p_t) and didn't show any indication of lack of fit $(\chi^2_{49} = 41.38, P = 0.77)$. Yet, because we fit a model with random year effects, we want to perform also a posterior predictive check to evaluate the goodness-of-fit and estimate a Bayesian p-value for that model. The data are already summarized in the m-array format, thus we will use the multinomial likelihood to fit the model.

```
m.leisleri <- matrix(c(4,1,0,0,0,0,0,0,0,0,0,0,0,0,0,0,0,0,3,
0,5,0,1,0,0,0,0,0,0,0,0,0,0,0,0,0,0,3,
0,0,9,2,0,0,0,0,0,0,0,0,0,0,0,0,0,0,3,
0,0,0,10,2,0,0,0,0,0,0,0,0,0,0,0,0,0,5,
0,0,0,0,10,2,1,0,0,0,0,0,0,0,0,0,0,0,6,
0,0,0,0,0,15,0,0,0,0,0,0,0,0,0,0,0,0,6,
0,0,0,0,0,0,11,2,0,1,0,0,0,0,0,0,0,0,19,
0,0,0,0,0,0,0,12,1,1,0,0,0,0,0,0,0,0,6,
0,0,0,0,0,0,0,0,13,2,0,0,0,0,0,0,0,0,4,
0,0,0,0,0,0,0,0,0,14,0,0,0,0,0,0,0,0,6,
0,0,0,0,0,0,0,0,0,0,13,1,0,0,0,1,0,0,8,
0,0,0,0,0,0,0,0,0,0,0,15,3,1,0,0,0,0,12,
0,0,0,0,0,0,0,0,0,0,0,0,12,4,0,1,0,0,7,
0,0,0,0,0,0,0,0,0,0,0,0,0,19,2,0,0,0,3,
0,0,0,0,0,0,0,0,0,0,0,0,0,0,28,1,0,0,4,
```

```
0,0,0,0,0,0,0,0,0,0,0,0,0,0,0,22,7,2,21,
0,0,0,0,0,0,0,0,0,0,0,0,0,0,0,0,12,2,21,
0,0,0,0,0,0,0,0,0,0,0,0,0,0,0,0,14,18), ncol = 19, nrow = 18,
    byrow = TRUE)
```

The BUGS code poses no additional difficulties; we merely have to add the hierarchical extension to the multinomial model to account for random year effects. This extension assumes that the annual survival probabilities are random draws from a normal distribution whose mean is the logit of mean survival and a variance. This variance (`sigma2` in the code below) is the temporal variance of survival on the logit scale. In case we prefer to express the temporal variance on the probability scale, we also have a parameter called `sigma2.real`.

```
# Specify model in BUGS language
sink("cjs-mnl-ran.bug")
cat("
model {

# Priors and constraints
for (t in 1:(n.occasions-1)){
    logit(phi[t]) <- mu + epsilon[t]
    epsilon[t] ~ dnorm(0, tau)
    p[t] <- mean.p
    }
mean.phi ~ dunif(0, 1)              # Prior for mean survival
mu <- log(mean.phi / (1-mean.phi))  # Logit transformation
sigma ~ dunif(0, 5)                 # Prior for standard deviation
tau <- pow(sigma, -2)
sigma2 <- pow(sigma, 2)
# Temporal variance on real scale
sigma2.real <- sigma2 * pow(mean.phi, 2) * pow((1-mean.phi), 2)
mean.p ~ dunif(0, 1)                # Prior for mean recapture

# Define the multinomial likelihood
for (t in 1:(n.occasions-1)){
    marr[t,1:n.occasions] ~ dmulti(pr[t,], r[t])
    }

# Calculate the number of birds released each year
for (t in 1:(n.occasions-1)){
    r[t] <- sum(marr[t,])
    }

# Define the cell probabilities of the m-array:
# Main diagonal
for (t in 1:(n.occasions-1)){
    q[t] <- 1-p[t]
    pr[t,t] <- phi[t]*p[t]
    # Above main diagonal
    for (j in (t+1):(n.occasions-1)){
        pr[t,j] <- prod(phi[t:j])*prod(q[t:(j-1)])*p[j]
        } #j
```

```
    # Below main diagonal
    for (j in 1:(t-1)){
        pr[t,j]<-0
        } #j
    } #t
# Last column: probability of non-recapture
for (t in 1:(n.occasions-1)){
    pr[t,n.occasions] <- 1-sum(pr[t,1:(n.occasions-1)])
    } # t

# Assess model fit using Freeman-Tukey statistic

# Compute fit statistics for observed data
for (t in 1:(n.occasions-1)){
    for (j in 1:n.occasions){
        expmarr[t,j] <- r[t]*pr[t,j]
        E.org[t,j] <- pow((pow(marr[t,j], 0.5)-pow(expmarr[t,j],
            0.5)), 2)
        }
    }

# Generate replicate data and compute fit stats from them
for (t in 1:(n.occasions-1)){
    marr.new[t,1:n.occasions] ~ dmulti(pr[t,], r[t])
    for (j in 1:n.occasions){
        E.new[t,j] <- pow((pow(marr.new[t,j], 0.5)-pow(expmarr[t,j],
            0.5)), 2)
        }
    }
fit <- sum(E.org[,])
fit.new <- sum(E.new[,])
}
",fill = TRUE)
sink()

# Bundle data
bugs.data <- list(marr = m.leisleri, n.occasions = dim(m.leisleri)[2])

# Initial values
inits <- function(){list(mean.phi = runif(1, 0, 1), sigma = runif(1, 0,
    5), mean.p = runif(1, 0, 1))}

# Parameters monitored
parameters <- c("phi", "mean.p", "mean.phi", "sigma2", "sigma2.real",
    "fit", "fit.new")

# MCMC settings
ni <- 5000
nt <- 3
nb <- 1000
nc <- 3

# Call WinBUGS from R (BRT 3 min)
leis.result <- bugs(bugs.data, inits, parameters, "cjs-mnl-ran.bug",
    n.chains = nc, n.thin = nt, n.iter = ni, n.burnin = nb, debug = TRUE,
    bugs.directory = bugs.dir, working.directory = getwd())
```

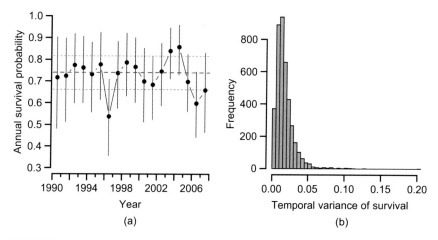

FIGURE 7.12   (a) Annual survival probability of adult female Leisler's bats (closed symbols, with 95% CRIs) and mean survival (red line; with 95% CRI dotted). (b) Posterior distribution of the temporal variance of adult survival.

The Markov chains converge quickly; with just 5000 iterations, we obtain satisfactory Rhat values (all <1.01). Mean annual survival is about 74%. Interestingly, and by chance, the recapture probability is numerically almost identical. Figure 7.12 plots the posterior distributions of the annual and mean survival probabilities as well as of the temporal variance. Annual survival probabilities were similar in most years, but in some, they were unusually low (1996–1997, 2006–2007) or unusually high (2003–2005). A next step in the demographic analysis of this population might be to find out which environmental factor is correlated with the temporal variation in survival, as shown in Section 7.4.3.

```
# Summarize posteriors
print(leis.result, digits = 3)
```

	mean	sd	2.5%	25%	50%	75%	97.5%	Rhat	n.eff
phi[1]	0.716	0.106	0.481	0.653	0.726	0.789	0.904	1.001	4000
[...]									
phi[18]	0.658	0.093	0.464	0.600	0.661	0.723	0.832	1.004	590
mean.p	0.747	0.029	0.689	0.728	0.748	0.766	0.800	1.001	4000
mean.phi	0.739	0.038	0.661	0.715	0.739	0.763	0.815	1.003	2700
sigma2	0.467	0.340	0.062	0.235	0.386	0.610	1.341	1.012	390
sigma2.real	0.017	0.013	0.002	0.009	0.014	0.022	0.048	1.013	450
fit	21.047	2.279	17.260	19.410	20.850	22.400	26.279	1.003	830
fit.new	18.950	3.458	12.950	16.450	18.705	21.100	26.370	1.001	4000

```
# Produce figure of female survival probabilities
par(mfrow = c(1, 2), las = 1, mar=c(4, 4, 2, 2), mgp = c(3, 1, 0))
lower <- upper <- numeric()
T <- dim(m.leisleri)[2]-1
```

```
for (t in 1:T) {
    lower[t] <- quantile(leis.result$sims.list$phi[,t], 0.025)
    upper[t] <- quantile(leis.result$sims.list$phi[,t], 0.975)
    }
plot(y = leis.result$mean$phi, x = (1:T)+0.5, type = "b", pch = 16, ylim =
    c(0.3, 1), ylab = "Annual survival probability", xlab = "", axes = F)
axis(1, at = seq(1, (T+1), 2), labels = seq(1990, 2008, 2))
axis(1, at = 1:(T+1), labels = rep("", T+1), tcl = -0.25)
axis(2, las = 1)
mtext("Year", 1, line = 2.25)
segments((1:T)+0.5, lower, (1:T)+0.5, upper)
segments(1, leis.result$mean$mean.phi, T+1, leis.result$mean$mean.phi,
    lty = 2, col = "red", lwd = 2)
segments(1, quantile(leis.result$sims.list$mean.phi,0.025), T+1,
    quantile(leis.result$sims.list$mean.phi, 0.025), lty = 2, col = "red")
segments(1, quantile(leis.result$sims.list$mean.phi, 0.975), T+1,
    quantile(leis.result$sims.list$mean.phi, 0.975), lty = 2, col = "red")
hist(leis.result$sims.list$sigma2.real, nclass = 45, col = "gray",
    main = "", las = 1, xlab = "")
mtext("Temporal variance of survival", 1, line = 2.25)
```

The GOF evaluation of the model shows a good fit (Fig. 7.13) with a Bayesian *p*-value of 0.27. The result is thus qualitatively the same as the GOF test performed in the frequentist framework (see above). Yet, the frequentist goodness-of-fit test evaluates the model with fixed year effects

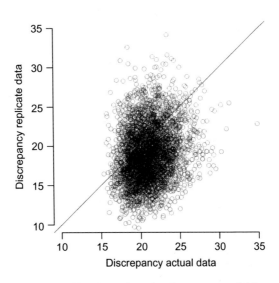

FIGURE 7.13   Scatter plot of replicate (simulated) versus actual (observed) discrepancy measures of model for female Leisler's bats. The Bayesian *p*-value is the proportion of points above the 1:1 equality line.

(ϕ_t, p_t), whereas the Bayesian test evaluates the model actually used for the estimation, that is, a model with random year effects on survival and constant recapture probabilities (ϕ_t, p.).

```
# Evaluation of fit
plot(leis.result$sims.list$fit, leis.result$sims.list$fit.new,
    main = "", xlab = "Discrepancy actual data", ylab = "Discrepancy
    replicate data", las = 1, ylim = c(10, 35), xlim = c(10, 35), frame = FALSE)
abline(0, 1, col = "black")
```

7.12 SUMMARY AND OUTLOOK

This chapter presents models of the Cormack–Jolly–Seber (CJS) class for analysis of capture–recapture data in the Bayesian framework to estimate probabilities of survival and recapture. We introduced two different approaches, based on a state-space or a multinomial likelihood. The state-space likelihood has the advantage that it is very flexible and especially enables us to fit models with individual effects, including random effects. The downside is that the Markov chains of these models take much longer per iteration and mix less well, resulting sometimes in a big computational burden. With the multinomial likelihood, we cannot fit models with individual effects, but otherwise the same models are possible as under a state-space likelihood. Use of the multinomial likelihood results in quicker updates and better mixing of the chains. We therefore recommend using the multinomial likelihood unless individual effects need to be fitted.

This chapter contains very important material for the broad class of capture–recapture models because we have introduced several key concepts. We have shown how we can model survival (and recapture) along the "time" as well as along the "individual" axes using GLM formulations (see also Chapter 6 for the analoguous concept to model detection probability). The corresponding models can have fixed or random effects, and there is great flexibility in combining them. In addition, we have introduced age-dependent models, which are a specific combination of effects along the time and the individual axes. We also have introduced goodness-of-fit testing using posterior predictive checks (Bayesian p-values). All these key concepts can be applied to the capture–recapture models in later chapters and indeed in an analogous way to all the models in the rest of the book.

Capture–recapture data could also be analyzed with the Jolly–Seber model (JS model; Williams et al., 2002), which is similar to the Cormack–Jolly–Seber model of this chapter. The main difference is that the CJS model conditions on first capture, whereas the JS model describes the complete capture-history. This means that the zeros before the first capture are not modeled in the CJS model, but they are in the JS model. The latter allows the estimation of additional parameters such as recruitment and population size, at the expense of additional assumptions. We describe the JS model in Chapter 10. Further extensions to this class of model include the robust design model (Kendall et al., 1997; Schofield et al., 2009), reverse-time modeling to estimate population growth rate (Pradel, 1996), or the relative contribution of survival and recruitment to population growth (Nichols et al., 2000). These could be implemented in WinBUGS as well.

This chapter was the first to introduce models for estimation of survival and related demographic parameters. Much of the material (e.g., m-array, state-space likelihood, random and fixed effects in survival) also carries over to similar models in Chapters 8–10. In Chapter 11, we will combine the CJS model with other models into an integrated population model.

7.13 EXERCISES

1. For reasons of greater generality, we always specify CJS models with a likelihood that allows all parameters to potentially vary by individual and time. For a beginner, this may not be the simplest way to fit a CJS model. Consider the constant model in Section 7.3 and adapt the BUGS model code so that we fit that model directly, without constraining the parameter matrices.

2. Simulate capture–recapture data of a species for males and females. The study is conducted for 15 years; the mean survival of males is 0.6 that of females is 0.5, and recapture is 0.4 for both. Assume that each year 30 individuals of each sex are newly marked. Fit the model $\{\phi_{sex}, p\}$ to the data using the multinomial likelihood.

3. Simulate capture–recapture data of a species for males and females. The study is conducted for 10 years, and each year 30 young and 20 adults of each sex are newly marked. The mean survival of young males is 0.3 (0.2 for females) and mean survival of adults of both sexes is 0.7. Further assume that the recapture probability of males is time-dependent [0.5, 0.6, 0.4, 0.4, 0.7, 0.5, 0.8, 0.3, 0.8]. Recapture probability of females varies in parallel to that of the males, it is a bit higher than that of males (difference on the logit scale: 0.3). Analyze these data with the data-generating model.

4. For the model in Section 7.3, do a simulation-based assessment of bias and precision. Generate a data set and then fit the model 500 times (perhaps for smaller sample size to save time) and each time save the estimates. On completion, print out the mean and the standard deviation of the estimates and also plot the distribution of these estimates. Is the estimator from the model biased? Where in the graph

can you see the standard error of the estimates? Are there other methods to check whether a model produces unbiased parameter estimates than simulation?

5. Take the data where survival of young and adult individuals is different (Section 7.7), but where only individuals of exact known age (marked as young) are included. Fit a model, in which survival after the second year changes linearly with increasing age.

6. Simulate data of a study that is running for 15 years, and each year 100 young individuals are marked. Survival in the first year is 0.4 on average with a temporal variability of 0.5 (on the logit scale), survival of older individuals is 0.8 without variability. Recapture probability is 0.6 for all individuals. Analyze these data with the data-generating model using the state-space and the multinomial likelihood.

Estimation of Survival Using Mark-Recovery Data

8.1 INTRODUCTION

Data on marked individuals that are reencountered alive formed the basis for the estimation of survival probabilities in the CJS models in Chapter 7. Here, we deal with another kind of data provided by marked individuals that serve the same goal: mark-recovery data. These data arise from animals that die and whose mark (typically a ring, but other marks are also possible) is recovered. As not all dead individuals will be found, the probability that a marked, dead individual is found (the recovery probability) must be estimated in addition to the survival probability. Thus, the dead-recovery probability takes the place of the live detection probability in the CJS models.

The sampling protocol is as follows: a number of individuals are marked, preferably over several years or other defined periods, and information is collected about the time of death from the marked individuals, which typically comes from members of the public, who find and report dead individuals. For each reported individual, we know the place and year of death and thus can compute its longevity. For all marked individuals that are not found or reported, we do not know when they die. However, the number of marked individuals that are never recovered is known and can be expressed as a function of the same survival and recovery probabilities that act on the recovered individuals. Hence, individuals that are not recovered contribute information about survival as well.

The unknown parameters are the survival probability (s) and the recovery probability (r). In theory, dead individuals can be found anywhere, not only in the study area. Hence, this survival probability is the true, rather than the apparent survival probability (ϕ) of the capture–recapture models in Chapter 7, where reencounters are usually restricted to fairly small areas. Apparent and true survival are linked by the fidelity probability (F, probability to remain within the study area), that is, $\phi = sF$. The recovery probability can be decomposed into a series of conditional binary events, such as the probability that an individual is found and the probability that the mark is reported. Sometimes, it is useful to consider them separately, resulting in a different parameterization of the mark-recovery model (Brownie et al., 1985).

Mark-recovery models are sometimes called dead-recovery or band-recovery models. They are primarily used for birds and in particular for hunted species because these have a much higher recovery probability than nongame species. The first treatise on these models was the handbook of Brownie et al. (1985), and a recent overview is provided in Williams et al. (2002). The Bayesian approach to these models is presented by Brooks et al. (2000a, 2000b, 2002), Barry et al. (2003), and Gimenez et al. (2007).

Here, we first show how the mark-recovery model can be fitted with a state-space formulation, the advantage of which is that we can apply exactly the same concepts (modeling along the time and individual axes; fixed and random effects) as introduced in Chapters 6 and 7; thus, we have great flexibility in modeling. However, we will not repeat these concepts here, but we just stress once more that all the key features introduced so far can be combined in a creative way. Second, we show the multinomial likelihood, which again enjoys great benefits in terms of computational efficiency.

8.2 THE MARK-RECOVERY MODEL AS A STATE-SPACE MODEL

Let us assume a newly marked individual at time t. It may survive until time $t + 1$ with probability s_t ($t = 1, ..., T - 1$; T being the number of occasions). Conceptually, we can imagine the individual tossing a coin to determine whether it survives (with probability s_t) or dies (with probability $1 - s_t$). Given that the individual is still alive at time $t + 1$, it may again survive until $t + 2$ with probability s_{t+1}. This is continued until either the individual is dead or the study ends. Clearly, once an individual is dead, its further fate is no longer a stochastic event, that is, it will remain dead with probability 1. What we have just described is the state process, that is, the possible states of an individual over time: dead or alive. As you may have noticed, this is exactly the same state process as in CJS models. The sole difference is a slightly different definition of the survival parameter: we use true survival in the ring-recovery model, whereas in the CJS model, it is the probability of surviving *and* remaining in the sampling area. The observation process for the mark-recovery model is different from the CJS model because only individuals that have just died can be observed (with probability r_t). Once an individual has been dead for a while, it cannot be recovered anymore because it has typically decayed. Another assumption of the model is that the time of death of a recovered individual is known to the accuracy of the temporal interval of the occasions (typically 1 year). In Fig. 8.1, the state and the observation processes are shown graphically.

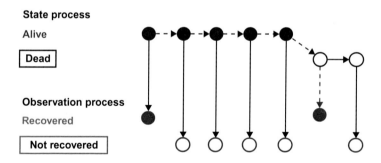

--- → Stochastic processes (survival and recovery)
——→ Deterministic process

FIGURE 8.1   Example of the state and observation process of a marked individual over time in the mark-recovery model. The sequence of true states in this individual is $z = [1, 1, 1, 1, 1, 0, 0]$, and the observed capture-history is $y = [1, 0, 0, 0, 0, 1, 0]$. The occasion at which the individual is marked produces a "recovery". This is just a convention to ensure that each capture-history starts with a 1.

The analysis of mark-recovery data with the state-space formulation is very similar to that of the CJS model. Again, we define the latent variable $z_{i,t}$, which takes value 1 if individual i is alive at time t and value 0 if it is dead. Thus, $z_{i,t}$ denotes the true state of individual i at time t. We also define the vector f_i that contains the occasion at which individual i is marked (its first encounter). The state of individual i at first encounter z_{i,f_i} is 1 with probability 1, that is, the individual is alive with certainty. The states at subsequent occasions are Bernoulli trials: conditional on being alive at occasion t, individual i survives until occasion $t+1$ with probability $s_{i,t}$. The following two equations define the state process:

$$z_{i,f_i} = 1$$

$$z_{i,t+1} \mid z_{i,t} \sim \text{Bernoulli}(z_{i,t}s_{i,t}).$$

The parameter of the Bernoulli trial is the product of the survival probability and the state variable z. The inclusion of z ensures that dead individuals (with $z = 0$) remain dead.

Given that individual i is "recently dead" at occasion t (i.e., has died between $t-1$ and t), it may be recovered with probability $r_{i,t}$ ($t = 2, \ldots, T$). The recovery, or observation, process is modeled as another Bernoulli trial with success probability $r_{i,t}$:

$$y_{i,t} \mid z_{i,t}, z_{i,t-1} \sim \text{Bernoulli}((z_{i,t-1} - z_{i,t})r_{i,t}).$$

The inclusion of the difference between the two successive values of latent variable z ensures that only individuals that are "recently dead" can be recovered. Matrix **y** contains the observed data, that is, the capture-histories. The state and the observation processes are both defined for $t \geq f_i$. The implementation of the model in the BUGS language now only requires the translation of these equations.

The mark-recovery model makes a number of assumptions that must be met to ensure unbiased parameter estimators. They are similar to those made in the CJS model. The survival and recovery probabilities are required to be identical for all individuals in the same group, cohort, or age class, and the fates of individuals must be independent. These assumptions can be tested with appropriate goodness-of-fit tests (Brownie et al., 1985). Furthermore, individuals must be reported without error (no misreading of the marks), and no mark loss is allowed.

8.2.1 Simulation of Mark-Recovery Data

We mimic a study of common terns (Fig. 8.2). Common terns live along rivers or coasts and breed in colonies, preferably on small islands. Adults are captured and marked, and some of them are found dead on migration

FIGURE 8.2   Common terns (*Sterna hirundo*), Finland, 2004 (Photograph by J. Peltomäki).

or at the breeding grounds. We assume that over 14 years, we mark 50 adults every year. We assume annual adult survival of 0.8 and a recovery probability of 0.2. The following R code simulates a mark-recovery matrix. The initial capture and the recovery event are both denoted with 1. The mark-recovery data matrix has 15 columns because common terns can still be recovered after the last year of marking.

```
# Define parameter values
n.occasions <- 14               # Number of release occasions
marked <- rep(50, n.occasions)  # Annual number of marked individuals
s <- rep(0.8, n.occasions)
r <- rep(0.2, n.occasions)

# Define matrices with survival and recovery probabilities
S <- matrix(s, ncol = n.occasions, nrow = sum(marked))
R <- matrix(r, ncol = n.occasions, nrow = sum(marked))

# Define function to simulate mark-recovery data
simul.mr <- function(S, R, marked){
    n.occasions <- dim(S)[2]
    MR <- matrix(NA, ncol = n.occasions+1, nrow = sum(marked))
    # Define a vector with the occasion of marking
    mark.occ <- rep(1:n.occasions, marked)
    # Fill the CH matrix
    for (i in 1:sum(marked)){
        MR[i, mark.occ[i]] <- 1    # Write an 1 at the release occasion
        for (t in mark.occ[i]:n.occasions){
```

```
# Bernoulli trial: has individual survived occasion?
sur <- rbinom(1, 1, S[i,t])
if (sur==1) next        # If still alive, move to next
                          occasion
# Bernoulli trial: has dead individual been recovered?
rp <- rbinom(1, 1, R[i,t])
if (rp==0){
  MR[i,t+1] <- 0
  break
  }
if (rp==1){
  MR[i,t+1] <- 1
  break
  }
      } #t
   } #i
      # Replace the NA in the file by 0
      MR[which(is.na(MR))] <- 0
      return(MR)
}

# Execute function
MR <- simul.mr(S, R, marked)
```

8.2.2 Analysis of a Model with Constant Parameters

To fit the dead-recovery model, we also need a vector indicating the occasion of marking for each individual.

```
# Create vector with occasion of marking
get.first <- function(x) min(which(x!=0))
f <- apply(MR, 1, get.first)
```

We define the model and run the analysis.

```
# Specify model in BUGS language
sink("mr.ss.bug")
cat("
model {

# Priors and constraints
for (i in 1:nind){
    for (t in f[i]:(n.occasions-1)){
        s[i,t] <- mean.s
        r[i,t] <- mean.r
        } #t
    } #i
mean.s ~ dunif(0, 1)        # Prior for mean survival
mean.r ~ dunif(0, 1)        # Prior for mean recapture

# Likelihood
for (i in 1:nind){
```

```
# Define latent state at first capture
z[i,f[i]] <- 1
for (t in (f[i]+1):n.occasions){
    # State process
    z[i,t] ~ dbern(mu1[i,t])
    mu1[i,t] <- s[i,t-1] * z[i,t-1]
    # Observation process
    y[i,t] ~ dbern(mu2[i,t])
    mu2[i,t] <- r[i,t-1] * (z[i,t-1] - z[i,t])
    } #t
} #i
}
",fill = TRUE)
sink()
```

For parameter estimation, we can either use the dead-recovery data matrix only or in addition provide information about the partly known latent state variable z (see Section 7.3.1). The latter results in faster computation and quicker convergence. In the dead-recovery model, the latent state variable is unknown for all individuals that are never recovered dead. However, for those that are recovered dead, the latent state is 1 for all occasions between marking and just prior to the recovery occasion and is 0 afterwards. The following function creates the known state variables from the dead-recovery matrix.

```
# Define function to create a matrix with information about known latent
    state z
known.state.mr <- function(mr){
    state <- matrix(NA, nrow = dim(mr)[1], ncol = dim(mr)[2])
    rec <- which(rowSums(mr)==2)
    for (i in 1:length(rec)){
        n1 <- min(which(mr[rec[i],]==1))
        n2 <- max(which(mr[rec[i],]==1))
        state[rec[i],n1:n2] <- 1
        state[rec[i],n1] <- NA
        state[rec[i],n2:dim(mr)[2]] <- 0
        }
    return(state)
    }
```

```
# Bundle data
bugs.data <- list(y = MR, f = f, nind = dim(MR)[1], n.occasions =
    dim(MR)[2], z = known.state.mr(MR))
```

```
# Define function to create a matrix of initial values for latent
    state z
mr.init.z <- function(mr){
    ch <- matrix(NA, nrow = dim(mr)[1], ncol = dim(mr)[2])
    rec <- which(rowSums(mr)==1)
    for (i in 1:length(rec)){
```

```
    n1 <- which(mr[rec[i],]==1)
    ch[rec[i],n1:dim(mr)[2]] <- 0
    ch[rec[i],n1] <- NA
    }
 return(ch)
 }
```

```
# Initial values
inits <- function() {list(z = mr.init.z(MR), mean.s = runif(1, 0, 1),
   mean.r = runif(1, 0, 1))}
```

```
# Parameters monitored
parameters <- c("mean.s", "mean.r")
```

```
# MCMC settings
ni <- 5000
nt <- 6
nb <- 2000
nc <- 3
```

```
# Call WinBUGS from R (BRT 4 min)
mr.ss <- bugs(bugs.data, inits, parameters, "mr.ss.bug", n.chains =
   nc, n.thin = nt, n.iter = ni, n.burnin = nb, debug = TRUE,
   bugs.directory = bugs.dir)
```

The posterior means obtained with the state-space likelihood are nearly identical to those obtained with the multinomial likelihood (see Section 8.3). However, the state-space likelihood is computationally more demanding, and we need longer chains to achieve convergence.

```
print(mr.ss, digits = 3)
          mean     sd   2.5%    25%    50%    75%  97.5%   Rhat  n.eff
mean.s   0.754  0.027  0.699  0.737  0.755  0.773  0.802  1.008    400
mean.r   0.190  0.019  0.157  0.177  0.190  0.202  0.230  1.000   1500
```

As mentioned already, we can apply all the modeling encountered in the CJS within the framework of this basic model (i.e., the likelihood part). The changes required in the BUGS code are restricted to the model section entitled "Priors and constraints".

8.3 THE MARK-RECOVERY MODEL FITTED WITH THE MULTINOMIAL LIKELIHOOD

8.3.1 Constant Parameters

The multinomial likelihood is the classical way to analyze mark-recovery data (Brownie et al., 1985; Williams et al., 2002). For this, the mark-recovery data are first summarized in the m-array (see Section 7.10). In this matrix, rows represent the release (marking) years, and the columns represent recovery years. The only difference between the mark-recovery and the capture–recapture m-array is that in the former, all individuals that are released in a year (i.e., form a release cohort) remain in the same row of the matrix because they can be reencountered at most once; they are not released after recovery (difficult if they are dead …). In the capture–recapture m-array, some individuals are released again in subsequent occasions and thus appear in more than one row of the matrix.

The following R code produces the necessary m-array for the mark-recovery data.

```
# Define function to create an m-array based for mark-recovery (MR) data
marray.dead <- function(MR) {
    nind <- dim(MR)[1]
    n.occasions <- dim(MR)[2]
    m.array <- matrix(data = 0, ncol = n.occasions+1, nrow =
        n.occasions)
    # Create vector with occasion of marking
    get.first <- function(x) min(which(x!=0))
    f <- apply(MR, 1, get.first)
    # Calculate the number of released individuals at each time period
    first <- as.numeric(table(f))
    for (t in 1:n.occasions) {
        m.array[t,1] <- first[t]
    }
    # Fill m-array with recovered individuals
    rec.ind <- which(apply(MR, 1, sum)==2)
    rec <- numeric()
    for (i in 1:length(rec.ind)) {
        d <- which(MR[rec.ind[i], (f[rec.ind[i]]+1):n.occasions]==1)
        rec[i] <- d+f[rec.ind[i]]
        m.array[f[rec.ind[i]],rec[i]] <- m.array[f[rec.ind[i]],
            rec[i]] +1
    }
    # Calculate the number of individuals that are never recovered
    for (t in 1:n.occasions) {
        m.array[t,n.occasions+1] <- m.array[t,1]-sum(m.array[t,2:
            n.occasions])
    }
    out <- m.array[1:(n.occasions-1),2:(n.occasions+1)]
    return(out)
}
```

We produce the m-array for the simulated data by executing the function:

```
marr <- marray.dead(MR)
```

This m-array contains the observed response. Each row is modeled as a multinomial trial with index equal to the cohort size, that is, the number of individuals released in that year. The multinomial cell probabilities are functions of the parameters for survival and recovery (s and r).

We first fit a model with constant parameters over time, but we have introduced an index of time (subscript) here in order to understand the model better. The cell probabilities are as follows:

Released at Occasion	Recovered at Occasion			
	2	3	4	Never Recovered
1	$(1-s_1)r_1$	$s_1(1-s_2)r_2$	$s_1s_2(1-s_3)r_3$	$(1-s_1)(1-r_1) + s_1(1-s_2)(1-r_2) +$ $s_1s_2(1-s_3)(1-r_3) + s_1s_2s_3 =$ $1 - \Sigma$ (Released at Occasion 1)
2	0	$(1-s_2)r_2$	$s_2(1-s_3)r_3$	$(1-s_2)(1-r_2) + s_2(1-s_3)(1-r_3) +$ $s_2s_3 = 1 - \Sigma$ (Released at Occasion 2)
3	0	0	$(1-s_3)r_3$	$(1-s_3)(1-r_3) + s_3 =$ $1 - \Sigma$ (Released at Occasion 3)

To fit this model in BUGS, we essentially have to define these cell probabilities. The probability for individuals never recovered may look complicated but is simply 1 minus the sum of the other probabilities in each row.

```
# Specify model in BUGS language
sink("mr-mnl.bug")
cat("
model {

# Priors and constraints
for (t in 1:n.occasions){
    s[t] <- mean.s
    r[t] <- mean.r
    }
mean.s ~ dunif(0, 1)          # Prior for mean survival
mean.r ~ dunif(0, 1)          # Prior for mean recovery

# Define the multinomial likelihood
for (t in 1:n.occasions){
    marr[t,1:(n.occasions+1)] ~ dmulti(pr[t,], rel[t])
    }

# Calculate the number of birds released each year
for (t in 1:n.occasions){
    rel[t] <- sum(marr[t,])
    }

# Define the cell probabilities of the m-array
# Main diagonal
for (t in 1:n.occasions){
    pr[t,t] <- (1-s[t])*r[t]
    # Above main diagonal
    for (j in (t+1):n.occasions){
        pr[t,j] <- prod(s[t:(j-1)])*(1-s[j])*r[j]
        } #j
```

```
# Below main diagonal
for (j in 1:(t-1)){
    pr[t,j] <- 0
    } #j
} #t
# Last column: probability of non-recovery
for (t in 1:n.occasions){
    pr[t,n.occasions+1] <- 1-sum(pr[t,1:n.occasions])
    } #t
}
",fill = TRUE)
sink()
```

Now, we run the mark-recovery model using the m-array data.

```
# Bundle data
bugs.data <- list(marr = marr, n.occasions = dim(marr)[2]-1)

# Initial values
inits<- function(){list(mean.s = runif(1, 0, 1), mean.r = runif(1, 0, 1))}

# Parameters monitored
parameters <- c("mean.s", "mean.r")

# MCMC settings
ni <- 5000
nt <- 6
nb <- 2000
nc <- 3

# Call WinBUGS from R (BRT <1 min)
mr <- bugs(bugs.data, inits, parameters, "mr-mnl.bug", n.chains = nc,
    n.thin = nt, n.iter = ni, n.burnin = nb, debug = TRUE, bugs.directory =
    bugs.dir)

# Summarize posteriors
print(mr, digits = 3)
          mean     sd   2.5%    25%    50%    75%  97.5%    Rhat  n.eff
mean.s   0.758  0.033  0.691  0.736  0.757  0.782  0.823   1.003    910
mean.r   0.192  0.020  0.156  0.179  0.191  0.204  0.236   1.001   1500
```

Convergence of the chains is not difficult to achieve. The posterior distributions of both parameters include the input values of 0.8 and 0.2 (Fig. 8.3).

```
par(mfrow = c(1, 2), las = 1)
hist(mr$sims.list$mean.s, nclass = 25, col = "gray", main = "", ylab =
    "Frequency", xlab = "Survival probability")
abline(v = 0.8, col = "red", lwd = 2)
hist(mr$sims.list$mean.r, nclass = 25, col = "gray", main = "", ylab =
    "", xlab = "Recovery probability")
abline(v = 0.2, col = "red", lwd = 2)
```

It is straightforward to build more complicated models, for example, with different groups, or fixed or random temporal variation. The BUGS

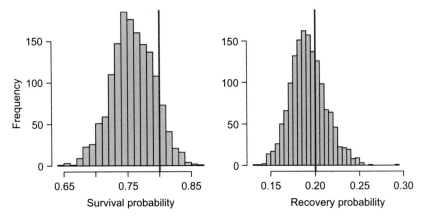

FIGURE 8.3 Posterior distributions of survival and recovery probabilities in the analysis of the simulated data (red line: values used for simulating the data).

code just has to be adapted in exactly the same way as explained for the capture–recapture models (Chapter 7). Basically, the only changes are made in the model section entitled "Priors and constraints".

8.3.2 Age-Dependent Parameters

Survival typically changes with age; hence, age-dependent models are often important. Sometimes, even recovery probability may change with age. Age-dependent recovery probabilities can occur if the main mortality cause changes with age, and different mortality causes are associated with differential recovery probabilities. For example, individuals dying from human-related causes are more likely found by humans than individuals dying from natural causes. As an example, the recovery probability of white storks (*Ciconia ciconia*) dying from power line collisions is significantly higher than for other causes of mortality (Schaub and Pradel, 2004).

We stay with our common tern example, and assume that young (nestlings) and adults are marked. We assume survival to be 0.3 for juveniles and 0.8 for adults. The recovery probabilities for juveniles and adults are 0.25 and 0.15, respectively. We simulate two data sets: one for individuals marked as young and another for individuals marked as adults. We summarize both data sets independently as an m-array.

```
n.occasions <- 15                    # Number of occasions
marked.j <- rep(200, n.occasions)    # Annual number of newly marked
                                       young
marked.a <- rep(20, n.occasions)     # Annual number of newly marked
                                       adults
sjuv <- 0.3                          # Juvenile survival probability
sad <- 0.8                           # Adult survival probability
```

```
rjuv <- 0.25                    # Juvenile recovery probability
rad <- 0.15                     # Adult recovery probability
sj <- c(sjuv, rep(sad, n.occasions-1))
rj <- c(rjuv, rep(rad, n.occasions-1))

# Define matrices with survival and recovery probabilities
SJ <- matrix(0, ncol = n.occasions, nrow = sum(marked.j))
for (i in 1:length(marked.j)){
    SJ[(sum(marked.j[1:i])-marked.j[i]+1):sum(marked.j[1:i]),
        i:n.occasions] <- matrix(rep(sj[1:(n.occasions-i+1)],
        marked.j[i]), ncol = n.occasions-i+1, byrow = TRUE)
    }
SA <- matrix(sad, ncol = n.occasions, nrow = sum(marked.a))
RJ <- matrix(0, ncol = n.occasions, nrow = sum(marked.j))
for (i in 1:length(marked.j)){
    RJ[(sum(marked.j[1:i])-marked.j[i]+1):sum(marked.j[1:i]),
        i:n.occasions] <- matrix(rep(rj[1:(n.occasions-i+1)],
        marked.j[i]), ncol = n.occasions-i+1, byrow = TRUE)
    }
RA <- matrix(rad, ncol = n.occasions, nrow = sum(marked.a))

# Execute simulation function
MRj <- simul.mr(SJ, RJ, marked.j)
MRa <- simul.mr(SA, RA, marked.a)

# Summarize data in m-arrays
marr.j <- marray.dead(MRj)
marr.a <- marray.dead(MRa)
```

The cell probabilities in the modeling of the m-array for adults are exactly the same as before except for s_i and r_i, which we now denote sa_i and ra_i, respectively. In contrast, the cell probabilities for the model of individuals marked as nestlings differ: for them, we have to include an age structure for the survival and recovery probabilities. These cell probabilities are as follows:

Released at Occasion	Recovered at Occasion			Never Recovered
	2	**3**	**4**	
1	$(1 - sj_1)rj_1$	$sj_1(1 - sa_2)ra_2$	$sj_1sa_2(1 - sa_3)ra_3$	$1 - \Sigma$ (Released at Occasion 1)
2	0	$(1 - sj_2)rj_2$	$sj_2(1 - sa_3)ra_3$	$1 - \Sigma$ (Released at Occasion 2)
3	0	0	$(1 - sj_3)rj_3$	$1 - \Sigma$ (Released at Occasion 3)

In the model, we define the probabilities of both m-arrays separately, with some parameters (sa and ra) shared.

```
# Specify model in BUGS language
sink("mr-mnl-age.bug")
cat("
model {
```

```
# Priors and constraints
for (t in 1:n.occasions){
    sj[t] <- mean.sj
    sa[t] <- mean.sa
    rj[t] <- mean.rj
    ra[t] <- mean.ra
    }
mean.sj ~ dunif(0, 1)              # Prior for mean juv.survival
mean.sa ~ dunif(0, 1)              # Prior for mean ad.survival
mean.rj ~ dunif(0, 1)              # Prior for mean juv.recovery
mean.ra ~ dunif(0, 1)              # Prior for mean ad.recovery

# Define the multinomial likelihoods
for (t in 1:n.occasions){
    marr.j[t,1:(n.occasions+1)] ~ dmulti(pr.j[t,], rel.j[t])
    marr.a[t,1:(n.occasions+1)] ~ dmulti(pr.a[t,], rel.a[t])
    }

# Calculate the number of birds released each year
for (t in 1:n.occasions){
    rel.j[t] <- sum(marr.j[t,])
    rel.a[t] <- sum(marr.a[t,])
    }

# Define the cell probabilities of the juvenile m-array
# Main diagonal
for (t in 1:n.occasions){
    pr.j[t,t] <- (1-sj[t])*rj[t]
    # Further above main diagonal
    for (j in (t+2):n.occasions){
        pr.j[t,j] <- sj[t]*prod(sa[(t+1):(j-1)])*(1-sa[j])*ra[j]
        } #j
    # Below main diagonal
    for (j in 1:(t-1)){
        pr.j[t,j] <- 0
        } #j
    } #t
for (t in 1:(n.occasions-1)){
    # One above main diagonal
    pr.j[t,t+1] <- sj[t]*(1-sa[t+1])*ra[t+1]
    } #t
# Last column: probability of non-recovery
for (t in 1:n.occasions){
    pr.j[t,n.occasions+1] <- 1-sum(pr.j[t,1:n.occasions])
    } #t

# Define the cell probabilities of the adult m-array
# Main diagonal
for (t in 1:n.occasions){
    pr.a[t,t] <- (1-sa[t])*ra[t]
    # Above main diagonal
    for (j in (t+1):n.occasions){
        pr.a[t,j] <- prod(sa[t:(j-1)])*(1-sa[j])*ra[j]
        } #j
```

```
     # Below main diagonal
     for (j in 1:(t-1)){
          pr.a[t,j] <- 0
          } #j
        } #t
   # Last column: probability of non-recovery
   for (t in 1:n.occasions){
        pr.a[t,n.occasions+1] <- 1-sum(pr.a[t,1:n.occasions])
        } #t
   }
   ",fill = TRUE)
   sink()
```

We prepare the remainder of the analysis and run the mark-recovery model.

```
# Bundle data
bugs.data <- list(marr.j = marr.j, marr.a = marr.a, n.occasions =
   dim(marr.j)[2]-1)

# Initial values
inits <- function(){list(mean.sj = runif(1, 0, 1), mean.sa =
   runif(1, 0, 1), mean.rj = runif(1, 0, 1), mean.ra = runif(1, 0, 1))}

# Parameters monitored
parameters <- c("mean.sj", "mean.rj", "mean.sa", "mean.ra")

# MCMC settings
ni <- 5000
nt <- 6
nb <- 2000
nc <- 3

# Call WinBUGS from R (BRT <1 min)
mr.age <- bugs(bugs.data, inits, parameters, "mr-mnl-age.bug",
   n.chains = nc, n.thin = nt, n.iter = ni, n.burnin = nb, debug =
   TRUE, bugs.directory = bugs.dir)
```

As before, convergence is achieved fairly quickly.

```
print(mr.age, digits = 3)
          mean     sd  2.5%    25%    50%    75% 97.5%   Rhat  n.eff
mean.sj  0.289  0.051  0.205  0.252  0.283  0.319  0.402  1.000   1500
mean.rj  0.254  0.022  0.219  0.239  0.250  0.265  0.304  1.001   1500
mean.sa  0.797  0.025  0.748  0.779  0.797  0.814  0.848  1.000   1500
mean.ra  0.192  0.029  0.140  0.171  0.190  0.210  0.251  1.000   1500
```

8.4 REAL-DATA EXAMPLE: AGE-DEPENDENT SURVIVAL IN SWISS RED KITES

The red kite (Fig. 8.4) is a large bird of prey that is declining in many parts of Europe but widespread in the Swiss lowlands. During the past 50 years, 1480 nestlings and 152 adults (>2 years old) have been marked,

FIGURE 8.4   Red kite (*Milvus milvus*), Switzerland (Photograph by P. Keusch).

of which 107 individuals were recovered dead. Our interest was to estimate age-specific survival probabilities; we were not interested in any changes over time. Therefore, we considered all individuals marked at the same age as a single release cohort. Here, we have two age classes at marking: juveniles and adults. Since we drop the time index, the resulting m-array of both age classes consists only of a single line, with "columns" referring to the age at which individuals are recovered. Strictly speaking, only in the m-array for individuals marked as juveniles do the columns correspond to true age because in these individuals true age is known. In the m-array of the adults, columns refer to the age since marking (in years) because the age of these individuals at marking is unknown. For example, in the data given below, we see that 1388 of all individuals marked as juveniles are never found, whereas five individuals are found dead in their third year of life. Here are the data for the individuals marked as juveniles and those marked as adults.

```
marray.juv <- c(42, 18, 5, 7, 4, 3, 2, 1, 2, 2, 1, 0, 1, 3, 0, 0, 1, 1388)
marray.ad <- c(3, 1, 1, 3, 0, 2, 1, 0, 1, 1, 0, 1, 1, 0, 0, 0, 0, 137)
```

In long-lived birds, survival usually varies with age. Here, we fit a survival model with three age classes. The first age class (juveniles) covers one year from fledging, the second age class (subadults) also covers one year from one to two years of age, and the last age class (adults) contains all ages 2 years and greater. For recovery probability, we only assume two age classes and distinguish the first year after fledging from all ages thereafter. Juvenile survival in mark-recovery models is sometimes difficult to estimate (see discussion below), and therefore, we will also try to utilize a priori information on juvenile survival. Few estimates of juvenile survival in red kites are available, and most of them were obtained using dated methods, that is, ignoring imperfect detection. On average, juvenile survival is likely to be about 0.6 but with a large uncertainty (Aebischer, 2009). We translated this knowledge into a beta prior distribution with parameters 4.2 and 2.8. This ensured a mean of 0.6 and a relatively wide spread of the prior (standard deviation $\cong 0.173$). To assess prior sensitivity, we also fitted a model with a flat uniform prior (U(0,1)). The BUGS code above needs some adaptations because we now have three age classes, but only two release cohorts: juveniles and adults.

```
# Specify model in BUGS language
sink("mr-mnl-age3.bug")
cat("
model {

# Priors and constraints
sjuv ~ dbeta(4.2, 2.8)      # Informative prior for juv. survival:
                            Analysis A
#sjuv ~ dunif(0, 1)         # Non-informative for juv. survival prior:
                            Analysis B
ssub ~ dunif(0, 1)          # Prior for subad. survival
sad ~ dunif(0, 1)           # Prior for ad. survival
rjuv ~ dunif(0, 1)          # Prior for juv. recovery
rad ~ dunif(0, 1)           # Prior for ad. recovery

# Define the multinomial likelihoods
marr.j[1:(n.age+1)] ~ dmulti(pr.j[], rel.j)
marr.a[1:(n.age+1)] ~ dmulti(pr.a[], rel.a)

# Calculate the number of birds released each year
rel.j <- sum(marr.j[])
rel.a <- sum(marr.a[])

# Define the cell probabilities of the juvenile m-array
# First element
pr.j[1] <- (1-sjuv)*rjuv
# Second element
pr.j[2] <- sjuv*(1-ssub)*rad
# Third and further elements
for (t in 3:n.age){
    pr.j[t] <- sjuv*ssub*pow(sad,(t-3))*(1-sad)*rad
    }
# Probability of non-recovery
pr.j[n.age+1] <- 1    sum(pr.j[1:n.age])
```

```
# Define the cell probabilities of the adult m-array
# All elements
for (t in 1:n.age){
    pr.a[t] <- pow(sad, (t-1))*(1-sad)*rad
    }
# Probability of non-recovery
pr.a[n.age+1] <- 1-sum(pr.a[1:n.age])
}
",fill = TRUE)
sink()
```

 # Bundle data
```
bugs.data <- list(marr.j = marray.juv, marr.a = marray.ad, n.age =
    length(marray.juv)-1)
```

 # Initial values
```
inits <- function(){list(sjuv = runif(1, 0, 1), ssub = runif(1, 0, 1),
    sad = runif(1, 0, 1), rjuv = runif(1, 0, 1), rad = runif(1, 0, 1))}
```

 # Parameters monitored
```
parameters <- c("sjuv", "ssub", "sad", "rjuv", "rad")
```

 # MCMC settings
```
ni <- 30000
nt <- 10
nb <- 10000
nc <- 3
```

 # Call WinBUGS from R (BRT <1 min)
```
rk.ageA <- bugs(bugs.data, inits, parameters, "mr-mnl-age3.bug",
    n.chains = nc, n.thin = nt, n.iter = ni, n.burnin = nb, debug =
    TRUE, bugs.directory = bugs.dir)
```

Convergence is reached quickly. Here are the posterior summaries for the estimated parameters.

```
print(rk.ageA, digits = 3)
```

	mean	sd	2.5%	25%	50%	75%	97.5%	Rhat	n.eff
sjuv	0.450	0.128	0.248	0.358	0.431	0.525	0.751	1.003	1100
ssub	0.655	0.067	0.521	0.611	0.658	0.702	0.780	1.001	2800
sad	0.841	0.032	0.778	0.820	0.842	0.863	0.904	1.001	4900
rjuv	0.057	0.027	0.033	0.043	0.051	0.062	0.119	1.002	1700
rad	0.090	0.024	0.051	0.073	0.088	0.104	0.143	1.002	1700

As shown below, parameter estimates under the model with noninformative priors are similar (for this, we repeat the analysis with one prior statement switched) to those under the model with informative priors. Two exceptions are the posterior mean of juvenile survival (lower) and the standard deviation of the juvenile recovery probability (higher). Thus, the prior information introduced for juvenile survival affected also juvenile recovery probability (and even adult recovery probability). This is not very surprising.

```
print(rk.ageB, digits = 3)
       mean     sd   2.5%    25%    50%    75%  97.5%   Rhat  n.eff
sjuv  0.406  0.139  0.216  0.309  0.378  0.473  0.773  1.003    920
ssub  0.656  0.067  0.518  0.612  0.660  0.703  0.779  1.001   6000
sad   0.842  0.032  0.779  0.820  0.842  0.864  0.906  1.001   6000
rjuv  0.057  0.060  0.031  0.040  0.047  0.057  0.129  1.001   3500
rad   0.099  0.027  0.052  0.080  0.097  0.116  0.159  1.003   1000
```

Inspection of the posterior distributions of the five parameters under the model with noninformative priors shows that subadult and adult survival and adult recovery probability are estimated precisely (Fig. 8.5). By contrast, the posterior distribution of juvenile survival is quite wide and has some of its mass extending to 1, whereas that of juvenile recovery is skewed. This does not mean that we cannot trust the estimates; it simply indicates that there is considerable uncertainty about the values of these parameters. This behavior is due to intrinsic identifiability problems. When survival and recovery probabilities are age dependent and only data of individuals marked as juveniles are available, only adult survival is identifiable (Anderson et al., 1985). Here, we have a different number of age classes for survival and recovery, and we included also data on individuals marked as adults; thus, the parameters in the model are intrinsically identifiable. Yet, from the posterior distributions of juvenile survival in particular, we see that the available information is a bit scarce.

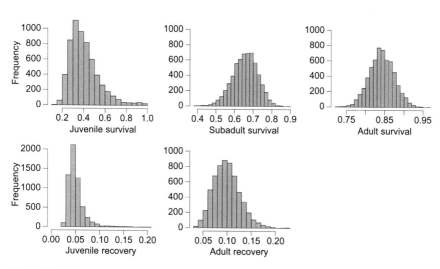

FIGURE 8.5   Posterior distributions of survival and recovery probabilities of Swiss red kites under model B with noninformative priors.

```
par(mfrow = c(2, 3), las = 1)
hist(rk.ageB$sims.list$sjuv, breaks = 20, col = "gray", main = "",
    xlab = "Juvenile survival")
hist(rk.ageB$sims.list$ssub, breaks = 20, col = "gray", main = "",
    xlab = "Subadult survival")
hist(rk.ageB$sims.list$sad, breaks = 20, col = "gray", main = "",
    xlab = "Adult survival")
hist(rk.ageB$sims.list$rjuv, breaks = 20, col = "gray", main = "",
    xlab = "Juvenile recovery", xlim = c(0, 0.2))
hist(rk.ageB$sims.list$rad, breaks = 20, col = "gray", main = "",
    xlab = "Adult recovery")
```

Comparison of the posterior distributions of juvenile survival under the two priors shows that both are similar (Fig. 8.6). Thus, existing information from the literature did not have a very strong impact, and the uncertainty about juvenile survival was not much reduced. We would just like to note that the specification of informative priors can be a challenge, and there may be better ways than the ad hoc approach in our example (e.g., McCarthy and Masters, 2005; Servanthy et al., 2010).

```
plot(density(rk.ageA$sims.list$sjuv), ylim = c(0, 5), lwd = 2,
    main = "", xlab = "Juvenile survival", las = 1)
points(density(rk.ageB$sims.list$sjuv), col = "red", type = "l",
    lwd = 2)
text(x = 0.5, y = 4.8, "Prior distributions", pos = 4, font = 3)
legend(x = 0.6, y = 4.7, legend = c("U(0,1)", "beta(4.2,2.8)"),
    lwd = c(2, 2), col = c("black", "red"), bty = "n")
```

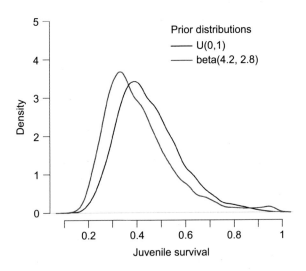

FIGURE 8.6 Posterior distributions of juvenile red kite survival with an informative (beta(4.2, 2.8), red) and a noninformative (U(0, 1), black) prior.

Finally, we reiterate the ease with which derived quantities are estimated in a Bayesian framework with posterior sampling: just compute the derived quantity for every MCMC iteration and summarize that new MCMC sample. For instance, here are the 95% CRI for the differences between juvenile and subadult and between subadult and adult survival:

```
quantile(rk.ageA$sims.list$ssub-rk.ageA$sims.list$sjuv, prob =
  c(0.025, 0.975))
     2.5%        97.5%
 -0.1106200   0.4867075

quantile(rk.ageA$sims.list$sad-rk.ageA$sims.list$ssub, prob =
  c(0.025, 0.975))
     2.5%        97.5%
  0.0595925   0.3242150
```

8.5 SUMMARY AND OUTLOOK

We have introduced an important class of models for estimation of survival and recovery probabilities from mark-recovery data, typically for birds. We have shown two different parameterizations of the model. The model based on the multinomial likelihood is computationally cheaper and can be extended to include groups, temporal covariates, as well as age classes. The model based on the state-space likelihood is required if we want to fit individual covariates, but this comes at the expense of much longer computational time. The combination of age-effects and individual covariates is best done with multistate models (Chapter 9).

Mark-recovery models have a long history, and many variants exist. They include models for the estimation of seasonal survival probabilities (Tavecchia et al., 2002), kill rates (Nichols et al., 1991), the proportion of animals dying from different mortality causes (Schaub and Pradel, 2004), and spatial variation of recovery probabilities (Royle and Dubovsky, 2001), to name just a few. Williams et al. (2002) provide a recent review of mark-recovery models and include plenty of additional information, such as different parameterizations, study design, or goodness-of-fit testing.

Mark-recovery data can also be analyzed with multistate models (Lebreton et al., 1999; Gauthier and Lebreton, 2008; see also Section 9.5). Moreover, it is possible to jointly analyze mark recovery and capture–recapture data, although they provide different measures of survival. Multistate capture–recapture models are the best tool to conduct such a joint analysis (see Section 9.5).

8.6 EXERCISES

1. Simulate mark-recovery data of two groups: both groups have a survival probability of 0.5, the first group has a recovery probability of 0.1, and the second group has a recovery probability of 0.2. The study is

conducted for 10 years, and each year, 50 individuals are marked in each group. Fit the model (s, r_g) using (1) the multinomial and (2) the state-space likelihoods.

2. It is quite typical for population studies that only nestlings are marked but no adult individuals. This is because the capture of adults is often much more time consuming than the marking of nestlings, which can be easily marked in the nest. Simulate data from a study on a common tern population in which only nestlings are marked. The study duration is 15 years; in each year, 200 nestlings are marked, and the parameters are $sj = 0.3$, $sa = 0.8$, $rj = 0.25$, and $ra = 0.15$. Analyze these data with (1) the data-generating model and (2) using a model in which the recovery probability is the same in both age classes. Comment on the parameter estimates that you obtain from both models.

3. Simulate mark-recovery data with the following characteristics: one group, during each of the 20 study years 500 individuals are released, the survival probability declines linearly from 0.8 in the first year to 0.6 in the last study year, whereas the recovery probability is constant at 0.05. Analyze these data with the multinomial model.

4. Because of differential behavior, the recovery probability may show strong individual variation. Simulate mark-recovery data for a population with mean survival of 0.7 and a mean recovery probability of 0.2. The variance of the recovery probability among individuals is 0.7 (on the logit scale). Assume that the study lasts 10 years and that each year 100 individuals are released. Analyze the data with (1) the data-generating model and (2) with a model that assume a common recovery probability for all individuals. What is the impact on the estimate of the survival probability?

CHAPTER

9

Estimation of Survival and Movement from Capture–Recapture Data Using Multistate Models

9.1 INTRODUCTION

When an individual is encountered, it is often possible to assign it to a certain *state*. A state may be described as a categorical individual covariate that can change over time. A state may be a geographical location, a class of reproductive success, or a disease status, to name just a few. Stratification of individuals according to their state then allows estimation of state-dependent survival and recapture probabilities, as well as state-transition probabilities. In this chapter, we extend the seminal CJS model from Chapter 7 to more than a single state. Perhaps not surprisingly, the resulting model is called a multistate (or historically also multistrata) model (Lebreton et al., 2009).

Depending on how the states are defined, a vast array of research questions can be addressed using this broad class of capture–recapture models. For example, if states represent geographic locations, we can estimate movement probabilities among locations, that is, dispersal. We may test whether movement is symmetrical or is related to habitat quality of a location. If states represent "not infected by a disease" and "infected by a disease", we may study whether survival is related to disease status or identify conditions that are positively correlated with the infection probability, that is, the transition probability from "not infected" to "infected". State definitions may also be less obvious. States could be age classes, which allows estimation of age-dependent survival probabilities, they could be "dead" and "alive" enabling modeling of mark-recovery data or the joint analysis of capture–recapture and mark-recovery data, they could be "present" and "absent" allowing estimation of temporary emigration, or they could be "captured" and "not captured", which enables fitting of models with immediate trap response. In fact, multistate capture–recapture models are extremely useful and should be used for many interesting ecological questions. Multistate models represent a unification of many different kinds of capture–recapture model (Lebreton et al., 1999, 2009).

There are many applications of multistate models in the frequentist framework. As an example, see the seminal papers by Arnason (1972, 1973), Hestbeck et al. (1991), Schwarz et al. (1993), Lebreton and Pradel (2002) and the review by Lebreton et al. (2009). Much fewer authors have adopted the Bayesian framework so far (e.g., Dupuis, 1995; King and Brooks, 2002; Gimenez et al., 2003; King and Brooks, 2004; Clark et al., 2005; Dupuis and Schwarz, 2007; Calvert et al., 2009; Schofield et al., 2009; King et al., 2010; Schaub et al., 2010).

As the single-state capture–recapture and mark-recovery models in Chapters 7 and 8, multistate capture–recapture models can be analyzed either in a state-space modeling framework or using a multinomial like-lihood. Frequentist analyses typically use the multinomial likelihood applied to the multistate m-array (Williams et al., 2002). This approach requires definition of all cell probabilities in the multistate m-array, which is straightforward when matrix multiplication is available in a soft-ware. Unfortunately, matrix multiplication is not available in WinBUGS (though it is in JAGS); hence, we will only use the state-space formulation here. It has the advantage that exactly the same concepts (modeling along the time and individual axis, with fixed and random effects) as introduced in Chapters 6 and 7 can be applied providing great flexibility in modeling. We will not repeat these concepts in this chapter anymore, but refer to Chapters 6 and 7 and to the exercises. The state equation of the state-space formulation describes the true development of the states, that is, it describes the state of an individual at time $t + 1$, given its state at time t. The observation equation maps the true state at time t on to the observed state. Since there are more than two possible true and observed states, the likelihood is not based on the Bernoulli distribution, as is the case with single-state capture–recapture models, but on the categorical distribution. The categorical distribution is the extension of a Bernoulli distribution to more than two categories. It is a special case of the multinomial distribu-tion with trial size equal to 1.

For a description of the state process in a system with two geographic locations, let us assume that a marked individual is at location 1 (referred to as state 1) at time t. At the next sampling occasion, $t + 1$, this individual may still be alive, and at location 1 with probability $\Phi_{11,t}$, it may still be alive but has moved to location 2 (state 2) with probability $\Phi_{12,t}$, or it may be dead with probability $1 - \Phi_{11,t} - \Phi_{12,t}$. If the individual is still alive at time $t + 1$, it may again survive and move among locations. If the indivi-dual is at location 2 at time $t + 1$, then the corresponding probability to survive and move to location 1 is $\Phi_{21,t+1}$, the probability to survive and remain at location 2 is $\Phi_{22,t+1}$, and the probability to die is the complement of the two, that is, $1 - \Phi_{21,t+1} - \Phi_{22,t+1}$. This is continued until the individual is either dead or a study ends. Once an individual is dead, its fate is no longer stochastic; the individual will remain dead with probability 1 until the end of the study. These probabilities define the state process, and we would like to know the parameters governing this process. Yet, inevitably, we cannot observe the state process without errors. Instead, we augment our system description with a component that describes the observation process. A marked individual that is alive at time t in state 1 may be encountered in state 1 with probability $p_{1,t}$, whereas an individual that is alive at time t and in state 2 may be encountered in state 2 with probability $p_{2,t}$. We can imagine that for each individual and occasion, a coin is tossed determining whether the individual is encountered (with probability $p_{1,t}$ or $p_{2,t}$) or not (with probability $1 - p_{1,t}$ or $1 - p_{2,t}$). We here assume the absence of state assignment errors; thus, an individual in state s can only be encountered in state s (or be not encountered), but not encountered in another state. In other words, we allow only false-negative, but no false-positive errors. Once dead, an individual can no longer be encountered. This completes our mostly verbal description of the observation process, which is conditional on the state process, and thus the model is conceptually hierarchical. The model is conditional on first capture, that is, we do not model and estimate the initial capture probability. In Fig. 9.1, the two processes are shown graphically for an example.

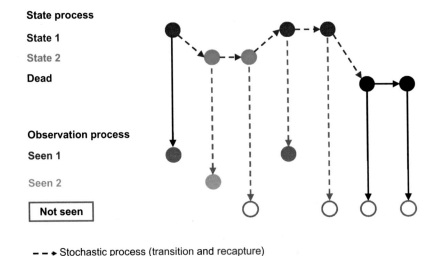

FIGURE 9.1   Example of the state and observation process of a marked individual over time for the multistate model. The sequence of true states in this individual is $z = [1, 2, 2, 1, 1, 3, 3]$, and the observed capture-history is $y = [1, 2, 0, 1, 0, 0, 0]$.

For an algebraic description of our two-location model, assume matrix z with element $z_{i,t}$, which indicates the true state of individual i at time t. States are numbered from 1 to S; S is the number of true states. Moreover, let us assume that vector fs_i denotes the true state of individual i at its first encounter. As we assume there are no state assignment errors, fs_i is identical to the observed state at first encounter. Furthermore, we define the four-dimensional state-transition matrix (Ω). The first and second dimension of Ω denote the states of departure and of arrival, respectively, the third dimension the individual (i), and the fourth dimension time (t). Element $\omega_{n,m,i,t}$ of Ω is the probability that individual i, which is in state n at time t, is in state m at $t + 1$. The observation matrix (Θ) also has four dimensions, the first denotes the true state of an individual, the second the observed state, and the remaining two dimensions are for individual and time. The element $\varphi_{n,m,i,t}$ of Θ is the probability that individual i, which is in state n at time t, is observed in state m at time t. The first two dimensions of the state-transition matrix Ω are identical ($S \times S$), but this need not be the case for the observation matrix (Θ). The first dimension of Θ must also be S (the true number of states), but the second dimension is O (the number of observed states) which can be smaller or larger than S. As usual, the state-space model then consists of two model parts. The set of state equations is

$$z_{i,f_i} = fs_i$$

$$z_{i,t+1} \,|\, z_{i,t} \sim \text{categorical}(\Omega_{z_{i,t},1\ldots S,i,t}).$$

The first equation describes the state at the first encounter that is assumed to be assigned without error. Note that the argument of the categorical distribution is a vector of length S, that is, it is the complete row of the matrix Ω for given values of the first ($z_{i,t}$), third (i), and fourth (t) dimension. The second equation describes the development of the state membership over time. The observation equation links the true state with the observed state:

$$y_{i,t} \,|\, z_{i,t} \sim \text{categorical}(\Theta_{z_{i,t},1\ldots O,i,t})$$

where y is the observed multistate capture–recapture data. Similarly as before, the argument of the categorical distribution is a vector of length O, that is, it is the complete row of the matrix Θ for given values of the first ($z_{i,t}$), third (i), and fourth (t) dimension. The state and the observation process are both defined for $t \geq f_i$.

The multistate capture–recapture model makes similar assumptions as the CJS model (Chapter 7): the transition and observation probabilities must be the same for all individuals at a given occasion and state and individuals must be independent of each other. Individuals and states are recorded without error, and no marks must be lost. Of course, it is possible to relax some of these assumptions by adopting a more general model. For example, by incorporating age or group effects, the assumption of equal transition and observation probabilities is no longer required for all individuals, but only for the individuals within an age class or group. Some of these assumptions can be tested with appropriate goodness-of-fit tests (Pradel et al., 2003; Choquet et al., 2009).

Because multistate capture–recapture models are so extremely flexible, there is a host of possible models that we might present. We have selected a few models that we think represent frequently encountered problems. In our presentation, we first give a description of the model by showing the first two dimensions of the state-transition (Ω) and observation (Θ) matrices. The formulation of these matrices requires the definition of exhaustive sets of true and observed states. Typically, state-transition probabilities may be composed of several parameters that we want to estimate separately, for example, state-specific survival and movement probabilities. These matrices form the heart of multistate modeling. They are essential for your understanding of this model class in principle and for the way in which these models are written in the BUGS language in particular. After presentation of the matrices, we either simulate data or use a real-data example and fit the model. Throughout, we denote state-transition matrices with rows representing states at occasion t and column states at occasion $t + 1$. Sometimes states at time t (rows) are also called "states of departure", whereas states at time $t + 1$ (columns) are named "states of arrival". For the observation matrix, true states are in rows and the observed states are in columns. In the list of true states, we always include the state "dead" and in the list of observed states the state "not seen/encountered". This is because both matrices need to be row stochastic, that is, the probabilities in a row must sum to 1. In Appendix 2, we show two additional useful multistate models along with the BUGS code for their analysis.

9.2 ESTIMATION OF MOVEMENT BETWEEN TWO SITES

9.2.1 Model Description

This is one of the simplest multistate models. Consider individuals that are marked and recaptured at two sites (A and B) and that there is movement between sites. Recapture is not perfect, and we want to estimate site-specific survival, as well as movement probabilities between sites. This is a common problem, and for this very situation, multistate capture–recapture models were originally developed (Arnason, 1972; Hestbeck et al., 1991; Brownie et al., 1993).

We start by defining the three true states: "alive at site A", "alive at site B", and "dead". Here is the state-transition matrix:

		True State at Time $t+1$		
		Site A	**Site B**	**Dead**
True State at Time t	**Site A**	$\phi_A(1-\psi_{AB})$	$\phi_A\psi_{AB}$	$1-\phi_A$
	Site B	$\phi_B\psi_{BA}$	$\phi_B(1-\psi_{BA})$	$1-\phi_B$
	Dead	0	0	1

or simply

$$
\begin{array}{c}
\text{site A} \\
\text{site B} \\
\text{dead}
\end{array}
\begin{array}{ccc}
\text{site A} & \text{site B} & \text{dead} \\
\end{array}
\left[
\begin{array}{ccc}
\phi_A(1-\psi_{AB}) & \phi_A\psi_{AB} & 1-\phi_A \\
\phi_B\psi_{BA} & \phi_B(1-\psi_{BA}) & 1-\phi_B \\
0 & 0 & 1
\end{array}
\right]
$$

States are ordered from top to bottom and from left to right in the order as given above ("site A", "site B", and "dead"). For example, the probability of being in state "site B" at time $t+1$, given presence in state "site A" at time t, is $\phi_A\psi_{AB}$. The parameters in this matrix are the site-specific survival probabilities (ϕ_A, ϕ_B) and the movement probabilities (ψ_{AB}, ψ_{BA}).

When written in this way, we make a crucial assumption: survival from t to $t+1$ refers to the state in which the individual is at time t, and there is no mortality during movement. Thus, ψ_{AB} is the probability that an individual, which survived at site A from time t to $t+1$, moves to site B shortly before $t+1$. This is the typical way how the survival and movement parameters are defined. If we wish, we could also define that movement comes first and then the individual survives with the site-specific survival probability of the new site, in which case the transition matrix is this:

$$
\begin{array}{c}
\text{site A} \\
\text{site B} \\
\text{dead}
\end{array}
\begin{array}{ccc}
\text{site A} & \text{site B} & \text{dead} \\
\end{array}
\left[
\begin{array}{ccc}
(1-\psi_{AB})\phi_A & \psi_{AB}\phi_B & 1-\sum row_1 \\
\psi_{BA}\phi_A & (1-\psi_{BA})\phi_B & 1-\sum row_2 \\
0 & 0 & 1
\end{array}
\right].
$$

Joe and Pollock (2002) developed a general model in which the time of movement is a random variable with a known distribution.

Regardless of how the state matrix is defined, the list of observed states includes "seen in A", "seen in B", and "not seen". The observation matrix links the true states with the observed states:

		Observation at Time t		
		Seen in A	Seen in B	Not seen
True State at Time t	Site A	p_A	0	$1 - p_A$
	Site B	0	p_B	$1 - p_B$
	Dead	0	0	1

or simply

$$
\begin{array}{c}
 \\
\text{site A} \\
\text{site B} \\
\text{dead}
\end{array}
\begin{array}{ccc}
\text{seen in A} & \text{seen in B} & \text{not seen} \\
\left[\begin{array}{ccc}
p_A & 0 & 1 - p_A \\
0 & p_B & 1 - p_B \\
0 & 0 & 1
\end{array}\right]
\end{array}
$$

The parameters in this matrix are the site-specific recapture probabilities (p_A, p_B). The true states at time t correspond to the rows of the observation matrix in the order "site A", "site B", and "dead" from top to bottom, and the observed states are in columns in the order "seen in A", "seen in B", and "not seen" from left to right. For example, the probability that an individual in true state "site A" at time t is in the observed state "not seen" at time t is $1 - p_A$.

For ease of presentation, we have dropped several indices in these matrices. In reality, however, both matrices could have an index t for time and i for individual.

9.2.2 Generation of Simulated Data

Imagine that we sampled capture–recapture data of little ringed plovers (Fig. 9.2) at two sites (A and B). Habitat quality at site A is higher than at site B, and thus annual survival in A is higher (0.8) than that in B (0.7), and movements from A to B are less likely ($\psi_{AB} = 0.3$) than movements from B to A ($\psi_{BA} = 0.5$). We assume that capture effort was higher at A than at B. In the data sets, captures of an individual at site A are labeled "1" and captures at site B "2".

To generate multistate capture–recapture data, we first need to define the probabilities in both the state-transition and the observation matrix. For individual i released at time t in state m, we simulate its state at time $t + 1$ using a categorical distribution. The probabilities of the categorical distribution are taken from row m of the state-transition matrix

FIGURE 9.2   Little ringed plover (*Charadrius dubius*) (Photograph by D. Occhiato).

(PSI.STATE) of individual *i* at time *t*. We then simulate the observation for individual *i* at time *t* + 1. Assume that individual *i* is in state *n* at time *t* + 1. We then simulate the observation using a categorical distribution again. The probabilities of the categorical distribution are taken this time from row *n* of the observation matrix (PSI.OBS) for individual *i* at time *t* + 1. These steps are first repeated for individual *i* until the end of the study and then for all released individuals. In program R, we specify the categorical distribution as a multinomial distribution with trial size equal to 1. In the following code, we first define the simulation parameters, the state-transition and observation matrix and then apply the function simul.ms, which simulates multistate capture–recapture data as described earlier.

```
# Define mean survival, transitions, recapture, as well as number of
  occasions, states, observations and released individuals
phiA <- 0.8
phiB <- 0.7
psiAB <- 0.3
psiBA <- 0.5
pA <- 0.7
pB <- 0.4
n.occasions <- 6
n.states <- 3
```

```
n.obs <- 3
marked <- matrix(NA, ncol = n.states, nrow = n.occasions)
marked[,1] <- rep(100, n.occasions)
marked[,2] <- rep(60, n.occasions)
marked[,3] <- rep(0, n.occasions)
```

```
# Define matrices with survival, transition and recapture probabilities
# These are 4-dimensional matrices, with
    # Dimension 1: state of departure
    # Dimension 2: state of arrival
    # Dimension 3: individual
    # Dimension 4: time
```

```
# 1. State process matrix
totrel <- sum(marked)*(n.occasions-1)
PSI.STATE <- array(NA, dim=c(n.states, n.states, totrel, n.occasions-1))
for (i in 1:totrel){
    for (t in 1:(n.occasions-1)){
        PSI.STATE[,,i,t] <- matrix(c(
        phiA*(1-psiAB), phiA*psiAB,    1-phiA,
        phiB*psiBA,     phiB*(1-psiBA), 1-phiB,
        0,              0,              1         ), nrow = n.states,
            byrow = TRUE)
        } #t
    } #i
```

```
# 2.Observation process matrix
PSI.OBS <- array(NA, dim=c(n.states, n.obs, totrel, n.occasions-1))
for (i in 1:totrel){
    for (t in 1:(n.occasions-1)){
        PSI.OBS[,,i,t] <- matrix(c(
        pA, 0,  1-pA,
        0,  pB, 1-pB,
        0,  0,  1         ), nrow = n.states, byrow = TRUE)
        } #t
    } #i
```

```
# Define function to simulate multistate capture-recapture data
simul.ms <- function(PSI.STATE, PSI.OBS, marked, unobservable = NA){
    # Unobservable: number of state that is unobservable
    n.occasions <- dim(PSI.STATE)[4] + 1
    CH <- CH.TRUE <- matrix(NA, ncol = n.occasions, nrow = sum(marked))
    # Define a vector with the occasion of marking
    mark.occ <- matrix(0, ncol = dim(PSI.STATE)[1], nrow = sum(marked))
    g <- colSums(marked)
    for (s in 1:dim(PSI.STATE)[1]){
    if (g[s]==0) next # To avoid error message if nothing to replace
        mark.occ[(cumsum(g[1:s])-g[s]+1)[s]:cumsum(g[1:s])[s],s] <-
        rep(1:n.occasions, marked[1:n.occasions,s])
        }#s
    for (i in 1:sum(marked)){
        for (s in 1:dim(PSI.STATE)[1]){
            if (mark.occ[i,s]==0) next
            first <- mark.occ[i,s]
```

```
      CH[i,first] <- s
      CH.TRUE[i,first] <- s
      } #s
    for (t in (first+1):n.occasions){
      # Multinomial trials for state transitions
      if (first==n.occasions) next
      state <- which(rmultinom(1, 1, PSI.STATE[CH.TRUE[i,t-1],,
        i,t-1])==1)
      CH.TRUE[i,t] <- state
      # Multinomial trials for observation process
      event <- which(rmultinom(1, 1, PSI.OBS[CH.TRUE[i,t],,i,
        t-1])==1)
      CH[i,t] <- event
      } #t
    } #i
  # Replace the NA and the highest state number (dead) in the file by 0
  CH[is.na(CH)] <- 0
  CH[CH==dim(PSI.STATE)[1]] <- 0
  CH[CH==unobservable] <- 0
  id <- numeric(0)
  for (i in 1:dim(CH)[1]){
    z <- min(which(CH[i,]!=0))
    ifelse(z==dim(CH)[2], id <- c(id,i), id <- c(id))
    }
  return(list(CH=CH[-id,], CH.TRUE=CH.TRUE[-id,]))
  # CH: capture-histories to be used
  # CH.TRUE: capture-histories with perfect observation
  }

# Execute function
sim <- simul.ms(PSI.STATE, PSI.OBS, marked)
CH <- sim$CH
```

The multistate capture–recapture data simulated may look like this (first five rows shown):

```
[1,]  1  2  0  0  0  0
[2,]  1  0  0  0  0  0
[3,]  1  0  1  1  0  0
[4,]  1  0  2  0  0  0
[5,]  1  0  2  0  0  0
```

A "1" denotes capture at site A, a "2" capture at site B, and a "0" denotes noncapture. To fit a multistate model in the state-space formulation, we need to compute a vector indicating the occasion of marking for each individual. Furthermore, we must replace the "0" in the data with a "3" to match the observed states, which are numbered "1" (seen at site A), "2" (seen at site B), and "3" (not seen).

```
# Compute vector with occasion of first capture
get.first <- function(x) min(which(x!=0))
f <- apply(CH, 1, get.first)
```

```
# Recode CH matrix: note, a 0 is not allowed in WinBUGS!
# 1 = seen alive in A, 2 = seen alive in B, 3 = not seen
rCH <- CH # Recoded CH
rCH[rCH==0] <- 3
```

The final multistate capture–recapture data ready to be analyzed in BUGS is named rCH and may look like this:

```
[1,]   1   2   3   3   3   3
[2,]   1   3   3   3   3   3
[3,]   1   3   1   1   3   3
[4,]   1   3   2   3   3   3
[5,]   1   3   2   3   3   3
```

9.2.3 Analysis of the Model

As so often, the BUGS code to analyze the multistate capture–recapture data closely resembles the way in which we simulate the data. In addition, we define priors for each parameter and can impose constraints on them. Then, we define the state-transition and the observation matrices using the model parameters. They are named ps and po, respectively, in the BUGS code, and correspond to Ω and Θ of Section 9.1. These matrices have four dimensions because they not only indicate states of departure and arrival but also time and individual. Finally, the state-space likelihood section of code is similar to that introduced for CJS models. The state-transition process describes the probability of the state at time $t + 1$ (stored in matrix Z) conditional on the state at time t, and the observation process describes the mapping of the state at time $t + 1$ on the observed data. The only difference with the CJS model is that in the likelihood we now use a categorical instead of a Bernoulli distribution. Note that the categorical distribution in WinBUGS needs the empty index in the last position; hence, the matrix dimensions are ordered differently from the formulas in Section 9.1.

```
# Specify model in BUGS language
sink("ms.bug")
cat("
model {

# --------------------------------------------------
# Parameters:
# phiA: survival probability at site A
# phiB: survival probability at site B
# psiAB: movement probability from site A to site B
# psiBA: movement probability from site B to site A
# pA: recapture probability at site A
# pB: recapture probability at site B
# --------------------------------------------------
# States (S):
# 1 alive at A
```

```
# 2 alive at B
# 3 dead
# Observations (O):
# 1 seen at A
# 2 seen at B
# 3 not seen
# -------------------------------------------------

# Priors and constraints
for (t in 1:(n.occasions-1)){
    phiA[t] <- mean.phi[1]
    phiB[t] <- mean.phi[2]
    psiAB[t] <- mean.psi[1]
    psiBA[t] <- mean.psi[2]
    pA[t] <- mean.p[1]
    pB[t] <- mean.p[2]
    }
for (u in 1:2){
    mean.phi[u] ~ dunif(0, 1)    # Priors for mean state-spec. survival
    mean.psi[u] ~ dunif(0, 1)    # Priors for mean transitions
    mean.p[u] ~ dunif(0, 1)      # Priors for mean state-spec. recapture
    }

# Define state-transition and observation matrices
for (i in 1:nind){
    # Define probabilities of state S(t+1) given S(t)
    for (t in f[i]:(n.occasions-1)){
        ps[1,i,t,1] <- phiA[t] * (1-psiAB[t])
        ps[1,i,t,2] <- phiA[t] * psiAB[t]
        ps[1,i,t,3] <- 1-phiA[t]
        ps[2,i,t,1] <- phiB[t] * psiBA[t]
        ps[2,i,t,2] <- phiB[t] * (1-psiBA[t])
        ps[2,i,t,3] <- 1-phiB[t]
        ps[3,i,t,1] <- 0
        ps[3,i,t,2] <- 0
        ps[3,i,t,3] <- 1

        # Define probabilities of O(t) given S(t)
        po[1,i,t,1] <- pA[t]
        po[1,i,t,2] <- 0
        po[1,i,t,3] <- 1-pA[t]
        po[2,i,t,1] <- 0
        po[2,i,t,2] <- pB[t]
        po[2,i,t,3] <- 1-pB[t]
        po[3,i,t,1] <- 0
        po[3,i,t,2] <- 0
        po[3,i,t,3] <- 1
        } #t
    } #i

# Likelihood
for (i in 1:nind){
    # Define latent state at first capture
    z[i,f[i]] <- Y[i,f[i]]
    for (t in (f[i]+1):n.occasions){
```

```
    # State process: draw S(t) given S(t-1)
    z[i,t] ~ dcat(ps[z[i,t-1], i, t-1,])
    # Observation process: draw O(t) given S(t)
    y[i,t] ~ dcat(po[z[i,t], i, t-1,])
    } #t
  } #i
}
",fill = TRUE)
sink()
```

Before we load the data, we may again compute a matrix with known latent states *z*. This will reduce computation time and improve convergence; see Section 7.3.1. The latent state *z* now contains information not only about survival as in the CJS or the mark-recovery model but also about a location (or "state"). Therefore, the latent state is always unknown during occasions when an individual is not encountered. Care must also be taken when computing the known-state matrix when the names of the true and the observed states differ. The following function creates the required matrix for the current example.

```
# Function to create known latent states z
known.state.ms <- function(ms, notseen){
    # notseen: label for 'not seen'
    state <- ms
    state[state==notseen] <- NA
    for (i in 1:dim(ms)[1]){
        m <- min(which(!is.na(state[i,])))
        state[i,m] <- NA
        }
    return(state)
    }
```

Initial values need to be given only for the unknown *z*; the following function creates these values.

```
# Function to create initial values for unknown z
ms.init.z <- function(ch, f){
    for (i in 1:dim(ch)[1]){ch[i,1:f[i]] <- NA}
    states <- max(ch, na.rm = TRUE)
    known.states <- 1:(states-1)
    v <- which(ch==states)
    ch[-v] <- NA
    ch[v] <- sample(known.states, length(v), replace = TRUE)
    return(ch)
    }
```

Now, we are ready to fit the model.

```
# Bundle data
bugs.data <- list(y = rCH, f = f, n.occasions = dim(rCH)[2], nind =
    dim(rCH)[1], z = known.state.ms(rCH, 3))
```

```
# Initial values
inits <- function () {list (mean.phi = runif (2, 0, 1), mean.psi = runif (2,
    0, 1), mean.p = runif (2, 0, 1), z = ms.init.z (rCH, f)) }

# Parameters monitored
parameters <- c ("mean.phi", "mean.psi", "mean.p")

# MCMC settings
ni <- 10000
nt <- 6
nb <- 2000
nc <- 3

# Call WinBUGS from R (BRT 8 min)
ms <- bugs (bugs.data, inits, parameters, "ms.bug", n.chains = nc,
    n.thin = nt, n.iter = ni, n.burnin = nb, debug = TRUE, bugs.directory =
    bugs.dir, working.directory = getwd ())
```

This model converges relatively quickly.

```
print (ms, digits = 3)
```

	mean	sd	2.5%	25%	50%	75%	97.5%	Rhat	n.eff
mean.phi [1]	0.808	0.030	0.753	0.786	0.806	0.826	0.872	1.005	550
mean.phi [2]	0.690	0.031	0.627	0.670	0.691	0.711	0.748	1.001	4000
mean.psi [1]	0.422	0.079	0.271	0.363	0.423	0.485	0.559	1.007	480
mean.psi [2]	0.419	0.069	0.311	0.367	0.412	0.460	0.578	1.005	660
mean.p [1]	0.803	0.102	0.626	0.723	0.795	0.888	0.985	1.009	310
mean.p [2]	0.288	0.062	0.201	0.242	0.277	0.322	0.430	1.008	590

The posterior distributions of the six model parameters look reasonably good (Fig. 9.3). However, the posteriors for transitions and recapture parameters are wide, indicating that these parameters are not estimated precisely. This is probably because the study duration was short in our example, so the data contained little information about these parameters.

```
par (mfrow = c (3, 2), las = 1)
hist (ms$sims.list$mean.phi [,1], col = "gray", main = "", xlab =
    expression (phi [A]), ylim=c (0,1300))
abline (v = phiA, col = "red")
hist (ms$sims.list$mean.phi [,2], col = "gray", main = "", xlab =
    expression (phi [B]), ylim=c (0,1300), ylab="")
abline (v = phiB, , col="red")
hist (ms$sims.list$mean.psi [,1], col = "gray", main = "", xlab =
    expression (psi [AB]), ylim=c (0,1300))
abline (v = psiAB, col="red")
hist (ms$sims.list$mean.psi [,2], col = "gray", main = "", xlab =
    expression (psi [BA]), ylab="", ylim=c (0,1300))
abline (v = psiBA, col="red")
hist (ms$sims.list$mean.p [,1], col = "gray", main = "", xlab =
    expression (p [A]), ylim=c (0,1300))
abline (v = pA, col = "red")
hist (ms$sims.list$mean.p [,2], col = "gray", main = "", xlab =
    expression (p [B]), ylab="", ylim=c (0,1300))
abline (v = pB, col = "red")
```

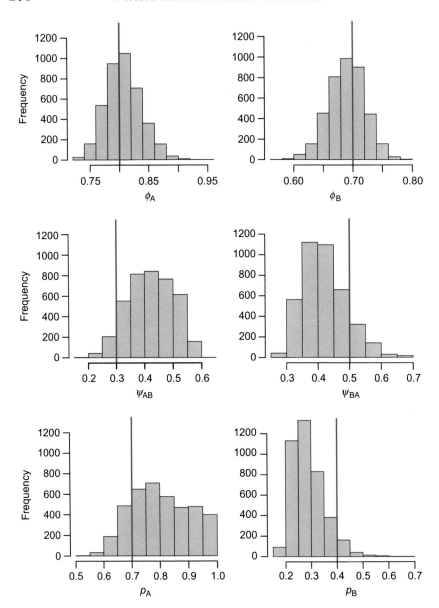

FIGURE 9.3 Posterior distributions of survival, movement, and recapture probabilities. Red lines give the values of the data generating parameters.

This basic model can now be extended in the same way as we saw for the CJS model in Chapter 7. Thus, it is straightforward to add fixed time effects, group effects, or to include individual or temporal random effects. As mentioned earlier, all we need to do is to modify the code sections called "Priors and constraints" and "Define parameters". You may want to check the examples given for the CJS models to understand how to make these changes and study exercises 1 and 2 in Section 9.9.

The same model structure may be used when states A and B denote disease states, classes of reproductive success, or "breeder" and "non-breeder", to name a few possibilities. Moreover, this model easily extends to a larger number of locations (see Section 9.5).

This multistate model is written in such a way that the inclusion of temporal and individual effects is straightforward, that is, only the model section called "Priors and constraints" needs to be modified. However, without individual effects, the model could be written in a more efficient way, which would reduce computing time somewhat. In particular, the definition of the state-transition and observation matrices (ps and po) does not need the index for individual in that case. Thus, an alternative way to write the model for this case is as follows:

```
# Specify model in BUGS language
sink("ms.alternative1.bug")
cat("
model {

# Priors and constraints
for (t in 1:(n.occasions-1)){
    phiA[t] <- mean.phi[1]
    phiB[t] <- mean.phi[2]
    psiAB[t] <- mean.psi[1]
    psiBA[t] <- mean.psi[2]
    pA[t] <- mean.p[1]
    pB[t] <- mean.p[2]
    }
for (u in 1:2){
    mean.phi[u] ~ dunif(0, 1)    # Priors for mean state-spec. survival
    mean.psi[u] ~ dunif(0, 1)    # Priors for mean transitions
    mean.p[u] ~ dunif(0, 1)      # Priors for mean state-spec. recapture
    }

# Define state-transition and observation matrices
    # Define probabilities of state S(t+1) given S(t)
    for (t in 1:(n.occasions-1)){
        ps[1,t,1] <- phiA[t] * (1-psiAB[t])
        ps[1,t,2] <- phiA[t] * psiAB[t]
        ps[1,t,3] <- 1-phiA[t]
        ps[2,t,1] <- phiB[t] * psiBA[t]
        ps[2,t,2] <- phiB[t] * (1-psiBA[t])
        ps[2,t,3] <- 1-phiB[t]
        ps[3,t,1] <- 0
        ps[3,t,2] <- 0
        ps[3,t,3] <- 1

    # Define probabilities of O(t) given S(t)
        po[1,t,1] <- pA[t]
        po[1,t,2] <- 0
```

```
      po[1,t,3] <- 1-pA[t]
      po[2,t,1] <- 0
      po[2,t,2] <- pB[t]
      po[2,t,3] <- 1-pB[t]
      po[3,t,1] <- 0
      po[3,t,2] <- 0
      po[3,t,3] <- 1
      } #t

# Likelihood
for (i in 1:nind){
   # Define latent state at first capture
   z[i,f[i]] <- Y[i,f[i]]
   for (t in (f[i]+1):n.occasions){
      # State process: draw S(t) given S(t-1)
      z[i,t] ~ dcat(ps[z[i,t-1], t-1,])
      # Observation process: draw O(t) given S(t)
      y[i,t] ~ dcat(po[z[i,t], t-1,])
      } #t
   } #i
}
",fill = TRUE)
sink()
```

If in addition we do not need temporal effects, there is an even more efficient way to write the model: the index for time in the matrices ps and po is no longer needed. We then define priors directly for the quantities of interest (phiA, phiB, ...), and we also need to change the initial values accordingly.

```
# Specify model in BUGS language
sink("ms.alternative2.bug")
cat("
model {

# Priors and constraints
   phiA ~ dunif(0, 1)      # Prior for mean survival in A
   phiB ~ dunif(0, 1)      # Prior for mean survival in B
   psiAB ~ dunif(0, 1)     # Prior for mean movement from A to B
   psiBA ~ dunif(0, 1)     # Prior for mean movement from B to A
   pA ~ dunif(0, 1)        # Prior for mean recapture in A
   pB ~ dunif(0, 1)        # Prior for mean recapture in B

# Define state-transition and observation matrices
   # Define probabilities of state S(t+1) given S(t)
      ps[1,1] <- phiA * (1-psiAB)
      ps[1,2] <- phiA * psiAB
      ps[1,3] <- 1-phiA
      ps[2,1] <- phiB * psiBA
      ps[2,2] <- phiB * (1-psiBA)
      ps[2,3] <- 1-phiB
      ps[3,1] <- 0
      ps[3,2] <- 0
      ps[3,3] <- 1
```

```
# Define probabilities of O(t) given S(t)
    po[1,1] <- pA
    po[1,2] <- 0
    po[1,3] <- 1-pA
    po[2,1] <- 0
    po[2,2] <- pB
    po[2,3] <- 1-pB
    po[3,1] <- 0
    po[3,2] <- 0
    po[3,3] <- 1

# Likelihood
for (i in 1:nind){
  # Define latent state at first capture
  z[i,f[i]] <- Y[i,f[i]]
  for (t in (f[i]+1):n.occasions){
    # State process: draw S(t) given S(t-1)
    z[i,t] ~ dcat(ps[z[i,t-1],])
    # Observation process: draw O(t) given S(t)
    y[i,t] ~ dcat(po[z[i,t],])
    } #t
  } #i
}
",fill = TRUE)
sink()
```

The reduction in computing time is about 30% for the first and about 40% for the second alternative model. Despite these computational benefits, we will not use these parameterizations in the following examples but stick to the more general parameterization. However, we recommend using alternative parameterizations when computing time is an issue.

9.3 ACCOUNTING FOR TEMPORARY EMIGRATION

9.3.1 Model Description

Sometimes individuals are not available for capture at certain occasions, although they are alive *somewhere*. An example of this is when individuals skip reproduction in a particular year, and sampling is conducted only at breeding sites, or plants that are dormant in some years when they are only surveyed above ground. If the temporary absence is random (i.e., does not depend on whether an individual was available for capture at the previous occasion), then temporary emigration does not bias estimates of survival probability. It does lower recapture probability, but this parameter is usually not of direct interest. By contrast, if temporary absence is Markovian, that is, depends on whether an individual was absent one time step ago, then it does cause bias in the estimated survival probability, unless accounted for (Kendall et al., 1997; Schaub et al., 2004a). Note that temporary emigration is different from permanent emigration. When individuals emigrate permanently, they become permanently unavailable for capture and the estimated survival probability is always biased low. That is why all survival estimated from CJS and multistate models should more accurately be called "apparent survival" (see Chapter 7).

To model temporary emigration, we define the states "alive and present", "alive and absent", and "dead". The state-transition matrix is

$$
\begin{array}{cc}
 & \begin{array}{ccc} \text{present} & \text{absent} & \text{dead} \end{array} \\
\begin{array}{c} \text{present} \\ \text{absent} \\ \text{dead} \end{array} &
\begin{bmatrix}
\phi(1-\psi_{\text{IO}}) & \phi\psi_{\text{IO}} & 1-\phi \\
\phi\psi_{\text{OI}} & \phi(1-\psi_{\text{OI}}) & 1-\phi \\
0 & 0 & 1
\end{bmatrix},
\end{array}
$$

where ϕ is survival probability, ψ_{IO} is the probability that an individual present ("in") at time t is absent ("out") at time $t + 1$, and ψ_{OI} is the probability that an individual absent at time t is present at time $t + 1$. If $\psi_{\text{IO}} = 1 - \psi_{\text{OI}}$, temporary emigration is random.

The list of possible observations is "seen" and "not seen". Therefore, we have a 3 × 2 observation matrix,

$$
\begin{array}{cc}
 & \begin{array}{cc} \text{seen} & \text{not seen} \end{array} \\
\begin{array}{c} \text{present} \\ \text{absent} \\ \text{dead} \end{array} &
\begin{bmatrix}
p & 1-p \\
0 & 1 \\
0 & 1
\end{bmatrix},
\end{array}
$$

where p is recapture probability (conditional on being alive and available for capture).

The model of temporary emigration is an example of a model with two unobserved states ("alive and absent" and "dead"). Such models often have identifiability problems. Kendall and Nichols (2002), Schaub et al. (2004a), and Bailey et al. (2010) studied the identifiability and the performance of this and more complex models with additional states, and give catalogues of which parameters can be estimated under which conditions.

9.3.2 Generation of Simulated Data

Let us assume that we have repeatedly photographed fire salamanders (Fig. 9.4) at a hibernation site in a cave. The black and yellow pattern is extremely variable among individuals; hence, these photos allow one to determine individual identity. Annual adult survival of fire salamanders is high (Schmidt et al., 2005); we here assume $\phi = 0.85$. Since salamanders do not hibernate every year at the same place, they may temporarily be absent, that is, unavailable for capture (which means, being

FIGURE 9.4 Fire salamander (*Salamandra salamandra*), Switzerland, 2008 (Photograph by T. Ott).

photographed), when sampling only takes place at one cave. We assume that the probability an individual that is present becomes absent in the next year is $\psi_{IO} = 0.2$, and that the probability a salamander that is absent becomes present the next year is $\psi_{OI} = 0.3$. Given presence in the cave, recapture probability is $p = 0.7$.

```
# Define mean survival, transitions, recapture, as well as number of
   occasions, states, observations and released individuals
phi <- 0.85
psiIO <- 0.2
psiOI <- 0.3
p <- 0.7
n.occasions <- 8
n.states <- 3
n.obs <- 2
marked <- matrix(NA, ncol = n.states, nrow = n.occasions)
marked[,1] <- rep(70, n.occasions) # Present
marked[,2] <- rep(0, n.occasions)  # Absent
marked[,3] <- rep(0, n.occasions)  # Dead

# Define matrices with survival, transition and recapture probabilities
# These are 4-dimensional matrices, with
   # Dimension 1: state of departure
```

```
# Dimension 2: state of arrival
# Dimension 3: individual
# Dimension 4: time
# 1. State process matrix
totrel <- sum(marked)*(n.occasions-1)
PSI.STATE <- array(NA, dim=c(n.states, n.states, totrel,
  n.occasions-1))
for (i in 1:totrel){
  for (t in 1:(n.occasions-1)){
    PSI.STATE[,,i,t] <- matrix(c(
    phi*(1-psiIO), phi*psiIO,      1-phi,
    phi*psiOI,     phi*(1-psiOI),  1-phi,
    0,             0,              1        ), nrow=n.states,
      byrow = TRUE)
    } #t
  } #i

# 2.Observation process matrix
PSI.OBS <- array(NA, dim=c(n.states, n.obs, totrel, n.occasions-1))
for (i in 1:totrel){
  for (t in 1:(n.occasions-1)){
    PSI.OBS[,,i,t] <- matrix(c(
    p, 1-p,
    0, 1,
    0, 1       ), nrow=n.states, byrow = TRUE)
    } #t
  } #i

# Execute simulation function
sim <- simul.ms(PSI.STATE, PSI.OBS, marked)
CH <- sim$CH

# Compute vector with occasion of first capture
get.first <- function(x) min(which(x!=0))
f <- apply(CH, 1, get.first)

# Recode CH matrix: note, a 0 is not allowed!
# 1 = seen alive, 2 = not seen
rCH <- CH # Recoded CH
rCH[rCH==0] <- 2
```

The elements of the capture-history matrix are equal to "1" at occasions when an individual was seen and "2" otherwise. So far, we always removed the zeroes in the capture-histories; however, this would not really be necessary for zeroes that occur before first capture. Remember that in the CJS, mark-recovery, and multistate models of Chapters 7–9, the data before first capture are not modeled, that is, they do not enter the likelihood.

9.3.3 Analysis of the Model

Again, the BUGS code is straightforward to write in terms of the state-transition and observation matrices. Both matrices are specified along with the priors; no change is required in the remaining code.

```
# Specify model in BUGS language
sink("tempemi.bug")
cat("
model {

# ------------------------------
# Parameters:
# phi: survival probability
# psiIO: probability to emigrate
# psiOI: probability to immigrate
# p: recapture probability
# ------------------------------
# States (S):
# 1 alive and present
# 2 alive and absent
# 3 dead
# Observations (O):
# 1 seen
# 2 not seen
# ------------------------------

# Priors and constraints
for (t in 1:(n.occasions-1)){
   phi[t] <- mean.phi
   psiIO[t] <- mean.psiIO
   psiOI[t] <- mean.psiOI
   p[t] <- mean.p
   }
mean.phi ~ dunif(0, 1)        # Prior for mean survival
mean.psiIO ~ dunif(0, 1)      # Prior for mean temp. emigration
mean.psiOI ~ dunif(0, 1)      # Prior for mean temp. immigration
mean.p ~ dunif(0, 1)          # Prior for mean recapture

# Define state-transition and observation matrices
for (i in 1:nind){
    # Define probabilities of state S(t+1) given S(t)
    for (t in f[i]:(n.occasions-1)){
      ps[1,i,t,1] <- phi[t] * (1-psiIO[t])
      ps[1,i,t,2] <- phi[t] * psiIO[t]
      ps[1,i,t,3] <- 1-phi[t]
      ps[2,i,t,1] <- phi[t] * psiOI[t]
      ps[2,i,t,2] <- phi[t] * (1-psiOI[t])
      ps[2,i,t,3] <- 1-phi[t]
      ps[3,i,t,1] <- 0
      ps[3,i,t,2] <- 0
      ps[3,i,t,3] <- 1

      # Define probabilities of O(t) given S(t)
      po[1,i,t,1] <- p[t]
      po[1,i,t,2] <- 1-p[t]
      po[2,i,t,1] <- 0
      po[2,i,t,2] <- 1
      po[3,i,t,1] <- 0
      po[3,i,t,2] <- 1
        } #t
    } #i
```

```
# Likelihood
for (i in 1:nind) {
    # Define latent state at first capture
    z[i,f[i]] <- Y[i,f[i]]
    for (t in (f[i]+1):n.occasions) {
        # State process: draw S(t) given S(t-1)
        z[i,t] ~ dcat(ps[z[i,t-1], i, t-1,])
        # Observation process: draw O(t) given S(t)
        y[i,t] ~ dcat(po[z[i,t], i, t-1,])
        } #t
    } #i
}
",fill = TRUE)
sink()

# Bundle data
bugs.data <- list(y = rCH, f = f, n.occasions = dim(rCH)[2],
    nind = dim(rCH)[1], z = known.state.ms(rCH, 2))

# Initial values
inits <- function(){list(mean.phi = runif(1, 0, 1), mean.psiIO = runif(1,
    0, 1), mean.psiOI = runif(1, 0, 1), mean.p = runif(1, 0, 1), z = ms.init.z
    (rCH, f))}

# Parameters monitored
parameters <- c("mean.phi", "mean.psiIO", "mean.psiOI", "mean.p")

# MCMC settings
ni <- 50000
nt <- 10
nb <- 10000
nc <- 3

# Call WinBUGS from R (BRT 35 min)
tempemi <- bugs(bugs.data, inits, parameters, "tempemi.bug", n.chains =
    nc, n.thin = nt, n.iter = ni, n.burnin = nb, debug = TRUE, bugs.directory =
    bugs.dir, working.directory = getwd())
```

The analysis of this simulated data set requires long Markov chains to achieve convergence. This model has identifiability problems, the degree of which depends on the parameter values. Recapture and transition probabilities are not identifiable and biased if temporary emigration is random (i.e., $\psi_{IO} = 1 - \psi_{OI}$); see Kendall and Nichols (2002) and Schaub et al. (2004a). In our case, however, the posterior distributions of all parameters match up well with the values used for generating the data set, with the exception of the probability of moving back to the study area (temporary immigration; Fig. 9.5). Again, the discrepancy stems from the fact that the simulated data set is relatively small. Repeated simulations would show that the estimators are unbiased, but that their precision is low (Schaub et al., 2004a). Low precision of transition parameters is typical for multistate models with unobservable states.

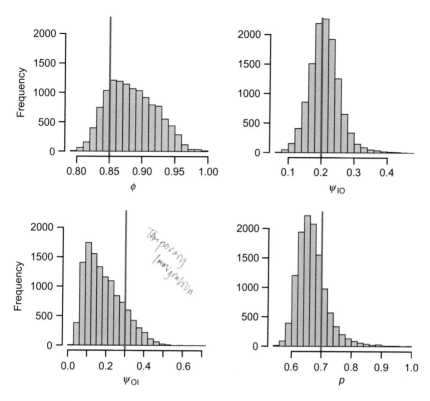

FIGURE 9.5 Posterior distributions of the estimated parameters along with the values used to simulate the data (red vertical lines).

```
print(tempemi, digits = 3)

              mean    sd   2.5%   25%    50%    75%  97.5%   Rhat  n.eff
mean.phi     0.884 0.037 0.823 0.855 0.880 0.910 0.956 1.011    260
mean.psiIO   0.210 0.046 0.126 0.180 0.207 0.235 0.310 1.004    610
mean.psiOI   0.189 0.096 0.057 0.111 0.170 0.252 0.407 1.008    370
mean.p       0.669 0.052 0.592 0.634 0.661 0.693 0.796 1.003  12000

par(mfrow = c(2, 2), las = 1)
hist(tempemi$sims.list$mean.phi, col = "gray", main = "", xlab =
    expression(phi))
abline(v = phi, col = "red", lwd = 2)
hist(tempemi$sims.list$mean.psiIO, col = "gray", main = "", xlab =
    expression(psi[IO]), ylab = "")
abline(v = psiIO, col = "red", lwd = 2)
hist(tempemi$sims.list$mean.psiOI, col = "gray", main = "", xlab =
    expression(psi[OI]))
abline(v = psiOI, col = "red", lwd = 2)
hist(tempemi$sims.list$mean.p, col = "gray", main = "", xlab =
    expression(p), ylab = "")
abline(v = p, col = "red", lwd = 2)
```

9.4 ESTIMATION OF AGE-SPECIFIC PROBABILITY OF FIRST BREEDING

9.4.1 Model Description

For many long-lived species, there is an interest in estimating age-specific probability of first breeding (reproduction). This requires that newborn individuals are marked and later resighted/recaptured when they breed. The state associated with a resighting event is "seen, no breeder yet" if an individual is observed but is not breeding in a given year, nor has it ever been observed breeding before, or "seen as breeder" if the individual is seen breeding in a year. If an individual is resighted as a non-breeder in a year but was observed to breed earlier, it is also assigned to the state "seen as breeder". (Note that this assumption could be relaxed by the inclusion of a further state allowing the estimation of breeding frequency of experienced breeders.) If such data are analyzed without accounting for imperfect detection, age at first breeding is overestimated because some individuals may have first bred *before* they were first *observed* breeding. The multistate capture–recapture model described here avoids this bias by accounting for imperfect detection.

The model makes the assumption that the age at which all previous non-breeders start to breed is known. In our example, we assume that all individuals 3 years old have become breeders and define the following states in the model: "juvenile", "not yet breeding at age 1", "not yet breeding at age 2", "breeder", and "dead". The resulting state-transition matrix is

	juvenile	non-breeder 1	non-breeder 2	breeder	dead
juvenile	0	$\phi_1(1-\alpha_1)$	0	$\phi_1\alpha_1$	$1-\phi_1$
non-breeder 1	0	0	$\phi_2(1-\alpha_2)$	$\phi_2\alpha_2$	$1-\phi_2$
non-breeder 2	0	0	0	ϕ_{ad}	$1-\phi_{ad}$
breeder	0	0	0	ϕ_{ad}	$1-\phi_{ad}$
dead	0	0	0	0	1

Here, ϕ denotes the age-specific survival probability and α_x the probabilities of starting to breed at age x. We define three age classes for survival, but other definitions would also be possible.

The possible observations are "seen as juv", "seen as non-breeder", "seen as breeder", and "not seen". The observation matrix is

	seen as juv	seen non-breeder	seen breeder	not seen
juvenile	0	0	0	1
non-breeder 1	0	p_{NB}	0	$1-p_{NB}$
non-breeder 2	0	p_{NB}	0	$1-p_{NB}$
breeder	0	0	p_B	$1-p_B$
dead	0	0	0	1

where p_{NB} is the probability of re-encountering an individual that is not yet breeding and p_B is the probability of re-encountering a breeder. Depending on the study, p_{NB} may be zero.

The parameters estimated in this model allow the estimation of the mean age at first reproduction or of age-specific recruitment probabilities. Pradel and Lebreton (1999) show the connections between these quantities.

9.4.2 Generation of Simulated Data

Let us assume that we studied survival and age-specific recruitment in little ringed plovers (Fig. 9.2). We color-mark chicks in a population and resight them in subsequent years. For all resighted birds, we record their breeding status. In the simulation, we assume the following parameters: $\phi_1 = 0.4$, $\phi_2 = 0.7$, $\phi_{ad} = 0.8$, $\alpha_1 = 0.2$, $\alpha_2 = 0.6$, $p_{NB} = 0.5$, and $p_B = 0.7$.

```
# Define mean survival, transitions, recapture, as well as number of
   occasions, states, observations and released individuals
phi.1 <- 0.4
phi.2 <- 0.7
phi.ad <- 0.8
alpha.1 <- 0.2
alpha.2 <- 0.6
p.NB <- 0.5
p.B <- 0.7
n.occasions <- 7
n.states <- 5
n.obs <- 4
marked <- matrix(0, ncol = n.states, nrow = n.occasions)
marked[,1] <- rep(100, n.occasions) # Releases only as juveniles

# Define matrices with survival, transition and recapture probabilities
# These are 4-dimensional matrices, with
    # Dimension 1: state of departure
    # Dimension 2: state of arrival
    # Dimension 3: individual
    # Dimension 4: time
# 1. State process matrix
totrel <- sum(marked) * (n.occasions-1)
PSI.STATE <- array(NA, dim=c(n.states, n.states, totrel, n.occasions-1))
for (i in 1:totrel){
   for (t in 1:(n.occasions-1)){
      PSI.STATE[,,i,t] <- matrix(c(
      0, phi.1*(1-alpha.1), 0,       phi.1*alpha.1, 1-phi.1,
      0, 0,       phi.2*(1-alpha.2), phi.2*alpha.2, 1-phi.2,
      0, 0,       0,                 phi.ad,        1-phi.ad,
      0, 0,       0,                 phi.ad,        1-phi.ad,
      0, 0,       0,                 0,             1), nrow =
                                              n.states, byrow = TRUE)
      } #t
   } #i
```

```
# 2.Observation process matrix
PSI.OBS <- array(NA, dim=c(n.states, n.obs, totrel, n.occasions-1))
for (i in 1:totrel){
   for (t in 1:(n.occasions-1)){
      PSI.OBS[,,i,t] <- matrix(c(
      0, 0,    0,    1,
      0, p.NB, 0,    1-p.NB,
      0, p.NB, 0,    1-p.NB,
      0, 0,    p.B,  1-p.B,
      0, 0,    0,    1), nrow = n.states, byrow = TRUE)
      } #t
   } #i
```

```
# Execute simulation function
sim <- simul.ms(PSI.STATE, PSI.OBS, marked)
CH <- sim$CH
```

```
# Compute vector with occasion of first capture
get.first <- function(x) min(which(x!=0))
f <- apply(CH, 1, get.first)
```

```
# Recode CH matrix: note, a 0 is not allowed!
# 1 = seen as juv, 2 = seen no rep, 3 = seen rep, 4 = not seen
rCH <- CH   # Recoded CH
rCH[rCH==0] <- 4
```

The capture-histories have a "1" when a chick was marked, a "2" when an as yet non-breeding individual is observed, and a "3" when an individual is either observed breeding or it is observed non-breeding but has been observed breeding already at previous occasions. Finally, at occasions when an individual is not observed, the capture-history contains a "4".

9.4.3 Analysis of the Model

Here is the BUGS code for the analysis of the model.

```
# Specify model in BUGS language
sink("agerecruitment.bug")
cat("
model {

# --------------------------------------------------
# Parameters:
# phi.1: first year survival probability
# phi.2: second year survival probability
# phi.ad: adult survival probability
# alpha.1: probability to start breeding when 1 year old
# alpha.2: probability to start breeding when 2 years old
# p.NB: recapture probability of non-breeders
# p.B: recapture probability of breeders
# --------------------------------------------------
# States (S):
# 1 juvenile
# 2 not yet breeding at age 1 year
```

```
# 3 not yet breeding at age 2 years
# 4 breeder
# 5 dead
# Observations (O):
# 1 seen as juvenile
# 2 seen as not yet breeding
# 3 seen breeding
# 4 not seen
# ------------------------------------------------

# Priors and constraints
for (t in 1:(n.occasions-1)){
   phi.1[t] <- mean.phi1
   phi.2[t] <- mean.phi2
   phi.ad[t] <- mean.phiad
   alpha.1[t] <- mean.alpha1
   alpha.2[t] <- mean.alpha2
   p.NB[t] <- mean.pNB
   p.B[t] <- mean.pB
   }
mean.phi1 ~ dunif(0, 1)      # Prior for mean 1y survival
mean.phi2 ~ dunif(0, 1)      # Prior for mean 2y survival
mean.phiad ~ dunif(0, 1)     # Prior for mean ad survival
mean.alpha1 ~ dunif(0, 1)    # Prior for mean 1y breeding prob.
mean.alpha2 ~ dunif(0, 1)    # Prior for mean 2y breeding prob.
mean.pNB ~ dunif(0, 1)       # Prior for mean recapture non-breeders
mean.pB ~ dunif(0, 1)        # Prior for mean recapture breeders

# Define state-transition and observation matrices
for (i in 1:nind){
   # Define probabilities of state S(t+1) given S(t)
   for (t in f[i]:(n.occasions-1)){
      ps[1,i,t,1] <- 0
      ps[1,i,t,2] <- phi.1[t] * (1-alpha.1[t])
      ps[1,i,t,3] <- 0
      ps[1,i,t,4] <- phi.1[t] * alpha.1[t]
      ps[1,i,t,5] <- 1-phi.1[t]
      ps[2,i,t,1] <- 0
      ps[2,i,t,2] <- 0
      ps[2,i,t,3] <- phi.2[t] * (1-alpha.2[t])
      ps[2,i,t,4] <- phi.2[t] * alpha.2[t]
      ps[2,i,t,5] <- 1-phi.2[t]
      ps[3,i,t,1] <- 0
      ps[3,i,t,2] <- 0
      ps[3,i,t,3] <- 0
      ps[3,i,t,4] <- phi.ad[t]
      ps[3,i,t,5] <- 1-phi.ad[t]
      ps[4,i,t,1] <- 0
      ps[4,i,t,2] <- 0
      ps[4,i,t,3] <- 0
      ps[4,i,t,4] <- phi.ad[t]
      ps[4,i,t,5] <- 1-phi.ad[t]
      ps[5,i,t,1] <- 0
```

```
       ps[5,i,t,2] <- 0
       ps[5,i,t,3] <- 0
       ps[5,i,t,4] <- 0
       ps[5,i,t,5] <- 1

     # Define probabilities of O(t) given S(t)
       po[1,i,t,1] <- 0
       po[1,i,t,2] <- 0
       po[1,i,t,3] <- 0
       po[1,i,t,4] <- 1
       po[2,i,t,1] <- 0
       po[2,i,t,2] <- p.NB[t]
       po[2,i,t,3] <- 0
       po[2,i,t,4] <- 1-p.NB[t]
       po[3,i,t,1] <- 0
       po[3,i,t,2] <- p.NB[t]
       po[3,i,t,3] <- 0
       po[3,i,t,4] <- 1-p.NB[t]
       po[4,i,t,1] <- 0
       po[4,i,t,2] <- 0
       po[4,i,t,3] <- p.B[t]
       po[4,i,t,4] <- 1-p.B[t]
       po[5,i,t,1] <- 0
       po[5,i,t,2] <- 0
       po[5,i,t,3] <- 0
       po[5,i,t,4] <- 1
       } #t
    } #i

 # Likelihood
 for (i in 1:nind){
    # Define latent state at first capture
    z[i,f[i]] <- Y[i,f[i]]
    for (t in (f[i]+1):n.occasions){
       # State process: draw S(t) given S(t-1)
       z[i,t] ~ dcat(ps[z[i,t-1], i, t-1,])
       # Observation process: draw O(t) given S(t)
       y[i,t] ~ dcat(po[z[i,t], i, t-1,])
       } #t
    } #i
 }
 ",fill = TRUE)
 sink()
```

It is again possible to provide the known values of the latent states z as data and to estimate only the unknown values of z. However, this is trickier in this example because the labels of the observed states do not correspond with the labels of the latent states (see observation matrix above). For example, individuals that are observed and do not yet breed are labeled with "2", while they are in the latent state "2" or "3", depending on age. Furthermore, individuals that are observed breeding are labeled with "3", while they are in latent state "4". Some serious bookkeeping is necessary to get the correct latent states for the observed capture-histories, and we avoid this here.

```
# Bundle data
bugs.data <- list(y = rCH, f = f, n.occasions = dim(rCH)[2], nind =
  dim(rCH)[1])

# Initial values (note: function ch.init is defined in section 7.3)
inits <- function(){list(mean.phi1 = runif(1, 0, 1), mean.phi2 =
  runif(1, 0, 1), mean.phiad = runif(1, 0, 1), mean.alpha1 = runif(1, 0,
  1), mean.alpha2 = runif(1, 0, 1), mean.pNB = runif(1, 0, 1), mean.pB =
  runif(1, 0, 1), z = ch.init(rCH, f))}

# Parameters monitored
parameters <- c("mean.phi1", "mean.phi2", "mean.phiad", "mean.alpha1",
  "mean.alpha2", "mean.pNB", "mean.pB")

# MCMC settings
ni <- 2000
nt <- 3
nb <- 1000
nc <- 3

# Call WinBUGS from R (BRT 2 min)
agefirst <- bugs(bugs.data, inits, parameters, "agerecruitment.bug",
  n.chains = nc, n.thin = nt, n.iter = ni, n.burnin = nb, debug = TRUE,
  bugs.directory = bugs.dir, working.directory = getwd())
```

Convergence is achieved quickly, and all parameter estimates are reasonably precise (Fig. 9.6).

```
par(mfrow = c(3, 3), las = 1)
hist(agefirst$sims.list$mean.phi1, col = "gray", main = "",
  xlab = expression(phi[1]))
abline(v = phi.1, col = "red", lwd = 2)
hist(agefirst$sims.list$mean.phi2, col = "gray", main = "",
  xlab = expression(phi[2]), ylab = "")
abline(v = phi.2, col = "red", lwd = 2)
hist(agefirst$sims.list$mean.phiad, col = "gray", main = "",
  xlab = expression(phi[ad]), ylab = "")
abline(v = phi.ad, col = "red", lwd = 2)
hist(agefirst$sims.list$mean.alpha1, col = "gray", main = "",
  xlab = expression(alpha[1]))
abline(v = alpha.1, col = "red", lwd = 2)
hist(agefirst$sims.list$mean.alpha2, col = "gray", main = "",
  xlab = expression(alpha[2]), ylab = "")
abline(v = alpha.2, col = "red", lwd = 2)
plot(0, type = "n", axes = F, ylab = "", xlab = "")
hist(agefirst$sims.list$mean.pNB, col = "gray", main = "",
  xlab = expression(p[NB]))
abline(v = p.NB, col = "red", lwd = 2)
hist(agefirst$sims.list$mean.pB, col = "gray", main = "",
  xlab = expression(p[B]), ylab = "")
abline(v = p.B, col = "red", lwd = 2)
```

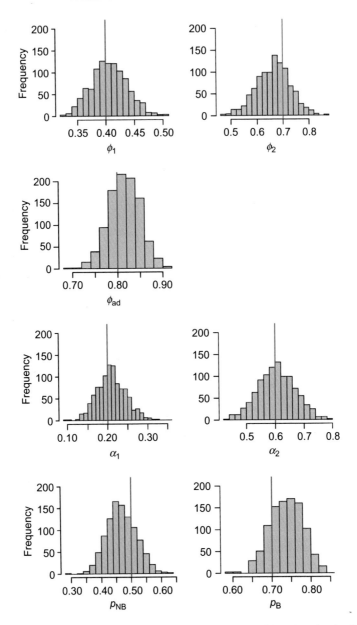

FIGURE 9.6 Posterior distribution of survival, probability of breeding for the first time, and recapture. The vertical red lines show the values used for the simulations.

9.5 JOINT ANALYSIS OF CAPTURE–RECAPTURE AND MARK-RECOVERY DATA

9.5.1 Model Description

Both capture–recapture and mark-recovery data contain information about survival. Sometimes both data types are available in the same study, for example, in bird population studies (Frederiksen and Bregnballe, 2000; Altwegg et al., 2007). It is then sensible to analyze them jointly to make use of all information about survival. The multinomial joint likelihood of this model was originally developed by Burnham (1993), Lebreton et al. (1995), and Barker (1997). More recently, Lebreton et al. (1999) showed how a joint analysis can be performed within the multistate modeling framework, and this is what we do here.

An important difference between capture–recapture and mark-recovery data is that they are often informative about two different kinds of survival probability. As we have seen in Chapter 7, capture–recapture data provide an estimate of apparent survival, which is the probability of surviving *and* remaining in the study area. By contrast, true survival can be estimated from mark-recovery data (Chapter 8). The difference between the two estimates of survival arises because sampling of marked individuals in capture–recapture studies is restricted to the study area (an exception might be studies using color marks), whereas dead recoveries can be obtained from anywhere. Apparent survival (ϕ) and true survival (s) are linked through site fidelity (F) via the relationship $\phi = s*F$. A joint analysis allows one to estimate all three parameters.

The multistate model for the joint analysis of capture–recapture and mark-recovery data has four states: "alive in the study area", "alive outside the study area", "recently dead", and "dead". It may seem strange to have two dead states; however, this is necessary because only individuals recently dead can be recovered. An individual in the state "recently dead" at occasion t has died between occasions $t - 1$ and t. From occasion $t + 1$ onwards, the individual can no longer be recovered. This assumption applies to the analysis of mark-recovery data as well (Section 8.2). Therefore, "recently dead" individuals move to the state "dead" at the next occasion. One says that "dead" is an absorbing state; once individuals are in it, they cannot get out anymore. The transition matrix of the joint model looks like the following:

	alive, inside	alive, outside	recently dead	dead
alive, inside	sF	$s(1-F)$	$1-s$	0
alive, outside	0	s	$1-s$	0
recently dead	0	0	0	1
dead	0	0	0	1

The parameters in the transition matrix are the true survival probability (s) and fidelity probability (F). Fidelity is defined as the probability to remain in the study area, given that an individual is alive. Thus, it is the complement of the probability to emigrate permanently from the study population ($1 - F$). Permanent emigration denotes the permanent movement of individuals outside the study area. It is different from temporary emigration, which allows multiple exits and entries to the study population (see Section 9.3). The distinction between these two types of emigration is crucial.

The possible observations are "seen alive", "recovered dead", and "not seen or recovered", and the observation matrix is

	seen alive	recovered dead	not seen or recovered
alive, inside	p	0	$1-p$
alive, outside	0	0	1
recently dead	0	r	$1-r$
dead	0	0	1

The parameters in the observation matrix are the recapture (p) and the recovery probabilities (r). The recapture probability is the probability to encounter an individual alive and in the study area, whereas the recovery probability is the probability to find and report an individual in the state "recently dead". Both parameters are defined in the same way as the corresponding parameters of the CJS (Chapter 7) and the mark-recovery model (Chapter 8).

9.5.2 Generation of Simulated Data

We assume we want to estimate the adult survival of little ringed plovers (Fig. 9.2) that are marked with ordinary rings but also with colored wing tags, so that individuals can be encountered both live and dead. We imagine that adult survival (s) is 0.8, and study site fidelity is high ($F = 0.6$). The resighting probability is moderate ($p = 0.5$), whereas the recovery probability is low ($r = 0.1$). We simulate a study over 10 years, with 100 individuals marked each year.

```
# Define mean survival, transitions, recapture, as well as number of
   occasions, states, observations and released individuals
s <- 0.8
F <- 0.6
r <- 0.1
p <- 0.5
n.occasions <- 10
n.states <- 4
n.obs <- 3
marked <- matrix(0, ncol = n.states, nrow = n.occasions)
marked[,1] <- rep(100, n.occasions)       # Releases in study area
```

```
# Define matrices with survival, transition and recapture probabilities
# These are 4-dimensional matrices, with
    # Dimension 1: state of departure
    # Dimension 2: state of arrival
    # Dimension 3: individual
    # Dimension 4: time
# 1. State process matrix
totrel<- sum(marked)*(n.occasions-1)
PSI.STATE<- array(NA, dim=c(n.states, n.states, totrel, n.occasions-1))
for (i in 1:totrel){
    for (t in 1:(n.occasions-1)){
        PSI.STATE[,,i,t] <- matrix(c(
        s*F, s*(1-F), 1-s, 0,
        0,   s,       1-s, 0,
        0,   0,       0,   1,
        0,   0,       0,   1), nrow = n.states, byrow = TRUE)
        } #t
    } #i
```

2.Observation process matrix

```
PSI.OBS <- array(NA, dim=c(n.states, n.obs, totrel, n.occasions-1))
for (i in 1:totrel){
    for (t in 1:(n.occasions-1)){
        PSI.OBS[,,i,t] <- matrix(c(
        p, 0, 1-p,
        0, 0, 1,
        0, r, 1-r,
        0, 0, 1), nrow = n.states, byrow = TRUE)
        } #t
    } #i
```

Execute simulation function

```
sim <- simul.ms(PSI.STATE, PSI.OBS, marked)
CH <- sim$CH
```

Compute date of first capture

```
get.first <- function(x) min(which(x!=0))
f <- apply(CH, 1, get.first)
```

Recode CH matrix: note, a 0 is not allowed!
1 = alive and in study are, 2 = recovered dead, 3 = not seen or recovered

```
rCH <- CH # Recoded CH
rCH[rCH==0] <- 3
```

9.5.3 Analysis of the Model

In principle, it should be possible to analyze the model in WinBUGS with code that directly translates the two matrices of the previous section, and thus in an analogous way as we have done for the other models in this chapter. However, due to a reason unknown to us, WinBUGS does not update the parameters properly, in particular the latent states z. It seems that the problem has to do with the recoveries; if they are excluded, the problem goes away. By educated trial and error, we found out that a reparameterization of the model works fine, where the recovery probability is included in the state transition matrix:

$$\begin{bmatrix} s^F & s(1-F) & (1-s)r & (1-s)(1-r) \\ 0 & s & (1-s)r & (1-s)(1-r) \\ 0 & 0 & 0 & 1 \\ 0 & 0 & 0 & 1 \end{bmatrix}$$

The observation matrix then no longer contains the recovery probability:

$$\begin{bmatrix} p & 0 & 1-p \\ 0 & 0 & 1 \\ 0 & 1 & 0 \\ 0 & 0 & 1 \end{bmatrix}$$

This model is then fitted in WinBUGS:

```
# Specify model in BUGS language
sink("lifedead.bug")
cat("
model {

# -------------------------------------------------
# Parameters:
# s: true survival probability
# F: fidelity probability
# r: recovery probability
# p: recapture/resighting probability
# -------------------------------------------------
# States (S):
# 1 alive in study area
# 2 alive outside study area
# 3 recently dead and recovered
# 4 recently dead, but not recovered, or dead (absorbing)
# Observations (O):
# 1 seen alive
# 2 recovered dead
# 3 neither seen nor recovered
# -------------------------------------------------

# Priors and constraints
for (t in 1:(n.occasions-1)){
   s[t] <- mean.s
   F[t] <- mean.f
   r[t] <- mean.r
   p[t] <- mean.p
   }
mean.s ~ dunif(0, 1)      # Prior for mean survival
mean.f ~ dunif(0, 1)      # Prior for mean fidelity
```

```
mean.r ~ dunif(0, 1)        # Prior for mean recovery
mean.p ~ dunif(0, 1)        # Prior for mean recapture

# Define state-transition and observation matrices
for (i in 1:nind){
   # Define probabilities of state S(t+1) given S(t)
   for (t in f[i]:(n.occasions-1)){
      ps[1,i,t,1] <- s[t]*F[t]
      ps[1,i,t,2] <- s[t]*(1-F[t])
      ps[1,i,t,3] <- (1-s[t])*r[t]
      ps[1,i,t,4] <- (1-s[t])*(1-r[t])
      ps[2,i,t,1] <- 0
      ps[2,i,t,2] <- s[t]
      ps[2,i,t,3] <- (1-s[t])*r[t]
      ps[2,i,t,4] <- (1-s[t])*(1-r[t])
      ps[3,i,t,1] <- 0
      ps[3,i,t,2] <- 0
      ps[3,i,t,3] <- 0
      ps[3,i,t,4] <- 1
      ps[4,i,t,1] <- 0
      ps[4,i,t,2] <- 0
      ps[4,i,t,3] <- 0
      ps[4,i,t,4] <- 1

      # Define probabilities of O(t) given S(t)
      po[1,i,t,1] <- p[t]
      po[1,i,t,2] <- 0
      po[1,i,t,3] <- 1-p[t]
      po[2,i,t,1] <- 0
      po[2,i,t,2] <- 0
      po[2,i,t,3] <- 1
      po[3,i,t,1] <- 0
      po[3,i,t,2] <- 1
      po[3,i,t,3] <- 0
      po[4,i,t,1] <- 0
      po[4,i,t,2] <- 0
      po[4,i,t,3] <- 1
      } #t
   } #i

# Likelihood
for (i in 1:nind){
   # Define latent state at first capture
   z[i,f[i]] <- Y[i,f[i]]
   for (t in (f[i]+1):n.occasions){
      # State process: draw S(t) given S(t-1)
      z[i,t] ~ dcat(ps[z[i,t-1], i, t-1,])
      # Observation process: draw O(t) given S(t)
      y[i,t] ~ dcat(po[z[i,t], i, t-1,])
      } #t
   } #i
}
",fill = TRUE)
sink()
```

(handwritten annotation: lower case — pointing to Y)

```
# Bundle data
bugs.data <- list(y = rCH, f = f, n.occasions = dim(rCH)[2], nind = dim
    (rCH)[1])

# Initial values (note: function ch.init is defined in section 7.3)
inits <- function(){list(mean.s = runif(1, 0, 1), mean.f = runif(1, 0, 1),
    mean.p = runif(1, 0, 1), mean.r = runif(1, 0, 1), z = ch.init(CH, f))}

# Parameters monitored
parameters <- c("mean.s", "mean.f", "mean.r", "mean.p")

# MCMC settings
ni <- 40000
nt <- 10
nb <- 10000
nc <- 3

# Call WinBUGS from R (BRT 80 min)
lifedead <- bugs(bugs.data, inits, parameters, "lifedead.bug",
    n.chains = nc, n.thin = nt, n.iter = ni, n.burnin = nb, debug = TRUE,
    bugs.directory = bugs.dir)
```

The model does not converge easily, and long chains are necessary to obtain satisfactory results.

```
print(lifedead, digit = 3)
          mean    sd    2.5%    25%    50%    75%  97.5%  Rhat  n.eff
mean.s  0.843  0.051  0.746  0.808  0.841  0.882  0.935  1.004    590
mean.f  0.606  0.041  0.533  0.576  0.605  0.634  0.692  1.003    770
mean.r  0.145  0.045  0.089  0.114  0.133  0.162  0.262  1.004    730
mean.p  0.515  0.028  0.461  0.496  0.515  0.534  0.572  1.001   4600
```

This model can be extended in several ways, for instance, by including mortality causes (Schaub and Pradel, 2004; Schaub, 2009; Servanthy et al., 2010), movement between sites (Kendall et al., 2006; Duriez et al., 2009), or age structures, to name just a few. Obviously, a multistate model could be used when the goal is to analyze single-state capture–recapture data alone (the true states being "alive" and "dead", and the observed states being "seen" and "not seen"), or if the goal is to analyze mark-recovery data alone (the true states being "alive", "recently dead and recovered", and "recently dead (not recovered) or dead", and the observed states being "recovered" and "not recovered").

9.6 ESTIMATION OF MOVEMENT AMONG THREE SITES

9.6.1 Model Description

In this example, we estimate movement among three sites. The list of states includes "alive at site A", "alive at site B", "alive at site C", and "dead", and the list of observations is "seen at A", "seen at B", "seen at C", and "not seen". The state transition matrix is

$$
\begin{array}{c}
& \text{site A} & \text{site B} & \text{site C} & \text{dead} \\
\begin{array}{c} \text{site A} \\ \text{site B} \\ \text{site C} \\ \text{dead} \end{array} &
\left[\begin{array}{cccc}
\phi_A(1-\psi_{AB}-\psi_{AC}) & \phi_A\psi_{AB} & \phi_A\psi_{AB} & 1-\phi_A \\
\phi_B\psi_{BA} & \phi_B(1-\psi_{BA}-\psi_{BC}) & \phi_B\psi_{BC} & 1-\phi_B \\
\phi_C\psi_{CA} & \phi_C\psi_{CB} & \phi_C(1-\psi_{CA}-\psi_{CB}) & 1-\phi_C \\
0 & 0 & 0 & 1
\end{array}\right]
\end{array},
$$

and the observation matrix is

$$
\begin{array}{c}
& \text{seen at A} & \text{seen at B} & \text{seen at C} & \text{not seen} \\
\begin{array}{c} \text{site A} \\ \text{site B} \\ \text{site C} \\ \text{dead} \end{array} &
\left[\begin{array}{cccc}
p_A & 0 & 0 & 1-p_A \\
0 & p_B & 0 & 1-p_B \\
0 & 0 & p_C & 1-p_C \\
0 & 0 & 0 & 1
\end{array}\right]
\end{array}
$$

We here extend the multistate model for two sites (Section 9.2) because there is an additional challenge in the constraints that need to be put on the movement probabilities. For each site, we now have three movement probabilities. For instance, from site A, we have ψ_{AA}, ψ_{AB}, and ψ_{AC}. Two sets of constraints must be imposed on their estimates: first, each of them must be in the interval [0, 1] and second, they must sum to 1. With only two transition probabilities as in all examples before, this is easy to achieve: we give a uniform or a beta prior to one of them and calculate the other as the complement to 1. With more than two states, this is no longer so easy, but there are two possible solutions: the use of a multi-nomial logit link function for the transition probabilities or the use of a Dirichlet distribution as a prior for the transition probabilities. Below, we illustrate both.

For a multinomial link function, we specify a normal prior distribution for $n-1$ transition parameters (α). These correspond to the transition probabilities on the logit scale, and they can be modeled using the GLM framework. This is exactly equivalent to the use of the logit function when the parameters on the logit scale are modeled with a GLM. The back-transformation for each of the $n-1$ parameters is calculated as

$$
\beta_j = \frac{\exp(\alpha_j)}{1+\sum_{i=1}^{n-1}\exp(\alpha_i)},
$$

which ensures that each of them, as well as their sum, is <1. The last parameter is calculated as $\beta_n = 1-\sum_{i=1}^{n-1}\beta_i$. In this model, only $n-1$ parameters can be modeled directly with a GLM, and the last parameter is modified indirectly, being a function of the covariates used in the GLM for the $n - 1$ modeled parameters.

The second option is the use of a Dirichlet prior for the βs, which automatically ensures that they are in the interval [0, 1] and sum to 1. For the Dirichlet prior distribution, hyperparameters must be chosen. With three transition probabilities that must sum to one, a vector [1, 1, 1] induces a noninformative Dirichlet prior. This vector of hyperparameters is best given as data.

The Dirichlet prior for the βs can also be specified indirectly. This option works well in WinBUGS by specification of a set of gamma (1, 1) hyperprior random variables, say, $\alpha_j \sim$ gamma(1, 1), followed by the relation $\beta_j = \alpha_j \Big/ \sum_{i=1}^{n} \alpha_i$ (Royle and Dorazio, 2008).

In the following example, we use the multinomial logit link function, whereas for the model in Section 9.7, we construct the Dirichlet prior distribution using gamma hyperpriors. The latter results in faster convergence, at least in our examples.

9.6.2 Generation of Simulated Data

We extend the previous little ringed plover example to three sites. We assume that habitat quality at site A is higher than at sites B and C, and thus annual survival at site A is higher ($\phi_A = 0.85$) than at site B ($\phi_B = 0.75$) and C ($\phi_C = 0.65$). Furthermore, movement away from A is less likely ($\psi_{AB} = 0.3$, $\psi_{AC} = 0.2$) than movement to A ($\psi_{BA} = 0.5$, $\psi_{CA} = 0.6$). Movement rates between B and C are identical ($\psi_{BC} = 0.1$, $\psi_{CB} = 0.1$). Capture effort is greater at site A than at B or C resulting in the following recapture probabilities: $p_A = 0.7$, $p_B = 0.4$, and $p_C = 0.5$. Captures at site A are labeled "1", at site B "2", and at site C "3".

```
# Define mean survival, transitions, recapture, as well as number of
   occasions, states, observations and released individuals
phiA <- 0.85
phiB <- 0.75
phiC <- 0.65
psiAB <- 0.3
psiAC <- 0.2
psiBA <- 0.5
psiBC <- 0.1
psiCA <- 0.6
psiCB <- 0.1
pA <- 0.7
pB <- 0.4
pC <- 0.5
```

```
n.occasions <- 6
n.states <- 4
n.obs <- 4
marked <- matrix(NA, ncol = n.states, nrow = n.occasions)
marked[,1] <- rep(50, n.occasions)
marked[,2] <- rep(50, n.occasions)
marked[,3] <- rep(50, n.occasions)
marked[,4] <- rep(0, n.occasions)

# Define matrices with survival, transition and recapture probabilities
# These are 4-dimensional matrices, with
   # Dimension 1: state of departure
   # Dimension 2: state of arrival
   # Dimension 3: individual
   # Dimension 4: time
# 1. State process matrix
totrel <- sum(marked)*(n.occasions-1)
PSI.STATE <- array(NA, dim=c(n.states, n.states, totrel, n.occasions-1))
for (i in 1:totrel){
   for (t in 1:(n.occasions-1)){
      PSI.STATE[,,i,t] <- matrix(c(
      phiA*(1-psiAB-psiAC), phiA*psiAB,          phiA*psiAC,          1-phiA,
      phiB*psiBA,           phiB*(1-psiBA-psiBC), phiB*psiBC,          1-phiB,
      phiC*psiCA,           phiC*psiCB,          phiC*(1-psiCA-psiCB), 1-phiC,
      0,                    0,                   0,                   1),
         nrow = n.states, byrow = TRUE)
        } #t
     } #i

# 2.Observation process matrix
PSI.OBS <- array(NA, dim=c(n.states, n.obs, totrel, n.occasions-1))
for (i in 1:totrel){
   for (t in 1:(n.occasions-1)){
      PSI.OBS[,,i,t] <- matrix(c(
      pA, 0, 0, 1-pA,
      0, pB, 0, 1-pB,
      0, 0, pC, 1-pC,
      0, 0, 0, 1), nrow = n.states, byrow = TRUE)
        } #t
     } #i

# Execute simulation function
sim <- simul.ms(PSI.STATE, PSI.OBS, marked)
CH <- sim$CH

# Compute vector with occasions of first capture
get.first <- function(x) min(which(x!=0))
f <- apply(CH, 1, get.first)

# Recode CH matrix: note, a 0 is not allowed in WinBUGS!
# 1 = seen alive in A, 2 = seen alive in B, 3, seen alive in C, 4 = not seen
rCH <- CH # Recoded CH
rCH[rCH==0] <- 4
```

9.6.3 Analysis of the Model

We first write the model with the multinomial logit link.

```
# Specify model in BUGS language
sink("ms3-multinomlogit.bug")
cat("
model {

# --------------------------------------------------
# Parameters:
# phiA: survival probability at site A
# phiB: survival probability at site B
# phiC: survival probability at site C
# psiAB: movement probability from site A to site B
# psiAC: movement probability from site A to site C
# psiBA: movement probability from site B to site A
# psiBC: movement probability from site B to site C
# psiCA: movement probability from site C to site A
# psiCB: movement probability from site C to site B
# pA: recapture probability at site A
# pB: recapture probability at site B
# pC: recapture probability at site C
# --------------------------------------------------
# States (S):
# 1 alive at A
# 2 alive at B
# 3 alive at C
# 4 dead
# Observations (O):
# 1 seen at A
# 2 seen at B
# 3 seen at C
# 4 not seen
# --------------------------------------------------

# Priors and constraints
   # Survival and recapture: uniform
   phiA ~ dunif(0, 1)
   phiB ~ dunif(0, 1)
   phiC ~ dunif(0, 1)
   pA ~ dunif(0, 1)
   pB ~ dunif(0, 1)
   pC ~ dunif(0, 1)
   # Transitions: multinomial logit
      # Normal priors on logit of all but one transition prob.
      for (i in 1:2){
         lpsiA[i] ~ dnorm(0, 0.001)
         lpsiB[i] ~ dnorm(0, 0.001)
         lpsiC[i] ~ dnorm(0, 0.001)
         }
      # Constrain the transitions such that their sum is < 1
      for (i in 1:2){
         psiA[i] <- exp(lpsiA[i]) / (1 + exp(lpsiA[1]) + exp(lpsiA[2]))
```

```
          psiB[i] <- exp(lpsiB[i]) / (1 + exp(lpsiB[1]) + exp(lpsiB[2]))
          psiC[i] <- exp(lpsiC[i]) / (1 + exp(lpsiC[1]) + exp(lpsiC[2]))
          }
      # Calculate the last transition probability
      psiA[3] <- 1-psiA[1]-psiA[2]
      psiB[3] <- 1-psiB[1]-psiB[2]
      psiC[3] <- 1-psiC[1]-psiC[2]

# Define state-transition and observation matrices
for (i in 1:nind){
   # Define probabilities of state S(t+1) given S(t)
   for (t in f[i]:(n.occasions-1)){
      ps[1,i,t,1] <- phiA * psiA[1]
      ps[1,i,t,2] <- phiA * psiA[2]
      ps[1,i,t,3] <- phiA * psiA[3]
      ps[1,i,t,4] <- 1-phiA
      ps[2,i,t,1] <- phiB * psiB[1]
      ps[2,i,t,2] <- phiB * psiB[2]
      ps[2,i,t,3] <- phiB * psiB[3]
      ps[2,i,t,4] <- 1-phiB
      ps[3,i,t,1] <- phiC * psiC[1]
      ps[3,i,t,2] <- phiC * psiC[2]
      ps[3,i,t,3] <- phiC * psiC[3]
      ps[3,i,t,4] <- 1-phiC
      ps[4,i,t,1] <- 0
      ps[4,i,t,2] <- 0
      ps[4,i,t,3] <- 0
      ps[4,i,t,4] <- 1

      # Define probabilities of O(t) given S(t)
      po[1,i,t,1] <- pA
      po[1,i,t,2] <- 0
      po[1,i,t,3] <- 0
      po[1,i,t,4] <- 1-pA
      po[2,i,t,1] <- 0
      po[2,i,t,2] <- pB
      po[2,i,t,3] <- 0
      po[2,i,t,4] <- 1-pB
      po[3,i,t,1] <- 0
      po[3,i,t,2] <- 0
      po[3,i,t,3] <- pC
      po[3,i,t,4] <- 1-pC
      po[4,i,t,1] <- 0
      po[4,i,t,2] <- 0
      po[4,i,t,3] <- 0
      po[4,i,t,4] <- 1
      } #t
   } #i

# Likelihood
for (i in 1:nind){
   # Define latent state at first capture
   z[i,f[i]] <- Y[i,f[i]]
   for (t in (f[i]+1):n.occasions){
```

```
    # State process: draw S(t) given S(t-1)
    z[i,t] ~ dcat(ps[z[i,t-1], i, t-1,])
    # Observation process: draw O(t) given S(t)
    y[i,t] ~ dcat(po[z[i,t], i, t-1,])
      } #t
   } #i
}
",fill = TRUE)
sink()
```

Bundle data
```
bugs.data <- list(y = rCH, f = f, n.occasions = dim(rCH)[2], nind = dim
   (rCH)[1], z = known.state.ms(rCH, 4))
```

Initial values
```
inits <- function(){list(phiA = runif(1, 0, 1), phiB = runif(1, 0, 1),
   phiC = runif(1, 0, 1), lpsiA = rnorm(2), lpsiB = rnorm(2), lpsiC =
   rnorm(2), pA = runif(1, 0, 1) , pB = runif(1, 0, 1) , pC = runif(1, 0, 1),
   z = ms.init.z(rCH, f))}
```

Parameters monitored
```
parameters <- c("phiA", "phiB", "phiC", "psiA", "psiB", "psiC", "pA",
   "pB", "pC")
```

MCMC settings
```
ni <- 50000
nt <- 6
nb <- 20000
nc <- 3
```

Call WinBUGS from R (BRT 56 min)
```
ms3 <- bugs(bugs.data, inits, parameters, "ms3-multinomlogit.bug",
   n.chains = nc, n.thin = nt, n.iter = ni, n.burnin = nb, debug = TRUE,
   bugs.directory = bugs.dir, working.directory = getwd())
```

This model runs slowly and convergence is hard to achieve. To increase computation speed, we have provided the known values of the latent state z (see bugs.data). The parameter estimates look like the following:

```
print(ms3, digits = 3)
```

	mean	sd	2.5%	25%	50%	75%	97.5%	Rhat	n.eff
phiA	0.833	0.029	0.780	0.813	0.832	0.851	0.893	1.001	8600
phiB	0.730	0.033	0.664	0.708	0.731	0.753	0.791	1.001	15000
phiC	0.676	0.036	0.607	0.651	0.676	0.699	0.747	1.001	15000
psiA[1]	0.546	0.080	0.395	0.491	0.546	0.602	0.702	1.001	15000
psiA[2]	0.310	0.070	0.173	0.262	0.310	0.357	0.449	1.002	1300
psiA[3]	0.144	0.040	0.091	0.115	0.135	0.165	0.240	1.007	320
psiB[1]	0.551	0.097	0.373	0.482	0.546	0.616	0.751	1.001	15000
psiB[2]	0.375	0.088	0.189	0.317	0.381	0.438	0.531	1.001	8400
psiB[3]	0.074	0.030	0.032	0.051	0.068	0.089	0.151	1.003	1000
psiC[1]	0.740	0.072	0.572	0.697	0.750	0.793	0.849	1.001	13000
psiC[2]	0.096	0.044	0.034	0.065	0.089	0.119	0.205	1.002	1300
psiC[3]	0.164	0.053	0.089	0.125	0.153	0.193	0.292	1.004	570
pA	0.671	0.085	0.535	0.610	0.662	0.720	0.870	1.001	15000
pB	0.456	0.132	0.280	0.366	0.427	0.514	0.817	1.002	1600
pC	0.732	0.170	0.398	0.601	0.749	0.877	0.988	1.005	450

9.7 REAL-DATA EXAMPLE:
THE SHOWY LADY'S SLIPPER

Here, we want to estimate the survival probability of a plant species, the beautiful showy lady's slipper (Fig. 9.7). You may ask yourself why there is a need to apply multistate capture–recapture models to plant data; after all, don't plants just stand still and wait to be counted (Harper, 1977)? Couldn't we simply use logistic regression models for survival estimation? Well, this is only partly true. If a plant remains aboveground throughout its life, such as an oak, then this may be true. However, some plants are temporally unobservable because they are dormant and thus live underground for one or several years. Since individuals may also die when they are dormant, we have to use probabilistic models. Moreover, there is an interest in modeling the transition probabilities to and from the dormant state, as well as between different aboveground states, such as vegetative and reproductive. Knowing these transition probabilities is important for setting up matrix projection models for such species. Examples of the application of capture–recapture models (both single- and multistate models) for plants are Shefferson et al. (2001) and Kéry et al. (2005a).

FIGURE 9.7   Showy lady's slipper (*Cypripedium reginae*), West Virginia, 2010 (Photograph by K. Gregg).

The multistate capture–recapture data analyzed here were collected by Kathy Gregg in Big Draft (West Virginia) from 1989 to 1999. Kéry and Gregg (2004) analyzed them in the frequentist framework. Three live states can be distinguished for the showy lady's slipper: dormant, vegetative, and flowering. We would like to estimate the probabilities of state transition and of survival of this species. For the state-transition matrix, we define four states: "vegetative", "flowering", "dormant", and "dead".

$$
\begin{array}{c}
\\
\text{vegetative} \\
\text{flowering} \\
\text{dormant} \\
\text{dead}
\end{array}
\begin{array}{cccc}
\text{vegetative} & \text{flowering} & \text{dormant} & \text{dead} \\
\left[\begin{array}{c} s\psi_{VV} \\ s\psi_{FV} \\ s\psi_{DV} \\ 0 \end{array}\right. &
\begin{array}{c} s\psi_{VF} \\ s\psi_{FF} \\ s\psi_{DF} \\ 0 \end{array} &
\begin{array}{c} s(1-\psi_{VV}-\psi_{VF}) \\ s(1-\psi_{FV}-\psi_{FF}) \\ s(1-\psi_{DV}-\psi_{DF}) \\ 0 \end{array} &
\left.\begin{array}{c} 1-s \\ 1-s \\ 1-s \\ 1 \end{array}\right]
\end{array}
$$

Permanent emigration is impossible, so we can estimate true survival; hence, the symbol s instead of ϕ. For the observation matrix, we define the observations "seen vegetative", "seen flowering", and "not seen". We assume that no plants were missed in the states "vegetative" and "flowering", but they cannot be observed when they are either "dormant" or "dead". Thus, the observation matrix is completely deterministic:

$$
\begin{array}{c}
\\
\text{vegetative} \\
\text{flowering} \\
\text{dormant} \\
\text{dead}
\end{array}
\begin{array}{ccc}
\text{seen veg.} & \text{seen flow.} & \text{not seen} \\
\left[\begin{array}{c} 1 \\ 0 \\ 0 \\ 0 \end{array}\right. &
\begin{array}{c} 0 \\ 1 \\ 0 \\ 0 \end{array} &
\left.\begin{array}{c} 0 \\ 0 \\ 1 \\ 1 \end{array}\right]
\end{array}
$$

In the data, the vegetative state is coded as 1, the flowering state as 2, and failure to observe an individual as 0. We now read the data in an R workspace

```
CH <- as.matrix(read.table("orchids.txt", sep=" ", header = F))
n.occasions <- dim(CH)[2]

# Compute vector with occasion of first capture
f <- numeric()
for (i in 1:dim(CH)[1]){f[i] <- min(which(CH[i,]!=0))}

# Recode CH matrix: note, a 0 is not allowed by WinBUGS!
# 1 = seen vegetative, 2 = seen flowering, 3 = not seen
rCH <- CH # Recoded CH
rCH[rCH==0] <- 3
```

Kéry and Gregg (2004) found that a model with year-specific survival and constant transition probabilities was most parsimonious, and we will use this parameter structure here. Since movement is possible among three live states, the transition probabilities must meet the constraints that each of them is between 0 and 1 and that they sum to 1. Here, we implement the Dirichlet prior distribution using elemental gamma random variables as described in Section 9.6.1.

```
# Specify model in BUGS language
sink("ladyslipper.bug")
cat("
model {

# -----------------------------------------------
# Parameters:
# s: survival probability
# psiV: transitions from vegetative
# psiF: transitions from flowering
# psiD: transitions from dormant
# -----------------------------------------------
# States (S):
# 1 vegetative
# 2 flowering
# 3 dormant
# 4 dead
# Observations (O):
# 1 seen vegetative
# 2 seen flowering
# 3 not seen
# -----------------------------------------------

# Priors and constraints
  # Survival: uniform
  for (t in 1:(n.occasions-1)){
     s[t] ~ dunif(0, 1)
     }
  # Transitions: gamma priors
  for (i in 1:3){
     a[i] ~ dgamma(1, 1)
     psiD[i] <- a[i]/sum(a[])
     b[i] ~ dgamma(1, 1)
     psiV[i] <- b[i]/sum(b[])
     c[i] ~ dgamma(1, 1)
     psiF[i] <- c[i]/sum(c[])
     }

# Define state-transition and observation matrices
for (i in 1:nind)
  # Define probabilities of state S(t+1) given S(t)
  for (t in 1:(n.occasions-1)){
     ps[1,i,t,1] <- s[t] * psiV[1]
     ps[1,i,t,2] <- s[t] * psiV[2]
     ps[1,i,t,3] <- s[t] * psiV[3]
     ps[1,i,t,4] <- 1-s[t]
     ps[2,i,t,1] <- s[t] * psiF[1]
     ps[2,i,t,2] <- s[t] * psiF[2]
     ps[2,i,t,3] <- s[t] * psiF[3]
     ps[2,i,t,4] <- 1-s[t]
```

```
    ps[3,i,t,1] <- s[t] * psiD[1]
    ps[3,i,t,2] <- s[t] * psiD[2]
    ps[3,i,t,3] <- s[t] * psiD[3]
    ps[3,i,t,4] <- 1-s[t]
    ps[4,i,t,1] <- 0
    ps[4,i,t,2] <- 0
    ps[4,i,t,3] <- 0
    ps[4,i,t,4] <- 1

    # Define probabilities of O(t) given S(t)
    po[1,i,t,1] <- 1
    po[1,i,t,2] <- 0
    po[1,i,t,3] <- 0
    po[2,i,t,1] <- 0
    po[2,i,t,2] <- 1
    po[2,i,t,3] <- 0
    po[3,i,t,1] <- 0
    po[3,i,t,2] <- 0
    po[3,i,t,3] <- 1
    po[4,i,t,1] <- 0
    po[4,i,t,2] <- 0
    po[4,i,t,3] <- 1
      } #t
  } #i

# Likelihood
for (i in 1:nind){
  # Define latent state at first capture
  z[i,f[i]] <- Y[i,f[i]]
  for (t in (f[i]+1):n.occasions){

    # State process: draw S(t) given S(t-1)
    z[i,t] ~ dcat(ps[z[i,t-1], i, t-1,])

    # Observation process: draw O(t) given S(t)
    y[i,t] ~ dcat(po[z[i,t], i, t-1,])
      } #t
    } #i
}
",fill=TRUE)
sink()

# Bundle data
bugs.data <- list(y = rCH, f = f, n.occasions = dim(rCH)[2],
    nind = dim(rCH)[1], z = known.state.ms(rCH, 3))

# Initial values
inits <- function(){list(s = runif((dim(rCH)[2]-1),0,1),
    z = ms.init.z(rCH, f))}

# Parameters monitored
parameters <- c("s", "psiV", "psiF", "psiD")

# MCMC settings
ni <- 5000
nt <- 3
```

```
nb <- 2000
nc <- 3

# Call WinBUGS from R (BRT 3 min)
ls <- bugs(bugs.data, inits, parameters, "ladyslipper.bug", n.chains =
    nc, n.thin = nt, n.iter = ni, n.burnin = nb, debug = TRUE,
    bugs.directory = bugs.dir, working.directory = getwd())
print(ls, digits = 3)
          mean    sd   2.5%    25%    50%    75%  97.5%   Rhat  n.eff
s[1]     0.984 0.013  0.952  0.977  0.986  0.993  0.999  1.001   3000
[...]
s[10]    0.982 0.013  0.951  0.975  0.984  0.992  0.999  1.001   3000
psiV[1]  0.830 0.012  0.806  0.822  0.830  0.838  0.852  1.001   3000
psiV[2]  0.151 0.011  0.130  0.143  0.151  0.159  0.174  1.002   1400
psiV[3]  0.019 0.005  0.011  0.016  0.019  0.022  0.030  1.002   1800
psiF[1]  0.183 0.018  0.149  0.171  0.183  0.195  0.221  1.001   3000
psiF[2]  0.803 0.019  0.763  0.790  0.803  0.816  0.838  1.001   3000
psiF[3]  0.014 0.006  0.005  0.010  0.013  0.018  0.028  1.001   3000
psiD[1]  0.554 0.101  0.348  0.486  0.557  0.625  0.742  1.005    990
psiD[2]  0.172 0.069  0.059  0.122  0.166  0.212  0.327  1.001   3000
psiD[3]  0.274 0.099  0.106  0.200  0.265  0.337  0.484  1.002   2000
```

Note how the estimated transitions relate to those presented in the state-transition matrix above. The estimate psiV[1] is ψ_{VV}, psiV[2] is ψ_{VF}, psiV[3] is $1 - \psi_{VV} - \psi_{VF}$, and so on. The estimated parameter estimates match very well the results from the published frequentist analysis of the model for this data set (Kéry and Gregg, 2004).

9.8 SUMMARY AND OUTLOOK

In this chapter, we have introduced an important class of capture–recapture models: multistate models. Multistate models represent a very general framework and other models such as the CJS (Chapter 7), the mark-recovery (Chapter 8), and the JS model (Chapter 10) can be described as special cases (Lebreton et al., 1999, 2009). Multistate models are extremely flexible and can be used to address a large array of very diverse ecological questions. The flexibility stems from the fact that the definition of states can involve many different quantities, as seen in the examples, which go far beyond the classical geographic locations. In addition to the examples that we have provided in this chapter, we present some further models in Appendix 2 (including data simulation and BUGS model code). To analyze multistate models in the Bayesian framework, we use the state-space formulation.

Multistate capture–recapture models can be extended in exactly the same ways as we have shown for the single-state models. Thus, we may model several groups, time-dependent parameters, and individual or temporal covariates, and group effects can be assumed fixed or random. The data and most parts of the BUGS model code remain the same, but there are modifications in the "Priors and constraints" part of the model, in exactly the same way as was shown in Chapters 6 and 7. The exercises and their solutions provide some examples of such extensions. Multistate models have also been combined with other model classes, such as site-occupancy models (Section 13.6).

Multistate capture–recapture models sometimes suffer from identifiability problems, both intrinsic and extrinsic. Hence, it is important to check for identifiability, in particular when adopting less well-known multistate model variants. To check identifiability, the method introduced in Section 7.9 can be used. Moreover, we recommend assessing the goodness of fit using χ^2-decompositions developed by Pradel et al. (2003).

Recently, an extremely general extension of the general multistate model to include state uncertainty has been developed (Pradel, 2005). E-SURGE (Choquet et al. 2009b) is a flexible software to fit such models using maximum likelihood. These so-called multievent models belong to the class of hidden Markov models and can also be fitted using WinBUGS. An important difference is that in the conventional multistate models of this chapter, there is no error in the state assignment, whereas in multievent models, state assignment errors can occur. In other words, multistate models allow only false-negative errors, while multievent models allow both false-negative and false-positive errors. The state-space formulation used here to fit multistate models can be adapted to include state assignment errors; see also Section 13.6. The observation matrix must then be written in such a way that false state assignments are possible. A further difference is that there is also uncertainty about the state at first observation in the multievent model. We can model this uncertainty by estimating a probability of state membership at first encounter based on the observed states. This means that we have several additional parameters in the model that require priors.

9.9 EXERCISES

1. Simulate multistate capture–recapture data for two sexes (m, f) in two populations (A, B) that are connected by dispersal. Assume that movement rates between populations are the same for both sexes, but that site-specific survival and recapture differ among populations. The simulation parameters are $\phi_{A,m} = 0.5$, $\phi_{B,m} = 0.6$, $\phi_{A,f} = 0.7$, $\phi_{B,f} = 0.6$, $\psi_{AB} = 0.2$, $\psi_{BA} = 0.5$, $p_{A,m} = 0.3$, $p_{B,m} = 0.7$, $p_{A,f} = 0.4$, $p_{B,f} = 0.8$, occasions = 6, and 20 males and females are released at each population in each year. Simulate the data and analyze them.
2. Simulate multistate capture–recapture data from two populations observed over 8 occasions that exchange individuals with the following

parameter values: $\phi_A = [0.5, 0.6, 0.3, 0.7, 0.5, 0.65, 0.55]$, $\phi_B = 0.6$, $\psi_{AB} = 0.2$, $\psi_{BA} = 0.5$, $p_A = 0.3$, $p_B = 0.7$, and 20 individuals are released at each population in each year. Thus, we assume that the annual survival probabilities vary among years at location A, but not at location B. Simulate data and analyze them, a) assuming fixed year effects and b) assuming random year effects.

3. In a population of salamanders, there is nonrandom temporary emigration (with respect to one breeding site). In addition, there is strong individual heterogeneity in capture probability. Assume a 10-years study and the following parameter values: survival = 0.7, $\psi_{IO} = 0.4$, $\psi_{OI} = 0.8$, mean recapture = 0.5, and the variance among individuals of the logit of recapture $\sigma_i^2 = 0.4$. Further assume that 100 salamanders are newly marked each year. Simulate data with these characteristics and analyze them.

Estimation of Survival, Recruitment, and Population Size from Capture–Recapture Data Using the Jolly–Seber Model

10.1 INTRODUCTION

Capture–recapture data contain information not only about the disappearance of marked individuals from a study population (i.e., mortality and permanent emigration) but also about their arrival into the population (i.e., recruitment by locally born individuals and immigration). Estimation of these recruitment-related parameters is possible when the *complete* capture-histories of the marked individuals are analyzed, not just the part following first capture, as for the CJS model (Chapter 7). The leading capture-history zeros (those before initial capture) along with the first capture contain the information about the arrival process. A leading zero is observed either because an individual has not yet arrived (recruited or immigrated) in the population or because it was already in the population but has not been captured. The part of the capture-histories after the initial capture contains information about survival, which is modeled by the CJS model (Chapter 7). All open-population capture–recapture types of models described in the Chapters 7–9 condition on first capture. This means that only the part of a capture-history *after* first capture is modeled; the information about entry of individuals is discarded. In this chapter, we introduce the Jolly–Seber (JS) model (Jolly, 1965; Seber, 1965), which allows estimation of gains to and losses from the population by *not* conditioning on first capture. Additionally, population size and the number of recruits per occasion can be estimated. The JS model is an extension of the closed-population models in Chapter 6, which do not condition on first capture either but assume demographic closure (i.e., the absence of mortality, recruitment, or dispersal), and of the CJS model.

Since the JS model uses the complete capture-history, additional assumptions are necessary. All assumptions listed for the CJS model (Section 7.1) also apply to the JS model. In addition, the JS model requires that *all* individuals (marked *and* unmarked) in the population have the same capture probability. In other words, newly captured individuals must be a random sample of all unmarked individuals in a population (Williams et al., 2002). This assumption is likely to be met when the same sampling protocol is applied for capture and recapture, but not when protocols differ. In many studies where color marks are applied, initial capture is a physical capture, whereas recaptures are just sightings from a distance. In this case, the equal-capturability assumption is likely to be violated. Moreover, the assumption of homogeneous capture is violated in the presence of a permanent trap effect. Violation of the equal-catchability assumption biases estimates of population size and recruitment, but not of survival (Nichols et al., 1984). Therefore, permanent trap effects do not violate the CJS assumptions. Williams et al. (2002) provide an in-depth overview of JS model assumptions and consequences of their failure for the parameter estimates.

There are a number of different parameterizations of the JS model, which differ basically in the way how recruitment is modeled. They include the original parameterizations of Jolly (1965) and Seber (1965), the superpopulation approach (Crosbie and Manly, 1985; Schwarz and Arnason, 1996), the reverse-time formulation (Pradel, 1996), the parameterization of Link and Barker (2005), and finally the formulation as a restricted dynamic occupancy model (Royle and Dorazio, 2008). All JS model parameterizations are related and should give the same estimates of population size and recruitment parameters. Here, we illustrate three JS model variants: the restricted occupancy formulation, the description as a multistate model, and the superpopulation formulation (Royle and Dorazio, 2008). We make extensive use of parameter-expanded data augmentation (introduced in Chapter 6) because it makes the modeling much easier (Royle et al., 2007a; Royle and Dorazio, 2011).

Numerous JS model variants have been described in the frequentist framework (e.g., Pollock et al., 1990; Pradel, 1996; Schwarz and Arnason, 1996; Williams et al., 2002) and implemented in software such as MARK (White and Burnham, 1999) or POPAN (Arnason and Schwarz, 1999). In contrast, Bayesian applications are still relatively rare (but see Link and Barker, 2005; Dupuis and Schwarz, 2007; Schofield and Barker, 2008; Royle and Dorazio, 2008; Gardner et al., 2010; Link and Barker, 2010; Royle and Dorazio, 2011).

10.2 THE JS MODEL AS A STATE-SPACE MODEL

We formulate the JS model in the hierarchical state-space framework. As mentioned repeatedly, the observed capture–recapture data are described as the result of a state process (the ecological process) and the observation process, which depends on the result of the state process. We denote the number of individuals ever alive during the study N_s and call it the superpopulation size (Schwarz and Arnason, 1996). We further assume that a fraction of N_s is already alive and in the study area at the first capture occasion, and that all remaining individuals have entered the population by the end of the study. The probability that a member of N_s enters the population at occasion t is b_t ($t = 1, \ldots, T$) and is called the entry probability (Schwarz and Arnason, 1996). It is the probability that an individual is new in the population, that is, it has entered the population since the preceding occasion. Entry could result either from in situ recruitment (locally born individuals) or from immigration. Sometimes the entry probability is called recruitment probability, but this is inaccurate. The number of individuals entering the population at t is $B_t = N_s b_t$. The fraction of individuals already present at the first occasion is b_1; this "entry" probability has no clear ecological meaning because it is a complex function of all entries before the first occasion. All entry probabilities must sum to 1 to ensure that all N_s individuals enter the population sometime during the study. The number of individuals entering at each occasion can be modeled with a multinomial distribution as $\mathbf{B} \sim$ multinomial(N_s, $\mathbf{b}$) (note that $\mathbf{B}$ and $\mathbf{b}$ are vectors).

As in the CJS model, we denote the latent state of individual i at occasion t as $z_{i,t} = 1$, if it is alive and present in the population, and as $z_{i,t} = 0$, if it is either dead or has not yet entered the population. Thus, if individual i enters the population at t, its latent state changes from $z_{i,t-1} = 0$ to $z_{i,t} = 1$ (Fig. 10.1). On entry, the survival process starts, which is a simple coin flip and identical to that in the CJS model (Chapter 7). Technically, the latent state $z_{i,t+1}$ at $t + 1$ is determined by a Bernoulli trial with success probability $\phi_{i,t}$ ($t = 1, \dots, T - 1$). The two processes defined so far, the entry and the survival process, represent the latent state processes. The observation process is defined for individuals that are alive ($z = 1$). As usual, we assume that the detection of individual i at occasion t is determined by another coin flip with success probability $p_{i,t}$ ($t = 1, \dots, T$), that is, by another Bernoulli trial.

The resulting capture–recapture data consist of the capture-histories of n individuals. When capture probability is < 1, typically not all individuals in a population are captured; hence, $n < N_s$. If N_s were known, the capture–recapture data would contain in addition N_s-n all-zero capture-histories, and the model specification would be relatively easy. We could just use a multinomial distribution to estimate entry probabilities. However, N_s is unknown and so the multinomial index is also unknown and must be estimated. Moreover, parameters such as entry and capture probabilities refer to the complete population (N_s), not just

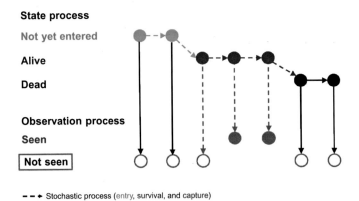

FIGURE 10.1   Example of the state and observation process of a marked individual over time in the JS model. The sequence of true states for this individual under the restricted occupancy and superpopulation formulation is $z = [0, 0, 1, 1, 1, 0, 0]$, and the observed capture-history is $y = [0, 0, 0, 1, 1, 0, 0]$. In the multistate formulation, $z = [1, 1, 2, 2, 2, 3, 3]$ and $y = [2, 2, 2, 1, 1, 2, 2]$.

to the n individuals ever captured. To deal with these challenges, we use parameter-expanded data augmentation (PX-DA; Tanner and Wong, 1987; Liu and Wu, 1999; Royle et al., 2007a; Royle and Dorazio, 2011), as we did in Chapter 6. The key idea is to fix the dimension of the parameter space in the analysis by augmenting the observed data with a large number of all-zero capture-histories, resulting in a larger data set of fixed dimension M, and to analyze the augmented data set using a reparameterized (zero-inflated) version of the model that would be applied if N_s were known. For a useful recent review of PX-DA, see Royle and Dorazio (2011).

10.3 FITTING THE JS MODEL WITH DATA AUGMENTATION

After augmentation, the capture–recapture data set contains M individuals, of which N_s are genuine and M-N_s are pseudo-individuals (Fig. 10.2). We do not know the proportions of genuine and pseudo-individuals, but we can estimate them. There are different ways to parameterize a JS model, and we present three here. First, the entry to the population is described as a removal process from M so that at the end of the study, N_s $(N_s \leq M)$ individuals have entered. This model can be developed either as a restricted version of a dynamic occupancy model

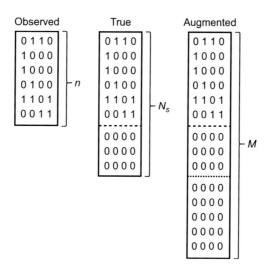

FIGURE 10.2 Observed, true, and augmented capture-history matrix. The observed number of capture-histories is n, true population size N_s, and the size of the augmented data set M; n and M are known, and N_s can be estimated.

(Section 13.5) or as a multistate model (Chapter 9). As a third approach, we use a zero-inflated version of the superpopulation formulation.

10.3.1 The JS Model as a Restricted Dynamic Occupancy Model

Royle and Dorazio (2008) showed that the JS model can be formulated as a restricted dynamic occupancy model. The entry process is defined slightly differently from what we described earlier. We imagine that individuals can be in one of three possible states: "not yet entered", "alive", and "dead" (Fig. 10.1). The state transitions are governed by two ecological processes, entry and survival, which we estimate. We denote as γ_t ($t = 1, \ldots, T$), the probability that an available individual in M enters the population at occasion t. This corresponds to the transition probability from state "not yet entered" to the state "alive". Importantly, γ refers to available individuals, that is, to those in M that have not yet entered. The entry process is thus a removal process; over time, fewer and fewer individuals will be in the state "not yet entered" and thus available to entering the population. As a result, γ will increase over time on average, even with constant per-capita recruitment. It is a pure "nuisance parameter", which is needed to describe the system, but without an ecological meaning. We refer to γ as a removal entry probability. The expected number of individuals present at the first occasion is $E(B_1) = M\gamma_1$. The expected number of individuals entering at the second occasion is the product of the number of individuals still available to enter and γ_2, thus $E(B_2) = M(1 - \gamma_1)\gamma_2$. More generally, the expected number of individuals entering the population at t is $E(B_t) = M\prod_{i=1}^{t-1}(1 - \gamma_i)\gamma_t$, and the total number of individuals that ever enter is $N_s = \sum \mathbf{B}$.

The state of individual i at the first occasion is

$$z_{i,1} \sim \text{Bernoulli}(\gamma_1).$$

Subsequent states are determined either by survival, for an individual already entered ($z_{i,t} = 1$), or by entry for one that has not ($z_{i,t} = 0$). Thus,

$$z_{i,t+1} \,|\, z_{i,t}, \ldots, z_{i,1} \sim \text{Bernoulli}\left(z_{i,t}\phi_{i,t} + \gamma_{t+1}\prod_{k=1}^{t}(1 - z_{i,k})\right).$$

Survival probability between occasion t and $t + 1$ for individual i is denoted as $\phi_{i,t}$. In contrast, γ_t is only indexed by time because an index for individual would not be meaningful. The two equations above describe the state process of the JS model. The observation process is the same as in the CJS model (Section 7.2). It conditions on the state process and is

$$y_{i,t} \,|\, z_{i,t} \sim \text{Bernoulli}(z_{i,t}p_{i,t}).$$

This model is very similar to the dynamic occupancy model (Section 13.5). In the JS model, we just need to add a constraint that recruitment is not possible after death, whereas in occupancy models, recolonization after local extinction is possible.

Several quantities of interest can be derived from the latent state variable z. Population size at t is $N_t = \sum_{i=1}^{M} z_{i,t}$, the number of "fresh recruits" (newly entered individuals) at t is $B_t = \sum_{i=1}^{M} (1 - z_{i,t-1})z_{i,t}$, and superpopulation size is $N_S = \sum B$.

In a Bayesian analysis of the model, the following parameters require priors: survival (ϕ), capture (p) and removal entry probabilities (γ). To express ignorance, we might specify a uniform prior U(0, 1) on all of them. The superpopulation size is a derived parameter; hence, a prior for N_s is defined implicitly, but it is not clear how it would have to look like. In any case, it is not a discrete uniform prior such as U(0, M), which is what we might like to use (Royle and Dorazio, 2008), and what we use in the closed-population case (Chapter 6).

The BUGS code for this model is not difficult conceptually, but relatively long, because several quantities of interest are calculated (all after "Calculate derived population parameters"). This could be removed from the code and calculated outside BUGS; it just requires monitoring of the latent variable z. We present the code of a model with constant survival and recapture probabilities and time-dependent recruitment (entry).

```
# Specify model in BUGS language
sink("js-rest.occ.bug")
cat("
model {

# Priors and constraints
for (i in 1:M) {
    for (t in 1:(n.occasions-1)) {
        phi[i,t] <- mean.phi
        } #t
    for (t in 1:n.occasions) {
        p[i,t] <- mean.p
        } #t
    } #i
mean.phi ~ dunif(0, 1)
mean.p ~ dunif(0, 1)

for (t in 1:n.occasions) {
    gamma[t] ~ dunif(0, 1)
    } #t

# Likelihood
for (i in 1:M) {
    # First occasion
    # State process
```

```
z[i,1] ~ dbern(gamma[1])
mu1[i] <- z[i,1] * p[i,1]
# Observation process
y[i,1] ~ dbern(mu1[i])
# Subsequent occasions
for (t in 2:n.occasions){
    # State process
    q[i,t-1] <- 1-z[i,t-1]          # Availability for recruitment
    mu2[i,t] <- phi[i,t-1] * z[i,t-1] + gamma[t] * prod(q[i,1:(t-1)])
    z[i,t] ~ dbern(mu2[i,t])
    # Observation process
    mu3[i,t] <- z[i,t] * p[i,t]
    y[i,t] ~ dbern(mu3[i,t])
    } #t
} #i

# Calculate derived population parameters
for (t in 1:n.occasions){
    qgamma[t] <- 1-gamma[t]
    }
cprob[1] <- gamma[1]
for (t in 2:n.occasions){
    cprob[t] <- gamma[t] * prod(qgamma[1:(t-1)])
    } #t
psi <- sum(cprob[])                       # Inclusion probability
for (t in 1:n.occasions){
    b[t] <- cprob[t] / psi                 # Entry probability
    } #t
for (i in 1:M){
    recruit[i,1] <- z[i,1]
    for (t in 2:n.occasions){
        recruit[i,t] <- (1-z[i,t-1]) * z[i,t]
        } #t
    } #i
for (t in 1:n.occasions){
    N[t] <- sum(z[1:M,t])                   # Actual population size
    B[t] <- sum(recruit[1:M,t])             # Number of entries
    } #t
for (i in 1:M){
    Nind[i] <- sum(z[i,1:n.occasions])
    Nalive[i] <- 1-equals(Nind[i], 0)
    } #i
Nsuper <- sum(Nalive[])                     # Superpopulation size
}
",fill=TRUE)
sink()
```

10.3.2 The JS Model as a Multistate Model

It is obvious from Fig. 10.1 that the JS model can also be viewed as a multistate model (Royle and Dorazio, 2011). This formulation has the advantage that it can be extended flexibly to include age classes, multiple sites, dead recoveries, or others, as we showed in Chapter 9. To fit the JS as a multistate model in BUGS, we again first have to define lists of true and observed states and to describe the transitions between them with appropriate parameters. For the JS model, the true states are "not yet entered", "alive", and "dead" (Fig. 10.1), and the state transition matrix therefore is

$$
\begin{array}{c}
\\
\text{not yet entered} \\
\text{alive} \\
\text{dead}
\end{array}
\begin{array}{ccc}
\text{not yet entered} & \text{alive} & \text{dead} \\
\begin{bmatrix}
1-\gamma & \gamma & 0 \\
0 & \phi & 1-\phi \\
0 & 0 & 1
\end{bmatrix}
\end{array}
$$

The parameters are the same as in the restricted occupancy formulation; thus, γ is the removal entry probability and ϕ is survival. The observation process maps the three true states on the two observed states "seen" and "not seen":

$$
\begin{array}{c}
\\
\text{not yet entered} \\
\text{alive} \\
\text{dead}
\end{array}
\begin{array}{cc}
\text{seen} & \text{not seen} \\
\begin{bmatrix}
0 & 1 \\
p & 1-p \\
0 & 1
\end{bmatrix}
\end{array}
$$

The implementation as a state-space model works similarly as for other multistate models (Chapter 9). However, since the traditional multistate models condition on initial capture, there is no way to estimate γ_1 at the first occasion. This can be overcome easily by adding a dummy occasion that contains only "0" before the first real occasion in the data. In the model specification, we then need to ensure that all individuals in the augmented data set are in state "not yet entered" at this first dummy occasion with probability 1. In this way, we solve two problems. First, the proportion of individuals present already at the first real occasion is estimated by the first transition, and second, the analyzed capture-histories condition on the first dummy occasion, which means that the model becomes unconditional for all real occasions.

The BUGS code to implement this model is given below. As discussed earlier, we assume constant survival and capture and time-dependent entry probability. The same quantities as before can be derived, we just have to remember that the latent state variable z now takes values 1 ("not yet entered"), 2 ("alive"), and 3 ("dead"), and thus these quantities must be calculated slightly differently. Priors are specified in the same way as for the restricted occupancy formulation.

```
# Specify model in BUGS language
sink("js-ms.bug")
cat("
model {

# -----------------------------------
# Parameters:
# phi: survival probability
# gamma: removal entry probability
# p: capture probability
# -----------------------------------
# States (S):
# 1 not yet entered
# 2 alive
# 3 dead
# Observations (O):
# 1 seen
# 2 not seen
# -----------------------------------

# Priors and constraints
for (t in 1:(n.occasions-1)){
    phi[t] <- mean.phi
    gamma[t] ~ dunif(0, 1)  # Prior for entry probabilities
    p[t] <- mean.p
    }

mean.phi ~ dunif(0, 1)       # Prior for mean survival
mean.p ~ dunif(0, 1)         # Prior for mean capture

# Define state-transition and observation matrices
for (i in 1:M){
    # Define probabilities of state S(t+1) given S(t)
    for (t in 1:(n.occasions-1)){
        ps[1,i,t,1] <- 1-gamma[t]
        ps[1,i,t,2] <- gamma[t]
        ps[1,i,t,3] <- 0
        ps[2,i,t,1] <- 0
        ps[2,i,t,2] <- phi[t]
        ps[2,i,t,3] <- 1-phi[t]
        ps[3,i,t,1] <- 0
        ps[3,i,t,2] <- 0
        ps[3,i,t,3] <- 1

        # Define probabilities of O(t) given S(t)
        po[1,i,t,1] <- 0
        po[1,i,t,2] <- 1
        po[2,i,t,1] <- p[t]
        po[2,i,t,2] <- 1-p[t]
        po[3,i,t,1] <- 0
        po[3,i,t,2] <- 1
        } #t
    } #i

# Likelihood
for (i in 1:M){
```

```
# Define latent state at first occasion
z[i,1] <- 1      # Make sure that all M individuals are in state 1 at t=1
for (t in 2:n.occasions){
    # State process: draw S(t) given S(t-1)
    z[i,t] ~ dcat(ps[z[i,t-1], i, t-1,])
    # Observation process: draw O(t) given S(t)
    y[i,t] ~ dcat(po[z[i,t], i, t-1,])
    } #t
  } #i

# Calculate derived population parameters
for (t in 1:(n.occasions-1)){
    qgamma[t] <- 1-gamma[t]
    }
cprob[1] <- gamma[1]
for (t in 2:(n.occasions-1)){
    cprob[t] <- gamma[t] * prod(qgamma[1:(t-1)])
    } #t
psi <- sum(cprob[])                # Inclusion probability
for (t in 1:(n.occasions-1)){
    b[t] <- cprob[t] / psi          # Entry probability
    } #t

for (i in 1:M){
    for (t in 2:n.occasions){
        al[i,t-1] <- equals(z[i,t], 2)
        } #t
    for (t in 1:(n.occasions-1)){
        d[i,t] <- equals(z[i,t]-al[i,t],0)
        } #t
    alive[i] <- sum(al[i,])
    } #i

for (t in 1:(n.occasions-1)){
    N[t] <- sum(al[,t])             # Actual population size
    B[t] <- sum(d[,t])              # Number of entries
    } #t
for (i in 1:M){
    w[i] <- 1-equals(alive[i],0)
    } #i
Nsuper <- sum(w[])                 # Superpopulation size
}
",fill = TRUE)
sink()
```

10.3.3 The Superpopulation Parameterization

An important parameterization of the JS model was developed by Crosbie and Manly (1985), extended by Schwarz and Arnason (1996), and implemented as a hierarchical model by Royle and Dorazio (2008) and Link and Barker (2010). This parameterization uses entry probabilities b and an inclusion parameter ψ. To keep the sequential specification of the state process model, we reexpress the entry probabilities (b) as conditional entry probabilities (η), and thus

$$\eta_1 = b_1, \quad \eta_2 = \frac{b_2}{1 - b_1}, \quad \ldots, \quad \eta_t = \frac{b_t}{1 - \sum\limits_{i=1}^{t-1} b_i}$$

The conditional entry probabilities (η) are not the same as the removal entry probabilities (γ) in Sections 10.3.1 and 10.3.2. Nevertheless, the state process is identical to that in the restricted occupancy parameterization, except that it contains η instead of γ. For the observation process, we suppose that each individual of M has an associated latent variable $w_i \sim$ Bernoulli(ψ). Individuals with $w_i = 1$ are exposed to sampling if alive, whereas individuals with $w_i = 0$ are not exposed to sampling. Thus, the observation model is

$$y_{i,t} \mid z_{i,t} \sim \text{Bernoulli}(w_i z_{i,t} p_{i,t}).$$

This observation model formally admits the zero-inflation of the augmented data set.

Here, we can derive some population estimates of interest as well. The vector of latent state variables z is inflated under the superpopulation formulation because it has length M, rather than N_s. We calculate $u_{i,t} = z_{i,t} w_i$ to account for this. By using u instead of z, we can use the same formulas as for the restricted occupancy formulation to calculate the derived population estimates.

We need to specify priors for the survival and capture probabilities as before, but not for the conditional entry probabilities (η). Instead, we specify priors for the entry probabilities (b), and a convenient one is the Dirichlet prior: $b_t \sim$ Dirichlet(α). To express ignorance and allocate the entries of all individuals uniformly over the T occasions, we set $\alpha_t = 1$ for all t. In addition, we give a U(0, 1) prior for the inclusion probability ψ. This induces a discrete U(0, M) prior for the superpopulation size N_s (Royle and Dorazio, 2008), as we did for the closed-population models (Chapter 6).

The BUGS code for the superpopulation parameterization again has constant survival and capture probabilities and time-dependent entry probabilities.

```
# Specify model in BUGS language
sink("js-super.bug")
cat("
model {

# Priors and constraints
for (i in 1:M){
    for (t in 1:(n.occasions-1)){
        phi[i,t] <- mean.phi
        } #t
```

```
    for (t in 1:n.occasions){
        p[i,t] <- mean.p
        } #t
    } #i
```

```
mean.phi ~ dunif(0, 1)          # Prior for mean survival
mean.p ~ dunif(0, 1)            # Prior for mean capture
psi ~ dunif(0, 1)               # Prior for inclusion probability
```

```
# Dirichlet prior for entry probabilities
for (t in 1:n.occasions){
    beta[t] ~ dgamma(1, 1)
    b[t] <- beta[t] / sum(beta[1:n.occasions])
    }
```

```
# Convert entry probs to conditional entry probs
nu[1] <- b[1]
for (t in 2:n.occasions){
    nu[t] <- b[t] / (1-sum(b[1:(t-1)]))
    } #t
```

```
# Likelihood
for (i in 1:M){
    # First occasion
    # State process
    w[i] ~ dbern(psi)                # Draw latent inclusion
    z[i,1] ~ dbern(nu[1])
    # Observation process
    mu1[i] <- z[i,1] * p[i,1] * w[i]
    y[i,1] ~ dbern(mu1[i])

    # Subsequent occasions
    for (t in 2:n.occasions){
        # State process
        q[i,t-1] <- 1-z[i,t-1]
        mu2[i,t] <- phi[i,t-1] * z[i,t-1] + nu[t] * prod(q[i,1:(t-1)])
        z[i,t] ~ dbern(mu2[i,t])
        # Observation process
        mu3[i,t] <- z[i,t] * p[i,t] * w[i]
        y[i,t] ~ dbern(mu3[i,t])
        } #t
    } #i
```

```
# Calculate derived population parameters
for (i in 1:M){
    for (t in 1:n.occasions){
        u[i,t] <- z[i,t]*w[i]      # Deflated latent state (u)
        }
    }
for (i in 1:M){
    recruit[i,1] <- u[i,1]
    for (t in 2:n.occasions){
        recruit[i,t] <- (1-u[i,t-1]) * u[i,t]
        } #t
    } #i
```

```
for (t in 1:n.occasions){
    N[t] <- sum(u[1:M,t])            # Actual population size
    B[t] <- sum(recruit[1:M,t])      # Number of entries
    } #t
for (i in 1:M){
    Nind[i] <- sum(u[i,1:n.occasions])
    Nalive[i] <- 1-equals(Nind[i], 0)
    } #i
Nsuper <- sum(Nalive[])              # Superpopulation size
}
",fill=TRUE)
sink()
```

Under the restricted occupancy or the multistate JS model and assuming T capture occasions and time-dependent parameters, we estimate T γ parameters, $T-1$ survival, and T capture parameters. Under the superpopulation approach, we estimate the same number of survival and capture parameters, but only $T-1$ entry parameters are separately estimable (note that b_T is 1 minus the sum of the other b) plus the inclusion parameter ψ. Thus, the total number of parameters is the same in all three formulations. This illustrates the fact that the different formulations are reparameterizations of the same basic model. In Section 10.6, we provide a summary of the relationships between the quantities in each. The parameterization with the least impact of the priors can then be specified.

Naturally, all model formulations can be extended using the GLM or GLMM framework, as we did for the models in Chapters 6 and 7. Care must be taken, however, with age-dependent models (Brownie et al., 1986; Williams et al., 2002). The age of all individuals at initial capture must be known, and the entry time to the population must be somewhere between the birth of the individual and its initial capture. Capture probabilities depend on age, but the capture probability of the first age class and therefore also the population size for this age class cannot be estimated. The multistate formulation of the JS model seems to be a framework with which age-dependent models can be fitted in the Bayesian paradigm, but the problem remains that population size of the first age class cannot be estimated. Care must also be taken when entry probabilities are modeled because they need to sum to 1, and therefore not all of them can independently be modeled.

10.4 MODELS WITH CONSTANT SURVIVAL AND TIME-DEPENDENT ENTRY

We start with a simple example to illustrate the application of all three model formulations. We first simulate data using function `simul.js` and then analyze them. The simulation code needs the parameter of the superpopulation formulation as input, and thus we specify the superpopulation size, entry, survival and capture probabilities, as well as the number of occasions. With T occasions, T entry probabilities must be defined, and they have to sum to 1. In the absence of any individual heterogeneity, there are T capture probabilities and $T-1$ survival probabilities that need to be determined.

We assume a 7-year study of survival and recruitment in black grouse (Fig. 10.3). Each spring black grouse are captured at a lek. They are marked and may be captured again in later years. We assume that annual survival is 0.7, and capture probability is 0.5; both are constant over time. Superpopulation size is 400 individuals. We assume the entry probability to be 0.11 for all occasions but the first one, when it is given by $1 - 6 * 0.11 = 0.34$.

```
# Define parameter values
n.occasions <- 7                          # Number of capture occasions
N <- 400                                  # Superpopulation size
phi <- rep(0.7, n.occasions-1)            # Survival probabilities
b <- c(0.34, rep(0.11, n.occasions-1))    # Entry probabilities
p <- rep(0.5, n.occasions)                # Capture probabilities
```

FIGURE 10.3   Displaying black grouse cock (*Tetrao tetrix*), Finland, 2005 (Photograph by J. Peltomäki).

```
PHI <- matrix(rep(phi, (n.occasions-1)*N), ncol = n.occasions-1,
   nrow = N, byrow = T)
P <- matrix(rep(p, n.occasions*N), ncol = n.occasions, nrow = N,
   byrow = T)

# Function to simulate capture-recapture data under the JS model
simul.js <- function(PHI, P, b, N){
   B <- rmultinom(1, N, b) # Generate no. of entering ind. per occasion
   n.occasions <- dim(PHI)[2] + 1
   CH.sur <- CH.p <- matrix(0, ncol = n.occasions, nrow = N)

   # Define a vector with the occasion of entering the population
   ent.occ <- numeric()
   for (t in 1:n.occasions){
      ent.occ <- c(ent.occ, rep(t, B[t]))
      }

   # Simulate survival
   for (i in 1:N){
      CH.sur[i, ent.occ[i]] <- 1    # Write 1 when ind. enters the pop.
      if (ent.occ[i] == n.occasions) next
      for (t in (ent.occ[i]+1):n.occasions){
         # Bernoulli trial: has individual survived occasion?
         sur <- rbinom(1, 1, PHI[i,t-1])
         ifelse (sur==1, CH.sur[i,t] <- 1, break)
         } #t
      } #i

   # Simulate capture
   for (i in 1:N){
      CH.p[i,] <- rbinom(n.occasions, 1, P[i,])
      } #i

   # Full capture-recapture matrix
   CH <- CH.sur * CH.p

   # Remove individuals never captured
   cap.sum <- rowSums(CH)
   never <- which(cap.sum == 0)
   CH <- CH[-never,]
   Nt <- colSums(CH.sur)     # Actual population size
   return(list(CH=CH, B=B, N=Nt))
   }

# Execute simulation function
sim <- simul.js(PHI, P, b, N)
CH <- sim$CH
```

In our case, the resulting capture–recapture matrix has the dimension of 7×294, and thus 294 among the 400 individuals were captured. Besides the capture-histories, the function returns the number of individuals that newly entered the population and the actual population size at each occasion. We analyze the simulated data with all three model formulations, thus illustrating the advantages and disadvantages of each.

10.4.1 Analysis of the JS Model as a Restricted Occupancy Model

We first need to augment the observed capture–recapture data. We must make sure that we augment the data by a large enough number of pseudo-individuals (see Section 6.2.1).

```
# Augment the capture-histories by nz pseudo-individuals
nz <- 500
CH.aug <- rbind(CH, matrix(0, ncol = dim(CH)[2], nrow = nz))
```

Then, we define initial values and parameters we want to monitor, set the MCMC specifications, run the model and print the results.

```
# Bundle data
bugs.data <- list(y = CH.aug, n.occasions = dim(CH.aug)[2],
  M = dim(CH.aug)[1])

# Initial values
inits <- function(){list(mean.phi = runif(1, 0, 1),
  mean.p = runif(1, 0, 1), z = CH.aug)}

# Parameters monitored
parameters <- c("psi", "mean.p", "mean.phi", "b", "Nsuper", "N", "B",
  "gamma")

# MCMC settings
ni <- 5000
nt <- 3
nb <- 2000
nc <- 3

# Call WinBUGS from R (BRT 11 min)
js.occ <- bugs(bugs.data, inits, parameters, "js-rest.occ.bug",
  n.chains = nc, n.thin = nt, n.iter = ni, n.burnin = nb, debug = TRUE,
  bugs.directory = bugs.dir, working.directory = getwd())

print(js.occ, digits = 3)
```

	mean	sd	2.5%	25%	50%	75%	97.5%	Rhat	n.eff
psi	0.522	0.032	0.465	0.500	0.522	0.543	0.590	1.002	1800
mean.p	0.473	0.035	0.407	0.448	0.472	0.497	0.542	1.003	930
mean.phi	0.718	0.025	0.668	0.701	0.719	0.736	0.768	1.001	2400
b[1]	0.328	0.040	0.252	0.300	0.327	0.354	0.408	1.003	870
[...]									
b[7]	0.089	0.029	0.036	0.068	0.088	0.108	0.150	1.004	3000
Nsuper	406.364	21.013	369.975	391.000	405.000	419.000	451.000	1.001	2500
N[1]	134.027	15.971	106.000	123.000	132.000	144.000	169.000	1.003	760
[...]									
N[7]	150.457	14.373	126.000	140.000	149.000	159.000	183.000	1.002	1800
B[1]	134.027	15.971	106.000	123.000	132.000	144.000	169.000	1.003	760
[...]									
B[7]	35.751	11.451	14.975	28.000	35.000	43.000	59.000	1.001	2100
[...]									

10.4.2 Analysis of the JS Model as a Multistate Model

⸙ We need to add a dummy occasion before the first real occasion, augment the data set, and recode that data to match the codes of the observed states.

```
# Add dummy occasion
CH.du <- cbind(rep(0, dim(CH)[1]), CH)

# Augment data
nz <- 500
CH.ms <- rbind(CH.du, matrix(0, ncol = dim(CH.du)[2], nrow = nz))

# Recode CH matrix: a 0 is not allowed in WinBUGS!
CH.ms[CH.ms==0] <- 2              # Not seen = 2, seen = 1
```

Then, we run the analysis.

```
# Bundle data
bugs.data <- list(y = CH.ms, n.occasions = dim(CH.ms)[2],
    M = dim(CH.ms)[1])

# Initial values
inits <- function(){list(mean.phi = runif(1, 0, 1),
    mean.p = runif(1, 0, 1), z = cbind(rep(NA, dim(CH.ms)[1]),
    CH.ms[,-1]))}

# Parameters monitored
parameters <- c("mean.p", "mean.phi", "b", "Nsuper", "N", "B")

# MCMC settings
ni <- 20000
nt <- 3
nb <- 5000
nc <- 3

# Call WinBUGS from R (BRT 32 min)
js.ms <- bugs(bugs.data, inits, parameters, "js-ms.bug", n.chains = nc,
    n.thin = nt, n.iter = ni, n.burnin = nb, debug = TRUE, bugs.directory =
    bugs.dir, working.directory = getwd())

print(js.ms, digits = 3)
```

	mean	sd	2.5%	25%	50%	75%	97.5%	Rhat	n.eff
mean.p	0.473	0.036	0.403	0.449	0.473	0.497	0.542	1.009	360
mean.phi	0.720	0.026	0.668	0.702	0.720	0.737	0.770	1.001	15000
b[1]	0.328	0.040	0.254	0.300	0.326	0.354	0.410	1.002	1500
[...]									
b[7]	0.088	0.029	0.032	0.068	0.087	0.107	0.146	1.001	11000
Nsuper	405.668	19.807	370.000	392.000	405.000	419.000	447.000	1.015	170
N[1]	133.950	16.146	106.000	122.000	133.000	144.000	169.000	1.010	280
[...]									
N[7]	150.550	14.173	126.000	140.000	150.000	160.000	181.000	1.003	970
B[1]	133.950	16.146	106.000	122.000	133.000	144.000	169.000	1.010	280
[...]									
B[7]	35.503	11.277	13.000	28.000	35.000	43.000	58.000	1.001	15000
[...]									

10.4.3 Analysis of the JS Model Under the Superpopulation Parameterization

This analysis requires the same preparation as the restricted occupancy formulation. We augment the observed capture–recapture data and run the analysis.

```
# Augment capture-histories by nz pseudo-individuals
nz <- 500
CH.aug <- rbind(CH, matrix(0, ncol = dim(CH)[2], nrow = nz))

# Bundle data
bugs.data <- list(y = CH.aug, n.occasions = dim(CH.aug)[2],
   M = dim(CH.aug)[1])

# Initial values
inits <- function(){list(mean.phi = runif(1, 0, 1),
   mean.p = runif(1, 0, 1), psi = runif(1, 0, 1), z = CH.aug)}

# Parameters monitored
parameters <- c("psi", "mean.p", "mean.phi", "b", "Nsuper",
   "N", "B", "nu")

# MCMC settings
ni <- 5000
nt <- 3
nb <- 2000
nc <- 3

# Call WinBUGS from R (BRT 40 min)
js.super <- bugs(bugs.data, inits, parameters, "js-super.bug",
   n.chains = nc, n.thin = nt, n.iter = ni, n.burnin = nb, debug = TRUE,
   bugs.directory = bugs.dir, working.directory = getwd())

print(js.super, digits = 3)
```

	mean	sd	2.5%	25%	50%	75%	97.5%	Rhat	n.eff
psi	0.504	0.029	0.449	0.484	0.504	0.524	0.563	1.001	3000
mean.p	0.483	0.034	0.417	0.459	0.482	0.506	0.548	1.002	1700
mean.phi	0.720	0.026	0.671	0.702	0.719	0.737	0.773	1.002	1500
b[1]	0.323	0.040	0.251	0.295	0.320	0.348	0.408	1.017	180
[...]									
b[7]	0.087	0.029	0.034	0.067	0.087	0.106	0.145	1.007	300
Nsuper	396.991	18.199	364.975	384.000	396.000	408.000	436.000	1.001	3000
N[1]	129.561	15.079	103.000	119.000	128.000	139.000	161.000	1.010	240
[...]									
N[7]	147.403	13.196	125.000	138.000	146.000	156.000	176.000	1.001	2300
B[1]	129.561	15.079	103.000	119.000	128.000	139.000	161.000	1.010	240
[...]									
B[7]	34.215	10.768	14.000	27.000	34.000	41.000	56.000	1.006	380
[...]									

10.4.4 Comparison of Estimates

Posterior means and standard deviations are nearly identical under all three parameterizations. This is shown graphically for the superpopulation

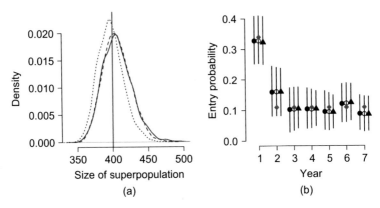

FIGURE 10.4   (a) Posterior distributions of the size of the number of black grouses ever alive during the study (superpopulation size, N_s) using the restricted occupancy (solid), multistate (dashed), and superpopulation parameterizations (dotted). The vertical red line shows the data generating size of the superpopulation. (b) Estimates of annual entry probabilities under the restricted occupancy (closed circle), multistate (open circle), and superpopulation parameterization (closed triangle), as well as the data-generating parameters (red diamond). The vertical lines are 95% CRI.

size and the entry probabilities (Fig. 10.4). We would expect to get exactly the same results for the restricted occupancy and the multistate formulation, but not for the superpopulation formulation. The latter uses different priors than the two former. This may make a difference with a small data set. The three approaches differ in terms of computing time, which is much shorter for the restricted occupancy formulation. The main advantage of the multistate formulation is its flexibility to model different age classes, movement between sites or to integrate other data types such as dead recoveries. The main advantage of the superpopulation formulation is the ability to specify directly a prior for the superpopulation size and to model entry probabilities directly. Entry probabilities are parameters of direct biological interest, whereas removal entry probabilities are mere mathematical constructs. Thus, if the goal of an analysis is to understand the arrival of individuals as a function of covariates, the superpopulation formulation is the best choice. A difficulty could be that the entry probabilities must sum to 1, so not all parameters can be freely modeled. This is the same difficulty as for multistate models with movements among three or more sites (Section 9.6). In order to improve computation speed, it is again possible to provide as data information about the latent state variable z (see Section 7.3.1). We have not done this here explicitly because the specification of them and of the corresponding initial values differs for each approach. However, we make use of this information in the solutions of the exercises (Section 10.9).

```
# Code to produce Fig. 10.4
par(mfrow = c(1,2), mar = c(5, 6, 2, 1), mgp=c(3.4, 1, 0), las = 1)
plot(density(js.occ$sims.list$Nsuper), main = "", xlab = "",
    ylab = "Density", frame = FALSE, lwd = 2, ylim=c(0, 0.023),
    col = "blue")
points(density(js.ms$sims.list$Nsuper), type = "l", lty = 2,
    col = "blue", lwd = 2)
points(density(js.super$sims.list$Nsuper), type = "l", lty = 3,
    col = "blue", lwd = 2)
abline(v = N, col = "red", lwd = 2)
mtext("Size of superpopulation", 1, line = 3)

b1.lower <- b2.lower <- b3.lower <- b1.upper <- b2.upper <- b3.upper <-
    numeric()
for (t in 1:n.occasions){
    b1.lower[t] <- quantile(js.occ$sims.list$b[,t], 0.025)
    b2.lower[t] <- quantile(js.ms$sims.list$b[,t], 0.025)
    b3.lower[t] <- quantile(js.super$sims.list$b[,t], 0.025)
    b1.upper[t] <- quantile(js.occ$sims.list$b[,t], 0.975)
    b2.upper[t] <- quantile(js.ms$sims.list$b[,t], 0.975)
    b3.upper[t] <- quantile(js.super$sims.list$b[,t], 0.975)
    }
time <- 1:n.occasions
plot(x = time-0.25, y = js.occ$mean$b, xlab = "", ylab = "Entry
    probability", frame = FALSE, las = 1, xlim = c(0.5, 7.5), pch = 16,
    ylim = c(0, max(c(b1.upper, b2.upper)))))
segments(time-0.25, b1.lower, time-0.25, b1.upper)
points(x = time, y = js.ms$mean$b, pch = 1)
segments(time, b2.lower, time, b2.upper)
points(x = time+0.25, y = js.super$mean$b, pch = 17)
segments(time+0.25, b3.lower, time+0.25, b3.upper)
points(x = time, y = b, pch = 18, col = "red")
mtext("Year", 1, line = 3)
```

10.5 MODELS WITH INDIVIDUAL CAPTURE HETEROGENEITY

Here, we show how an individual random effect on capture probability can be included to avoid negative bias in population size estimates (Pledger and Efford, 1998; Link, 2003; Royle and Dorazio, 2008); also see Chapter 6. We assume an 8-year study of grey-headed woodpeckers (Fig. 10.5), where birds are attracted with playback calls and caught in mist nets. There is individual variation in the aggressive reaction to the calls; hence, capture probability differs by individual. We assume a superpopulation size of 300, mean survival probability of 0.75, and annual entry probability of 0.09, except for 0.37 at the first occasion. Mean capture probability is 0.6, with an individual variance of 1 on the logit scale. We first simulate one data set and then analyze it with the superpopulation formulation.

FIGURE 10.5 Male grey-headed woodpecker (*Picus canus*), Finland, 2002 (Photograph by T. Muukkonen).

```
# Define parameter values
n.occasions <- 8                        # Number of capture occasions
N <- 300                                # Size of the superpopulation
phi <- rep(0.75, n.occasions-1)         # Survival probabilities
b <- c(0.37, rep(0.09, n.occasions-1))  # Entry probabilities
mean.p <- 0.6                           # Mean capture probability
var.p <- 1                              # Indv. Variance of capture
                                          prob.
p <- plogis(rnorm(N, qlogis(mean.p), var.p^0.5))
PHI <- matrix(rep(phi, (n.occasions-1)*N), ncol = n.occasions-1,
   nrow = N, byrow = T)
P <- matrix(rep(p, n.occasions), ncol = n.occasions, nrow = N, byrow = F)

# Execute simulation function
sim <- simul.js(PHI, P, b, N)
CH <- sim$CH
```

Here is the BUGS code.

```
# Specify model in BUGS language
sink("js-super-indran.bug")
cat("
model {
```

```
# Priors and constraints
for (i in 1:M){
    for (t in 1:(n.occasions-1)){
        phi[i,t] <- mean.phi
        } #t
    for (t in 1:n.occasions){
        logit(p[i,t]) <- mean.lp + epsilon[i]
        } #t
    } #i

mean.phi ~ dunif(0, 1)              # Prior for mean survival
mean.lp <- log(mean.p / (1-mean.p))
mean.p ~ dunif(0, 1)               # Prior for mean capture
for (i in 1:M){
    epsilon[i] ~ dnorm(0, tau)I(-15,15)
    }
tau <- pow(sigma, -2)
sigma ~ dunif(0, 5)                # Prior for sd of indv. variation of p
sigma2 <- pow(sigma, 2)
psi ~ dunif(0, 1)                  # Prior for inclusion probability

# Dirichlet prior for entry probabilities
for (t in 1:n.occasions){
    beta[t] ~ dgamma(1, 1)
    b[t] <- beta[t] / sum(beta[1:n.occasions])
    }

# Convert entry probs to conditional entry probs
nu[1] <- b[1]
for (t in 2:n.occasions){
    nu[t] <- b[t] / (1-sum(b[1:(t-1)]))
    } #t

# Likelihood
for (i in 1:M){
    # First occasion
    # State process
    w[i] ~ dbern(psi)              # Draw latent inclusion
    z[i,1] ~ dbern(nu[1])
    # Observation process
    mu1[i] <- z[i,1] * p[i,1] * w[i]
    y[i,1] ~ dbern(mu1[i])

    # Subsequent occasions
    for (t in 2:n.occasions){
        # State process
        q[i,t-1] <- 1-z[i,t-1]
        mu2[i,t] <- phi[i,t-1] * z[i,t-1] + nu[t] * prod(q[i,1:(t-1)])
        z[i,t] ~ dbern(mu2[i,t])
        # Observation process
        mu3[i,t] <- z[i,t] * p[i,t] * w[i]
        y[i,t] ~ dbern(mu3[i,t])
        } #t
    } #i
```

```
# Calculate derived population parameters
for (i in 1:M){
    for (t in 1:n.occasions){
        u[i,t] <- z[i,t]*w[i]          # Deflated latent state (u)
        }
    }
for (i in 1:M){
    recruit[i,1] <- u[i,1]
    for (t in 2:n.occasions){
        recruit[i,t] <- (1-u[i,t-1]) * u[i,t]
        } #t
    } #i
for (t in 1:n.occasions){
    N[t] <- sum(u[1:M,t])              # Actual population size
    B[t] <- sum(recruit[1:M,t])        # Number of entries
    } #t
for (i in 1:M){
    Nind[i] <- sum(u[i,1:n.occasions])
    Nalive[i] <- 1-equals(Nind[i], 0)
    } #i
Nsuper <- sum(Nalive[])               # Superpopulation size
}
",fill=TRUE)
sink()
```

Finally, we augment the data set and run the analysis in BUGS.

```
# Augment the capture-histories by nz pseudo-individuals
nz <- 300
CH.aug <- rbind(CH, matrix(0, ncol = dim(CH)[2], nrow = nz))

# Bundle data
bugs.data <- list(y = CH.aug, n.occasions = dim(CH.aug)[2],
    M = dim(CH.aug)[1])

# Initial values
inits <- function(){list(mean.phi = runif(1, 0, 1),
    mean.p = runif(1, 0, 1), sigma = runif(1, 0, 1), z = CH.aug)}

# Parameters monitored
parameters <- c("sigma2","psi","mean.p","mean.phi", "N", "Nsuper",
    "b", "B")

# MCMC settings
ni <- 20000
nt <- 6
nb <- 5000
nc <- 3

# Call WinBUGS from R (BRT 179 min)
js.ran <- bugs(bugs.data, inits, parameters, "js-super-indran.bug",
    n.chains = nc, n.thin = nt, n.iter = ni, n.burnin = nb, debug = TRUE,
    bugs.directory = bugs.dir, working.directory = getwd())
```

```
print(js.ran, digits = 3)
```

	mean	sd	2.5%	25%	50%	75%	97.5%	Rhat	n.eff
sigma2	0.191	0.281	0.001	0.019	0.083	0.242	0.980	1.135	23
psi	0.542	0.033	0.483	0.520	0.540	0.562	0.613	1.002	2000
mean.p	0.629	0.037	0.550	0.607	0.631	0.655	0.696	1.003	1100
mean.phi	0.746	0.021	0.704	0.732	0.746	0.760	0.787	1.005	520
N[1]	121.716	10.153	104.000	115.000	121.000	128.000	143.000	1.005	520
[...]									
N[8]	113.286	9.498	97.000	107.000	113.000	119.000	134.000	1.005	490
Nsuper	291.239	13.436	270.000	282.000	290.000	298.000	323.000	1.003	780
b[1]	0.410	0.039	0.335	0.383	0.409	0.436	0.485	1.003	770
[...]									
b[8]	0.155	0.030	0.099	0.135	0.154	0.175	0.215	1.003	800
B[1]	121.716	10.153	104.000	115.000	121.000	128.000	143.000	1.005	520
[...]									
B[8]	45.505	7.246	32.000	40.000	45.000	50.000	61.000	1.002	1200
[...]									

The posterior means match up quite well with the data-generating parameters. Survival, capture and the entry probabilities are estimated well, whereas the estimate for the individual variation is lower than the data-generating parameter. Yet, as always, in order to study whether the model produces unbiased estimates, the exercise would have to be repeated many times and the average behavior of estimates studied.

10.6 CONNECTIONS BETWEEN PARAMETERS, FURTHER QUANTITIES AND SOME REMARKS ON IDENTIFIABILITY

All three approaches to the JS model under data augmentation are related. The restricted occupancy and the multistate formulation are exactly equivalent in terms of parameterization and priors. In contrast, the superpopulation formulation has a different parameterization (in terms of b and ψ instead of γ) and consequently needs priors for other parameters. Here, we summarize connections between different parameters in the three approaches and also their relation to further quantities of interest.

The expected number of newly entered individuals per occasion is

$$E(B_1) = M\gamma_1 = N_s b_1$$
$$E(B_2) = M(1 - \gamma_1)\gamma_2 = N_s b_2$$
$$\ldots$$
$$E(B_t) = M\prod_{i=1}^{t-1}(1 - \gamma_i)\gamma_t = N_s b_t$$

Let us denote the probability that an "individual" within the augmented data M is a member of the true individuals N_s with $\psi = N_s/M$. After some algebra, we see that

$$\gamma_1 = \psi b_1, \quad \gamma_2 = \psi \frac{b_2}{1 - b_1}, \quad \dots, \quad \gamma_t = \psi \frac{b_t}{1 - \sum_{i=1}^{t-1} b_i}$$

Likewise, we can calculate b from γ as

$$b_1 = \frac{1}{\psi}\gamma_1, \quad b_2 = \frac{1}{\psi}(1 - \gamma_1)\gamma_2, \dots$$

Because all b sum to 1, b_T at the last occasion T is

$$b_T = \frac{1}{\psi}\gamma_T \prod_{i=1}^{T-1}(1 - \gamma_i) = 1 - \frac{1}{\psi}\left(\gamma_1 + \sum_{i=1}^{T-1}\left(\gamma_{i+1}\prod^{i}(1 - \gamma_i)\right)\right)$$

Therefore, we can directly calculate ψ from γ as

$$\psi = 1 - \prod_{i=1}^{T}(1 - \gamma_i)$$

Pradel (1996) and Link and Barker (2005) used a further parameterization to model the recruitment process. Instead of an entry probability that refers either to the size of the augmented data set (γ, restricted occupancy parameterization and multistate model) or to the size of the superpopulation (b, superpopulation parameterization), they defined a per-capita entry probability (f). This quantity is computed as

$$f_t = \frac{B_t}{N_t}$$

and expresses the fraction of new individuals at t per individual alive at t. Expressing recruitment in this way results in the biologically most meaningful quantity. For the three models in this chapter, the per-capita entry probability can easily be estimated as a derived parameter, but to model this quantity directly, a different model parameterization is needed (Link and Barker, 2010).

The population growth rate (λ) is easily computed as a derived quantity from the estimated population sizes or survival and per-capita entry probability:

$$\lambda_t = \frac{N_{t+1}}{N_t} = \phi_t + f_t.$$

As almost always with complex models, not all parameters may be separately identifiable. It is well known that some parameters are not identifiable in a JS model with a time-dependent structure on survival, capture, and entry probabilities: the first entry and capture probabilities and the last survival and capture probabilities, respectively, are only estimable as products (i.e., $b_1 p_1$, $\phi_{T-1} p_T$; Schwarz and Arnason, 1996). This confounding occurs for all three parameterizations in this chapter. To verify parameter estimability, we can inspect the prior/posterior overlap (see Section 7.9) or see whether an analysis of simulated data yields estimates that resemble the input parameters.

10.7 ANALYSIS OF A REAL DATA SET: SURVIVAL, RECRUITMENT AND POPULATION SIZE OF LEISLER'S BATS

As a real-world example, we reanalyze capture–recapture data from adult female Leisler's bat (Fig. 7.11) from Section 7.11 (see also Schorcht et al., 2009) under the JS model. We only use a homogenous subset of these data consisting of locally born adult females. We are interested in population size and in the variability of local recruitment over time. Our data set consists of 181 individuals. Initial modeling suggested that adult survival was subject to strong temporal variation, whereas recapture probability was constant over time. We therefore fit a model with temporal random effects in survival, fixed time effects in recruitment, and a constant capture rate. We denote this model as $(\phi_t, b_t, p.)$.

We first specify the BUGS model. We use the restricted occupancy formulation because of its advantage in terms of computation speed. The model code needs an adaptation: annual survival is now specified as a random effect.

```
# Specify model in BUGS language
sink("js-tempran.bug")
cat("
model {

# Priors and constraints
for (i in 1:M){
   for (t in 1:(n.occasions-1)){
      logit(phi[i,t]) <- mean.lphi + epsilon[t]
      } #t
   for (t in 1:n.occasions){
      p[i,t] <- mean.p
      } #t
   } #i
mean.p ~ dunif(0, 1)            # Prior for mean capture
mean.phi ~ dunif(0, 1)          # Prior for mean survival
mean.lphi <- log(mean.phi / (1-mean.phi))
for (t in 1:(n.occasions-1)){
   epsilon[t] ~ dnorm(0, tau)
   }
```

```
tau <- pow(sigma, -2)
sigma ~ dunif(0, 5)           # Prior for sd of indv. variation of phi
sigma2 <- pow(sigma, 2)

for (t in 1:n.occasions){
    gamma[t] ~ dunif(0, 1)
    } #t

# Likelihood
for (i in 1:M){
    # First occasion
    # State process
    z[i,1] ~ dbern(gamma[1])
    mu1[i] <- z[i,1] * p[i,1]
    # Observation process
    y[i,1] ~ dbern(mu1[i])

    # Subsequent occasions
    for (t in 2:n.occasions){
        # State process
        q[i,t-1] <- 1-z[i,t-1]
        mu2[i,t] <- phi[i,t-1] * z[i,t-1] + gamma[t] * prod(q[i,1:
            (t-1)])
        z[i,t] ~ dbern(mu2[i,t])
        # Observation process
        mu3[i,t] <- z[i,t] * p[i,t]
        y[i,t] ~ dbern(mu3[i,t])
        } #t
    } #i

# Calculate derived population parameters
for (t in 1:n.occasions){
    qgamma[t] <- 1-gamma[t]
    }
cprob[1] <- gamma[1]
for (t in 2:n.occasions){
    cprob[t] <- gamma[t] * prod(qgamma[1:(t-1)])
    } #t
psi <- sum(cprob[])                # Inclusion probability
for (t in 1:n.occasions){
    b[t] <- cprob[t] / psi         # Entry probability
    } #t
for (i in 1:M){
    recruit[i,1] <- z[i,1]
    for (t in 2:n.occasions){
        recruit[i,t] <- (1-z[i,t-1]) * z[i,t]
        } #t
    } #i
for (t in 1:n.occasions){
    N[t] <- sum(z[1:M,t])          # Actual population size
    B[t] <- sum(recruit[1:M,t])    # Number of entries
    } #t
for (i in 1:M){
    Nind[i] <- sum(z[i,1:n.occasions])
    Nalive[i] <- 1-equals(Nind[i], 0)
    } #i
```

```
Nsuper <- sum(Nalive[])        # Size of superpopulation
}
",fill=TRUE)
sink()
```

Next, we load the capture–recapture data and augment the data.

```
leis <- as.matrix(read.table("leisleri.txt", sep = " ",
   header = FALSE))
nz <- 300
CH.aug <- rbind(leis, matrix(0, ncol = dim(leis)[2], nrow = nz))
```

Then, we run the analysis.

```
# Bundle data
bugs.data <- list(y = CH.aug, n.occasions = dim(CH.aug)[2],
   M = dim(CH.aug)[1])

# Initial values
inits <- function(){list(mean.phi = runif(1, 0, 1),
   mean.p = runif(1, 0, 1), sigma = runif(1, 0, 1), z = CH.aug)}

# Parameters monitored
parameters <- c("psi", "mean.p", "sigma2", "mean.phi", "N", "Nsuper",
   "b", "B")

# MCMC settings
ni <- 10000
nt <- 6
nb <- 5000
nc <- 3

# Call WinBUGS from R (BRT 127 min)
nl <- bugs(bugs.data, inits, parameters, "js-tempran.bug", n.chains =
   nc, n.thin = nt, n.iter = ni, n.burnin = nb, debug = TRUE,
   bugs.directory = bugs.dir, working.directory = getwd())

print(nl, digits = 3)
             mean      sd    2.5%     25%     50%     75%   97.5% Rhat n.eff
mean.p      0.725   0.030   0.665   0.704   0.726   0.746   0.782 1.001  2500
sigma2      0.477   0.350   0.064   0.247   0.397   0.613   1.363 1.012   260
mean.phi    0.743   0.039   0.669   0.717   0.743   0.768   0.821 1.003   690
[ ...]
Nsuper    205.896   6.576 194.000 201.000 205.000 210.000 220.000 1.003  2500
[ ... ]
```

The model runs quite slowly, but relatively few MCMC samples are
sufficient to obtain convergence. Estimates of mean survival and its
temporal variability are close to those obtained under the CJS model (see
Section 7.11), and also the capture probabilities differ only very slightly
(JS: 0.725 vs. CJS: 0.747). Such a difference is not unusual since the
parameters are not exactly the same: in the CJS model, it is the recapture
probability, whereas in the JS, it is the capture probability for all occasions,
including the first. The estimated population sizes suggest that bat

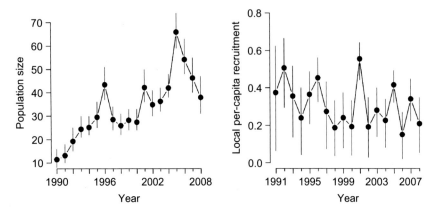

FIGURE 10.6   Posterior means of population sizes and of per-capita recruitment of adult female Leisler's bats. The vertical lines are 95% CRI.

population increased until 2005 and declined afterwards (Fig. 10.6). The per-capita recruitment seemed to have declined slightly over time, but showed strong annual fluctuations (Fig. 10.6). Note that the per-capita recruitment refers to local recruitment only because the data set consisted only of locally born bats.

```r
# Code to produce Fig. 10.6
# Calculate per-capita recruitment
T <- dim(leis)[2]
f <- matrix(NA, ncol = T, nrow = length(nl$sims.list$B[,1]))
for (t in 1:(T-1)){
    f[,t] <- nl$sims.list$B[,t+1] / nl$sims.list$N[,t+1]
    }
n.lower <- n.upper <- f.lower <- f.upper <- f.mean <- numeric()
for (t in 1:T){
    n.lower[t] <- quantile(nl$sims.list$N[,t], 0.025)
    n.upper[t] <- quantile(nl$sims.list$N[,t], 0.975)
    }
for (t in 1:(T-1)){
    f.lower[t] <- quantile(f[,t], 0.025)
    f.upper[t] <- quantile(f[,t], 0.975)
    f.mean[t] <- mean(f[,t])
    }

par(mfrow = c(1, 2))
plot(nl$mean$N, type = "b", pch = 19, ylab = "Population size", xlab = "",
    axes = F, cex = 1.5, ylim = c(10, max(n.upper)))
axis(1, at = seq(1, T, 2), labels = seq(1990, 2008, 2))
axis(1, at = 1:T, labels = rep("", T), tcl = -0.25)
axis(2, las = 1)
segments(1:T, n.lower, 1:T, n.upper)

plot(f.mean, type = "b", pch = 19, ylab = "Local per capita recruitment",
    xlab = "", axes = F, cex = 1.5, ylim = c(0, 0.8))
```

```
axis(1, at=seq(1, (T-1), 2), labels=seq(1991, 2008, 2))
axis(1, at=1:(T-1), labels=rep("", T-1), tcl=-0.25)
axis(2, las=1)
segments(1:(T-1), f.lower, 1:(T-1), f.upper)
```

10.8 SUMMARY AND OUTLOOK

We have described the Jolly-Seber (JS) model to estimate population size, survival and recruitment from capture–recapture data. The main difference to the CJS model (Chapter 7) is that the JS does not condition on first capture, that is, leading zeros before initial capture and the initial capture are modeled as well. There are several variants (parameterizations) of JS models that differ in the way how recruitment-related parameters are defined and estimated. We have illustrated three different parameterizations, showed advantages and disadvantages, as well as the connection between the parameters in them. The formulation of the JS model as a restricted occupancy model has advantages of relatively fast speed and a simple model code. The superpopulation formulation runs relatively slowly, but it is possible to directly model the entry probability and to specify a natural prior for the size of the superpopulation. We also showed that the JS model can be formulated as a multistate model. This formulation is appealing because it allows extensions in many directions. For all three formulations, we use parameter-expanded data augmentation (Royle et al., 2007a; Royle and Dorazio, 2011).

The GLM concept and random effects can be applied to all structural parameters in all three formulations of the JS model. Particular care must be taken, however, with age-dependent models and when the entry process is modeled.

Sometimes capture–recapture data arise under the robust design, that is, under a two-stage temporal sampling scheme, where the population is assumed open between primary occasions but closed between secondary, within-primary, occasions (Pollock, 1982; Kendall et al., 1997). The multiseason metapopulation estimation models in Chapters 12 and 13 also require the robust design data format. The JS model to analyze capture–recapture data sampled under the robust design is a combination of open- and closed-population models and has many advantages. First, it allows the estimation of survival, recruitment-related parameters, and population sizes as does the traditional JS model. Yet, because there is more information about the capture process, the robust design model can deal with certain violations of the basic JS model assumptions, such as permanent trap response. It also provides the basis to decompose entry probability into in situ recruitment and immigration (Nichols and Pollock, 1990) and to estimate population size of all age classes. The restricted occupancy and the superpopulation formulations of the JS model only require a small modification in the observation model to fit the robust design model. In its simplest version, we just need to model the observation with the Binomial instead of the Bernoulli distribution

$$Y_{i,t} \,|\, z_{i,t} \sim \text{Binomial}(K, z_{i,t}p_{i,t})$$

where the binomial total (K) is the number of secondary occasions (Royle and Dorazio, 2008; Royle and Dorazio, 2011). The observed data for individual i and each primary occasion t ($Y_{i,t}$) is then the number of times individual i was captured during the primary occasion t. Of course, more complex models with binary response require more adaptations.

10.9 EXERCISES

1. Simulate capture–recapture data of a species for males and females. The study is conducted for 8 years; the mean survival of males is 0.75 and of females 0.5, and capture is 0.4 for both. The entry probability after the first occasion is 0.1 in both sexes. The size of the superpopulation is 300 in both sexes. Simulate one data set and analyze it with the model ($\phi_{\text{sex}}, b_t, p$).

2. Simulate capture–recapture data of a species collected over 7 years. Mean survival is 0.5, mean capture is 0.6, and entry probability is 0.1 for all but the first occasion. The size of the superpopulation is assumed to be 500. Analyze the data with the model that explicitly uses constant entry probability for all occasions, but the first.

3. Simulate data for a species for which capture–recapture data are sampled and recoveries of dead individuals are available. The study runs for 10 years, mean survival is 0.5, mean capture is 0.6, mean recovery is 0.2, and entry probability is 0.1 for all but the first occasion. The size of the superpopulation is assumed to be 500. Analyze the simulated data with an appropriate model.

CHAPTER

11

Estimation of Demographic Rates, Population Size, and Projection Matrices from Multiple Data Types Using Integrated Population Models

OUTLINE

11.1 INTRODUCTION

Chapters 6–10 introduced models to separately estimate population size, recruitment, survival, or movement probabilities from various types of data. Often, studies focus on population dynamics, that is, changes in abundance over time and demographic causes of those changes. In that case, the obvious thing to do is to combine different available data sets to get deeper insights into population dynamics and better estimates of the demographic quantities. The link between population size and demographic, or vital, rates is straightforward because the change in population size over time is the direct result of these demographic rates. More formally, we have

$$N_{t+1} = N_t \times g(s, f)$$

where N_t is population size in year t, s is survival, f is productivity, and g is some function. When a study population is geographically open, the argument of g also includes terms for immigration and emigration. Looking at this link between population size and demographic rates, an important point becomes evident: time-series data on the size of a population contain information about the underlying demographic processes. When data on population size and demographic rates are analyzed jointly, three benefits accrue:

1. There is information about demographic rates both from explicit data on demographic rates (e.g., mark-recoveries for survival) and from data on population size. As a result, demographic rates are estimated with increased precision in a combined analysis. At the same time, changes in population size are the result of four demographic rates, and incorporation of data on demographic rates will likely improve population size estimates.
2. When explicit data about a demographic rate (such as productivity) is lacking, it may be possible to estimate the demographic rate by exploiting the information about it from the data on population size.
3. A combined analysis of data on demographic rates and population size allows the simultaneous study of population processes (demographic rates) and the result of these processes (population size). This can be important as we are often interested in the demographic causes for population change in population ecology, conservation biology, or wildlife management. Thus, a joint analysis allows a comprehensive assessment of the state and the dynamics of a population (Baillie, 1991).

A relatively new modeling framework, which uses different types of data to simultaneously estimate trajectories of population size and demographic parameters, is usually called an integrated population model (Besbeas et al., 2002; reviewed by Schaub and Abadi, 2011). This analytical framework uses a population model for the time-series data on population size and combines it with additional data to inform certain elements of the population model, such as survival, fecundity, or dispersal. The use of integrated population models in animal population ecology is relatively recent (Besbeas et al., 2002, 2003; Brooks et al., 2004; Thomas et al., 2005; Schaub et al., 2007; Baillie et al., 2009; Borysiewicz et al., 2009; King et al., 2010) although some varieties of these models have been used in fisheries (e.g., Elliott and Little, 2000; Maunder, 2004). Here, we focus on the Bayesian analysis of these models, although frequentist analyses using maximum likelihood are also possible and historically came before Bayesian analyses (see, e.g., Besbeas et al., 2002, 2003, 2005; Besbeas and Freeman, 2006; Gauthier et al., 2007; Tavecchia et al., 2009; Péron et al., 2010; De Valpine, 2011). Most frequentist analyses use Kalman filter techniques (Harvey, 1989) with the advantage that numerical optimization of the likelihood function is faster than posterior sampling by MCMC. Furthermore, model selection using AIC is straightforward when using maximum likelihood; however, this comes at the cost of stronger assumptions about distributional forms and linearity of the model (Brooks et al., 2004; De Valpine, 2011).

Developing an integrated population model involves three basic steps (Schaub and Abadi, 2011). First, we need to develop a population model that links the demographic rates with changes in population size. Typically, an age- or stage-classified matrix population model (Caswell, 2001) is used. Second, we write down the likelihood of all data sets available. One data set that is always required for a classical integrated population model is a time series of estimated population sizes or of population indices (counts). To separate process variability from observation errors in these data, we can use a state-space model as used in Chapter 5. Other data sets may be capture–recapture data, for which we may adopt the CJS model, or ring-recovery data. Third, we construct the joint likelihood—the likelihood of the complete model—and make inferences. Under the assumption of independence of all data sets, the joint likelihood is the product of the likelihoods of the individual data sets. In the frequentist framework, the joint likelihood would be maximized, while in a Bayesian analysis of the model, we combine it with prior distributions for all unknowns and use MCMC to sample the joint posterior distribution. To see more clearly how such a model is constructed and analyzed, we will walk through an example and comment each step.

We first use a simulated data set. We will not show or explain the simulation code, as this would take too much room. However, you can find R code for the simulation of our data in Web appendix 2, and comments on simulating these data are given in the study by Abadi et al. (2010a). Our data mimic the dynamics of a population of ortolan buntings (Fig. 11.1), a small passerine

FIGURE 11.1 Singing male ortolan bunting (*Emberiza hortulana*), Switzerland (Photograph by P. Keusch).

species. We assume a 10-year study in a large study area, where the population is closely surveyed. Each year we record the number of singing males and the number of fledglings produced in nests that are found. Both nestlings and adults are caught and ringed. Thus, we have three data sets that contain information about the dynamics of this population: population size (the number of singing males), fecundity (the total number of fledglings produced in the surveyed broods), and survival (capture–recapture data from juveniles and adults). We chose the following parameter values for the simulation of the data sets: 0.26 for juvenile survival, 0.5 for adult survival, 0.6 for recapture, and 4.0 for productivity. We assumed constant parameters over time, which results in a population growth rate of 1.02.

11.2 DEVELOPING AN INTEGRATED POPULATION MODEL (IPM)

11.2.1 First Step: Define the Link between Changes in Population Size and Demographic Rates

First, we need to link changes in population size with the demographic parameters. We use a simple female-based, age-classified population projection matrix model (Caswell, 2001). We assume that all individuals start

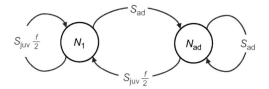

FIGURE 11.2   Life-cycle graph of an ortolan bunting population. The nodes show two age classes (N_1: 1-year-old females; N_{ad}: females older than 1 year) and the arrows the transition probabilities based on the vital rates (S_{juv}: juvenile survival; S_{ad}: adult survival; f: productivity).

to reproduce at the age of 1 year and distinguish two age classes: 1-year-old individuals (1) and individuals older than one year (ad). Each year we survey the population immediately before the young are born, hence, we assume a prebreeding census. A life-cycle graph of the model is shown in Fig. 11.2. A mathematical description of a deterministic version of the model is

$$\begin{bmatrix} N_1 \\ N_{ad} \end{bmatrix}_{t+1} = \begin{bmatrix} S_{juv}\dfrac{f}{2} & S_{juv}\dfrac{f}{2} \\ S_{ad} & S_{ad} \end{bmatrix}_t \begin{bmatrix} N_1 \\ N_{ad} \end{bmatrix}_t,$$

where S_{juv} and S_{ad} are the annual survival probabilities of juvenile and adult females, respectively, f is the number of offspring produced per female, and N_1 and N_{ad} are the number of 1-year-old and adult females in the population. Fecundity is divided by 2, reflecting our assumption of an even sex ratio and because our model only keeps track of females. Care must be taken with the time indices of the demographic rates. When using a prebreeding census, as here, the projection matrix is parameterized with survival from year t to year $t + 1$ and with fecundity in year t. With a post-breeding census, the matrix would still contain survival from year t to $t + 1$ but fecundity in year $t + 1$ and also a different parameterization of the projection matrix.

Another way to write the above model is in terms of the expected numbers of 1-year-old and adult individuals, respectively:

$$E(N_{1,t+1} \mid N_{1,t}, N_{ad,t}) = N_{1,t}S_{juv,t}\frac{f_t}{2} + N_{ad,t}S_{ad,t}\frac{f_t}{2}$$

$$E(N_{ad,t+1} \mid N_{ad,t}) = N_{1,t}S_{ad,t} + N_{ad,t}S_{ad,t}$$

These are the expected numbers; now we want to write these equations in such a way that all relevant sources of uncertainty are included. One form of variability that is always present is demographic stochasticity. Demographic stochasticity is particularly important when population size is small (Lande, 2002). To include demographic stochasticity, we use appropriate distributions to describe the number of individuals in year $t + 1$. To estimate the number of 1-year-old individuals, we must find a distribution that yields an integer value between 0 (if reproduction is 0 or all individuals die) and some big number (if reproduction is great and many survive) and whose expected value is $N_{1,t}S_{juv,t}f_t/2 + N_{ad,t}S_{ad,t}f_t/2$. The Poisson distribution is an appropriate candidate:

$$N_{1,t+1} \sim \text{Poisson}\left(N_{1,t}S_{juv,t}\frac{f_t}{2} + N_{ad,t}S_{ad,t}\frac{f_t}{2} \right).$$

For the adults, we must find a distribution that generates an integer value between 0 (if no individual survives) and $N_{ad,t}$ (if all individuals survive) and whose expected value is $N_{1,t}S_{ad,t} + N_{ad,t}S_{ad,t}$. Here, the binomial distribution is appropriate for modeling such bounded counts:

$$N_{ad,t+1} \sim \text{Binomial}(N_{1,t} + N_{ad,t}, S_{ad,t}).$$

By relating the adult and juvenile population sizes between successive years among each other in a stochastic manner, we account for demographic stochasticity.

11.2.2 Second Step: Define the Likelihoods of Each Individual Data Set

Now we have defined the link between the population size and the demographic parameters. The next step is to write the likelihood of all available data sets. Here we have three different data sets, and we start with the likelihood of population counts.

Likelihood of the Population Count Data

A powerful way to model population counts is a state-space model (Chapter 5). The state process describes the true but unknown population trajectory under the model defined in step 1, and the observation process links the observed population counts to the true population sizes by allowing for observation error. Thus, the state-process model is defined by the two equations developed in Section 11.2.1:

$$N_{1,t+1} \sim \text{Poisson}\left(N_{1,t}S_{juv,t}\frac{f_t}{2} + N_{ad,t}S_{ad,t}\frac{f_t}{2} \right)$$

$$N_{ad,t+1} \sim \text{Binomial}(N_{1,t} + N_{ad,t}, S_{ad,t}).$$

The age-specific number of individuals present in the first study year must be estimated from the data (see below). There are different possibilities to write the observation model that differ in the assumed distribution of the observation errors. Often, a normal error assumption is made; thus, the count data (y) are modeled as

$$y_t = (N_{1,t} + N_{\text{ad},t}) + \eta_t$$
$$\eta_t \sim \text{Normal}(0, \sigma_y^2)$$

where σ_y^2 is the observation error. Another possibility is to adopt a Poisson distribution for the observation error in population counts:

$$y_t \sim \text{Poisson}(N_{1,t} + N_{\text{ad},t}).$$

A feature of the Poisson distribution is that the variance is equal to its mean, implying that the observation error increases with the population size. A third possibility is a log-normal distribution:

$$\log(y_t) = \log(N_{1,t} + N_{\text{ad},t}) + \eta_t$$
$$\eta_t \sim \text{Normal}(0, \sigma_y^2).$$

Modeling the log population counts ensures that the observation error increases with population size and allows for counts that are skewed on the arithmetic scale.

Some comments are in order on the observation model. First, in our experience, the choice of the observation model (i.e., between the three variants given above) often has no strong effect on the parameter estimates (but see Knape et al., 2011). Second, all the models can only adjust for random observation errors, that is, some sort of binomial sampling error as shown in Section 5.3. Any systematic patterns such as a trend (e.g., when observers become better over time) cannot be properly accounted for by this type of model. The general discussion about state-space models for inference about population size (see Chapter 5) also applies for this component of integrated models. Third, none of the above-mentioned observation models allows estimation of detection probability, and, consequently, the true population size remains unknown. So if the average detection probability of an individual is 0.9, then the estimated population size (N) will on average be 0.9 times the true population size. If we want to estimate detection probability, different survey protocols must be used (see Chapters 6, 10, 12, and 13). If detection probability is stationary (i.e., fluctuates around a constant mean), this caveat does not apply for conclusions about population dynamics and for the estimation of the demographic parameters. Fourth, the survey may be restricted to certain age classes or other segments of the population or it may not differentiate between age classes, and yet, we are usually still able to estimate age-specific population sizes (see also Link et al., 2003, for an impressive example of this, although not in the context of an integrated population model). Finally, it may be possible to get separate counts of different age classes, with the advantage of being able to extract more detailed information from the counts (Tavecchia et al., 2009). The observation equation then needs a slight adaptation.

In what follows, we will use the normal approximation for the observation error. The likelihood of the state-space model is the product of the likelihood of the observation and the process equations:

$$L_{SS}(\mathbf{y} \mid \mathbf{N}, \mathbf{S_{juv}}, \mathbf{S_{ad}}, \mathbf{f}, \sigma_y^2) = L_O(\mathbf{y} \mid \mathbf{N}, \sigma_y^2) \times L_S(\mathbf{N} \mid \mathbf{S_{juv}}, \mathbf{S_{ad}}, \mathbf{f}).$$

The state-space likelihood already contains all parameters that we would like to estimate. So one might wonder why not just use the state-space model alone to estimate these parameters; that is, why aren't the count data enough? The reason is that the parameters in this model would not be identifiable, unless we impose strong constraints on the parameters (King et al., 2010), use informative prior distributions (Thomas et al., 2005; Newman et al., 2006; Buckland et al., 2007), or have counts from several stage/age classes (Link et al., 2003; David et al., 2010). Otherwise, the parameters would not be identifiable. However, if we add more (independent) information about some or all of the parameters, the model typically becomes identifiable. Therefore, we have to go on with the definition of likelihoods of other kinds of data.

Likelihood of the Capture–Recapture Data

For the capture–recapture data, we can use the likelihood of the CJS model introduced in Section 7.9, that is, the multinomial likelihood, $L_{CJS}(\mathbf{m} \mid \mathbf{S_{juv}}, \mathbf{S_{ad}}, \mathbf{p})$. Whenever possible, we recommend the multinomial likelihood to estimate survival, because of the resulting computational benefits compared with the state-space likelihood. It requires that the capture–recapture data are summarized in the m-array format ($\mathbf{m}$).

Likelihood of Reproductive Success Data

We use a simple Poisson regression to model productivity (see Chapters 3 and 4). We assume that the total number of nestlings counted in year t, (J_t), follows a Poisson distribution with parameters that are the product of the number of surveyed broods (R_t) and productivity (f_t), hence, $J_t \sim \text{Poisson}(R_t f_t)$. Thus, the likelihood is $L_P(\mathbf{J}, \mathbf{R} \mid \mathbf{f})$.

11.2.3 Third Step: Formulate the Joint Likelihood

The last step is to formulate the likelihood of the complete model. This is in fact simple, if we can assume independence among the component data sets of the integrated analysis. Then, the joint likelihood is just the product of the component likelihoods:

$$L_{IPM}(\mathbf{y}, \mathbf{m}, \mathbf{J}, \mathbf{R} \mid \mathbf{N}, \mathbf{S_{juv}}, \mathbf{S_{ad}}, \mathbf{f}, \mathbf{p}, \sigma_y^2) = L_O(\mathbf{y} \mid \mathbf{N}, \sigma_y^2) \times L_S(\mathbf{N} \mid \mathbf{S_{juv}}, \mathbf{S_{ad}}, \mathbf{f})$$
$$\times L_{CJS}(\mathbf{m} \mid \mathbf{S_{juv}}, \mathbf{S_{ad}}, \mathbf{p}) \times L_P(\mathbf{J}, \mathbf{R} \mid \mathbf{f})$$

A graph of this model is shown in Fig. 11.3a. The independence of the data sets is a crucial assumption. Under one—restrictive—view, this would mean that no animal in the population count data must occur in the capture–recapture data or in the productivity data. This could be achieved if different (sub)populations are sampled: in one population we collect population count data, in another the capture–recapture data, and in the third productivity data. Alternatively, we could sample a single very large population (e.g., living in a whole country) where it is unlikely that the same individual appears in more than one data set. Although the independence assumption may then hold, we would need a new assumption that the dynamics as well as the link between population size and demography is identical in all sampled (sub)populations or across the large spatial scale. This may well be an unrealistic assumption too.

In practice, we often have different kinds of demographic data from a single and rather small population. After all, it is for small populations with limited data where the combination of multiple data sets is particularly fruitful in terms of the increased precision of parameter estimates (Schaub et al., 2007). Therefore, it is important to understand whether the violation of the independence assumption has a strong impact on the parameter estimates. Abadi et al. (2010a) have recently studied this issue. In principle, if the data sets are not independent, we would not expect biased parameter estimates, but spuriously high precision of the estimates. This is a classical result in statistics when nonindependent data are analyzed as if they were independent: the information from one individual is used multiple times, and hence, the genuine sample size is not as large as it seems. For example, if an individual is included in the population count data, it contributes to the estimation of survival in the state-space likelihood. The same individual might be included in the capture–recapture data and thus again provide information about survival via the multinomial likelihood of the CJS model. The result of this is a kind of overdispersion due to lack of independence.

Abadi et al. (2010a) simulated data types similar to the ones we use here with different degrees of nonindependence. They found that violation of the independence assumption had almost no effect on the accuracy of the parameter estimates. In contrast, Besbeas et al. (2009) found that the violation of the independence assumption had an effect when population count and mark-recovery data were combined. These divergent conclusions likely stem from the fact that different data sets contribute differently to the joint likelihood. In fact, in these classical applications, violation of independence can only occur between the state-space likelihood and another likelihood because in the state-space likelihood all demographic parameters are included. Generally, the amount of information about demographic parameters in the state-space likelihood is small. If it is combined with a likelihood that contains plenty of information about

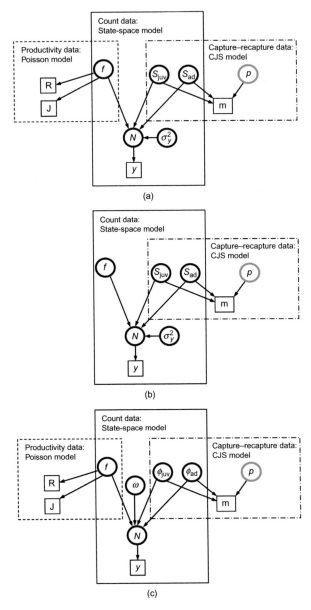

FIGURE 11.3 Graphical representation of different integrated population models. This graph is similar to an acyclic directed graph (DAG) without the priors. Small squares represent the data, circles the parameters (blue: target parameters, green: nuisence parameters), large squares the individual submodels, and arrows the flux of information. Circles appearing in two submodels indicate that they are informed from two data sources. (a) Model of Section 11.3; (b) same model as (a), but without the availability of productivity data (Section 11.4); (c) model of Section 11.6. For the notation of the parameters and data see text.

a demographic parameter, as is the case with the capture–recapture data and survival, the joint likelihood in terms of survival is dominated by the capture–recapture likelihood. Consequently, nonindependence plays a minor role. In contrast, if the state-space likelihood is combined with a likelihood that contains little information about a demographic parameter, as is the case with the mark-recovery likelihood and survival, the joint likelihood with respect to survival contains similar amounts of information from both the population count and the mark-recovery data. In that case, violation of the independence assumption can have a more serious effect on parameter accuracy. Thus, whether the violation of the independence assumption has an effect on parameter accuracy needs to be evaluated for each model separately.

11.3 EXAMPLE OF A SIMPLE IPM (COUNTS, CAPTURE–RECAPTURE, REPRODUCTION)

11.3.1 Load Data

We will load one data set from the ortolan bunting population that was simulated using the code in Web appendix 2.

```
# Population counts (from years 1 to 10)
y <- c(45, 48, 44, 59, 62, 62, 55, 51, 46, 42)

# Capture-recapture data (in m-array format, from years 1 to 10)
m <- matrix(c(11,  0,  0,  0,  0,  0,  0,  0,  0, 70,
               0, 12,  0,  1,  0,  0,  0,  0,  0, 52,
               0,  0, 15,  5,  1,  0,  0,  0,  0, 42,
               0,  0,  0,  8,  3,  0,  0,  0,  0, 51,
               0,  0,  0,  0,  4,  3,  0,  0,  0, 61,
               0,  0,  0,  0,  0, 12,  2,  3,  0, 66,
               0,  0,  0,  0,  0,  0, 16,  5,  0, 44,
               0,  0,  0,  0,  0,  0,  0, 12,  0, 46,
               0,  0,  0,  0,  0,  0,  0,  0, 11, 71,
              10,  2,  0,  0,  0,  0,  0,  0,  0, 13,
               0,  7,  0,  1,  0,  0,  0,  0,  0, 27,
               0,  0, 13,  2,  1,  1,  0,  0,  0, 14,
               0,  0,  0, 12,  2,  0,  0,  0,  0, 20,
               0,  0,  0,  0, 10,  2,  0,  0,  0, 21,
               0,  0,  0,  0,  0, 11,  2,  1,  1, 14,
               0,  0,  0,  0,  0,  0, 12,  0,  0, 18,
               0,  0,  0,  0,  0,  0,  0, 11,  1, 21,
               0,  0,  0,  0,  0,  0,  0,  0, 10, 26), ncol = 10,
            byrow = TRUE)
```

The last column in matrix **m** contains the number of released individuals that are never recaptured. The top half of the array contains the data on birds marked as juveniles and the bottom half on those marked as adults.

```
# Productivity data (from years 1 to 9)
J <- c(64, 132, 86, 154, 156, 134, 116, 106, 110)
R <- c(21, 28, 26, 38, 35, 33, 31, 30, 33)
```

Vector **J** contains the total number of nestlings recorded, and vector **R** is the annual number of surveyed broods. The numbers recorded in the last year are not considered here because they are not needed in the population model.

11.3.2 Analysis of the Model

We find it useful to highlight three sections in the BUGS code for analyzing the integrated population model. First, we define the priors of the unknowns (parameters, latent effects). This includes the latent population size of each class in the first year, the demographic parameters, and the observation error. As always in this book, we can specify vague priors with little prior information if we wish. We must ensure that the priors have support only for values that are possible at all (e.g., positive numbers for the initial population sizes). In our model, all demographic rates are constant over time; hence, we define priors for their means. When using vague priors for the initial population sizes, BUGS may not even start to update or, if it does, the chains may struggle to converge. Thus, with integrated population models, it is often advisable to use slightly more informative priors. King et al. (2010) suggest normal priors centered on the observed count in the first year and with a variance that is equal to the observation error.

Second, we may compute various derived parameters. As we have seen many times, one of the big assets of an MCMC-based Bayesian analysis is the ease with which derived quantities can be computed along with a full assessment of their uncertainty. In our example, we are interested in the population growth rate.

Third, our code contains likelihoods of the different data sets whose modeling we integrate in our analysis. These likelihoods are more or less identical to the BUGS code given for the different data sets so far, for example, in Chapters 5 and 7. You may ask yourself the following question: where is that ugly joint likelihood that we saw in Section 11.2.3? Does it lurk in some terrifying BUGS code that we have yet to disclose? No, what you see is all that is necessary to define the joint likelihood of the model in the BUGS language. To us, as ecologists, this is another great asset of Bayesian population analyses using BUGS: instead of defining huge likelihoods at once, you decompose them and describe them by defining the quantities in the model and their stochastic and deterministic local relationships. The joint likelihood is then defined implicitly by using the same names for some parameters that co-occur in different component likelihoods. We believe that a good grasp of reasonably complex statistical models such as an IPM is much more within the reach of most ecologists than it is when you want to use the method of maximum likelihood to fit the same model. Thus, again, BUGS frees the modeler in you.

```
# Specify model in BUGS language
sink("ipm.bug")
cat("
model {

# -----------------------------------------------
# Integrated population model
# - Age structured model with 2 age classes:
#        1-year old and adults (at least 2 years old)
# - Age at first breeding = 1 year
# - Prebreeding census, female-based
# - All vital rates assumed to be constant
# -----------------------------------------------

# -----------------------------------------------
# 1. Define the priors for the parameters
# -----------------------------------------------

# Observation error
tauy <- pow(sigma.y, -2)
sigma.y ~ dunif(0, 50)
sigma2.y <- pow(sigma.y, 2)

# Initial population sizes
N1[1] ~ dnorm(100, 0.0001)I(0,)      # 1-year
Nad[1] ~ dnorm(100, 0.0001)I(0,)     # Adults

# Survival and recapture probabilities, as well as productivity
for (t in 1:(nyears-1)){
    sjuv[t] <- mean.sjuv
    sad[t] <- mean.sad
    p[t] <- mean.p
    f[t] <- mean.fec
    }

mean.sjuv ~ dunif(0, 1)
mean.sad ~ dunif(0, 1)
mean.p ~ dunif(0, 1)
mean.fec ~ dunif(0, 20)

# -----------------------------------------------
# 2. Derived parameters
# -----------------------------------------------
# Population growth rate
for (t in 1:(nyears-1)){
    lambda[t] <- Ntot[t+1] / Ntot[t]
    }
```

```
# ---------------------------------------------------
# 3. The likelihoods of the single data sets
# ---------------------------------------------------
# 3.1. Likelihood for population population count data (state-space
  model)
    # 3.1.1 System process
    for (t in 2:nyears) {
        mean1[t] <- f[t-1] / 2 * sjuv[t-1] * Ntot[t-1]
        N1[t] ~ dpois(mean1[t])
        Nad[t] ~ dbin(sad[t-1], Ntot[t-1])
        }
    for (t in 1:nyears) {
        Ntot[t] <- Nad[t] + N1[t]
        }

    # 3.1.2 Observation process
    for (t in 1:nyears) {
        y[t] ~ dnorm(Ntot[t], tauy)
        }

# 3.2 Likelihood for capture-recapture data: CJS model (2 age classes)
# Multinomial likelihood
for (t in 1:2*(nyears-1)) {
    m[t,1:nyears] ~ dmulti(pr[t,], r[t])
    }

# Calculate the number of released individuals
for (t in 1:2*(nyears-1)) {
    r[t] <- sum(m[t,])
    }

# m-array cell probabilities for juveniles
for (t in 1:(nyears-1)) {
    # Main diagonal
    q[t] <- 1-p[t]
    pr[t,t] <- sjuv[t] * p[t]
    # Above main diagonal
    for (j in (t+1):(nyears-1)) {
        pr[t,j] <- sjuv[t]*prod(sad[(t+1):j])*prod(q[t:(j-1)])*p[j]
        } #j
    # Below main diagonal
    for (j in 1:(t-1)) {
        pr[t,j] <- 0
        } #j
    # Last column: probability of non-recapture
    pr[t,nyears] <- 1-sum(pr[t,1:(nyears-1)])
    } #t

# m-array cell probabilities for adults
for (t in 1:(nyears-1)) {
    # Main diagonal
    pr[t+nyears-1,t] <- sad[t] * p[t]
    # Above main diagonal
    for (j in (t+1):(nyears-1)) {
```

```
        pr[t+nyears-1,j] <- prod(sad[t:j])*prod(q[t:(j-1)])*p[j]
        } #j
    # Below main diagonal
    for (j in 1:(t-1)){
        pr[t+nyears-1,j] <- 0
        } #j
    # Last column
    pr[t+nyears-1,nyears] <- 1 - sum(pr[t+nyears-1,1:(nyears-1)])
        } #t

# 3.3. Likelihood for productivity data: Poisson regression
for (t in 1:(nyears-1)){
    J[t] ~ dpois(rho[t])
    rho[t] <- R[t]*f[t]
    }
}
",fill = TRUE)
sink()

# Bundle data
bugs.data <- list(m = m, y = y, J = J, R = R, nyears = dim(m)[2])

# Initial values
inits <- function(){list(mean.sjuv = runif(1, 0, 1), mean.sad = runif
    (1, 0, 1), mean.p = runif(1, 0, 1), mean.fec = runif(1, 0, 10),
    N1 = rpois(dim(m)[2], 30), Nad = rpois(dim(m)[2], 30), sigma.y = runif
    (1, 0, 10))}

# Parameters monitored
parameters <- c("mean.sjuv", "mean.sad", "mean.p", "mean.fec", "N1",
    "Nad", "Ntot", "lambda", "sigma2.y")

# MCMC settings
ni <- 20000
nt <- 6
nb <- 5000
nc <- 3

# Call WinBUGS from R (BRT 2 min)
ipm <- bugs(bugs.data, inits, parameters, "ipm.bug", n.chains = nc,
    n.thin = nt, n.iter = ni, n.burnin = nb, debug = TRUE, bugs.directory =
    bugs.dir, working.directory = getwd())
```

The chains converge fairly quickly. Here are the posterior summaries:

```
print(ipm, digits = 3)
```

	mean	sd	2.5%	25%	50%	75%	97.5%	Rhat	n.eff
mean.sjuv	0.257	0.018	0.223	0.245	0.257	0.269	0.294	1.001	7500
mean.sad	0.519	0.026	0.468	0.501	0.519	0.536	0.570	1.001	7500
mean.p	0.619	0.037	0.548	0.594	0.618	0.644	0.691	1.001	7500
mean.fec	3.829	0.115	3.603	3.752	3.826	3.907	4.055	1.003	1000
N1[1]	22.757	13.264	1.127	11.440	22.600	34.052	45.310	1.009	320
[...]									
N1[10]	20.237	3.563	13.630	17.880	20.050	22.490	27.565	1.001	4900
Nad[1]	22.955	13.209	1.359	11.330	23.050	34.052	45.180	1.005	540
[...]									

```
Nad[10]     22.831   3.230  17.000  21.000  23.000  25.000  29.000  1.002  1400
Ntot[1]     45.711   3.101  39.990  44.260  45.220  46.870  53.137  1.001  5100
[ ... ]
Ntot[10]    43.068   3.240  37.540  41.480  42.400  44.310  51.241  1.001  3000
lambda[1]    1.047   0.071   0.893   1.008   1.055   1.082   1.192  1.001  7500
[ ... ]
lambda[9]    0.930   0.068   0.804   0.893   0.920   0.960   1.096  1.001  7500
sigma2.y    14.580  28.382   0.016   1.550   6.087  16.480  79.205  1.010   740
```

Estimated population sizes are quite close to the counts in our example (Fig. 11.4). As expected, the estimates are less variable than the counts, illustrating the smoothing that results from separating out state and observation processes, the autoregressive nature of the population model, and adding more information (from the other data sets). We could also plot the age-specific population sizes, but in our study example this is not very interesting since both age classes have about the same size. This is because the stable age distribution (obtained as the right eigenvector of the Leslie matrix) in this population is 50% 1-year-old individuals and 50% adults. Yet, generally, this is an advantage of integrated models: one may obtain estimates of the size of population segments (such as age classes) that are never even observed.

```
# Produce Fig. 11-4
par(cex = 1.2)
lower <- upper <- numeric()
for (i in 1:10){
    lower[i] <- quantile(ipm$sims.list$Ntot[,i], 0.025)
    upper[i] <- quantile(ipm$sims.list$Ntot[,i], 0.975)
    }
```

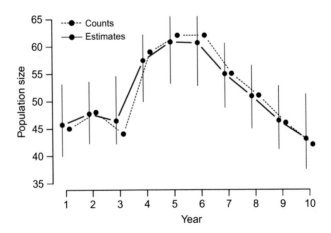

FIGURE 11.4 Observed (black) and estimated population sizes (blue) with 95% CRI under an integrated population model for the simulated ortolan bunting data set.

```
plot(ipm$mean$Ntot, type = "b", ylim = c(35, 65), ylab = "Population size",
   xlab = "Year", las = 1, pch = 16, col = "blue", frame = F, cex = 1.5)
segments(1:10, lower, 1:10, upper, col = "blue")
points(y, type = "b", col = "black", pch = 16, lty = 2, cex = 1.5)
legend(x = 1, y = 65, legend = c("Counts", "Estimates"), pch = c(16, 16),
   col = c("black", "blue"), lty = c(2, 1), bty = "n")
```

11.4 ANOTHER EXAMPLE OF AN IPM: ESTIMATING PRODUCTIVITY WITHOUT EXPLICIT PRODUCTIVITY DATA

One very important advantage of integrated population models is that they typically allow one to estimate demographic parameters for which no explicit data are available (e.g., Besbeas et al., 2002; Schaub et al., 2007). This is possible because the population count data contain information about all demographic parameters, and this information is exploited with the integrated population model. Here, we aim to estimate productivity (f) in a study in which no explicit data on productivity are available. We focus on the same ortolan bunting population as in the previous section, but this time only use the population count data and the capture–recapture data (Fig. 11.3b), and we adopt the same model structure as before (e.g., constant demographic rates). Essentially, the BUGS code requires one simple change: just remove the definition of the likelihood of the productivity data.

```
# Specify model in BUGS language
sink("ipm-prod.bug")
cat("
model {

# -----------------------------------------------
# Integrated population model
# - Age structured model with 2 age classes:
#        1-year old and adults (at least 2 years old)
# - Age at first breeding = 1 year
# - Prebreeding census, female-based
# - All vital rates assumed to be constant
# -----------------------------------------------

# -----------------------------------------------
# 1. Define the priors for the parameters
# -----------------------------------------------
# Observation error
tauy <- pow(sigma.y, -2)
sigma.y ~ dunif(0, 50)
sigma2.y <- pow(sigma.y, 2)

# Initial population sizes
N1[1] ~ dnorm(100, 0.0001)I(0,)        # 1-year
Nad[1] ~ dnorm(100, 0.0001)I(0,)       # Adults
```

```
# Survival and recapture probabilities, as well as productivity
for (t in 1:(nyears-1)){
    sjuv[t] <- mean.sjuv
    sad[t] <- mean.sad
    p[t] <- mean.p
    f[t] <- mean.fec
    }

mean.sjuv ~ dunif(0, 1)
mean.sad ~ dunif(0, 1)
mean.p ~ dunif(0, 1)
mean.fec ~ dunif(0, 20)

# -------------------------------------------------
# 2. Derived parameters
# -------------------------------------------------
# Population growth rate
for (t in 1:(nyears-1)){
    lambda[t] <- Ntot[t+1] / Ntot[t]
    }

# -------------------------------------------------
# 3. The likelihoods of the single data sets
# -------------------------------------------------
# 3.1. Likelihood for population population count data (state-space
  model)
    # 3.1.1 System process
    for (t in 2:nyears){
        mean1[t] <- f[t-1] / 2 * sjuv[t-1] * Ntot[t-1]
        N1[t] ~ dpois(mean1[t])
        Nad[t] ~ dbin(sad[t-1], Ntot[t-1])
        }
    for (t in 1:nyears){
        Ntot[t] <- Nad[t] + N1[t]
        }

    # 3.1.2 Observation process
    for (t in 1:nyears){
        y[t] ~ dnorm(Ntot[t], tauy)
        }

# 3.2 Likelihood for capture-recapture data: CJS model (2 age classes)
# Multinomial likelihood
for (t in 1:2*(nyears-1)){
    m[t,1:nyears] ~ dmulti(pr[t,], r[t])
    }

# Calculate the number of released individuals
for (t in 1:2*(nyears-1)){
    r[t] <- sum(m[t,])
    }

# m-array cell probabilities for juveniles
for (t in 1:(nyears-1)){
    # Main diagonal
    q[t] <- 1-p[t]
```

```
        pr[t,t] <- sjuv[t] * p[t]
        # Above main diagonal
        for (j in (t+1):(nyears-1)){
            pr[t,j] <- sjuv[t]*prod(sad[(t+1):j])*prod(q[t:(j-1)])*p[j]
            } #j
        # Below main diagonal
        for (j in 1:(t-1)){
            pr[t,j] <- 0
            } #j
        # Last column: probability of non-recapture
        pr[t,nyears] <- 1-sum(pr[t,1:(nyears-1)])
        } #t

# m-array cell probabilities for adults
for (t in 1:(nyears-1)){
        # Main diagonal
        pr[t+nyears-1,t] <- sad[t] * p[t]
        # Above main diagonal
        for (j in (t+1):(nyears-1)){
            pr[t+nyears-1,j] <- prod(sad[t:j])*prod(q[t:(j-1)])*p[j]
            } #j
        # Below main diagonal
        for (j in 1:(t-1)){
            pr[t+nyears-1,j] <- 0
            } #j
        # Last column
        pr[t+nyears-1,nyears] <- 1 - sum(pr[t+nyears-1,1:(nyears-1)])
        } #t
}
",fill = TRUE)
sink()

# Bundle data
bugs.data <- list(m = m, y = y, nyears = dim(m)[2])

# Initial values
inits <- function(){list(mean.sjuv = runif(1, 0, 1), mean.sad = runif(1,
    0, 1), mean.p = runif(1, 0, 1), mean.fec = runif(1, 0, 10), N1 = rpois
    (dim(m)[2], 30), Nad = rpois(dim(m)[2], 30), sigma.y = runif(1, 0,
    10))}

# Parameters monitored
parameters <- c("mean.sjuv", "mean.sad", "mean.p", "mean.fec", "N1",
    "Nad", "Ntot", "lambda", "sigma2.y")

# MCMC settings
ni <- 20000
nt <- 6
nb <- 5000
nc <- 3

# Call WinBUGS from R (BRT 1 min)
ipm.prod <- bugs(bugs.data, inits, parameters, "ipm-prod.bug",
    n.chains = nc, n.thin = nt, n.iter = ni, n.burnin = nb, debug = TRUE,
    bugs.directory = bugs.dir, working.directory = getwd())
```

```
# Summarize posteriors
print(ipm.prod, digits = 3)
            mean      sd    2.5%     25%     50%     75%   97.5%   Rhat  n.eff
mean.sjuv  0.266   0.024   0.222   0.250   0.265   0.282   0.317  1.001   7500
mean.sad   0.527   0.029   0.471   0.507   0.527   0.546   0.584  1.002   1900
mean.p     0.611   0.040   0.531   0.584   0.610   0.639   0.689  1.001   3500
mean.fec   3.547   0.487   2.673   3.209   3.515   3.858   4.557  1.001   5400
N1[1]     23.363  13.252   1.184  12.557  23.275  34.402  45.535  1.014    170
[ ... ]
N1[10]    19.499   3.631  12.699  17.090  19.400  21.750  26.870  1.004    680
Nad[1]    22.561  13.274   1.233  11.390  22.590  33.230  45.305  1.022    120
[ ... ]
Nad[10]   23.398   3.313  17.000  21.000  23.000  26.000  30.000  1.002   1500
Ntot[1]   45.925   3.244  40.600  44.450  45.260  46.960  53.905  1.001   7500
[ ... ]
Ntot[10]  42.898   3.130  37.519  41.470  42.290  43.940  50.430  1.002   1600
lambda[1]  1.044   0.069   0.891   1.007   1.054   1.078   1.187  1.001   7500
[ ... ]
lambda[9]  0.928   0.066   0.804   0.894   0.917   0.957   1.091  1.001   7100
sigma2.y  14.000  31.952   0.003   1.268   5.318  15.167  78.404  1.025    210
```

Most parameter estimates are nearly identical in both models. Overall, the precision of the estimates is slightly reduced now since we have ignored part of the available information by not using the productivity data. The most striking difference occurs for the productivity parameter. Under the model without productivity data, the estimate is slightly lower (3.547 vs. 3.829) and much less precise (sd = 0.487 vs. 0.115). A simulation study shows that the productivity estimator from both models is unbiased, but if no productivity data are available the precision is understandably lower (Abadi et al., 2010a).

11.5 IPMs FOR POPULATION VIABILITY ANALYSIS

One particularly useful feature of integrated population models is that predictions of the size of "unobserved populations" (e.g., age classes) can be made. We have already mentioned that we may estimate the size of unobserved segments of a population. However, we may just as well estimate the size of (as yet) unobserved populations in the future. In particular, Bayesian population analysis using posterior sampling is strikingly useful for a full assessment of all uncertainties involved in such forecasts. To project the model into the future and forecast population size, we extend the loops of the state process and adapt the prior definitions of the demographic rates to cover the additional years. Within the MCMC samples, the future population sizes are estimated with full accounting for all uncertainty in the parameter estimates. The posterior distributions of the predicted future population sizes can be directly used to compute population extinction probabilities or population prediction intervals, both typical inferential targets in population viability analyses (Beissinger, 2002). We illustrate predictions with the ortolan bunting example.

```
# Specify model in BUGS language
sink("ipm-pred.bug")
cat("
model {
# -------------------------------------------------
# Integrated population model
# - Age structured model with 2 age classes:
#    1-year old and adults (at least 2 years old)
# - Age at first breeding = 1 year
# - Prebreeding census, female-based
# - All vital rates assumed to be constant
# -------------------------------------------------

# -------------------------------------------------
# 1. Define the priors for the parameters
# -------------------------------------------------
# Observation error
tauy <- pow(sigma.y, -2)
sigma.y ~ dunif(0, 50)
sigma2.y <- pow(sigma.y, 2)

# Initial population sizes
N1[1] ~ dnorm(100, 0.0001)I(0,)        # 1-year
Nad[1] ~ dnorm(100, 0.0001)I(0,)       # Adults

# Survival and recapture probabilities, as well as productivity
for (t in 1:(nyears-1+t.pred)){
    sjuv[t] <- mean.sjuv
    sad[t] <- mean.sad
    p[t] <- mean.p
    f[t] <- mean.fec
    }

mean.sjuv ~ dunif(0, 1)
mean.sad ~ dunif(0, 1)
mean.p ~ dunif(0, 1)
mean.fec ~ dunif(0, 20)

# -------------------------------------------------
# 2. Derived parameters
# -------------------------------------------------
# Population growth rate
for (t in 1:(nyears-1+t.pred)){
    lambda[t] <- Ntot[t+1] / Ntot[t]
    }
```

```
# ------------------------------------------------
# 3. The likelihoods of the single data sets
# ------------------------------------------------
# 3.1. Likelihood for population population count data (state-space
  model)
    # 3.1.1 System process
    for (t in 2:nyears+t.pred){
        mean1[t] <- f[t-1] / 2 * sjuv[t-1] * Ntot[t-1]
        N1[t] ~ dpois(mean1[t])
        Nad[t] ~ dbin(sad[t-1], Ntot[t-1])
        }
    for (t in 1:nyears+t.pred){
        Ntot[t] <- Nad[t] +N1[t]
        }

    # 3.1.2 Observation process
    for (t in 1:nyears){
        y[t] ~ dnorm(Ntot[t], tauy)
        }

# 3.2 Likelihood for capture-recapture data: CJS model (2 age classes)
# Multinomial likelihood
for (t in 1:2*(nyears-1)){
    m[t,1:nyears] ~ dmulti(pr[t,], r[t])
    }

# Calculate the number of released individuals
for (t in 1:2*(nyears-1)){
    r[t] <- sum(m[t,])
    }

# m-array cell probabilities for juveniles
for (t in 1:(nyears-1)){
    # Main diagonal
    q[t] <- 1-p[t]
    pr[t,t] <- sjuv[t] * p[t]
    # Above main diagonal
    for (j in (t+1):(nyears-1)){
        pr[t,j] <- sjuv[t]*prod(sad[(t+1):j])*prod(q[t:(j-1)])*p[j]
        } #j
    # Below main diagonal
    for (j in 1:(t-1)){
        pr[t,j] <- 0
        } #j
    # Last column: probability of non-recapture
    pr[t,nyears] <- 1-sum(pr[t,1:(nyears-1)])
    } #t

# m-array cell probabilities for adults
for (t in 1:(nyears-1)){
    # Main diagonal
    pr[t+nyears-1,t] <- sad[t] * p[t]
    # Above main diagonal
    for (j in (t+1):(nyears-1)){
        pr[t+nyears-1,j] <- prod(sad[t:j])*prod(q[t:(j-1)])*p[j]
        } #j
```

```
# Below main diagonal
for (j in 1:(t-1)){
    pr[t+nyears-1,j] <- 0
    } #j
# Last column
pr[t+nyears-1,nyears] <- 1 - sum(pr[t+nyears-1,1:(nyears-1)])
    } #t

# 3.3. Likelihood for productivity data: Poisson regression
for (t in 1:(nyears-1)){
    J[t] ~ dpois(rho[t])
    rho[t] <- R[t]*f[t]
    }
}
",fill = TRUE)
sink()

# Give the number of future years for which population size shall be
  estimated
t.pred <- 5

# Bundle data
bugs.data <- list(m = m, y = y, J = J, R = R, nyears = dim(m)[2],
    t.pred = t.pred)

# Initial values
inits <- function(){list(mean.sjuv = runif(1, 0, 1), mean.sad = runif
    (1, 0, 1), mean.p = runif(1, 0, 1), mean.fec = runif(1, 0, 10), N1 =
    rpois(dim(m)[2]+ t.pred, 30), Nad = rpois(dim(m)[2]+ t.pred, 30),
    sigma.y = runif(1, 0, 10))}

# Parameters monitored
parameters <- c("mean.sjuv", "mean.sad", "mean.p", "mean.fec", "N1",
    "Nad", "Ntot", "lambda", "sigma2.y")

# MCMC settings
ni <- 20000
nt <- 6
nb <- 5000
nc <- 3

# Call WinBUGS from R (BRT 1 min)
ipm.pred <- bugs(bugs.data, inits, parameters, "ipm-pred.bug",
    n.chains = nc, n.thin = nt, n.iter = ni, n.burnin = nb, debug = TRUE,
    bugs.directory = bugs.dir, working.directory = getwd())
```

The estimated population sizes for the entire 15 years are shown in Fig. 11.5. We notice that 95% CRIs increase over time after year 10, reflecting an increased uncertainty when projecting further ahead. This makes intuitive sense.

```
# Produce Fig. 11-5
par(cex = 1.2)
lower <- upper <- numeric()
for (i in 1:15){
```

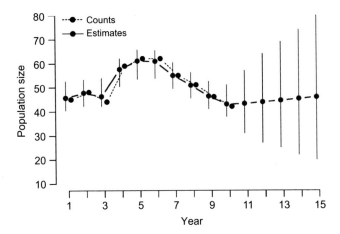

FIGURE 11.5   Observed (black) and estimated population sizes (blue) along with the 95% CRI. For years 11–15, projected population is shown.

```
    lower[i] <- quantile(ipm.pred$sims.list$Ntot[,i], 0.025)
    upper[i] <- quantile(ipm.pred$sims.list$Ntot[,i], 0.975)
    }
plot(ipm.pred$mean$Ntot, type = "b", ylim = c(10, max(upper)), ylab =
    "Population size", xlab = "Year", las = 1, pch = 16, col = "blue",
    frame = F)
segments(1:15, lower, 1:15, upper, col = "blue")
points(y, type = "b", col = "black", lty = 2, pch = 16)
legend(x = 1, y = 80, legend = c("Counts", "Estimates"), pch = c(16, 16),
    col = c("black", "blue"), lty = c(2, 1), bty = "n")
```

The estimation of extinction probabilities is straightforward. In the example, we might be interested to know the probability that population size falls below 30 pairs in 5 years from now. Our model provides the answer to that based on the assumption that the demographic processes modeled remain the same as observed in the past. We only need to evaluate the posterior distribution of population size in year 15:

```
mean(ipm.pred$sims.list$Ntot[,15]<30)
[1] 0.140
```

Forecasting population size is slightly more complicated if the demographic parameters are not constant but vary over time. The best way to achieve this goal is to estimate a mean and a temporal variance of the demographic parameters from the observed data (see Section 11.6), that is, fit random year effects. Future realizations of the demographic rates can then be sampled from these distributions. When specifying random year effects in WinBUGS, process variability is automatically accounted for.

11.6 REAL DATA EXAMPLE: HOOPOE POPULATION DYNAMICS

We look at a real example using data types that are typically collected in demographic population studies. We studied a local population of hoopoes (Fig. 11.6) in the SW Swiss Alps (Valais; Arlettaz et al. 2010). In an area of 62 km², the vast majority of hoopoes use nest boxes for reproduction. From 2002 to 2009, these nest boxes were repeatedly checked every year to record the breeding success, and all the nestlings were ringed. In addition, adults were marked and recaptured. Thus, we obtained the following three types of demographic data: (1) a population count (the maximal number of simultaneously occupied nest boxes in each year), (2) capture–recapture data of adults and young, and (3) data on reproductive output. The goal of our study was to estimate the demographic parameters as well as their temporal variability to understand the dynamics of the hoopoe population (Schaub et al., 2011).

Although the study area is fairly large, the population is not geographically closed. Therefore, emigration and immigration need to be considered. We have already seen in Chapter 7 that capture–recapture data allow estimation of apparent survival probabilities, that is, the product of true survival and site fidelity. By modeling apparent survival in a CJS model as a part of

FIGURE 11.6 Happy hoopoes (*Upupa epops*), Switzerland (Photograph by P. Keusch). Note that both individuals are ringed; they belong to the study population in the Valais (Schaub et al., 2011).

the integrated population model, we automatically account for emigration, even if we cannot estimate it. On the other hand, information on immigration is very elusive. In our study, the population counts contain information about immigration because the annual change in population size is a result of all four demographic processes operating in a population: survival, productivity, immigration, and emigration. We have independent data for the other demographic processes (capture–recapture for apparent survival, reproductive output for productivity); hence, the combined analysis should enable us to obtain an estimate of immigration. This neat idea was brought up by Abadi et al. (2010b).

To write the BUGS code for our model, we take the three steps outlined earlier. First, we describe the link between population change and demographic rates. Hoopoes are short-lived, and we therefore assume two age classes only. We survey the population just before reproduction; that is, we conduct a prebreeding census. Hence, we differentiate 1-year-old individuals from older individuals. We include demographic stochasticity by using appropriate distributions. Since we want to estimate immigration, the population can be divided into three components: surviving philopatric adults (N_{ad}), locally produced young that survived and recruited into our population (N_1), and immigrants (N_{im}). We model the numbers of individuals in these population segments with binomial and Poisson distributions:

$$N_{ad,t+1} \sim \text{Binomial}(N_{1,t} + N_{ad,t} + N_{im,t}, \phi_{ad,t})$$

$$N_{1,t+1} \sim \text{Poisson}\left((N_{1,t} + N_{ad,t} + N_{im,t})\phi_{juv,t}\frac{f_t}{2} \right)$$

$$N_{im,t+1} \sim \text{Poisson}\left((N_{1,t} + N_{ad,t} + N_{im,t})\omega_t \right).$$

Here, $\phi_{juv,t}$ and $\phi_{ad,t}$ are apparent survival probabilities from year t to $t + 1$ of young (from fledging to age 1) and adults, respectively, f_t is productivity in year t, and ω_t is the immigration rate. The latter is expressed as a ratio, that is, as the number of immigrants in year $t + 1$ per individual in year t. We could estimate the annual number of immigrants using a Poisson distribution, but we prefer the rate, because we are interested in the temporal variation of the demographic rates and in the temporal variation of components of population size.

The second step is to write the likelihood of the individual data sets. As before, we use a state-space model for the population counts, with the state-process equations given above. The assumed observation process is slightly different from the earlier one: we now adopt a Poisson observation error (i.e., $y_t \sim \text{Poisson}(N_{1,t} + N_{ad,t} + N_{im,t})$). Hence, the relative observation error is constant, but the absolute observation error increases with population size, because in the Poisson distribution the variance is equal to the mean. Compared to the log-normal distribution used by Schaub et al. (2011) for the same data, convergence of Markov chains is obtained faster with a Poisson observation error. Parameter estimates are almost identical regardless of the distribution chosen for the observation error (you can try this out for the lognormal or even the normal). The state-space model further requires prior distributions for the initial sizes of all population components $(N_{1,1}, N_{ad,1}, N_{im,1})$. For the capture–recapture data, we use the CJS model with a multinomial likelihood and for the productivity data a Poisson regression. We assume independence among the three data sets, and consequently, the joint likelihood, the definition of which is our third step, is the product of the three individual data likelihoods. This model is depicted graphically in Fig. 11.3c.

We are particularly interested in assessing the temporal variability of all demographic parameters, and we formulate a model that includes environmental stochasticity. We specify random time effects for all demographic parameters as discussed in Section 7.4.2. Thus, we imagine that the annual values of all demographic rates (on an appropriately transformed scale) are realizations from normal distributions with means and variances that we estimate. We use the logit link for survival probabilities and the log link for productivity and immigration rates. When adopting a hierarchical model for the demographic parameters in each year, we no longer need priors and initial values for each of them in each year. Rather, we specify a prior and an initial value for their mean and variance, that is, for the hyperparameters. We use vague normal priors for the logit of the mean survival probabilities and the log of mean fecundity and immigration and uniform priors for the variance parameters on the standard deviation scale.

Now, we are ready! We load the data, write the model in BUGS language, and run it.

```
# Load data
nyears <- 9       # Number of years

# Capture-recapture data: m-array of juveniles and adults (these are
  males and females together)
marray.j <- matrix (c(15, 3, 0, 0, 0, 0, 0, 0, 198, 0, 34, 9, 1, 0, 0, 0, 0,
    287, 0, 0, 56, 8, 1, 0, 0, 0, 455, 0, 0, 0, 48, 3, 1, 0, 0, 518, 0, 0, 0, 0,
    45, 13, 2, 0, 463, 0, 0, 0, 0, 0, 27, 7, 0, 493, 0, 0, 0, 0, 0, 0, 37, 3,
    434, 0, 0, 0, 0, 0, 0, 39, 405), nrow = 8, ncol = 9, byrow = TRUE)
marray.a <- matrix(c(14, 2, 0, 0, 0, 0, 0, 0, 43, 0, 22, 4, 0, 0, 0, 0, 0,
    44, 0, 0, 34, 2, 0, 0, 0, 0, 79, 0, 0, 0, 51, 3, 0, 0, 0, 94, 0, 0, 0, 0, 45,
    3, 0, 0, 118, 0, 0, 0, 0, 0, 44, 3, 0, 113, 0, 0, 0, 0, 0, 0, 48, 2, 99, 0,
    0, 0, 0, 0, 0, 0, 51, 90), nrow = 8, ncol = 9, byrow = TRUE)

# Population count data
popcount <- c(32, 42, 64, 85, 82, 78, 73, 69, 79)

# Productivity data
J <- c(189, 274, 398, 538, 520, 476, 463, 438)  # Number of offspring
R <- c(28, 36, 57, 77, 81, 83, 77, 72)           # Number of surveyed
                                                   broods
```

```
# Specify model in BUGS language
sink("ipm.hoopoe.bug")
cat("
model {

# ----------------------------------------------------------
# Integrated population model
# - Age structured model with 2 age classes:
#       1-year old and adults (at least 2-years old)
# - Age at first breeding = 1 year
# - Prebreeding census, female-based
# - All vital rates are assumed to be time-dependent (random)
# - Explicit estimation of immigration
# ----------------------------------------------------------

# --------------------------------------
# 1. Define the priors for the parameters
# --------------------------------------
# Initial population sizes
N1[1] ~ dnorm(100, 0.0001)I(0,)           # 1-year old individuals
NadSurv[1] ~ dnorm(100, 0.0001)I(0,)      # Adults >= 2 years
Nadimm[1] ~ dnorm(100, 0.0001)I(0,)       # Immigrants

# Mean demographic parameters (on appropriate scale)
l.mphij ~ dnorm(0, 0.0001)I(-10,10)          # Bounded to help with
                                             #  convergence
l.mphia ~ dnorm(0, 0.0001)I(-10,10)
l.mfec ~ dnorm(0, 0.0001)I(-10,10)
l.mim ~ dnorm(0, 0.0001)I(-10,10)
l.p ~ dnorm(0, 0.0001)I(-10,10)

# Precision of standard deviations of temporal variability
sig.phij ~ dunif(0, 10)
tau.phij <- pow(sig.phij, -2)
sig.phia ~ dunif(0, 10)
tau.phia <- pow(sig.phia, -2)
sig.fec ~ dunif(0, 10)
tau.fec <- pow(sig.fec, -2)
sig.im ~ dunif(0, 10)
tau.im <- pow(sig.im, -2)

# Distribution of error terms (bounded to help with convergence)
for (t in 1:(nyears-1)){
    epsilon.phij[t] ~ dnorm(0, tau.phij)I(-15,15)
    epsilon.phia[t] ~ dnorm(0, tau.phia)I(-15,15)
    epsilon.fec[t] ~ dnorm(0, tau.fec)I(-15,15)
    epsilon.im[t] ~ dnorm(0, tau.im)I(-15,15)
    }

# ----------------------
# 2. Constrain parameters
# ----------------------
for (t in 1:(nyears-1)){
    logit(phij[t]) <- l.mphij + epsilon.phij[t] # Juv. apparent survival
    logit(phia[t]) <- l.mphia + epsilon.phia[t] # Adult apparent
                                                #  survival
```

```
    log(f[t]) <- l.mfec + epsilon.fec[t]      # Productivity
    log(omega[t]) <- l.mim + epsilon.im[t]    # Immigration
    logit(p[t]) <- l.p                        # Recapture probability
    }

# ----------------------
# 3. Derived parameters
# ----------------------
mphij <- exp(l.mphij)/(1+exp(l.mphij))    # Mean juvenile survival
                                            probability
mphia <- exp(l.mphia)/(1+exp(l.mphia))    # Mean adult survival
                                            probability
mfec <- exp(l.mfec)                       # Mean productivity
mim <- exp(l.mim)                         # Mean immigration rate

# Population growth rate
for (t in 1:(nyears-1)){
    lambda[t] <- Ntot[t+1] / Ntot[t]
    logla[t] <- log(lambda[t])
    }
mlam <- exp((1/(nyears-1))*sum(logla[1:(nyears-1)]))   # Geometric
                                                         mean

# -----------------------------------------
# 4. The likelihoods of the single data sets
# -----------------------------------------
# 4.1. Likelihood for population population count data (state-space
  model)
    # 4.1.1 System process
    for (t in 2:nyears){
        mean1[t] <- 0.5 * f[t-1] * phij[t-1] * Ntot[t-1]
        N1[t] ~ dpois(mean1[t])
        NadSurv[t] ~ dbin(phia[t-1], Ntot[t-1])
        mpo[t] <- Ntot[t-1] * omega[t-1]
        Nadimm[t] ~ dpois(mpo[t])
        }

    # 4.1.2 Observation process
    for (t in 1:nyears){
        Ntot[t] <- NadSurv[t] + Nadimm[t] + N1[t]
        y[t] ~ dpois(Ntot[t])
        }

# 4.2 Likelihood for capture-recapture data: CJS model (2 age classes)
# Multinomial likelihood
for (t in 1:(nyears-1)){
    marray.j[t,1:nyears] ~ dmulti(pr.j[t,], r.j[t])
    marray.a[t,1:nyears] ~ dmulti(pr.a[t,], r.a[t])
    }

# Calculate number of released individuals
for (t in 1:(nyears-1)){
    r.j[t] <- sum(marray.j[t,])
    r.a[t] <- sum(marray.a[t,])
    }
```

```
# m-array cell probabilities for juveniles
for (t in 1:(nyears-1)){
    q[t] <- 1-p[t]
    # Main diagonal
    pr.j[t,t] <- phij[t]*p[t]
    # Above main diagonal
    for (j in (t+1):(nyears-1)){
        pr.j[t,j] <- phij[t]*prod(phia[(t+1):j])*prod(q[t:(j-1)])*p[j]
        } #j
    # Below main diagonal
    for (j in 1:(t-1)){
        pr.j[t,j] <- 0
        } #j
    # Last column
    pr.j[t,nyears] <- 1-sum(pr.j[t,1:(nyears-1)])
    } #t

# m-array cell probabilities for adults
for (t in 1:(nyears-1)){
    # Main diagonal
    pr.a[t,t] <- phia[t]*p[t]
    # above main diagonal
    for (j in (t+1):(nyears-1)){
        pr.a[t,j] <- prod(phia[t:j])*prod(q[t:(j-1)])*p[j]
        } #j
    # Below main diagonal
    for (j in 1:(t-1)){
        pr.a[t,j] <- 0
        } #j
    # Last column
    pr.a[t,nyears] <- 1-sum(pr.a[t,1:(nyears-1)])
    } #t

# 4.3. Likelihood for productivity data: Poisson regression
for (t in 1:(nyears-1)){
    J[t] ~ dpois(rho[t])
    rho[t] <- R[t] * f[t]
    }
}
",fill = TRUE)
sink()
```

```
# Bundle data
bugs.data <- list(nyears = nyears, marray.j = marray.j, marray.a =
    marray.a, y = popcount, J = J, R = R)
```

```
# Initial values
inits <- function(){list(l.mphij = rnorm(1, 0.2, 0.5), l.mphia = rnorm
    (1, 0.2, 0.5), l.mfec = rnorm(1, 0.2, 0.5), l.mim = rnorm(1, 0.2,
    0.5), l.p = rnorm(1, 0.2, 1), sig.phij = runif(1, 0.1, 10), sig.phia =
    runif(1, 0.1, 10), sig.fec = runif(1, 0.1, 10), sig.im = runif(1, 0.1,
    10), N1 = round(runif(nyears, 1, 50), 0), NadSurv = round(runif
    (nyears, 5, 50), 0), Nadimm = round(runif(nyears, 1, 50), 0))}
```

```
# Parameters monitored
parameters <- c("phij", "phia", "f", "omega", "p", "lambda", "mphij",
    "mphia", "mfec", "mim", "mlam", "sig.phij", "sig.phia", "sig.fec",
    "sig.im", "N1", "NadSurv", "Nadimm", "Ntot")

# MCMC settings
ni <- 20000
nt <- 6
nb <- 10000
nc <- 3

# Call WinBUGS from R (BRT 5 min)
ipm.hoopoe <- bugs(bugs.data, inits, parameters, "ipm.hoopoe.bug",
    n.chains = nc, n.thin = nt, n.iter = ni, n.burnin = nb, debug = TRUE,
    bugs.directory = bugs.dir, working.directory = getwd())
```

With the chosen MCMC settings, we achieve convergence, though for a research paper, we may decide to run longer chains. Next, we inspect posterior distributions of the parameters of interest. Figure 11.7 is a graphical summary of what we learn about the dynamics of our hoopoe population (see Web appendix 1 for R code). The estimated population size is close to the population counts; that is, the observation error appears small. This is not surprising because the vast majority of hoopoes in our study use nest boxes, and the count of occupied nest boxes is unaffected by the observation error. Yet, there is still some uncertainty because some hoopoes conduct two broods in a year, and first and second broods may overlap. By modeling the maximal number of simultaneously occupied nest boxes, we strictly model an index of the actual population size, though probably a rather accurate one. The uncertainty around the population size estimates is quite large. This may reflect uncertainty due to the estimation of the demographic parameters and especially the uncertainty introduced by accounting for annual variability in all rates. Survival and productivity are estimated quite precisely; that is, they have a narrow CRI. In contrast, the immigration rate is not estimated very precisely because we have no explicit data on immigration (compare this with the similar situation in Section 11.4, in which we estimated productivity without productivity data). Immigration rate is one of the hardest demographic parameters to estimate in a demographic population analysis.

Specification of annual rates as random effects allowed us to estimate the temporal variance in the demographic rates and to get better estimates of the annual demographic rates (Gelman and Hill, 2007). The annual parameter estimates are shrunken toward the mean of their prior distribution, and the degree of shrinkage depends on the precision and the temporal variance (Burnham and White, 2002). Shrinkage pulls back outlying estimates toward more "sensible" values (see Section 4.1).

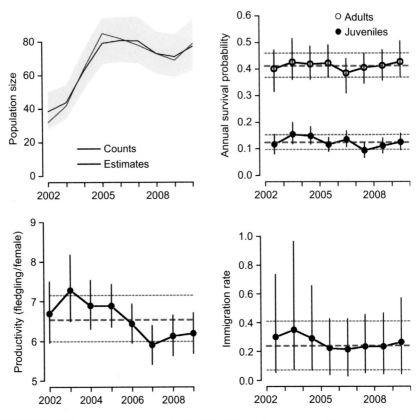

FIGURE 11.7 Posterior means (with 95% CRI) of the demographic parameters in a hoopoe population in SW Switzerland under a population model with random year effects for all demographic rates. Red lines show the mean and the 95% CRI of the mean hyperparameters (see Web appendix 1 for R code to create this figure).

To study the link between demographic rates and population growth, we can correlate the estimates of annual population growth rates with those of each demographic rate. These correlations provide indications about the strength of the contributions of the temporal variation in demographic rates to the temporal variation in the population growth rate (Robinson et al., 2004; Schaub et al., 2011). These correlations were positive for all demographic rates (Fig. 11.8; for R code see Web appendix 1). The correlation was highest for productivity and lowest for adult survival, suggesting that variation in productivity contributed more to the variation in population growth rates than the variation in adult survival. Credible intervals for correlation coefficients and the incidence of a positive correlation can easily be computed as derived quantity from the MCMC output of the analysis (see Web appendix 1).

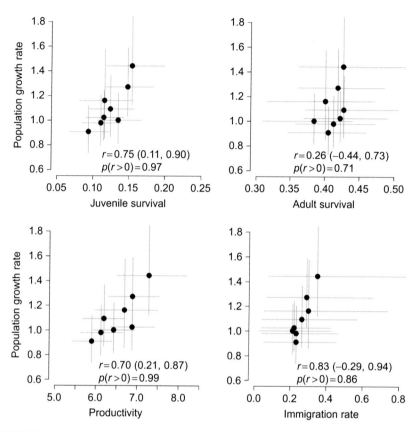

FIGURE 11.8 Estimates of annual demographic rates plotted against the estimates of interannual population growth. Black dots show posterior means and grey lines 95% CRI. Inset we print the posterior mode of the correlation coefficients (r, with 95% CRI) and the probability of a positive correlation (p(r > 0)) (see Web appendix 1 for R code to create this figure).

11.7 SUMMARY AND OUTLOOK

In this chapter, we have introduced integrated population models. In this recently developed modeling framework, population counts are combined coherently with data on demographic rates, such as survival or productivity, in a sort of stochastic Leslie matrix model. There are many advantages of using an integrated population model: the precision of parameter estimates is increased and parameters that are not estimable otherwise may become estimable. Thus, an integrated population model is much more powerful than many traditional approaches to population analysis, in which counts and data on demographic rates are analyzed separately. The core of any integrated model is a population projection matrix model, which provides the explicit link between changes in population size and demographic rates. A state-space formulation for the counts separates the dynamics of the true population size from observation error.

Using integrated population models allows one to make rigorous inference about unobserved quantities, such as the sizes of all age (or stage) classes defined, even if we cannot distinguish them in the field. As one caveat, though, we must not forget that what is called "population size" in state-space models such as those in this chapter and in Chapter 5 is really a smoothed index of population size; see Chapter 5. If our goal is to get unbiased estimates of population size, additional information about the population count data is necessary, combined with a different model for the observation process (i.e., as in Chapters 6, 10, 12, and 13).

So far no goodness-of-fit test is available for integrated population models (Schaub and Abadi, 2011). The best that can be done at the moment is to assess the goodness of fit of individual likelihoods to single data set using established procedures. If these tests are satisfactory, we may assume that the integrated model is also a satisfactory description of the complete data.

Integrated population models are a powerful and flexible framework to understand population dynamics (Schaub and Abadi, 2011). Our examples combined rather simple Leslie matrix state-space, capture–recapture, and Poisson regression models. Yet, it is easy to either make these models more complicated and realistic, consider multistate models or likelihoods of different data types. For example, Brooks et al. (2004) used mark-recovery data of lapwings instead of capture–recapture data to get independent information about true rather than apparent survival (see Exercise 4 in Section 11.8). Schaub et al. (2010) used age-at-death data to inform survival in an eagle owl population. The basic structure of the integrated model remains the same; you just need to replace the different modules in the joint likelihood, and you can make creative use of all the Lego pieces that we have described in this book. Thus, the models featured in this chapter provide some sort of synthesis of all other models, which makes them extremely flexible and powerful!

11.8 EXERCISES

1. Predict the hoopoe population size in 3 years. How large is the extinction probability (assume an extinction threshold of five pairs)?
2. Assume that population count data from years 3 and 5 are missing in the hoopoe example. Use an integrated population model to estimate these missing data. What do you observe?

3. Fit an integrated population model with time-dependent parameters to the ortolan bunting data (Section 11.3). Compare the population size estimates with those from a model with constant demographic parameters and explain.

4. Use an integrated population model to study population dynamics of British lapwings (Besbeas et al., 2002; Brooks et al., 2004). The data consist of a national population index (1965–1998) and of mark recoveries from individuals marked as hatchings (1963–1997). No data on productivity is available. Construct a model with two age classes for survival and where (1) first breeding occurs at the age of 2 years and (2) where it occurs at the age of 3 years. Further, (3) make a model where survival is a function of the number of frost days. The data file lapwing.txt (population index, m-array, normalized number of frost days; from Brooks et al. 2004) can be found on the book website (www.vogelwarte.ch/bpa).

Estimation of Abundance from Counts in Metapopulation Designs Using the Binomial Mixture Model

12.1 INTRODUCTION

The last two chapters of this book deal with the modeling of abundance and occurrence in a metapopulation design. We show how a sort of non-standard generalized linear mixed model (GLMM), a logistic regression with Poisson or with Bernoulli random effects, can be used to estimate population size or species occurrence in systems of spatial replicate populations. At least some of them must be surveyed more than once during a short period, that is, replication is required in space *and* in time. Short means that the dynamics of the collection of populations (extinction, colonization, or emigration and immigration, as well as survival and recruitment) must be negligible over the time period over which replicate surveys are conducted. We call the design of studies with such systems of spatial replicate populations with temporally replicated samples a *metapopulation design* (Royle, 2004c; Kéry and Royle, 2010). The system of spatial replicates may or may not be inhabited by a metapopulation in the biological sense (Hanski, 1994, 1998).

In Chapters 4 and 5, we used two variants of hierarchical model that attempt to partition the observed data into contributions from the dynamics of the true ecological state and from an observation process. These models are useful because failure to distinguish between the two processes that generate the observed data will often lead to severely biased inferences, for example, about the presence or magnitude of density dependence. However, if any further information is absent (e.g., covariates informative about the observation process), these models cannot account for patterns in detection probability (see Link and Sauer, 1998 for good examples of such covariate modeling as a partial remedy for imperfect and patterned detection probability). The models in Chapters 4 and 5 are unable in principle to fully correct for the observation error. We have shown that with a single count per time interval, this framework simply models the expectation Np, where N is population size, and p is the average detection probability. What in these models is called "observation error" is simply the ups and downs around Np of the observed counts due to binomial sampling error. Therefore, such hierarchical models have been called implicit hierarchical models (Royle and Dorazio, 2008): the product Np is not a quantity with an explicit biological meaning.

In the present chapter, we extend these implicit hierarchical models for counts to become explicit hierarchical models for counts so that the two main parameters have the interpretation of local abundance N and of detection probability p. The binomial (also called N-) mixture model of Royle (2004c) jointly estimates local abundance and detection probability (Dodd and Dorazio, 2004; Royle, 2004a, 2004c; Kéry et al., 2005b; Dorazio, 2007; Royle and Dorazio, 2008; Wenger and Freeman, 2008; Joseph et al., 2009; Kéry et al., 2009a; Kéry and Royle, 2010; Post van der Burg et al., 2011). It takes as input spatially and temporally replicated counts of independent individuals within a period of closure and yields estimates of the parameters of the ecological and the observation processes. The parameters of the ecological process describe the spatial or spatio-temporal variation in latent abundance. Abundance is a latent state because it is incompletely observed owing to detection error. The observation process is the process of detecting (or overlooking) individuals and is described by a binomial process as we have seen so many times.

The binomial mixture model has great appeal, since it allows us to estimate abundance, corrected for imperfect detection, from fairly "cheap" data: simple counts without any extra information, such as individual identification or distance measurements. Therefore, this model may be more widely applicable than capture–recapture methods or distance sampling. What the model does require, though, is replication in two dimensions, both spatially (at >10–20 sites, say) and temporally within a period of closure (at least two observations per site, though not necessarily at every site). Hence, it requires counts $y_{i,j}$ for a number of sites i and temporal replicates j.

Conceptually, such replicated counts arise from two distinct processes, one ecological and another observational. Accordingly, the simplest binomial mixture model for a single period of closure (season) can be written succinctly in just two lines:

$$N_i \sim \text{Poisson}(\lambda) \qquad \text{1. Ecological process yields latent state}$$

$$y_{i,j} \mid N_i \sim \text{Binomial}(N_i, p) \qquad \text{2. Observation process yields observations}$$

First, the spatial variation of local abundance at site i, N_i, for a collection of sites is described by a Poisson distribution with mean λ. Second, the observed counts $y_{i,j}$ (given N_i) at site i and during replicate survey j are described by a binomial distribution with sample size N_i and detection probability p. This model is sometimes also called a Poisson-binomial mixture model.

If we think of it, few things could be more natural than making these two distributional assumptions. The Poisson is the standard distribution assumed for spatial or temporal variation in abundance (McCullagh and Nelder, 1989), and the binomial distribution underlies a vast array of capture–recapture models as a formal description of the coin-flip-like detection process of individuals (Williams et al., 2002; see also Section 1.3). Thus, the binomial mixture model can be called a hierarchical Poisson regression, since the basic model for abundance is Poisson, but there is a logistic regression attached to account for imperfect detection. Several important extensions are possible, among them the adoption of distributions other than the Poisson for abundance or the binomial for detection, the introduction of covariates, and the relaxation of the independence of detection and of the closure assumption. We next briefly sketch each one in turn.

First, we could specify distributions other than a Poisson for the ecological part of the model, for instance, a negative binomial (Royle, 2004b, 2004c; Kéry et al., 2005b; Joseph et al., 2009), or a zero-inflated Poisson (Wenger and Freeman, 2008; Joseph et al., 2009). We will see a zero-inflated Poisson in Section 12.3.2 and the Poisson log-normal as an alternative to a negative binomial distribution in Section 12.3.3.

Second, since the binomial mixture model consists simply of two linked GLMs, it is natural to introduce the effects of covariates through a log- and a logit-link function, respectively, for abundance and detection. This means that neither the mean local abundance λ nor detection probability p needs to be constant; indeed, they rarely ever are! Rather, we can specify covariate relationships such as these:

$$\log(\lambda_i) = \alpha_0 + \alpha_1 * x_i \text{ and}$$

$$\text{logit}(p_{i,j}) = \beta_0 + \beta_1 * x_{i,j}$$

In the first case, mean abundance at site i, on the scale of the natural logarithm, is a linear function of site-specific covariate x_i (a "site covariate"), with intercept α_0 and slope α_1. Thus, the binomial mixture model allows one to model habitat relationships in abundance while accounting for detection error; for examples, see Kéry (2008), Webster et al. (2008), Chandler et al. (2009a, b), and Schlossberg et al. (2010). In the second case, the logit transform of detection probability at site i during survey j is a logit-linear function of the site- and survey-specific covariate $x_{i,j}$ (a "survey covariate"), with intercept β_0 and slope β_1. Of course, a site covariate (x_i) is also possible for detection.

Similarly, for abundance or detection, latent structure can be added by the introduction of random effects on the scale of the linear predictor. These account for additional variation in abundance or detection that is not accounted for by the nominal distributional assumptions along with the specified covariates. For instance, we can model extra-Poisson dispersion in the latent abundance parameters N_i by specifying the following Poisson-log-normal binomial mixture model (only linear predictor shown):

$$\log(\lambda_i) = \alpha_0 + \alpha_1 * x_i + \varepsilon_i,$$

$$\text{with } \varepsilon_i \sim \text{Normal}(0, \sigma_\lambda^2)$$

This modeling can be seen as a sort of correction for overdispersion in abundance (see also Section 4.2). Its result will be similar to the adoption of a negative binomial distribution instead of a Poisson. Random effects can likewise be introduced into the linear predictor for detection. Both will account for the increased uncertainty in parameter estimates owing to the effects of unmodeled covariates by spreading out the posterior distributions and, hence, increasing uncertainty intervals. We see an example in Section 12.3.3.

Third, the model assumes that all N_i individuals in each local population i behave and are detected independently. This assumption may be violated for animals that live in groups so that when one individual in a group is detected, others in the same group are more likely to be detected as well. An extension of the basic binomial mixture model to this situation has recently been described by Martin et al. (2011).

Fourth, the model as described so far is for static situations where replicate counts are available for a single, closed population of size N_i at each site i. This ideal will be impossible to attain in many situations, and indeed, in many cases, changes in abundance, for instance trends, are the focus of the modeling. The binomial mixture model can easily be extended to dynamic situations, for example, to several breeding seasons k, provided that data are available in the so-called robust design (Williams et al., 2002), with temporal replicate observations within each of multiple seasons. We then model counts $y_{i,j,k}$ from site i, replicate j, and season k and estimate different parameters for each season in the ecological process and possibly also for the observation process. The abundance parameters may be related to each other across years, for instance, to model a trend (Royle and Dorazio, 2008; Kéry and Royle, 2010; Kéry et al., 2010a). We will see an example of this in Section 12.3. In principle, it would also be possible to model dynamic (autoregressive) population models, such as the Ricker or Gompertz equations (Dennis et al., 2006), or the models in Chapter 5, within a binomial mixture framework, but this has not been done so far.

Key assumptions of the model are the following:

1. The ecological state is constant during the period over which replicate surveys are conducted (the traditional closure assumption). Its violation will lead to inflated abundance estimates. In benign cases, this may mean that N estimates the size of some superpopulation, that is, the number of all individuals that *ever* use a sample site during the surveys. In severe cases, though, N estimates may no longer be meaningful.

2. Detection probability is constant for all N_i individuals present at time j and equal to $p_{i,j}$. The model does not require individual identification but is not able to accommodate individual variation in detection probability either. In analogy to closed models (Chapter 6), intuition suggests that individual heterogeneity in detection probability at site i during period j leads to a negative bias in the abundance estimator (see Efford and Dawson (2009) for the special case of distance-related heterogeneity in detection).

3. The distribution of abundance N_i is adequately described by the chosen parametric form (e.g., a Poisson, possibly with covariates and latent effects). Similarly, detection probability is modeled adequately by the chosen parametric distribution (including possible covariates and other model structure). Especially the assumption about N_i is likely to be

more difficult to meet than the analogous assumption about occurrence in the site-occupancy models in Chapter 13. Effects of deviations of the data from the parametric model assumptions are hard to gauge, but posterior predictive checks (Section 12.3.) enable one to diagnose whether a model fits adequately.

4. There are no false positives such as double counts. The effect of the violation of this assumption has not been studied so far but is likely to induce a positive bias in the abundance estimator.

In Section 12.2, we first generate and analyze data from a single season (i.e., period of closure). In Section 12.3, we look at real-world data from multiple seasons in an insect species. A season may be one annual breeding season (for instance, for birds or reptiles, Kéry et al., 2005b, 2009a) or a single day, as in our insect example. We will fit a progression of increasingly complex models and see examples of zero-inflation and overdispersion correction. We will revisit (after their introduction in Chapter 7) an important and very general technique for goodness-of-fit assessment called a posterior predictive check (or Bayesian p-value).

12.2 GENERATION AND ANALYSIS OF SIMULATED DATA

12.2.1 The Simplest Case with Constant Parameters

To see the conceptual simplicity and beauty of the binomial mixture model, we first look at the simplest possible case, where both the ecological and the observation processes are described by an intercept only. To generate count data y under this Null model for $R = 200$ spatial replicates (sites) and $T = 3$ temporal replicates, we execute the following R commands:

```
# Determine sample sizes (spatial and temporal replication)
R <- 200
T <- 3

# Create structure to contain counts
y <- array(dim = c(R, T))

# Sample abundance from a Poisson(lambda = 2)
N <- rpois(n = R, lambda = 2)

# Sample counts from a Binomial(N, p = 0.5)
for (j in 1:T){
    y[,j] <- rbinom(n = R, size = N, prob = 0.5)
    }

# Look at realization of biological and observation processes
cbind(N, y)
```

We have assumed a mean abundance per site of 2 and mean detection per individual of 0.5. Note that in this model, the detection parameter refers to each individual, whereas in the site-occupancy model (Chapter 13) it refers to the collection of *all* individuals inhabiting a site, that is, to an occupied site. Now, we will try to recover these parameter values when fitting the model in WinBUGS. Note how similar the BUGS code for this model is to the hierarchical way the data were created. Also, note that for this class of models, initial values for the latent states (the Ns) must sometimes be close to the solution; otherwise, WinBUGS may not achieve convergence or only do so very slowly. As our best guess, we choose the observed maximum count at each site, increased by 1, to save WinBUGS from having to update a Binomial with index 0.

```
# Specify model in BUGS language
sink("model.txt")
cat("
model {

# Priors
lambda ~ dgamma(0.005, 0.005)    # Standard vague prior for lambda
# lambda ~ dunif(0, 10)          # Other possibility
p ~ dunif(0, 1)

# Likelihood
# Biological model for true abundance
for (i in 1:R) {
    N[i] ~ dpois(lambda)
    # Observation model for replicated counts
    for (j in 1:T) {
        y[i,j] ~ dbin(p, N[i])
        } #j
    } #i
}
",fill = TRUE)
sink()

# Bundle data
win.data <- list(y = y, R = nrow(y), T = ncol(y))

# Initial values
Nst <- apply(y, 1, max) + 1 # This line is important
inits <- function() list(N = Nst)

# Parameters monitored
params <- c("lambda", "p")

# MCMC settings
ni <- 1200
nt <- 2
nb <- 200
nc <- 3

# Call WinBUGS from R (BRT 0.1 min)
out <- bugs(win.data, inits, params, "model.txt", n.chains = nc,
    n.thin = nt, n.iter = ni, n.burnin = nb, debug = TRUE, bugs.directory =
    bugs.dir, working.directory = getwd())
```

[handwritten annotation:] — OpenBUGS does not use shape/scale parameterization, but shape/mu. Try something like dgamma(0.05, 0.05²)

```
# Summarize posteriors
print(out, dig = 2)
          mean   sd   2.5%    25%    50%    75%  97.5%  Rhat  n.eff
lambda    2.20  0.18  1.89   2.08   2.19   2.30  2.57   1.01   440
p         0.48  0.03  0.42   0.46   0.49   0.51  0.55   1.03   120
```

This looks good. There is a fair amount of sampling variance and so repeated realizations of the analysis will yield fairly variable estimates.

12.2.2 Introducing Covariates

Next, we simulate more complex data for a single season. We introduce a single covariate that acts on both the ecological and the observation process. We model the effect of the covariate on the scale of the log and the logit, as is customary for generalized linear models. This example illustrates a so-called site covariate, that is, a covariate that varies by site only, but not among individual surveys (this would be called a survey or sampling covariate). Sampling covariates may be weather condition or survey duration, that is, something that may affect detection but not abundance. For sampling covariates, see the exercises at the end of this chapter. OpenBUGS (Examples > Ecology examples > Lizards) also contains an example of a binomial mixture model with covariates for both abundance and detection.

```
# Define function for generating binom-mix model data
data.fn <- function(R = 200, T = 3, xmin = -1, xmax = 1, alpha0 = 1,
   alpha1 = 3, beta0 = 0, beta1 = -5){

# R: number of sites at which counts were made (= number of spatial reps)
# T: number of times that counts were made at each site
# (= number of temporal reps)
# xmin, xmax: define range of the covariate X
# alpha0 and alpha1: intercept and slope of log-linear regression
# relating abundance to the site covariate A
# beta0 and beta1: intercept and slope of logistic-linear regression
# of detection probability on A

   y <- array(dim = c(R, T)) # Array for counts

   # Ecological process
   # Covariate values: sort for ease of presentation
   X <- sort(runif(n = R, min = xmin, max = xmax))

   # Relationship expected abundance - covariate
   lam <- exp(alpha0 + alpha1 * X)

   # Add Poisson noise: draw N from Poisson(lambda)
   N <- rpois(n = R, lambda = lam)
   table(N)            # Distribution of abundances across sites
   sum(N > 0) / R      # Empirical occupancy
   totalN <- sum(N) ; totalN
```

```
# Observation process
# Relationship detection prob - covariate
p <- plogis(beta0 + beta1 * X)

# Make a 'census' (i.e., go out and count things)
for (i in 1:T){
    y[,i] <- rbinom(n = R, size = N, prob = p)
    }

# Naïve regression
naive.pred <- exp(predict(glm(apply(y, 1, max) ~ X + I(X^2),
    family = poisson)))

# Plot features of the simulated system
par(mfrow = c(2, 2))
plot(X, lam, main = "Expected abundance", xlab = "Covariate",
    ylab = "lambda", las = 1, type = "l", col = "red", lwd = 3,
    frame.plot = FALSE)
plot(X, N, main = "Realised abundance", xlab = "Covariate", ylab =
    "N", las = 1, frame.plot = FALSE, col = "red", cex = 1.2)
plot(X, p, ylim = c(0, 1), main = "Detection probability", xlab =
    "Covariate", ylab = "p", type = "l", col = "red", lwd = 3, las = 1,
    frame.plot = FALSE)
plot(X, naive.pred, main = "Actual counts \n and naïve regression",
    xlab = "Covariate", ylab = "Relative abundance", ylim = c(min(y),
    max(y)), type = "l", lty = 2, lwd = 4, col = "blue", las = 1,
    frame.plot = FALSE)
points(rep(X, T), y, col = "black", cex = 1.2)

# Return stuff
return(list(R = R, T = T, X = X, alpha0 = alpha0, alpha1 = alpha1,
    beta0 = beta0, beta1 = beta1, lam = lam, N = N, totalN = totalN,
    p = p, y = y))
}
```

We execute this function once to generate one data set and produce an overview of the simulation.

```
data <- data.fn()
str(data)
```

Figure 12.1 shows the main features of this stochastic system and its observation, that is, the data set generated. Abundance has a positive relation with the covariate (Fig. 12.1a and b). In contrast, detection probability has a negative relationship with that same covariate (Fig. 12.1c). The result of this is that the observed counts (Fig. 12.1d) suggest an intermediate optimum value of the covariate for abundance, and this false impression is confirmed by fitting a quadratic covariate effect in a Poisson regression of the max count at each site. The dashed blue line shows the prediction from that naïve analysis.

Next, we use a binomial mixture model to see whether we can tease apart the opposing effects of the covariate on the ecological state and on

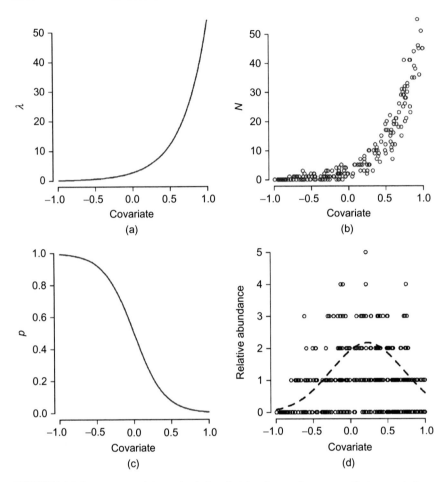

FIGURE 12.1   Features of the ecological and of the observation process that generated our data set and a conventional (naïve) analysis of counts in relation to an environmental covariate (dashed blue line in (d)): (a) Expected abundance, (b) realized abundance, (c) detection probability, (d) actual counts and naïve regression. The truth is shown in red and observed data in black. See text and R code for further explanations.

the observation of that state or, in plain English, whether we can recover estimates of the two GLM regressions that resemble the known input values. We are also interested in an estimate of the total population size across all surveyed plots, which, in our simulated data, was 1938.

```
# Specify model in BUGS language
sink("model.txt")
cat("
model {
```

```
# Priors
alpha0 ~ dunif(-10, 10)
alpha1 ~ dunif(-10, 10)
beta0 ~ dunif(-10, 10)
beta1 ~ dunif(-10, 10)

# Likelihood
# Ecological model for true abundance
for (i in 1:R){
    N[i] ~ dpois(lambda[i])
    log(lambda[i]) <- alpha0 + alpha1 * X[i]

    # Observation model for replicated counts
    for (j in 1:T){
        y[i,j] ~ dbin(p[i,j], N[i])
        p[i,j] <- exp(lp[i,j])/(1+exp(lp[i,j]))
        lp[i,j] <- beta0 + beta1 * X[i]
        } #j
    } #i

# Derived quantities
totalN <- sum(N[])
}
",fill = TRUE)
sink()

# Bundle data
y <- data$y
win.data <- list(y = y, R = nrow(y), T = ncol(y), X = data$X)

# Initial values
Nst <- apply(y, 1, max) + 1 # Important to give good inits for latent N
inits <- function() list(N = Nst, alpha0 = runif(1, -1, 1), alpha1 = runif
    (1, -1, 1), beta0 = runif(1, -1, 1), beta1 = runif(1, -1, 1))

# Parameters monitored
params <- c("totalN", "alpha0", "alpha1", "beta0", "beta1")

# MCMC settings
ni <- 22000
nt <- 20
nb <- 2000
nc <- 3

# Call WinBUGS from R (BRT 4 min)
out <- bugs(win.data, inits, params, "model.txt", n.chains = nc,
    n.thin = nt, n.iter = ni, n.burnin = nb, debug = TRUE, bugs.directory =
    bugs.dir, working.directory = getwd())

# Summarize posteriors
print(out, dig = 3)
```

	mean	sd	2.5%	25%	50%	75%	97.5%	Rhat	n.eff
totalN	1866.708	574.032	982.975	1464.750	1759.000	2192.000	3214.225	1.068	37
alpha0	0.981	0.123	0.736	0.900	0.983	1.064	1.223	1.027	83

alpha1	2.941	0.319	2.303	2.726	2.931	3.151	3.575	1.060	39
beta0	0.191	0.187	-0.178	0.064	0.192	0.319	0.551	1.023	98
beta1	-5.078	0.370	-5.806	-5.328	-5.078	-4.834	-4.339	1.040	58
deviance	853.819	14.566	826.897	843.875	853.000	863.300	883.700	1.013	160

We recover estimates that appear unbiased. The estimate of total population size is fairly imprecise, but will often, and here does, contain the true value (1938) within its 95% CRI. The sum of the maximum counts at each site, a conventional estimator of total population size, is only 240 individuals (type `sum(apply(data$y, 1, max))`). It is remarkable that the binomial mixture model gets so close to the truth! Let us look at further inferences and plot the posterior distribution for the four regression parameters (Fig. 12.2).

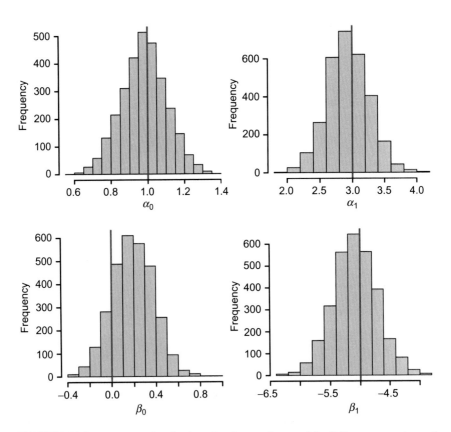

FIGURE 12.2 Posterior distributions for the two log- and logit-linear regressions of expected abundance and detection probability on a covariate. The red lines show the values used for these parameters in the simulation of the data.

Typically, an ecologist would want estimates of abundance for each site also. Within the Bayesian framework, this is trivial: just add N to the list of quantities monitored!

```
# Plot posteriors
par(mfrow = c(2, 2))
hist(out$sims.list$alpha0, col = "gray", main = "", xlab = "alpha0",
   las = 1)
abline(v = data$alpha0, lwd = 3, col = "red")
hist(out$sims.list$alpha1, col = "gray", main = "", xlab = "alpha1",
   las = 1)
abline(v = data$alpha1, lwd = 3, col = "red")
hist(out$sims.list$beta0, col = "gray", main = "", xlab = "beta0", las=1)
abline(v = data$beta0, lwd = 3, col = "red")
hist(out$sims.list$beta1, col = "gray", main = "", xlab = "beta1", las = 1)
abline(v = data$beta1, lwd = 3, col = "red")
```

How well can the naive and the binomial mixture analysis recover the covariate relationship? Figure 12.3 shows that for the conventional model, the answer is: not very well! In contrast, the binomial mixture model seems to do an excellent job at recovering the true positive relationship between abundance and the covariate.

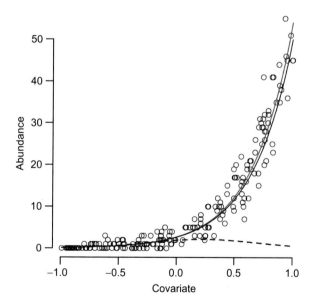

FIGURE 12.3   Relationship between abundance and covariate in a simulated system. The red line shows truth, with realized abundance at 200 sites in black. The blue lines show the estimates under a binomial mixture model (solid line) and under a conventional nonhierarchical Poisson regression (dashed).

```
# Plot predicted covariate relationship with abundance
plot(data$X, data$N, main = "", xlab = "Covariate", ylab = "Abundance",
    las = 1, ylim = c(0, max(data$N)), frame.plot = FALSE)
lines(data$X, data$lam, type = "l", col = "red", lwd = 3)
GLM.pred <- exp(predict(glm(apply(data$y, 1, max) ~ X + I(X^2),
    family = poisson, data = data)))
lines(data$X, GLM.pred, type = "l", lty = 2, col = "blue", lwd = 3)
Nmix.pred <- exp(out$mean$alpha0 + out$mean$alpha1 * data$X)
points(data$X, Nmix.pred, type = "l", col = "blue", lwd = 3)
```

12.3 ANALYSIS OF REAL DATA: OPEN-POPULATION BINOMIAL MIXTURE MODELS

Frequently, counts are made at two temporal scales. That is, one does not only have count data from a single period of closure, but in addition from several seasons. For instance, for birds, we may have repeated samples within a breeding season (visits within a year are secondary occasions) that are repeated across several years (years are primary occasions). In capture–recapture, this sampling design is called the robust design (Williams et al., 2002): a population is repeatedly sampled over a short period, during which the population is considered to be closed, and these sampling sessions are repeated over a longer period, over which the population is considered to be open. The primary occasions may also consist of (much) shorter time intervals than years if the population dynamics of the study organism is fast relative to the duration of a study.

In our real-world example, we will estimate population size of a butterfly, the silver-washed fritillary (Fig. 12.4), over an entire summer. The information for application of the binomial mixture model comes from the fact that each of 95 sites was surveyed twice along a 2.5 km transect on each of 4–7 survey days (Kéry et al., 2009a; Dorazio et al., 2010). Survey days are separated by at least two weeks, and butterflies are rather short-lived; hence, it would not be sensible to assume a constant population size at each site over repeated days or even during the entire summer. Hence, we shall consider each day a primary occasion and model different parameters for each day. The two replicate observations of each transects within a day represent the secondary occasions between which the populations are assumed constant. We will apply the open-population binomial mixture model of Dorazio and Royle (2008), Kéry et al. (2009a), and Kéry and Royle (2010) to estimate population size during each day.

We denote as $y_{i,j,k}$ the count from site i ($i = 1 \ldots 95$), within-day temporal replicate j ($j = 1, 2$), and day k ($k = 1 \ldots 7$). Note that both j and k index temporal replicates, but the population is assumed to be static over the former and allowed to change over the latter. In program R, we format

FIGURE 12.4 Silver-washed fritillary *Argynnis paphia*, Switzerland, 2005 (Photograph by T. Marent).

the counts into a three-dimensional array, since this is convenient for the modeling. In our experience, one of the most difficult things about statistical modeling in WinBUGS is to keep track of the dimensions of multi-dimensional arrays, including putting data into such arrays in the first place. So, expect some time to learn how to do this, either in a clumsy way like we do here or using R functions like those in the reshape package.

We will revisit posterior predictive distributions and Bayesian p-values in this example, introduced in Section 7.10, a very general method of checking the goodness-of-fit of a model fit using Bayesian posterior sampling (see Gelman et al., 2004; Gelman et al., 1996, Kéry, 2010). The posterior predictive distribution is the distribution of replicate data sets or statistics computed from data sets, given the model, its parameter values, and the observed data set. We do a posterior predictive check of whether the model used to analyze the observed data fits them, in the sense that the model, with the estimated parameters, could plausibly have generated data such as the data set that we actually observed. The idea behind a posterior predictive check is rather similar to a parametric bootstrap: use the parameter values estimated from the actual data set under a given model to generate new data sets. Then, calculate some discrepancy measure for the new data set (e.g., chi-squared) and repeat that many times to get the reference distribution for that discrepancy measure for a model that fits. Then, compare the fit of the model with the actual data with that reference distribution. For example, we see whether a, say, chi-squared test statistic computed for the actual data set falls within the distribution of chi-squared statistics that was computed for the replicate data sets.

We load the data, put them into a 3D array, and look at some summary statistics.

```
# Get the data and put them into 3D array
bdat <- read.table("fritillary.txt", header = TRUE)
y <- array(NA, dim = c(95, 2, 7))    # 95 sites, 2 reps, 7 days

for(k in 1:7){
    sel.rows <- bdat$day == k
    y[,,k] <- as.matrix(bdat)[sel.rows, 3:4]
    }
y                       # Look at data set in 3D layout
str(y)
```

```
# Have a look at raw data
day.max <- apply(y, c(1, 3), max, na.rm = TRUE)   # Max count each site
                                                    and day

day.max
site.max <- apply(day.max, 1, max, na.rm = TRUE)  # Max count each site
site.max
table(site.max)          # Frequency distribution of max counts
plot(table(site.max))
table(site.max>0)        # Observed occupancy is only 56%
```

```
# Sum of observed max as conventional estimator of total abundance
max1 <- apply(y, c(1, 3), max)
obs.max.sum <- apply(max1, 2, sum, na.rm = TRUE)

obs.max.sum
[1]  4  0  15  32  99  85  63
```

Very few butterflies were observed during the first day and none during the second day.

12.3.1 Simple Poisson Model

We start with the simplest binomial mixture model that appears to make sense in this case. It has time-specific, constant parameters for both abundance and detection probability. Note that in the computation of the chi-squared discrepancy measure for the posterior predictive check, a small constant (0.5) is added in the denominator to avoid possible divisions by zero.

```
# Specify model in BUGS language
sink("Nmix0.txt")
cat("
model {
```

```
# Priors
for (k in 1:7) {
    alpha.lam[k] ~ dnorm(0, 0.01)
    p[k] ~ dunif(0, 1)
    }

# Likelihood
# Ecological model for true abundance
for (k in 1:7) {                              # Loop over days (7)
    lambda[k] <- exp(alpha.lam[k])
    for (i in 1:R) {                          # Loop over R sites (95)
        N[i,k] ~ dpois(lambda[k])             # Abundance

        # Observation model for replicated counts
        for (j in 1:T) {                      # Loop over temporal reps (2)
            y[i,j,k] ~ dbin(p[k], N[i,k])     # Detection

            # Assess model fit using Chi-squared discrepancy
            # Compute fit statistic E for observed data
            eval[i,j,k] <- p[k] * N[i,k]      # Expected values
            E[i,j,k] <- pow((y[i,j,k] - eval[i,j,k]),2) / (eval[i,j,k] +
                0.5)
            # Generate replicate data and compute fit stats for them
            y.new[i,j,k] ~ dbin(p[k], N[i,k])
            E.new[i,j,k] <- pow((y.new[i,j,k] - eval[i,j,k]),2) /
                (eval[i,j,k] + 0.5)

            } #j
        } #i
    } #k

# Derived and other quantities
for (k in 1:7) {
    totalN[k] <- sum(N[,k])      # Total pop. size across all sites
    mean.abundance[k] <- exp(alpha.lam[k])
    }
fit <- sum(E[,,])
fit.new <- sum(E.new[,,])
}
",fill = TRUE)
sink()

# Bundle data
R = nrow(y)
T = ncol(y)
win.data <- list(y = y, R = R, T = T)

# Initial values
Nst <- apply(y, c(1, 3), max) + 1
Nst[is.na(Nst)] <- 1
inits <- function() {list(N = Nst, alpha.lam = runif(7, -1, 1))}

# Parameters monitored
params <- c("totalN", "mean.abundance", "alpha.lam", "p", "fit",
    "fit.new")
```

```
# MCMC settings
ni <- 10000
nt <- 8
nb <- 2000
nc <- 3
```

```
# Call WinBUGS from R (BRT 1 min)
out0 <- bugs(win.data, inits, params, "Nmix0.txt", n.chains = nc,
    n.thin = nt, n.iter = ni, n.burnin = nb, debug = TRUE, bugs.directory =
    bugs.dir, working.directory = getwd())
```

```
# Summarize posteriors
print(out0, dig = 3)
```

	mean	sd	2.5%	25%	50%	75%	97.5%	Rhat	n.eff
totalN[1]	35.133	59.426	4.000	8.000	15.000	32.000	233.148	1.090	49
totalN[2]	0.162	0.902	0.000	0.000	0.000	0.000	2.000	1.132	330
totalN[3]	20.003	5.097	15.000	17.000	19.000	22.000	34.000	1.002	1800
totalN[4]	39.511	5.117	33.000	36.000	38.000	42.000	52.000	1.003	2400
totalN[5]	135.943	13.689	115.000	126.000	134.000	144.000	168.000	1.001	3000
totalN[6]	99.653	6.869	90.000	95.000	99.000	103.000	116.000	1.004	750
totalN[7]	90.296	10.605	74.000	83.000	89.000	96.000	115.000	1.001	3000
mean.abundance[1]	0.371	0.631	0.030	0.088	0.163	0.348	2.447	1.077	56
mean.abundance[2]	0.003	0.010	0.000	0.000	0.000	0.001	0.023	1.001	3000
mean.abundance[3]	0.211	0.071	0.109	0.165	0.201	0.245	0.389	1.002	1900
mean.abundance[4]	0.415	0.086	0.271	0.356	0.407	0.465	0.608	1.001	3000
mean.abundance[5]	1.430	0.191	1.091	1.299	1.415	1.549	1.843	1.001	3000
mean.abundance[6]	1.048	0.128	0.820	0.960	1.040	1.127	1.316	1.003	930
mean.abundance[7]	0.952	0.151	0.686	0.850	0.939	1.041	1.277	1.001	3000
[...]									
p[1]	0.212	0.167	0.012	0.077	0.170	0.312	0.625	1.070	60
p[2]	0.485	0.291	0.017	0.229	0.489	0.731	0.972	1.003	1300
p[3]	0.545	0.124	0.282	0.465	0.552	0.634	0.766	1.002	3000
p[4]	0.600	0.087	0.416	0.543	0.605	0.661	0.761	1.002	1700
p[5]	0.515	0.057	0.401	0.475	0.518	0.556	0.619	1.001	3000
p[6]	0.653	0.054	0.539	0.619	0.656	0.692	0.750	1.002	1500
p[7]	0.550	0.068	0.416	0.505	0.552	0.597	0.677	1.001	3000
fit	147.924	15.887	121.000	136.675	146.400	157.625	183.102	1.001	3000
fit.new	97.796	11.908	76.427	89.490	97.220	104.900	123.000	1.002	3000
deviance	765.186	42.162	689.300	735.575	763.400	792.200	855.505	1.001	2700

We note that the estimates for the first two days, when very few or no butterflies were observed, are very imprecise and entirely driven by the priors, respectively: the 95% CRI for p at day 2 extends almost from 0 to 1. We look at the posterior predictive check of goodness-of-fit for this model (Fig. 12.5a).

```
# Evaluation of fit
plot(out0$sims.list$fit, out0$sims.list$fit.new, main = "", xlab =
    "Discrepancy actual data", ylab = "Discrepancy replicate data",
    frame.plot = FALSE)
abline(0, 1, lwd = 2, col = "black")
```

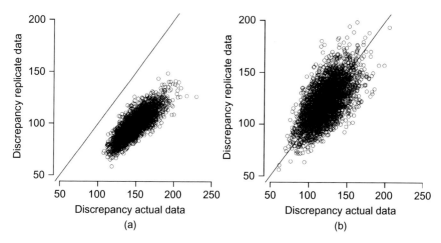

FIGURE 12.5 Posterior predictive checks of model adequacy of two binomial mixture models fit to the Swiss fritillary data; (a) Null model, (b) model with random effects in abundance and detection (see Section 12.3.3.).

```
mean(out0$sims.list$fit.new > out0$sims.list$fit)
[1] 0

mean(out0$mean$fit) / mean(out0$mean$fit.new)
[1] 1.512573
```

The model does not fit well at all (Fig. 12.5a). Indeed, there is a "lack-of-fit ratio" of 1.51. This informal quantity compares the mean of the fit statistic for the actual data with that for the perfect data sets and thus gives a numerical expression of how bad the lack of fit is. What could be wrong? The fritillary was never detected at 42 sites and detected at least once at 53; yielding an observed occupancy of 56%. It may well be that a Poisson distribution for the spatial variation in abundance is not flexible enough to account for that many zeroes. Therefore we will next model abundance with a zero-inflated Poisson distribution (Wenger and Freeman, 2008; Joseph et al., 2009).

12.3.2 Zero-Inflated Poisson Binomial Mixture Model (ZIP Binomial Mixture Model)

The ZIP binomial mixture model appears like a sensible model for these data. It divides the sites into those that are suitable and those that are not suitable. A Poisson distribution for abundance is assumed for suitable sites only. To obtain a ZIP binomial mixture model, we simply add another hierarchical layer to the model. This additional layer is binary: we decide by a coin flip whether a site is suitable in principle or not. Only if a site is suitable in principle will Nature roll her Poisson die to determine the actual number of butterflies living there. Here is the resulting hierarchical model:

Level 1 (suitability of site i): $z_i \sim \text{Bernoulli}(\Omega)$
Level 2 (realized abundance at i, k): $N_{i,k} \mid z_i \sim \text{Poisson}(z_i \lambda_k)$
Level 3 (observed count at i, j, k): $y_{i,j,k} \mid N_{i,k} \sim \text{Binomial}(N_{i,k}, p_{i,j,k})$

We have three main structural parameters (Ω, λ_k, $p_{i,j,k}$), one for each level in the model hierarchy. We could model each of them as a function of covariates through a GLM link function. In our case, we do not have any covariates, so we simply fit group effects, that is, estimate a separate parameter for abundance and detection at every time period.

To describe the model in the BUGS language, we want to define the latent suitability indicators z first, that is, in the outermost loop of the likelihood definition. Thus, we simply flip the order in which we loop over the dimensions of the site-by-rep-by-day data array $y_{i,j,k}$.

```
# Specify model in BUGS language
sink("Nmix1.txt")
cat("
model {

# Priors
omega ~ dunif(0, 1)
for (k in 1:7){
    alpha.lam[k] ~ dnorm(0, 0.01)
    p[k] ~ dunif(0, 1)
    }

# Likelihood
# Ecological model for true abundance
for (i in 1:R){                          # Loop over R sites (95)
    z[i] ~ dbern(omega)                  # Latent suitability state
    for (k in 1:7){                      # Loop over survey periods (seasons)
        N[i,k] ~ dpois(lam.eff[i,k]) # Latent abundance state
        lam.eff[i,k] <- z[i] * lambda[i,k]
        log(lambda[i,k]) <- alpha.lam[k]
        # Observation model for replicated counts
        for (j in 1:T){                         # Loop over temporal reps (2)
            y[i,j,k] ~ dbin(p[k], N[i,k])   # Detection
            # Assess model fit using Chi-squared discrepancy
            # Compute fit statistic for observed data
            eval[i,j,k] <- p[k] * N[i,k]
            E[i,j,k] <- pow((y[i,j,k] - eval[i,j,k]),2) / (eval[i,j,k] +
                0.5)
            # Generate replicate data and compute fit stats for them
            y.new[i,j,k] ~ dbin(p[k], N[i,k])
            E.new[i,j,k] <- pow((y.new[i,j,k] - eval[i,j,k]),2) /
                (eval[i,j,k]+0.5)
            } #j
        } #k
    } #i
```

```
# Derived and other quantities
for (k in 1:7){
    # Estimate total pop. size across all sites
    totalN[k] <- sum(N[,k])
    mean.abundance[k] <- exp(alpha.lam[k])
    }
fit <- sum(E[,,])
fit.new <- sum(E.new[,,])
}
",fill = TRUE)
sink()
```

```
# Bundle data
R = nrow(y)
T = ncol(y)
win.data <- list(y = y, R = R, T = T)
```

```
# Initial values
Nst <- apply(y, c(1, 3), max) + 1
Nst[is.na(Nst)] <- 1
inits <- function(){list(N = Nst, alpha.lam = runif(7, -1, 1))}
```

```
# Parameters monitored
params <- c("omega", "totalN", "alpha.lam", "p", "mean.abundance",
    "fit", "fit.new")
```

```
# MCMC settings
ni <- 30000
nt <- 15
nb <- 15000
nc <- 3
```

```
# Call WinBUGS from R (BRT 3 min)
out1 <- bugs(win.data, inits, params, "Nmix1.txt", n.chains = nc,
    n.thin = nt, n.iter = ni, n.burnin = nb, debug = TRUE, bugs.directory =
    bugs.dir, working.directory = getwd())
```

```
# Summarize posteriors
print(out1, dig = 3)
```

	mean	sd	2.5%	25%	50%	75%	97.5%	Rhat	n.eff
omega	0.561	0.050	0.464	0.527	0.561	0.594	0.655	1.001	3000
totalN[1]	21.063	31.485	4.000	7.000	11.000	21.000	99.025	1.050	57
totalN[2]	0.145	0.756	0.000	0.000	0.000	0.000	2.000	1.068	300
totalN[3]	21.074	6.506	15.000	17.000	19.000	23.000	38.000	1.005	1000
totalN[4]	40.953	7.002	33.000	36.747	39.000	43.000	59.000	1.003	1900
totalN[5]	154.783	23.744	122.000	139.000	151.000	166.000	212.000	1.003	760
totalN[6]	105.251	9.486	91.975	99.000	104.000	110.000	128.000	1.002	3000
totalN[7]	91.561	14.688	72.000	81.000	89.000	98.000	129.025	1.002	2500
[...]									
p[1]	0.235	0.170	0.017	0.096	0.197	0.342	0.647	1.043	63
p[2]	0.479	0.295	0.016	0.212	0.474	0.736	0.970	1.001	3000
p[3]	0.527	0.132	0.262	0.437	0.535	0.624	0.766	1.006	580
p[4]	0.585	0.094	0.384	0.526	0.591	0.651	0.748	1.001	3000
p[5]	0.458	0.067	0.322	0.415	0.459	0.504	0.582	1.003	1000
p[6]	0.621	0.060	0.496	0.582	0.623	0.665	0.725	1.001	3000
p[7]	0.503	0.079	0.338	0.452	0.507	0.558	0.651	1.001	2400
[...]									

```
fit          147.329  16.573 119.900 135.700 145.800 157.000 184.500 1.003    780
fit.new       97.575  11.791  76.604  89.475  96.855 105.000 122.902 1.003    990
deviance     751.830  38.437 680.582 725.000 749.800 775.825 834.300 1.004    610
```

Under this model, the deviance is somewhat improved (here, from 765 to 752). The proportion of suitable sites, omega, is estimated identically with the proportion of sites at which the butterfly was ever detected. But does this model fit?

```
# Evaluation of fit
plot(out1$sims.list$fit, out1$sims.list$fit.new, main = "", xlab =
    "Discrepancy actual data", ylab = "Discrepancy replicate data",
    frame.plot = FALSE)
abline(0, 1, lwd = 2, col = "black")
mean(out1$sims.list$fit.new > out1$sims.list$fit)
[1] 0
mean(out1$mean$fit) / mean(out1$mean$fit.new)
[1] 1.509898
```

Unfortunately, the model still does not fit the data according to our chosen discrepancy measure, which is much greater for the actual data set than for the replicate data sets (i.e., the reference distribution of the test statistic). The Bayesian p-value, the proportion of symbols above the 1:1 line in the figure, is equal to zero. Compared with the model without zero-inflation, the lack-fit-ratio has barely gone down (from 1.513 to 1.510). Hence, a zero-inflated binomial mixture model is not flexible enough to capture the variability in the system adequately.

12.3.3 Binomial Mixture Model with Overdispersion in Both Abundance and Detection

Finally, we drop zero-inflation and instead try a model that accounts for extra-Poisson dispersion in both abundance and detection. The introduction of latent (random) effects into either or both linear predictors can be seen as sort of overdispersion correction, and it increases the uncertainty in the estimates. Thus, as in overdispersion correction in capture–recapture for instance (Burnham and Anderson, 2002), we buy a fitting model by losing precision in our estimates.

Level 1 (realized abundance at i, k): $N_{i,k} \sim \text{Poisson}(\lambda_{i,k})$
GLM for level 1: $\log(\lambda_{i,k}) = \alpha_k + \varepsilon_i$
Level 1b (random site effects): $\varepsilon_i \sim \text{Normal}(0, \sigma_\lambda^2)$

Level 2 (observed count at i, j, k): $y_{i,j,k} \mid N_{i,k} \sim \text{Binomial}(N_{i,k}, p_{i,j,k})$

GLM for level 2: $\text{logit}(p_{i,j,k}) = \beta_k + \delta_{i,j,k}$
Level 2b (random survey effects): $\delta_{i,j,k} \sim \text{Normal}(0, \sigma_p^2)$

So, we combine a naturally hierarchical model with two additional hierarchical levels, one for the sites in the ecological process and another for the individual surveys in the observation process. We assume the presence of "residual" site- and site-day-replicate-specific contributions to abundance (ε) and detection probability (δ), respectively. By specifying a Poisson-log-normal (Millar, 2009) model for the ecological state description, we account for the fact that there may be extra-Poisson dispersion in the distribution used to model spatio-temporal variation in the latent abundance parameters. Similarly, observation conditions may vary among sites, days, and replicates, and the random effect $\delta_{i,j,k}$ adequately accounts for that additional variability. As is customary for this type of modeling, we assume a normal distribution for both random noise terms. Note that for the extra variability in detection (delta), we could model $\delta_{i,j,k}$, $\delta_{i,k}$, or δ_i. Our treatment here is consistent with the published analyses in Kéry et al. (2009a) and Kéry and Royle (2010) as well as with an unpublished study by L. Tanadini and M. Kéry.

```
# Specify model in BUGS language
sink("Nmix2.txt")
cat("
model{

# Priors
for (k in 1:7){
    alpha.lam[k] ~ dnorm(0, 0.1)
    beta[k] ~ dnorm(0, 0.1)
    }

# Abundance site and detection site-by-day random effects
for (i in 1:R){
    eps[i] ~ dnorm(0, tau.lam)              # Abundance noise
    }
tau.lam <- 1 / (sd.lam * sd.lam)
sd.lam ~ dunif(0, 3)
tau.p <- 1 / (sd.p * sd.p)
sd.p ~ dunif(0, 3)

# Likelihood
# Ecological model for true abundance
for (i in 1:R){                            # Loop over R sites (95)
    for (k in 1:7){                        # Loop over days (7)
        N[i,k] ~ dpois(lambda[i,k])        # Abundance
        log(lambda[i,k]) <- alpha.lam[k] + eps[i]

        # Observation model for replicated counts
        for (j in 1:T){                    # Loop over temporal
                                           reps (2)
```

```
y[i,j,k] ~ dbin(p[i,j,k], N[i,k])    # Detection
p[i,j,k] <- 1 / (1 + exp(-lp[i,j,k]))
lp[i,j,k] ~ dnorm(beta[k], tau.p)    # Random delta defined
                                       implicitly

# Assess model fit using Chi-squared discrepancy
# Compute fit statistic for observed data
eval[i,j,k] <- p[i,j,k] * N[i,k]
E[i,j,k] <- pow(((y[i,j,k] - eval[i,j,k]),2) / (eval[i,j,k]
    +0.5)
# Generate replicate data and compute fit stats for them
y.new[i,j,k] ~ dbin(p[i,j,k], N[i,k])
E.new[i,j,k] <- pow((y.new[i,j,k] - eval[i,j,k]),2) /
    (eval[i,j,k]+0.5)
    } #j
    ik.p[i,k] <- mean(p[i,,k])
  } #k
} #i

# Derived and other quantities
for (k in 1:7){
    totalN[k] <- sum(N[,k])    # Estimate total pop. size across all
        sites
    mean.abundance[k] <- mean(lambda[,k])
    mean.N[k] <- mean(N[,k])
    mean.detection[k] <- mean(ik.p[,k])
    }
fit <- sum(E[,,])
fit.new <- sum(E.new[,,])
}
",fill = TRUE)
sink()

# Bundle data
R = nrow(y)
T = ncol(y)
win.data <- list(y = y, R = R, T = T)

# Initial values
Nst <- apply(y, c(1, 3), max) + 1
Nst[is.na(Nst)] <- 1
inits <- function(){list(N = Nst, alpha.lam = runif(7, -3, 3), beta =
    runif(7, -3, 3), sd.lam = runif(1, 0, 1), sd.p = runif(1, 0, 1))}

# Parameters monitored
params <- c("totalN", "alpha.lam", "beta", "sd.lam", "sd.p",
    "mean.abundance", "mean.N", "mean.detection", "fit", "fit.new")
```

Models with lots of random effects always need much longer to enable the Markov chains to mix properly. Hence, we greatly increase the number of MCMC iterations (obviously, we did this after some initial experimenting). We also increase the thinning rate to avoid having to save huge results files.

```
# MCMC settings
ni <- 350000
nt <- 300
nb <- 50000
nc <- 3
# Call WinBUGS from R (BRT 215 min)
out2 <- bugs(win.data, inits, params, "Nmix2.txt", n.chains = nc,
    n.thin = nt, n.iter = ni, n.burnin = nb, debug = TRUE, bugs.directory =
    bugs.dir, working.directory = getwd())
```

We get done after almost 4 h. First, we evaluate the fit of the model (Fig. 12.5b): it does fit now!

```
# Evaluation of fit
plot(out2$sims.list$fit, out2$sims.list$fit.new, main = "", xlab =
    "Discrepancy actual data", ylab = "Discrepancy replicate data",
    frame.plot = FALSE, xlim = c(50, 200), ylim = c(50, 200))
abline(0, 1, lwd = 2, col = "black")
mean(out2$sims.list$fit.new > out2$sims.list$fit)
[1] 0.505
mean(out2$mean$fit) / mean(out2$mean$fit.new)
[1] 0.999935
```

```
# Summarize posteriors
print(out2, dig = 2)
```

	mean	sd	2.5%	25%	50%	75%	97.5%	Rhat	n.eff
totalN[1]	94.48	163.99	5.00	13.00	35.00	95.00	593.05	1.01	370
totalN[2]	120.22	461.11	0.00	0.00	2.00	18.00	1762.90	1.36	25
totalN[3]	225.13	381.69	19.00	45.00	101.00	234.25	1537.05	1.06	55
totalN[4]	55.89	26.21	34.00	41.00	48.00	61.00	126.02	1.00	1100
totalN[5]	830.35	575.54	204.97	395.00	640.50	1119.25	2353.15	1.02	180
totalN[6]	128.36	30.90	96.00	109.00	121.00	138.00	209.00	1.01	390
totalN[7]	158.64	86.42	83.00	107.00	131.00	178.00	402.05	1.00	630
[...]									
sd.lam	1.87	0.23	1.46	1.70	1.84	2.01	2.37	1.00	1000
sd.p	1.05	0.21	0.70	0.91	1.03	1.17	1.50	1.00	980
mean.abundance[1]	1.00	1.73	0.04	0.14	0.37	1.00	6.30	1.01	340
mean.abundance[2]	1.27	4.86	0.00	0.01	0.03	0.18	18.73	1.07	48
mean.abundance[3]	2.37	4.01	0.18	0.48	1.07	2.46	16.44	1.06	55
mean.abundance[4]	0.59	0.29	0.31	0.43	0.52	0.66	1.38	1.00	1100
mean.abundance[5]	8.72	6.06	2.10	4.16	6.78	11.68	24.91	1.02	190
mean.abundance[6]	1.35	0.35	0.93	1.14	1.29	1.48	2.10	1.01	420
mean.abundance[7]	1.67	0.92	0.83	1.13	1.38	1.88	4.32	1.00	760
mean.N[1]	0.99	1.73	0.05	0.14	0.37	1.00	6.24	1.01	370
mean.N[2]	1.27	4.85	0.00	0.00	0.02	0.19	18.55	1.36	25
mean.N[3]	2.37	4.02	0.20	0.47	1.06	2.47	16.18	1.06	55
mean.N[4]	0.59	0.28	0.36	0.43	0.51	0.64	1.33	1.00	1100
mean.N[5]	8.74	6.06	2.16	4.16	6.74	11.78	24.77	1.02	180
mean.N[6]	1.35	0.33	1.01	1.15	1.27	1.45	2.20	1.01	390
mean.N[7]	1.67	0.91	0.87	1.13	1.38	1.87	4.23	1.00	630
mean.detection[1]	0.12	0.14	0.00	0.02	0.06	0.16	0.49	1.01	310

mean.detection[2]	0.23	0.32	0.00	0.01	0.04	0.39	0.99	1.06	62
mean.detection[3]	0.14	0.14	0.01	0.04	0.08	0.19	0.52	1.06	55
mean.detection[4]	0.47	0.14	0.18	0.38	0.48	0.56	0.71	1.01	810
mean.detection[5]	0.14	0.08	0.03	0.07	0.12	0.18	0.34	1.02	200
mean.detection[6]	0.51	0.10	0.29	0.45	0.52	0.58	0.69	1.01	460
mean.detection[7]	0.34	0.11	0.12	0.27	0.35	0.43	0.55	1.00	610
fit	121.41	18.67	88.48	108.60	120.20	133.22	161.41	1.01	240
fit.new	121.42	19.04	86.02	108.07	120.60	134.20	161.40	1.01	240
deviance	640.44	49.86	540.00	607.37	641.30	674.42	737.21	1.01	250

We note that convergence for some quantities associated with day 2 (when no fritillaries were observed at all) is less good. This illustrates the fact that often, though not always, lack of identifiability is associated with lack of convergence.

Since we have a fitting model now, we produce some plots of the estimates. In particular, we compare the mean count per day with the estimated mean abundance of the fritillary on each day. For mean daily abundance, we use the posterior median as our measure of central tendency, since the posterior is highly skewed (you can check that by typing hist(out2$sims.list$mean.abundance[,4], breaks = 40)).

```
max.day.count <- apply(y, c(1, 3), max, na.rm = TRUE)
max.day.count[max.day.count == "-Inf"] <- NA
mean.max.count <- apply(max.day.count, 2, mean, na.rm = TRUE)
mean.max.count

par(mfrow = c(2, 1))
plot(1:7, mean.max.count, xlab = "Day", ylab = "Mean daily abundance",
    las = 1, ylim = c(0, 16), type = "b", main = "", frame.plot = FALSE,
    pch = 16, lwd = 2)
lines(1:7, out2$summary[24:30,5], type = "b", pch = 16, col = "blue",
    lwd = 2)
segments(1:7, out2$summary[24:30,3], 1:7, out2$summary[24:30,7],
    col = "blue")

plot(1:7, out2$summary[38:44,1], xlab = "Day", ylab = "Detection
    probability ", las = 1, ylim = c(0, 1), type = "b", col = "blue",
    pch = 16, frame.plot = FALSE, lwd = 2)
segments(1:7, out2$summary[38:44,3], 1:7, out2$summary[38:44,7],
    col = "blue")
```

In Fig. 12.6, we see well that we now have a model that fits the fritillary counts, but that the fit comes at the expense of much less precision. Indeed, the Bayesian credible intervals are huge; much larger at any rate than under the two simpler models. This uncertainty around the estimates is a direct consequence of the introduction of the two sets of random effects. Thus, a refined analysis might try to get rid of one or both of them by introducing covariates that are informative about that variation in abundance or detection.

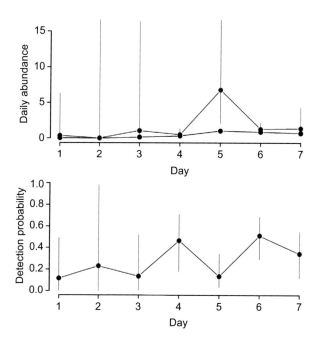

FIGURE 12.6 Abundance and detection of silver-washed fritillary in the Swiss biodiversity monitoring program under a binomial mixture model with random effects in the linear predictors of both abundance and detection. Top: Mean daily abundance per transect (black: raw counts, blue: posterior median with 95% CRI, upper bound on day 5 (23) truncated). Bottom: Detection probability per individual fritillary during each of two passes on a transect.

12.4 SUMMARY AND OUTLOOK

Abundance N is the key numerical descriptor of a central concept in ecology, the population. Since we virtually always overlook individuals, we must usually estimate N and can not directly observe it. Classical capture–recapture methods (Williams et al., 2002; and in Chapters 6 and 10), distance sampling (Buckland et al., 2001), and spatial capture–recapture methods young (Royle and Young, 2008; Borchers and Efford, 2008; Royle et al., 2011) are well developed and can be applied to data from a single site or also to data from multiple sites. However, they are costly, in the sense that extra information in the form of individual identification or accurate distance or location measurements is needed. Frequently, ecologists are interested in abundance within a metapopulation design, where the size of a collection of local populations is needed. When replicate counts are conducted over a reasonably short period of time, the binomial mixture model (or N-mixture model) is useful for estimation of abundance based on such relatively cheap count data. This model is an extension of the Poisson models in Chapters 3 and 4 to account for imperfect detection. The binomial mixture model is a powerful model with a big scope of application in ecology and management, such as monitoring. However, we saw that it can be difficult to find models that fit the data. Furthermore, the standard Bayesian AIC-analog, DIC, should not be used for hierarchical models such as this mixture model (Millar, 2009). Hence, in the Bayesian framework, model selection can be a challenge. A somewhat ad hoc alternative might then consist in doing model selection in the frequentist framework using AIC, for example, using functions in the new R package **unmarked** (Fiske and Chandler 2011), and then fit the best model in the Bayesian framework.

Recently, an exciting generalization of the binomial mixture model to fully open metapopulation designs has been developed by Dail and Madsen (2011); see Chandler and King (2011) for an application. This model describes the openness of local populations between successive sample periods as a function of parameters for local survival and recruitment and hence, achieves two things at the same time: providing a framework of estimating abundance, corrected for detection, without any period of closure and estimating two key parameters of population dynamics from comparatively "cheap" data. This model is an important conceptual advance for attempts at making inferences about population abundance from counts of unmarked individuals. This opens up exciting possibilities for the study of spatial population dynamics. Unfortunately, the model has so far resisted to all attempts at fitting it in WinBUGS (D. Dail, R. Chandler, A. Royle, pers. comm.), but it can be fitted using maximum likelihood in the R package **unmarked** (Fiske and Chandler, 2011).

All previous applications of open-population binomial mixture models have been more or less naive in terms of the modeled biological process. That is, explicit population dynamics models such as the Ricker model for density-dependence or a dynamics description in terms of survival and recruitment processes await to be couched within the framework of binomial mixture models. Such an integration of large-scale population dynamics modeling within an estimation framework for the latent states appears to have much promise for population ecology (Buckland et al., 2007; Hooten et al., 2007; see also Pagel and Schurr, 2011). It would open up the avenue towards the study of spatial population dynamics.

Abundance is the key state variable in ecology, so when possible we would always try to model abundance rather than simply the occurrence (distribution, "presence/absence") of an organism in a metapopulation. However, there may be doubts about the validity of the closure assumption (i.e., whether $N_{i,j}$ remains constant over replicates j). In this case, it may be adequate to reduce count data to detection/nondetection data and use another variant of a hierarchical metapopulation model called a site-occupancy model. This is the topic of the final main chapter in this book.

12.5 EXERCISES

1. With hierarchical models such as the binomial mixture model, we have several kinds of covariates: here, we have covariates that vary among sites (site covariates) and those that vary among individual surveys (sampling covariates). It is important in practice to know how to fit both kinds. Invent a sampling covariate in the example of Section 12.2.2 and fit it also to see how this works.
2. In the fritillary data, fit a simpler binomial mixture model than the one in Section 12.3.3 with detection random effects specific to day and site (i.e., drop the index j in the $\delta_{i,j,k}$). See whether that model also fits.
3. In the fritillary data, fit a more complex binomial mixture model by introducing (in addition to the random site-day-rep effect) a random site effect in the linear predictor for detection in the model in Section 12.3.3. Compare the estimates under the model in Section 12.3.3 and those in exercises 2 and 3. Explain.

Estimation of Occupancy and Species Distributions from Detection/Nondetection Data in Metapopulation Designs Using Site-Occupancy Models

OUTLINE

13.1 INTRODUCTION

In much of ecology, abundance (N) is the most interesting state variable when analyzing a population. Abundance is usually estimated from capture–recapture data or counts using the methods in Chapters 6, 10 or 12, or else strong assumptions are made about the count-abundance relationship. However, sometimes we do not have counts but only less information-rich data of the detection/nondetection kind (also misleadingly called presence/absence data). These are binary data indicating whether a species is detected (1) or not (0) at a site. We may then want to characterize one or several sites using occupancy: the probability that a site is occupied, that is, that local abundance is greater than zero. Often, occupancy is not of direct interest and merely a proxy for abundance, in which one is really interested. Indeed, it is often hard to think about occupancy separately from the abundance at the occupied sites.

However, there are also important fields in ecology that do focus on occupancy rather than abundance. Outstanding examples include meta-population ecology (Hanski, 1994, 1998), niche and species distribution (Guisan and Thuiller, 2005), and disease modeling (Thompson, 2007; McClintock et al., 2010). In addition, there is a sense in which, at a small spatial scale, occupancy and abundance coincide; when a site is chosen so small that at most one individual or pair can occupy it. The spotted owl data set in MacKenzie et al. (2003) and our Section 13.5.1 provide examples for this. A similar example is given by Bled et al. (2011a), who studied the habitat selection of kittiwakes in breeding cliffs. Here, a potential nest site is a straightforward site definition, and it can be occupied by two birds at most.

This chapter deals with a class of hierarchical models known as "site-occupancy models". In the statistical literature, these models are also called zero-inflated binomial models. In the context of distribution modeling in ecology, they have been introduced independently by MacKenzie et al. (2003) and Tyre et al. (2003), though they have important roots in earlier approaches as summarized in MacKenzie et al. (2006). "Site-occupancy model" is a fairly uninformative name for this extremely flexible modeling framework. We believe that this has helped to hide its usefulness for inference about any kind of occurrence ("presence/absence") data at discrete sites. Essentially, site-occupancy models are hierarchical logistic regression models that jointly model the probability of occupancy and detection in animals or plants.

As usual, we believe that a hierarchical view of occurrence data is important to properly separate the ecological component and the observation component that combine to produce the observed data. However, this has not been a widely-held opinion in ecology so far. For instance, in classical species distribution modeling (e.g., Guisan and Thuiller, 2005), it is typically ignored what is actually being modeled: it is *not* the distribution of a species. Rather, it is the *apparent species distribution* (unless detection probability is estimated). The apparent distribution is a function of both the true species distribution and of the detection probability of the species (Kéry and Schmidt, 2008; Kéry et al., 2010a; Kéry, 2011b).

There are three concerns when apparent instead of true distribution is modeled:

1. The extent of species distributions will be underestimated when $p < 1$,
2. Estimates of covariate relationships will be biased towards zero when $p < 1$,
3. Factors that affect the difficulty with which a species is found may end up in predictive models of species occurrence or may mask factors that do affect species occurrence.

The first is intuitively clear: if a species is not found at all sites where it occurs, the perceived range will be smaller than the actual range. However, the second is not so intuitive, especially perhaps, because it seems to be different from the modeling of abundance when detection probability is ignored. Yet, this effect has been demonstrated very clearly by Tyre et al. (2003) and in the next section, we conduct a little simulation to illustrate it. Finally, as an example of the third effect, assume that a species is more detectable in habitat A than in habitat B, for instance, because habitat A is more open and B is more wooded. In this case, open habitat may be identified as a factor that positively affects the occupancy probability/distribution of the species. For an example of the converse, see Section 13.3.2.

As always, to account for imperfect detection, extra data about the observation process are required. This means temporally replicated "presence/absence" observations, where the pattern of detection/ nondetection at a site contains the information about the observation process. We note that spatial replication at a small scale is informative about detection probability as well (Nichols et al., 1998a, 1998b; Kendall and White, 2009; Hines et al., 2010), but we focus on temporal replication here. Site-occupancy models require data collected in a metapopulation design (Royle, 2004c; Kéry and Royle, 2010), where (temporally or small-scale spatially) replicated detection/nondetection observations are available for a number of spatial replicates (for instance, > 20). As in Chapter 12, analyzing such a data set does not mean to imply that it represents a metapopulation in the ecological sense of the term.

In the simplest case, we consider detection/nondetection observation $y_{i,j}$ at site i during survey j: $y_{i,j}$ takes on a value of 1 when a species is detected at site i on survey j and value of 0 when it is *not* detected.

It is useful to consider the genesis of all species distribution or metapopulation data as a combination of two processes: one (ecological) process determines whether a site is occupied or not and the other (observation) process determines whether the species is found or not, given that a site is occupied. Correspondingly, in a site-occupancy model, we formally distinguish between a first submodel for the partly observed true state (occurrence, the result of the ecological process) and second submodel for the actual observations. The actual observations result from both the particular realization of the ecological process and of the observation process.

$$z_i \sim \text{Bernoulli}(\psi) \qquad \text{1. Ecological process yields true state}$$

$$y_{i,j} \mid z_i \sim \text{Bernoulli}(z_i p) \qquad \text{2. Observation process yields observations}$$

We naturally model true occurrence z_i ($z_i = 1$, if site i is occupied; $z_i = 0$ if site i is not occupied) as a Bernoulli random variable governed by the parameter ψ (occupancy probability); ψ is the parameter that distribution modelers would wish they were modeling but only do so when detection is perfect or detection probability can be estimated. (Note that we denote probability of occupancy by ψ and the latent occurrence state of a site as z.) However, z_i is not what we usually get to see; instead, our actual observations, $y_{i,j}$, detection or not at site i during survey j (or "presence/absence" datum $y_{i,j}$), are another Bernoulli random variable with a success rate that is the product of the actual occurrence at site i, z_i, and detection probability p at site i during survey j. At a site where a study species does not occur, z equals 0, and y must be 0, unless there are false-positive errors. Conversely, at an occupied site, we have $z = 1$, and the species is detected with probability p. That is, in the site-occupancy model, detection probability is expressed *conditional on actual occurrence*, and the two parameters ψ and p are separately estimable if replicate visits are available. We could call this model a Bernoulli-Bernoulli mixture model. Moreover, recognizing that the modeling of the latent occurrence (z) in the first level of the hierarchy accommodates additional zeroes in the data set (beyond those coming from the Bernoulli observation process), we see that it is also zero-inflated binomial (ZIB) model.

We have claimed that the term "presence/absence" for data $y_{i,j}$ is misleading. The preceding equations clarify why this is so: $y_{i,j}$ is a function of two processes, and only one of them has to do with occurrence and the other one is a nuisance process owing to the imperfect nature of the observation process. The true presence/absence data are the z_i, and they are only imperfectly observed and therefore latent: $z = 1$ can be observed as $y = 0$ or as $y = 1$. Site-occupancy models allow one to make a formal distinction between the two latter cases.

Two important assumptions of the model are closure and lack of false-positive errors. Closure in the context of the site-occupancy model means that over the duration of surveys, the occurrence state of a site must not change. Each site is either occupied or it is not, but there is no extinction or colonization. This sounds like a rather strong assumption; however, it is not always that problematic. Lack of closure is akin to temporary emigration (see Chapter 9), so if temporary emigration is random, it will be confounded with detection probability. This means that temporary (but not permanent) absence of a species from a site will be one component of imperfect detection. Consequently, the estimate of the occupancy parameter will describe the proportion of sites ever occupied or used during the study period, rather than of sites that are permanently occupied, as it would in the absence of temporary emigration. If there is colonization/extinction, for instance when surveys are spread over several years, we could simply model occupancy separately for each period of closure, as we did for the open-population binomial mixture model in Section 12.3. Alternatively, we can use the dynamic occupancy model described in Section 13.5, which expresses changes in occurrence over multiple "seasons" as a function of colonization and extinction.

Absence of false positives means that no other species must be mistakenly identified as our focal species, or more generally, we must be sure that a 1 really means that our focal species was present. False positives can seriously bias occupancy estimates (Royle and Link, 2006); hence, they should be avoided for instance by good training of field personnel or by discarding doubtful records. If we discard doubtful sightings that in reality refer to our focal species, we simply lower detection probability but do not incur biased estimators. However, our models are able to deal with imperfect detection very well. When different kinds of occupancy data are available and false positives can be excluded for at least one of them, multistate occupancy models (see Section 13.6) can be used to account for both false negatives and for false positives (Miller et al., 2011).

One way to look at site-occupancy models is as a hierarchical, coupled logistic regression. One logistic regression describes true occurrence, and the other describes detection, given that the species occurs. Remember that conventional methods for distribution modeling (GLM, GAM, boosted regression trees: Elith et al., 2008; Maxent: Phillips and Dudik, 2008) would pool the temporal replicates j and model the maximal observation, that is, site i will get a value of 1 if the species was ever detected there. Those approaches discard the information available about the observation process and thus in principle cannot model true, but only apparent species distributions (Kéry et al., 2010a). In contrast, site-occupancy models exploit all the available information about both ecological and observation process contained in detection/nondetection data.

The two Bernoulli distributions above describe the simplest possible site-occupancy model, where both occupancy (ψ) and detection probability (p)

are constant (see Section 13.3.1). This simple model can be extended in many ways. Most importantly, we need to be able to model the effects of measured covariates on one or both parameter(s). Both the ecological and the observation processes represent a logistic regression (with an intercept only so far), so it is natural to include covariate effects via a logit link function. Hence, we can add statements of the following kind to the model description

$$\text{logit}(\psi_i) = \alpha + \beta * x_i.$$

Here, x_i is the value of some occurrence-relevant covariate measured at site i, and α and β are the intercept and slope parameters of this logit-linear regression. We can do the same for the observation model, where we distinguish between "site covariates" and "sampling covariates". Site covariates vary among sites only and are constant across repeated surveys to a site, that is, they will be indexed by i only. In contrast, survey covariates vary by site *and* by survey; hence, they will be indexed by i and j. This is a minor distinction but in practice, the modeling of sampling covariates requires a little more book-keeping effort. Explicitly couching site-occupancy models within the GLM framework makes it clear that other GLM extensions might be applied, too. For instance, overdispersion in detection probability could be modeled by the introduction of random site effects (Royle, 2006). Of course, we could model the effects of many explanatory variables, of polynomial terms, or of splines (Gimenez et al., 2006a, b; Collier et al., 2011).

In Section 13.2, we conduct a simulation to understand what happens to the estimates of regression coefficients in conventional species distribution models when detection probability is not perfect. In Section 13.3, we analyze simulated data sets and in Section 13.4 a real data set using single-season site-occupancy models. In Section 13.5, we extend the model to multiple "seasons" and thus arrive at an extended metapopulation model. In Section 13.6, we extend the single-season model to multiple states of occurrence, which in our example are owl territories occupied with or without reproduction.

We emphasize that we will not conduct any goodness-of-fit assessments based on posterior predictive checks in this chapter. The reason for this is that with a binary response, the deviance or other discrepancy measures based directly on the response are uninformative about the fit of a model (McCullagh and Nelder, 1989). Kéry (2010) erroneously showed such posterior predictive checks for site-occupancy models. These checks are meaningless because regardless of the model structure, they will always and thus sometimes spuriously indicate a fitting model. To do a goodness-of-fit test, the binary responses have to be aggregated.

13.2 WHAT HAPPENS WHEN $p < 1$ AND CONSTANT AND p IS NOT ACCOUNTED FOR IN A SPECIES DISTRIBUTION MODEL?

We use simulation to understand what happens when there is a constant degree of imperfect detection and this is not accounted for in an analysis. We simulate 100,000 data sets from 250 sites, with a constant $p < 1$ (here, $p = 0.60$), and analyze them with a conventional species distribution model (here, a nonhierarchical logistic regression). We have a single explanatory variable (think of it as a habitat or environmental covariate) that links the habitat to occurrence probability on the logit-linear scale with intercept -3 and slope 1. (You may want to change nreps in the code to 1000.)

```
nreps <- 10^5                              # No. replicates
estimates <- array(NA, dim = c(nreps, 2))  # Array to contain the
                                             estimates
R <- 250                                   # No. sites

for (i in 1:nreps) {
    cat(i, "\n"); flush.console()
    x <- runif(R, 0, 10) # choose covariate values
    state<-rbinom(n = R, size = 1, prob = plogis(-3 + 1 * x)) # Occ. state
    obs <- rbinom(n = R, size = 1, prob = 0.6) * state       # Observations
    fm <- glm(obs~x, family = binomial)
    estimates[i,] <- fm$coef
    }

par(mfrow = c(3, 1))
hist(estimates[,1], col = "gray", nclass = 50, main = "",
    xlab = "Intercept estimates", las = 1, ylab = "", freq = FALSE)
abline(v = -3, col = "red", lwd = 3)        # Truth
hist(estimates[,2], col = "gray", nclass = 50, main = "", xlab = "Slope
    estimates", xlim = c(0,1), las = 1, ylab = "", freq = FALSE)
abline(v = 1, col = "red", lwd = 3)         # Truth

plot(1:10, plogis(estimates[1,1] + estimates[1,2] * (1:10)), col =
    "gray", lwd = 1, ylab = "Occupancy probability", xlab = "Covariate
    value", type = "l", ylim = c(0, 1), frame.plot = FALSE, las = 1)
samp <- sample(1:nreps, 1000)
for (i in samp) {
    lines(1:10, plogis(estimates[i,1] + estimates[i,2] * (1:10)),
        col = "gray", lwd = 1, type = "l")
    }
lines(1:10, plogis(-3 + 1 * (1:10)), col = "red", lwd = 3, type = "l")
```

When failing to account for a constant nondetection error, slope estimates of a covariate are biased towards zero (Fig. 13.1, middle panel). The intercept (Fig. 13.1, top panel) is not necessarily estimated too low; rather, here, it is overestimated. However, the combined effect is such

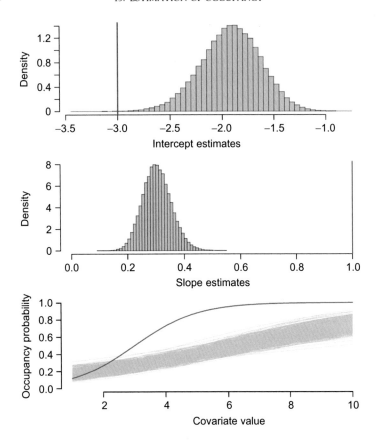

FIGURE 13.1 Effect of imperfect detection on a conventional species distribution model: slope estimates become biased low with imperfect detection even if detection probability is constant (here, 0.60). In the bottom panel, the red lines show the truth and the gray lines show a random sample of 1000 estimated regression lines: the extent of the distribution is always underestimated. See also Tyre et al. (2003).

that the total extent of a distribution is underestimated. The latter is represented by the area under the red curve in the bottom panel. The area under the gray curves (the estimated distribution) is always less than the area under the red curve (true distribution).

13.3 GENERATION AND ANALYSIS OF SIMULATED DATA FOR SINGLE-SEASON OCCUPANCY

13.3.1 The Simplest Possible Site-Occupancy Model

To fully grasp how the site-occupancy model "works", we first look at the simplest possible case: both the ecological and the observation process are described by an intercept only. To generate detection/nondetection data $y_{i,j}$ under this Null model for $R = 200$ spatial replicates (sites) and $T = 3$ temporal replicates, we simply do this.

```
# Select sample sizes (spatial and temporal replication)
R <- 200
T <- 3

# Determine process parameters
psi <- 0.8      # Occupancy probability
p <- 0.5        # Detection probability

# Create structure to contain counts
y <- matrix(NA, nrow = R, ncol = T)

# Ecological process: Sample true occurrence (z, yes/no) from a
  Bernoulli (occurrence probability = psi)
z <- rbinom(n = R, size = 1, prob = psi) # Latent occurrence state

# Observation process: Sample detection/nondetection observations
  from a Bernoulli(with p) if z=1
for (j in 1:T) {
    y[,j] <- rbinom(n = R, size = 1, prob = z * p)
    }

# Look at truth and at our imperfect observations
sum(z)                   # Realized occupancy among 200 surveyed sites
[1] 169
sum(apply(y, 1, max))  # Observed occupancy
[1] 151
```

Note that in the simulation of the observation process, we have multiplied the Bernoulli draw with z. This means that the result will be zero whenever $z = 0$, that is, whenever the species does not occur. Next, we analyze this data set.

```
# Specify model in BUGS language
sink("model.txt")
cat("
model {

# Priors
psi ~ dunif(0, 1)
p ~ dunif(0, 1)

# Likelihood
# Ecological model for true occurrence
for (i in 1:R) {
    z[i] ~ dbern(psi)
    p.eff[i] <- z[i] * p

    # Observation model for replicated detection/nondetection
      observations
    for (j in 1:T) {
        y[i,j] ~ dbern(p.eff[i])
```

```
        } #j
      } #i

# Derived quantities
occ.fs <- sum(z[])          # Number of occupied sites among the 200
}
",fill = TRUE)
sink()

# Bundle data
win.data <- list(y = y, R = nrow(y), T = ncol(y))

# Initial values
zst <- apply(y, 1, max)     # Observed occurrence as starting values for z
inits <- function() list(z = zst)

# Parameters monitored
params <- c("psi", "p", "occ.fs")

# MCMC settings
ni <- 1200
nt <- 2
nb <- 200
nc <- 3

# Call WinBUGS from R (BRT < 1 min)
out <- bugs(win.data, inits, params, "model.txt", n.chains = nc,
   n.thin = nt, n.iter = ni, n.burnin = nb, debug = TRUE, bugs.directory =
   bugs.dir, working.directory = getwd())

# Summarize posteriors
print(out, dig = 2)
[...]
```

	mean	sd	2.5%	25%	50%	75%	97.5%	Rhat	n.eff
psi	0.89	0.04	0.80	0.86	0.89	0.92	0.97	1.01	340
p	0.47	0.03	0.41	0.45	0.47	0.49	0.53	1.00	870
occ.fs	178.29	7.59	165.00	173.00	178.00	183.00	195.00	1.01	510
deviance	739.37	28.50	686.50	719.00	738.20	758.05	798.75	1.01	470

```
[...]
```

This looks good. You will note quite a bit of sampling variability in this system. The estimates may be fairly different among repeated generations of the data set or among the replicate data sets of different people. This basic model is a good starting point for running simulation exercises to find out about how good inferences can be in marginal data situations; see exercises and Guillera-Arroita et al. (2010).

13.3.2 Site-Occupancy Models with Covariates

Next, we look into the case where covariates affect the ecological and the observation process. We model covariate effects on a parameter θ through the canonical GLM link function, the logit $= \log(\theta/(1 - \theta))$. As in the previous chapter, we will look at a worst-case scenario for a species distribution model, where opposing effects of a single covariate on the two processes generating the observed data effectively cancel each other out in the observations. The result will be that in a conventional species distribution model, the effect of this covariate on the species distribution will not be identified correctly. We next define a function that creates species distribution data (detection/nondetection data) for us.

```
# Define function for generating species distribution data
data.fn <- function(R = 200, T = 3, xmin = -1, xmax = 1, alpha.psi = -1,
  beta.psi = 3, alpha.p = 1, beta.p = -3) {

  y <- array(dim = c(R, T)) # Array for counts

  # Ecological process
  # Covariate values
  X <- sort(runif(n = R, min = xmin, max = xmax))

  # Relationship expected occurrence - covariate
  psi <- plogis(alpha.psi + beta.psi * X)     # Apply inverse logit

  # Add Bernoulli noise: draw occurrence indicator z from
    Bernoulli(psi)
  z <- rbinom(n = R, size = 1, prob = psi)
  occ.fs <- sum(z)     # Finite-sample occupancy (see
                         Royle and Kéry, 2007)

  # Observation process
  # Relationship detection prob - covariate
  p <- plogis(alpha.p + beta.p * X)

  # Make a 'census'
  p.eff <- z * p
  for (i in 1:T) {
      y[,i] <- rbinom(n = R, size = 1, prob = p.eff)
      }

  # Naïve regression
  naive.pred <- plogis(predict(glm(apply(y, 1, max) ~ X + I(X^2),
    family = binomial)))

  # Plot features of the simulated system
  par(mfrow = c(2, 2))
  plot(X, psi, main = "Expected occurrence", xlab = "Covariate",
    ylab = "Occupancy probability", las = 1, type = "l", col = "red",
    lwd = 3, frame.plot = FALSE)
  plot(X, z, main = "Realised (true) occurrence", xlab = "Covariate",
    ylab = "Occurrence", las = 1, frame.plot = FALSE, col = "red",)
  plot(X, p, ylim = c(0,1), main = "Detection probability",
    xlab = "Covariate", ylab = "p", type = "l", lwd = 3, col = "red",
    las = 1, frame.plot = FALSE)
  plot(X, naive.pred, main = "Detection/nondetection observations \n
    and conventional SDM", xlab = "Covariate", ylab = "Apparent
    occupancy", ylim = c(min(y), max(y)), type = "l", lwd = 3, lty = 2,
    col = "blue", las = 1, frame.plot = FALSE)
  points(rep(X, T), y)
```

```
# Return stuff
return(list(R = R, T = T, X = X, alpha.psi = alpha.psi, beta.psi =
  beta.psi, alpha.p = alpha.p , beta.p = beta.p, psi = psi, z = z,
  occ.fs = occ.fs, p = p, y = y))
}
```

We obtain one realization from the stochastic system just defined and conduct a conventional species distribution model (Fig. 13.2):

```
sodata <- data.fn()
str(sodata)                    # Look at data

summary(glm(apply(y, 1, max) ~ X + I(X^2), family = binomial,
  data = sodata))

Call:
glm(formula = apply(y, 1, max) ~ X + I(X^2), family = binomial,
  data = sodata)

Deviance Residuals:
     Min         1Q      Median         3Q        Max
 -1.10984   -0.83363   -0.28985   -0.04219    2.45653

Coefficients:
              Estimate  Std. Error   z value   Pr(>|z|)
(Intercept)    -1.0439      0.2624    -3.978   6.95e-05 ***
X               3.3989      0.8348     4.072   4.67e-05 ***
I(X^2)         -3.2680      1.1757    -2.780    0.00544 **
---
Signif. codes: 0 '***' 0.001 '**' 0.01 '*' 0.05 '.' 0.1 ' ' 1

(Dispersion parameter for binomial family taken to be 1)

    Null deviance: 213.27 on 199 degrees of freedom
Residual deviance: 170.95 on 197 degrees of freedom
AIC: 176.95

Number of Fisher Scoring iterations: 6
```

Hence, in this simulated data set and with a conventional species distribution model, we identify an optimum value of the covariate for the occupancy probability of the study species (see blue curve in bottom right panel of Fig. 13.2). Let us see what a site-occupancy model can do.

```
# Specify model in BUGS language
sink("model.txt")
cat("
model {

# Priors
alpha.occ ~ dunif(-10, 10)
beta.occ ~ dunif(-10, 10)
alpha.p ~ dunif(-10, 10)
beta.p ~ dunif(-10, 10)

# Likelihood
for (i in 1:R) {
```

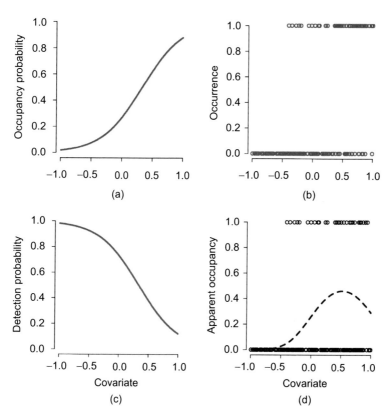

FIGURE 13.2   Features of the simulated data set, and truth behind it, and inference about the system based on a conventional species distribution model (blue line in bottom right panel). The truth is shown in red and observed data in black. (a) Occupancy probability, (b) realized (true) occurrence, (c) detection probability, and (d) detection/nondetection ("presence/absence") observations and estimated occupancy probability under a conventional species distribution model.

```
# True state model for the partially observed true state
z[i] ~ dbern(psi[i])        # True occupancy z at site i
logit(psi[i]) <- alpha.occ + beta.occ * X[i]

for (j in 1:T) {

    # Observation model for the actual observations
    y[i,j] ~ dbern(p.eff[i,j]) # Detection-nondetection at i and j
    p.eff[i,j] <- z[i] * p[i,j]
    logit(p[i,j]) <- alpha.p + beta.p * X[i]
    } #j
} #i

# Derived quantities
occ.fs <- sum(z[]) # Number of occupied sites among those studied
}
",fill = TRUE)
sink()
```

```
# Bundle data
win.data <- list(y = sodata$y, X = sodata$X, R = nrow(sodata$y),
    T = ncol(sodata$y))

# Initial values
zst <- apply(sodata$y, 1, max) # Good inits for latent states essential
inits <- function(){list(z = zst, alpha.occ = runif(1, -3, 3),
    beta.occ = runif(1, -3, 3), alpha.p = runif(1, -3, 3), beta.p = runif
    (1, -3, 3))}

# Parameters monitored
params <- c("alpha.occ", "beta.occ", "alpha.p", "beta.p", "occ.fs")

# MCMC settings
ni <- 10000
nt <- 8
nb <- 2000
nc <- 3

# Call WinBUGS from R (BRT 1 min)
out <- bugs(win.data, inits, params, "model.txt", n.chains = nc,
    n.thin = nt, n.iter = ni, n.burnin = nb, debug = TRUE, bugs.directory =
    bugs.dir, working.directory = getwd())
```

We compare the known truth in the data-generating mechanism with our estimates of truth under the site-occupancy species distribution model. We find that the model does a decent job at recovering the parameters for the habitat relationships of the probability of occupancy (alpha.occ and beta.occ) and of detection (alpha.p and beta.p), but that the estimates are much more precise for the relationship with detection. This makes sense because there is more data ($n = 600$ instead of $n = 200$) from which to estimate those regression parameters. A total of 59 sites were occupied in our simulated data set, and at 45 of those, the study species was discovered. Our model estimated 67 occurrences (95% CRI 57–78). This number, finite-sample occurrence, is not a function of population occupancy probability, but of the latent occurrence states z, which we can easily estimate in an MCMC-based analysis (Royle and Kéry, 2007).

```
TRUTH <- c(sodata$alpha.psi, sodata$beta.psi, sodata$alpha.p, sodata
    $beta.p, sum(sodata$z))
print(cbind(TRUTH, out$summary[1:5, c(1,2,3,7)]), dig = 3)
              TRUTH    mean      sd    2.5%    97.5%
alpha.occ        -1  -1.269   0.274   -1.81   -0.738
beta.occ          3   4.084   0.854    2.58    5.939
alpha.p           1   0.925   0.330    0.28    1.584
beta.p           -3  -2.942   0.546   -4.00   -1.865
occ.fs           59  67.335   5.291   57.00   78.000

sum(apply(sodata$y, 1, sum) > 0) # Apparent number of occupied sites
[1] 45
```

We graphically compare the conclusions from the two species distribution models (Fig. 13.3). We see again that the conventional approach,

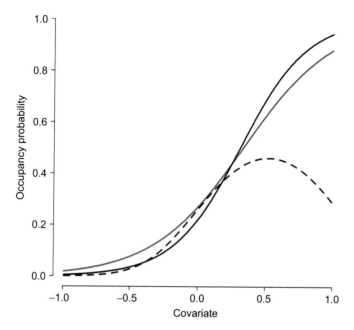

FIGURE 13.3   Comparison of true and estimated relationship between occupancy probability and an environmental covariate under a site-occupancy model (solid blue) and under the conventional approach that ignores detection probability (dashed blue). Truth is shown in red.

which ignores the effects of the observation process in the generation of detection/nondetection data, models apparent rather than true species distributions only (Kéry, 2011b).

```
naive.pred <- plogis(predict(glm(apply(sodata$y, 1, max) ~ X + I(X^2),
   family = binomial, data = sodata)))
lin.pred2 <- out$mean$alpha.occ + out$mean$beta.occ * sodata$X

plot(sodata$X, sodata$psi, ylim = c(0, 1), main = "", ylab = "Occupancy
   probability", xlab = "Covariate", type = "l", lwd = 3, col = "red",
   las = 1, frame.plot = FALSE)
lines(sodata$X, naive.pred, ylim = c(0 ,1), type = "l", lty = 2, lwd = 3,
   col = "blue")
lines(sodata$X, plogis(lin.pred2), ylim = c(0, 1), type = "l", lty = 1,
   lwd = 2, col = "blue")
```

13.4 ANALYSIS OF REAL DATA SET: SINGLE-SEASON OCCUPANCY MODEL

We will next analyze a small, but typical real-world occurrence data set: surveys to breeding sites of the endangered beetle *Rosalia alpina* (Fig. 13.4; see also the cover of Kéry, 2010) during a single flight period (July–August

FIGURE 13.4   The remarkable "blue bug", the cerambycid beetle *Rosalia alpina*, Switzerland, 2009 (Photograph by T. Marent).

2009). In Switzerland, this striking blue bug lays its eggs into the wood of dead beech trees *Fagus sylvatica*, preferentially in tall and old logs, but unfortunately also in piles of firewood stocked in the forest only temporarily. Larvae develop over 3–4 years; hence, eggs laid in firewood are normally doomed. Nevertheless, checking firewood piles in forests is an efficient search strategy for this rare and elusive beetle. In 2009, one of us (MK) surveyed one of the few Swiss areas where the species is known to occur, the hills around Movelier in the Swiss Jura mountains.

The complete data set ("bluebug.txt") contains replicated counts at a total of 27 sites (woodpiles) in the Movelier region in 2009. There were up to six replicate counts at each woodpile; the count result of which is called detX. Woodpiles were either at the forest edge or more in the interior of a forest (covariate forest_edge), and individual visits took place at varying dates (covariate dateX) and times of day (hours in the afternoon, covariates hX).

A summary of these data is shown in Table 13.1. We see that *Rosalia* was detected at 10 of 27 woodpiles and from 1 to 5 times. Clearly, detection probability at an occupied woodpile is not perfect; for instance, the woodpile in row 10 was surveyed six times and *Rosalia* was seen only once. It is natural to wonder whether other woodpiles might have been occupied but *Rosalia* was simply missed. Another question might be to ask how many times a woodpile might have to be checked in order to detect *Rosalia* at least once when it occurs. And finally, we may wonder

TABLE 13.1   A Summary of the Blue Bug Data Set (`bluebug.txt`) That Keeps Track Only of Detections and Nondetections.

0	1	1	1	1	1	5
1	1	1	1	1	–	5
1	0	1	0	0	1	3
1	0	0	0	1	1	3
1	1	–	–	–	–	2
1	–	–	–	–	–	1
0	0	0	0	1	0	1
1	–	–	–	–	–	1
1	–	–	–	–	–	1
1	0	0	0	0	0	1
0	0	0	0	0	–	0
0	0	0	0	0	–	0
0	0	0	0	0	–	0
0	–	–	–	–	–	0
0	–	–	–	–	–	0
0	–	–	–	–	–	0
0	–	–	–	–	–	0
0	0	–	–	–	–	0
0	0	–	–	–	–	0
0	–	–	–	–	–	0
0	0	–	–	–	–	0
0	0	–	–	–	–	0
0	0	–	–	–	–	0
0	0	0	–	–	–	0
0	–	–	–	–	–	0
0	–	–	–	–	–	0
0	–	–	–	–	–	0

Note: Rows denote woodpiles and columns, except for the right-most column, denote survey occasions. The total number of surveys with detections is shown in the right-most column. Surveys with *Rosalia* detections are shown in buff color, those without *Rosalia* detections in yellow, and missing values shown as dashes. For pure convenience, sites have been ordered by decreasing number of surveys with detections.

whether the location of a woodpile, at the forest edge or in the interior, may affect the probability of it being occupied, and similarly, whether there were relationships between detection probability and the date and time of day, respectively, at which a survey took place, or whether *Rosalia* was detected before (behavioral effect, see Section 6.2.3.). We will answer these questions with a site-occupancy species distribution model now.

```
# Read in the data
data <- read.table("bluebug.txt", header = TRUE)

# Collect the data into suitable structures
y <- as.matrix(data[,4:9])        # as.matrix essential for WinBUGS
y[y>1] <- 1                       # Reduce counts to 0/1
edge <- data$forest_edge
dates <- as.matrix(data[,10:15])
hours <- as.matrix(data[,16:21])

# Standardize covariates
mean.date <- mean(dates, na.rm = TRUE)
sd.date <- sd(dates[!is.na(dates)])
DATES <- (dates-mean.date)/sd.date        # Standardise date
DATES[is.na(DATES)] <- 0                   # Impute zeroes (means)

mean.hour <- mean(hours, na.rm = TRUE)
sd.hour <- sd(hours[!is.na(hours)])
HOURS <- (hours-mean.hour)/sd.hour         # Standardise hour
HOURS[is.na(HOURS)] <- 0                    # Impute zeroes (means)
```

In the BUGS code below, we "stabilize" the logit to avoid numerical under- or overflow by truncating values more extreme than $(-999, 999)$ on the logit scale. This should hardly affect the inference because this restricts the value of the linear predictor to the range (plogis(-999), plogis(999)).

```
# Specify model in BUGS language
sink("model.txt")
cat("
model {

# Priors
alpha.psi ~ dnorm(0, 0.01)
beta.psi ~ dnorm(0, 0.01)
alpha.p ~ dnorm(0, 0.01)
beta1.p ~ dnorm(0, 0.01)
beta2.p ~ dnorm(0, 0.01)
beta3.p ~ dnorm(0, 0.01)
beta4.p ~ dnorm(0, 0.01)

# Likelihood
# Ecological model for the partially observed true state
for (i in 1:R) {
    z[i] ~ dbern(psi[i]) # True occurrence z at site i
    psi[i] <- 1 / (1 + exp(-lpsi.lim[i]))
    lpsi.lim[i] <- min(999, max(-999, lpsi[i]))
    lpsi[i] <- alpha.psi + beta.psi * edge[i]
```

```
# Observation model for the observations
for (j in 1:T) {
    y[i,j] ~ dbern(mu.p[i,j]) # Detection-nondetection at i and j
    mu.p[i,j] <- z[i] * p[i,j]
    p[i,j] <- 1 / (1 + exp(-lp.lim[i,j]))
    lp.lim[i,j] <- min(999, max(-999, lp[i,j]))
    lp[i,j] <- alpha.p + beta1.p * DATES[i,j] + beta2.p *
        pow(DATES[i,j], 2) + beta3.p * HOURS[i,j] + beta4.p *
        pow(HOURS[i,j], 2)
    } #j
  } #i

# Derived quantities
occ.fs <- sum(z[])                        # Number of occupied sites
mean.p <- exp(alpha.p) / (1 + exp(alpha.p)) # Average detection
}
",fill = TRUE)
sink()

# Bundle data
win.data <- list(y=y, R=nrow(y), T=ncol(y), edge=edge, DATES=
    DATES, HOURS=HOURS)

# Initial values
zst <- apply(y, 1, max, na.rm=TRUE)    # Good starting values crucial
inits <- function(){list(z=zst, alpha.psi=runif(1, -3, 3), alpha.p=
    runif(1, -3, 3))}

# Parameters monitored
params <- c("alpha.psi", "beta.psi", "mean.p", "occ.fs", "alpha.p",
    "beta1.p", "beta2.p", "beta3.p", "beta4.p")

# MCMC settings
ni <- 30000
nt <- 10
nb <- 20000
nc <- 3

# Call WinBUGS from R (BRT < 1 min)
out <- bugs(win.data, inits, params, "model.txt", n.chains=nc,
    n.thin=nt, n.iter=ni, n.burnin=nb, debug=TRUE, bugs.directory=
    bugs.dir, working.directory=getwd())
```

We inspect the estimates and then illustrate.

```
# Summarize posteriors
print(out, dig=2)
              mean    sd   2.5%    25%    50%    75%  97.5%  Rhat  n.eff
alpha.psi     5.83  5.26  -0.10   1.73   4.26   8.67  17.98  1.10     46
beta.psi     -6.61  5.26 -18.83  -9.38  -5.13  -2.60  -0.44  1.10     48
mean.p        0.56  0.15   0.27   0.46   0.56   0.67   0.85  1.01    200
occ.fs       17.02  2.38  11.00  16.00  17.00  18.00  21.00  1.01    220
alpha.p       0.29  0.66  -0.97  -0.15   0.26   0.72   1.71  1.01    160
beta1.p       0.34  0.40  -0.42   0.06   0.33   0.60   1.13  1.00   2400
beta2.p       0.21  0.47  -0.71  -0.10   0.19   0.51   1.17  1.01    230
beta3.p      -0.48  0.42  -1.37  -0.75  -0.46  -0.20   0.31  1.01    330
beta4.p      -0.59  0.32  -1.28  -0.79  -0.57  -0.37   0.00  1.00   1600
```

We note that convergence for the occupancy parameters could be better (Rhat = 1.10). We also note (not shown) that parameter estimates are quite sensitive to the priors chosen in the model. This is not quite unexpected, given the small size of the data set. Thus, we should state our inferences with caution.

Earlier on, we asked a series of questions that we wanted to answer with the site-occupancy model. The first was "How many woodpiles were likely occupied by *Rosalia alpina*, given the detection probability estimated?". We find the answer in the tabular summary of the estimates above, it is 17.02 (95% CRI 11–21). Since this is a key quantity in our analysis, we want to visualize its entire posterior distribution (Fig. 13.5).

```
# Posterior distribution of the number of occupied woodpiles in actual
  sample
hist(out$sims.list$occ.fs, nclass = 30, col = "gray", main = "", xlab =
  "Number of occupied woodpiles (occ.fs)", xlim = c(9, 27))
abline(v = 10, lwd = 2) # The observed number
```

The second question of interest was "Given that we may overlook the species at occupied woodpiles, how many times must we survey a

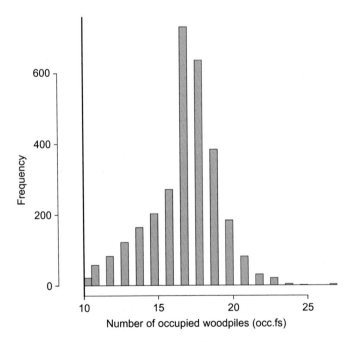

FIGURE 13.5 Posterior distribution of the number of woodpiles occupied by the cerambycid beetle *Rosalia alpina* in the Movelier region in 2009 among the 27 surveyed woodpiles. Vertical line indicates the observed number of 10.

woodpile before we can be "almost certain" to detect it at least once, when it occurs?". We can answer this question by using a simple binomial argument put forwards in Kéry (2002) and many times elsewhere: the probability P^* to detect the species during n identical and independent surveys is $P^* = 1 - (1 - p)^n$, where p is the detection probability from a site-occupancy model. Since detection varies in all sorts of ways (see below), we have to decide on one "useful" value of p. We take the mean.p monitored in the analysis. Using the MCMC samples for that quantity, we can incorporate our uncertainty about detection probability into the answer to our question. We will compute P^* for values of n between 1 and 10 and see where it is at least 95%, which will be our definition of "almost certain".

```
Pstar <- array(NA, dim = c(out$n.sims, 10))
x <- cbind(rep(1, 3000), rep(2, 3000), rep(3, 3000), rep(4, 3000), rep
    (5, 3000), rep(6, 3000), rep(7, 3000), rep(8, 3000), rep(9, 3000),
    rep(10, 3000))
for (i in 1:out$n.sims) {
    for (j in 1:10){
        Pstar[i,j] <- 1 - (1 - out$sims.list$mean.p[i])^j
        } #j
    } #i

boxplot(Pstar ~ x, col = "gray", las = 1, ylab = "Pstar", xlab = "Number of
    surveys", outline = FALSE)
abline(h = 0.95, lty = 2, lwd = 2)
```

Hence, 3–4 "average" surveys were required to be almost certain to detect *Rosalia alpina* at a woodpile where it occurred (Fig. 13.6).

What about the occupancy at woodpiles at the forest edge as compared to the forest interior? Our parameter beta.psi represents the difference in occupancy probability, on the logit scale between woodpiles at the forest edge and those in the interior. The 95% CRI of its estimate does not cover 0; hence, we can be rather confident in that *Rosalia* was more widespread at woodpiles in the forest interior. We convert the occupancy parameters into an estimate of occupancy in both locations and plot that.

```
par(mfrow = c(2, 1))
hist(plogis(out$sims.list$alpha.psi), nclass = 40, col = "gray", main =
    "Forest interior", xlab = "Occupancy probability", xlim = c(0, 1))
hist(plogis(out$sims.list$alpha.psi+ out$sims.list$beta.psi),
    nclass = 40, col = "gray", main = "Forest edge", xlab = "Occupancy
    probability", xlim = c(0, 1))
```

So, indeed, there appears to be a big effect of the location of a woodpile on the probability that it is occupied by *Rosalia alpina*: the forest interior is much preferred (Fig. 13.7).

Finally, we want to answer the questions about a relationship between detection probability and date and time of day, respectively. We can see from the 95% CRI in the summary results table above that the regression

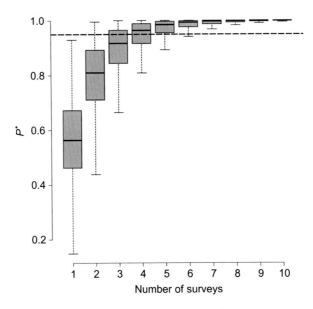

FIGURE 13.6 The relationship between P^*, the probability to detect *Rosalia alpina* at a woodpile at least once during n surveys, and n for the blue bug data set. The dashed line indicates 95% certainty to detect the species when present.

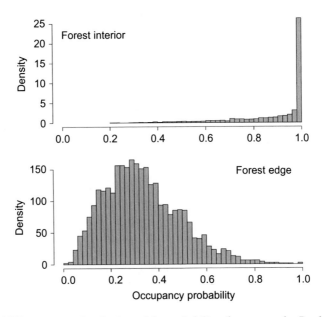

FIGURE 13.7 Posterior distributions of the probability of occupancy by *Rosalia alpina* for a woodpile in the forest interior (top) and at the forest edge (bottom) in Movelier, 2009.

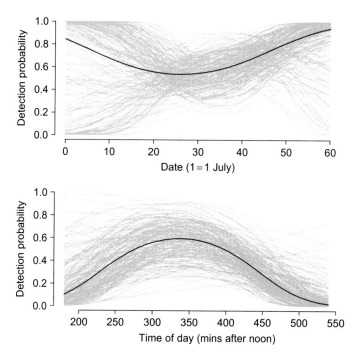

FIGURE 13.8 Predictions of the covariate relationships that account for estimation uncertainty. Top, effect of date; bottom, effect of time of day. Blue lines show the posterior mean, and gray lines show the relationships based on a random posterior sample of size 200 to visualize estimation uncertainty.

parameters for date, `beta1.p` and `beta2.p`, largely overlap zero but that those for time of day, `beta3.p` and `beta4.p`, do not do this so clearly (at least not `beta4.p`, which just about straddles 0). We will plot the predicted relationship in a figure that also shows the uncertainty in the estimates by plotting the relationships for a random MCMC sample of the regression coefficients involved in their computation (Fig. 13.8). This again suggests the absence of a date effect on detection probability (top panel); however, detection probability seems to be highest around 5 – 6 pm (bottom panel). These results can be interesting for designing a monitoring program for this endangered species.

```
# Predict effect of time of day with uncertainty
mcmc.sample <- out$n.sims

original.date.pred <- seq(0, 60, length.out = 30)
original.hour.pred <- seq(180, 540, length.out = 30)
date.pred <- (original.date.pred – mean.date)/sd.date
hour.pred <- (original.hour.pred – mean.hour)/sd.hour
p.pred.date <- plogis(out$mean$alpha.p + out$mean$beta1.p *
    date.pred + out$mean$beta2.p * date.pred^2 )
```

```
p.pred.hour <- plogis(out$mean$alpha.p + out$mean$beta3.p *
    hour.pred + out$mean$beta4.p * hour.pred^2 )

array.p.pred.hour <- array.p.pred.date <- array(NA, dim = c(length
    (hour.pred), mcmc.sample))
for (i in 1:mcmc.sample){
    array.p.pred.date[,i] <- plogis(out$sims.list$alpha.p[i] +
        out$sims.list$beta1.p[i] * date.pred + out$sims.list$beta2.p[i] *
        date.pred^2)
    array.p.pred.hour[,i] <- plogis(out$sims.list$alpha.p[i] +
        out$sims.list$beta3.p[i] * hour.pred + out$sims.list$beta4.p[i] *
        hour.pred^2)
    }

# Plot for a subsample of MCMC draws
sub.set <- sort(sample(1:mcmc.sample, size = 200))

par(mfrow = c(2, 1))
plot(original.date.pred, p.pred.date, main = "", ylab = "Detection
    probability", xlab = "Date (1 = 1 July)", ylim = c(0, 1), type = "l",
    lwd = 3, frame.plot = FALSE)
for (i in sub.set){
    lines(original.date.pred, array.p.pred.date[,i], type = "l",
        lwd = 1, col = "gray")
    }
lines(original.date.pred, p.pred.date, type = "l", lwd = 3,
    col = "blue")

plot(original.hour.pred, p.pred.hour, main = "", ylab = "Detection
    probability", xlab = "Time of day (mins after noon)", ylim = c(0, 1),
    type = "l", lwd = 3, frame.plot = FALSE)
for (i in sub.set){
    lines(original.hour.pred, array.p.pred.hour[,i], type = "l",
        lwd = 1, col = "gray")
    }
lines(original.hour.pred, p.pred.hour, type = "l", lwd = 3,
    col = "blue")
```

13.5 DYNAMIC (MULTISEASON)
SITE-OCCUPANCY MODELS

So far we have been modeling detection/nondetection observations from R sites and J replicate surveys, yielding data $y_{i,j}$ for site i and survey j. We required a so-called closed population, which in the occupancy context means that the occurrence state of site i must not change over the J replicates. The closure assumption is often a reasonable approximation for studies that are short relative to the dynamics of the system investigated. However, in other cases, closure may not hold for all replicate surveys, for instance, when animals randomly move onto and off study sites. This specific form of nonclosure is called random temporary emigration, and the models of the preceding sections may still be applied. The probability of random temporary emigration, that is, of being temporarily unavailable for detection, is confounded with the probability of detection given availability (Kendall, 1999). In other words, the detection parameter refers to the product of the probability of being available for detection and that of being detected, given being present. According to conventional wisdom, the interpretation of the occupancy parameter simply changes from the *probability of permanent presence* to the *probability of use sometime* during the study period (MacKenzie, 2005).

However, there may be cases when temporary emigration (dispersal) is so strong as to make the resulting estimates of probability of use meaningless, for example, effectively 1. In other cases, temporary emigration may be Markovian: whether a site is occupied at time $t = 2$ depends on whether it was so at $t = 1$. Probability of (un-)availability is then no longer confounded with the probability of detection given availability, and naive application of single-season occupancy models results in biased estimates of occupancy (Kendall, 1999; Rota et al., 2009).

As a remedy, the J survey occasions may be assigned to subgroups and closure assumed only within each such subgroup. Owing to the seasonality of nature in most parts of the world, seasons over a series of years represent an extremely common, natural grouping factor. As an example, for birds or amphibians, replicate surveys are often conducted during the breeding season and this may be repeated over multiple years. Such a sampling at two temporal scales is called the robust design (Williams et al., 2002); each year, or breeding season, is called a primary sampling occasion, and the surveys within each season are called secondary sampling occasions. It is natural then to assume closure among secondary seasons only, that is, within each primary season, and allow change in the occurrence state among primary seasons. In the context of site-occupancy models, we then have observations from R sites, J replicate surveys (secondary sampling occasions), and K primary seasons (such as years), yielding detection/nondetection data $y_{i,j,k}$ for site i, within-season survey j, and season k. Note that up to now in this chapter, index j was for all occasions, while in this section j will index secondary occasions only.

Given our expectation that occupancy changes among seasons k, how should we model occupancy dynamics? It would be simplest to treat season as a group and fit separate parameters for each, as we did in Section 12.3 in the context of abundance estimation in an open population. This is a reasonable approach, but there may be two issues with it. First, it treats observations from a site surveyed in different seasons as independent. However, whether a site is occupied at one time may depend on whether it was occupied previously, violating the independence assumption and representing a form of pseudoreplication (Hurlbert, 1984). This may result in too short standard error estimates, so it may be desirable to account for the repeated-measures nature of

treating
season as
a covariate
results in
pseudorep.

multiseason
models allow
for patch
dynamics
to be
estimated

multiseason data. Second, the interest of a study may focus on the parameters that govern occupancy dynamics, that is, colonization and extinction/survival. Occupancy is the quantity that metapopulation ecologists also call incidence (Hanski, 1994). Rather than simply describing changes of incidence over time, a metapopulation ecologist is interested in estimating probabilities of patch survival (or extinction) and patch colonization. This provides us with the motivation to explicitly model occupancy dynamics in terms of parameters describing the demographic components of that dynamics. This is achieved by the multiseason, or dynamic, site-occupancy model of MacKenzie et al. (2003). Moving from a single-season to a dynamic site-occupancy model is analogous to moving from a closed capture–recapture model (Chapter 6) to a Jolly-Seber model (Chapter 10) or from a classic binomial mixture model (Chapter 12) to the generalized binomial mixture model of Dail and Madsen (2011).

To describe detection/nondetection data $y_{i,j,k}$ for site i and (within-season) replicate survey j in season k, we follow the hierarchical, or state-space, formulation of the model by Royle and Kéry (2007). We describe the observed data in a two-level random-effects model, that is, as a set of two linked stochastic processes or equations. The first equation describes the ecological process, that is, the evolution of the latent occurrence state $z_{i,k}$ of site i over season k. Occurrence is latent because it is only partly observable and hence must be estimated from the observations $y_{i,j,k}$. The second equation describes the observation process, that is, the mapping of the latent state $z_{i,k}$ on observation $y_{i,j,k}$. The basic model is thus the following:

$$z_{i,k} \sim \text{Bernoulli}(\psi_{i,k}) \qquad \text{1. Ecological process yields true state}$$

$$y_{i,j,k} \mid z_{i,k} \sim \text{Bernoulli}(z_{i,k}p_{i,j,k}) \qquad \text{2. Observation process yields observations}$$

The sole change to the single-season occupancy model is the addition of an index for season, k. The model now describes the latent occurrence state $z_{i,k}$ at site i in season k as a Bernoulli trial with occupancy parameter $\psi_{i,k}$. Observation $y_{i,j,k}$ is equal to 1 if a species is detected during temporal replicate j at site i in season k, and zero otherwise, and is another Bernoulli trial governed by the product of the occurrence state at i and k and detection probability $p_{i,j,k}$.

As said above, we could model $y_{i,j,k}$ by simply treating season k as a group, which would be equivalent to fitting separate occupancy models to the data from each season. This is how we modeled changes in abundance over multiple seasons in Section 12.3. But now, we will describe the state dynamics in an explicit, Markovian way instead: we will specify an initial state and two sets of parameters that govern subsequent changes in a first-order autoregressive manner. This is a simple extension of the ecological process model above. For clarity, we will drop the site index (i).

$z_1 \sim \text{Bernoulli}(\psi_1)$ 1a. Initial ecological state in first season

$z_{k+1} \mid z_k \sim \text{Bernoulli}(z_k\phi_k + (1 - z_k)\gamma_k)$ 1b. Markovian transitions in later seasons

[margin note: Markovian transitions in occupancy state among seasons]

Hence, in season 1, occurrence is a simple Bernoulli trial as before. In all later seasons, the occurrence state z_{k+1} of a site in season $k + 1$ is a Bernoulli trial with a success parameter that depends on two things: whether the site was occupied at time k and on the value of either a survival or a colonization parameter. Hence, if a site was occupied during season k (i.e., $z_k = 1$ and therefore, $1 - z_k = 0$), it will be re-occupied in the following season with probability ϕ_k; this is the (site) survival probability. Of course, we could equivalently describe this in terms of the complement of survival, extinction probability $1 - \phi_k$. On the other hand, if a site was unoccupied during season k (i.e., $z_k = 0$ and therefore, $1 - z_k = 1$), it will be occupied at $k + 1$ with probability γ_k; this is the (site) colonization probability.

The state process of the dynamic site-occupancy model is exactly equivalent to a classical metapopulation model (Hanski, 1998), which expresses changes between time t and $t + 1$ in the occurrence state of a collection of patches as a function of the probabilities of colonization of patches unoccupied at time k, and of survival (or alternatively, of extinction) of patches that were occupied at time k. This model makes the important assumption that the occurrence state of each patch can be determined perfectly, that is, that detection probability is equal to 1. Dynamic site-occupancy models represent an extended metapopulation model: the extension lies in an explicit accounting for imperfect detection (MacKenzie et al., 2003; Royle and Kéry, 2007), which becomes possible whenever replicated detection/nondetection observations are available within single periods of closure for at least some sites and/or such periods. Not accounting for imperfect detection in conventional metapopulation models will lead to biased estimates of *all* estimated quantities: incidence will be estimated too low and the probabilities of extinction, colonization, and turnover will all be estimated too high (Moilanen (2002); Royle and Dorazio (2008); see also Risk et al. (2011), for a robust-design incidence function model).

[margin note: Equivalence to metapopulation modeling]

We will next simulate a data set under the dynamic site-occupancy model and analyze that. Afterwards, we will analyze a real data set. You will find another example of a dynamic occupancy model in the OpenBUGS manual (Examples > Ecology examples > Sparrowhawks).

13.5.1 Generation and Analysis of Simulated Data

We assume that we have data from a typical population study of a (nocturnal) bird of prey, the Long-eared owl (Fig. 13.9). Each of a total of R territories was surveyed on J occasions during each of K breeding seasons (years), and it was recorded whether any sign of territory occupation was

FIGURE 13.9   Long-eared owl (*Asio otus*), Finland, 2008 (Photograph by T. Muukkonen).

detected. Our data $y_{i,j,k}$ represent detection ($y = 1$) or nondetection ($y = 0$) of an owl in territory i, during replicate survey j in breeding season (year) k. Note that here, occupancy is equivalent to abundance because the number of occupied sites is exactly the local population size of owls.

We define a function to generate a data set. As always, apart from generating a data set to be analyzed later, this function may be used to get insights into the structure of the model used to analyze the data, issues of parameter estimation, or required samples sizes (see Section 1.5).

```
data.fn <- function(R = 250, J = 3, K = 10, psi1 = 0.4, range.p =
  c(0.2, 0.4), range.phi = c(0.6, 0.8), range.gamma = c(0, 0.1)) {
# Function to simulate detection/nondetection data for dynamic
  site-occ model
# Annual variation in probabilities of patch survival, colonization and
# detection is specified by the bounds of a uniform distribution.
# Function arguments:
# R – Number of sites
# J – Number of replicate surveys
# K – Number of years
# psi1 – occupancy probability in first year
# range.p – bounds of uniform distribution from which annual p drawn
# range.psi and range.gamma – same for survival and colonization
  probability
```

```r
# Set up some required arrays
site <- 1:R                        # Sites
year <- 1:K                        # Years
psi <- rep(NA, K)                  # Occupancy probability
muZ <- z <- array(dim = c(R, K))   # Expected and realized occurrence
y <- array(NA, dim = c(R, J, K))   # Detection histories

# Determine initial occupancy and demographic parameters
psi[1] <- psi1                     # Initial occupancy probability
p <- runif(n = K, min = range.p[1], max = range.p[2])
phi <- runif(n = K-1, min = range.phi[1], max = range.phi[2])
gamma <- runif(n = K-1, min = range.gamma[1], max = range.gamma[2])

# Generate latent states of occurrence
# First year
z[,1] <- rbinom(R, 1, psi[1])      # Initial occupancy state

# Later years
for(i in 1:R){                     # Loop over sites
    for(k in 2:K){                 # Loop over years
        muZ[k] <- z[i, k-1]*phi[k-1] + (1-z[i, k-1])*gamma[k-1]
            # Prob for occ.
        z[i,k] <- rbinom(1, 1, muZ[k])
        } #k
    } #i

# Plot realised occupancy
plot(year, apply(z, 2, mean), type = "l", xlab = "Year", ylab =
  "Occupancy or Detection prob.", col = "red", xlim = c(0,K+1),
  ylim = c(0,1), lwd = 2, lty = 1, frame.plot = FALSE, las = 1)
lines(year, p, type = "l", col = "red", lwd = 2, lty = 2)

# Generate detection/nondetection data
for(i in 1:R){
    for(k in 1:K){
        prob <- z[i,k] * p[k]
        for(j in 1:J){
            y[i,j,k] <- rbinom(1, 1, prob)
            } #j
        } #k
    } #i

# Compute annual population occupancy
for (k in 2:K){
    psi[k] <- psi[k-1]*phi[k-1] + (1-psi[k-1])*gamma[k-1]
    }

# Plot apparent occupancy
psi.app <- apply(apply(y, c(1,3), max), 2, mean)
lines(year, psi.app, type = "l", col = "black", lwd = 2)
text(0.85*K, 0.06, labels = "red solid - true occupancy\n red
  dashed - detection\n black - observed occupancy")

# Return data
return(list(R = R, J = J, K = K, psi = psi, psi.app = psi.app, z = z,
  phi = phi, gamma = gamma, p = p, y = y))
}
```

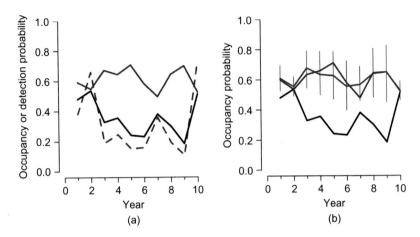

FIGURE 13.10 (a) Simulated territory occupancy data for long-eared owls. Truth is shown in red (solid, occupancy probability; dashed, detection probability) and the observed occupancy probability in black. The difference between the red and the black lines is due to detection error. (b) Comparison between true, observed, and estimated occupancy probability. Truth is shown in red, estimates under the site-occupancy model (with 95% CRI) are in blue, and naïve estimates (observed values) are in black. (Note: Using the R code in the book, you will generate each plot separately.)

We execute the function once to obtain a data set for 250 owl territories with three surveys in each of 10 years (Fig. 13.10a).

```
data <- data.fn(R = 250, J = 3, K = 10, psi1 = 0.6, range.p = c(0.1, 0.9),
    range.phi = c(0.7, 0.9), range.gamma = c(0.1, 0.5))
```

We attach the data set and produce a simple summary.

```
attach(data)
str(data)
> str(data)
List of 10
 $ R       : num 250
 $ J       : num 3
 $ K       : num 10
 $ psi     : num [1:10] 0.6 0.535 0.635 0.658 0.71 ...
 $ psi.app : num [1:10] 0.48 0.536 0.328 0.356 0.24 0.232 0.38 0.3 0.184 0.512
 $ z       : num [1:250, 1:10] 0 1 0 1 1 1 1 1 0 1 ...
 $ phi     : num [1:9] 0.791 0.761 0.805 0.879 0.772 ...
 $ gamma   : num [1:9] 0.151 0.489 0.403 0.384 0.105 ...
 $ p       : num [1:10] 0.382 0.659 0.19 0.246 0.151 ...
 $ y       : num [1:250, 1:3, 1:10] 0 0 0 1 1 0 1 0 0 0 ...
```

We conduct the analysis using code from Royle and Kéry (2007), which includes the estimation of the actual number of occupied territories (among the 250), the occupancy-based population growth rate, and the turnover rate.

```
# Specify model in BUGS language
sink("Dynocc.txt")
cat("
model {

# Specify priors
psi1 ~ dunif(0, 1)
for (k in 1:(nyear-1)){
    phi[k] ~ dunif(0, 1)
    gamma[k] ~ dunif(0, 1)
    p[k] ~ dunif(0, 1)
    }
p[nyear] ~ dunif(0, 1)

# Ecological submodel: Define state conditional on parameters
for (i in 1:nsite){
    z[i,1] ~ dbern(psi1)
    for (k in 2:nyear){
        muZ[i,k]<- z[i,k-1]*phi[k-1] + (1-z[i,k-1])*gamma[k-1]
        z[i,k] ~ dbern(muZ[i,k])
        } #k
    } #i

# Observation model
for (i in 1:nsite){
    for (j in 1:nrep){
        for (k in 1:nyear){
            muy[i,j,k] <- z[i,k]*p[k]
            y[i,j,k] ~ dbern(muy[i,j,k])
            } #k
        } #j
    } #i

# Derived parameters: Sample and population occupancy, growth rate
  and turnover
psi[1] <- psi1
n.occ[1]<-sum(z[1:nsite,1])
for (k in 2:nyear){
    psi[k] <- psi[k-1]*phi[k-1] + (1-psi[k-1])*gamma[k-1]
    n.occ[k] <- sum(z[1:nsite,k])
    growthr[k] <- psi[k]/psi[k-1]
    turnover[k-1] <- (1 - psi[k-1]) * gamma[k-1]/psi[k]
    }
}
",fill = TRUE)
sink()

# Bundle data
win.data <- list(y = y, nsite = dim(y)[1], nrep = dim(y)[2], nyear = dim
    (y)[3])

# Initial values
Zst <- apply(y, c(1, 3), max) # Observed occurrence as inits for z
inits <- function(){ list(z = zst)}

# Parameters monitored
params <- c("psi", "phi", "gamma", "p", "n.occ", "growthr",
    "turnover")
```

```
# MCMC settings
ni <- 2500
nt <- 4
nb <- 500
nc <- 3
```

```
# Call WinBUGS from R (BRT 3 min)
out <- bugs(win.data, inits, params, "Dynocc.txt", n.chains = nc,
    n.thin = nt, n.iter = ni, n.burnin = nb, debug = TRUE, bugs.directory =
    bugs.dir, working.directory = getwd())
```

```
# Summarize posteriors
print(out, dig = 2)
[...]
```

	mean	sd	2.5%	25%	50%	75%	97.5%	Rhat	n.eff
psi[1]	0.61	0.04	0.53	0.58	0.61	0.64	0.69	1.00	720
[...]
psi[10]	0.53	0.03	0.46	0.50	0.53	0.55	0.59	1.00	810
phi[1]	0.83	0.04	0.75	0.81	0.83	0.86	0.90	1.00	1500
[...]
phi[9]	0.67	0.06	0.55	0.63	0.68	0.71	0.80	1.00	1500
gamma[1]	0.12	0.06	0.01	0.08	0.12	0.17	0.25	1.00	1500
[...]
gamma[9]	0.24	0.12	0.02	0.15	0.24	0.33	0.44	1.00	1500
p[1]	0.40	0.03	0.35	0.38	0.40	0.42	0.47	1.00	1100
[...]
p[10]	0.71	0.03	0.66	0.69	0.71	0.72	0.75	1.00	1500
n.occ[1]	152.32	7.48	138.00	147.00	152.00	158.00	166.00	1.00	1500
[...]
n.occ[10]	131.51	2.18	128.00	130.00	131.00	133.00	137.00	1.00	1100
growthr[2]	0.91	0.06	0.80	0.87	0.91	0.95	1.04	1.00	1500
[...]
growthr[10]	0.83	0.14	0.62	0.73	0.81	0.90	1.16	1.00	1400
turnover[1]	0.09	0.05	0.01	0.05	0.08	0.12	0.20	1.00	1500
[...]
turnover[9]	0.17	0.11	0.01	0.09	0.16	0.24	0.41	1.00	1500
[...]

We compare truth and estimates of truth (posterior mean, sd, and 95% CRI) in tables …

```
print(cbind(data$psi, out$summary[1:K, c(1, 2, 3, 7)]), dig = 3)
print(cbind(data$phi, out$summary[(K+1):(K+(K-1)), c(1, 2, 3, 7)]),
    dig = 3)
print(cbind(data$gamma, out$summary[(2*K):(2*K+(K-2)), c(1, 2, 3,
    7)]), dig = 3)
print(cbind(data$p, out$summary[(3*K-1):(4*K-2), c(1, 2, 3, 7)]),
    dig = 3)
```

… and in a picture (Fig. 13.10b).

```
plot(1:K, data$psi, type = "l", xlab = "Year", ylab = "Occupancy
    probability", col = "red", xlim = c(0,K+1), ylim = c(0,1), lwd = 2,
    lty = 1, frame.plot = FALSE, las = 1)
```

```
lines(1:K, data$psi.app, type = "l", col = "black", lwd = 2)
points(1:K, out$mean$psi, type = "l", col = "blue", lwd = 2)
segments(1:K, out$summary[1:K,3], 1:K,out$summary[1:K,7],
    col = "blue", lwd = 1)
```

We are rather satisfied with the performance of the metapopulation estimators of the model.

13.5.2 Dynamic Occupancy Modeling in a Real Data Set

As another illustration of the dynamic occupancy model of MacKenzie et al. (2003), we will use data from the Six-spot burnet (Fig. 13.11) collected in the Swiss butterfly monitoring program. Remember that we have 95 sites with two replications in each of 7 seasons, and that a "season"

FIGURE 13.11 The Six-spot burnet *Zygaena filipendulae*, a day-flying moth, Switzerland, 2004 (Photograph by T. Marent).

represents one day, within which a transect is surveyed back and forth (for further description, see Section 12.3; Kéry et al. (2009b); Dorazio et al. (2010)). This is a more typical example of an occupancy model, where a "site" represents a 2.5 km transect in a 1 km^2 square and is so large relative to the space requirements of the study species that is can be inhabited by many (hundred) individuals. Thus, there is no longer a 1:1 relationship between occupancy and abundance as in the owl example.

After reading the count data into R, we will first reformat the data into a 3-dimensional array, as we did for the multiseason binomial mixture model in Section 12.3. We start with a format where butterfly counts from different "seasons" (days) are stacked. For this code to work, the data must be balanced, that is, we must have the same number of surveyed sites in each "season" (day). This is not a requirement of the model, simply of our code. If you have variation in the number of sites surveyed, then you have to "fill in" the data using NAs to make them balanced or else vectorize the BUGS model description (see chapter 21 in Kéry, 2010).

```
# Read in the data and put it into 3D array
bdat <- read.table(file = "burnet.txt", header = T)
str(bdat)

y <- array(NA, dim = c(95, 2, 7)) # 95 sites, 2 reps, 7 days

for (i in 1:7) {
    sel.rows <- bdat$day == i
    y[,,i] <- as.matrix(bdat)[sel.rows, 3:4]
    }
str(y)

# Convert counts to detection/nondetection data
y[y>0] <- 1

# Look at the number of sites with detections for each day
tmp <- apply(y, c(1,3), max, na.rm = TRUE)
tmp[tmp == "-Inf"] <- NA
apply(tmp, 2, sum, na.rm = TRUE)
 [1] 0 0 3 10 17 17 6
```

There are no detections of burnets at all during the first two days. We are now ready to fit the dynamic occupancy model in WinBUGS. The code is the same as before (Section 13.5.1) so we simply recycle the BUGS model description from there.

```
# Bundle data
win.data <- list(y = y, nsite = dim(y)[1], nrep = dim(y)[2], nyear = dim
    (y)[3])

# Initial values
inits <- function() { list(z = apply(y, c(1, 3), max)) }

# Parameters monitored
params <- c("psi", "phi", "gamma", "p", "n.occ", "growthr",
    "turnover")
```

```
# MCMC settings
ni <- 5000
nt <- 4
nb <- 1000
nc <- 3

# Call WinBUGS from R (BRT 1 min)
out1 <- bugs(win.data, inits, params, "Dynocc.txt", n.chains = nc,
    n.thin = nt, n.iter = ni, n.burnin = nb, debug = TRUE, bugs.directory =
    bugs.dir, working.directory = getwd())

# Summarize posteriors
print(out1, dig = 3)
```

	mean	sd	2.5%	25%	50%	75%	97.5%	Rhat	n.eff
psi[1]	0.106	0.208	0.001	0.009	0.025	0.078	0.895	1.048	60
[...]									
psi[7]	0.117	0.052	0.044	0.080	0.106	0.142	0.246	1.005	490
phi[1]	0.442	0.294	0.014	0.177	0.419	0.687	0.969	1.007	870
[...]									
phi[6]	0.447	0.183	0.170	0.313	0.415	0.551	0.900	1.002	1000
gamma[1]	0.151	0.230	0.001	0.014	0.050	0.171	0.905	1.025	100
[...]									
gamma[6]	0.026	0.026	0.001	0.008	0.018	0.036	0.095	1.004	650
p[1]	0.294	0.296	0.002	0.038	0.179	0.497	0.948	1.037	79
[...]									
p[7]	0.536	0.183	0.195	0.398	0.540	0.679	0.864	1.005	430
n.occ[1]	9.268	19.972	0.000	0.000	1.000	6.000	85.000	1.171	32
[...]									
n.occ[7]	9.515	3.971	6.000	7.000	8.000	11.000	20.000	1.009	300
growthr[2]	21.130	257.481	0.078	0.841	2.037	6.563	117.412	1.026	88
[...]									
growthr[7]	0.548	0.230	0.222	0.384	0.504	0.671	1.101	1.003	710
turnover[1]	0.714	0.287	0.054	0.539	0.826	0.953	0.998	1.011	260
[...]									
turnover[6]	0.172	0.139	0.005	0.061	0.137	0.251	0.505	1.003	940

We see that some of the parameters associated with the first two days, when no burnets were observed, are not estimable. An indication of this is that their posterior distributions cover (almost) the entire range of their prior distributions, that is, the 95% CRI essentially covers the range from 0 to 1 for the probability parameters. This means that the data contain no information about these parameters. The parameters describing the dynamics of occupancy, survival (phi), colonization (gamma), and the growth rate, may all offer interesting insights into the factors that drive the population dynamics of a species in the context of occurrence.

Apart from the third day, when very few burnets were observed (and during the first two, see above), detection probability appears to be similar. Hence, we pool the detection parameters and fit a model with constant detection probability. In addition, as an exercise we aggregate the binary response over the two replicates per day and specify a binomial(2, p) data distribution instead of a Bernoulli(p). When there is no modeled structure among replicate surveys, this model parameter-ization is computationally more efficient than the one with a Bernoulli response.

```
# Specify model in BUGS language
sink("Dynocc2.txt")
cat("
model {

# Specify priors
psi1 ~ dunif(0, 1)
for (k in 1:(nyear-1)){
    phi[k] ~ dunif(0, 1)
    gamma[k] ~ dunif(0, 1)
    }
p ~ dunif(0, 1)

# Both models at once
for (i in 1:nsite){
    z[i,1] ~ dbern(psi1)      # State model 1: Initial state
    for (k in 2:nyear){       # State model 2: State dynamics
        muZ[i,k] <- z[i,k-1]*phi[k-1] + (1-z[i,k-1])*gamma[k-1]
        z[i,k] ~ dbern(muZ[i,k])

        # Observation model
        muy[i,k] <- z[i,k]*p
        y[i,k] ~ dbin(muy[i,k], 2)
        } #k
    } #i

# Derived parameters: Sample and population occupancy, growth
    rate and turnover
psi[1] <- psi1
n.occ[1] <- sum(z[1:nsite,1])
for (k in 2:nyear){
    psi[k] <- psi[k-1]*phi[k-1] + (1-psi[k-1])*gamma[k-1]
    n.occ[k] <- sum(z[1:nsite,k])
    growthr[k] <- psi[k]/psi[k-1]
    turnover[k-1] <- (1 - psi[k-1]) * gamma[k-1]/psi[k]
    }
}
",fill = TRUE)
sink()

# Aggregate detections over reps within a day and bundle data
yy <- apply(y, c(1, 3), sum, na.rm = TRUE)
win.data <- list(y = yy, nsite = dim(yy)[1], nyear = dim(yy)[2])

# Initial values
inits <- function(){list(z = apply(y, c(1, 3), max))}

# Parameters monitored
params <- c("psi", "phi", "gamma", "p", "n.occ", "growthr",
    "turnover")
```

```
# MCMC settings
ni <- 2500
nt <- 2
nb <- 500
nc <- 3

# Call WinBUGS from R (BRT 1 min)
out2 <- bugs(win.data, inits, params, "Dynocc2.txt", n.chains = nc,
    n.thin = nt, n.iter = ni, n.burnin = nb, debug = TRUE, bugs.directory =
    bugs.dir, working.directory = getwd())

# Summarize posteriors
print(out2, dig = 3)
```

	mean	sd	2.5%	25%	50%	75%	97.5%	Rhat	n.eff
psi[1]	0.461	0.394	0.003	0.058	0.387	0.902	0.997	1.122	21
[...]									
psi[7]	0.093	0.032	0.040	0.070	0.090	0.114	0.165	1.002	1700
phi[1]	0.121	0.207	0.001	0.008	0.026	0.121	0.778	1.087	28
[...]									
phi[6]	0.368	0.120	0.154	0.280	0.362	0.447	0.625	1.001	3000
gamma[1]	0.108	0.202	0.001	0.007	0.020	0.083	0.790	1.070	33
[...]									
gamma[6]	0.017	0.017	0.000	0.005	0.012	0.024	0.063	1.001	3000
p	0.646	0.059	0.525	0.608	0.648	0.687	0.756	1.001	3000
n.occ[1]	43.739	38.086	0.000	5.000	36.000	87.000	95.000	1.176	16
[...]									
n.occ[7]	7.241	1.301	6.000	6.000	7.000	8.000	10.000	1.001	3000
growthr[2]	0.742	4.958	0.004	0.021	0.060	0.327	5.190	1.096	26
[...]									
growthr[7]	0.433	0.139	0.196	0.334	0.422	0.517	0.742	1.002	1900
turnover[1]	0.507	0.300	0.016	0.244	0.507	0.777	0.981	1.002	1400
[...]									
turnover[6]	0.143	0.126	0.004	0.048	0.108	0.206	0.464	1.001	3000

We plot what we have learnt about the occupancy, or incidence, of Swiss burnets over the season (Fig. 13.12).

```
DAY <- cbind(rep(1, out2$n.sims), rep(2, out2$n.sims), rep(3,
    out2$n.sims), rep(4, out2$n.sims), rep(5, out2$n.sims), rep(6,
    out2$n.sims), rep(7, out2$n.sims))
boxplot(out2$sims.list$psi ~ DAY, col = "gray", ylab = "Occupancy
    probability", xlab = "Day of survey", las = 1, frame.plot = FALSE)
```

We see the typical unimodal phenology of an insect in temperate latitudes (Kéry et al., 2009). Six-spot burnets are most widespread in Switzerland during the period in which survey number 5 is made. Interestingly, although no burnets were seen during either the first or the second day, the posterior distribution for occupancy was quite different for the two days. There are two reasons for this. First, the Markovian model propagates information backwards in time and so occurrence at $k = 2$ ($z_{i,2}$) is informed directly by $z_{i,3}$ because there are data at $k = 3$. Conversely, $z_{i,1}$ gets no direct information

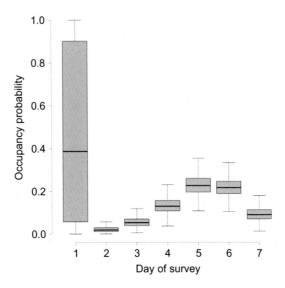

FIGURE 13.12   Occupancy probability of the burnet over a season: summary of posterior distributions for survey day 1 through survey day 7. No burnets at all were seen during the first two days.

at all from $k = 2$ because there were no observations (J.A. Royle, pers. comm.). Second, different amounts of information are available for occupancy on the two days. There were only 75 sites with surveys on the first, but 87 sites with surveys on the second day. As a consequence, the occupancy parameter was not estimable on the first day; the posterior samples simply reflected the prior. In contrast, on the second day, occupancy was estimated at effectively zero. You can compare the sample sizes for each day like the following:

```
apply(apply(y, c(1, 3), max), 2, function(x){sum(!is.na(x))})
[1] 75 87 95 95 95 95 87
```

In summary, the dynamic site-occupancy model is a powerful extension to the classical metapopulation model. Depending on the definition of a site and the state of occurrence, dynamic occupancy models can be used to describe the dynamics of a vast array of systems. Covariates can be introduced for all parameters via the usual GLM link functions. The main challenge when applying the model may be a data management and parameter bookkeeping one: to put the data in the required multidimensional arrays and not to get confused with multidimensional model code.

13.6 MULTISTATE OCCUPANCY MODELS

So far, we have been treating occurrence as a binary variable. However, frequently we can distinguish different states of occurrence. Examples include "single bird", "nonreproductive pair", and "reproductive pair" when studying territory occupancy, "breeding possible", "breeding probable", or "breeding confirmed" in bird atlas studies (Schmid et al., 1998), different population size classes in the monitoring of vocal amphibians (Royle and Link, 2005), or "occupied by species A only", "occupied by species B only", or "occupied by both species" in studies of species interactions. Apart from detection uncertainty, there is an additional potential component of uncertainty in these examples: state uncertainty, that is, whether a site observed in one state truly is in that state. For example, when species A is observed at a site, the true state of that site could either be "occupied by species A only" or "occupied by both species".

The multistate site-occupancy model is used for inference about multiple states of occupancy in the presence of both state and detection uncertainty. This model seems to have been independently developed by Royle and Link (2005) and Nichols et al. (2007), providing another example for the independent and (more or less) simultaneous development of a model, such as the Cormack-Jolly-Seber model (Cormack, 1964; Jolly, 1965; Seber, 1965), single-state site-occupancy models (MacKenzie et al., 2002; Tyre et al., 2003), and spatial capture–recapture models (Borchers and Efford, 2008; Royle and Young, 2008). The explicit merging of site-occupancy models with multistate models (Chapter 9) holds promise because the combination of two already very general model classes likely results in even more flexible models. It is likely that many ideas that are well understood and applied in the multistate arena may be taken over to site-occupancy models as well.

In the following, we focus on the simplest possible multistate occupancy model, where two occurrence states along with the third state "unoccupied" are distinguished in a closed population. The generalization to more than two states is straightforward. We illustrate with data from a survey of long-eared owls (Fig. 13.9), where either hooting adult males or begging young are detected, or nothing at all. If a hooting male is heard, we are unsure about whether reproduction is taking place at a site. If we fail to hear anything, we are unsure about whether a site is occupied at all as well as whether there is reproduction. In contrast, when hearing begging young, there is no uncertainty about state and occurrence.

The development of the model is nearly identical to that of the multistate model (Chapter 9). First, we need to define lists of true and of observed states. The true states in our example are "not occupied", "occupied without reproduction", and "occupied with reproduction". The list of observed states comprises "not seen", "seen without reproduction", and "seen with reproduction". A hierarchical model for data from this system distinguishes a description of the state and another of the observation process. We therefore introduce the latent variable z, which defines the true state of each site and can take values 1 (site not occupied), 2 (site occupied without reproduction), or 3 (site occupied with reproduction). The probability of the state of site i is modeled using a categorical distribution as

$$z_i \sim \text{categorical}(\Omega_i),$$

where Ω_i is the state vector. The state vector has as many elements as there are states and each element is the probability that site i is in a given state. In our example, we have

$$\Omega_i = \begin{bmatrix} 1 - \psi_{1,i} - \psi_{2,i} \\ \psi_{1,i} \\ \psi_{2,i} \end{bmatrix},$$

where $\psi_{1,i}$ is the probability that site i is occupied without reproduction, $\psi_{2,i}$ is the probability that site i is occupied and reproduction takes place, and $1 - \psi_{1,i} - \psi_{2,i}$ is the probability that site i is unoccupied. Obviously, the three probabilities need to sum to 1, and we often assume that the probabilities are the same at all sites (no index i).

Given the true state z_i of site i, the observation process links the true state with the observations $(y_{i,j})$. We write

$$y_{i,j} \mid z_i \sim \text{categorical}(\Theta_{z_i,1...O,i,j}),$$

where Θ is the observation array and O is the number of observed states. The array has four dimensions; the last two refer to site (i) and survey (j). If detection is assumed to be the same at all sites and constant among surveys, the observation array becomes a two-dimensional matrix. The first dimension refers to the true state and the second to the observed states. The elements of the matrix are the probabilities of an observation given a state. Assuming constancy over sites and surveys, the most general observation matrix Θ is

	not seen	seen without rep.	seen with rep.
not occupied	$\pi_{1,1}$	$\pi_{1,2}$	$\pi_{1,3}$
occupied without reproduction	$\pi_{2,1}$	$\pi_{2,2}$	$\pi_{2,3}$
occupied with reproduction	$\pi_{3,1}$	$\pi_{3,2}$	$\pi_{3,3}$

The true states are in the rows and the observed states in the columns. Thus, $\pi_{m,k}$ denotes the probability of classifying a site in state m as being in state k. These probabilities are either detection or genuine classification probabilities or both. Clearly, the probabilities of correct classification are in the diagonal, while the off-diagonals contain the probabilities of incorrect classification. The matrix is row-stochastic, so the three probabilities in the same row are not independent; rather, they sum to one.

   This matrix defines the most general multistate model that could be fitted in a site-occupancy context. Given sufficient data, all parameters should be estimable. However, frequently, there is a natural order in the modeled states and some errors are unlikely or impossible. Typically, it can be assumed that classification errors only occur in one direction, so that a "higher" state can be erroneously taken to be a lower state, but not the other way round. For instance, a site with reproduction could be classified as having no reproduction if only an adult is heard hooting and no begging young are heard, but not the other way round. The result of this is that we model a restricted version of the fully general observation matrix (now we also make explicit the relationships among cell probabilities within a row):

$$
\begin{array}{ccc}
 & \text{not} & \text{seen without} \quad \text{seen with} \\
 & \text{seen} & \text{rep.} \qquad\qquad \text{rep.}
\end{array}
$$

$$
\begin{array}{c}
\text{not occupied} \\
\text{occupied without reproduction} \\
\text{occupied with reproduction}
\end{array}
\begin{bmatrix}
1 & 0 & 0 \\
1 - \pi_{2,2} & \pi_{2,2} & 0 \\
1 - \pi_{3,2} - \pi_{3,3} & \pi_{3,2} & \pi_{3,3}
\end{bmatrix}
$$

Both Royle and Link (2005) and Nichols et al. (2007) describe restricted models of this kind, where a site in state 1 (unoccupied) can only be observed in state 1 (we assume there are no false positives), but sites in state 2 can be observed in state 1 or 2 and sites in state 3 in all three states (1, 2, or 3).

   This model can be re-expressed in various parameterizations. What this means is that the elements of the state vector and the elements $\pi_{m,k}$ in the observation matrix can be rewritten as functions of other parameters that may be more interesting biologically or that may allow a more natural formulation of covariate effects; see Royle and Link (2005) and Nichols et al. (2007). Our parameterization in this chapter is as follows:

$$
\begin{array}{cc}
\text{State vector} & \text{Observation matrix} \\[4pt]
\begin{bmatrix} 1 - \psi \\ \psi(1 - r) \\ \psi r \end{bmatrix} &
\begin{bmatrix} 1 & 0 & 0 \\ 1 - p_2 & p_2 & 0 \\ p_{3,1} & p_{3,2} & p_{3,3} \end{bmatrix}
\end{array}
$$

Here, ψ is the probability of occupancy, regardless of reproduction, and r is the probability that reproduction takes place at an occupied site. In the observation matrix, p_2 is the detection probability of a site without reproduction, $p_{3,3}$ is the probability that at a site with reproduction, the species is detected and reproduction is observed (i.e., the state is correctly classified), $p_{3,2}$ is the probability that at a site with reproduction, the species is detected but reproduction is not observed (i.e., the state is misclassified), and $p_{3,1}$ is the probability that the species is not detected at a site with reproduction. The three probabilities, $p_{3,k}$, must sum to one, and this is accounted for by our choice of a Dirichlet prior in the BUGS model description; see below.

To illustrate this model, we use data on territory occupancy of the long-eared owl (Fig. 13.9) from a long-term population study of our colleague Simon Birrer at the Swiss Ornithological Institute. Birrer has been surveying 40 owl territories repeatedly in every breeding season since 1989. Not all sites were checked in every year and we chose the data from 2009, when 31 sites were checked up to 5 times. We read in the data and briefly look at them.

```
owls <- read.table("owls.txt", header = TRUE)
str(owls)
```

The variables entitled obs1-obs5 denote the result of each survey: detection of no owl at all (0), of a hooting owl (1) or of begging young (2). The variables entitled date1-date5 give the Julian date of each survey. To fit the model, we must relabel the states because WinBUGS does not allow indices of 0. Hence, we denote the states in the same way as defined above. This relabeling is done in the data bundle statement below.

We specify the model with default vague priors for all parameters. The beta terms are used to specify a vague Dirichlet prior for the multinomial distribution represented by row three in the observation matrix above (see also Section 9.6). Our model could accommodate time variation in the observation matrix, but at first we will assume constancy of parameters over time.

```
# Specify model in BUGS language
sink("model1.txt")
cat("
model {

# Priors
p2 ~ dunif(0, 1)
psi ~ dunif(0, 1)
r ~ dunif(0, 1)
for (i in 1:3) {
    beta[i] ~ dgamma(1, 1) # Induce Dirichlet prior
    p3[i] <- beta[i]/sum(beta[])
    }

# Define state vector
for (s in 1:R) {
    phi[s,1] <- 1 - psi           # Prob. of nonoccupation
    phi[s,2] <- psi * (1 - r)     # Prob. of occupancy without repro
    phi[s,3] <- psi * r           # Prob. of occupancy and repro
    }
```

```
# Define observation matrix
# Order of indices: true state, time, observed state
for (t in 1:T) {
    p[1,t,1] <- 1
    p[1,t,2] <- 0
    p[1,t,3] <- 0
    p[2,t,1] <- 1-p2
    p[2,t,2] <- p2
    p[2,t,3] <- 0
    p[3,t,1] <- p3[1]
    p[3,t,2] <- p3[2]
    p[3,t,3] <- p3[3]
    }

# State-space likelihood
# State equation: model of true states (z)
for (s in 1:R) {
    z[s] ~ dcat(phi[s,])
    }

# Observation equation
for (s in 1:R) {
    for (t in 1:T) {
        y[s,t] ~ dcat(p[z[s],t,])
        } #t
    } #s

# Derived quantities
for (s in 1:R) {
    occ1[s] <- equals(z[s], 1)
    occ2[s] <- equals(z[s], 2)
    occ3[s] <- equals(z[s], 3)
    }
n.occ[1] <- sum(occ1[]) # Sites in state 1
n.occ[2] <- sum(occ2[]) # Sites in state 2
n.occ[3] <- sum(occ3[]) # Sites in state 3
}
",fill=TRUE)
sink()
```

We analyze rows 2–6 in the owls data frame and convert them to a matrix called **y**.

```
# Bundle data
y <- as.matrix(owls[, 2:6])
y <- y + 1
win.data <- list(y = y, R = dim(Y)[1], T = dim(Y)[2])

# Initial values
zst <- apply(y, 1, max, na.rm = TRUE)
zst[zst == "-Inf"] <- 1
inits <- function() {list(z = zst)}

# Parameters monitored
params <- c("p2", "p3", "r", "psi", "n.occ") # Might want to add "z"
```

```
# MCMC settings
ni <- 2500
nt <- 2
nb <- 500
nc <- 3

# Call WinBUGS from R (BRT <1 min)
out1 <- bugs(win.data, inits, params, "model1.txt", n.chains = nc,
    n.thin = nt, n.iter = ni, n.burnin = nb, debug =TRUE, bugs.directory =
    bugs.dir, working.directory = getwd())

# Summarize posteriors
print(out1, dig = 2)
            mean    sd   2.5%    25%    50%    75%  97.5%  Rhat  n.eff
p2          0.35  0.19   0.04   0.21   0.33   0.46   0.82  1.00   2400
p3[1]       0.55  0.12   0.30   0.47   0.56   0.64   0.77  1.00   3000
p3[2]       0.21  0.09   0.05   0.14   0.20   0.26   0.40  1.00    530
p3[3]       0.24  0.12   0.07   0.16   0.22   0.31   0.51  1.00    550
r           0.64  0.21   0.24   0.48   0.64   0.81   0.98  1.01    350
psi         0.52  0.15   0.28   0.42   0.50   0.61   0.86  1.00   1900
n.occ[1]   19.11  5.39   5.00  16.00  20.00  23.00  27.00  1.00   1100
n.occ[2]    7.51  5.46   0.00   3.00   7.00  10.00  21.03  1.01    260
n.occ[3]   13.38  5.10   6.00  10.00  13.00  16.00  25.00  1.00    600
```

We estimate that 52% of sites are occupied, of which 64% by reproductive owls. For our specific sample of 40 sites, this translates into an estimated 13.4 occupied sites with and 7.5 sites without reproduction and 19.1 unoccupied sites. Detection probability of a site without reproduction is estimated at 0.35 and for a site with reproduction at 0.24. There is a probability of 0.21 to detect only hooting adults at a site with reproduction and one of 0.55 to miss it altogether. The parameters describing state uncertainty and detection error all refer to a single survey.

This model assumes that all parameters are constant, but the surveys take place over an extended time period (early March–early September), so this assumption may be unlikely. For instance, begging young will not be available over the entire period. Therefore, a more realistic model may be one that allows for these parameters to vary by occasion (i.e., survey 1–5).

```
# Specify model in BUGS language
sink("model2.txt")
cat("
model {

# Priors
psi ~ dunif(0, 1)
r ~ dunif(0, 1)

for (t in 1:T) {
    p2[t] ~ dunif(0, 1)
    for (i in 1:3) {
        beta[i,t] ~ dgamma(1, 1)      # Induce Dirichlet prior
        p3[i,t] <- beta[i,t]/sum(beta[,t])
        } #i
    } #t
```

```
# Define state vector
for (s in 1:R) {
    phi[s,1] <- 1 - psi          # Prob. of nonoccupation
    phi[s,2] <- psi * (1 - r)    # Prob. of occupancy without repro.
    phi[s,3] <- psi * r          # Prob. of occupancy and repro.
    }


# Define observation matrix
# Order of indices: true state, time, observed state
for (t in 1:T) {
    p[1,t,1] <- 1
    p[1,t,2] <- 0
    p[1,t,3] <- 0
    p[2,t,1] <- 1-p2[t]
    p[2,t,2] <- p2[t]
    p[2,t,3] <- 0
    p[3,t,1] <- p3[1,t]
    p[3,t,2] <- p3[2,t]
    p[3,t,3] <- p3[3,t]
    }


# State-space likelihood
# State equation: model of true states (z)
for (s in 1:R) {
    z[s] ~ dcat(phi[s,])
    }


# Observation equation
for (s in 1:R) {
    for (t in 1:T) {
        y[s,t] ~ dcat(p[z[s],t,])
        } #t
    } #s


# Derived quantities
for (s in 1:R) {
    occ1[s] <- equals(z[s], 1)
    occ2[s] <- equals(z[s], 2)
    occ3[s] <- equals(z[s], 3)
    }
n.occ[1] <- sum(occ1[]) # Sites in state 1
n.occ[2] <- sum(occ2[]) # Sites in state 2
n.occ[3] <- sum(occ3[]) # Sites in state 3
}
",fill=TRUE)
sink()
```

We recycle the remaining "ingredients" for the call to bugs() below.

```
# Call WinBUGS from R (BRT 1 min)
out2 <- bugs(win.data, inits, params, "model2.txt", n.chains = nc,
    n.thin = nt, n.iter = ni, n.burnin = nb, debug =TRUE, bugs.directory =
    bugs.dir, working.directory = getwd())
```

```
# Summarize posteriors
print(out2, dig = 2)
            mean    sd   2.5%    25%    50%    75%  97.5%   Rhat  n.eff
p2[1]       0.76  0.19   0.32   0.65   0.80   0.92   0.99   1.01    440
p2[2]       0.57  0.21   0.17   0.41   0.57   0.72   0.94   1.00   3000
p2[3]       0.16  0.16   0.00   0.05   0.12   0.23   0.58   1.00   1600
p2[4]       0.34  0.20   0.04   0.19   0.32   0.47   0.78   1.01    670
p2[5]       0.27  0.21   0.01   0.09   0.22   0.39   0.78   1.00   3000
p3[1,1]     0.53  0.17   0.20   0.40   0.53   0.65   0.84   1.00   1300
p3[1,2]     0.33  0.17   0.06   0.20   0.32   0.44   0.68   1.00   3000
p3[1,3]     0.41  0.19   0.08   0.26   0.40   0.55   0.80   1.00   3000
p3[1,4]     0.53  0.22   0.11   0.36   0.54   0.70   0.91   1.00   3000
p3[1,5]     0.37  0.25   0.02   0.16   0.34   0.55   0.87   1.00   3000
p3[2,1]     0.37  0.16   0.09   0.25   0.36   0.48   0.70   1.00   3000
p3[2,2]     0.14  0.12   0.00   0.04   0.10   0.19   0.44   1.00   1300
p3[2,3]     0.15  0.13   0.00   0.04   0.11   0.21   0.48   1.00   1000
p3[2,4]     0.24  0.19   0.01   0.09   0.20   0.36   0.69   1.00   3000
p3[2,5]     0.31  0.23   0.01   0.11   0.27   0.47   0.82   1.00   2000
p3[3,1]     0.10  0.09   0.00   0.03   0.08   0.14   0.35   1.00   3000
p3[3,2]     0.54  0.18   0.20   0.41   0.54   0.67   0.86   1.00   2000
p3[3,3]     0.45  0.19   0.11   0.30   0.44   0.58   0.82   1.01    600
p3[3,4]     0.23  0.19   0.01   0.08   0.19   0.33   0.69   1.00   3000
p3[3,5]     0.32  0.23   0.01   0.13   0.28   0.48   0.83   1.00   3000
r           0.58  0.17   0.27   0.47   0.59   0.70   0.91   1.00   3000
psi         0.40  0.10   0.22   0.33   0.40   0.47   0.62   1.00   3000
n.occ[1]   24.13  2.94  17.00  22.00  25.00  26.00  29.00  1.00   1100
n.occ[2]    6.33  2.48   1.00   5.00   6.00   8.00  11.03  1.00   3000
n.occ[3]    9.54  2.90   5.00   7.00   9.00  11.00  16.00  1.00   1900
```

Many parameters are estimated with little precision, but we see that occupancy (psi) and the conditional (on occupancy) probability of successful reproduction (r) are estimated at higher values under model 2 than under model 1. We could also specify a model with covariate effects (Julian date in our data set) on these time-dependent parameters, but leave this for the exercises.

The multistate occupancy model can be extended in two important ways. First, the generalization to more than two occupancy states is straightforward. Second, a dynamic multistate occupancy model has been developed recently (MacKenzie et al., 2009). Similar to the multistate models of Chapter 9, these models estimate state transition probabilities. Technically, the state transition is an element of the state equation and can be included in WinBUGS by using a categorical distribution. The parameters of the state transition matrix may then be, for example, the probability that a site with reproduction in year t is abandoned in year $t + 1$, or the probability that a site without reproduction in year t produces young in year $t + 1$. Dynamic multistate occupancy models are conceptually analogous to multievent models (Pradel, 2005).

13.7 SUMMARY AND OUTLOOK

We have introduced site-occupancy models, a class of hierarchical logistic regression model for occurrence data that jointly estimate detection probability to account for imperfect detection. Occurrence may be a proxy for the local metapopulation abundance, which is the focus of interest in the binomial mixture model of the previous chapter. Alternatively, occupancy may be the focus of interest such as in species distribution models, disease ecology, or metapopulation ecology. When detection of occupied sites (patches) is not perfect, the extent of occurrence of species will be underestimated and covariate relationships will be estimated with bias, regardless of whether there are patterns in detection probability or whether it is constant. Given suitable data (occurrence observations that are replicated in both space and time within a short period), occupancy probability can be estimated separately from detection probability, and covariate relationships with either parameter can be estimated, even when the same covariate is affecting both occurrence and detection. Knowing typical values of detection probability and how the latter varies with measurable covariates can be invaluable for the planning of surveys.

We have furthermore illustrated a dynamic, multiseason version of a site-occupancy model (MacKenzie et al., 2003; Royle and Kéry, 2007), which is precisely a generalization of a classical metapopulation model for incidence, colonization, and extinction probability that accounts for imperfect detection; imperfect detection biases virtually all parameter estimates in classical metapopulation models unless corrected for. Static and especially dynamic site-occupancy models have increasingly been used to correct for variation in effort over long time scales when studying changes in species distributions from historic data (Altwegg et al., 2008; Moritz et al., 2008; Tingley and Beissinger, 2009; Tingley et al., 2009; Kéry et al., 2010b; van Strien et al., 2011). We have also illustrated another important generalization, the multistate site-occupancy model (Royle and Link, 2005; Nichols et al., 2007). These models allow one to simultaneously deal with detection error and state uncertainty and thus considerably extend the range of possible applications of this model class. For instance, Miller et al. (2011) use multistate occupancy models to deal with false-negative (detection) *and* false-positive (misclassification) errors in occupancy data.

Further extensions of the basic model include Royle and Nichols (2003), who describe a heterogeneity site-occupancy model that allows one, under certain conditions, to estimate the mean abundance at a collection of sites from detection/nondetection data alone (see also Dorazio (2007); Conroy et al. (2008) for a Bayesian implementation). In an exciting new development, Bled et al. (2011b) describe complex, spatially explicit, dynamic occupancy model for the spread of invasive species. Roth and Amrhein (2009) have developed a site-occupancy model to estimate local survival and recruitment from territory occupancy data with unmarked animals. Dorazio and Royle (2005) have described a multispecies site-occupancy model that enables one, among other things, to estimate species richness for each site (i.e., community size) as well as for the collection of sites (i.e., metacommunity size). The Bayesian implementation of this model using data augmentation (Dorazio et al., 2006) has been very seminal for community studies; see series of papers by Kéry and Royle (2008, 2009), Russell et al. (2009), Zipkin et al. (2009, 2010), and Ruiz-Gutiérrez and Zipkin (2011). This model has been extended to open population by Kéry et al. (2009; not including dynamics) and Dorazio et al. (2010; including occurrence dynamics); Yamaura et al. (2011) developed a version of the open multispecies site-occupancy model with the Royle-Nichols (2003) formulation of detection heterogeneity. In addition, MacKenzie et al. (2009) developed a multistate, dynamic occupancy model, which appears to be a very general and unifying model—most other occupancy models can be described as special cases of this overarching model. In summary, site-occupancy models represent an extremely powerful and flexible class of models for inference about populations of animals and plants.

13.8 EXERCISES

1. In the blue bug example, fit a "behavioral response" effect, that is, fit a separate detection probability dependent on whether the species has been detected ever before at a site or not. Hint, you can use the following R code to generate the "seen-before" covariate matrix. How do you interpret the results? Would you use the behavioral response model for inference about the system behind the blue bug data set? Discuss.

```
# Generate a 'seen-before' covariate
sb <- array(NA, dim = dim(y))
for (i in 1:27){
    for (j in 1:6){
        sb[i,j] <- max(y[i, 1:(j-1)])
        }
    }
sb[is.na(y)] <- 0                    # Impute 'irrelevant' zeroes
```

2. In the dynamic occupancy model of Section 13.5.1, ignore the detection process and aggregate the temporal within-day replicates. Adapt the WinBUGS code to fit a conventional metapopulation model and see

how the estimated quantities are biased; see also Ruiz-Gutiérrez and Zipkin (2011).

3. Fit a multiseason, nondynamic version of the site-occupancy model to the burnet data. That is, treat days as a group and model occupancy independent between successive days (similar to how we modeled abundance in Section 12.3). In this way, you commit some pseudoreplication, but treating days as a group allows you to model occupancy as a function of temporally varying covariates.

4. Site-occupancy models represent the only currently available species distribution modeling framework that can estimate true, rather than apparent distributions (Kéry et al., 2010a; Kéry, 2011b). However, modeling occurrence and observation jointly can be difficult in marginal data situations. Devise a simulation study, where you vary the number of sites, occupancy, and detection probability as well as the number of replicate visits per site to see that in small-data situations, occupancy estimates will be biased high, and sometimes severely so. Do so in a model with constant detection and occurrence probability. Hint: this is a somewhat larger project.

5. In the multistate occupancy model, add an effect of Julian date on detection probability of hooting adults and begging young, that is, p_2, $p_{3,2}$ and $p_{3,3}$. Do not forget to standardize the covariate.

Concluding Remarks

We have given an overview of the Bayesian analysis of models for population analysis using WinBUGS. By population analysis, we mean the analysis of data from populations and communities, especially data on distribution and abundance, and the four vital rates governing their dynamics: survival, recruitment, immigration, and emigration probability. We almost always use hierarchical models, which are fitted very naturally in a Bayesian framework of inference using the simple and flexible BUGS language. In particular, hierarchical models enable direct modeling of the observation process, thereby accounting for false-negative observation errors. We have extensively used capture–recapture-type models, which achieve a partitioning of an observed response into one component describing the ecological process of interest and another representing its imperfect observation. In this concluding chapter, we first reflect on the power and beauty of hierarchical models (Section 14.1) and on the importance of accounting for the observation process in any inference about populations and communities from ecological field data (Section 14.2). We continue with remarks on possible future avenues for population analysis (Section 14.3) and finally emphasize some of the applications in which rigorous population analyses appear to be particularly important (Section 14.4).

14.1 THE POWER AND BEAUTY OF HIERARCHICAL MODELS

The concept of hierarchical models runs as a common thread throughout this book. In this respect, we owe a great debt to Royle and Dorazio (2008), who have laid much of the intellectual groundwork for us and from which many code examples are taken. As we have seen many times in our book, the use of hierarchical models, especially when fitted in WinBUGS, has many advantages; some of which we discuss in the following.

14.1.1 Hierarchical Models Make the Fitting of Complex Statistical Models Easier

Hierarchical models express the observed data as a result of a sequence of linked, simpler probabilistic systems, with each random variable being dependent on the outcome of the random variable preceding it in the hierarchy of a model. A neat example is that for the dynamic occupancy model (Section 13.5). It consists of three linked Bernoulli random variables, or logistic regressions, describing the initial occupancy state, occupancy dynamics, and the observation process, respectively. Ignoring site indices, this model can be written as follows:

Random variable 1 (initial state): $z_1 \sim \text{Bernoulli}(\psi_1)$
Random variable 2 (state dynamics): $z_{t+1} \mid z_t \sim \text{Bernoulli}(z_t \phi_t + (1 - z_t)\gamma_t)$
Random variable 3 (observation process): $y_t \mid z_t \sim \text{Bernoulli}(z_t p_t)$

The hierarchical model decomposes a complicated stochastic system into a sequence of three dependent subprocesses. In this way, a complex model becomes much easier to understand and fit. The beauty of hierarchical models lies in the almost unbelievable simplicity when a complex model is decomposed into its individual component models. The entire model may be difficult to understand and fit for an ecologist, but each individual submodel is really simple. For example, the incorporation of additional complexity, such as covariate or random effects, is straightforward.

14.1.2 Hierarchical Models Foster a Synthetic Understanding of a Large Array of Models

A big advantage of the hierarchical specification of complex models in population analysis is that it fosters a whole new and synthetic understanding of a vast array of models, which may often be thought of as being unrelated. For instance, in the capture–recapture literature a big divide is typically made between models for closed and models for open populations. However, when written as a hierarchical model, we cannot avoid recognizing the similarities rather than seeing the differences between them. For instance, Table 14.1a shows the hierarchical specification of a closed-population model for abundance estimation implemented by data augmentation (Chapter 6) and that for an open population (dynamic occupancy model, Section 13.5).

In both the closed- and the open-population model, the initial state is modeled as a Bernoulli trial with a success parameter (ψ_1). In the closed model, $z_1 = 1$ denotes a genuinely existing individual, whereas in the open model $z_1 = 1$ denotes an occupied site. The description of the state dynamics in the closed model is simply that there is none: the state at occasion $t + 1$ is identical to the state at occasion t. In contrast, in the open model, the state at occasion $t + 1$ is a function of the state at occasion t and parameters for survival (ϕ) and colonization (γ). Finally, the observation process is again identical in both models: at time t, all existing individuals or occupied sites flip a coin to determine whether they are detected or not.

As another example, Table 14.1b shows the relationships between two superficially very different models, one an implicit and the other an explicit hierarchical model (Royle and Dorazio 2008). The first is a

TABLE 14.1　Two examples of The Power of Hierarchical Models to Clarify the Relationships among Model Classes

(a) Conceptual Similarity between a Closed-Population Model (see Chapter 6) and an Open-Population Model (dynamic occupancy model; see Chapter 13)*

Submodel	Closed-Population Model	Open-Population Model
Initial State	$z_1 \sim \text{Bernoulli}(\psi_1)$	$z_1 \sim \text{Bernoulli}(\psi_1)$
State Dynamics	$z_{t+1} \mid z_t = z_t$	$z_{t+1} \mid z_t \sim \text{Bernoulli}(z_t \phi_t + (1 - z_t)\gamma_t)$
Observation Process	$y_t \mid z_t \sim \text{Bernoulli}(z_t p_t)$	$y_t \mid z_t \sim \text{Bernoulli}(z_t p_t)$

(b) Conceptual Similarity between a State-Space Model (see Chapter 5) and the Cormack–Jolly–Seber Model (see Chapter 7)**

Submodel	State-Space Model	CJS Model
Initial State	$N_1 \sim f(\theta_1)$	$z_1 = 1$
State Dynamics	$N_{t+1} \mid N_t \sim g(N_t, \theta_2)$	$z_{t+1} \mid z_t \sim g(z_t, \theta_2)$
Observation Process	$y_t \mid N_t \sim h(N_t, \theta_3)$	$y_t \mid z_t \sim h(z_t, \theta_3)$

*t indexes occasions in the closed-population model and primary occasions in the open-population model. To make all parameters in the latter identifiable, data are required from secondary occasions during a period of closure.
**To clarify the difference between states in the two models, the relative abundance state at time t in the state-space model is denoted as N_t, whereas the "alive" state in the CJS model is denoted as z_t.

state-space model for a single time series of population counts (Chapter 5) and the second is the Cormack–Jolly–Seber (CJS) model for multiple time series of survival events (Chapter 7). The initial state is modeled using a distribution f with parameter θ_1 in the state-space model. In contrast, the initial state is not modeled in the CJS model but is 1 by definition because the CJS model conditions on initial capture. In both models, for all later time steps, the state at time $t + 1$ is a random variable that depends on the state at time t and on parameter θ_2 via a distribution g. For g, we use a normal distribution with a mean and a variance parameter for the state-space model and a Bernoulli distribution with a parameter representing the success probability for the CJS model. Finally, as a description of the observation error at time t, we use a distribution h, which depends on the true state at time t and on parameter θ_3. The statistical description of the observation process is another normal for the state space and a Bernoulli distribution for the CJS model. Similar schemes can be devised for all hierarchical models.

Hence, a hierarchical specification of models for population analysis emphasizes the similarities among models that appear to be very different at a first glance. We believe that the unified perspective on a large number of models provided by their hierarchical description will be very beneficial for your population modeling. Moreover, we have seen at many places how the specification of a model in the BUGS language is almost a direct translation of a hierarchical model described in algebra, as in Table 14.1. Thus, we believe that statistical modeling in BUGS will foster in you a more synthetic understanding of large classes of models: they may *appear* quite different, but in fact they share many commonalities!

Throughout this book, we have emphasized the algebraic description of hierarchical models. There is another, very general way to describe hierarchical models: by directed acyclic graphs (DAGs; Spiegelhalter, 1998). We have not used DAGs in this book, except for Fig. 11.3, but if you have experience in reading and drawing DAGs, it can be very enlightening to draw them for the models in this book (R. A. Hutchinson, pers. comm.). This will also allow you to see the surprising similarities among these models.

14.1.3 Hierarchical Models Lead to Cleaner Thinking

We believe that hierarchical models foster a unified way of thinking about statistical modeling. For instance, for ecological field data, it becomes completely natural to think in terms of a hierarchical model that separates the ecological and the observation processes. Indeed, after a while of being in that mode of thinking, it becomes hard *not* to partition in your mind any kind of field data into the result of an ecological process and that of an observation process. So, indirectly, working with WinBUGS can be an act of intellectual hygiene that leads to a more mechanistic thinking about the systems we study.

14.1.4 Hierarchical Models Lead to a Step-Up Approach in Tackling a Problem

Although conceptually easy, fitting hierarchical models using WinBUGS can be complicated in practice and many things can go wrong. Hence, we always favor a modeling strategy where we start from a simple model and increasingly add in complexity until we are at the desired model (see Appendix 1, tip 28). This step-up approach may force on us a whole new way of thinking, where we start thinking about a problem in a very simplified way. Once we have understood the problem in that setting, we incrementally add in more complexity until we (hopefully) understand the model we wanted to fit to start with. We believe that this is exactly the way in which successful science should work: we must first understand a simple version of a problem before we can go on to try and understand the more complex ones. Often, we see people who immediately want to attack a very complex version of a problem, without first even trying to understand its simpler versions. We believe that this is a recipe for failure. Thus, modeling in WinBUGS trains us to think in a more disciplined way about doing science in general.

14.1.5 What Kind of Hierarchical Model? Primary Model Selection in WinBUGS

One of the aims of this book is to provide an accessible entry point to the literature on a large number of models that are useful for population analysis and to illustrate their implementation in WinBUGS. So which one in this bewildering multitude of models should we choose to answer our ecological questions? Obviously, the best choice among these models will depend on many things, including modeling objectives, data, sampling design and the assumptions one is willing to make.

The first criterion for primary model choice should always be our scientific or management questions, that is, the *objectives of the model*. This cannot be stressed enough: we ought to be very clear about the objective behind every modeling exercise. For example, prediction may require quite a different model than explanation. Further, model choice may depend on how similar the inferences (for instance, the estimate of the effect of a management intervention) under different models are and whether these differences are of practical importance given the modeling objectives. It may be reasonable to choose a second-best model when the inferences are practically identical to those under the best model and when the second-best model has other advantages (e.g., runs much faster).

Second, model choice depends on the data at hand. For instance, if data are available to estimate detection probability in a time series of counts, we would not use the rather simplistic description of the observation process of the models in Chapter 5. Rather, we might use a binomial or other suitable distribution to explicitly model false-negative detection errors (see Section 1.3). If no such information on detection probability is available, the implicit hierarchical models in Chapters 4 and 5 may be the best that can be done. Similarly, occurrence data such as territory occupancy or species distribution could be modeled using a variant of a binomial GLM (Chapters 3 and 4). Such an approach balls up in a single parameter the probabilities of occupancy and detection (Kéry et al. 2010a, Kéry 2011b). However, often we *do* have extra information on the observation process, for example, replicated detection or nondetection observations within a short time period. If this is the case, we find it hard to understand how one would choose *not* to jointly model the ecological process and the observation process in an explicit hierarchical model (i.e., a site-occupancy model, Chapter 13).

Sampling design is intimately linked to the previous point as are the assumptions that we may want or have to make. Often, we must make assumptions to compensate for deficiencies in the design and the data. For instance, absent data that are directly informative about the observation process, we must make strong assumptions about detection probability, for example, that it is constant on average or even that it is equal to 1.

Such primary decisions in the selection among broad classes of models require a great flexibility in our modeling and indeed an "organic" approach to statistical modeling, where the model can be tailored exactly to one's needs. Fitting hierarchical models in WinBUGS typically gives one this flexibility.

14.1.6 Secondary Model Selection: Hierarchical Models and Variable Selection

Once we have made the primary decision about the general class of model for population analysis, there are additional decisions to take, for instance about the types or the form of covariates to incorporate. These secondary modeling decisions are often called model selection. Over the last decades, Burnham and Anderson (e.g., 2002) have been very influential in population ecology and management with their ideas about model building by a certain form of model selection. In a way, they advocate the opposite approach from the one that we are almost forced to adopt when using WinBUGS. Burnham and Anderson argue that, first, one must think hard about a problem and come up with a set of models that each represent a distinct biological hypothesis that we want to compare and test. Second, one must fit exactly these models to the data and use the Akaike's information criterion (AIC) as a referee as to which model explains the observed data best.

We endorse this general strategy of doing science and like the emphasis on a priori thinking, instead of rushing into the data and doing data dredging. However, it appears to us that a strict adherence to the recipe of Burnham and Anderson is difficult with complicated models regardless of whether they are fitted in a frequentist or Bayesian way. As described in Section 14.1.4, there is much heuristic value in an incremental model building strategy. Thus, with WinBUGS, we are almost forced to do something that *resembles* data dredging, in which our fitting of a desired ultimate model often means that we have to fit several similar neighboring models as well. We believe that the ideal of Burnham and Anderson could still be upheld when a set of different a priori hypotheses are formulated before the start of the modeling exercise.

When teaching WinBUGS workshops to ecologists, one of the biggest disappointments we see is always the lack of an automated variable selection strategy that can be as easily implemented as AIC in maximum likelihood analyses. In hierarchical models, use of the standard DIC (Spiegelhalter et al., 2002) is controversial (Celeux et al., 2006) or downright wrong for at least some hierarchical models (Millar, 2009)—and most interesting models in this book are hierarchical. Furthermore, Bayesian variable selection is more involved and computationally demanding (O'Hara and Sillanpää, 2009).

The lack of an automated variable selection procedure can be seen as a good or as a bad thing. Of course, we would like to be able to filter through a large number of hierarchical models and have an easily computed criterion to help us pick the most useful one. On the other hand, we believe that the very ease with which AIC does variable selection has defeated part of the intentions of its advocates, Burnham and Anderson: since model comparison is made so easy, AIC may often lead to more rather than less data dredging. So, it may be that only when variable selection is difficult, do we actually think hard about which models we want to fit!

14.1.7 Hierarchical Models and MARK, unmarked, E-SURGE, and PRESENCE

Hierarchical models can be fitted using frequentist and Bayesian methods. We believe that the choice between a frequentist and a Bayesian analysis of a model should in a large part be made on the basis of how practical it is and how well each one meets the objectives of the modeling. In this sense, we argue for a pragmatic choice between frequentist and Bayesian approaches (Little, 2006; Gelman and Hill, 2007; Gelman, 2008). Our own preference for Bayesian modeling using WinBUGS is, first and foremost, due to the fact that the BUGS language and the automated generation of MCMC algorithms in WinBUGS (and OpenBUGS or JAGS) have given us such a remarkable modeling freedom, one we have never experienced with any other software.

So, what about other frequentist software to fit population models as illustrated in this book? Examples of such software include MARK (White and Burnham, 1999), the new R package unmarked (Fiske and Chandler, 2011), E-SURGE (Choquet et al., 2009b), and PRESENCE (Hines, 2006). These useful software programs allow you to fit a very large number of models, many of them hierarchical, at least in concept (see Section 2.8). For instance, somebody commented to us that software MARK, along with its free and constantly evolving, excellent online manual of E. Cooch and G. White (www.phidot.org/software/mark/docs/book), is a competitor with our book or the way we do population modeling. We are not convinced that this is true. MARK, as well as unmarked, E-SURGE, and PRESENCE, represent tremendous endeavors that have done and continue to do an immeasurable service to the community of population ecologists to enhance the level of analyses that are possible and are conducted. For instance, MARK has about 100 different kinds of models that can be fitted by click and point techniques, and it has a reasonably unified layout of data entry and model building.

We think that MARK, unmarked, E-SURGE and PRESENCE and the modeling advocated in our book serve different audiences and targets:

for first-timers in population modeling or for someone who wants to fit some sort of standard model (which may be very sophisticated!), MARK or one of these other packages surely represent an ideal tool. By contrast, for users who want to fit nonstandard models, combine different models (integration of information) or use prior information, WinBUGS is the appropriate choice.

Finally, WinBUGS gives you a new way of thinking about statistical modeling in population analysis that comes with the model specification in the BUGS language. WinBUGS frees the modeler in you and allows for a fully "organic way" of model building. In WinBUGS, quick and easy jumps can often be made to totally different model classes by simply adding a line of code or two. In contrast, in software such as MARK, the same modification to a model might require one to start the whole modeling project anew, right from reading in the data into the software. Thereby, it is easy to lose sight of the underlying similarities of many of the models (as illustrated, for instance, in Table 14.1).

14.1.8 Hierarchical Models and Study Design

Study design is an important topic that we have not covered in this book. We heard the comment that we ought to include in our book a chapter on study design. We first agreed, but in the end did not do this. The reason was simply that we thought the topic would be too daunting. We thought that the kinds of designs underlying the data featured in this book are too diverse and that we could not have said anything useful within a single book chapter. Instead, we refer to useful (non-Bayesian) books by Borchers et al. (2001), Buckland et al. (2001), Thompson (2002), and Williams et al (2002).

We would never want to downplay the importance of design in population ecology and wildlife management—actually, design is very important, and important first principles of good study design are almost always violated in ecological field studies, for example, random sampling. Nevertheless, with the great modeling freedom given by modern software such as WinBUGS, study design is perhaps a *little* less important nowadays than it was for the older, more rigid ways of analyzing data, for example, using ANOVA for designed experiments. The new modeling freedom brings with it a certain design freedom because even quite nonstandard designs can still be rigorously accommodated in a nonstandard analysis. Modeling in WinBUGS is perfect for nonstandard analyses (see also the Foreword by J. D. Nichols in Kéry, 2010).

One important design that we have only touched upon very superficially (see Section 10.8) is the robust design of sampling capture–recapture data (Pollock, 1982; Kendall et al., 1997; Williams et al., 2002). Except for demographic analyses of abundance and occurrence data from metapopulation designs (Chapters 12 and 13), we have not illustrated this powerful design in this book. The robust design can be used also for demographic analyses of single populations to get improved estimates of population size and population dynamics (e.g., Karanth et al., 2006; Link and Barker, 2010). Often, data can be collected in the robust design with little added costs in the field. The robust design should be adopted whenever possible to improve inference in population analysis.

14.2 THE IMPORTANCE OF THE OBSERVATION PROCESS

We have emphasized a hierarchical perspective on models for population analysis. This is a reflection of the hierarchical processes that generate the observed data: an ecological process, which is usually of primary interest, and a dependent observation process, which often is a mere nuisance, but must be modeled to avoid spurious inferences about the ecological process. We have also emphasized what we believe is an important conceptual distinction between explicit and implicit hierarchical models (Royle and Dorazio, 2008); the former have parameters with an explicit ecological meaning and the latter do not. Typically, the distinction between explicit and implicit hierarchical models boils down to the question of whether our model contains an explicit description of the observation process, often in the form of a binomial distribution for a response representing a count or a Bernoulli for a response representing an event.

The direct interpretation of observed data, without accounting for the observation process, can be seriously misleading, even with constant detection probability. For instance, in Section 1.3, we saw that the average count seriously underestimated the true population size of sparrows in our yard. Moreover, repeated counts suggested that population size varies, whereas in reality, the variation in the counts was merely a consequence of the chance element inherent in any count based on an observation process characterized by imperfect detection. As another example, in Section 13.2, we saw how inferences from species distribution models can be quite wrong when imperfect detection is not accounted for. These difficulties may be aggravated severely when detectability is not constant but varies in response to environmental variables (see Sections 12.2.2 and 13.3.2).

But do we really always need to model the observation process in population analyses? After all, this usually requires additional data and more complex models. For instance, we need replicated counts for inference about abundance under an binomial mixture model (Chapter 12), whereas unreplicated counts suffice to model relative abundance under a simple Poisson regression (Chapter 3) or state-space model (Chapter 5).

We believe that explicit modeling of the observation process may not always be required or even possible. Most importantly, whether our models need a component for the observation process or not depends on the goals of our modeling exercise as well as on the available data. If we are satisfied with detecting *patterns* in abundance, occurrence, or survival, for instance, and courageous enough to assume that detection probability is constant over the desired dimensions of comparison (e.g., time), then we may well forego modeling of detection probability. Alternatively, we may have measured covariates that explain some or much of the variation in detection probability, and their inclusion in the model may standardize detection probability analytically (Link and Sauer, 2002; Sauer and Link, 2002). This may often be satisfactory. However, as soon as we want to interpret our data as true distribution, abundance, or survival, as opposed to relative distribution, relative abundance, and return rates, we must model detection probability explicitly and then also need the required data to do this (Kéry et al., 2010a). There is no escaping that. Treating a response in a model as relative abundance (i.e., not estimating detection probability as part of the model) and then reporting the results as "abundance" or "population size" is misleading and can be downright dishonest. When the required data to model detection explicitly are lacking (e.g., there are no replicated counts or no individual identification), then the model chosen should be as realistic as possible, but it must always be kept in mind that the model parameters confound the ecological and the observation process. The results of such an analysis must then be reported with due caution.

Perhaps, one ought to take a model-selection view of detection probability. Its inclusion in a model is associated with a cost as we need more and different data and a more complex model, so we ought to include it in the model only when its inclusion is warranted or practically feasible from a design standpoint. However, at the start, any rigorous population analysis ought to consider inclusion of detection probability as an essential model component. Only when we have reasons to exclude it should this be done. In other words, we believe that the choice of whether or not to include in a model a component for detection probability should be an active and conscious one and must be described and justified.

These considerations are also important at the design state of a study. We think that it should become much more natural to choose a design that includes collection of data informative on the observation process. To the extent possible, each ecological field study should be as follows:

1. Try to maximize detection probability and make it stable (eliminate as much variation in detection probability as possible, for instance, among observers, sites, and over time). Responses will still be variable (see Section 1.3), but at least some noise is eliminated.

2. Record the values of covariates that could be informative about the observation process, for instance, the experience and age of an observer, wind speed, and other measures of the conditions during a survey, and adjust your response variable for the effects of these nuisance variables.
3. Choose a design that enables explicit hierarchical models to be fitted, that is, collect data that allow detection probability to be estimated.

14.3 WHERE WILL WE GO?

In our book, we have presented a broad array of models useful for population analysis, but obviously, it was not possible to include everything. Population analysis is an extremely active field at the interface of ecology and statistics, so many new developments are foreseeable in the near future. Here, we highlight some new developments which we think are particularly relevant.

14.3.1 Combination of Information

The issue of combining different kinds of information in a single model is very general and includes the combined analysis of capture–recapture and mark-recovery data (Section 9.5) and integrated population models (Chapter 11). Such combinations represent the most efficient use of all available data from a study system and result in improved precision and increased number of parameters that can be estimated. This is especially important for rare and elusive species, where the increase from an effectively very small to a moderate amount of information may yield great benefits (Schaub et al., 2007; Kéry et al., 2011). Bayesian modeling is ideally suited for making such integrated modeling available to ecologists. We are likely to see increasing numbers of studies that combine all available data into a single model.

14.3.2 Population and Community Models for Metapopulation Designs

The development of site-occupancy models (MacKenzie et al. 2002; Tyre et al., 2003; Chapter 13) has started a rush in the development of models for the analysis of population and community data from metapopulation designs—collections of sites that are surveyed repeatedly. Models have been described for different kinds of responses (e.g., detection or nondetection data, counts), diverse ecological states (e.g., distribution, abundance, species richness), and static and dynamic systems. Metapopulation designs are extremely common especially in biodiversity monitoring, but are frequently adopted also in ecological studies, and many new developments are likely for this kind of models in the near future. One example of a novel idea that combines metapopulation designs and the issue of combining information is an integrated metapopulation model (Conroy et al., 2008). Their model merges in a single analysis expensive data that directly inform on abundance (capture–recapture data), with cheaper data (detection/nondetection data), which can be collected over large areas for cheaper money.

14.3.3 Spatial Models

Spatial models describe the spatial dependence in a response or parameters due to neighborhood relations. Recent developments in statistics and computing increasingly allow modeling spatial relationships explicitly, rather than assuming them away or perhaps trying to eliminate them by careful study design. One example is occupancy modeling, where Royle and Dorazio (2008), Hines et al. (2010), and Bled et al. (2011) have described models where the occurrence of a species in one pixel, and possibly the associated colonization and extinction probabilities, depends on the state of neighboring pixels. This appears like an important and very obvious way of taking occupancy modeling to the next level of realism and ecological relevance. The same can also be undertaken for other types of spatially indexed data, for instance, for modeling abundance (Royle et al., 2007; Webster et al., 2008; Post van der Burg et al., 2011) and survival (Royle and Dubovsky, 2001; Saracco et al., 2010). We are certain to see a great increase of this type of models in the future.

One special case of spatial models is spatially explicit capture–recapture models (Efford, 2004; Borchers and Efford, 2008; Royle and Young, 2008; see also Section 6.5). Essentially, all individual capture–recapture data are spatially indexed. Explicitly taking into account this spatial information allows to obtain less-biased estimators for quantities such as density or survival (Gardner et al., 2010) and to directly estimate other interesting quantities, such as the radius of a home-range or a dispersal kernel. This is a very active field of research with much to hope for in the near future.

14.3.4 Relaxing the Closure Assumption

Many ecological models of the capture–recapture type rely on the closure assumption: they assume that replicated observations can be made over some short time interval, when the system state is approximately constant. Obviously, no population in the field is ever entirely constant, so this assumption can only ever hold approximately. Violation of the closure assumption must be common and has various biasing effects on estimators of models that assume closure (Kendall, 1999; Rota et al., 2009).

Development of study designs and of models that do not need the closure assumption is therefore interesting. For counts from metapopulation designs, Dail and Madsen (2011) have developed a Jolly–Seber kind of binomial mixture model. Their model yields estimates of the population dynamics (abundance, survival, and recruitment) from temporally and spatially replicated counts that do not conform to the robust design (i.e., there is no replication for a site and year combination, say). This model is a great conceptual advantage and similar extensions may be possible in other situations.

14.3.5 More Flexible Covariate Modeling

Modeling of nonlinear covariate relationships by using polynomials (e.g., Section 4.2) often gives sufficient flexibility. However, in many cases, more flexible covariate modeling is desirable, for instance, in the exploratory phase of an analysis, where one would like to "let the data speak for themselves". Splines, general additive modeling and boosted regression trees have recently been developed within models illustrated in this book (Gimenez et al., 2006a,b; Collier et al., 2011; R. A. Hutchinson, personal communication). This is likely to become an ongoing development. Similarly, simpler parametric assumptions like the Poisson for the state in the binomial mixture models may be replaced with more flexible "nonparametric" assumptions (Dorazio et al., 2008).

14.3.6 Accounting for Misclassification Error

A final topic we would like to highlight is the explicit modeling of misclassification. This had long had to be assumed away in capture–recapture models because simultaneous modeling of false-negative and false-positive errors proved too challenging. However, in recent years, there has been a surge of papers that deal with false-positive errors in addition to false-negative errors, for instance, in multistate models (Kendall et al., 2003; Pradel, 2005), for data from genetic analyses (Wright et al., 2009; Yoshizaki et al., 2009; Link et al., 2010) and in site-occupancy models (Royle and Link, 2006; Miller et al., 2011).

14.4 THE IMPORTANCE OF POPULATION ANALYSIS FOR CONSERVATION AND MANAGEMENT

In Chapter 1, we have claimed, perhaps with a little wink of our eyes, that for us the following equation is valid to a good approximation:

$$\text{Ecology} = \text{Population ecology} = \text{Population analysis}$$

The reason for this belief of ours is the central conceptual and practical importance of the population for all of ecology. In addition, population analysis is a pillar in many applied branches of ecology, such as wildlife and fisheries management and especially conservation biology. A rigorous scientific approach to conservation must be based on quantitative evidence and rely on the best available assessments of quantities such as distribution, abundance, species richness, population trend, and extinction probability or sustainability of a given harvest level (Caughley, 1994; Norris, 2004). These and other demographic quantities must be estimated, as well as possible, along with a full assessment in their uncertainty.

Unfortunately, the scientific standards of decision making in the arena of wildlife management and conservation in many countries are still extremely poor. Rather than basing decisions on hard evidence and rigorous science, unquantified claims and beliefs of stakeholders may be the sole basis for decisions. As an example, in 2011, the Swiss parliament approved of a change in the law that governs the control of predators of ungulates, such as wolf, bear, and lynx. It is now planned that complaints by one party of stakeholders, recreational hunters, about a decline in ungulate stocks be enough to trigger culling of these predators. The implementation details of the new law have yet to be worked out, but it is very likely that the decision to take action against these large predators will not be based on scientific standards of evidence, such as any scientifically defensible population analysis. In most Swiss cantons, there is not even a rigorous population monitoring of ungulates in place of the kind that is now commonplace for many taxa across Europe, including birds, plants, butterflies, and snails in Switzerland (Weber et al., 2004). Thus, even in countries such as Switzerland we still have a far way to go in making wildlife management evidence-based, rigorous, and scientifically defensible.

Recurring themes in population analyses for conservation biology are small sample sizes, data sets collected under nonstandard sampling designs or with no specified design at all, disparate data types, multiple levels of uncertainty, and stochasticity. As seen throughout this book, Bayesian population analysis using WinBUGS is extremely well suited for these challenges. Bayesian inference is exact for any sample size (Little, 2006). The remarkable modeling freedom given to the ecologist when using WinBUGS lets him or her adapt a model very flexibly to many idiosyncrasies of such data sets. The integration of information from disparate data types occurs very naturally (Chapter 11). Furthermore, multiple levels of uncertainty can be modeled flexibly using random effects. Thereby, all known components of uncertainty can be incorporated into an analysis and the combined uncertainty is propagated into all estimates and forecasts. Thus, we sincerely hope that Bayesian population analysis using WinBUGS not only makes you enjoy population modeling even more but also that it leads to better conclusions in science and to better decisions in wildlife management and conservation.

A List of WinBUGS TRICKS

The appendix provides a list of tips that hopefully allow you to love WinBUGS more unconditionally. It is based on an appendix in the book *Introduction to WinBUGS for Ecologists* by Marc Kéry (2010), but also includes new stuff. We would suggest you skim over the list when you start working with WinBUGS and then refer back to it later as necessary.

1. Do read the manual: WinBUGS may not have the best documentation available for a software, but its manual is nevertheless very useful. Be sure to at least skim over most of it once when you start getting into WinBUGS, so you may remember that the manual has something to say about a particular topic when you need it. Do not forget the sections entitled "Tricks: Advanced Use of the BUGS Language" and "Tips and Troubleshooting".
2. Always begin from a template: When starting a new analysis, *always* start from a template of a similar analysis. Only ever try to write an analysis from scratch if you want to test yourself.
3. Make a clear distinction between BUGS and R code: We use the R function `sink()` to write into the R working directory (which you can set yourself using `setwd()`) a text file containing the model description in the BUGS language. We find it practical to have all our codes in a single document. Here is a sketch example of how this looks like (you see this kind of code for each example where we use WinBUGS in the book).

```
# Define the model in the BUGS language
sink("modelname.txt")
cat("
    model {          # BUGS model starts on this line

    # Priors
    some priors
```

```
# Likelihood
for (i in 1:n){
    some description of the likelihood
    }
    }                    # BUGS model ends with this line
",fill = TRUE)
sink()
```

Here, R code is left-aligned and BUGS code is indented one level and in bold. We neither show this indentation nor the bold type in the book, but show it here to clarify how everything inside the two quotes after "cat" and before ",fill" is BUGS code and everything outside these two quotes is R code. You have to be totally clear about which part of the code is in the BUGS language and which is in the R language. This may be a little confusing at first, especially because the two languages are quite similar: R is a dialect of S and BUGS is strongly inspired by S. Moreover, this way of writing the BUGS model sometimes seems to cause problems when using the R editor Tinn-R (see trick 17).

4. Give initial values: The wise choice of initial values can be the key to success or failure of an analysis in WinBUGS. With complex models, WinBUGS needs to start the Markov chains not too far away from their stationary distribution or it will crash or not even start to update. Of course, the requirement to start the chains close to the solution goes counter the requirement to start them at dispersed places in order to assess convergence, so some reasonable intermediate choice is important.

5. Do not select initial values that contradict the priors: Initial values must not be outside of the possible range of a parameter. For instance, negative initial values for a parameter that has prior mass only for positive values (such as a variance) will cause WinBUGS to crash and so do initial values outside of the range of a uniform prior.

6. Only provide initial values for quantities that appear in the model: Otherwise the "incompatible copy" error may appear.

7. Do not provide initial values for fixed elements of a vector-valued parameter: Sometimes some elements of a vector-valued parameter are known or fixed at a certain value. Then, they are no longer a parameter that is estimated and initial values must not be given for them. An example is a two-way fixed-effects ANOVA, where you must set to zero the effect of one level (e.g., the first) of one factor to avoid overparameterisation. In this case, no initial value is required for that effect. For a factor beta with four levels, the first of which is set to zero, you can do this as follows: beta = c(NA, rnorm(3)).

8. In your prior choice, be ignorant, but not too ignorant: When you want your Bayesian inference to be dominated by your data and choose

priors intended to be vague, do not specify too much ignorance, otherwise traps may result or convergence may not be achieved. For instance, do not specify the limits of a uniform prior or the variance of a normal prior to be too wide.

9. How to deal with missing values (NAs): In WinBUGS, NAs are dealt with less automatically than in conventional stats programs with which you are likely familiar; hence, it is important to know how to deal with them: briefly, missing responses (i.e., missing y s) are not a problem, but NAs in the explanatory variables (the x s) need attention. A missing response is simply estimated, and indeed, adding missing responses for selected covariate values is one of the simplest ways to form predictions for desired values of explanatory variables (see Sections 5.4 and 11.5). On the other hand, a missing explanatory variable must either be replaced with some number, for example, the mean observed value for that variable, or else given some prior distribution. In general, the former is easier and should not pose a problem unless the number of missing x s is large.

10. NAs and NaNs: When dealing with data in multidimensional arrays, a very useful R package is "reshape". The newer versions of the reshape package in R 2.9 use an NaN to fill in NAs. This makes WinBUGS very unhappy—you must have NA, not NaN. In general, this is probably good to know about BUGS, and newer versions of other packages may be doing the same thing. So, if you use the `melt/cast` functions in reshape to organize data, then you will need to update your code in the newer R versions by adding `"fill=NA_real_"`. Example: `Ymat=cast(data.melt, SppCode~JulianDate~GridCellID, fun.aggregate=mean, fill=NA_real_)` (Beth Gardner, personal communication).

11. Data in arrays; think in a box (and know your box): When coding an analysis in WinBUGS, you often will have to deal with data that come in arrays, and these may have more than one dimension. For instance, when analyzing animal counts from different sites, over several years and taken at various months in a year, it may be useful to format them into a three-dimensional array. Some covariates of such an analysis will then have two or even three dimensions, too. You must then be absolutely clear about the dimensions of theses "boxes" in which your data are and not get confused by the indexing of the data. In our experience, knowing how to format data into such arrays and then not getting lost is one of the most difficult things to learn about the routine use of WinBUGS.

12. Loop order in arrays: In "serious" analyses, your modeling will often require the data to be formatted in some multidimensional array. For instance, for a multispecies version of a site-occupancy model (Dorazio and Royle, 2005), you will have at least three dimensions

corresponding to species (*i*), site (*j*), and replicate survey (*k*). It appears that how you build your array and, especially, how you loop over that array in the definition of the likelihood can make a huge difference in terms of the speed with which your Markov chains in WinBUGS evolve. You should loop over the longest dimension first and over the shortest last. For instance, if you have data from 450 sites, 100 species, and for two surveys each, then it appears best to format the data as $y[j, i, k]$ and then loop over sites (*j*) first, then over species (*i*), and finally over replicate surveys (*k*) (Beth Gardner and Elise Zipkin, personal communication).

13. Do not define things twice: Every parameter in WinBUGS can only be defined once. For instance, writing `y ~ dnorm(mu, tau)` and then adding `y[3] <- 5` will cause an error. There is a single exception to this rule, and that is the transformation of the response by some function such as the `log()` or `abs()`. So in order to conduct an analysis of a log-transformed response, you may write `log.y <- log(y)` and then `log.y ~ dnorm(mu, tau)`. Beware of inadvertently defining quantities multiple times when erroneously putting them within a loop that they do not belong.

14. Problems with WinBUGS' own logit function: We have sometimes experienced problems when using WinBUGS' own logit function, for instance, with achieving convergence. Therefore, it is often better to specify that transformation explicitly by `logit.p[i] <- log(p[i] / (1 - p[i]))`, `p[i] <- exp(logit.p[i]) / (1 + exp(logit.p[i]))` or `p[i] <- 1 / (1 + exp(-logit.p[i]))`.

15. "Stabilizing" the logit: To avoid numerical over- or underflow, you may "stabilize" the logit function by excluding extreme values (Brendan Wintle, personal communication). Here's a sketch of how to do that. The Gibbs sampling will typically get slower, but at least WinBUGS will be less likely to crash:

```
logit(psi.lim[i]) <- lpsi.lim[i]
lpsi.lim[i] <- min(999, max(-999, lpsi[i]))
lpsi[i] <- alpha.occ + beta.occ * something[i]
```

16. Truncated priors for normal random effects: Similarly, in log- or logit-normal mixtures (which we see when introducing a normal random effect into the linear predictor), you can truncate the zero-mean normal distribution, e.g., at ± 20 (Kéry and Royle, 2009): `e[i] ~ dnorm(0, tau) I(-20,20))`. This can greatly help convergence of the Markov chains.

17. Problems with Tinn-R: Users of the popular R editor Tinn-R 2.0 (or newer) may have problems writing the text file containing the BUGS model description with the `sink()` function; Tinn-R adds to that file some gibberish that will cause WinBUGS to crash. You must then

use an alternative way of writing the model file. As an example, here is a workaround that should be compatible with Tinn-R (Wesley Hochachka, personal communication):

```
modelFilename = 'model.txt'
cat("
model {
# Here is the model in BUGS language
}
",fill=TRUE, file=modelFilename)
```

An alternative solution due to Jérôme Guélat is this: The "R send" functions available in Tinn-R allow sending commands into R. However, the "(echo=TRUE)" versions of these functions should not be used when sending the sink() function and its content into R. For example: one should use "R send: selection" instead of "R send: selection (echo=TRUE)".

18. Run trial analyses first: Run very short chains first, for example, of length 12 with a burnin of 2, just to confirm that there are no coding or other errors. Only when you are satisfied that your code works and your model does what it should, increase the chain length to get a production run.

19. How to choose the burnin length: We have chosen Markov chain lengths so that convergence appears to be achieved. You may ask yourself how we decided on adequate chain lengths. The answer is simple: we always conduct trial runs first and based on that decide on the chain length for a production run of the analysis.

20. Avoid long Windows addresses: WinBUGS does not seem to like very long Windows addresses (C:\My harddisk\Important stuff\Less important stuff\ ...) for its working directory. Hence, you should not bury your WinBUGS analyses too far down in a tree hierarchy.

21. Use of native WinBUGS (1): A feature of both Kéry (2010) and this book is that WinBUGS is run exclusively from within program R. We believe that this is much more efficient than running native WinBUGS. However, with some complex models and/or large data sets, WinBUGS will be extremely slow. This may be the one exception where it is perhaps more efficient to run WinBUGS natively. You may still prepare the analysis in R as shown in this book, but only request WinBUGS to run very short Markov chains. When you set the option DEBUG = TRUE in the function bugs(), then WinBUGS will stay open after the requested number of iterations have been conducted. Then, you can request more iterations to be executed directly in WinBUGS (i.e., using the Update Tool; see chapter 4 in Kéry, 2010). You can then incrementally increase the total chain length and monitor convergence

as you go. Once convergence has been achieved, do the required additional number of iterations and save them into coda files. You must do this latter, since when exiting WinBUGS, the `bugs()` function will only import back into R the (small) number of iterations that you originally requested. When you have your valuable samples of your complex model's posterior distribution in coda files, use facilities provided by R packages `boa` or `coda` to import them into R and process them (e.g., compute Brooks–Gelman–Rubin convergence tests or posterior summaries for inference about the parameters).

22. Use of native WinBUGS (2): Use of native WinBUGS can also be helpful to diagnose why a model does not run properly or produces unexpected results. If WinBUGS has been successfully called from R, there will be three (or more) text files in your current directory. If you have specified `working.directory = getwd()` in "bugs", the files will be stored in the working directory (type `getwd()` if you are not sure which one this is). Otherwise, the files will be in a temporary directory (type `tempdir()` to see the path). The file stored first is the BUGS model and has the name that you have specified just after the `sink` command. The second file with the name `data.txt` contains the data in WinBUGS format. Finally, the third file contains the initial values in WinBUGS format and is named `inits1.txt`. If you have specified more than one chain, there will be more files of this type. To make use of native WinBUGS, you open WinBUGS, and select "file" –> "new". Then you copy the model text file, the data text file, and the text file(s) with the initial values into the empty window. You have then all information to start with a native WinBUGS analysis. See the WinBUGS documentation and chapter 4 in Kéry (2010) if you do not know how to proceed within WinBUGS.

23. Be flexible in your modeling: Try out different priors, for example, for parameters representing probabilities try a uniform(0,1), a flat normal for the logit transform, or a beta(1,1). Sometimes, one may work while another does not. Similarly, WinBUGS is very sensitive to changes in the parameterization of a model (see Gelman and Hill, 2007, for some good examples). Sometimes, one way of writing the model may work and the other does not, or one works much faster than the other.

24. Don't know how to specify the linear model? If you have trouble seeing how to specify a linear model in WinBUGS, use of the very handy R function `model.matrix()` may help. For instance, if you want to fit a model with four factors, A, B, C, and D, with all main effects and interactions A.B and C.D, do this to see how the linear model looks like: `model.matrix(~ A + B + C + D + A:B + C:D)`.

25. Scale continuous covariates: Scaling continuous covariates so that their range does not extend too far away on either side of zero, can greatly

improve mixing of the chains and often makes convergence possible (see, e.g., Section 11.4. in Kéry, 2010, and Section 3.3.1 in this book).

26. What if WinBUGS hangs after compiling? Try a restart and if that does not work, find better starting values (this tip is from the manual).

27. How to debug a WinBUGS analysis (1): If something went wrong, you need to attentively read through the entire WinBUGS log file from the top to identify the first thing that went wrong. Other errors may follow, but they may not be the actual cause of the failure.

28. How to debug a WinBUGS analysis (2): When something does not work, the simplest and best advice (see also Gelman and Hill, 2007) is to go back to a simpler version of the same model, or to a similar model, that did work, and then incrementally increase the complexity of that model until you arrive at the desired model. That is, from less complex models *sneak up* on the model you want. Indeed, when using WinBUGS, you learn to always start from the simplest version of a problem and gradually build in more complexity until you are at the level of complexity that you require. We think that this is actually a very good approach to learning in general.

29. DIC problems: Surprisingly, sometimes when getting a trap (including one with the very informative title "NIL dereference (read)"), setting the argument DIC = FALSE in the bugs() function has helped.

30. What if R chokes on too much results from WinBUGS? Sometimes the R object created by R2WinBUGS is too big for one's computer. Then, use boa or coda to read in the coda files directly and use their facilities to produce your inference in this way (e.g., convergence diagnostics, posterior summaries). Also see trick 37.

31. Check of identifiability/estimability of parameters: To see whether two or more parameters are difficult to estimate separately, you can plot the values of their Markov chains against each other.

32. Check of model adequacy: Do residual analysis, posterior predictive checks, and cross validation to see whether your model appears to be an adequate representation of the main features in the data.

33. Predictions: The estimation of unobserved or future data is a very important part of inference. One particularly useful way to examine predictions is to estimate what a response would look like for a chosen combination of values of the explanatory variables. The generation and examination of such predicted values is an important method to understand complex models (for instance, to see what a particular interaction means) and also needed to illustrate the results of an analysis, for example, as a figure in a paper.

34. Sensitivity analysis for priors: Consider assessing prior sensitivity, that is, repeat your analyses, or those for key models, with different prior specifications and see whether your inference is robust in this respect.

If it is not, then not all is lost, but you must report on that in the methods section of your paper.

35. VISTA problems: Windows VISTA has caused all sorts of "challenges" in workshops taught—be prepared! One problem was that the default BUGS directory is not the same as that stated in the preface.

36. Windows 7 problems: We experienced problems when WinBUGS is installed in a folder like "C:\Program Files\...". WinBUGS runs fine when directly installed on "C:\".

37. Use of the coda package: Some prefer to work with coda objects than with the results returned by `bugs()` as we do throughout the book. Here is some R sample code to summarize the posterior samples and to check convergence and sample autocorrelation (from Richard B. Chandler):

```
outmc <- as.mcmc.list(out)
summary(outmc)
plot(outmc, ask=TRUE)
outmc[, "alpha"]
autocorr.plot(outmc, ask=TRUE)
gelman.plot(outmc, ask=TRUE)
gelman.diag(outmc)
window(outmc, thin=5)
```

38. Free choice among the sisters: When a model does not run in WinBUGS, you may try (and succeed) in OpenBUGS or JAGS, or vice versa (Mike Meredith, personal communication).

39. Beware of the dreaded "tiefschutz and probefahrt error" (Scott Sillett, Andy Royle, personal communication): It means that your computer has been invaded by space aliens. Stay calm, shut the door, leave the building, and set it on fire.

40. Last but not least, you must have a healthy distrust in your solutions: Always inspect your inference to see whether the WinBUGS solution makes sense with respect to what you know about the modeled system. For instance, look at tables of estimates and plot predictions against observed values for quantities that can be observed. Also watch out for unexplained differences in parameter estimates between neighboring models, for example, those that differ by only one covariate or some other rather minor model characteristic. This can be an indication that something went wrong (e.g. convergence was not reached or you made a coding error) or that there are estimability problems with the model for your data set.

Two Further Useful Multistate Capture–Recapture Models

This appendix contains code for data simulation and analysis of two further multistate capture–recapture models.

2.1 ESTIMATION OF AGE-SPECIFIC SURVIVAL PROBABILITIES

2.1.1 Model Description

Age is one of the main predictors of survival in animal populations, and hence, estimation of age-specific survival is important in population analysis. Multistate models can be used to estimate age-specific survival; we define states as age classes. As a simple example, we consider the estimation of juvenile and adult survival. Juvenile survival refers to the interval from birth until the age of 1, and adult survival refers to all annual intervals after age 1. The states in this model are therefore "juvenile", "adult", and "dead". Here is the state-transition matrix:

$$
\begin{array}{c}
 \\
\text{juvenile} \\
\text{adult} \\
\text{dead}
\end{array}
\begin{array}{ccc}
\text{juvenile} & \text{adult} & \text{dead} \\
\left[\begin{array}{ccc}
0 & \phi_{\text{juv}} & 1 - \phi_{\text{juv}} \\
0 & \phi_{\text{ad}} & 1 - \phi_{\text{ad}} \\
0 & 0 & 1
\end{array}\right]
\end{array}
$$

where ϕ_{juv} is juvenile, and ϕ_{ad} is adult apparent survival probability. As always, states are ordered from top down and from left to right in the same order as above. Juvenile survival is not on the diagonal of the transition matrix because juveniles become adult if they survive their first year of life.

The vector of observed states includes "seen as juvenile", "seen as adult", and "not seen"; hence, the observation matrix is

$$
\begin{array}{c}
\\
\text{juvenile} \\
\text{adult} \\
\text{dead}
\end{array}
\begin{array}{ccc}
\text{seen as juvenile} & \text{seen as adult} & \text{not seen} \\
\left[\begin{array}{ccc}
0 & 0 & 1 \\
0 & p & 1-p \\
0 & 0 & 1
\end{array}\right]
\end{array}
$$

where p is recapture probability. The true states at time t correspond to the rows of the observation matrix in the order "alive as juvenile", "alive as adult", and "dead" from top down, and the observed states are in columns in the order "seen as juvenile", "seen as adult", and "not seen" from left to right. It may seem strange at first that juveniles cannot be seen—but if you think about it, the reason for it becomes clear juveniles may well be captured and marked, but the only possibility for them to be recaptured is in the following occasion at 1-year old and thus in the adult state.

2.1.2 Generation of Simulated Data

Let us assume that we marked young and adult little owls. Survival probability is 0.65 for adults and 0.3 for juveniles (from fledgling to their first anniversary), and recapture probability is 0.5 (note recapture refers only to adults). First, we simulate a data set, where juveniles are denoted as 1 and adults as 2.

```
# Define mean survival, transitions, recapture, as well as number of
  occasions, states, observations and released individuals
phi.juv <- 0.3
phi.ad <- 0.65
p <- 0.5
n.occasions <- 6
n.states <- 3
n.obs <- 3
marked <- matrix(NA, ncol = n.states, nrow = n.occasions)
marked[,1] <- rep(200, n.occasions)     # Juveniles
marked[,2] <- rep(30, n.occasions)      # Adults
marked[,3] <- rep(0, n.occasions)       # Dead individuals

# Define matrices with survival, transition and recapture
  probabilities
# These are 4-dimensional matrices, with
    # Dimension 1: state of departure
    # Dimension 2: state of arrival
    # Dimension 3: individual
    # Dimension 4: time
# 1. State process matrix
totrel <- sum(marked) * (n.occasions-1)
PSI.STATE <- array(NA, dim=c(n.states, n.states, totrel,
  n.occasions-1))
```

```
for (i in 1:totrel){
    for (t in 1:(n.occasions-1)){
        PSI.STATE[,,i,t] <- matrix(c(
        0, phi.juv, 1-phi.juv,
        0, phi.ad,  1-phi.ad,
        0, 0,       1              ), nrow = n.states, byrow = TRUE)
        } #t
    } #i
# 2.Observation process matrix
PSI.OBS <- array(NA, dim=c(n.states, n.obs, totrel, n.occasions-1))
for (i in 1:totrel){
    for (t in 1:(n.occasions-1)){
        PSI.OBS[,,i,t] <- matrix(c(
        0, 0, 1,
        0, p, 1-p,
        0, 0, 1       ), nrow = n.states, byrow = TRUE)
        } #t
    } #i

# Execute simulation function
sim <- simul.ms(PSI.STATE, PSI.OBS, marked)
CH <- sim$CH

# Compute vector with occasion of first capture
get.first <- function(x) min(which(x!=0))
f <- apply(CH, 1, get.first)

# Recode CH matrix: note, a 0 is not allowed in WinBUGS!
# 1 = seen alive as juvenile, 2 = seen alive as adult, 3 = not seen
rCH <- CH # Recoded CH
rCH[rCH==0] <- 3
```

We create only one data set, although we mark juveniles and adults. The capture-histories of individuals marked as juveniles start with a "1" and those of adults with a "2". If we analyzed these data with a single-state capture–recapture (CJS) model, we would have to create an individual covariate containing the age (class) at first capture (see Section 7.7).

2.1.3 Analysis of the Model

```
# Specify model in BUGS language
sink("age.bug")
cat("
model {
# --------------------------------------
# Parameters:
# phi.juv: juvenile survival probability
# phi.ad: adult survival probability
# p: recapture probability
# --------------------------------------
# States (S):
# 1 alive as juvenile
# 2 alive as adult
```

```
# 3 dead
# Observations (O):
# 1 seen as juvenile
# 2 seen as adult
# 3 not seen
# -------------------------------------

# Priors and constraints
for (t in 1:(n.occasions-1)){
    phi.juv[t] <- mean.phijuv
    phi.ad[t] <- mean.phiad
    p[t] <- mean.p
    }
mean.phijuv ~ dunif(0, 1)
mean.phiad ~ dunif(0, 1)
mean.p ~ dunif(0, 1)

# Define state-transition and observation matrices
for (i in 1:nind){
    # Define probabilities of state S(t+1) given S(t)
    for (t in f[i]:(n.occasions-1)){
        ps[1,i,t,1] <- 0
        ps[1,i,t,2] <- phi.juv[t]
        ps[1,i,t,3] <- 1-phi.juv[t]
        ps[2,i,t,1] <- 0
        ps[2,i,t,2] <- phi.ad[t]
        ps[2,i,t,3] <- 1-phi.ad[t]
        ps[3,i,t,1] <- 0
        ps[3,i,t,2] <- 0
        ps[3,i,t,3] <- 1

        # Define probabilities of O(t) given S(t)
        po[1,i,t,1] <- 0
        po[1,i,t,2] <- 0
        po[1,i,t,3] <- 1
        po[2,i,t,1] <- 0
        po[2,i,t,2] <- p[t]
        po[2,i,t,3] <- 1-p[t]
        po[3,i,t,1] <- 0
        po[3,i,t,2] <- 0
        po[3,i,t,3] <- 1
        } #t
    } #i

# State-space model likelihood
for (i in 1:nind){
    z[i,f[i]] <- Y[i,f[i]]
    for (t in (f[i]+1):n.occasions){
        # State equation: draw S(t) given S(t-1)
        z[i,t] ~ dcat(ps[z[i,t-1], i, t-1,])
        # Observation equation: draw O(t) given S(t)
        Y[i,t] ~ dcat(po[z[i,t], i, t-1,])
        } #t
    } #i
}
```

```
", fill = TRUE)
sink()


# Bundle data
bugs.data <- list(Y = rCH, f = f, n.occasions = dim(rCH)[2], nind =
    dim(rCH)[1])

# Initial values
inits <- function(){list(mean.phijuv = runif(1, 0, 1), mean.phiad =
    runif(1, 0, 1), mean.p = runif(1, 0, 1), z = ch.init(rCH, f))}

# Parameters monitored
parameters <- c("mean.phijuv", "mean.phiad", "mean.p")

# MCMC settings
ni <- 2000
nt <- 3
nb <- 1000
nc <- 3

# Call WinBUGS from R (BRT 2 min)
age <- bugs(bugs.data, inits, parameters, "age.bug", n.chains = nc,
    n.thin = nt, n.iter = ni, n.burnin = nb, debug = TRUE,
    bugs.directory = bugs.dir, working.directory = getwd())
```

The chains converge quite quickly.

```
print(age, digits = 3)
```

	mean	sd	2.5%	25%	50%	75%	97.5%	Rhat	n.eff
mean.phijuv	0.287	0.022	0.244	0.272	0.287	0.301	0.331	1.000	1000
mean.phiad	0.634	0.026	0.584	0.615	0.634	0.651	0.684	1.002	1000
mean.p	0.517	0.031	0.456	0.497	0.516	0.538	0.577	1.000	1000

The same model structure (age-dependent survival with two age classes) can be used to account for transients in the analyzed population and to estimate the probability that a newly caught individual is a transient (Pradel et al., 1997; Schaub et al., 2004b).

2.2 ACCOUNTING FOR IMMEDIATE TRAP RESPONSE

2.2.1 Model Description

One assumption of standard capture–recapture models in Chapters 7 and 9 is that all marked animals alive and available for capture at a given occasion have the same recapture probability. Sometimes this assumption is violated in a very specific way, namely that individuals captured at time $t - 1$ have a different recapture probability at time t than individuals not captured at time $t - 1$. This is called trap response or behavioral response (see Sections 6.2.3 and 7.8). If recapture probability at time t for individuals captured at $t-1$ is higher, trap response is called "trap happiness", if recapture probability is lower, then it is called "trap shyness". There are several mechanisms that may induce one or the other effect. Sometimes the effects are also induced by the sampling and do not reflect a behavioral change of the individuals. Nevertheless, trap response must be modeled; otherwise estimates for the other parameters will be biased. To account for immediate trap response, a multistate model can be used (Schaub et al., 2009). For a solution for the CJS model, see Section 7.8 and Pradel (1993b).

The states in this model are "alive and seen", "alive and not seen" and "dead". By this definition of the states, the observation process is included in the state-transition process. This is necessary, because the trap-response is a Markovian process which can be implemented in the state-transition matrix, but not in the observation matrix. The state-transition matrix is then

$$
\begin{array}{c}
\text{alive, seen} \\
\text{alive, not seen} \\
\text{dead}
\end{array}
\begin{array}{c}
\text{alive, seen} \quad\ \text{alive, not seen} \quad\ \text{dead} \\
\begin{bmatrix}
\phi p_{ss} & \phi(1-p_{ss}) & 1-\phi \\
\phi p_{ns} & \phi(1-p_{ns}) & 1-\phi \\
0 & 0 & 1
\end{bmatrix}.
\end{array}
$$

Here, ϕ is survival probability, p_{ss} is recapture probability if captured at the previous occasion ("seen", "seen"), and p_{ns} is recapture probability if not captured at the previous occasion ("not seen", "seen").

The possible observations are "seen" and "not seen". Because "seen" and "not seen" are defined and modeled the previous matrix, which formally describes the state process, assignment in the observation process is now deterministic. The observation transition matrix becomes

$$
\begin{array}{c}
\text{alive, seen} \\
\text{alive, not seen} \\
\text{dead}
\end{array}
\begin{array}{c}
\text{seen} \quad \text{not seen} \\
\begin{bmatrix}
1 & 0 \\
0 & 1 \\
0 & 1
\end{bmatrix}.
\end{array}
$$

This model has identifiability problems. For example, when both recapture probabilities vary independently from each other over time, the model (often termed p_{t*m}) is parameter-redundant (Gimenez et al., 2003). By contrast, models where both recapture probabilities are either linked with an additive time structure (p_{t+m}) or are constant over time (p_m) are not parameter redundant.

2.2.2 Generation of Simulated Data

We now generate the data as used in Section 7.8. Recall that we estimate survival of adult red-backed shrikes. We catch adults during the breeding season and mark them with color rings to facilitate resighting and identification in the subsequent years. We survey all potential breeding territories each year. Typically we focus on breeding territories that were occupied by shrikes in previous years. If time allows, we search for other, newly established territories. Thus, marked individuals that survived and are philopatric to their territory have a higher chance of being resighted, while individuals that establish new territories are less likely to be found. However, once they are found, their chances of being resighted in the next year increases again. Such a sampling protocol induces a trap effect that biases survival unless accounted for. For data simulation, we assume survival $\phi = 0.55$ and resighting probabilities $p_{ss} = 0.75$ following a sighting in the preceding year and $p_{ns} = 0.35$ if there was no sighting in the preceding occasion.

```
# Define mean survival, transitions, recapture, as well as number of
    occasions, states, observations and released individuals
phi <- 0.55
pss <- 0.75
pns <- 0.3
n.occasions <- 10
n.states <- 3
n.obs <- 2
marked <- matrix(NA, ncol = n.states, nrow = n.occasions)
marked[,1] <- rep(100, n.occasions)    # Alive, seen
marked[,2] <- rep(0, n.occasions)      # Alive, not seen
marked[,3] <- rep(0, n.occasions)      # Dead

# Define matrices with survival, transition and recapture
    probabilities
# These are 4-dimensional matrices, with
    # Dimension 1: state of departure
    # Dimension 2: state of arrival
    # Dimension 3: individual
    # Dimension 4: time
# 1. State process matrix
totrel <- sum(marked)*(n.occasions-1)
PSI.STATE <- array(NA, dim=c(n.states, n.states, totrel,
    n.occasions-1))
for (i in 1:totrel){
    for (t in 1:(n.occasions-1)){
        PSI.STATE[,,i,t] <- matrix(c(
        phi*pss, phi*(1-pss), 1-phi,
        phi*pns, phi*(1-pns), 1-phi,
        0,       0,           1      ), nrow = n.states, byrow =
            TRUE)
        } #t
    } #i

# 2.Observation process matrix
PSI.OBS <- array(NA, dim=c(n.states, n.obs, totrel, n.occasions-1))
for (i in 1:totrel){
    for (t in 1:(n.occasions-1)){
        PSI.OBS[,,i,t] <- matrix(c(
```

```
        1, 0,
        0, 1,
        0, 1 ), nrow = n.states, byrow = TRUE)
        } #t
    } #i
```

```
# Execute simulation function
sim <- simul.ms(PSI.STATE, PSI.OBS, marked, unobservable = 2)
CH <- sim$CH
```

```
# Compute vector with occasion of first capture
get.first <- function(x) min(which(x!=0))
f <- apply(CH, 1, get.first)
```

```
# Recode CH matrix: note, a 0 is not allowed in WinBUGS!
# 1 = seen, 2 = not seen
rCH <- CH # Recoded CH
rCH[rCH==0] <- 2
```

The capture–recapture data now consist only of 1 at occasions when an individual was seen and of a 2 at occasions when an individual was not seen.

2.2.3 Analysis of the Model

Again, to fit the trap response model in the BUGS code, we only alter the definition of matrices, priors, and possibly of the constraints.

```
# Specify model in BUGS language
sink("immtrap.bug")
cat("
model {
# ----------------------------------------------------------------
# Parameters:
# phi: survival probability
# pss: recapture probability at t, given captured at t-1
# pns: recapture probability at t, given not captured at t-1
# ----------------------------------------------------------------
# States (S):
# 1 alive, seen at t-1
# 2 alive, not seen at t-1
# 3 dead
# Observations (O):
# 1 seen
# 2 not seen
# ----------------------------------------------------------------

# Priors and constraints
for (t in 1:(n.occasions-1)){
    phi[t] <- mean.phi
    pss[t] <- mean.pss
    pns[t] <- mean.pns
    }
mean.phi ~ dunif(0, 1)
```

```
mean.pss ~ dunif(0, 1)
mean.pns ~ dunif(0, 1)

# Define state-transition and observation matrices
for (i in 1:nind){
   # Define probabilities of state S(t+1) given S(t)
   for (t in f[i]:(n.occasions-1)){
        ps[1,i,t,1] <- phi[t]*pss[t]
        ps[1,i,t,2] <- phi[t]*(1-pss[t])
        ps[1,i,t,3] <- 1-phi[t]
        ps[2,i,t,1] <- phi[t]*pns[t]
        ps[2,i,t,2] <- phi[t]*(1-pns[t])
        ps[2,i,t,3] <- 1-phi[t]
        ps[3,i,t,1] <- 0
        ps[3,i,t,2] <- 0
        ps[3,i,t,3] <- 1

        # Define probabilities of O(t) given S(t)
        po[1,i,t,1] <- 1
        po[1,i,t,2] <- 0
        po[2,i,t,1] <- 0
        po[2,i,t,2] <- 1
        po[3,i,t,1] <- 0
        po[3,i,t,2] <- 1
        } #t
   } #i
# State-space model likelihood
for (i in 1:nind){
   z[i,f[i]] <- Y[i,f[i]]
   for (t in (f[i]+1):n.occasions){
       # State equation: draw S(t) given S(t-1)
       z[i,t] ~ dcat(ps[z[i,t-1], i, t-1,])
       # Observation equation: draw O(t) given S(t)
       Y[i,t] ~ dcat(po[z[i,t], i, t-1,])
       } #t
   } #i
}
",fill = TRUE)
sink()

# Bundle data
bugs.data <- list(Y = rCH, f = f, n.occasions = dim(rCH)[2], nind =
   dim(rCH)[1], z = known.state.ms(rCH, 2))

# Initial values
inits <- function(){list(mean.phi = runif(1, 0, 1), mean.pss =
   runif(1, 0, 1), mean.pns = runif(1, 0, 1), z = ms.init.z(rCH, f))}

# Parameters monitored
parameters <- c("mean.phi", "mean.pss", "mean.pns")

# MCMC settings
ni <- 20000
nt <- 6
nb <- 10000
nc <- 3
```

```
# Call WinBUGS from R (BRT 33 min)
immtrap <- bugs(bugs.data, inits, parameters, "immtrap.bug",
    n.chains = nc, n.thin = nt, n.iter = ni, n.burnin = nb, debug = TRUE,
    bugs.directory = bugs.dir, working.directory = getwd())
```

```
print(immtrap, digits = 3)
           mean    sd   2.5%    25%    50%    75%  97.5%   Rhat  n.eff
mean.phi  0.558 0.028 0.513 0.538 0.555 0.575 0.621 1.006   1000
mean.pss  0.776 0.040 0.692 0.750 0.779 0.805 0.847 1.006    660
mean.pns  0.312 0.097 0.145 0.239 0.307 0.376 0.517 1.006    790
```

Convergence is not obtained very quickly, so long MCMC runs are necessary. The use of information about the latent state variable z helps to obtain convergence more swiftly.

References

Abadi, F., Gimenez, O., Arlettaz, R., Schaub, M., 2010a. An assessment of integrated population models: bias, accuracy, and violation of the assumption of independence. Ecology 91, 7–14.

Abadi, F., Gimenez, O., Ullrich, B., Arlettaz, R., Schaub, M., 2010b. Estimation of immigration rate using integrated population modeling. J. Appl. Ecol. 47, 393–400.

Aebischer, A., 2009. Der Rotmilan. Haupt Verlag, Bern.

Altwegg, R., Schaub, M., Roulin, A., 2007. Age-specific fitness components and their temporal variation in the barn owl. Am. Nat. 169, 47–61.

Altwegg, R., Wheeler, M., Erni, B., 2008. Climate and the range dynamics of species with imperfect detection. Biol. Lett. 4, 581–584.

Anderson, D.R., Burnham, K.P., White, G.C., 1985. Problems in estimating age-specific survival rates from recovery data of birds ringed as young. J. Anim. Ecol. 54, 89–98.

Anderson, D.R., Burnham, K.P., White, G.C., 1994. AIC model selection in overdispersed capture-recapture data. Ecology 75, 1780–1793.

Andrewartha, H.G., Birch, L.C., 1954. The Distribution and Abundance of Animals. University of Chicago Press, Chicago, IL.

Arlettaz, R., Schaub, M., Fournier, J., Reichlin, T.S., Sierro, A., Watson, J.E.M., et al., 2010. From publications to public actions: when conservation biologists bridge the gap between research and implementation. BioScience 60, 835–842.

Arnason, A.N., 1972. Parameter estimates from mark-recapture experiments on two populations subject to migration and death. Res. Pop. Ecol. 13, 97–113.

Arnason, A.N., 1973. The estimation of population size, migration rates and survival in a stratified population. Res. Pop. Ecol. 15, 1–8.

Arnason, A.N., Schwarz, C.J., 1999. Using POPAN-5 to analyse banding data. Bird Study 46, 157–168.

Bailey, L.L., Converse, S.J., Kendall, W.L., 2010. Bias, precision and parameter redundancy in complex multistate models with unobservable states. Ecology 91, 1598–1604.

Baillie, S.R., 1991. Integrated population monitoring of breeding birds in Britain and Irland. Ibis 132, 151–166.

Baillie, S.R., Brooks, S.P., King, R., Thomas, L., 2009. Using a state-space model of the British song trush *Turdus pilomenos* population to diagnose the causes of a population decline. Thomson, D.L., Cooch, E.G., Conroy, M.J. (Eds.), Modeling Demographic Processes in Marked Populations. Springer, New York, pp. 541–561.

Balmford, A., Green, R.E., Jenkins, M., 2003. Measuring the changing state of nature. Trend. Ecol. Evol. 18, 326–330.

Barker, R.J., 1997. Joint modeling of live-recapture, tag-resight, and tag-recovery data. Biometrics 53, 666–677.

Barry, S.C., Brooks, S.P., Catchpole, E.A., Morgan, B.J.T., 2003. The analysis of ring-recovery data using random effects. Biometrics 59, 54–65.

Bayes, T., 1763. An essay towards solving a problem in the doctrine of chances. Phil. Trans. R. Soc. A 53, 370–418.

Begon, M., Harper, J.L., Townsend, C.R., 1986. Ecology: Individuals, Populations and Communities. Blackwell, Oxford.

Beissinger, S.R., 2002. Population viability analysis: past, present, future. In: Beissinger, S.R. (Ed.), Population Viability Analysis. The University of Chicago Press, Chicago, IL, pp. 5–17.

Besbeas, P., Borysiewicz, R.S., Morgan, B.J.T., 2009. Completing the ecological jigsaw. In: Thomson, D.L., Cooch, E.G., Conroy, M.J. (Eds.), Modeling Demographic Processes in Marked Populations. Springer, New York, pp. 513–539.

Besbeas, P., Freeman, S.N., 2006. Methods for joint inference from panel survey and demographic data. Ecology 87, 1138–1145.

Besbeas, P., Freeman, S.N., Morgan, B.J.T., 2005. The potential of integrated population modelling. Aust. N. Z. J. Stat. 47, 35–48.

Besbeas, P., Freeman, S.N., Morgan, B.J.T., Catchpole, E.A., 2002. Integrating mark-recapture-recovery and census data to estimate animal abundance and demographic parameters. Biometrics 58, 540–547.

Besbeas, P., Lebreton, J.D., Morgan, B.J.T., 2003. The efficient integration of abundance and demographic data. App. Stat. 52, 95–102.

Bled, F., Royle, J.A., Cam, E., 2011a. Assessing hypotheses about nesting site occupancy dynamics. Ecology 92, 938–951.

Bled, F., Royle, J.A., Cam, E., 2011b. Hierarchical modeling of an invasive spread: case of the Eurasian collared dove *Streptopelia decaocto* in the USA. Ecol. Appl. 21, 290–302.

Bolker, B.M., 2008. Ecological Models and Data in R. Princeton University Press, Princeton, NJ.

Bonner, S.J., Schwarz, C.J., 2006. An extension of the Cormack-Jolly-Seber model for continuous covariates with application to *Microtus pennsylvanicus*. Biometrics 62, 142–149.

Borchers, D.L., Buckland, S.T., Zucchini, W., 2002. Estimating Animal Abundance. Springer, London.

Borchers, D.L., Efford, M.G., 2008. Spatially explicit maximum likelihood methods for capture-recapture studies. Biometrics 64, 377–385.

Borysiewicz, R.S., Morgan, B.J.T., Hénaux, V., Bregnballe, T., Lebreton, J.D., Gimenez, O., 2009. An integrated analysis of multisite recruitment, mark-recapture-recovery and multisite census data. In: Thomson, D.L., Cooch, E.G., Conroy, M.J. (Eds.), Modeling Demographic Processes in Marked Populations. Springer, New York, pp. 579–591.

Boulinier, T., Nichols, J.D., Sauer, J.R., Hines, J.E., Pollock, K.H., 1998. Estimating species richness: the importance of heterogeneity in species detectability. Ecology 79, 1018–1028.

Boyce, M.S., MacKenzie, D.I., Manly, B.F.J., Haroldson, M.A., Moody, D.S., 2001. Negative binomial models for abundance estimation of multiple closed populations. J. Wildl. Manage. 65, 498–509.

Brooks, S.P., 2003. Bayesian computation: a statistical revolution. Phil. Trans. R. Soc. A. 361, 2681–2697.

Brooks, S.P., Catchpole, E.A., Morgan, B.J.T., 2000a. Bayesian animal survival estimation. Stat. Sci. 15, 357–376.

Brooks, S.P., Catchpole, E.A., Morgan, B.J.T., Barry, S.C., 2000b. On the Bayesian analysis of ring-recovery data. Biometrics 56, 951–956.

Brooks, S.P., Catchpole, E.A., Morgan, B.J.T., Harris, M.P., 2002. Bayesian methods for analysing ringing data. J. Appl. Stat. 29, 187–206.

Brooks, S.P., Gelman, A., 1998. Alternative methods for monitoring convergence of iterative simulations. J. Comput. Graph. Stat. 7, 434–455.

Brooks, S.P., King, R., Morgan, B.J.T., 2004. A Bayesian approach to combining animal abundance and demographic data. Anim. Biodiv. Cons. 27.1, 515–529.

Brown, J.H., Maurer, B.A., 1989. Macroecology: the division of food and space among species on continents. Science 243, 1145–1150.

Brownie, C., Anderson, D.R., Burnham, K.P., Robson, D.S., 1985. Statistical Inference from Band Recovery Data: A Handbook. US Fish and Wildlife Service, Resource Publication 156, Washington, DC.

Brownie, C., Hines, J.E., Nichols, J.D., 1986. Constant-parameter capture-recapture models. Biometrics 42, 561–574.

Brownie, C., Hines, J.E., Nichols, J.D., Pollock, K.H., Hestbeck, J.B., 1993. Capture-recapture studies for multiple strata including non-Markovian transitions. Biometrics 49, 1173–1187.

Buckland, S.T., Anderson, D.R., Burnham, K.P., Laake, J.L., Borchers, D.L., Thomas, L., 2001. Introduction to Distance Sampling. Oxford University Press, Oxford.

Buckland, S.T., Newman, K.B., Fernandez, C., Thomas, L., Harwood, J., 2007. Embedding population dynamics models in inference. Stat. Sci. 22, 44–58.

Buckland, S.T., Newman, K.B., Thomas, L., Koesters, N.B., 2004. State-space models for the dynamics of wild animal populations. Ecol. Mod. 171, 157–175.

Burnham, K.P., 1993. A theory for combined analysis of ring recovery and recapture data. In: Lebreton, J.D. (Ed), Marked Individuals in the Study of Bird Populations. Birkhäuser, Basel, pp. 199–213.

Burnham, K.P., Anderson, D.R., 2002. Model Selection and Multimodel Inference: A Practical Information Theoretic Approach. Springer, New York.

Burnham, K.P., Anderson, D.R., White, G.C., Brownie, C., Pollock, K.H., 1987. Design and analysis methods for fish survival experiments based on release-recapture. Am. Fish. Soc. Monogr. 5, 1–437.

Burnham, K.P., White, G.C., 2002. Evaluation of some random effects methodology applicable to bird ringing data. J. Appl. Stat. 29, 245–264.

Calvert, A.M., Bonner, S.J., Jonsen, I.D., Mills Flemming, J., Walde, S.J., Taylor, P.D., 2009. A hierarchical Bayesian approach to multi-state mark-recapture: simulations and applications. J. Appl. Ecol. 46, 610–620.

Cam, E., Link, W.A., Cooch, E.G., Monnat, J.Y., Danchin, E., 2002. Individual covariation in life-history traits: seeing the trees despite the forest. Am. Nat. 159, 96–105.

Carlin, B.P., Louis, T.A., 2009. Bayesian Methods for Data Analysis. CRC Press/Taylor & Francis Group, Boca Raton, FL.

Caswell, H., 1988. Theory and models in ecology: a different perspective. Ecol. Mod. 43, 33–44.

Caswell, H., 2001. Matrix Population Models. Construction, Analysis, and Interpretation. Sinauer Associates, Sunderland, MA.

Catchpole, A.E., Morgan, B.J.T., Tavecchia, G., 2008. A new method for analysing discrete life history data with missing covariate values. J. R. Stat. Soc. B 70, 445–460.

Catchpole, E.A., Kgosi, P.M., Morgan, B.J.T., 2001. On the near-singularity of models for animal recovery data. Biometrics 57, 720–726.

Catchpole, E.A., Morgan, B.J.T., 1997. Detecting parameter redundancy. Biometrika 84, 187–196.

Caughley, G., 1994. Directions in conservation biology. J. Anim. Ecol. 63, 215–244.

Celeux, G., Forbes, F., Robert, C.P., Titterington, D.M., 2006. Deviance information citeria for missing data models. Bayesian Anal. 1, 651–674.

Chandler, R.B., King, D.I., 2011. Golden-winged warbler habitat selection and habitat quality in Costa Rica: an application of hierarchical models for open populations. J. Appl. Ecol. 48, 1038–1047.

Chandler, R.B., King, D.I., Chandler, C.C., 2009a. Effects of management regime on the abundance and nest survival of shrubland birds in wildlife openings in northern New England, USA. Forest Ecol. Manage. 258, 1669–1676.

Chandler, R.B., King, D.I., DeStefano, S., 2009b. Scrub-shrub bird habitat associations at multiple spatial scales in beaver meadows in Massachusetts. Auk 126, 186–197.

Choquet, R., Lebreton, J.D., Gimenez, O., Reboulet, A.M., Pradel, R., 2009a. U-CARE: utilities for performing goodness of fit tests and manipulating CApture-REcapture data. Ecography 32, 1071–1074.

Choquet, R., Rouan, L., Pradel, R., 2009b. Program E-SURGE: a software application for fitting multievent models. In: Thomson, D.L., Cooch, E.G., Conroy, M.J. (Eds.), Modeling Demographic Processes in Marked Populations. Springer, New York, pp. 845–865.

Choquet, R., Reboulet, A.M., Pradel, R., Lebreton, J.D., 2001. U-CARE (Utilities-Capture-Recapture) User's Guide. CEFE/CNRS, Montpellier, France.

Clark, J.S., 2005. Why environmental scientists are becoming Bayesians. Ecol. Lett. 8, 2–14.

Clark, J.S., Björnstad, O.N., 2004. Population time series: process variability, observation errors, missing values, lags, and hidden states. Ecology 85, 3140–3150.

Clark, J.S., Ferraz, G., Oguge, N., Hays, H., DiCostanzo, J., 2005. Hierarchical Bayes for structured, variable populations: from recapture data to life-history prediction. Ecology 86, 2232–2244.

Clobert, J., Lebreton, J.D., 1991. Estimation of demographic parameters in bird populations. In: Perrins, C.M. (Ed.), Bird Population Studies. Oxford University Press, Oxford, pp. 75–104.

Collier, B.A., Groce, J.E., Morrison, M.L., Newnam, J.C., Campomizzi, A.J., Farrell, S.L., et al., 2011. Predicting patch occupancy in fragmented landscapes at the rangewide scale for endangered species: an example of an American warbler. Div. Dist. (in press).

Conn, P.B., Cooch, E.G., 2009. Multistate capture-recapture analysis under imperfect state observation: an application to disease models. J. Appl. Ecol. 46, 486–492.

Conroy, M.J., Runge, J.P., Barker, R.J., Schofield, M.R., Fonnesbeck, C.J., 2008. Efficient estimation of abundance for patchily distributed populations via two-phase, adaptive sampling. Ecology 89, 3362–3370.

Cormack, R.M., 1964. Estimates of survival from the sighting of marked animals. Biometrika 51, 429–438.

Coull, B.A., Agresti, A., 1999. The use of mixed logit models to reflect heterogeneity in capture-recapture studies. Biometrics 55, 294–301.

Crawley, M.J., 2005. Statistics. An Introduction Using R. Wiley, Chinchester, West Sussex.

Cressie, N., Calder, C.A., Clark, J.S., Ver Hoef, J.M., Wikle, C.K., 2009. Accounting for uncertainty in ecological analysis: the strengths and limitations of hierarchical statistical modeling. Ecol. Appl. 19, 553–570.

Crosbie, S.F., Manly, B.F.J., 1985. Parsimonious modeling of capture-mark-recapture studies. Biometrics 41, 385–398.

Dail, D., Madsen, L., 2011. Models for estimating abundance from repeated counts of an open population. Biometrics 67, 577–587.

David, O., Garnier, A., Larédo, C., Lecomte, J., 2010. Estimation of plant demographic parameters from stage-structured censuses. Biometrics 66, 875–882.

De Valpine, P., 2011. Frequentist analysis of hierarchical models for population dynamics and demographic data. J. Ornithol. (in press).

De Valpine, P., Hastings, A., 2002. Fitting population models incorporating process noise and observation error. Ecol. Monogr. 72, 57–76.

Dennis, B., 1996. Discussion: should ecologists become Bayesian? Ecol. Appl. 6, 1095–1103.

Dennis, B., Munholland, P.L., Scott, J.M., 1991. Estimation of growth and extinction parameters for endangered species. Ecol. Monogr. 61, 115–143.

Dennis, B., Ponciano, J.M., Lele, S.R., Taper, M.L., Staples, D.F., 2006. Estimating density dependence, process noise, and observation error. Ecol. Monogr. 76, 323–341.

Dennis, B., Taper, M.L., 1994. Density dependence in time series observations of natural populations: estimation and testing. Ecol. Monogr. 64, 205–224.

Dobson, A., Barnett, A., 2008. An Introduction to Generalized Linear Models. CRC/Chapmann & Hall, Boca Raton, FL.

Dodd, C.K., Dorazio, R.M., 2004. Using counts to simultaneously estimate abundance and detection probabilities in salamander surveys. Herpetologica 60, 468–478.

Dorazio, R.M., 2007. On the choice of statistical models for estimating occurrence and extinction from animal surveys. Ecology 88, 2773–2782.

Dorazio, R.M., Kéry, M., Royle, J.A., Plattner, M., 2010. Models for inference in dynamic metacommunity systems. Ecology 91, 2466–2475.

Dorazio, R.M., Mukherjee, B., Zhang, L., Ghosh, M., Jelks, H.L., Jordan, F., 2008. Modeling unobserved sources of heterogeneity in animal abundance using a Dirichlet process prior. Biometrics 64, 635–644.

Dorazio, R.M., Royle, J.A., 2003. Mixture models for estimating the size of a closed population when capture rates vary among individuals. Biometrics 59, 351–364.

Dorazio, R.M., Royle, J.A., 2005. Estimating size and composition of biological communities by modeling the occurrence of species. J. Am. Stat. Assoc. 100, 389–398.

Dorazio, R.M., Royle, J.A., Söderström, B., Glimskär, A., 2006. Estimating species richness and accumulation by modeling species occurrence and detectability. Ecology 87, 842–854.

Dupuis, J.A., 1995. Bayesian estimation of movement and survival probabilities from capture-recapture data. Biometrika 82, 761–772.

Dupuis, J.A., Schwarz, C.J., 2007. A Bayesian approach to the multistate Jolly-Seber capture-recapture model. Biometrics 63, 1015–1022.

Duriez, O., Saether, S.A., Ens, B.J., Choquet, R., Pradel, R., Lambeck, R.H.D., et al., 2009. Estimating survival and movements using both live and dead recoveries: a case study of oystercatchers confronted with habitat change. J. Appl. Ecol. 46, 144–153.

Efford, M., 2004. Density estimation in live-trapping studies. Oikos 106, 598–610.

Efford, M.G., Borchers, D.L., Byrom, A.E., 2009a. Density estimation by spatially explicit capture-recapture: likelihood-based methods. In: Thomson, D.L., Cooch, E.G., Conroy, M.J. (Eds.), Modeling Demographic Processes in Marked Populations. Springer, New York, pp. 255–269.

Efford, M.G., Dawson, D.K., 2009. Effect of distance-related heterogeneity on population size estimates from point counts. Auk 126, 100–111.

Efford, M.G., Dawson, D., Borchers, D.L., 2009b. Population density estimated from locations of individuals on a passive detector array. Ecology 90, 2676–2682.

Elith, J., Leathwick, J.R., Hastie, T., 2008. A working guide to boosted regression trees. J. Anim. Ecol. 77, 802–813.

Elliott, M.R., Little, R.J.A., 2000. A Bayesian approach to combining information from a census, a coverage measurement survey, and demographic analysis. J. Am. Stat. Assoc. 95, 351–362.

Ellison, A.M., 2004. Bayesian inference in ecology. Ecol. Lett. 7, 509–520.

Engen, S., Saether, B.E., Sverdrup-Thygeson, A., Grotan, V., Odegaard, F., 2008. Assessment of species richness from species abundance distributions at different localities. Oikos 117, 738–748.

Fewster, R.M., Buckland, S.T., Siriwardena, G.M., Baillie, S.R., Wilson, J.D., 2000. Analysis of population trends for farmland birds using generalized additive models. Ecology 81, 1970–1984.

Fiske, I.J., Chandler, R., 2011. Unmarked: An R package for the analysis of wildlife occurrence and abundance data. J. Stat. Softw. (in press).

Fletcher, D., 1994. A mark-recapture model in which sighting probability depends on the number of sightings on the previous occasion. In: Fletcher, D., Manly, B.F.J. (Eds.), Statistics in Ecology and Environmental Monitoring. Otago University Press, Dunedin, pp. 105–110.

Franklin, A.B., Anderson, D.R., Gutierrez, R.J., Burnham, K.P., 2000. Climate, habitat quality, and fitness in Northern spotted owl populations in Northwestern California. Ecol. Monogr. 70, 539–590.

Freckleton, R.P., Watkinson, A.R., Green, R.E., Sutherland, B.J., 2006. Census error and the detection of density dependence. J. Anim. Ecol. 75, 837–851.

Frederiksen, M., Bregnballe, T., 2000. Evidence for density-dependent survival in adult cormorants from a combined analysis of recoveries and resightings. J. Anim. Ecol. 69, 737–752.

Gaillard, J.M., Viallefont, A., Loison, A., Festa-Bianchet, M., 2004. Assessing senescence patterns in populations of large mammals. Anim. Biodiv. Cons. 27.1, 47–58.

Gardner, B., Reppucci, J., Lucherini, M., Royle, J.A., 2010. Spatially explicit inference for open populations: estimating demographic parameters from camera-trap studies. Ecology 91, 3376–3383.

Gardner, B., Royle, J.A., Wegan, M.T., 2009. Hierarchical models for estimating density from DNA mark-recapture studies. Ecology 90, 1106–1115.

Gaston, K.J., Blackburn, T.M., 2000. Pattern and Process in Macroecology. Blackwell Science, Oxford.

Gauthier, G., Besbeas, P., Lebreton, J.D., Morgan, B.J.T., 2007. Population growth in snow geese: a modeling approach integrating demographic and survey information. Ecology 88, 1420–1429.

Gauthier, G., Lebreton, J.D., 2008. Analysis of band-recovery data in a multistate capture-recapture framework. Can. J. Stat. 36, 59–73.

Gelman, A., 2005. Analysis of variance: why is it more important than ever (with discussion). Ann. Stat. 33, 1–53.

Gelman, A., 2006. Prior distributions for variance parameters in hierarchical models. Bayesian Anal. 1, 515–534.

Gelman, A., 2008. Objections to Bayesian statistics (with discussion). Bayesian Anal. 3, 445–450.

Gelman, A., Carlin, J.P., Stern, H.S., Rubin, D.B., 2004. Bayesian Data Analysis. CRC/Chapman & Hall, Boca Raton, FL.

Gelman, A., Hill, J., 2007. Data Analysis Using Regression and Multilevel/Hierarchical Models. Cambridge University Press, Cambridge.

Gelman, A., Meng, X.-L., Stern, H.S., 1996. Posterior predictive assessment of model fitness via realized discrepancies (with discussion). Stat. Sinica. 6, 733–807.

Geman, S., Geman, D., 1984. Stochastic relaxion, Gibbs distributions, and the Bayesian restoration of images. IEEE Trans. Pat. Anal. Mach. Intell. 6, 721–741.

Gibbons, D.W., Donald, P.F., Bauer, H.G., Fornasari, L., Dawson, I.K., 2007. Mapping avian distributions: the evolution of bird atlases. Bird Study. 54, 324–334.

Gilks, W.R., Thomas, A., Spiegelhalter, D.J., 1994. A language and program for complex Bayesian modelling. Statistician 43, 169–177.

Gimenez, O., Bonner, S.J., King, R., Parker, R.A., Brooks, S.P., Jamieson, L.E., et al., 2009a. WinBUGS for population ecologists: Bayesian modeling using Markov Chain Monte Carlo methods. In: Thomson, D.L., Cooch, E.G., Conroy, M.J. (Eds.), Modeling Demographic Processes in Marked Populations. Springer, New York, pp. 883–915.

Gimenez, O., Choquet, R., Lebreton, J.D., 2003. Parameter redundancy in multistate capture-recapture models. Biomet. J. 45, 704–722.

Gimenez, O., Covas, R., Brown, C.R., Anderson, M.D., Bomberger Brown, M., Lenormand, T., 2006a. Nonparametric estimation of natural selection on a quantitative trait using mark-recapture data. Evolution 60, 460–466.

Gimenez, O., Crainiceanu, C., Barbraud, C., Jenouvrier, S., Morgan, B.J.T., 2006b. Semiparametric regression in capture-recapture modeling. Biometrics 62, 691–698.

Gimenez, O., Morgan, B.J.T., Brooks, S.P., 2009b. Weak identifiability in models for mark-recapture-recovery data. In: Thomson, D.L., Cooch, E.G., Conroy, M.J. (Eds.), Modeling Demographic Processes in Marked Populations. Springer, New York, pp. 1055–1067.

Gimenez, O., Rossi, V., Choquet, R., Dehais, C., Doris, B., Varella, H., et al., 2007. State-space modelling of data on marked individuals. Ecol. Mod. 206, 431–438.

Gimenez, O., Viallefont, A., Catchpole, A.E., Choquet, R., Morgan, B.J.T., 2004. Methods for investigating parameter redundancy. Anim. Biodiv. Cons. 27.1, 561–572.

Gimenez, O., Viallefont, A., Charmantier, A., Pradel, R., Cam, E., Brown, C.R., et al., 2008. The risk of flawed inference in evolutionary studies when detectability is less than one. Am. Nat. 172, 441–448.

Gotelli, N.J., McGill, B.J., 2006. Null versus neutral models: what's the difference? Ecography 29, 793–800.

Gould, W.R., Nichols, J.D., 1998. Estimation of temporal variability of survival in animal populations. Ecology 79, 2531–2538.

Grosbois, V., Gimenez, O., Gaillard, J.M., Pradel, R., Barbraud, C., Clobert, J., et al., 2008. Assessing the impact of climate variation on survival in vertebrate populations. Biol. Rev. 83, 357–399.

Grosbois, V., Harris, M.P., Anker-Nilssen, T., McCleery, R.H., Shaw, D.N., Morgan, B.J.T., et al., 2009. Modeling survival at multi-population scales using mark-recapture data. Ecology 90, 2922–2932.

Guillera-Arroita, G., Ridout, M.S., Morgan, B.J.T., 2010. Design of occupancy studies with imperfect detection. Meth. Ecol. Evol. 1, 131–139.

Guisan, A., Thuiller, W., 2005. Predicting species distribution: offering more than simple habitat models. Ecol. Lett. 8, 993–1009.

Hagemeijer, W., Blair, M., 1998. The EBCC Atlas of European Breeding Birds. T. & A.D. Poyser, London.

Hanski, I., 1994. A practical model for metapopulation dynamics. J. Anim. Ecol. 63, 151–162.

Hanski, I., 1998. Metapopulation dynamics. Nature 396, 41–49.

Hargrove, J.W., Borland, C.H., 1994. Pooled population parameter estimates from mark-recapture data. Biometrics 50, 1129–1141.

Harper, J.L., 1977. Population Biology of Plants. Academic Press, London.

Harvey, A.C., 1989. Forecasting, Structural Time Series Models and Kalman Filter. Cambridge University Press, Cambridge.

Hastie, T.J., Tibshirani, R.J., 1990. Generalized Additive Models. Chapman & Hall/CRC, Boca Raton, FL.

Hastings, W.K., 1970. Monte Carlo sampling methods using Markov chains and their applications. Biometrika 57, 97–109.

Hendriks, I.E., Deudero, S., Basso, L., Cabanellas-Reboredo, M., Alvarez, E., 2011. Growth rates of juvenile and adult *Pinna nobilis* around Majorca (Mediterranean, Spain). (in prep.).

Hestbeck, J.B., Nichols, J.D., Malecki, R.A., 1991. Estimates of movement and site fidelity using mark-resight data of wintering Canada Geese. Ecology 72, 523–533.

Hines, J.E., 2006. PRESENCE2: Software to estimate patch occupancy and related parameters. USGS-PWRC, Laurel, MD.

Hines, J.E., Nichols, J.D., Royle, J.A., MacKenzie, D.I., Gopalaswamy, A.M., Samba Kumar, N., et al., 2010. Tigers on trails: occupancy modeling for cluster sampling. Ecol. Appl. 20, 1456–1466.

Hooten, M.B., Wikle, C.K., Dorazio, R.M., Royle, J.A., 2007. Hierarchical spatiotemporal matrix models for characterizing invasions. Biometrics 63, 558–567.

Hubbell, S.P., 2001. A Unified Theory of Biodiversity and Biogeography. Princeton University Press, Princeton, NJ.

Huntley, B., Green, R.E., Collingham, Y.C., Willis, S.G., 2007. A Climatic Atlas of European Breeding Birds. Lynx Edicions, Barcelona.

Hurlbert, S.H., 1984. Pseudoreplication and the design of ecological field experiments. Ecol. Monogr. 54, 187–211.

Jetz, W., Rahbek, C., 2002. Geographic range size and the determinants of vaian species richness. Science 297, 1548–1551.

Joe, M., Pollock, K.H., 2002. Separation of survival and movement rates in multi-state tag-return and capture-recapture models. J. Appl. Stat. 29, 373–384.

Jolly, G.M., 1965. Explicit estimates from capture-recapture data with both death and immigration-stochastic model. Biometrika 52, 225–247.

Joseph, L.N., Elkin, C., Martin, T.G., Possingham, H., 2009. Modeling abundance using N-mixture models: the importance of considering ecological mechanisms. Ecol. Appl. 19, 631–642.

Kadane, J.B., Lazar, N.A., 2004. Methods and criteria for model selection. J. Am. Stat. Assoc. 99, 279–290.

Kalman, R.E., 1960. A new approach to linear filtering and prediction problems. J. Basic Eng. D 82, 35–45.

Karanth, K.U., Nichols, J.D., Kumar, N.S., Hines, J.E., 2006. Assessing tiger population dynamics using photographic capture-recapture sampling. Ecology 87, 2925–2937.

Kendall, W.L., 1999. Robustness of closed capture-recapture methods to violations of the closure assumption. Ecology 80, 2517–2525.

Kendall, W.L., Conn, P.B., Hines, J.E., 2006. Combining multistate capture-recapture data with tag recoveries to estimate demographic parameters. Ecology 87, 169–177.

Kendall, W.L., Hines, J.E., Nichols, J.D., 2003. Adjusting multistate capture-recapture models for misclassification bias: manatee breeding proportions. Ecology 84, 1058–1066.

Kendall, W.L., Nichols, J.D., 2002. Estimating state-transition probabilities for unobservable states using capture-recapture/resighting data. Ecology 83, 3276–3284.

Kendall, W.L., Nichols, J.D., Hines, J.E., 1997. Estimating temporary emigration using capture-recapture data with Pollock's robust design. Ecology 78, 563–578.

Kendall, W.L., White, G.C., 2009. A cautionary note on substituting spatial subunits for repeated temporal sampling in studies of site occupancy. J. Appl. Ecol. 46, 1182–1188.

Kéry, M., 2002. Inferring the absence of a species—a case study of snakes. J. Wildl. Manage. 66, 330–338.

Kéry, M., 2004. Extinction rate estimates for plant populations in revisitation studies: importance of detectability. Conserv. Biol. 18, 570–574.

Kéry, M., 2008. Estimating abundance from bird counts: binomial mixture models uncover complex covariate relationships. Auk 125, 336–345.

Kéry, M., 2010. Introduction to WinBUGS for Ecologists. A Bayesian Approach to Regression, ANOVA, Mixed Models and Related Analyses. Academic Press, Burlington, MA.

Kéry, M., 2011a. Species richness and community dynamics—a conceptual framework. In: O'Connell, A.F., Nichols, J.D., Karanth, K.U. (Eds.), Camera Traps in Animal Ecology: Methods and Analyses. Springer, Tokyo, pp. 207–231.

Kéry, M., 2011b. Towards the modeling of true species distributions. J. Biogeogr. 38, 617–618.

Kéry, M., Dorazio, R.M., Soldaat, L., van Strien, A., Zuiderwijk, A., Royle, J.A., 2009a. Trend estimation in populations with imperfect detection. J. Appl. Ecol. 46, 1163–1172.

Kéry, M., Gardner, B., Monnerat, C., 2010a. Predicting species distributions from checklist data using site-occupancy models. J. Biogeogr. 37, 1851–1862.

Kéry, M., Gardner, B., Stoeckle, T., Weber, D., Royle, J.A., 2011. Use of spatial capture-recapture modeling and DNA data to estimate densities of elusive animals. Conserv. Biol. 25, 356–364.

Kéry, M., Gregg, K.B., 2003. Effects of life-state on detectablity in a demographic study of the terrestrial orchid Cleistes bifaria. J. Ecol. 91, 265–273.

Kéry, M., Gregg, K.B., 2004. Demographic analysis of dormancy and survival in the terrestrial orchid Cypripedium reginae. J. Ecol. 92, 686–695.

Kéry, M., Gregg, K.B., Schaub, M., 2005a. Demographic estimation methods for plants with unobservable life-states. Oikos 108, 307–320.

Kéry, M., Madsen, J., Lebreton, J.D., 2006. Survival of Svalbard pink-footed geese Anser brachyrhynchus in relation to winter climate, density and land-use. J. Anim. Ecol. 75, 1172–1181.

Kéry, M., Royle, J.A., 2008. Hierarchical Bayes estimation of species richness and occupancy in spatially replicated surveys. J. Appl. Ecol. 45, 589–598.

Kéry, M., Royle, J.A., 2009. Inference about species richness and community structure using species-specific occupancy models in the national Swiss breeding bird survey MHB. In: Thomson, D.L., Cooch, E.G., Conroy, M.J. (Eds.), Modeling Demographic Processes in Marked Populations, Springer, New York, pp. 639–656.

Kéry, M., Royle, J.A., 2010. Hierarchical modeling and estimation of abundance in metapopulation designs. J. Anim. Ecol. 79, 453–461.

Kéry, M., Royle, J.A., Plattner, M., Dorazio, R.M., 2009b. Species richness and occupancy estimation in communities subject to temporary emigration. Ecology 90, 1279–1290.

Kéry, M., Royle, J.A., Schmid, H., 2005b. Modeling avian abundance from replicated counts using binomial mixture models. Ecol. Appl. 15, 1450–1461.

Kéry, M., Royle, J.A., Schmid, H., Schaub, M., Volet, B., Häfliger, G., Zbinden, N., 2010b. Site-occupancy distribution modeling to correct population-trend estimates derived from opportunistic observations. Conserv. Biol. 24, 1388–1397.

Kéry, M., Schmidt, B.R., 2008. Imperfect detection and its consequences for monitoring for conservation. Comm. Ecol. 9, 207–216.

King, R., Brooks, S.P., 2002. Bayesian model discrimination for multiple strata capture-recapture data. Biometrika 89, 785–806.

King, R., Brooks, S.P., 2004. Bayesian analyses of the Hector's dolphin data. Anim. Biodiv. Cons. 27.1, 343–354.

King, R., Morgan, B.J.T., Gimenez, O., Brooks, S.P., 2010. Bayesian Analysis for Population Ecology. Chapmann & Hall, Boca Raton, FL.

Knape, J., 2008. Estimability of density dependence in models of time series data. Ecology 89, 2994–3000.

Knape, J., Jonzén, N., Sköld, M., 2011. On observation distributions for state space models of population survey data. J. Anim. Ecol. (in press).

Krebs, C.J., 2001. The Experimental Analysis of Distribution and Abundance. Benjamin Cummings, San Francisco, CA.

Krebs, C.J., Davies, N.B., 1993. An Introduction to Behavioural Ecology. Blackwell Scientific, Oxford.

Lande, R., 2002. Incorporating stochasticity in population viability analysis. In: Beissinger, S.R. (Eds.), Population Viability Analysis. The University of Chicago Press, Chicago, IL, pp. 18–40.

Lande, R., Engen, S., Saether, B.E., 2003. Stochastic Population Dynamics in Ecology and Conservation. Oxford University Press, Oxford.

Lebreton, J.D., 2009. Assessing density-dependence: where are we left? In: Thomson, D.L., Cooch, E.G., Conroy, M.J. (Eds.), Modeling Demographic Processes in Marked Populations. Springer, New York, pp. 19–42.

Lebreton, J.D., Almeras, T., Pradel, R., 1999. Competing events, mixtures of information and multistratum recapture models. Bird Study 46, 39–46.

Lebreton, J.D., Burnham, K.P., Clobert, J., Anderson, D.R., 1992. Modeling survival and testing biological hypothesis using marked animals: a unified approach with case studies. Ecol. Monogr. 62, 67–118.

Lebreton, J.D., Morgan, B.J.T., Pradel, R., Freeman, S.N., 1995. A simultaneous survival rate analysis of dead recovery and live recapture data. Biometrics 51, 1418–1428.

Lebreton, J.D., Nichols, J.D., Barker, R.J., Pradel, R., Spendelow, J.A., 2009. Modeling individual animal histories with multistate capture-recapture models. Adv. Ecol. Res. 41, 87–173.

Lebreton, J.D., Pradel, R., 2002. Multistate recapture models: modelling incomplete individual histories. J. Appl. Stat. 29, 353–369.

Le Cam, L., 1990. Maximum likelihood – an introduction. ISI Rev. 58, 153–171.

Lee, Y., Nelder, J.A., 2000. Two ways of modeling overdispersion in non-normal data. App. Stat. 49, 591–598.

Lee, Y., Nelder, J.A., 2006. Double hierarchical generalized linear models. App. Stat. 55, 139–185.

Lele, S.R., Dennis, B., Lutscher, F., 2007. Data cloning: easy maximum likelihood estimation for complex ecological models using Bayesian Markov chain Monte Carlo methods. Ecol. Lett. 10, 551–563.

Lindley, D.V., 1983. Theory and practice of Bayesian statistics. Statistician 32, 1–11.

Lindley, D.V., 2006. Understanding Uncertainty. Wiley, Hoboken, NJ.

Lindley, S.T., 2003. Estimation of population growth and extinction parameters from noisy data. Ecol. Appl. 13, 806–813.

Link, W.A., 1999. Modeling pattern in collections of parameters. J. Wildl. Manage. 63, 1017–1027.

Link, W.A., 2003. Nonidentifiability of population size from capture-recapture data with heterogeneous detection probabilities. Biometrics 59, 1123–1130.

Link, W.A., Barker, R.J., 2005. Modeling association among demographic parameters in analysis of open population capture-recapture data. Biometrics 61, 46–54.

Link, W.A., Barker, R.J., 2010. Bayesian Inference with Ecological Applications. Academic Press, London.

Link, W.A., Nichols, J.D., 1994. On the importance of sampling variance to investigations of temporal variations in animal population size. Oikos 69, 539–544.

Link, W.A., Royle, J.A., Hatfield, J.S., 2003. Demographic analysis from summaries of an age-structured population. Biometrics 59, 778–785.

Link, W.A., Sauer, J.R., 1996. Extremes in ecology: avoiding the misleading effects of sampling variation in summary analyses. Ecology 77, 1633–1640.

Link, W.A., Sauer, J.R., 1998. Estimating population change from count data: application to the North American breeding bird survey. Ecol. Appl. 8, 258–268.

Link, W.A., Sauer, J.R., 2002. A hierarchical analysis of population change with application to Cerulean warblers. Ecology 83, 2832–2840.

Link, W.A., Yoshizaki, J., Bailey, L.L., Pollock, K.H., 2010. Uncovering a latent multinomial: analysis of mark-recapture data with misidentification. Biometrics 66, 178–185.

Little, R.J.A., 2006. Calibrated Bayes: A bayes/frequentist roadmap. Am. Stat. 60, 213–223.

Liu, J.S., Wu, Y.N., 1999. Parameter expansion for data augmentation. J. Am. Stat. Assoc. 94, 1264–1274.

Lukacs, P.M., Burnham, K.P., 2005. Estimating population size from DNA-based closed capture–recapture data incorporating genotyping error. J. Wildl. Manage. 69, 396–403.

Lunn, D.J., Spiegelhalter, D., Thomas, A., Best, N., 2009. The BUGS project: evaluation, critique and future directions. Stat. Med. 28, 3049–3067.

Lunn, D.J., Thomas, A., Best, N., Spiegelhalter, D., 2000. WinBUGS—a Bayesian modelling framework: concepts, structure, and extensibility. Stat. Comput. 10, 325–337.

MacKenzie, D.I., 2005. What are the issues with presence-absence data for wildlife managers? J. Wildl. Manage. 69, 849–860.

MacKenzie, D.I., 2006. Modeling the probability of resource use: the effect of, and dealing with, detecting a species imperfectly. J. Wildl. Manage. 70, 367–374.

MacKenzie, D.I., Nichols, J.D., Hines, J.E., Knutson, M.G., Franklin, A.B., 2003. Estimating site occupancy, colonization, and local extinction when a species is detected imperfectly. Ecology 84, 2200–2207.

MacKenzie, D.I., Nichols, J.D., Lachman, G.B., Droege, S., Royle, J.A., Langtimm, C.A., 2002. Estimating site occupancy rates when detection probabilities are less than one. Ecology 83, 2248–2255.

MacKenzie, D.I., Nichols, J.D., Royle, J.A., Pollock, K.H., Hines, J.E., Bailey, L.L., 2006. Occupancy Estimation and Modeling: Inferring Patterns and Dynamics of Species Occurrence. Elsevier, San Diego, CA.

MacKenzie, D.I., Nichols, J.D., Seamans, M.E., Gutierrez, R.J., 2009. Modeling species occurrence dynamics with multiple states and imperfect detection. Ecology 90, 823–835.

Marra, P.P., Griffing, S., Caffrey, C., Kilpatrick, A.M., McLean, R., Brand, C., et al., 2004. West nile virus and wildlife. BioScience 54, 393–402.

Marshall, M.R., Diefenbach, D.R., Wood, L.A., Cooper, R.J., 2004. Annual survival estimation of migratory songbirds confounded by incomplete breeding site-fidelity: study designs that may help. Anim. Biodiv. Cons. 27.1, 59–72.

Martin, J.E., Royle, J.A., Gardner, B., MacKenzie, D.I., Edwards, H.H., Kéry, M., 2011. Accounting for non-independent detection when estimating abundance of organisms with a Bayesian approach. Meth. Ecol. Evol. (in press).

Martin, T.E., Clobert, J., Anderson, D.R., 1995. Return rates in studies of life history evolution: are biases large? J. Appl. Stat. 22, 863–875.

Maunder, M.N., 2004. Population viability analysis based on combining Bayesian, integrated, and hierarchical analyses. Acta Oecol. 26, 85–94.

McCarthy, M.A., 2007. Bayesian Methods for Ecology. Cambridge University Press, Cambridge.

McCarthy, M.A., Masters, P., 2005. Profiting from prior information in Bayesian analyses of ecological data. J. Appl. Ecol. 42, 1012–1019.

McClintock, B.T., Nichols, J.D., Bailey, L.L., MacKenzie, D.I., Kendall, W.L., Franklin, A.B., 2010. Seeking a second opinion: uncertainty in disease ecology. Ecol. Lett. 13, 659–674.

McCullagh, P., Nelder, J.A., 1989. Generalized Linear Models. Chapman & Hall, London.

Metropolis, N., Rosenbluth, A.W., Rosenbluth, M.N., Teller, A.H., Teller, E., 1953. Equation of state calculations by fast computing machines. J. Chem. Phys. 21, 1087–1092.

Millar, R.B., 2009. Comparison of hierarchical Bayesian models for overdispersed count data using DIC and Bayes' factors. Biometrics 65, 962–969.

Miller, D.A., Nichols, J.D., McClintock, B.T., Grant, E.H.C., Bailey, L.L., Weir, L., 2011. Improving occupancy estimation when two types of observational errors occur: non-detection and species misidentification. Ecology 92, 1422–1428.

Moilanen, A., 2002. Implications of empirical data quality to metapopulation model parameter estimation and application. Oikos 96, 516–530.

Monneret, R.-J., 2006. Le faucon pèlerin. Delachaux and Niestlé, Paris.

Moritz, C., Patton, J.L., Conroy, C.J., Parra, J.L., White, G.C., Beissinger, S.R., 2008. Impact of a century of climate change on small mammal communities in Yosemite National Park, USA. Science 322, 261–264.

Newman, K.B., Buckland, S.T., Lindley, S.T., Thomas, L., Fernandez, C., 2006. Hidden process models for animal population dynamics. Ecol. Appl. 16, 74–86.

Newton, I., 1998. Population Limitation in Birds. Academic Press, London.

Nichols, J.D., Blohm, R.J., Reynolds, R.E., Trost, R.E., Hines, J.E., Bladen, J.P., 1991. Band reporting rates for Mallards with reward bands of different Dollar values. J. Wildl. Manage. 55, 119–126.

Nichols, J.D., Boulinier, T., Hines, J.E., Pollock, K.H., Sauer, J.R., 1998a. Estimating rates of local species extinction, colonization, and turnover in animal communities. Ecol. Appl. 8, 1213–1225.

Nichols, J.D., Boulinier, T., Hines, J.E., Pollock, K.H., Sauer, J.R., 1998b. Inference methods for spatial variation in species richness and community composition when not all species are detected. Conserv. Biol. 12, 1390–1398.

Nichols, J.D., Hines, J.E., Lebreton, J.D., Pradel, R., 2000. Estimation of contributions to population growth: a reverse-time capture-recapture approach. Ecology 81, 3362–3376.

Nichols, J.D., Hines, J.E., MacKenzie, D.I., Seamans, M.E., Gutierrez, R.J., 2007. Occupancy estimation and modeling with multiple states and state uncertainty. Ecology 88, 1395–1400.

Nichols, J.D., Hines, J.E., Pollock, K.H., 1984. Effects of permanent trap response in capture probability on Jolly-Seber capture-recapture model estimates. J. Wildl. Manage. 48, 289–293.

Nichols, J.D., Kendall, W.L., Hines, J.E., Spendelow, J.A., 2004. Estimation of sex-specific survival from capture-recapture data when sex is not always known. Ecology 85, 3192–3201.

Nichols, J.D., Pollock, K.H., 1983. Estimation methodology in contemporary small mammal capture-recapture studies. J. Mamm. 64, 253–260.

Nichols, J.D., Pollock, K.H., 1990. Estimation of recruitment from immigration versus in situ reproduction using Pollock's Robust design. Ecology 71, 21–26.

Nichols, J.D., Thomas, L., Conn, P.B., 2009. Inferences about landbird abundance from count data: recent advances and future directions. In: Thomson, D.L., Cooch, E.G., Conroy, M.J. (Eds.), Modeling Demographic Processes in Marked Populations. Springer, New York, pp. 201–235.

Norris, K., 2004. Managing threatened species: the ecological toolbox, evolutionary theory and declining-population paradigm. J. Appl. Ecol. 41, 413–426.

Ntzoufras, I., 2009. Bayesian Modeling Using WinBUGS. Wiley, Hoboken, NJ.

O'Hara, R.B., Sillanpää, M.J., 2009. A review of Bayesian variable selection methods: what, how and which. Bayesian Anal. 4, 85–118.

Orme, C.D.L., Davies, R.G., Burgess, M., Eigenbrod, F., Pickup, N., Olson, V.A., et al., 2005. Global hotspots of species richness are not congruent with endemism or threat. Nature 436, 1019.

Otis, D.L., Burnham, K.P., White, G.C., Anderson, D.R., 1978. Statistical inference from capture data on closed animal populations. Wildl. Monogr. 62, 1–135.

Pagel, J., Schurr, F.M., 2011. Forecasting species ranges by statistical estimation of ecological niches and spatial population dynamics. Global Ecol. Biogeogr. (in press).

Pearman, P.B., Weber, D., 2007. Common species determine richness patterns in biodiversity indicator taxa. Biol. Cons. 138, 109–119.

Pellet, J., Schmidt, B.R., 2005. Monitoring distributions using call surveys: estimating site occupancy, detection probabilities and inferring absence. Biol. Cons. 123, 27–35.

Péron, G., Crochet, P.-A., Doherty, P.F., Lebreton, J.D., 2010. Studying dispersal at the landscape scale: efficient combination of population surveys and capture-recapture data. Ecology 91, 3365–3375.

Phillips, S.J., Dudik, M., 2008. Modeling of species distributions with Maxent: new extensions and a comprehensive evaluation. Ecography 31, 161–175.

Pigliucci, M., 2002. Denying Evolution: Creationism, Scientism, and the Nature of Science. Sinauer Associates, Sunderland, MA.

Pledger, S., 2000. Unified maximum likelihood estimates for closed capture-recapture models using mixtures. Biometrics 56, 434–442.

Pledger, S., Efford, M., 1998. Correction of bias due to heterogeneous capture probability in capture-recapture studies of open populations. Biometrics 54, 888–898.

Pledger, S., Efford, M., Pollock, K., Collazo, J., Lyons, J., 2009. Stopover duration analysis with departure probability dependent on unknown time since arrival. In: Thomson, D.L., Cooch, E.G., Conroy, M.J. (Eds.), Modeling Demographic Processes in Marked Populations. Springer, New York, pp. 349–363.

Pollock, K.H., 1982. A capture-recapture design robust to unequal probability of capture. J. Wildl. Manage. 46, 752–757.

Pollock, K.H., Nichols, J.D., Brownie, C., Hines, J.E., 1990. Statistical inference for capture-recapture experiments. Wildl. Monogr. 107, 1–97.

Post van der Burg, M., Bly, B., Vercauteren, T., Tyre, A.J., 2011. Making better use of monitoring data from low density species using a spatially explicit modeling approach. J. Appl. Ecol. 48, 47–55.

Powell, L.A., 2007. Approximating variance of demographic parameters using the delta method: a reference for avian biologists. Condor 109, 949–954.

Pradel, R., 1993. Flexibility in survival analysis from recapture data: handling trap-dependence. In: Lebreton, J.D. (Ed.), Marked Individuals in the Study of Bird Population. Birkhäuser-Verlag, Basel, pp. 29–37.

Pradel, R., 1996. Utilization of capture-mark-recapture for the study of recruitment and population growth rate. Biometrics 52, 703–709.

Pradel, R., 2005. Multievent: an extension of multistate capture-recapture models to uncertain states. Biometrics 61, 442–447.

Pradel, R., Hines, J.E., Lebreton, J.D., Nichols, J.D., 1997. Capture-recapture survival models taking account of transients. Biometrics 53, 60–72.

Pradel, R., Lebreton, J.D., 1999. Comparison of different approaches to the study of local recruitment of breeders. Bird Study 46, 74–81.

Pradel, R., Wintrebert, C.M.A., Gimenez, O., 2003. A proposal for a goodness-of-fit test to the Arnason-Schwarz multistate capture-recapture model. Biometrics 59, 43–53.

Purvis, A., Hector, A., 2000. Getting the measure of biodiversity. Nature 405, 212–219.

R Development Core Team, 2004. R: A Language and Environment for Statistical Computing. R Foundation for Statistical Computing, Vienna.

Reid, J.M., Bignal, E.M., Bignal, S., McCracken, D.I., Monaghan, P., 2003. Environmental variability, life-history covariation and cohort effects in the red-billed chough *Pyrrhocorax pyrrhocorax*. J. Anim. Ecol. 72, 36–46.

Reif, J., Storch, D., Simova, I., 2008. The effect of scale-dependent habitat gradients on the structure of bird assemblages in the Czech Republic. Acta Ornithol. 43, 197–206.

Rexstad, E., Burnham, K.P., 1991. User's Guide for Interactive Program CAPTURE. Colorado Cooperative Fish & Wildlife Research Unit, Colorado State University, Fort Collins, CO.

Risk, B.B., De Valpine, P., Beissinger, S.R., 2011. A robust-design formulation of the incidence function model of metapopulation dynamics applied to two rail species. Ecology 92, 462–474.

Robinson, R.A., Green, R.E., Baillie, S.R., Peach, W.J., Thomson, D.L., 2004. Demographic mechanisms of the population decline of the song trush *Turdus philomelos* in Britain. J. Anim. Ecol. 73, 670–682.

Rota, C.T., Fletcher Jr., R.J., Dorazio, R.M., Betts, M.G., 2009. Occupancy estimation and the closure assumption. J. Appl. Ecol. 46, 1173–1181.

Roth, T., Amrhein, V., 2009. Estimating individual survival using territory occupancy data on unmarked animals. J. Appl. Ecol. 47, 386–392.

Royle, J.A., 2004a. Generalized estimators of avian abundance from count survey data. Anim. Biodiv. Cons. 27.1, 375–386.

Royle, J.A., 2004b. Modeling abundance index data from anuran calling surveys. Conserv. Biol. 18, 1378–1385.

Royle, J.A., 2004c. N-mixture models for estimating population size from spatially replicated counts. Biometrics 60, 108–115.

Royle, J.A., 2006. Site occupancy model with heterogeneous detection probabilities. Biometrics 62, 97–102.

Royle, J.A., 2008. Modeling individual effects in the Cormack-Jolly-Seber model: a state-space formulation. Biometrics 64, 364–370.

Royle, J.A., 2009. Analysis of capture-recapture models with individual covariates using data augmentation. Biometrics 65, 267–274.

Royle, J.A., Dorazio, R.M., 2006. Hierarchical models of animal abundance and occurrence. JABES 11, 249–263.

Royle, J.A., Dorazio, R.M., 2008. Hierarchical Modeling and Inference in Ecology. The Analysis of Data from Populations, Metapopulations and Communities. Academic Press, New York.

Royle, J.A., Dorazio, R.M., 2011. Parameter-expanded data augmentation for Bayesian analysis of capture-recapture models. J. Ornithol. (in press).

Royle, J.A., Dorazio, R.M., Link, W.A., 2007a. Analysis of multinomial models with unknown index using data augmentation. J. Comput. Graph. Stat. 16, 67–85.

Royle, J.A., Dubovsky, J.A., 2001. Modeling spatial variation in waterfowl band-recovery data. J. Wildl. Manage. 65, 726–737.

Royle, J.A., Gardner, B., 2011. Hierarchical spatial capture-recapture models for estimating density from trap-arrays. In: O'Connell, A.F., Nichols, J.D., Karanth, K.U. (Eds.), Camera Traps in Animal Ecology—Methods and Analyses. Springer, New York, pp. 163–190.

Royle, J.A., Karanth, K.U., Gopalaswamy, A.M., Kumar, N.S., 2009a. Bayesian inference in camera trapping studies for a class of spatial capture-recapture models. Ecology 90, 3233–3244.

Royle, J.A., Kéry, M., 2007. A Bayesian state-space formulation of dynamics occupancy models. Ecology 88, 1813–1823.

Royle, J.A., Kéry, M., Gauthier, R., Schmid, H., 2007b. Hierarchical spatial models of abundance and occurrence from imperfect survey data. Ecol. Monogr. 77, 465–481.

Royle, J.A., Kéry, M., Guélat, J., 2011. Spatial capture-recapture models for search-encounter data. Meth. Ecol. Evol. (in press).

Royle, J.A., Link, W.A., 2005. A general class of multinomial mixture models for anuran calling survey data. Ecology 86, 2505–2512.

Royle, J.A., Link, W.A., 2006. Generalized site occupancy models allowing for false positive and false negative errors. Ecology 87, 835–841.

Royle, J.A., Nichols, J.D., 2003. Estimating abundance from repeated presence-absence data or point counts. Ecology 84, 777–790.

Royle, J.A., Nichols, J.D., Karanth, K.U., Gopalaswamy, A.M., 2009b. A hierarchical model for estimating density in camera-trap studies. J. Appl. Ecol. 46, 118–127.

Royle, J.A., Nichols, J.D., Kéry, M., 2005. Modelling occurrence and abundance of species when detection is imperfect. Oikos 110, 353–359.

Royle, J.A., Young, K.G., 2008. A hierarchical model for spatial capture-recapture data. Ecology 89, 2281–2289.

Rue, H., Martino, S., Chopin, N., 2009. Approximate Bayesian inference for latent Gaussian models by using integrated nested Laplace approximations (with discussion). J. R. Stat. Soc. B 71, 319–392.

Ruiz-Gutierrez, V., Zipkin, E.F., 2011. Detection biases yield misleading patterns of species persistence and colonization in fragmented landscapes. Ecosphere 2, Article 61.

Russell, R.E., Royle, J.A., Saab, V.A., Lehmkuhl, J.F., Block, W.M., Sauer, J.A., 2009. Modeling the effects of environmental disturbance on wildlife communities: avian responses to prescribed fire. Ecol. Appl. 19, 1253–1263.

Saether, B.E., Bakke, O., 2000. Avian life history variation and contribution of demographic traits to the population growth rate. Ecology 81, 642–653.

Saracco, J.F., Royle, J.A., DeSante, D.F., Gardner, B., 2010. Modeling spatial variation in avian survival and residency probabilities. Ecology 91, 1885–1891.

Sauer, J.R., Link, W.A., 2002. Hierarchical modeling of population stability and species group attributes from survey data. Ecology 86, 1743–1751.

Schaub, M., 2009. Estimation of cause-specific mortality rates from ring recovery data: a Bayesian evaluation. In: Thomson, D.L., Cooch, E.G., Conroy, M.J. (Eds.), Modeling Demographic Processes in Marked Populations. Springer, New York, pp. 1081–1097.

Schaub, M., Abadi, F., 2011. Integrated population models: A novel analysis framework for deeper insights into population dynamics. J. Ornithol. (in press).

Schaub, M., Aebischer, A., Gimenez, O., Berger, S., Arlettaz, R., 2010. Massive immigration balances high human induced mortality in a stable eagle owl population. Biol. Cons. 143, 1911–1918.

Schaub, M., Gimenez, O., Schmidt, B.R., Pradel, R., 2004a. Estimating survival and temporary emigration in the multistate capture-recapture framework. Ecology 85, 2107–2113.

Schaub, M., Gimenez, O., Sierro, A., Arlettaz, R., 2007. Use of integrated modeling to enhance estimates of population dynamics obtained from limited data. Conserv. Biol. 21, 945–955.

Schaub, M., Liechti, F., Jenni, L., 2004b. Departure of migrating European robins, *Erithacus rubecula*, from a stopover site in relation to wind and rain. Anim. Behav. 67, 229–237.

Schaub, M., Pradel, R., 2004. Assessing the relative importance of different sources of mortality from recoveries of marked animals. Ecology 85, 930–938.

Schaub, M., Reichlin, T.S., Abadi, F., Kéry, M., Jenni, L., Arlettaz, R., 2011. The demographic drivers of local population dynamics in two rare migratory birds. Oecologia (in press).

Schaub, M., Ullrich, B., Knötzsch, G., Albrecht, P., Meisser, C., 2006. Local population dynamics and the impact of scale and isolation: a study on different little owl populations. Oikos 115, 389–400.

Schaub, M., Zink, R., Beissmann, H., Sarrazin, F., Arlettaz, R., 2009. When to end releases in reintroduction programmes: demographic rates and population viability analysis of bearded vultures in the Alps. J. Appl. Ecol. 46, 92–100.

Schlossberg, S., King, D.I., Chandler, R.B., Mazzei, D.A., 2010. Regional synthesis of habitat relationships in shrubland birds. J. Wildl. Manage. 74, 1513–1522.

Schmid, H., Luder, R., Naef-Daenzer, B., Graf, R., Zbinden, N., 1998. Schweizer Brutvogelatlas. Schweizerische Vogelwarte, Sempach, Switzerland.

Schmid, H., Zbinden, N., Keller, V., 2004. Überwachung der Bestandsentwicklung häufiger Brutvögel in der Schweiz. Schweizerische Vogelwarte, Sempach, Switzerland.

Schmidt, B.R., 2005. Monitoring the distribution of pond-breeding amphibians when species are detected imperfectly. Aquat. Conserv.: Mar. Freshw. Ecosyst. 15, 681–692.

Schmidt, B.R., Feldmann, R., Schaub, M., 2005. Demographic processes underlying population growth and decline in *Salamandra salamandra*. Conserv. Biol. 19, 1149–1156.

Schofield, M.R., Barker, R.J., 2008. A unified capture-recapture framework. JABES 13, 458–477.

Schofield, M.R., Barker, R.J., MacKenzie, D.I., 2009. Flexible hierarchical mark-recapture modeling for open populations using WinBUGS. Environ. Ecol. Stat. 16, 369–387.

Schorcht, W., Bontadina, F., Schaub, M., 2009. Variation of adult survival drives population dynamics in a migrating forest bat. J. Anim. Ecol. 78, 1182–1190.

Schwarz, C.J., 2002. Real and quasi-experiments in capture-recapture studies. J. Appl. Stat. 29, 459–473.

Schwarz, C.J., Arnason, A.N., 1996. A general methodology for the analysis of capture-recapture experiments in open populations. Biometrics 52, 860–873.

Schwarz, C.J., Schweigert, J.F., Arnason, A.N., 1993. Estimating migration rates using tag recovery data. Biometrics 49, 177–193.

Scott, J.M., Heglund, P.J., Haufler, J.B., Morrsion, M., Raphael, M.G., Wall, W.B., et al., 2002. Predicting Species Occurrence: Issues of Accuracy and Scale. Island Press, Covelo, CA.

Seber, G.A.F., 1965. A note on the multiple recapture census. Biometrika 52, 249–259.

Seber, G.A.F., 1982. The Estimation of Animal Abundance and Related Parameters. Charles Griffin & Company Ltd, London.

Seber, G.A.F., Wild, C.J., 2003. Nonlinear Regression. Wiley, Hoboken, NJ.

Servanthy, S., Choquet, R., Baubet, E., Brandt, S., Gaillard, J.M., Schaub, M., et al., 2010. Assessing whether mortality is additive using marked animals: a Bayesian state-space modeling approach. Ecology 91, 1916–1923.

Service, P.M., 2000. Heterogeneity in individual mortality risk and its importance for evolutionary studies of senescence. Am. Nat. 156, 1–13.

Shefferson, R.P., Sandercock, B.K., Proper, J., Beissinger, S.R., 2001. Estimating dormancy and survival of a rare herbaceous perennial using mark-recapture models. Ecology 82, 145–156.

Sibly, R.M., Calow, P., 1986. Physiological Ecology of Animals: An Evolutionary Approach. Blackwell Scientific, Oxford.

Sibly, R.M., Hone, J., 2002. Population growth rate and its determinants: an overview. Phil. Trans. R. Soc. B 357, 1153–1170.

Smith, A.F.M., Gelfand, A., 1993. Bayesian statistics without tears. Am. Stat. 46, 84–88.

Smout, S., King, R., Pomeroy, P.P., 2011. Integrating heterogeneity of detection and mark loss to estimate survival and transience in UK grey seal colonies. J. Appl. Ecol. 48, 364–372.

Spiegelhalter, D.J., 1998. Bayesian graphical modelling: a case-study in monitoring health outcomes. App. Stat. 47, 115–133.

Spiegelhalter, D.J., Best, N.G., Carlin, B.P., van der Linde, A., 2002. Bayesian measure of model complexity and fit. J. R. Stat. Soc. B 64, 583–639.

Stearns, S.C., 1992. The Evolution of Life Histories. Oxford University Press, Oxford.

Sturtz, S., Ligges, U., Gelman, A., 2005. R2WinBUGS: a package for running WinBUGS from R. J. Stat. Softw. 12, 1–16.

Sutherland, B.J., Dolman, P.M., 1994. Combining behaviour and population dynamics with applications for predicting consequences of habitat loss. Proc. R. Soc. Lond. B 255, 133–138.

Talley, T.S., Fleishman, E., Holyoak, M., Murphy, D.D., Ballard, A., 2007. Rethinking a rare-species conservation strategy in an urban landscape: the case of the valley elderberry longhorn beetle. Biol. Cons. 135, 21–32.

Tanner, M.A., Wong, W.H., 1987. The calculation of posterior distributions by data augmentation. J. Am. Stat. Assoc. 82, 528–540.

Tavecchia, G., Besbeas, P., Coulson, T., Morgan, B.J.T., Clutton-Brock, T.H., 2009. Estimating population size and hidden demographic parameters with state-space modeling. Am. Nat. 173, 722–733.

Tavecchia, G., Pradel, R., Gossmann, F., Bastat, C., Ferrand, Y., Lebreton, J.D., 2002. Temporal variation in annual survival probability of the Eurasian woodcock Scolopax rusticola wintering in France. Wildl. Biol. 8, 21–30.

Thomas, C.D., Lennon, J.J., 1999. Birds extend their ranges northwards. Nature 399, 213.

Thomas, L., Buckland, S.T., Newman, K.B., Harwood, J., 2005. A unified framework for modelling wildlife population dynamics. Aust. N. Z. J. Stat. 47, 19–34.

Thompson, D.K., 2007. Use of site-occupancy models to estimate prevalence of Myxobolus cerebralis infection in trout. J. Anim. Health 19, 8–13.

Thompson, S.K., 2002. Sampling. Wiley, New York.

Tingley, M.W., Beissinger, S.R., 2009. Detecting range shifts from historical species occurrences: new perspectives on old data. Trend. Ecol. Evol. 24, 625–633.

Tingley, M.W., Monahan, W.B., Beissinger, S.R., Moritz, C., 2009. Birds track their Grinnellian niche through a century of climate change. Proc. Nat. Acad. Sci. USA 106, 19637–19643.

Tyre, A.J., Tenhumberg, B., Field, S.A., Niejalke, D., Parris, K., Possingham, H.P., 2003. Improving precision and reducing bias in biological surveys: estimating false-negative error rates. Ecol. Appl. 13, 1790–1801.

van de Pol, M., Verhulst, S., 2006. Age-dependent traits: a new statistical model to separate within- and between-individual effects. Am. Nat. 167, 766–773.

van Strien, A.J., van Swaay, C.A.M., Kéry, M., 2011. Metapopulation dynamics in the butterfly Hipparchia semele changed decades before decline in the Netherlands. Ecol. Appl. (in press).

Ver Hoef, J.M., Jansen, J.K., 2007. Space-time zero-inflated count models of harbour seals. Environmetrics 18, 697–712.

Weber, D., Hintermann, U., Zangger, A., 2004. Scale and trends in species richness: considerations for monitoring biological diversity for political purposes. Glob. Ecol. Biogeo. 13, 97–104.

Webster, R.A., Pollock, K.H., Simons, T.R., 2008. Bayesian spatial modeling of data from avian point surveys. JABES 13, 121–139.

Welham, S., Cullins, B., Gogel, B., Gilmour, A., Thompson, R., 2004. Prediction in linear mixed models. Aust. N. Z. J. Stat. 46, 325–347.

Wenger, S.J., Freeman, M.C., 2008. Estimating species occurrence, abundance, and detection probability using zero-inflated distributions. Ecology 89, 2953–2959.

White, G.C., Burnham, K.P., 1999. Program MARK: survival estimation from populations of marked animals. Bird Study 46, 120–139.

White, G.C., Garrott, R.A., 1990. Analysis of Wildlife Radio-Tracking Data. Academic Press, London.

Wikle, C.K., 2003. Hierarchical Bayesian models for predicting the spread of ecological processes. Ecology 84, 1382–1394.

Williams, B.K., Nichols, J.D., Conroy, M.J., 2002. Analysis and Management of Animal Populations. Academic Press, San Diego, CA.

Wright, J.A., Barker, R.J., Schofield, M.R., Frantz, A.C., Byrom, A.E., Gleeson, D.M., 2009. Incorporating genotype uncertainty into mark-recapture-type models for estimating abundance using DNA samples. Biometrics 65, 833–840.

Yamaura, Y., Royle, J.A., Kubio, K., Tada, T., Ikeno, S., Makino, S., 2011. Modelling community dynamics based on species-level abundance models from detection/nondetection data. J. Appl. Ecol. 48, 67–75.

Yoshizaki, J., Pollock, K.H., Brownie, C., Webster, R.A., 2009. Modeling misidentification errors in capture-recapture studies using photographic identification of evolving marks. Ecology 90, 3–9.

Zheng, C., Ovaskainen, O., Saastamoinen, M., Hanski, I., 2007. Age-dependent survival analyzed with Bayesian models of mark-recapture data. Ecology 88, 1970–1976.

Zipkin, E.F., DeWan, A., Royle, J.A., 2009. Impacts of forest fragmentation on species richness: a hierarchical approach to community modelling. J. Appl. Ecol. 46, 815–822.

Zipkin, E.F., Royle, J.A., Dawson, D.K., Bates, S., 2010. Multi-species occurrence models to evaluate the effects of conservation and management actions. Biol. Cons. 143, 479–484.

Index

Printed in the United States
By Bookmasters